The French Artillery Officer

Lawrence Fischman

Gram's Group, Ltd.
Dallas, Texas

The French Artillery Officer

Gram's Group, Ltd. books may be ordered through booksellers or by contacting:

Gram's Group, Ltd.
18 Royal Way
Dallas, Texas 75229
TheFrenchArtilleryOfficer.com
972/419-8318

ISBN: 978-0-6153-5346-3 (sc)
ISBN: 978-0-6153-5080-6 (dj)

Printed in the United States of America

Gram's Group, Ltd. rev. date: 03/04/2010

PROLOGUE

"My Captain, I am cold!"

Alfred Dreyfus was the second son of a well-to-do family in Alsace. His ambition in life was to serve his beloved France as a career officer in her army. Until the commencement of the infamous *Affaire* he had been on a fast career track. He had done well in officers' school. He took his commission in the artillery, then the cutting edge of the science of war, and thus among the more prestigious of service branches. He soon distinguished himself thereby earning an assignment to the General Staff, a choice posting for the upwardly mobile young officer.

On October 15, 1894, Dreyfus was secretly arrested by agents of the Section of Statistics, the French military intelligence branch organized in the aftermath of France's defeat in the war of 1870 at the hands of a newly united, Prussian-dominated Germany. Months earlier this unit had come into possession of a document—the infamous *bordereau*—purloined from the German military attaché, Count von Schwarzkoppen, by a French agent planted in the German Embassy by the Section. The *bordereau* consisted of a list of topics each comprising a subject of apparent military intelligence, such as the operating characteristics of certain field artillery pieces, a manual-at-arms and the like. No one could seriously doubt that it was the stuff of spies. Although possessed of conflicting opinions from both qualified and self-anointed forensic document examiners, the Section of Statistics head (a Colonel Jean Sandherr) attributed the writing to Dreyfus and based on this attribution accused him of treason. Dreyfus was held incommunicado for more than two months, all the while protesting his innocence and begging for the opportunity to prove it.

Meanwhile, the press—especially the anti-Semitic press—had gotten hold of the story and were agitating for Dreyfus to be tried for treason and for a general purge of Jews from the officer ranks. In this charged atmosphere Dreyfus was secretly tried in a proceeding that was lacking in due process even by court-martial standards. Despite representation by able counsel, to no one's surprise except for his own, Dreyfus was instantly and unanimously convicted. Again to no one's—this time including even Dreyfus's—surprise his appeal was turned down. Execution of the sentence, degradation and banishment from Metropolitan France for life, was set for January 5, 1895.

Until his trial Dreyfus had been confined at the Prison of Cherche-Midi. The degradation ceremony was fixed to take place at 8:45 in the morning in the parade ground of the Ecole Militarie in Place Fontenoy. A large, hostile crowd began to gather even before first light. The curiosity-seeking throng, goaded by the press which had just played so large a role in his conviction, was in a vicious mood. In order that the lesson not be lost upon any in the officer corps or the rank-and-file who might harbor seditious thoughts or contemplate similar treasonous acts, each regiment comprising the garrison of Paris was commanded to send a contingent comprised both of regular soldiers and recruits. Representatives of the press and of the Diplomatic Corps were sent and accepted invitations.

Dreyfus was up before dawn. A slight man of less than average height, Dreyfus had the light eyes and complexion of the typical Alsatian which had run in his family for generations. His blondish hair, cut extremely short in the French military fashion, was going to gray. He wore pince-nez which, when seen out of uniform, made him look like a severe school-master. What he lacked in size and other physical qualities, he more than compensated for in the dogged, matter-of-fact courage that often characterizes men of Dreyfus's physical stature. The night before, he had written to his wife and promised her, come-what-may, he would not take his own life. This was an option which was made available to him on a daily basis by his tormentors from the Section of Statistics. His declining this rather irrevocable opportunity to express contrition was the subject of much derisive comment among his "fellow" officers. He asked for and was granted permission to bathe and to put on fresh linen. He carefully trimmed his full mustache, shaved and saw to his boots, sword and uniform just as though he were about to stand a rigorous but routine inspection. Having satisfied himself in these things, he bade farewell to the Warden-Colonel and nodded to the four-man guard detail that he was ready.

The morning was damp and bone-chilling cold as Paris winters can be. It was the kind of cold that only those equipped with neither cloak nor hope can truly know. Carried by prison van to the Ecole, Dreyfus was deposited by the guard detail in a small administrative office and left in the custody of a Captain Lebrun-Renault of the Section of Statistics. Although much would later be made of the conversation between the two men, little was actually said. Dreyfus related that Commandant du Paty de Clam, also of the Section of Statistics and the nominal head of the investigation, had asked Dreyfus on the previous day whether he—Dreyfus—had possibly traded the admittedly inconsequential *bordereau* for more valuable information from the German Attaché. Dreyfus responded, as he informed Lebrun-Renault, that he had done no such thing and had passed nothing, regardless of value, to the Germans. He then spoke for a brief while of his family and how much he would miss them. Presently it was time to go. Lebrun-Renault, perhaps sensing that he was a part of history in the making, asked Dreyfus how he felt. Wishing that he were not a part of history in the making, Dreyfus's simple response was "My captain, I am cold!"

In the center of the parade ground General Darras, the grand marshal of the proceedings, presided astride his horse. Dreyfus entered flanked by the four-man guard detail, each of whom carried a drawn sabre and holstered revolver. General Darras drew his sword and with a grand downward gesture commanded that the ceremony begin. There was a drum roll which brought the assembled troops to attention. Dreyfus marched forward until he was standing but a few feet from the general and came to attention. The guard detail withdrew and at the general's command the verdict of the court-martial was read. As the verdict was read, the general glared down at Dreyfus and when the reading was concluded rose in his stirrups. Raising his sword he intoned the ritual words: "Alfred Dreyfus, you are unworthy of bearing arms for France. In the name and by the authority of Her People, I dishonor you."

Dreyfus began for the first time in public to proclaim his innocence. At the general's command a sergeant-major of the Garde Republicaine came forward and stood in front of Dreyfus. With what must have been a practiced hand, the non-commissioned officer ripped the braid from Dreyfus's cap and sleeves. With the swiftest of movements he then clawed off the epaulets and red officer's stripes from Dreyfus's trousers. The mob grew silent at the spectacle; the only sound was the rending of Dreyfus's uniform which by now was in tatters. For the ceremony's finale, the sergeant-major ripped Dreyfus's saber from its sheath and splintered it over his knee. As this was done, summoning his last reserves of dignity, Dreyfus cried out "Vive la France! I swear on the lives of my wife and children, I am an innocent man!" No reply was heard save from the general's horse who at that moment, as though impatient with contempt, snorted and stamped his foreleg.

To the sound of a dull drum tattoo, Dreyfus in his tattered rags was then marched around the parade ground before the ranks of troops whose stares spoke their hatred and contempt. The ceremony having been thus completed, Dreyfus was quickly frog-marched back into the prison van. He was returned to Cherche-Midi where he was searched for any weapon by which he might end his own life. Because he was no longer an officer, this genteel custom must be denied him as well. He was photographed and, appropriately enough, his Bertillon System measurements were taken. There he remained, in isolation, but otherwise just another convict awaiting transport to his place of exile.

Once at sea Dreyfus was confined in a cage-like cell exposed to the cold of the mid-Atlantic winter. Several days out the weather became warmer. As he ate the stale bread and drank the brackish water that made up his daily ration, it dawned on Dreyfus where he was to be confined. In the shark-infested waters just off the coast of French Guiana is a tiny volcanic archipelago comprised of three islands named, collectively, *"Iles du Salut"*. The last and smallest of the three, which was to be Dreyfus's home for the next four years and more, is named *"Ile du Diable"*— Devil's Island. Formerly a leper colony it was deemed the only fitting place to confine the moral leper Dreyfus. And so the *Dreyfus Affaire* ended, at least for the time being.

CHAPTER ONE

"You've been in the Sudan, I perceive."

*W*atson thought it had been a disappointing evening. The early dinner at the Savoy Hotel in The Strand was typical of the standards to which the establishment had declined since the departure of Ritz and Escoffier. The Dover sole was overcooked and instead of Escoffier's celebrated sauce of drawn butter and herbs, it was served with a dreadful congealed cheese-like substance whose name Watson could not recall. Holmes had reluctantly assented to Watson's suggestion of dinner and a concert and when they left Baker Street he seemed to be in a good if not effusive mood. But once they had ordered, Holmes seemed preoccupied and merely picked at his entrée, a rabbit stew. Watson, preoccupied with his own entree, barely listened as Holmes speculated as to whether the tarragon had overpowered the hare as the instrument *causa mortis* or the unhappy collision had occurred post-mortem. That in turn had led to a somewhat desultory conversation involving the chemistry of common herbs and what deadly new alkaloids might be derived by future practitioners of the art of the Borgias. The conversation, such as it was, wore itself out even before the dishes were cleared.

Nor, it seemed, was the service up to former standards. The waiter was either incompetent or had so fallen out of favor with the kitchen, that a red-faced D'Oyly Carte, the managing director of the establishment, had offered to adjust the bill. In remembrance of more pleasurable experiences past Holmes and Watson declined the offer and after bestowing a generous gratuity, departed for St. James's Hall, Picadilly, and what Watson greatly hoped would be a pleasant musical entertainment such as might help dispel the deepening ennui which was, to Watson's practiced eye, so evident in Holmes's affect.

Holmes's own violin playing over the years metamorphosed from a minor vice to what could fairly be said to be a not inconsiderable virtue. He had acquired a magnificent Amati, a gift from the family of Victor Emmanuel II for a small

1

service to the royal house and People of Italy. He had toured both in England and abroad with a major orchestra in order to recover a folio of priceless Bach manuscripts which had been purloined, so it turned out, by a woodwind player with a penchant for gambling, but alas little aptitude for the avocation. Watson too, though he could not play an instrument, had developed the ability to distinguish virtuosity from vulgarity.

With dinner only an annoying memory, Holmes and Watson settled in their concert-hall seats anticipating the evening's performance. Although the impresario had spent lavish sums in advertising the concert as the finest of the season, indeed of any season in memory, it proved, to be charitable, as insulting to the ear as the dinner had been to the palate. The highlight of the performance was to be Beethoven's *Violin Concerto* a favorite of both Holmes and Watson. But the soloist had gotten lost in his own cadenza and made such a pig's breakfast of the third-movement rondo that during the intermission Holmes had been constrained to remark that it was just as well that Beethoven was stone deaf, else he would no doubt be turning in his grave. By mutual consent, instead of returning to the stalls to witness an assault upon Bruch's *Scottish Fantasy,* the two men took their leave and hailed a cab for Baker Street.

They said little during the ride up Bond Street, other than Watson's remarking that the evening had gotten quite chilly and Holmes's concurring observation that it was just as well that they had left early since the competition for cabs at the concert's end would have been intense. Holmes, perhaps feeling a twinge of remorse, suggested that while he was not de Sarasate, he might try his own hand at the Bruch. But as the cab turned off Oxford Street into Baker Street, Watson demurred, allowing that he would just as soon have a brandy and a cigar, and call it an early night. As their cab rattled the last few yards up Baker Street, they both noticed another cab stopped in front of 221B.

As they came to a halt, Watson fished about for his coin purse in order to pay the driver. Just then a man scrambled from the waiting cab and fairly bounded the distance to where Holmes, who had been on the left-hand or kerb side, was just alighting. In the flickering light of the carriage lamp Watson could see Holmes assume a two-handed kendo grip on his walking stick for just the

2

briefest instant as the man came to an equally abrupt stop scarcely three feet away. Watson debated for a moment exiting on the street side, and if the stranger's intent was hostile, going round the front of the cab so as to catch him in a classic hammer-and-anvil movement suddenly remembered with striking clarity from some long-ago military tactics class at Netley.

"Never-mind, Watson." Holmes, as he so often did, had sensed Watson's intentions. "It's only a military man in mufti. He looks harmless enough."

"Mr. Holmes, sir. Dr. Watson. At last you've arrived. I've been waiting for hours and I'm afraid I've quite run out of shillings to keep the cabby waiting. I tried to persuade your redoubtable landlady to let me await your return inside, but she was quite adamant: no appointment, no entrance. Since it's become somewhat nippy, rather than risk catching my death, I detained the cabby so as to make use of his passenger compartment and its lap-rug. Could you, sir? It's of the utmost importance that I see you, and the fellow's threatening to call an officer to arrest me for theft of services."

"Nonsense, young man." Watson stepped forward brandishing his own walking stick. "Sherlock Holmes does not need to pay for people to bring him business; we have quite enough the other way 'round. Be off with you!"

Holmes deftly stepped between the advancing Watson and the by now backpedaling young man. Handing his stick to Watson he reached in his breast pocket, took out his wallet and handed the wide-eyed cabby a pound note. "Here, my good man. That should do for now. Do you have a time-piece? Good; be back here in..." Holmes paused and turned to the young man.

"Would an hour be too much to ask, sir?"

"That, I should think, remains to be seen." Turning to the cabby, Holmes held up another pound note. "Very well, be back here in an hour. You may either take our young friend where he wishes to go or you may haul him off to jail for theft of *my* services. Either way you shall have this note as well."

"As you wish, guv. I'll wager that pound note that it's off to gaol that I'll be takin' 'im. Don't say I din na warn you, gents. That 'un he'll be talkin' yer ears off, 'e will." With that Parthian shot the driver remounted his box, brought his horse smartly around and clattered back down Baker Street in the direction of Oxford Street.

Meanwhile, Watson and the young man were maintaining a cautious truce. By the light of the street-lamp, Watson appraised the fellow standing before him. Watson could see—now that the man had regained his composure—a pair of wide-set, blue-gray eyes which looked steadily back at Watson suggesting an intelligence beyond his callow appearance. As had Holmes, Watson immediately observed the man's obvious military bearing, and made note of the rather stiff manner in which he seemed to favor his right shoulder as well as an odd-shaped scar on his wrist.

Watson had mused to himself that Holmes's intuition was like lightning: leaping from point to point giving off a blue-white light so intense at times that all one could really see is the after-image that remained when he had gone on to the next thought. As Watson took out his door-key, Holmes grasped the young man by the elbow, and propelling him toward the door bade him "Come along, Lieutenant. You've been in the Sudan, I perceive." Mounting the steps, he spoke to Watson. "Whatever the nature of the problem that has prompted the lieutenant to bivouac on our door-step, it's bound to be more entertaining than our evening thus far. What say, Watson, are you game?" Affecting nonchalance, Watson shrugged and held open the door for the other men.

Once inside the house and up the stairs, the three men paused while Watson again did the door-unlocking honors. The previous autumn they had installed a solid-oak door equipped with a new Yale lock guaranteed by the locksmith to be impervious to anything, save its proper key or a high-explosive charge. This was done in the aftermath of an incursion late one night by an immense South-sea islander who burst through their door just as the two men were preparing to retire. The intruder, as they soon learned after the man was brought to his knees by Holmes's stiff right upper-cut and his full attention gained by means of Watson cocking his Webley revolver just next to the man's ear, had come to demand satisfaction from Holmes for alienating the affections of his favourite wife. The man, whose English was fluent with a discernible Midlands accent, was the reigning monarch of a remote Pacific island kingdom and considered by his people to be a temporal descendant of the principal god in their primitive pantheon. In a spirit of noblesse oblige he and his wives had learned English from a group of missionaries whom he had allowed to establish an outpost on one of the islands comprising his kingdom.

When the crews manning the vessels of the pearl and copra traders would come ashore, while the chief and the other tribal officials would tend to the business at hand with the ship's master and officers, the women-folk would entertain the mates and ordinary seamen with food and demonstrations of native dances. This led to a lively exchanging of gifts: native handicrafts on the one hand for whatever was deemed barter fare on the other. It was in this way that the chief's wife came into possession of a many-months-old edition of *Strand Magazine* and first read one of Watson's accounts. From this initial exposure she soon became enamoured of Holmes and demanded that her husband obtain for her the rest of Watson's writings, which she would spend each night reading and rereading by the meager light of a copra oil lamp.

The chief had become so exasperated that he bartered passage on a trading ship to Singapore, sold a cache of pearls and with the proceeds purchased his first suit of western clothes and a starboard stateroom on a P&O liner bound through Suez to London. Being bored with his other wives, he'd had the favoured wife read him aloud the complete collection of Watson's accounts. Thus he was able on his arrival to engage a cab and come straight-away to Baker Street and his encounter with the bane of his marital bliss. Once he had acceded to Holmes's and Watson's joint suggestion that he get hold of himself and he had poured out his story, the three men got on quite well. He stayed on in London for several weeks seeing the City and his new-found friends until the first deep cold-snap reminded him that it was time to return to his people.

Their present visitor, at Watson's bidding, arranged himself in a more relaxed posture on the sofa at right angles to the fire while Holmes and Watson took up their favored Queen Anne-style arm chairs opposite the sofa. He lighted a cigar and swirled his brandy around in the snifter like a practiced connoisseur. "Please tell me, Mr. Holmes, before I tell you why I'm here, I've read of your abilities, but how could you have known my rank and last posting?"

Watson, thoughts of an early night put behind, interjected, "Wait Holmes, I'll have a go this time." Holmes nodded his assent. "First of all," Watson intoned, "your erect bearing and the way you fairly stamped your right foot when you first addressed Holmes betrayed your occupation." Encouraged by a nod from Holmes, he continued. "Second, your age and accent made it obvious that you are a junior officer. You speak with an upper-class, public school accent, so you can't have been in the ranks. Yet you are by turns brash and also obviously deferential to authority, traits which mark you, in my experience, as a young barrister, physician, or in your case a junior officer."

"Excellent, Watson; well done." Holmes clapped his hands politely. "And what about the Sudan?"

"Elementary, my dear Holmes, elementary." Watson, his eyes narrowing as he delivered this long-repressed retort, continued, "surely you noticed the rectangular scar on his wrist when he held up his arm?"

"Indeed Watson, so I did. Do continue," Holmes replied. The young man, as though seeing it for the first time, looked in bewilderment at his own wrist.

"Notice that the rectangular shape of the scar belies a penetrating wound; these tend almost always to be either perfectly round or elliptical. Note how regular the margins are. No, this wound was not inflicted by a bullet or knife wielded in battle; it had to have been inflicted by a lancet in the hands of a surgeon. It can only be," he continued, "that our young visitor has recently allowed himself to be the donor of a skin-graft in order to heal the wound of some less fortunate comrade-in-arms."

Watson rose from his chair and gently took the man's forearm and held it near to the table-lamp in order to more closely examine the object of his discourse. "To my knowledge, no civilian surgeon is regularly using this procedure. The risk of infection is too great, and the procedure, which must be done without benefit of anesthesia, is both time-consuming and excruciatingly painful. The only institution where this operation is being done is the army. And the only recent combat theatre being the Sudan, it took no crystal ball to conclude where the chap had recently seen active duty."

"Bravo!" Holmes applauded again. "Watson, you do us both great honour. And did you notice that our young guest has American connexions as well? However, I must confess that something about him still puzzles me."

During this dialogue the visitor sat, as though in rigor mortis, his cigar ash growing perilously long. Watson broke the man's trance, "Mind your cigar, young man. Do continue, Holmes. I readily admit that the iatrogenic pathology presented by his arm more than absorbed my full attention and I missed any clews indicating America."

Holmes took a deliberate sip of his brandy. "See, Watson, how he holds his cigar. You and I by habit hold ours between thumb and forefinger, whereas he holds his between fore- and middle-fingers. You recall, no doubt, the monograph which I penned some years ago on the various types of cigar ash?" Watson nodded as he and the young man glanced self-consciously at their respective cigars and confirmed what Holmes had observed. Holmes, smiling slightly at the gesture, continued, "my research, being something of a labour of love, extended over quite some time. In its course I had many opportunities to delve into issues which were collateral to the main subject of my investigation. One of those areas was *how* men smoke, as contrasted with *what* they smoke."

"I learned that in America, because of the abundance of domestic tobacco and cigar-makers, the price and quality of cigars varies greatly, hence the habit is indulged in by all classes of men." Holmes tapped the ash on his own cigar. "Some of the less cultivated classes do not smoke their cigars, but merely clamp them in their teeth and chew them to extinction." The young man grimaced and nodded his head in confirmation. Holmes continued, "more to the point, I came across a fairly small sub-genre of cigar smokers who for occupational reasons hold their cigars as does our visitor."

"And what singular occupation might that be?" Watson asked.

Holmes rose and stood with his back to the fire warming himself. "Watson, I'm surprised you never encountered them. I refer of course to professional gamblers—card sharps, if you will. The custom originated amongst the card sharps who plied their trade on the packet boats traveling the Mississippi River up and back between New Orleans and St. Louis. It seems that it was necessary 'pon occasion, to hold one's cards and cigar in the same hand, thus freeing the other hand to be used for other purposes: to manipulate one's stake of chips, take a drink or, if necessary, reach for one's weapon. In the latter instance, of course, time was very much of the essence, and taking time to put down one's cigar might in the circumstances prove fatal.

"I would venture to say, therefore, that the lieutenant has spent considerable time in America where he learned to smoke cigars. But I cannot yet account for the ever-so-faint American accent. Obviously English as we speak it here is his mother tongue. And if he was old enough to pick up the cigar habit while traveling in some rather fast company, then he surely was too old to acquire an American accent. All in all, quite a mystery, Watson. Perhaps we should send him 'round to your friend Mr. G.B. Shaw and let him see what he can make of him."

"Seeing that my allotted time is nearly half gone, perhaps, if I may, I will be able to shed some light on the matter. You are quite correct, Mr. Holmes. Indeed, I did learn the pleasures of a good cigar in America. And my tutor in that endeavor was an older gentleman in New York City—a friend of my mother's—whose great passion is the gaming tables. As for the accent, I must say that it has been a good while since anyone has detected its presence enough to comment." Rising from his place on the sofa, the young man handed each of his hosts a plain calling card which read *Mr. Winston S. Churchill.* "You see," he went on, "my late father was Lord Randolph Churchill, and my mother, Lady Jennie Churchill, was born in America. It is to her that I am indebted for the accent which you so astutely detected."

"Ah-ha, Lieutenant Churchill." Holmes exclaimed. "Now you shall be able to tell the world that you managed to stump the *Great* Sherlock Holmes. The floor is yours. Pray, state your business. Hopefully it will prove to be more challenging than your recent travels, and less intractable than your accent."

Holmes poured another round of brandy, and after Holmes had retaken his chair, Churchill took a thoughtful sip of his drink.

"I must say gentlemen that the popular press, and especially your own accounts Dr. Watson, do not overstate yours and Mr. Holmes's powers of observation and ratiocination. But I must correct you in regard to one point: I have within the month resigned my commission and no longer am I able to claim either active rank or affiliation with my former regiment, the 4th Hussars. Much as I miss my stalwart company, I feel that there may yet be larger challenges awaiting me than whacking a polo ball up and down the dusty plains of India.

"I did see action at Omdurman while on detached duty with Kitchener's staff. You may have read my accounts of the final weeks of the campaign published in the *Daily Mail*."

"Yes, we certainly did," Watson interjected. "Your account of the cavalry charge that turned the battle in Kitchener's favor was well drawn I must say. It reminded me so keenly of my own experiences that a thrill ran through me as I read it. It should rank with the heart-pounding epic of the Eleventh Light Dragoons at Balaclava and the heroic if some-what ambiguous action of the Bulgarian regiment under Major Saranoff in the Serbo-Bulgarian war. Good work, sir. You are to be congratulated not only for your reportorial skill but for your bravery and clear-headedness in the midst of battle."

"I quite agree, said Holmes. "I thought your account of the cavalry charge was quite charming. I would venture to say that it may stand for all time as the definitive account of the last great horse-back battle in history. And your account of what was done with the corpse of the vanquished *Mahdi*—in full view of senior officers—was simply too, too poignant."

"I think, I pray, Mr. Holmes, that the incident of which you speak was merely an aberration and does not typify the honour code of British men-at-arms. If it does, then I cannot have resigned my commission a moment too soon."

"Well said, young man," Holmes replied. "Now, lest we digress further, kindly state your business."

Churchill leaned forward as though to convey by body language a sense of the importance and confidential nature of his mission. "You are, I'm sure, familiar with the business regarding the French artillery captain convicted of treason..."

"NO! NEVER AGAIN!" Holmes leaped out of his chair knocking over the small side-table situated between his chair and Watson's. "Do *NOT* even mention that wretched man's name in this house!"

"There, there, steady on old man." Watson moved quickly between Holmes and Churchill who, mouth agape, had recoiled against the back cushions of the sofa. Watson turned toward Holmes and grasped him firmly by the shoulders. "What in heaven's name is it Holmes? The man's our guest; what can he have possibly said to so offend you?"

Holmes tore himself away from Watson's grip and stood, fairly shaking with anger, the now-empty brandy decanter resting against his right foot. For nearly a full minute no one moved, Churchill scarcely daring even to breathe. Finally Holmes, a measure of composure restored, turned and reached for the cigarette box situated on the fire-place mantle in its familiar spot next to the Persian slipper containing his shag tobacco.

Hands trembling, he lit his cigarette and inhaled deeply. "Do take your chair, Watson; I'm al-right now. You're quite right old fellow. Please accept my apology, Mr. Churchill." After pausing to restore the table to its upright position and picking up the brandy decanter and ash tray, Holmes continued, "as you've no doubt discerned from my reaction, I am familiar—let me say too familiar—with the case of the unfortunate Captain Dreyfus." Returning to his place in front of the fire, Holmes took another drag on his cigarette. "You remember, Watson, upon my return from my absence following the business at the Reichenbach Falls, I gave you a brief synopsis of my travels abroad?"

"Yes, yes, of course I do," Watson responded in a tentative voice that betrayed his anticipation of what was to come. Petulantly, he went on, "and as you may recall, in keeping with my custom, I took extremely good notes." Churchill, his mind racing, sat completely still shifting his eyes back and forth between the two men as though watching a tennis match.

"So you did, dear friend, so you did." Holmes threw the stub of his cigarette into the fire and immediately lit a fresh one. "And your notes, insofar as I've been made privy to them, are entirely accurate. I must therefore confess that with regard to the Dreyfus business I deliberately deceived you. I told you, as you

10

must remember, that I spent several months in the South of France experimenting with coal-tar derivatives. You even made mention of that little scientific side-trip in your published version of the capture of Colonel Sebastian Moran."

Churchill interjected, "Yes, I remember reading..." Both men turned and glared at him and he lapsed once more into silence.

"*Version* indeed Holmes. You know full well that you approved every word of the account, and that every word reported either what I saw with my own eyes or what you yourself told me had occurred."

"That is quite true, old chap. Any errors were my responsibility, and mine alone. But if I deceived you, which I admit is the case, it was for reasons which at the time I thought to be both valid and of over-riding importance. You wrote that I had spent several months in Montpelier. If you will consult a current atlas, you will see that Montpelier is the capital of the State of Vermont, in America, whereas, Montpellier is a city in the South of France. I suspect that the spelling error was the result of lazy editing at your publisher's, since my recollection is that in your notes the name is spelt correctly.

"Be that as it may, the spelling error created even more confusion as to my whereabouts and doings, and obfuscation was in this instance my objective. For you see, Watson..." Holmes paused and looked at Churchill, "we may, I trust, count on your absolute discretion?"

"Yes, yes. Of course you may."

Holmes continued: "For you see, Watson, it was during this time that I was engaged, at the request of the *Sureté,* in trying to establish whether there was in fact a traitor, and if so, to learn his identity. As I soon enough learned, long before news of the case broke in the press and Dreyfus was arrested, the *Sureté,* the French civilian judicial police, were intensely jealous of the Section of Statistics, which is a military intelligence operation responsible for ferreting-out of foreign espionage agents and home-grown traitors. The *Sureté* wanted to either steal the military's thunder by conclusively proving that a traitor existed, or to embarrass the military by conclusively proving that there was no traitor and that the military had been foolishly dashing about for months on a wild-goose chase. In either case, until the issue was decided and the political winds thoroughly tested, the bureaucracy-wise mandarins running the show did not want their agency's interest to be found out. So they hired me and I idiotically accepted the engagement."

As he spoke, Holmes stood before the fire, his normally impassive face a mask of pain. Watson considered interrupting, but before he could choose the proper words, Holmes went on with his narrative. "The Section of Statistics is riddled with incompetents and, for all I know, German spies. It is, as a practical matter, a dumping ground for misfits whom the army for whatever reasons cannot dismiss, but cannot afford to have in positions of responsibility lest they do some real harm in a genuine crisis. My investigation established that the key piece of evidence, the *bordereau,* was a forgery calculated to implicate Dreyfus. Since anyone who'd ever had anything to do with Dreyfus knew him to be a chauvinist whose loyalty was beyond question, it should have been of the utmost importance to discover who the forger was and what was his motive.

"Rather than doing what had to be done, the Section Head, the numbskull Sandherr, was inclined to merely let the matter drop. However, someone, probably in the *Sureté,* gave the information to a lackey newspaper editor who, in the guise of seeking confirmation for a story about to be published, threatened Sandherr with publication of the story thereby openly branding him a fool for not having caught the dangerous traitor. This, of course, would have been unacceptable. So Sandherr was faced with a seemingly impossible dilemma: either he had to expose a non-existent traitor, or be publicly humiliated and probably sacked from his job because he was unable to catch-out the non-existent traitor.

"He chose, not surprisingly, to unmask the non-existent traitor. The next problem, then, was to select a victim. It had to be an officer, since only an officer could be expected to have sufficient access to obtain the information comprising the *bordereau's* list of topics. But he was loathe to inflict such a terrible blow on a brother officer. Finally, he hit upon the perfect solution: blame the Jews, or in this instance, a Jew, there being several of these who, despite the odds, had earned their positions in the officer corps. Although they were officers, no one would say they were *brother* officers, and it was unlikely that anyone of importance would either come to their defence or be too much concerned with such ambiguous concepts as guilt and innocence. The honor of the army was paramount, and if a sacrificial offering were required, who better to sacrifice than an outsider, a Jew? So even after my departure from France and re-emergence at the door-step of your consulting rooms, the perfidious chess game went on with Dreyfus now the pawn, and the knight, me, knocked off the board.

"As to the experimentation with coal-tar derivatives, it was an expedient in the cause of self-preservation. Somehow, possibly through an informer planted by the military in the *Sureté,* my involvement in the matter became known to the military group as well as the civilian. Once I'd made up my mind that I'd had quite enough of French political intrigue, I didn't want two bands of cutthroats after my head, so I decided to obliterate any mention of my part in the whole sordid affair.

"I'd spent several sleepless nights thinking how I might extricate myself from this mess. Suspecting that every port and egress point was probably alerted to be on the lookout for me, I did not want to run the risk, even in disguise, of a border crossing. I determined instead to hide more or less in plain sight until my pursuers either tired of the game or grew careless. Through my family contacts in the region, I arranged to work in an obscure chemistry laboratory at the University in Montpellier as an assistant to a professor whose colleagues, owing to his eccentricity, tended to avoid him and his work as much as possible. This situation was ideally suited to my circumstances. Moreover, the fellow actually was quite brilliant, and the work, given my interest in chemistry, was most stimulating. Lodging in a room in a relative's house, I spent most of my time, days and nights, in the laboratory working on coal-tar derivatives which were the professor's specialty and not of much interest to his colleagues. I bided my time, and when the professor's work was at a convenient stopping place, I took my leave. Through my family's passing me from village to village, I made my way to Cherbourg where I arranged passage back to England on a fishing vessel and hoped never again to hear those dread words '*Dreyfus Affair.*'"

Wearily Holmes sat back down, his elbows on his knees and his face cupped in his hands. Watson went to the liquor

13

cabinet, procured a fresh bottle of brandy and poured each man a generous measure. After a few moments, Holmes took a careful sip, "Thank you, Watson." Holmes sat back in his chair. His expression grew stern and his voice took on a determined timbre. "The problem, gentlemen, is that I have already solved this case once; Captain Dreyfus is innocent. But his innocence was then, and is even today, too inconvenient for too many people: the French government, the military, the religious establishment, the anti-Semitic press, and quite possibly even his own supporters who see him as a martyr. No, my good friends, this is one matter that can do just as well without our meddling. Mr. Churchill, I've enjoyed meeting you. Now I must bid you good-night. Please come again; I shall be glad to stand your cab-fare anytime."

Holmes rose and turned in the direction of his bed-chamber. Watson and Churchill both rose and Churchill reached in the breast pocket of his suit. "Please wait, Mr. Holmes. A moment, if you will. I was told that I should be prepared for a negative reaction on your part, although I must say that nothing could have prepared me for the depth of your feelings." He paused and handed Watson a sealed envelope addressed to both men. "I was also instructed that should your enthusiasm for the project not be manifest, I was to give you this envelope, and if you would allow me to do so, await your response." Churchill gestured toward his former place on the sofa, "May I?"

Watson recognized at once the crest imprinted in the old-fashion sealing wax as well as the tiny, precise handwriting of the author. He gestured Churchill to resume his seat and turned to Holmes. "I say, old man, I think you'd best have a look at this. I believe that duty is once again about to call."

"Blast it all, Watson. What is it now?" Holmes snatched the envelope from Watson's hand and took it over to a lamp. Holding the envelope under the light he bent down to more closely inspect the handwriting. Slowly he turned it over and peered even more closely at the waxen imprint. He lay the envelope on the lamp table unopened, turned and went into his bed-chamber. Churchill looked nervously at Watson who sat in his arm chair his face an enigma.

In a moment Holmes reappeared, a pair of reading glasses perched on the end of his nose. Holmes picked up the envelope, resumed his seat and carefully broke the wax seal. He removed the contents of the envelope which consisted of several pages in the same handwriting as the outside of the envelope. "Shall I, gentlemen?" Without waiting for a reply, Holmes adjusted his spectacles and began:

"Windsor Castle

20th May, 1899

My Dear Mr. Holmes and Dr. Watson,
For whatever your reasons, and I accept them whatever they may be, I am given to understand that you have expressed a strong reluctance to involve yourselves in what the press are pleased to call the 'Dreyfus Affair'. You have, I am sure, absorbed as much of the detail of this seemingly endless passion play as I have and perhaps you know a good deal more. Be that as it may, it is my duty to ask that you lay aside your predisposition and listen once again to the entreaty—for that's what it is, neither less nor more—of the 'Widow of Windsor'
You have made note, I'm sure, that I write to you in the first-person. I do so in deference to the constitutional limitations on the power of the crown. I have no authority to even ask, much less insist, that you undertake this mission. I know only that if you do, the matter will be in the most capable of hands. For reasons that I will explain presently, neither I nor the Government can be involved, nor can my or its involvement even be suspected. It is not generally known, but Lord Salisbury, owing to the state of his health, is head of the present Government in name only; his nephew, Mr. Balfour, presides over the cabinet, but at the moment it is your brother Mycroft, Mr. Holmes, who is in fact The Government.
We will, I am sure, soon be involved militarily in South Africa. This fellow Kruger, typically of the Dutch, is stubborn and determined, such that the lives and property of British subjects are gravely at risk. Your brother, Mr. Holmes, informs me that there is good reason to fear intervention by the Germans should hostilities ensue in South Africa. For myself I have always felt that my grandson too much enjoys cantering about with his troops, and would like nothing more than a nice neat little war in some far-off

place. *While I shall probably not live to see it, without a doubt we shall in his lifetime find ourselves in a war with the Germans on the Continent, if not on the seas and perhaps around the globe.*

I am also given to understand that there is a possibility the German military establishment may be at the bottom of this Dreyfus business. If there is a chance this is so, then we cannot allow your participation (assuming that I am able to persuade you to change your position) to be in the slightest way attributed to myself or to the Government. My own view is that if we fear confrontation with the Germans, our fear shall more likely than not become a grim reality. However, Mr. Mycroft Holmes, whose wise counsel in these matters I value most of all, persuades me otherwise. And with the Government in its present state, I gladly accept his advice.

As to the matter at hand, I need not remind you of the high esteem in which I hold the late Lord Beaconsfield. Of all my First Ministers, none has done more for England and Empire, and none has been so dear a friend. It must also be said, though, that for all his great intellect and diplomatic skills, without the financial resources of the House of Rothschild, much of what has been accomplished would have remained undone. I am aware of much agitation regarding the Dreyfus case in the press of late, but I do not profess to know in detail the evidence for and against the man. However, both Mr. Mycroft Holmes and I have no hesitation in accepting the representation of Lord Rothschild that Captain Dreyfus is the innocent victim of a vile plot, and we are equally convinced that our interests are in the long-run best served by his being cleared.

So I again in closing urge you to take up this cause, knowing that if you are persuaded, I have done as much as even I can do. Wishing you Godspeed and good hunting, I remain,

Your loyal and admiring friend,

V. R. I."

Holmes silently passed the letter to Watson as if inviting him to confirm with his own eyes what he had just heard read to him. For a while no one spoke. Watson absently shuffled the pages of the letter over and over in his hands, while Churchill sat nervously crossing and re-crossing his legs. Finally, Holmes pushed his reading glasses back on his forehead and gave his decision. "Mr. Churchill, you may report to my dear brother—I assume that it is him to whom you report—that he is more likely to secure Captain Dreyfus's freedom by sending a squadron of marines to storm Devil's Island than by sending his younger brother on this futile crusade. Moreover, the odds of the Government's role not coming to light are not much worse than if I do the job. I am no paladin, nor am I a magician; I do not work miracles. Yet I must also confess that when Captain Dreyfus and I departed France five years ago—he for his island, and I for mine—I knew somehow that this business was not done."

Turning to Watson, he went on. "Her Highness's letter brings to a head that which has been building for quite some time. Many's the time, old man, in the last five years that you have no doubt wondered, but were too polite or astute to ask, where my thoughts were as I sat in a state of semi-reverie. I must tell you that on many, many such occasions they were with that poor chap in his island prison striving each day to survive and to keep from going mad. Watson, I must finish this business once and for all. I know what your answer will be, but I must warn you that we'll be swimming in deep and shark-infested waters. I sense that there are deep undercurrents, deeper even than the bureaucratic machinations of which I spoke earlier. If I am correct, we shall be not unlike gladiators in ancient Rome; once we enter this coliseum, the price of failure may easily be our very lives. So what say you?"

Watson looked at Holmes for several long seconds, as if choosing his words with the utmost care. "In your company alone, not to mention my army service, I have faced death in several forms. I look forward to living out my three-score years and ten, and hopefully many more after that. But any man who will not go in harm's way just so he can say he died of old age, well..." Watson drained his snifter. "Besides, I flatter myself to think that in some way, should we find ourselves in a tight spot, you will be glad that I came along."

Holmes rose and rubbed his hands together, whether in glee or to warm them Watson could not be sure. "Very well, then, Mr. Churchill you may tell my brother that we are at his disposal."

"I don't think that will be necessary, sir. I do come as your brother's emissary. He sends his compliments and asks that you call on him at No. 10 Downing Street, where he is prepared to receive you at 10:30 in the morning. Mr. Holmes, Dr. Watson, thank you for the many courtesies you have shown me this evening, and goodnight."

CHAPTER TWO

"...if we miscalculate, we may find ourselves..,
with Wilhelm on his grosse-mutti's throne
and us conducting our business
in German rather than the language of
Shakespeare, Dickens and Austen."

After the ardours of the previous night Holmes and Watson, although relieved that the game was again afoot, scarcely touched their breakfasts and were in somber frame of mind as their hansom made its way in fits and starts with the mid-morning traffic in Parliament Street. At Watson's direction the driver left them off at Downing Street. They walked the short distance to Number 10; just minutes shy of the appointed time they passed under the curious wrought-iron arch and were admitted by a uniformed porter. Once inside they were relieved of their hats, coats and walking sticks and taken straight away to the cabinet ante-room. There they were invited to make themselves comfortable and asked if they would take tea or perhaps a glass of hunter's port. Mindful of the quantity of brandy consumed the previous night, both men replied that they would welcome a cup of tea.

Although neither man was a first-time visitor to Number 10, neither had been there in some time. As the porter excused himself, Watson appropriated the comfortable tufted leather chair placed at the round, leather-topped writing table in the center of the room. Holmes chose to remain standing and busied himself inspecting an oil-painting, apparently by a lesser artist of the Flemish school. It evidently had been acquired since Holmes's last visit and placed on the wall just to the left of the corner fire place. As Holmes was silently critiquing the piece, the grandfather clock which stood to the right of the fire place announced the time, and moments later the porter reappeared bearing a tray laden with a tea service. He opened the door and indicated that they should proceed before him through a secretarial office and into the cabinet room.

The cabinet room is situated more or less on the northwest corner of the ground floor, with its long dimension running west to east. The west wall has a window and door opening on to a terrace which overlooks a manicured lawn and beyond the garden, the Horse Guards Parade. Dividing the room at its terrace-end are several vertical structural columns which were added in the late 18th Century when the room was expanded. Elegant though they are, they give the room a sort of make-shift look not unlike so many other government offices of far humbler stature. The room is dominated by the cloth-covered Chippendale-style table which runs nearly the length of the room. The mid-point of the table is opposite the fire place on the north wall. It is at this point that the Prime Minister's chair is situated between the table and the fire place. The other chairs are arranged around the perimeter of the room and are drawn up to the table as needed.

As Holmes and Watson stood rather unsure of whether to be seated, the porter set down the tea tray on a deal-topped side table and with no further words left the room. No sooner than he had done so, then the east door opened and Mycroft Holmes barged in, one hand clutching several manila folders with papers poking out of all sides, and under his other arm a red dispatch case, its lid askew. Like many men of his corpulent stature, Mycroft Holmes had relatively tiny, virtually delicate hands and feet. In his case, all that was Mycroft Holmes was concentrated in his large head and substantial abdominal girth.

Somehow he made it to the cabinet table without dropping any of his paper burden. That having been accomplished, he pirouetted 'round, clasped his startled brother by the shoulders in what was intended as a filial embrace, presented his soft, tiny hand to Watson for a brief handshake. He bade the two men pull up chairs on either side of him at the end of the long table. Once seated, he pulled a large handkerchief from his coat pocket and mopped several beads of perspiration from his wide forehead. Watson, ever the physician, immediately noticed the gesture as well as the apparent dyspnea and ruddy complexion which are the well-recognized symptoms of essential hypertension. Mycroft self-consciously thrust the cloth back into his pocket.

As he made to pour the tea, Sherlock was the first to speak. "I'm surprised, dear brother, that you did not choose to seat yourself at mid-table, your back to the fire place. We are made to

understand that these days you are, *de facto, The* Government."
Pouring the first cup he offered it to his brother.

"Oh, no thank you. Dr. Watson is quite right; I am suffering
from hypertension. In fact I'm under the strictest of doctor's
orders: no caffeine, no rich foods, no more than two glasses of
wine per day. I tell you it's a case of the cure, if it is that, being
nearly worse than the disease. I subsist these days on a diet of
mush and par-boiled vegetables. But even in the face of this
adversity, when duty calls, I muddle on. What I wouldn't give for a
great slab of roast beef at Simpson's.

"Ah, but then you two have not been eating so well these
days either. From what I..."

"Confound it, Watson, I should have known." Sherlock set
down the cup and saucer so hard they nearly shattered. "Tell me,
Mycroft, did you also co-opt the violinist?"

Watson, not for the first time feeling out of his depth in the
midst of Holmesian internecine banter, asked, "Confound what,
Holmes? What on earth are you two talking about?"

"The waiter, man, the waiter. Last evening; at the Savoy.
You yourself remarked that he was about as qualified to wait table
as you were to be a circus acrobat." Sherlock jabbed his long, bony
index finger in the direction of Mycroft. "The waiter, Watson, was
an agent of my dear brother's. Enoch incarnate, if you will.
Mycroft, one day you will go too far."

Mycroft, laughing so hard that tears came to his eyes, held
up his hands in mock surrender "I give up! I give up! I do assure
you that it was not my intention to deliberately spoil your dinner,
or for that matter any part of your evening. Since you said 'one day
I shall go too far', may I assume that at least for the time being, I
remain in your good graces?"

"I should be inclined to confirm your good standing,"
Watson took a sip of his tea and peered over the rim of his cup at
Mycroft, "if you will kindly explain why a 'minor treasury
official', which is what you purport to be, would take such pains to
insinuate an agent into the Savoy Hotel dining room wait staff.
Surely D'Oyly Carte is not fiddling on his tax returns?"

Mycroft drew himself close to the table and motioned that
his brother and Watson should draw close as well. Lowering his
voice he began, "It's all quite hush, hush. In these matters one

21

cannot be too careful. Even here the walls may have un-welcome ears. Only the P.M., the First Lord, the Army C-I-C and small cadre working under me have any knowledge of what I'm about to tell you. You are the only two men outside of government and the military who will possess this knowledge. For some time," he went on, "I have been cognizant of a need for us to expand our intelligence gathering capability not only abroad, but also here at home. Even though we are more or less at peace..."

"Yes," Watson interjected, "but what of existing resources—Scotland Yard—I should think..."

"Hear me out." Mycroft placed his hand on Watson's arm. "The Home Secretary adamantly makes the very same argument. He wants to establish something which he is pleased to call 'Special Branch'—a sort of flying-squad of detectives to handle all domestic counter-espionage matters. I will not bore you with the details of the bureaucratic territorial war that ensued. I shall tell you only that the result was, as always, a compromise; all investigative work is to be done by my little cadre, but arrests can be made and prosecutions instigated only by The Yard under the direction of the Home Secretary. Whether this system will prove workable under the stress of an actual crisis remains to be seen. But there you have it."

"No, not quite all of it." Sherlock took out a vermeil cigarette case and held it toward the other two men. Mycroft pushed it away. "No, thank you. That's another habit I've been forced to give up. It's really too, too much. Not only am I forced to give up tobacco, but my physicians also insist that, weather permitting, I must walk at least half a mile per day. I do believe, Dr. Watson, that you medical men dream up these regimens as a means of testing your hapless patients' constitutions. If one can survive the treatment, one can surely survive the disease."

Sherlock, in deference to his brother's lament, snapped shut the case and, without taking a cigarette for himself, returned it to his pocket. "Tell us more about your 'little cadre'."

"There's not much more to tell. We're still in quite the formative stage. My idea is to recruit from the great universities a group of young men and, if I have my way, young women as well. These, among our best and brightest, would ordinarily go on to careers at the bar, or in medicine or industry. In some cases they

22

would opt anyway for careers in government service. In fact, I picked up your waiter from the foreign service examination list just a few weeks ago. Actually, he placed quite well, and had I not come along to save him from his fate, he would no doubt be preparing for his first posting as third-deputy-assistant to the commercial attaché at Her Majesty's Embassy in some pestilential hell-hole of a country half-way 'round the globe."

"Have you no qualms at all about this espionage business?" Watson asked. "Legal objections notwithstanding, while your brother and I have seen much of the seamy underside of society, it seems to me that spies, traitors, the whole sordid lot, are a cut or two below even the worst of the criminal class. The very idea of recruiting naive youths, no matter how well-educated, to catch-out or possibly themselves become espionage agents, I frankly find rather off-putting and certainly not a suitable enterprise in which Her Majesty's Government should be engaged. Really, Mr. Holmes."

Mycroft pushed back a bit from the table and locking his fingers together across his ample waist-coat turned to Sherlock. "And you, Sherlock, are those your sentiments as well?"

"You must admit, Mycroft, that Watson makes some valid points."

"Yes he does, Sherlock. And they are ones that have been debated in the Cabinet with the same ardor and articulateness as we have just heard. But before the two of you conclude that I'm some sort of Fagan picking innocent waifs off the street and turning them into pickpockets and footpads, let me make a few things plain to you. You would do well to keep them in mind because they bear directly on what you are about to undertake and forewarned, as they say, is forearmed."

Mycroft shifted in his seat. "I say, Watson, would you mind terribly pushing twice on that electrical call-button on the right-hand side of the P.M.'s desk pad. Watson rose to oblige and stepped to the mid-point of the table where the Prime Minister's chair and desk pad were situated. "Yes, yes. That's it. Just push the button twice. Good. Thank you." In a moment, the door through which Mycroft had entered the room opened and in came a young woman dressed in a simple gray dress with a bit of white trim around the neck and at the cuffs. "Yes, Mr. Holmes?" she asked, addressing Mycroft.

"Miss Davies," Mycroft twisted his bulk around in his chair so that he was nearly facing the young woman, "I believe I'm scheduled for a luncheon meeting with some sub-group or other of the inland revenue people?"

"Yes, sir. I believe it has to do with death duties and inheritance taxes."

"Well, ring up whomever is in charge and tell them I shan't be able to make it. By the way," turning back to his brother and Watson, "Sherlock, Dr. Watson, this is Miss Davies, my stenographer and type-writer operator. Be assured that I will not be sending her into the nether world of which we were just speaking. She's far too valuable to me in her present capacity. Although *I* am accused in some quarters of being the government, truth be known, it is really she who runs things." He looked down at the mass of papers still lying in a pile on the table in front of him. "It seems at times that all I do is sign these blasted papers. Sign this, initial that. I do it so much that I've taken to signing everything using just my first initial. My little group finds this curious practice so amusing that behind my back they've taken to referring to me simply as '*M*'."

At Mycroft's words of praise Miss Davies favored Sherlock and Watson with a smile that dimpled slightly blushing cheeks and showed even white teeth. "Very good, sir. Shall I also reschedule your 2:30 meeting at Admiralty House?"

"No, I think not, Miss Davies. That's one that I should like to keep. It will, I'm quite sure, be far more interesting than pouring over the Equitable Life Assurance Society's actuarial tables to determine how much revenue the government may anticipate from mortality taxes during the next fiscal year, or whatever may be on the agenda." After making a brief note on her pad, Miss Davies turned and left to carry out her appointed tasks.

Mycroft's demeanor once again turned serious. "Gentlemen, that bumbling waiter you saw last night, has a first in German literature, speaks German and at least three other languages fluently. He has in barely a fortnight learnt most of what there is that's useful to know about ciphers. Very soon he will begin training with an elite military group and will be taught

24

offensive and defensive unarmed combat techniques which even you, Sherlock, would find amazing. When it becomes necessary, he will become proficient in small arms and knife-fighting.

"Believe me, I know full-well the risks to which these young people are likely to be exposed. I do all that is possible to see that they are equipped to cope with those risks. I quite agree, Watson, this business of espionage and counter-espionage is a disgusting one and ought to be beneath the dignity of any civilized man or nation. The Foreign Office turns up its collective nose at the very idea, but to my mind they are feckless hypocrites. They condone without hesitation our training and employing Gurkhas and other indigenous troops, 'wogs', as they are pleased to call them. But they think it unseemly for us to train and employ our own to fight wars—not merely for some remote parcel of hardscrabble land—but wars which threaten our very existence as a nation. The military rails against it as well. Truthfully, I think they just want to run it. But despite all that, and the dubious legality as well, I assure you that the business is a necessary one.

"I apologise for babbling on like this, but I think it important that you know why it is that your government has felt it necessary to muck about in this most dismal swamp. We live in an era of rapid travel and communication. It sometimes frightens me to think what further innovations the coming century will bring. My meeting at Admiralty House this afternoon is with an Italian chap, name of Marconi, who claims to have invented, of all things, a wireless telegraph. If he's telling the truth, it's my task to sell the Royal Navy on giving it a try. Think of it: being able to communicate instantly with your fleet deployed at sea. With capability such as that, it will be possible to carry the battle to the enemy anywhere in the world in a matter of days.

"In this day and age, gentlemen, with such immense fire-power and logistical resources any potential enemy is a potentially deadly enemy. We simply cannot afford to remain ignorant of other possibly hostile nations' intentions and capabilities. The maxim that gentlemen do not read other gentlemen's correspondence, if ever it was valid, is today at best nostalgic, and at worst, treason by recklessness. It is with this prospect at hand that my little group was authorized and this 'minor treasury official' placed in charge. We have a budget, paltry though it is,

25

buried so deeply in the treasury estimates that even the permanent under-secretary is ignorant of its existence. Through my liaison with Admiralty and the CIC, I'm able from time to time to cage a bit of training or matériel out of their budgets which are nearly as penurious as mine."

"Thank you for the tour d' horizon," Sherlock said rising from his seat. "I trust that this officially-sanctioned paranoia will not lead us to seeing spies and agents-provocateur behind every elm tree and gorse-bush, or that our individual liberties will not be too greatly compromised in the process of preserving them."

"Your point is well-taken, Sherlock. But enough of this background. These ethical conundrums quite exhaust me. I can hear in them the faint echoes of the halcyon days of university debating societies. Come, gentlemen, the weather's tolerable for a change and it's time for my walk. Shall we adjourn to the garden?" Mycroft eased his body out of his chair and ambled toward the terrace door, Sherlock and Watson trailing dutifully behind.

Once outside, and having made his way somewhat laboriously down the steps to the gravel path, Mycroft noticed Sherlock glancing down at his breast-pocket. "Go on, Sherlock. You, too, Watson. You've been fondling your briar inside your coat pocket for the last half-hour at the least." As the two men lit up their respective smokes, Mycroft busied himself inspecting a bed of crocuses and daffodils that were just reaching the peak of their bloom.

As they resumed their walk, Mycroft took up the conversation. "I'm afraid I must begin with a further mention of last evening's dining experience. Although he does not know the reason, Mr. D'Oyly Carte has graciously agreed to train some of my people in the finer points of waiting table and housekeeping. He and I are friends, incidentally, out of our common interest in the so-called 'Savoy operas' of Sir William Gilbert and Sir Arthur Sullivan.

"The reason for this curious apprenticeship program is that hotels such as the Savoy and many restaurants are the best places we've found so far for picking up useful information. That is, of course, other than inside certain embassies where we have managed to insinuate a few of our people. Interesting though it is, I do not wish to burden you with any more knowledge in that direction.

"You are aware I'm sure that ever since his conviction, Dreyfus's family has never given up hope for his eventual exoneration. They are joined by a number of journalists and polemicists, as well as a growing number of influential persons both in France and here who are convinced that a great injustice has been done. You, of course," he paused and placed his arm across his brother's shoulders, "are more aware of the truth than anyone save Dreyfus himself and those responsible for his persecution."

"That is all too true," Sherlock replied. "As I confessed to Watson last night, no case in my entire career has caused me so much frustration for so long. I let it get the best of me last night and I took out my frustration on young Churchill. I trust he does not think too ill of me."

"Rest assured that he does not. In fact I should like to speak more of him before our business today is done. But do let me continue," Mycroft stopped and took out his watch. "Dear me. So much to do; so little time.

"Her Majesty's letter was quite frank. She feels a profound duty both to the memory of Disraeli—Lord Beaconsfield—and to the House of Rothschild. From my long years of service in Her Majesty's Government, it is my own view that her sentiment is amply warranted. Their respective contributions cannot be over-stated. Moreover, I wholly concur in her view that the Germans, in some Machiavellian fashion, are at the bottom of this Dreyfus business. So," he paused to more closely examine a budding rhododendron bush, "we have every reason, both moral and practical, to come to the aid of Captain Dreyfus and in so doing find out what it is that Grandson Willy and his monocled Visigoth band are up to. Not to put too fine a point on it, if we miscalculate, we may find ourselves in the not-too-distant future with Wilhelm on his *grosse-mutti's* throne, and we, gentlemen, will be conducting our business in German, rather than the language of Shakespeare, Dickens and Austen."

"You have seen the letter, then?" Sherlock asked.

"Yes I did," Mycroft replied. "I was flattered to have been asked to comment on it after it was written and before I placed it in

Churchill's hands for what I was certain would be delivery to the two of you. I did not, may I add, feel constrained to suggest that even one word be changed. Nor did Mr. Balfour with whom I discussed its contents."

"Why now?" Watson asked as he paused to refill his pipe. "Why after all these years? Would it not have been better to get at the truth when the evidence was fresh?"

Mycroft motioned toward a stone bench situated under a tree about six feet back from the gravel path. He took a seat on the bench and motioned for Watson to join him. Sherlock stood leaning against the tree. Turning to Watson, he continued, "There are several answers to your question. For one thing, Lord Rothschild was extremely reticent until just recently. For another, owing to the attitudes I described earlier, particularly in the case of the Foreign Office, no one within the government at the cabinet-secretary level thought there was any vital interest of ours at stake, although at the deputy and assistant level there was for a time some minor agitation in favor of finding out more. I was, I would say, the most outspoken in favour of pursuing the matter. The reason being, of course, that even before Sherlock reappeared at your consulting rooms, he had stopped off to let me know he was back, and thoroughly briefed me on what he had learnt. Since I could not risk compromising Sherlock, I was unable to provide the attribution which is necessary to lend credibility to so fantastic a story. Hence my views did not carry much weight. Based on bitter experience, I opted to live to fight another day. Finally, and most importantly, Sherlock had adamantly refused to get re-involved, and that left us with no one whose sponsorship we could plausibly deny, who had even the slightest chance of bringing the whole thing off and living to tell about it.

"As to why now, for one thing, Lord Rothschild has finally for whatever reasons determined to end his and his family's non-involvement. I don't know what his feelings may have been five years ago, but he has in the plainest terms made them known to us as well as Her Majesty. It was his idea to speak to The Queen, but he did so only after speaking with Mr. Balfour, who in turn consulted with me. Based on my advice, Balfour apprised Lord Rothschild that the Government would have no objection to his taking up the matter with her. I think Lord Rothschild is a practical man. He is mindful, as are we all, that Her Majesty is an elderly woman whose general health is not all that good. He fears, not without justification, that His Highness, The Prince of Wales, will be far less accessible to him, and if not totally indifferent to the special concerns of his Jewish subjects, at least not as sensitive as our beloved Queen. I do not like to use people," Watson and Sherlock, both gazed impassively at Mycroft as he said these words, "but I saw Lord Rothschild as the perfect agent to advance my own agenda. So when he came to Mr. Balfour, and Mr. Balfour asked my advice, I welcomed Lord Rothschild's initiative with arms wide-open. My soul is comforted in the knowledge that even though Lord Rothschild is serving my purposes, he is serving his own as well."

"No wonder," Sherlock remarked dryly, "that allusions to Machiavelli come so readily to your lips."

"Do not judge me too harshly, Sherlock, until you've heard me out." Mycroft, with Watson's aid, managed to stand up. "Come along, gentlemen, we've much ground, both territorial and conversational, yet to cover." Regaining the path, Mycroft continued his perambulation and discourse. "It has come to our attention that the French Government, with the reluctant acquiescence of the military, will soon succumb to the public pressure and grant Dreyfus a new trial. While the French President, *M.* Emile Loubet, is not what you would consider a 'Dreyfusard', neither is he to be counted among the lynch-mob, then or now."

Watson, busily reaming out his pipe bowl, asked, "Why not just let French military justice take its natural course? It seems to me that I read somewhere the fellow has a very able lawyer; what was his name? Oh yes. Demange, Edgar—or is it Edouard—Demange. Yes. That's it: *Maitre* Edgar Demange. Seems as though he's never given up either; stuck by his client all these years. He should, if you ask me, be held up as an example to some of the more reptilian denizens of our own Inns of Court."

Sherlock took the opportunity to light another cigarette. "Just so, Watson. I'm sure that Mycroft would quite agree with you but for the fact that in France, the term 'military justice', not unlike the corresponding systems in other countries, our own fair land included, is..." Sherlock paused, searching for a word, "an oxymoron."

Mycroft continued his brother's thought. "You are entirely correct. The military establishment is fundamentally incapable of grasping the many nuances embraced by the term 'justice.' The French military have learnt in the ensuing five years to live with Dreyfus's supposed treachery. Consider how Dreyfus came to be their scape-goat in the first place. It has been reported to me, through a channel I dare not name even to you, that someone remarked in Sandherr's presence that 'if he were wearing Dreyfus's skin, and were in fact innocent, he should shout his innocence to the world. Put up the fiercest struggle he knew how.' Sandherr, I'm told, responded that 'clearly you'—meaning his interlocutor—'do not know the mind of the Jew. The entire race,' he went on, 'is without pride, patriotism or honour. For centuries, to those who have offered them haven and allowed them to live freely in their midst, they have offered in return only betrayal.' Such, I fear, is still the prevailing mentality amongst the French military even today. They have their scape-goat and I expect they mean to stick with him.

"Gentlemen, we cannot rely on the French military to do the right thing today any more than we could five years ago. They'd sooner fall on their swords than admit that they were mistaken. No, my prediction is there will be some kind of 'white-wash' as the Americans say. I'd surmise that the government's already made some cowardly bargain that will free Dreyfus, but at the same time let the military save face."

Sherlock removed a cigarette and began absently tamping it on the case. "From what I know about Dreyfus, I shouldn't think that he'd have any part of such an under-handed deal as that."

Watson broke in, "You haven't considered what five years on Devil's Island can do to a man. Think of his wife and family. Why risk it? If four years on that miserable rock haven't robbed him of his reason, he'll take whatever deal is most likely to restore him to the embrace of his loving wife and children. What sane man wouldn't?"

Sherlock started to light his cigarette. "Nonsense, old man. Why he'd sooner..."

"Gentlemen, gentlemen." Mycroft held up his tiny palms. "My intuition tells me that it is improbable that Dreyfus himself will have any say in the matter. I think the decision is already

30

taken, and like it or not, Captain Dreyfus will soon be a free man, although it is unlikely to be on terms of his choosing."

His cigarette finally lighted, Sherlock asked, "Well, dear brother, if, to borrow yet another American term, the 'fix is in', what is our role in this farce? Are we to work the stalls hawking tea and sweets during intermission? Or did you have in mind something more substantive?"

"As it happens, I agree with you about Dreyfus. Given a say, Dreyfus is unlikely to accept a 'white-wash,' and when free will continue to try and clear his name. Nor do I think that the Rothchilds are willing to accept such a facile solution. They cannot accept a result which does not remove any and all stains on the character of Dreyfus, and by extension, on the character of Jews everywhere, and French Jews in particular. Anti-Semitism requires only the pretense of justification, if even that, to flare up in ways that are too monstrous to even contemplate. By way of example, look at what is happening in Russia. Those pogroms...well..."

Watson began once again to fill his pipe. "We surely take your point. But apart from being driven by concerns for justice and humanity, what national interests of ours are at stake? I don't want to appear obtuse, but..."

Mycroft came to a stop, clearly fatigued from the brief walk. He placed an arm around Sherlock's shoulders, leaning on him for support. Watson took Mycroft's free arm at the wrist and took out his watch in order to measure Mycroft's pulse. "Perhaps we should send for assistance?"

Mycroft took a couple of shallow breaths, "No, no, I'll be al-right in a few moments. I do not understand this obsession with exercise that seems to infect all physicians. Exercise..." he paused again for breath, "in my opinion, is the means by which we punish our bodies for the crime of growing old." He removed his arm from his brother's shoulders, and took a deep breath. "Thank you, I think we can resume now."

He hunched his shoulders and started walking again. "To continue what I was saying, the point of the matter is this: we need to know with certainty who's behind this farce and why. For all their resources and determination, the Dreyfuses and the Rothschilds are not very likely to ever find that out. They are amateurs. They haven't a clew where or even how to look for the

31

truth. They consult spiritualists, and for all I know, Gypsy fortune tellers; they'll be easy marks for every charlatan on the Continent.

"One of my operatives overheard a dinner conversation between two German diplomats at the Connaught within just the last week. Ostensibly, these two chaps are commercial attaches facilitating trade. My chap, affecting a Cockney accent, and being fully fluent in German, managed to listen to a good bit of their conversation which, for two innocent fellows helping flog office machines abroad, sounded to our chap awfully like a couple of clandestine agents talking shop. The gist of the dialogue, which my man memorized nearly verbatim as he has been trained to do, is that the Junkers who dominate the military high command are in a highly over-wrought state in contemplation of this latest chapter in the Dreyfus saga. The Germans mistakenly discount the 'white-wash' scenario, and are genuinely concerned that some deep dark secret or other will this time be exposed. Evidently, the Germans are so desperate that they have considered options including a commando-style raid on Devil's Island to kidnap Dreyfus, leaving behind various religious paraphernalia so as to suggest that Dreyfus's co-religionists were responsible, as well as plausible ideas such as murdering von Schwarzkoppen, making it look like a suicide in which he leaves behind a note confessing his role and implicating Dreyfus once more as the traitorous co-conspirator.

"Gentlemen," Mycroft rubbed the sides of his nose with his forefingers, "your Country wants..." he paused, shifting his gaze from Watson to Sherlock, "no, your Country *must* know what secret has gotten the Germans' wind up." In a surprising gesture, he seized a lapel of each man's jacket, "Find out what in damnation is going on!"

"And how," Sherlock asked mildly as he disengaged his lapels from Mycroft's fingers, "do you propose we go about doing that?"

"That, dear brother, is for you to say. You know how intensely I dislike the legwork that goes with your chosen occupation. No, I must have nothing to do with that. I'm afraid you're quite on your own. Moreover, should you and your retinue be exposed or captured, the Foreign Secretary—or the Government, I should say—will disavow any knowledge of your purpose."

"Retinue, Mycroft?" Sherlock's features hardened as he leaned toward his brother, his face pausing only inches away from his sibling, "And just what *retinue* would that..."

"Oh, yes," Mycroft glanced at his watch again, "I thought I might send Mr. Churchill along..."

Watson, who had just lighted his pipe, gasped and coughed, "Surely, sir, you must be joking. Why..."

Sherlock's face was a study in disbelief "You will, I trust, provide him with an ample supply of shillings for the trip? Or shall Watson and I have to feed and lodge him as well as change his nappies?".

Watson, his coughing fit nearly subsided, went on. "Why not a brass band to see us off? Perhaps a piece or two by Elgar. Why not a little Wagner to put us in the proper frame of mind?"

"Mycroft, you have impressed upon us the importance of this undertaking. For myself, and I believe that I speak for Watson as well," Watson, his pipe clenched in his teeth and his arms folded across his chest, nodded his assent, "Her Majesty's wish is our command. When our Country calls, we hear but one voice even if it chooses to speak through my addle-brained brother. But if you wish for the success of our mission and if in your heart you earnestly wish for the safe return of your mother's youngest son and his dearest companion, do not, I implore you, weight us down with the baggage of any of your trainees, including young Mr. Churchill. He seems bright and eager enough, and no doubt he'll go far in the world, that is unless he gets himself killed in some dare-devil adventure. Pack him off to South Africa; better yet, stand him for Parliament. Surely there's a nice, safe seat in a coming by-election..."

Mycroft consulted his watch again and tugged at the bottom of his waist-coat. "As you wish, Sherlock. "Turning to Watson he extended his hand, "Watson, Sherlock trusts no man more than you. Watch his back." Turning to Sherlock, he embraced him briefly once again and then held him at arms' length. "If I may borrow a phrase from a message you recently received, *'Godspeed and good hunting'.* "

CHAPTER THREE

*"I must confess I'm at a loss to know where to
begin to unravel this Gordian knot."*

After their meeting with Mycroft, the two men had returned to
Baker Street. Watson allowed that he'd had rather a restless night
and would find a nap most beneficial. Holmes, who when his mind
was engaged slept little if at all, indicated that he would like to
study some of his old notes and give some thought to how they
ought to go about dealing with the matter to which they were now
committed.

Some two hours later, refreshed by his nap, Watson filled
his pipe and ambled into the parlor intending to have a pre-prandial
gin and tonic, a habit acquired as a result of serving in India. He
found Holmes recumbent on the sofa, his head propped up by a
pillow made from a scrap of Kilim carpet. A jumble of papers lay
on his chest and stomach and still others were scattered on the
floor about him. He'd been smoking his calabash pipe. In the still
air a seemingly palpable layer of blue-white smoke hung over the
room just at Watson's eye-level. Wielding the edge of his hand like
a machete, he cleaved a path through the fog to the liquor cabinet,
leaving behind a wake of swirls and eddies.

"Fix you a drink, old man?"

"A bit of whisky and a splash of soda would do nicely.
Make it the single-malt. Lowland if we have it." Holmes yawned
and rotated his chin from one shoulder to the other to alleviate the
stiffness that comes from lying motionless for a long period of
time. By the time Watson handed him his drink, he'd managed to
make it to a sitting position and deposit his papers like
antimacassars on the arms and back of the sofa.

Drink in hand, Watson took his arm chair opposite the sofa.
"I must confess that I'm at a loss to know where to begin to
unravel this Gordian knot. As you yourself have remarked so many
times, a cold trail is no trail at all. And if memory serves, there
can't be but a mere handful of cases over the years which have

taken more than a few days. But I see by the state of your notes that you've been giving the problem a good bit of thought as well. Other than the fact that we obviously have to go to Paris, have you had any further ideas?"

"As a general proposition, I quite agree with you, and the general rule in this instance may yet prove to be applicable. But my sense is that whatever was going on then continues even today. Unless Mycroft's man's German is not as good as my brother is led to believe, one must conclude that the Germans are greatly concerned about something. To think that my fantastic suggestion about storming Devil's Island is actually being mooted about by them must be indicative of something."

"Even if the trail is still warm, and I'm prepared to accept that it is," Watson paused and took a sip of his cocktail, "isn't our going there openly and poking about going to drive the cockroaches back into the woodwork, as it were? I'd thought, as I'm sure you have, that disguises might do the job, but while you speak the language like a native, my French is limited to reading restaurant menus and wine labels and not much else and my accent is what is commonly described as 'atrocious'."

"Once again I'm dazzled by the agility of your mind. You're right on all counts." Holmes laid aside his pipe and took a taste of his scotch. "So unless you are prepared to learn your tenses and declensions overnight, we'll have to try an alternative approach. I think, perhaps we should turn our supposed weakness into a strength. Our weakness, obviously, is that my name and face—as is yours to nearly the same extent—are as well known in every capital on the Continent as they are known in London."

"True," Watson replied, "but how can we use that to our advantage? Surely, if we arrive in Paris under the present circumstances, no one—especially those whose purpose is to conceal the truth—will be misled as to our intentions."

"Just so, old chap. That's what we're counting on. Think about the grouse, a reasonably intelligent bird, as birds go. You've been grouse hunting. With their winter plumage they are nearly indistinguishable from the underbrush that is their habitat. Yet what do they do when the hunter approaches? Instead of relying on their camouflage, their best defence, their fear makes them take flight. And the result is one pull on your Purdy's 20-gauge, and in no time at all they're in your game-bag. If things go well, I expect that whomever is directing this 'passion play'—as Her majesty so aptly puts it—will behave exactly like your grouse."

"So you propose that we simply go to Paris, announce our mission and wait about the train station to see who leaves on the first north-bound train?" Watson took a generous pull on his drink and wondered to himself whether there was any truth to the cliché about there being a fine line between genius and madness.

Holmes lit a cigarette from the box on the mantle. Pleased as always by his friend's down-to-earth attitude, he paused as though pondering Watson's idea. "You know, old chap, it might work at that. We could disguise you as the conductor. Can you remember *'billet, si'l vous plait, billet...?'"* Watson, as he lit his pipe, was silently relieved to know that Holmes was indulging in a bit of drollery and had not gone "round the bend."

Holmes picked up his drink and began pacing the room. "No, I think that we shall have to be a bit more subtle than that. If we are too direct in making known our mission, whoever it is that will be reacting to us may just remain in the underbrush and wait us out. It's a strange game we're playing here, one whose rules are made up as the play progresses. And we have only the vaguest notion of who our opponents are. "'Pon my oath, Watson, it reminds me of the mind-games that I used to engage in with the late, unlamented Professor..." Holmes paused... "Moriarty. This business is equally complex and as I've already warned you, just as deadly.

"I think, Watson, we must go to Paris as a couple of innocents abroad. Two middle-age *bon vivants* tired of the miserable London weather. Think of it. May in Paris. Why I believe, if we're lucky, the chestnuts are still in blossom. Yes, that's it: May in Paris; chestnuts in blossom; perhaps a sidewalk-cafe table under a tree; a *Pernod* at hand; the lovely *mademoiselles* in their spring frocks..."

Watson, having third-thoughts about Holmes's mental state, finished his drink in a single swallow. "Charming, Holmes, charming. And how, pray tell, will our adversaries know that this idyll, the prospect of which—despite your overwrought description—does not seem at all unpleasant, is but a clever ruse calculated to mask our true purpose."

Holmes made a mock bow and resumed his seat on the sofa. "We shall, of course, have to help them without their knowing it. They shall have to figure out for themselves what the purpose of our sojourn to the 'City of Lights' truly is. We shall give them hints—broad ones at that—but unless they believe that they've seen through us without our knowing, I don't fancy the odds of our plan succeeding."

"I must say, Holmes, this is all quite beyond me. If I understand you rightly, you're proposing that we go to Paris for what to all outward appearances is a spring-time holiday, although those whom we seek to deceive, are unlikely to believe for a moment that our purpose is what it appears. Then, to make certain that our adversaries are not deceived, you plan to reveal to them in some subtle but unmistakable way that their suspicions are not unfounded. Will you be so kind, as we go along, to take care that I understand which role we are playing at any given time? I should hate to be caught in my natural *bon vivant* state when I should be playing the bumbling police inspector, or vice-versa. Just how is it that you propose we go about informing those whom we wish to inform of our intentions, without them knowing that we know we are informing them? Watson placed his hands on either side of his head, "I must confess that the task, as you've outlined it, seems even more daunting than your 'swimming with sharks' metaphor of last night."

"Let us hope then that there are others who are even more bewildered." During Watson's disquisition Holmes had begun picking up his papers and restoring them to some semblance of order. "I say, Watson, have you seen the telegraph message pad?"

"I think it's on the secretary; look under that stack of *Lancets*. Shall I go down and see if there's an 'Irregular' lurking about?"

"No, no... Ah! Here it is just where you said. We shall be wanting to go out to dine soon enough, so we just as well drop it off ourselves."

Watson had risen and started toward the bow window to see if there were any street arabs about, as there usually were, who for a shilling would have taken the message to the nearby telegraph office for dispatch. When Holmes declined his offer, he veered instead to the bar and fixed a fresh round of drinks. Handing

Holmes his whisky and soda, he prompted, "You were about to tell me how we are going to pretend to be what we are busy pretending not to be, and at the same time avoid looking like utter fools."

Holmes, seated at the secretary, was busily writing out a telegram. He held up his free hand, "A moment, old fellow. Let me finish this." A few moments later he lay down his pen, tore the message from the pad and folded it into his unbuttoned waist-coat. Removing his reading glasses, he returned to the sofa. "You recall, I'm sure, the good Dr. Mortimer of Devonshire." As Watson nodded, Holmes continued, "I'm equally sure that you remember his referring to me as the 'second highest expert in Europe.' And do you recall upon whom he saw fit to bestow the ultimate accolade?"

Watson leaned back in his chair, and pressed his finger tips to his forehead. "No... Wait! Yes, the Frenchman. Bertillon, *M'sieur* Alphonse Bertillon. The fellow who invented that business of measuring the circumference of one's head and the length of his nose, and I can't recall what else. Even wrote a book about it. Calls it 'anthropometric measurements'. Never did catch on here, although I seem to have read somewhere that the State of Illinois, in America, was trying to make use of it."

"If I recall," Watson paused and for a moment closed his eyes better to remember, "even you expressed a rather unbridled enthusiasm in describing its potential."

"You're referring, I assume, to the time we discussed *M'sieur* Bertillon during the train down to Woking to pull Percy Phelps's chestnuts out of the fire. I'm horrified to learn, after all these years, that you took my remarks literally and not sarcastically as I had intended."

"That occasion being ten years ago come this summer, perhaps I didn't know you as well as I fancy that I do today. I must admit as I recall the occasion I was quite taken aback by your effusiveness in praising the bloke. For my own part, I thought the whole concept was crack-brained. I feel the same even today. But what, may I ask, does *M'sieur* Bertillon have to do with what we're preparing to undertake? As we sit at our sidewalk table sipping our *Pernods,* are we to hail every tenth passer-by and ask him his hat size?"

Holmes replied with just the slightest tinge of asperity, "I surmise, dear fellow, that you've been reading Charles Sanders Peirce again."

"You make it seem as though reading Peirce is as disreputable as the salacious magazines the booksellers keep in their stockrooms or under the cash register stand. Actually, if you do not allow yourself to get bogged down in the drivel about 'semiotics', his 'pragmatist' philosophy has much to commend it."

"Whatever you say, Watson. I shall leave the realm of modern Western philosophers to you. In any case, I shall respond to your question in due course. For now, however, let it suffice that we're going to pay a call on the 'highest expert in Europe' day after tomorrow. In fact," Holmes patted the telegraph message sheet in his waist-coat pocket, "this telegram is to announce our coming visit and to beg him to receive us.

"With your permission, I will defer additional explanation tonight, but promise to enlighten you tomorrow. Just now, my brain is keenly feeling the effects of the last several hours of mental gymnastics, not to mention two whiskies, and my stomach tells me that it is quite ready to receive sustenance whilst I give my brain a rest. Ever since Mycroft made mention of Simpson's, I've been in a carnivorous mood. What say you to a slab of prime-rib?"

"Excellent idea, Holmes. Give me ten minutes and I shall be as ready as you. In the meantime, unless you've done so already, we ought to let Mrs. Hudson know of our impending departure. Shall I join you downstairs?"

Holmes adjusted the knot of his tie, buttoned his waist-coat and slipped into his suit jacket. Picking up his hat and walking stick he said, "Consider it done. I will see you downstairs. Perhaps we shall be lucky and find a cab without having to walk as far as Oxford Street."

Having apprised Mrs. Hudson that he and Watson had made a spur-of-the-moment decision to visit the Continent for a brief holiday and would be departing in the morning, Holmes went out the door to await Watson. As he stood on the step, a hansom ground to a stop just at the kerb, and Churchill debouched at the same time Watson was making his way out the door. "Gentlemen, 'looks as though I've arrived just in time. I should not want to spend another evening replicating last night's experience."

39

Watson gave Churchill his most disapproving look, the one normally reserved for patients who fail to adhere to his treatment regimen, "I say, young man, Mr. Holmes and I were just on our way to dinner, and..."

"Why thank you, Dr. Watson, I'd be delighted to join you. I've the most exciting news."

Holmes and Watson, both totally at a loss for words, looked at one another, shrugged and motioned Churchill to get back in the cab. Somehow the three men all managed to squeeze into the cab in varying degrees of discomfort. As the cab did an about-face, Watson instructed the driver as to their destination in The Strand across from Charing Cross Station.

Upon arriving at Simpson's they were seated straight away at a window table in the spacious, paneled first-floor dining room. Declining drinks, they each ordered the establishment's celebrated prime rib with Yorkshire pudding and vegetables *du jour*. Holmes selected a '92 claret from a small estate in the southern-most part of Bordeaux north of Pau where he had spent a portion of his early childhood.

Churchill turned toward Holmes, "You said something last night, Mr. Holmes, that I found most curious."

"Apart from my reaction to your mention of the unfortunate French artillery captain?"

"Yes, sir. When the discussion turned to the captain I quite forgot to ask you what you meant by your reference to Kitchener's triumph as the 'last great cavalry battle'. Perhaps I misunderstood..."

"No, you heard me correctly. Given the military's interest in the application of the newest technology to the development of even more efficient killing machines, how long will it take for the internal combustion engine to replace the horse?"

"I see what you're getting at, Holmes," Watson interjected. "Perhaps motorized lorries to carry troops and supplies. Horses are, after all, expensive to acquire and maintain and are not always reliable."

"That's true, Watson. But I was thinking also about cannon and machine guns mounted on motorized vehicles, perhaps even armoured vehicles."

"I understand now, Mr. Holmes, but I wonder..."

"Enough for now, Mr. Churchill. I see that the carving cart is about to arrive."

The beef carved and served *au jus,* and the wine poured, a toast was drunk to the health of each and the three men settled in to the business at hand. After the entree dishes were cleared a wedge of Stilton was ordered along with biscuits and port. Watson contemplating a biscuit spread with the Stilton, turned to Churchill, "Come now Mr. Churchill, what is this momentous news you bring us?"

His face slightly reddened from the wine, the excitement of the moment or both, Churchill sat erect in his chair, squared his shoulders and replied, "the most wonderful thing has happened. Mr. Robert Ascroft, one of the two Members for Oldham has died suddenly."

Holmes nudged Watson's leg under the table. "You don't say, Mr. Churchill. I shouldn't think the grieving widow would look upon it as such a joyous occasion. Or perhaps she's a young attractive second wife and he's left her a vast legacy. Do you and she plan to wed as soon as she can shed her widow's weeds without causing too great a scandal?"

"Oh no! Oh no!" Churchill, his hand shaking so that he could scarcely lift the glass to his lips, took a deep swallow of his port. "You misunderstand me, Mr. Holmes. I meant... no... I didn't... that didn't... come out as I intended. It's a great shame that Mr. Ascroft has died. He was a Party stalwart and served his constituency ably for many years. I know nothing of his personal life, but I'm sure his widow, if indeed he left one, is most terribly distraught."

"The *good* news, at least for me, is that the Party leadership has asked me to stand for his seat in the by-election which will be called for just a few weeks hence. I'm given to understand that it's a safe seat, but I shall campaign day and night anyway. My late father, as you know, served in Parliament for many years and was from time to time given responsible positions in the Government. I've always wanted to follow in his footsteps, and I suppose even surpass his accomplishments, if the truth be known. I have no idea whether my political career shall ever amount to much, but I shall certainly do my utmost. As this is my first opportunity, I hope you'll pardon my excitement."

As Churchill spoke of his aspirations, Watson and Holmes finished what was left of the cheese course and Watson signaled the waiter for sweets and coffee. "Tell me," Holmes asked, "how did you come to learn of this great news? Have you any idea to what or whom you owe your—as you put it—good fortune?"

"I'm afraid, sir that I can answer only your first question. Were it in my power to answer both, I should gladly do so. As to the first, I was requested to call on your brother, Mr. Holmes, late this afternoon in Downing Street. He gave me two... good heavens! In the excitement I've quite forgotten about them." Churchill reached inside his suit coat and brought out two envelopes which he handed to Holmes and Watson. "I was directed to bring these to you as I understand you'll be needing them tomorrow. Mr. Holmes, that is—I mean—your brother, Mr. Mycroft Holmes, informed me that before I left Mr. Balfour would like a word with me in the Cabinet Room."

"I was escorted up to the ground floor and shown straight-away into the Cabinet Room. Mr. Balfour himself informed me of my selection. But when I ventured to ask to whom I should be conveying my deep appreciation, all he would tell me is that certain very influential persons thought me 'a-comer' and that I should make the best of the opportunity. Except to wish me 'good luck' that's all he would say and the interview was concluded just that quickly. From there I came directly to Baker Street, where it was my further good fortune to meet up with you as I did."

"Well then, congratulations Mr. Churchill." Holmes motioned for the sommelier. "I should say that a toast is in order. Let us have a bottle of the...let's see...yes! The Pol Roger '97 will do nicely."

As the wine steward hurried off to fulfill Holmes's order, Watson, who was as relieved as Holmes, added his congratulations, "Congratulations indeed, Mr. Churchill. No doubt we shall soon be referring to you as 'The Right-Honourable Mr. Churchill.'"

Churchill's demeanor grew more serious. "I thank you, Dr. Watson, Mr. Holmes, for your good wishes and kind words. I hope that I shall continue to deserve them and to merit the continued confidence of the unseen hand or hands that have given such a dramatic boost to my career. I don't know whether I shall be elected, or if elected, whether I shall serve my entire incumbency as a back-bencher. I do fervently hope that I shall have the opportunity, some day, to help shape our nation's governing policy."

At Churchill's words, Holmes too grew serious. Planting his palms on the table, he leaned across toward Churchill, "Well-spoken, Mr. Churchill. Promise us that we shall be invited to hear your maiden speech.

"But now I see that our wine has arrived." After the sommelier had finished pouring, the three men raised their flutes, and Holmes made the toast, "To the late, lamented Mr. Ascroft, and to his soon-to-be most worthy successor."

"And may I add," Churchill intervened, "To the gallant French artillery captain whose plight has brought me to your door."

CHAPTER FOUR

"Merci, gentlemen. Merci, beaucoup. If your destination is Paris, possibly we shall see one another again."

*T*he car-porter stowed their *portmanteaux* in the overhead racks. Pocketing the proffered gratuity, he wished Holmes and Watson a pleasant journey. The two men settled into the brocade seats of their first-class compartment just as the departure whistle sounded and the morning London-to-Paris, via Folkestone and Boulogne, boat-train laboured its way out of Victoria Station. Each man carried in his pocket next to his passport and ready money, an international letter of credit in his favor issued by Cox & Co., Bankers, London, as well as a telegram confirming his reservation at The Hotel Ritz, No. 15 Place Vendome, Paris, for a stay of indeterminate length.

Following dinner, Churchill took his leave saying that he was off to his mother's residence in Great Cumberland Place as he had not had an opportunity to tell her his news. Wishing him well, and enjoining him, once again, not to mention their business to anyone, Holmes and Watson found a cab and returned to Baker Street, with a brief stop along the way to get off the telegram to *M'sieur* Bertillon. Upon reaching their rooms, they had examined the contents of the envelopes given them by Churchill during dinner. In addition to the letters of credit and reservation confirmations, the envelopes contained one-way, first-class tickets for the train which was now crossing the river and making its way through the wharves, warehouses and working-class precincts of South London.

"I can scarcely imagine," Watson remarked as he finished lighting his pipe, "what 2000 pounds expense money, first-class boat-train tickets and reservations at the Ritz must have done to Mycroft's *'paltry'* departmental budget."

Holmes, who had just begun perusing the agony columns of the *Daily Mail,* lowered his newspaper and peering over his reading glasses regarded his friend for a long moment before replying. "You might do well, if I may so suggest, to re-examine the assumption underlying your statement. Either Mycroft, through his years of service in the treasury department, has grown so inured to the public's anguish at tax-time that his fiscal compass is all but lost, or someone else, accountable only to himself, is the true source of my brother's apparent largesse.

"I suppose I do not mind spending the Rothschilds' money," Holmes continued, "assuming, that is, that there are no strings attached. That much we shall clear up upon our arrival in Paris. But what truly has me clenching my jaws—besides the enormity of the task facing us—is my dear brother's affecting the character and habits of the *Grand Pooh-Bah,* of his beloved Gilbert and Sullivan. Despite his self-deprecating facade, he fancies himself both omniscient and omnipotent. I trust that at least he will avoid the more avaricious aspects of his exalted role model.

"Although we are both middle-aged men, and there is less than six years difference in our ages, he still feels as though he must treat me like his younger brother. Did you notice, Watson, that our tickets were purchased and the letters of credit issued over a week ago? And I've no doubt that the reservations at the Ritz were made as early as two nights ago as a result of our dinner table comments at the Savoy. *Grand Pooh-Bah* indeed." Holmes readjusted his glasses and returned to his newspaper, leaving Watson to gaze at the passing Kentish country-side and ponder this latest revelation of his friend's persona.

By the time they finished a light luncheon in the dining car, the train had arrived at Folkestone. Their luggage was collected by the porter as they left the train for the short walk to the cross-channel ferry which would carry them to the port of Boulogne-sur-Mer. After once again presenting their passports and tickets, they were allowed to board the ferry where they found a comfortable banquette in the boat-deck saloon and soon settled in, cigars in hand, for the crossing.

As the ship got underway and cleared the mole, a stiff quartering wind blew up from the southwest serrating the gray-green channel waters and making the broad-beamed, shallow-draft vessel seem as though it were rolling across cobblestones instead of ocean waters. The sensation was accentuated by the vibration of the ship's engines as her captain attempted to maintain course and headway without coming full a-beam of the wind. Watson made a few attempts to hold his cigar between his forefinger and middle-finger, but finding it awkward, reverted to the more conventional practice. That too was soon abandoned as the effects of the captain's yielding more and more of his ship's keel to the wind began to be felt by the passengers. Holmes fared no better than Watson. He soon abandoned his cigar as well, exchanging it for a bicarbonate of soda which he obtained from a passing steward, and quickly downed in hopes of settling his stomach.

The experienced chief steward, recognizing that conditions were ripe for a general outbreak of *mal-de-mer*, prudently shut down the bar. And, he told himself, if the managing director back in London wants to complain about slow liquor sales in the first-class saloon, let him put up with the stench and the griping by the under-stewards as they tried to clean up the mess left by a gaggle of sea-sick passengers.

Holmes and Watson were seated on the port side of the saloon on a banquette which ran around the perimeter of the cabin beneath rows of windows in the starboard and port walls. Netting was strung among the ceiling joists, and suspended in the netting were life-jackets to be used by the first-class passengers in the event of a ship-abandoning emergency. These swayed back and forth in opposition to the rolling of the vessel, and tended to exacerbate the effect of the vessel's roll. Deciding that conversation under the circumstances was probably not the best of ideas, in a determined but largely futile effort to concentrate his attention on anything save the motion of the ship, Watson began looking about the cabin intending to practice his divining skills on his fellow passengers. At sailing time the saloon had been crowded with nearly all the seats being occupied. But, since the sea had turned rough, a fair number had gone below seeking out the water closets, and others, of perhaps a hardier constitution, had forsaken the somewhat close quarters of the cabin for the space and fresh air of the boat deck itself, so that barely half the original complement of passengers remained. Of those remaining only a few were of any particular interest.

To Watson's left on the banquette, was a pale, bespectacled man dressed in a long, black frock coat and broad-brimmed, beaver-trimmed hat from which protruded long, dark curls framing both sides of his face. He sat staring straight ahead, his knees pressed tightly together. In his lap he had a leather gladstone on top of which he held his hands, his thumbs threaded through the leather-clad metal handles. Not much challenge there, Watson thought to himself; obviously a Hassidic Jew; a diamond merchant, certainly; perhaps a rabbi; possibly both.

On the starboard banquette directly opposite Holmes and Watson a young man, judging by the quality of his traveling cloak and hat, a gentleman of some social status sat engrossed in reading a newspaper. There was not much to observe as he was wrapped in his traveling cloak and wore a hat pulled down low on his brow and gloves that covered his hands all the way above the wrists. Yet any diversion, like any port in a storm, would serve the purpose, so Watson focused his entire energy in trying to create a mental image of the young man out of an occasional glimpse of a rather smallish boot-clad foot peeking our from beneath the cloak, or a brief flash of chin and a somewhat incongruous-looking mustache and neatly-trimmed Van Dyke beard revealed whenever the fellow would lower the newspaper to turn the page.

Watson turned his attention back to Holmes thinking he would elicit his companion's opinion on the subjects of his scrutiny. Holmes, however, had left his seat and was standing at the bar in front of the aft bulkhead smoking a cigarette and gazing absently into the mirror behind the bar. Seeing that Holmes was evidently lost in his own thoughts, Watson continued his study of the other passengers in the hope of finding someone who was more challenging than the devout diamond merchant, yet less inscrutable than the young gentleman. There were two clerics of the Roman Church in cassocks and flat, wide-brim hats. From the red piping and sash worn by the older of the two, Watson judged him to be a monsignor and the younger man his aide or secretary. Two swarthy men in fezzes were seated in the forward facing rows of seats. Neither was handling the motion of the ship well at all, and were, by Watson's cursory reckoning, probably Turkish or Persian rug merchants.

Toward the starboard side near the young man there was an elderly man in a high-backed wooden wheel-chair. He was attended by a female nurse who had prudently aligned the chair wheels with the ship's keel, lest her charge careen back and forth with each roll of the vessel. The man, Watson concluded, was probably headed to Spa to take the waters, even though it was a bit early for the season. But the fellow was certainly going for his health and not the wretchedly-excessive social season for which the baths provided an opulent and slightly erotic setting.

Little could be seen of the man as he too wore a hat which was pulled down low over his forehead and cast his face in shadow. He was wrapped from his chin to his ankles in a dark, heavy robe from which protruded only his gloved hands and booted feet, these having been arranged in a splayed position on the wheel-chair footrests. Watson could tell he was an elderly man only from the wisps of thin white hair poking out from under his hat, the tufts of bristly hair protruding from his ear and the black and white stubble on his chin which occasionally became visible when the man raised his head from the folds of the paisley-patterned muffler wound round his neck.

Periodically, he would slump further and further down in his chair until Watson thought surely he would slide all the way to the floor and possibly break his fragile legs in the process. But each time, the nurse, at seemingly the last possible moment, would grasp him at his axilla and restore him to something approaching an upright posture. She would then produce a cloth which she would use to wipe the corners of his mouth and his chin where spittle would collect during each posture-righting interval.

The nurse was an interesting study herself. She was a large woman; indeed she would be considered a large man. She was dressed in the standard garb of her vocation and carried a reticule hanging from a strap on her shoulder. In her other hand she carried a newish-looking gladstone, which Watson surmised held medication and medical paraphernalia for her patient. Her hair was pinned up beneath her cap exposing her muscular neck. Watson also observed that even though the woman had evidently made some effort at grooming—plucking her eyebrows and applying a bit of rouge to her cheeks and lip-rouge to her mouth—the sum total was singularly unappealing from a man's perspective.

As Watson speculated about the nurse's ethnic background, the ship's captain decided he could make better headway by tacking rather than trying to maintain a linear course. Apparently unable to effect the desired course correction by steering alone, he

48

cut back the power to the starboard engine. This had the desired effect from a navigational perspective, and produced no untoward side-effects among the seasoned sailors on the bridge. The same could not, however, be said for the hapless passengers, at least those in the first-class saloon. The manoeuvre reduced the ship's speed to dead slow just as it came full a-beam of the wind and sea. This caused the vessel to heel violently first to port then to starboard, and back to port as the laws of physics applied themselves to restore the keel to equilibrium.

Being experienced passengers, Holmes and Watson had adjusted fairly well to the rough voyage. While they were not exactly enjoying themselves, their degree of discomfort was far less than the majority of their fellow passengers. The ill-executed course correction had caused several more of the passengers to dash from the saloon, hands-over-mouths, out to the boat deck. The young man, however, in keeping with his apparent genteel station, chose instead to pass out slowly rolling from his perch on the banquette to the cabin floor, coming to rest between the base of the banquette and the wheel-chair.

Seeing his predicament, Holmes and Watson both sprang to his aide crowding past the wheel-chair. Gently they lifted him from the floor and laid him out on the cushioned banquette. Oddly, his hat had not been dislodged in the fall. Holmes quickly un-fastened his cloak. As he did so Watson turned to the nurse who to that point had done nothing except to gape in the universal manner of witnesses to any sudden unfortunate event that happens to someone else. Instantly assuming his professional demeanor, Watson asked the nurse, "do you have any ammonium carbonate in your bag?" The woman looked at him blankly. "I'm a physician, but I'm on holiday so I haven't brought my bag. Please, madam. I asked for ammonium carbonate. Don't you hear?" Watson was becoming angry at the woman's indifference. "You are bound by the same oath as I. Are you as uncaring about the needs of your own patient? Nurse, this young man could be in great distress breathing. Indeed if not restored to consciousness immediately, he may asphyxiate in his own gastric fluids."

While Watson was imploring the nurse, Holmes had returned to the bar and located a water pitcher and drinking glass both of which he was bringing back to the banquette. Watson turned to the chair-bound man who at this point had slumped so far down as to be indistinguishable from a heap of old rags. He even gave off the aroma of naphthalene moth-proofing crystals the effect of which was to remind Watson of a pile of discarded clothing moldering in the bottom of his spare closet. "Please, sir, no medical bag is without smelling salts. Surely you can allow us to borrow them for this urgent purpose."

Wordlessly, the invalid raised a palsied hand in some sort of signal to the nurse who somehow interpreted it to mean acquiescence. She immediately opened the bag and after some rummaging within, finally produced a new vial of smelling salts which she silently handed to Watson. Having apparently received another signal from her charge, she snapped the bag shut and got up from her seat. Brushing past the returning Holmes she took her place behind the wheel-chair which she then proceeded to turn about and push to the front of the cabin.

Watson quickly opened the vial and passed it under the young man's nose as Holmes raised his head off the banquette. After a few moments, his eyelids began to flutter as he returned to sentience. Not quite recovered, he looked up and saw Watson and Holmes and attempted to scream. All he could manage, however, was a sort of gasping sob. The two men propped him up to a more-or-less sitting position, and Holmes handed him a glass of the water indicating that he should attempt to drink.

When his breathing had apparently returned to normal, Holmes asked him, *"comment allez vous?"*

"Je ne sais pas," he replied. Then, noticing the two men's English-style clothing, repeated in English, "I don't feel very well. But thanks to you gentlemen," he managed a wan smile, "I think, perhaps that I shall live."

"Je suis un... un...," Watson struggled for a word, "I am a doctor, a physician. I'm sorry my French is not so good. But if I can do anything further..."

"You are too kind, *M'sieur*. Both of you. I don't know what would have happened had you not come to my rescue. But I really feel much better now. I think that I shall go outside for a few minutes and take in the fresh air. Either I shall be restored, or I may decide to jump overboard." He managed another smile, and as he started to stand up, Holmes and Watson each took one of his hands and helped him to his feet. He held each man's hand perhaps a little tighter and a little longer than was absolutely necessary. "*Merci,* gentlemen. *Merci, beaucoup.* If your destination is Paris, possibly we shall see one another again." .

Watson was absently fingering the borrowed vial of smelling salts. "I say, Holmes, these salts are from Booth's—you know—the chemist's shop in Kensington where I used to purchase my surgical supplies. Ouch! Damn! I must have chipped the mouth of the vial, and now I've gone and nicked my finger. I'm becoming as clumsy as a first-year student." Watson took out his pocket-handkerchief and wiped off a large drop of blood from the vial and then wound the cloth tightly around his finger. "I'd best return this before I do any more damage. I wonder who is the old invalid's physician. If he trades at Booth's I most likely would know him."

Holding the vial in his uninjured hand, Watson went to the front of the cabin as Holmes retrieved the water glass and returned it to the bar where he resumed his earlier position resting his elbows on the bar and gazing absently in the mirror. He saw Watson tender the bottle to the nurse who returned it to her medical bag without examination and without so much as a civil nod to Watson. ..

The business done, Watson walked back to where Holmes was standing. "Not terribly sociable, were they, old man?" Holmes asked.

"That's rather an understatement don't you think? Would you mind lighting my cigarette, Holmes? If I try I'm just as likely to light my handkerchief and end up setting the entire ship aflame."

Holmes chuckled as he produced a match, which he lighted and applied to Watson's cigarette. "Oh well, old fellow. You're an experienced traveler. One can never tell what manner of ship-board companions one will be thrown amongst."

CHAPTER FIVE

"Holmes, what this fellow did is monstrous—
a few scoundrels like Bertillon
and the general acceptance of forensic science
will be set back fifty years."

*B*oulogne finally came into view, and by the time the captain sidled his ship along side the quay, the sun was nearly down. The waiting stevedores had hardly made the vessel fast before the passengers were streaming pell mell down the gangway overjoyed at the prospect of again feeling terra firma beneath their feet. Anxious to get home, the stevedores quickly unloaded the luggage from the ship to the waiting train as the passengers again went through the customs ritual. As soon as the passengers had cleared customs and settled themselves aboard, the train started up for the three hour run to Paris.

Ensconced in their compartment, the two men watched the town of Boulogne, with its white-washed cottages reflecting the golden hues of the last rays of sunlight, and slender-spired churches clinging to the purple hills, slide past their window and into the twilight darkness as the train gathered speed and the electric lamps in their compartment came to life.

As Watson fussed with his pipe, Holmes lit a cigarette from his vermeil case, "Unless you're ravenous, I would just as soon forego the pleasures of the dining car and trust that *M'sieur* Ritz's hospitality has survived the cross-channel trip and now flourishes in the Place Vendome. On the other hand, perhaps, you'd like to check on your happenstance patient from this afternoon."

"It pains me to admit it, Holmes, but I find the former alternative the more appealing. Ten years ago, even five years ago, not even *M'sieur* Escoffier's celebrated *magret de canard avec cepes et primeurs* could have kept me from discharging my professional duty to make a follow-up visit so as to be sure that the young man is completely recovered." Watson grimaced slightly as he pulled on his pipe and shifted his weight seeking a more comfortable perch on the bench-type seat which was neither as deep nor as padded as the standard British Railway first-class compartment seating. "At this stage in my life, I shall instead trust that his affliction was no more than a transient episode of sea-sickness, a diagnosis which is entirely consistent with the known circumstances, and just relax where I am. And while contemplating the promised delights of *M'sieur* Ritz's hospitality and *M'sieur* Escoffier's table, hopefully you will enlighten me as to what we can possibly gain by calling upon the *poseur* Bertillon."

"If memory serves," Holmes began, "when the Dreyfus saga first came to public notice, you were in the throes of winding down your Kensington practice, as well as compiling three volumes worth of manuscripts concerning cases undertaken during '94. I was in no mood to comment, especially on the Dreyfus case, mostly, I think, out of fear that if I so much as spoke the name aloud, I would allow myself to be goaded into becoming re-involved. Had I brought the matter to your attention, the entire story would have come out, and with one expression of outrage from you, we would have found ourselves then where we are today: returning, as it were, to the scene of the crime.

"Clearly, my stoic silence served its purpose. I don't recall your having made any mention of the case, except an occasional reference when the London newspapers would run a conspicuous article based on some new sensation or supposed newly-discovered evidence appearing in the French press. For the same reason that sealed my lips initially, if you will recall, I usually responded with some laconic remark that tended to discourage further discussion of the subject. In any event, it seems that between the demands of your regular pursuits, and my apparent lack of interest, your knowledge of the finer points of the case could stand a refresher."

For a long moment, Watson gazed out the window into the blackness of the French country-side, unwilling to look directly at Holmes, but instead contemplated Holmes's reflection in the window glass. Still without directly facing Holmes, Watson said, "Looking back, I can recall being curious as to why I was unable to draw you out more on the subject of the Dreyfus Case. It was, after all, fully as melodramatic as anything one could find in the agony columns of the daily newspapers, not to mention that it was as festooned with tid-bits of forensic science as ornaments on a Christmas tree. In hindsight, I'm sure I sensed that there was more to your un-responsiveness than mere non-interest. In deference to my instinct I quite likely allowed my own interest to ebb, although, as you yourself admit, no human endeavor is more difficult or less likely to succeed than trying not to think about a particular subject."

Turning now to face Holmes, Watson went on, "In the field of forensic science, you have no peer. In the discipline of deductive reasoning, your powers place you among the great philosophers of Western civilisation. You have an amazing faculty for finding the most elegantly simple explanation for the most seemingly disparate set of facts. Yet for all that I must wonder upon occasions such as these, building upon one of your pet theories, whether these formidable analytical skills are not maintained at the expense of skills in the area of human relationships. To put the matter most plainly, without putting too fine a point on it, I think you have done us both a considerable disservice."

"As always, old friend, your diagnosis is quite right. No matter how much anatomy, pathology and pharmacology I may have learnt over the years, I would never have amounted to much as a physician, since I am totally lacking in bedside manner. I cannot think how many times over the years that I have worked out the solution to a problem using you as a sounding board and on how many occasions you have consoled the inconsolable client or coaxed a nugget of useful information out of the most useless of sources."

This unlikely expression of feeling on Holmes part took Watson by surprise and caused him to blush noticeably. "I say, Holmes, such maudlin thoughts are best saved for a wake. When that day comes, be assured that I shall hold you to them. In the meantime, pray refresh my recollection regarding *M'sieur* Bertillon's role in this business."

"Bertillon," Holmes paused to light a cigarette, "as you know, although he didn't *invent* the concept of measuring a person's physical characteristics as a means of identification, was and is by far its leading proponent. In his Gallic egotism he has lent his name to what would otherwise be known generically as 'anthropometric measurement'. The name, I would concede, is fairly bestowed. The idea, if I recall, grew out of earlier experimentation by Bertillon's father and uncle, both physicians, who dabbled extensively in phrenology. But it was *our* Bertillon in his capacity as medical examiner for the judicial police that standardized the measurement techniques and developed the taxonomical system that is now in use.

"Last night you referred to the entire idea as 'crack-brain', and I would say your assessment is spot-on. That has not, however, deterred its chief proponent in the slightest. You correctly recalled that he has even published a book extolling the system and describing its methodology. For the last ten or so years that his book has been in print, he himself buys up most of the copies and goes about like some one-man Gideon Society foisting them upon official police agencies throughout the civilized world. I doubt that there is a single official of the rank inspector or above, in Europe or America, who has not had a copy thrust upon him as the ultimate weapon in the fight against crime. I would venture to say that a visit to any of the used-book stalls in Charing Cross Road would most probably yield no less than half a dozen copies, none of which is likely to show signs of excessive use.

"The point of the matter is," Holmes continued, "that Bertillon seeks by any and every means to inflate his own credentials and reputation. There is no branch of forensic science in which he does not claim to be a world-renown expert. The rigors of scientific method, and the solemn obligation of sworn testimony, constrain him not in the least. So it was that when Sandherr selected Dreyfus for his little 'frame-up', he engaged the complaisant *M'sieur* Bertillon as his accomplice in crime. You recall, I'm sure, that the chief evidence against Dreyfus—apart, that is, from the fact of his being of the Jewish persuasion—was the *bordereau*. Before enlisting Bertillon, Sandherr had taken the *bordereau* along with a known exemplar of Dreyfus's handwriting to virtually every recognized forensic questioned-document examiner in France. Although one or two were at best ambivalent about it, none was willing to swear that Dreyfus was the author of the damning document."

"Since Sandherr already knew that Dreyfus was not guilty anyway, he looked upon this lack of support by any credible expert as no more than a temporary inconvenience. As Bertillon was generally known to share Sandherr's anti-Semitic views, it took no great amount of persuasion by Sandherr to enlist Bertillon in the cause. Bertillon knows as much about scientific handwriting comparison as you and I know about the mating habits of the duck-billed platypus. Yet here was a heaven-sent opportunity for Bertillon to act upon his anti-Semitic beliefs, gain the respect of the army in which he had been unable to rise above the rank of corporal, and above all else place himself in the limelight once again as the 'highest expert in Europe', if I may borrow Dr. Mortimer's adulatory phrase."

"May providence protect us from corporals who would be generals, and conquer the world. But what of the trial, Holmes? Wasn't there a risk that Bertillon's incompetence would be exposed? Where was Demange? Why the greenest English barrister would have made the fellow a laughing-stock."

"Good questions all, Watson. But bear in mind this was no English court of law. No, I would be more inclined to call it an inquisition with epaulettes in place of ecclesiastical trappings. Demange was not permitted to cross examine Bertillon at all. He was not allowed to call expert witnesses on behalf of Dreyfus to contradict Bertillon's testimony. He was never even allowed to so much as see the crucial document. The night before the trial he was allowed to look at a copy which in all probability bore little resemblance to the actual document. No, I should say that the colonel and his co-conspirator, Europe's 'highest expert', were leaving nothing to chance."

"Holmes, what this fellow did is monstrous. A few scoundrels like Bertillon and the general acceptance of forensic science will be set back fifty years. The poor fellow Dreyfus; what a horror it must have been for him. Why on earth are we going to see such a charlatan? I trust that he speaks at least some English so that he'll be able to understand me when I call him a blackguard to his face." .

Holmes chuckled. "Steady on, Watson. Much as I would like to do the same, I'm afraid we'll have to do just the opposite. If the conspiracy against Dreyfus is still in progress, I'm assuming that Bertillon is still involved. Remember, Bertillon is like an anchovy; he's slippery and he leaves a bad taste in one's mouth. But it's not us that have to swallow him. He is only our bait, and we shall troll him in hopes of catching the barracuda."

"Do you think he's at the hub of the conspiracy? From what I recall, the man is one of those insufferable Francocentrics. Do you really think him capable of betrayal?"

"Not in the slightest," Holmes replied. "But the chauvinist thinks he and the state are one. And in Bertillon's case, his egocentrism leads him to the convenient conclusion that whatever he does is for the good of France. It is my belief that Bertillon, like so many others in this Greek tragedy, is being manipulated by some higher agency without his knowing it. It is through Bertillon that we must identify who in fact is the mastermind. So we shall pay our visit to 'Europe's highest expert'. I cannot imagine that he will be overly reticent in sharing his exploits with us, nor do I expect that our little visit will go unnoticed by those who will be most concerned with our nosing about."

CHAPTER SIX

"In the same way as the English gentleman is obsessively devoted to his equine pursuits, the French gentleman is equally infatuated with the pursuit of women."

*F*or the remainder of the ride, Watson, with his back resting against the outer wall of the carriage and his legs stretched out on the seat, pushed his derby down over his eyes and napped while Holmes, lost in thought, gazed out the window into the blackness that was becoming increasingly punctuated by lights from villages and farm houses as the train rolled on toward its destination. From time to time Holmes could see the lights from the passenger carriages of west-bound trains pulled over onto sidings yielding the right-of way on the single main track to the east-bound express.

Presently, the platform lights and overhead canopy slid into view and they came to a halt in the huge Gare du Nord station. They collected their baggage and got out of the carriage onto the platform. As they started toward the terminal they were met by a young man in black livery who presented himself with a well-practiced continental bow. Embroidered over his left breast and on the front of his gendarme-style cap was the single word "Ritz". *"M'sieur* Holmes, Doctor Watson. *M'sieur* Ritz presents his compliments." He took each man's portmanteau and gladstone and loaded them onto a small two-wheeled cart. "If you gentlemen will please come with me, I have transportation waiting just outside."

Transportation proved to be a Benz hotel bus, a motor-vehicle which looked like a barouche coach with an enclosed compartment for the passengers in which two sat facing front-wards and two back-wards. The engine was mounted in the rear behind the tonneau, and the driver sat in an unenclosed single seat in front on the left side. Steering was effected by a tiller mounted so as to be operable using the right hand. The luggage was soon secured on the tonneau roof and the passengers secured inside. The driver started the engine, turned on the single electric headlamp, and headed down the Rue Lafayette in the direction of the Place De L' Opera.

The grand plaza in front of the opera house, an urban scene much favoured by artists of every school from post-card painters to well-known impressionists, was choked with traffic. Motorcars, motorcycles, horse-drawn conveyances of every type, bicycles and pedestrians all seemed to be vying to occupy the same space at the same time, often, it appeared, for no better reason than to deny it to someone else. A marvel of poise and skill, the Ritz driver somehow managed to find a niche in the southerly flow of traffic big enough to accommodate the large Benz and eventually they made their way unscathed through the plaza into the narrower but less traffic-choked Rue De La Paix which in a few blocks brought them to the Place Vendome. The driver brought the bus to a stop in front of a rather unpretentious door beneath a simple canopy. As soon as the vehicle stopped, a uniformed *chassuer* appeared to open the door.

"*Bon soir, M'sieurs.* Welcome to the Ritz. The *portier* will tend to your baggage." The door-man held open the front door and Holmes and Watson went in to the surprisingly small lobby, followed by a bell-boy with their luggage. At the registration desk Holmes started to address the clerk, "*J'ai une reservation. Je m 'appelle...*"

"Welcome, Mr. Holmes, Dr. Watson. We received your telegraph message from Boulogne advising us that the boat was late and informing us of your arrival time."

"But we sent no..."

Holmes tapped Watson's leg with his walking stick. "Excellent, I assumed that to be the case since you were so kind as to have your bus meet us at the station. I wonder, do you still have the telegram? I was in such a hurry that I neglected to get a receipt, and I should like to keep track of expenses."

"*Mais oui, M'sieur* Holmes. I shall look at once. In the meantime would you and Dr. Watson be so kind as to sign the register? Also, gentlemen, I must ask that you leave your passports with us overnight. You can leave them now, or if you plan to go out you can leave them when you return for the night."

"What?" Watson sputtered. "That is an outrage. My good man we are British citizens, Her Majesty Queen Victoria's loyal subjects. I'll not surrender my passport to anyone."

. *"J suis desole, M'sieurs.* However it is the law. The *Sureté*: they come each night and check them against the registry and then again against the records compiled at each port of entry. It is the times, gentlemen. The government is in chaos over this Dreyfus *Affaire.* The civilian authorities and the military— especially the military—they see spies whereever they turn. And they turn every where. To them..."

"Cay est d'accord," Holmes interrupted, handing over his passport. "It's quite al-right. We're here on holiday and I'm sure we have nothing to fear from the authorities. Go ahead, Watson. There's more than enough for us to see and do than to spend our holiday in the custody of the *gendarmes.* We are, I believe, quite willing to leave French politics to the French." With a slight nudge from Holmes, Watson too handed his passport to the desk clerk.

"What? What is this talk about politics? It is all too, too boring." Cesár Ritz came up behind Holmes and Watson as Watson was handing over his passport. "Please do not let these insignificant matters trouble you. Welcome, *mon cher amis,* welcome to my little house. Of all my friends from my days at the Savoy, it is you whom I miss the most. And Auguste has been in a state all day awaiting your arrival."

Ritz was of medium height and his build was middle-age stout. He had the pallid complexion of one who spends all his time indoors. He had an odd, one might say almost obsequious, way of holding himself so that he seemed to always be bowing. He easily could have been taken for a prosperous Swiss banker, which he likely would have become had the hospitality business not captured his fancy as a young man. His normally stern features dissolved into a broad smile as he pumped each man's hand.

"Come, my friends; let me show you to your rooms. *Tout droit, s'il vous plait.* Ah," Ritz slapped his forehead with the heel of his hand, *"excusez moi.* I forget sometimes which language to speak. This way gentlemen..."

"But what about the telegram?" Watson asked the desk clerk.

The clerk replied somewhat nervously, *"Oui M'sieur le medicin,* er...*Docteur* Watson. I shall personally search for it and see that it is brought to you, *tout de suite."*

As Ritz led them to their rooms he remarked, as though apologizing, "I designed the lobby to be so small in order to discourage the loiterers. I am after all in the business of hiring out space. Small as it is, I still find it a problem to keep a certain class of—I hesitate to call them 'ladies'—from using the hotel facilities for arranging their assignations and, please pardon my indelicacy, consummating them in our guestrooms. Since many of their patrons are high civilian or military officials, the police do nothing about it."

Their rooms proved to be two beautifully furnished bedrooms, each with a large, comfortable bed and each with the ultimate in modern luxury, an *en suite* private bathroom and water closet. After the bell-boy had arranged their luggage in the proper rooms and they had reconvened in Holmes's room, Ritz asked, "Well, gentlemen, I trust you approve." Before either man could respond, he continued, "What do you think of the *salle de bain,...that* is, I mean,...the bathroom? Another one of my innovations. Every guest room in the hotel is so equipped. Some day perhaps all hotels will have these features. But now, only The Hotel Ritz can make such a claim."

Before Ritz could begin a discourse on the inner workings of the plumbing, Watson interjected, "Indeed, Mr. Ritz. It is without a doubt the most luxurious we've ever seen." Watson handed the bell-boy a ten-franc note. *"M'sieur* Escoffier, I'm sure grows impatient, and I know that Holmes and I are equally looking forward to seeing him." Watson grasped Ritz's hand and while pumping it used it to lever him to the door. "Everything is quite magnificent, Ritz. All these modern conveniences. I don't know how we shall ever be able to return to Baker Street. Now if you will give us a few minutes to change..."

*'Mais oui...*yes, but of course." Ritz managed to get in a few more words as Watson was closing the door. "I shall tell Auguste to expect you momentarily."

The two men adjourned to their respective rooms, and in a short while reemerged in proper, if somewhat wrinkled, dinner attire. As they made their way down to the grille-room, Watson remarked, "I say, Holmes, our friend Ritz seems to have become garrulous enough. He's almost as talkative as one of those estate agents. A few more minutes and I'd have been ready to draw on my letter of credit for earnest money. He certainly doesn't fit the taciturn Swiss-banker image."

"I expect." Holmes replied, "that he goes on as much as he does not only out of pride, but out of habit developed to acquaint the hotel guests with all the modern conveniences. Bear in mind, Watson, that more than half the people in France think that bathing more than once or twice annually is un-healthful and a waste of water. I would venture to say that an equally large percentage have never seen a water closet, or for that matter, running water."

In contrast to the utilitarian lobby, the dining room defined opulent luxury. From the floor covered by a thick-piled carpet in an art noveau pattern, to the mirrored walls framed in ceiling-high arches trimmed in gold molding, the room exuded a warm elegance at which the French excel and which the rest of the world, no matter how it tries, seems never to quite duplicate. The tables were covered in starched white over a pale mauve, with brocade chairs in a Louis Quinze rococo style. Lighting was provided by electric fixtures mounted on the wall columns so that the light was directed upwards and then reflected down off the white ceiling and wall columns. The effect was to give the room a burnished golden hue, and entering it was like walking through a gilt frame and into a Botticelli painting.

As did most people upon entering the room for the first time, Holmes and Watson paused at the door to take in the spectacle of the elegant room filled with elegantly dressed diners. Both men self-consciously tugged at their waist-coats and adjusted their ties in the mirror across the room on the far wall. As they waited for Ritz, who was talking with the patrons at a nearby table, and had not yet seen them, Holmes said, "I wish I'd taken time to have my dinner jacket pressed."

"Nonsense, old man, you look..." Watson paused, "...*tres elegant*. Ah Ritz, here we are. I trust that Escoffier has saved us a morsel or two."

"Gentlemen, gentlemen. But of course he has. Come, let me show you to your table. Would you prefer a nice quiet table by the window? Or..."

"Something perhaps closer to the center of the room?" Holmes replied. "I think to-night's a night to see and be seen. Watson, is that al-right with you?"

"H-m-m...Oh yes, whatever you say Holmes." Watson replied as Ritz led them to a table near the center of the room.

As they were seated, Ritz said, "Here, gentlemen, you shall be the center of attention. By tomorrow morning all Paris shall know that the world's most celebrated detective and his...his erudite companion are guests at the Ritz. Now, *M'sieurs,* perhaps a small *aperitif* while I tell Auguste that you are here. He forbids you to order anything, and insists that you allow him the pleasure of ordering for you."

The aperitifs were ordered and quickly brought; a Dubonnet for Holmes and a martini cocktail for Watson. These were soon followed by an appetizer of *truite fume* served cold, and then a light consommé, both of which were accompanied by a Montrachet that Holmes and Watson pronounced to be the best they'd ever tasted. As they were finishing the soup course Escoffier himself, assisted by Ritz and a retinue of waiters, brought out the main course on covered salvers. Overcome by his Gallic nature, and somewhat to his guests' discomfort, he insisted on embracing each man.

"For you, Mr. Holmes I have created the new dish: *roti selle d'agneau de pre sale;* roast saddle of young lamb grazed in fields bordering the sea. I call it, with your kind permission, *'Agneau a la Holmes'* And for you, my dear friend Dr. Watson, what else but your treasured *magret de canard avec cepes et primeurs,* which I have also taken the liberty of naming in your honor, *'Canard a la Watson.' Et Voila!* "He clapped his hands and the waiters placed the dishes on the table. With a flourish they simultaneously removed the domes as the *sommelier* presented for each man's inspection a venerable Chateau Latour which he had already decanted so that the sediment had settled and the wine fully opened.

During the meal, there was little conversation except to remark upon the subtle characteristics of the wine and to confirm that Escoffier was still the world's premier chef. If anything, they collectively opined, the return to his native land, with its greater variety of ingredients and vastly larger universe of sophisticated and venturesome palates, had inspired him to even greater achievements. Although, they were again of the same mind, the naming of dishes after one's patrons, while flattering, was perhaps a bit much.

With this thought in mind, it came as no surprise that as soon as the entree dishes were cleared, Ritz and Escoffier returned followed by a waiter bearing a tray laden with the ingredients for Escoffier's famous dessert creation *Peche Melba*, which the chef himself proceeded to prepare at the table. After Escoffier had poured his special sauce and topped the mound with a light sprinkling of diced almonds, Holmes and Watson dutifully—they both would have preferred a serving of the *crepes Suzette* which Ritz's *maitre d' hotel* had so expertly prepared for an adjoining table—consumed the concoction and pronounced it exquisite as always. Ritz summoned a waiter to bring cognac and cigars for three, and Escoffier, satisfied that his guests were satisfied, returned to his kitchen.

As the cigars were being lighted Ritz held his and looked at it with a wistful reverence as though contemplating a photograph of a favorite dog. "I hope you enjoy these as they are among the last of my stock of Uppmann's. The Romeo *y* Juliettas ran out a month ago and there's no prospect of getting any more for months."

"It's an absolute outrage," Watson nodded in agreement. "Davidoff's been out for weeks as well. In fact Davidoff himself told me that his man in Havana reported to him that just before the invasion, the American press baron, name of Hearst, I believe, bought up the entire export stock and shipped it back to the States."

"Would have served him right," Holmes added, "if he'd shipped them on the *Maine*. Perhaps the next time the Americans find it necessary to invade Cuba, their President will have a keener appreciation of fine cigars. I understand that the current incumbent, Mr. McKinley, smokes only the cheapest domestic brands either out of habit or political expediency. Indeed..." Holmes who was seated facing the entrance to the room paused and made a slight gesture indicating that Watson and Ritz, who were seated facing him, should look around in the direction of the entrance. Just as

Holmes had stopped in mid-sentence, the entire room went totally silent like on a music box whose lid had replaced.

Standing at the entrance were three of the most striking women Watson and Holmes had ever seen. All three were perfectly made up and coifed. One was gowned in deep purple, one in pale pink set off by ribbons and bows, and the third in a harmony of bright, primary colors. Each gown revealed a breathtaking décolletage which displayed more of its wearer's anatomy than it covered up. And to make certain that her natural charms would not go unnoticed each woman was bedecked in jewelry in every visible place. A tiara atop the head; long, dangling earrings; pearls, diamonds or both about the neck; bracelets on each wrist; and rings on nearly every finger. There was virtually no visable anatomical feature which had gone unadorned.

In no less than a full minute the tableau began to re-animate. The male diners affected to return to the pleasures of the palate. Their female counterparts glanced covertly in the nearest of the wall mirrors so as to check the state of repair of their own coiffure and make-up, not to mention the several who discreetly rearranged their own décolletage to better advantage. Ritz, sniffing the air—whether in contempt, or at the scent of ylang-ylang which wafted from the direction of the entrance—glanced at the three women somewhat irritably and took a substantial swallow of his cognac.

"Do you know them, Ritz?" Watson asked.

"*Oui,* unfortunately yes, my friends. *Les 'Demoiselles de la soir.* Ladies of the evening, I believe is the polite appellation. By name, in the purple gown, Emilienne d' Alencon; the vision in pink, Liane de Pougy, the 'leader' of the group and referred to as *'notre courtisane nationale'* and she of the *arc en ciel* gown, *Mlle.* Caroline Otero. I've heard them referred to collectively as *'Les Grandes Trois'* Most evenings you may find them at Maxim's restaurant. However, I believe that tonight, some Russian Grand Duke or another has booked the entire establishment for a private party at which these ladies' presence might have proved awkward."

Ritz's *maitre d'* escorted the three women in the direction of a table at the rear of the room near the kitchen door. Although the ensuing conversation could not be heard, even though the room had lapsed once again into near silence, the meaning, like a children's charade game, was unmistakable: the women were no more inclined to accept such an inferior table than the hapless *maitre d'* was on his own initiative going to offer them a better one. Not knowing what else to do, the unfortunate man looked pleadingly at Ritz. Rather than chance escalation, Ritz gave a slight nod in the direction of a table near the center of the room that had just been vacated. The *maitre d'* made a sweeping bow and bade the women precede him to the table indicated by Ritz.

With the seating of the women, the sounds of normalcy began to return. Ritz, however, leaned forward and lowered his voice, "It is absolutely scandalous my friends. Not only must I accommodate these women, but I must be humiliated in the process."

"You poor fellow," Watson placed a consoling hand on Ritz's forearm. "Is there nothing to be done?"

Flicking his cigar ash, Ritz lowered his voice even more. "It is as I mentioned earlier. Sometimes I think I am operating a...a...disorderly house rather than the world's finest hotel. And the authorities? *Phooey!* My friends, I am no philosopher; I am a simple inn-keeper. But I have, under the circumstances, been compelled of late to give the matter a great deal of thought. You no doubt have read or heard the term *'fin de siecle'?"*

"Yes," Holmes answered, "I'm familiar with the term, although less so its meaning."

"Sounds to me," Watson interjected, "Like one of those French expressions that are perhaps best left un-translated."

Ritz took a thoughtful puff on his cigar. "You are probably correct; however, do indulge me *cher ami.* As I use the term, and as I think it is commonly understood, it means *der zeitgeist...ach...nein.* No...excuse me. As a Swiss, I grew up speaking both languages, and of course since then I've learned English along with enough of other languages so as to be able to communicate the bare essentials to my guests. In any case, I frequently think in German while speaking in French. It sometimes gets confusing..."

"It's quite al-right; pray continue," Holmes said before holding his brandy snifter up to his nose to take in the aroma and to counteract the cloying scent of perfume wafting from the adjacent table.

"It means, as best I can put it in English, a world-weariness that is somehow justified by the coming end of the century. It's as though the world as we know it will come to an end merely by the turn of a calendar page. Here, in Paris, that is, one senses that this attitude pervades every aspect of life, at least among those who can afford such indulgence. Do you also know the expression *'nostalgie de la boue'?"*

Not waiting for an answer, Ritz continued, "literally, 'nostalgia for the mud'. It is used to convey an obsessive longing for decadence or depravity. Let me explain what I mean. What, my friends, is the primary indulgence of the English gentleman?" Ritz paused to puff his cigar.

"Er...why..." Watson, who had been following the conversation while studying the three women, "Er...I..."

"Let me hazard a guess," Holmes interjected, "gambling? sports? politics?"

"No, no and no, my friend." Ritz demeanor remained serious. "You could shut down every club and gambling house in London; turn Wembley and Lord's back into sheep meadows and pack the House of Commons *en masse* off to live among the Esquimois and the true English gentleman might sputter and spout for a day. However, by night-fall, they would all be quite forgotten. But take away an English gentleman's horses, and then...," Ritz struck his fist on the table for emphasis, "and then you truly would have gotten his attention.

"Think about it, my friends. They race them over flat courses and steeplechases; they bet on them compulsively; they ride them 'to hounds' as they say; they collect them in herds just to play polo; they will not have their portrait painted except astride a favorite; they die gallant mounted deaths in battle; and they spend countless hours and fortunes pouring over bloodlines, buying, selling and trading."

"What you say is certainly true," Watson conceded, "but what has that to do with *'nostalgie de la...*whatever?"

"Directly, nothing," Ritz replied. "I offer it merely by way of analogy. In the same way that the English gentleman is obsessively devoted to his equine pursuits, the French gentleman is equally infatuated with the pursuit of women."

"And is the converse true as well?" Watson asked as he cleaned his glasses with his napkin. "Do the women pursue the men with equal ardour?"

"Probably so, Dr. Watson, although as a gentleman I must decline to speak from personal experience. It is a game that all can and do play. It is not uncommon for an energetic army officer or politician to have not only a wife but one, two or even more mistresses. I cannot count the times I've seem Madame so-and-so here in the afternoon with a lover—who is himself married—and then seen her here again in the evening on the arm of her husband. It has even been known to happen that madame and her husband, and lover and his wife, will spend the evening dining together.

"This obsession with what was once thought by all to be a matter between husband and wife, has become in Paris—if not all of France—a major industry. What is there to compare? The cheese industry? The wine industry? Every country, even England, makes its own cheese. Every country, except England, makes a palatable wine. The automobile industry shows promise, but it is still very much a cottage industry. There is little standardization, and no modern manufacturing facilities; each machine is built by hand, so only the wealthy, or those such as myself who have a practical use for such machines, can afford them. The clever inventors and engineers in the industry are chronically short of capital, and don't know how to raise it. The entrepreneurs who know how to raise capital, don't know what to do with it. And each group holds the other in contempt."

"Ah, but the debauchery industry...that my friends is a different matter altogether." Ritz paused, and noticing that the brandy glasses, including his own, were empty, signaled a waiter for more cognac and to bring coffee as well. "Please excuse my running on like this. Except for Auguste, whose knowledge of and interest in matters outside his kitchen is virtually non-existent, there is no one with whom I can speak of these things with complete candor. I am, as you know, still a Swiss citizen, and my company—the owner of the hotel—is chartered in England and is allowed to do business here only as a foreign company. So if in an unguarded moment I express myself with such frankness, and my indiscretion reaches the wrong ears, I could easily find myself back at the Savoy or worse yet, waiting tables in the Zurich Bahnhof café. So when, as now, I have the opportunity to bend the ears of old friends upon whose discretion I can confidently rely I keep the cognac flowing and like the ancient mariner 'halt thee with a glittering eye' and let pour my tale of woe. But no, you both must be exhausted from your journey, and..."

Watson held up his refilled brandy glass. "Oh no, please do continue. After all, what are friends for?" Holmes nodded his encouragement.

"As you wish, my friends. But I too grow weary." Ritz tasted his coffee. "Just think of the commercial aspects, gentlemen. The couturier houses that flourish as a result of catering to these women," Ritz nodded slightly in the direction of the adjacent table, "and to those who would emulate them. Do you know that there are more than a thousand corset makers in Paris alone. Any one of the fifty or so gowns in this room costs more than a common laborer earns in a year. And the jewels. The Tsarina herself is said to be jealous of Otero's bauble collection. And her's is but one of who knows how many? Cornuche sets a fine table at Maxim's, but without the patronage of these charming ladies and the rest of the Sybaritic set, he'd probably be selling *pommesfrites et saucisses* on a street-corner from a push-cart. I tell you, for what it may be worth, licentiousness is the single engine that drives the Paris economy, if not all of France."

"But aren't you..." Watson began.

Ritz swirled his cognac. "Am I being cynical? hypocritical? Yes, perhaps both. But I am also practical. This establishment represents all I have in this world, and all I shall ever want. My financial supporters are entitled to a return on their investment. I have nearly one employee for every guest. These mouths too must be fed. Will Auguste compromise his standards? And our wine cellars? If I may say so, they are among the finest on the Continent. So, my friends," Ritz raised his glass, "let us drink to the *'Les Grandes Trois'*. May they, like recumbent Atlases, continue to support the world."

As Ritz clinked glasses with Holmes and Watson, a bell-man approached the table. *"Excusez-moi. M'sieurs Holmes?"*

"Oui. Je m'appelle Sherlock Holmes."

"Pour vous, M'sieur." The man held out a small tray bearing two envelopes the first of which contained the telegraph message, unsigned, informing *M'sieur Le Directeur* of Holmes's and Watson's arrival on the boat-train from Boulogne. Although pains had been taken to restore the message to a pristine state, it was evident that it had been crumpled up and had in all probability been retrieved from a trash can. The second bore simply a return address in the Avenue de Trocadero. Holmes quickly perused the second message which he then tucked inside his breast pocket along with the telegram. Seeing the expectant look on Watson's face, Holmes finished his cognac. "Oh it was only the telegram from Boulogne and a letter from a potential client who tried to contact us in London and upon learning that we'd left for Paris, assumed that we would stop only at the Ritz." Holmes turned and smiled at Ritz. "Ritz, my friend and host, you have set a new standard for elegance and taste. From now on, when one wishes to define the ultimate in luxury, describing something as 'Ritz-like' will be all that is necessary."

"Watson, we've much to see and do, and I think I'm quite prepared to call it a night. However, should you wish to remain and perhaps persuade *M.* Ritz to introduce you to *'Les Grandes Trois'* feel free to do so. I have observed, as you have, that for some time now we've been the principal topic of their conversation as they have of ours. *M.* Ritz, thank you. Everything is perfect. With your permission I shall take a moment to convey my thanks once more to Auguste and then I'm off to bed."

CHAPTER SEVEN

"I wanted to get a closer look at
the two chaps who've been following us
since we left the hotel."

*B*y mid-morning Watson had not arisen, so Holmes, with considerable trepidation, ventured to knock on his door to inquire as to his health. As he did, he could have sworn that he detected the faintest hint of ylang-ylang, but dismissed the idea as a trick of the olfactory senses. In due course Watson completed his morning ablutions and joined Holmes in the restaurant where Holmes had already ordered something called a "continental breakfast". This proved to be *croissants* and pots of strong coffee. Although Watson would have preferred a more traditional English breakfast, the *croissants* were edible, and the coffee helped somewhat to counter-act the lingering effects of the previous night's beverage consumption.

As they were finishing their coffee, a bell-man brought Holmes a message which he read with evident satisfaction. "Excellent news, Watson. The estimable *M'sieur* Bertillon has found time to receive us this afternoon at two o'clock. While you were still in the world of Morpheus, I sent a second message advising of our arrival and ensconcement at the Ritz, and expressing the hope that receiving us would not greatly inconvenience such a busy and important official. Since we have some time on our hands, shall we have a go at being a couple of *flanuers?"*

Watson looked at Holmes blankly. *"Flaneurs?"*

"Sorry. Difficult word to translate to English. 'Loafer', 'idler', these seem not to do it justice. Let's just say 'strolling about like a couple of tourists'."

"I'm game, I suppose, although I would not think it amiss if in our perambulations we were to encounter a chemist's shop. Partly out of professional curiosity and partly because I've rather a bad headache, I'd like to see what the French have for such a common yet debilitating malady."

"Then it's off we go. Remember the ancient Chinese proverb: 'a journey of a thousand miles begins with a single step'."

Watson gave Holmes a malevolent look as he struggled to his feet.

Leaving the hotel, they walked north back up the Rue de la Paix in the direction of the Place De L' Opera. The street was crowded, more so than the previous night. There was a seemingly endless procession of horse-drawn coaches attended by smartly turned out coachmen. There were as many vehicles standing at the margins of the street as there were trying to navigate the occluded middle. The sidewalks were nearly as crowded with elegantly dressed women, getting in or out of their coaches, entering and leaving the many shops crowding one another for frontage along the street. Each establishment catered to some facet of feminine adornment, from millinery to shoe-makers and all in between. From the corset-maker shops, to the purveyors of the newly fashionable sensuous lingerie—the window displays of which both men thought scandalous—to the studios of the *haute couture* designers there was every conceivable article of apparel to display *madame's* beauty to best advantage and to advertise her husband's or *papa's* affluence.

They paused for a minute or two in front of Cartier's, *primus inter pares*, of the *joailleries* interspersed with the other shops along the street musing about why such otherwise useless pieces of polished rock should be assigned so high a place in mankind's scale of values. As they approached the Rue Daunou they spotted a drab little shop which identified itself as a *pharmacie*, the local equivalent of a chemist's shop.

As they entered the shop Watson touched Holmes's arm, "Let me give it a try, Holmes. I may end up with corn plasters, but..."

"Bonjour, M'sieurs." A diminutive, elfin-like man in a white laboratory coat popped up from behind a low counter displaying patent medicines.

Watson addressed the man, *"Avez-vous... les...les...comprimes...pour le...".* Watson pointed to his head.

Holmes interceded, *"mal a la tete..."*

72

"Headache, *M'sieur? Oui, la-bas,* er...over there. Yes, over there." The little man pointed to a counter at the rear of the shop and motioned for Watson and Holmes to follow him as he scurried back toward his compounding table and cabinets with their row upon row of small drawers.

"Do you prefer to speak in English, *M'sieurs?"* He opened one of the cabinet drawers and extracted a small box bearing the name "Fabrikfarben Bayer" which he then handed to Watson. "Try some of these, *M'sieur."*

Watson opened the box which proved to contain a number of small, white pills. "I should like to know what they are, my good man, before I take them. As a physician I would hardly recommend a medication to my patient without knowing what it is and what it does, and whether there are any deleterious side effects."

"Ah, mais oui. Excusez-moi, M'sieur Le Medecin. It is called 'acetylsalicylic acid', or by its trade-name, 'Aspirin'. It is a coal-tar derivative." He lowered his voice to a near whisper. "It was first produced many years ago, but its medicinal properties were discovered only recently. As you can see from the brand-name, it is a German product. And because anything German is so offensive to many of my customers, especially with this dreadful *Dreyfus Affaire* so much on everyone's mind at present, I do not usually offer it unless specifically asked, even though it is quite safe and most effective. But since you gentlemen are English, I make so bold as to presume that you are neither infected with this Dreyfus business, nor did your fathers fight with and lose a war to the Germans."

The diminutive pharmacist produced a glass and bottle of *eau minerale* from under the counter. He filled the glass with the water and handed it to Watson. "Take two of the pills, *M'sieur Le Medecin.* It is best that you ingest them with water as the taste is quite bitter."

Watson complied. "How does the drug work?"

"No one knows for a certainty, *M'sieur.* There is speculation that somehow it acts as a blood thinner, but no one knows what effect that has. Research continues in Germany, but it is exceedingly difficult for the scientific community here to keep informed. If one is known to receive mail on a regular basis from

73

Germany, it is likely to lead to unwelcome scrutiny from the *Sureté,* the Section of Statistics, or both. If a dose of Aspirin could also cure this *espionitis,* then it would truly be a wonder drug."

"Espionitis?" Holmes asked.

The pharmacist looked Holmes and Watson over carefully as though to assure himself that they were what they appeared to be. *"Oui, M'sieur.* Spies everywhere, or so we are led to believe. It is far easier to blame our problems on sinister foreign intervention and on fifth-columnists, than to deal with the real causes. As your William Shakespeare so eloquently put it in the mouth of Julius Caesar, if I remember the speech correctly, Caesar says to Brutus: 'The fault, dear Brutus, lies not in our stars, but in ourselves.' So it is with France today, *M'sieurs."*

He produced two more glasses which he also filled with mineral water and topped off Watson's glass. "I would offer you something better, but it is perhaps best that *M'sieur Le Medecin* refrain at least until the drug has had its effect."

"Thank you, I'm sure." Watson took another sip of his mineral water. "But do not let us detain you from your duties. How much do I..." Watson reached for his wallet.

"No, no *M'sieur.* Please accept the medication with my complements. I would, in fact be glad for you to stay a few more minutes to be sure the drug is having the desired effect. I lived in England during a part of my student days. That, of course, is where I learned English and acquired a passion for Shakespeare. So I am always glad to have the opportunity to speak the language as well as merely read it. The government officially discourages the use of English. Indeed it is not even taught below the university level." He shrugged his shoulders and rolled his eyes upward. "The popular culture embraces everything Russian, even though the Russians are nothing more than barbarians who have traded their animal skins for silk and patent leather. But England, alas, shall always be 'Perfidious Albion'."

"How is it," Watson asked, "that you came to study in England?"

"A curious custom; but please, let me first introduce myself. I feel somehow that I know both of you, but I cannot recall when or where we met. I am Henri Lambert." He extended his hand which Watson had to lean over the counter to grasp.

"I am Dr. Watson, John Watson. And this is..."

"Yes, yes of course. I knew I recognized you *M'sieur* Holmes. I am one of your greatest admirers. I have not only followed Dr. Watson's reports of your cases, but I have also read with great interest your work in developing a human haemoglobin-specific reagent. I, myself am working on a theory that there are at least two or three types of human blood. I have been corresponding with a biochemist at the Hygiene Institute in Vienna, Karl Landsteiner, who is working on the same theory. But that is for another time." He continued to pump Holmes hand until Holmes nearly fell over the counter.

"In England, the custom among the minor nobility and landed gentry is to send a second son off to join the military or the church. In France, the curious custom among the *bourgeoisie*—that is the middle class—is to send the second or otherwise difficult son off to England. So it was in my case. I had shown no aptitude for any practical vocation, and was adamantly uninterested in a career in politics. I was given a passport, a visa and an exceedingly modest letter of credit. With a single tear in *maman's* eye to match those welling up in my own, I, like so many others in the same circumstance, was packed off to England to see what I could make of myself."

Watson nodded in agreement, recalling his own circumstances and silently reproaching himself for thinking ungenerous thoughts about his deceased elder brother.

"Fortunately," the pharmacist continued, "I found that I did enjoy the detail and precision which pharmacology demands, and I find considerable satisfaction when I am able to help restore someone to good health. Although I make no pretense of scientific genius, I do respect it."

"You spoke a moment ago," Holmes began, "about—I believe you referred to it as— *'espionitis'* ?"

Lambert gave Holmes an appraising look. "Was there something specific you wished to know, *M'sieur* Holmes? I doubt that I," he paused, "a simple *chemist"* he used the British word, "would know anything of use to you. Ones so famous and respected as yourselves," he made a sweeping gesture so as to indicate he was referring to both men, "surely would be treated most accommodatingly by the *Sureté..."*

Sensing Lambert's growing alarm, Holmes quickly interjected, "It is only a general curiosity, *M'sieur* Lambert, I assure you. Dr. Watson and I are nothing more than a couple of foot-loose tourists come to enjoy the pleasures of springtime in this most beautiful of cities." Turing to Watson, he asked, "I say, Watson, has *M'sieur* Lambert's miraculous coal-tar derivative," he smiled enigmatically,"cured your *mal a la tete?* "

Reading Holmes's mind, Watson replied, "Yes, indeed it has. Absolutely amazing. Thank you, Mr. Lambert, thank you. As soon as we return to London I shall write to the Bayer people to obtain the pertinent details regarding dosage and side-effects, and to secure a supply. If you wish, give me your address and I will pass along all the information I receive. Surely that's the least I can do. Are you sure you will not accept payment?"

"No, no *Docteur* Watson, I insist." Lambert handed Watson a card with the name and address of the apothecary. "I do, however, accept your kind offer."

"Well then. Watson, shall we be on our way? *Au revoir, M'sieur* Lambert." Lambert shook each man's hand several more times as they made their way back to the front of the shop. When they finally reached the street, Holmes suggested that they continue up the Rue Dc La Paix to the Place De L' Opera. Before resuming their walk, Holmes paused and took out his cigarette case. Turning toward the chemist's shop window, he lighted a cigarette. Although there was almost no breeze, it took a third match before he finally got it started.

Watson, making note of this, and recalling that Holmes almost never smoked during their perambulations about London, started to say something.

Holmes inhaled his cigarette. "Perfectly acceptable local custom, old chap. And, as they say, 'when in Rome....' Besides," he lowered his voice and moved a step closer to Watson, "I wanted to get a closer look at the two thugs who've been following us since we left the hotel. I thought at first they might be mere footpads hoping to prey on a pair of hapless tourists. However, if that were the case, I would think that by now, with as much time as we spent in the company of *M'sieur* Lambert, they would have gotten bored with the hunt and gone off in search of other victims.

Don't turn, Watson. I'd rather let this farce go on for a while, just to see what happens."

CHAPTER EIGHT

"Your little melodrama quite fascinates me.
I can hardly contain myself in contemplation
of the denouement"

*U*pon reaching the Place De L' Opera, they decided to take a cab back to the Ministrie de la Justice which is next door to the Ritz and soon found an available fiacre, a horse-drawn cab somewhat smaller and less comfortable than the standard London hansom. From the Place De L' Opera, they headed southwest on the Boulevard des Capuchines to the Rue Cambon entrance to the Ministry and the incongruously situated offices of Alphonse Bertillon, self-proclaimed world's foremost expert in all branches of forensic science, leading apostle of the anthropometric system of criminal identification and, so Watson reflected, prophet honoured in his own land alone.

A receptionist at the entrance verified their identities from their passports and gave them indifferent directions to Bertillon's offices. They wound their way through wide hallways and cramped corridors, up one flight of stairs and through more corridors, some in which the only sound was their own footsteps, and others bustling with clerks and various functionaries. From time to time Holmes would attempt to engage one of the clerk-types in conversation. Watson presumed that Holmes was asking directions. Sometimes Holmes's *"Pouvez-vous m' aider?"* or *"Est-ce que c'est bien le..."* would be met by a brusque *"Je ne sais pas"* or merely a curt *"non"*. Others, apparently actually trying to be helpful, would point *a droite* or *a gauche,* others *en haut,* still others *en bas* until Holmes was quite exasperated and Watson thoroughly bemused.

Eventually, by twenty minutes past two o'clock, through their own dogged persistence they located what proved to be Bertillon's offices, a suite of rooms above whose main entrance was a disarmingly straight-forward sign: *"Bureau d' Identification"*. The part of the suite which Holmes and Watson were able to see in the course of being escorted to Bertillon's private office consisted of a series of rooms the walls of which were lined with cabinets, eighty-one in all, comprised of row upon row of small drawers not unlike those in a chemist's shop or a library card-catalog. In the center of each room were several rows of high-legged desks with work surfaces slanted down-ward toward the user. Clerks sat on high stools or stood at the desks comparing single cards containing what presumably were individual anthropometric measurements with cards containing previously catalogued individual measurements culled from the peripheral cabinets. Each time a clerk would remove a drawer, he—they were in fact all men—would place a numbered tag in the space vacated by the drawer. By this means, Watson surmised, anyone else needing the same drawer would be able to locate it readily, although, Watson thought sceptically, even if one found the drawer for which one was looking, its contents were unlikely to be of much value.

Following their clerk-escort it took a few more minutes to make their way past the last of the cabinets which contained, as Holmes would later apprise Watson, two sets of torso measurements, each being further subdivided, as in the case of the other nine body measurements, into *grande, a pointe* and *petite,* to a small ante-room where the clerk bade them be seated in the arm-less straight-backed wooden chairs lining one of the walls. The opposite wall was taken up by a bookcase which contained dozens of volumes, all of which bore the same title, variously in French, English, German and either Italian or Spanish: *Alphonse Bertillon's Instructions For The Identification Of Criminals And Others By The Means Of Anthropometric Indications.* The wall opposite the entrance to the room had a single, dark-stained wooden door on which the name *Alphonse Bertillon* was painted in gilt script and beneath his name the word *"Privee"* On the wall to the right of the door at right-angles to the book-case wall hung a large photographic chest-to-head portrait of a man whom, they assumed, they would be meeting in-the-flesh momentarily. To the left of the door to Bertillon's private office there was another large picture frame containing a number of testimonial letters. These were mounted behind green baize-like matting cut out to fit each of the letters and surmounted by a pane of glass.

Momentarily proved to be twenty-three minutes. Having served the requisite amount of time in order to establish whose time was the more valuable and who was condescending to see whom, the clerk opened the door and they were ushered into the presence of the great man himself.

To their surprise, presumably in order to show that their inexcusable tardiness was forgiven, Bertillon arose from his chair and came around to the front of the desk. To Holmes's and Watson's relief, in keeping with English custom, he clasped each man's hand in a formal yet rather tepid hand-shake instead of the quotidian practice in that part of the world of men embracing one another in public as a means of greeting.

Bertillon was, for a Frenchman, unusually tall, nearly as tall as Holmes. Having anthropometric measurements very much on his mind, Watson could not help thinking that the man was several inches taller than his typical countryman. Otherwise, the anteroom photograph must have been from a fairly recent sitting as it portrayed its subject exactly as he appeared before them. Bertillon was considerably stouter than Holmes, although one would by no means describe him as portly. He had that erect posture-conscious bearing that is characteristic of French men—and women as well—that Watson surmised must be taught as a course, like history or geography, to every little French child upon entering grammar school, and which, Watson reflected, compared favorably to the nonchalant slouch affected by every English public school boy by the time he reached his teen-age years. Bertillon was dressed in a somber black suit over a soft-collared white shirt. He wore his suit buttoned nearly to his short, black gros-grain tie, the ends of which lay neatly beneath his collar. His thick, dark hair showing only a little gray had receded on both sides of his head above the temples almost all the way back toward his ears. His well-kept beard, in contrast to the hair on his head, showed as much gray as black. He wore a mustache the fullness of which almost covered his entire mouth. He had a large, straight nose and dark, deeply-recessed eyes which looked steadily back at his visitors from beneath prominent bushy eyebrows.

After Bertillon had returned to his desk chair and Holmes and Watson were seated in the visitors' chairs arranged in front of the desk, Bertillon and Holmes lit cigarettes and Watson fired up his briar. To Watson's surprise, Bertillon addressed them in English. "So at long last we meet. The renown Sherlock Holmes and his estimable chronicler, Dr. Watson. What brings you to Paris? Are the British Isles wholly devoid of miscreants so that you must now expand your environs to include my humble precincts as well? Perhaps Dr. Watson can be persuaded to publish accounts of some of my own notable cases."

Although Bertillon's last remark was in the form of a statement, the long pause at the end of the sentence made it clear that it was intended as an interrogatory with a question-mark at the end rather than a full-stop. It lay there like a ripe cherry atop a chocolate frappe waiting to be plucked-up and swallowed. Holmes gave Watson's foot a slight nudge with his own. "Indeed, perhaps we may, *M'sieur* Bertillon," Holmes replied enthusiastically.

The signal from Holmes having been unnecessary, Watson added, "Yes, yes, of course. I would be honoured if you would permit me to do so. Holmes has been quite the lay-about of late, and it's been months, I'm sure, since any interesting cases have come our way." Watson, not daring to risk the temptation of a side-ways glance at Holmes, went on, "But how is it *M'sieur* Bertillon that you do not publish your own accounts? I could not help but notice as we were awaiting the completion of your other more pressing business that your great treatise has been translated from your native French into a number of other languages. Did you yourself do the English translation? If I may say so, you speak the language remarkably well..."

"*Merci,* Dr. Watson. Coming from a fellow author, I am most flattered. While I have spoken English for virtually my entire adult life, the translation of my book was done ten years ago by Gallus Miller, an ardent admirer of mine. Mr. Miller, although he holds the somewhat modest position of clerk of the State Penitentiary for the State of Illinois, in America, is in actuality one of the foremost penologists in that country, a true genius and far ahead of his time."

"How did you come to learn English," Watson asked. "Why only this morning we were made to understand that it is not generally taught in the French school system."

"That is quite true, Dr. Watson." Bertillon, having stubbed out his cigarette, laced his fingers together across his middle and leaned back in his chair. "I learned to speak the language twenty-five years ago when, as a young man my parents sent me to England to broaden my education by first-hand experience. Such experience as can be gained only from living and working abroad in a foreign land with unfamiliar customs and language.

"My father procured a situation for me as a clerk in a banking house in 'The City'." Bertillon used the term as referring to the London financial district centered in the vicinity of the Bank of England and St. Paul's Cathedral. "However, even though I was in my child-hood considered something of a mathematics prodigy, my initial task was counting pence and shillings in the basement and I was soon bored to distraction. The menial nature of my duties, coupled with the fact that my supervisor was a Jew, and an arrogant one at that, soon impelled me to conclude that I was not cut out for a career in banking.

"With almost no English, my prospects were severely limited. I wrote to a certain professor whose work was known to me, and through his recommendation I obtained a position teaching French at a prominent public-school, the University School in Smithwyck. You are perhaps familiar with it?" Like a tenured professor impatient to conclude a lecture, he continued without pausing for an answer. "It was through this position that I eventually learned your native language. As I correspond with law enforcement officials in The United States and Canada, as well as England, Australia and India, I have of necessity maintained my proficiency.

"But enough, gentlemen, of ancient history." Bertillon leaned forward in his chair and lighted another cigarette. "What brings you to Paris and my *little* agency?" He said the word "little" so as to emphasize that he thought his agency was anything but little, but modesty prevented his saying so.

"We are hoping," Holmes replied, "that we may have the opportunity so see the anthropometric identification system in actual operation so as to better understand its finer aspects. And," he added, "perhaps you can clear up a few points regarding the system especially as to its usefulness in the investigation of crimes where the identity of the perpetrator is strongly suspected, but the challenge is to establish guilt to the requisite legal standard."

"I shall be delighted to show you the *Bertillon* System, gentlemen, although I cannot claim that what you will see here is the *entire* system in actual operation. This office is of course the central record repository where, as you have already seen, the records on each individual whose measurements have been taken are kept. And it is here that the measurements of the individual, living or deceased, whose identity is to be determined are sent for identification.

"Come this way, please, gentlemen," Bertillon arose, with Holmes and Watson following, "and I will explain as we walk." He led them through the door and back into the series of rooms containing the file-cabinets and researchers. "The *Bertillon* System," he again emphasized *Bertillon* in order to reinforce the point that The *Bertillon* System was the preferred form of reference, "as I'm sure you're both aware, measures eleven physical characteristics of the subject. These measurements are made, as you will soon see for yourselves, with the utmost precision.

"The measurements are recorded in the correct places on a standard, pre-printed card, along with the subject's name and, in recent years, photographs, both front and profile views. The cards are then filed here according to sub-classifications based upon size: large, average or medium, and small. I, myself, have calculated that the odds of two persons having all eleven measurements identical are greater than four million-to-one."

"Permit me, if I may," Watson interrupted, "to ask a question. Can one's measurements not be affected by changes in circumstances?"

"Not so, my learned friend. Not so at all. One's measurements are one's measurements."

Ignoring a warning glance from Holmes, Watson pressed on. "What then of a youth whose measurements are made before he achieves his full growth? And how infallible is the system in identifying a corpse that has been immersed in water or is in an advanced state of putrefaction so that anatomical features may be distorted or even missing? Could not a clever but ruthless criminal—I confess that I'm describing a homicidal maniac—find someone whose measurements closely approximate his own, do in the poor fellow, allow the corpse to decompose, and with the aid of confederates pass the victim off as himself?"

"Brilliant, Dr. Watson! Absolutely brilliant!" Bertillon clapped his hands together in mock applause. "What a superb imagination. How fortunate you are, *M'sieur* Holmes to have such creativity to enliven the accounts of your cases."

Watson bit down so hard on his pipestem that he could actually feel his molar sink into the ebonite. Even Holmes, the consummate actor, found it necessary to remind himself of the larger overriding purpose for cultivating this monomaniac. "You must indulge my physician colleague, *M'sieur* Bertillon. His professional training has as one of its side-effects a somewhat morbid curiosity which manifests itself from time to time in such hypothetical paradigms."

Content to let Watson's cross-questions remain unanswered, Bertillon led them through the series of rooms pausing from time to time to inspect the comparison work being performed by the clerks and to illustrate the comparison of various of the eleven measurements or to comment on how a particular anatomical feature, such as the length of a nose or the shape of an ear was a reliable sign-post in the science of physiognomy, superior even to such hallmarks as shoes, clothing and personal effects so often relied upon by Holmes.

He took them back out into the main corridor, through a series of turns until they came to another door also marked *"Bureau d' Identification"* which opened into a large, gymnasium-like room. The wall opposite the door was taken up with windows. At right angles to each of the two lateral walls there were three wooden panels which were about six feet high and protruded out from the walls toward the center of the room so as to create four separate areas along each wall. Similar partitions flanked either side of the door so that the corridor wall was also divided into four areas, two on each side of the door. In most of the segments there was a plain wooden bench, evidently for seating, and a small, flat-topped cabinet on rollers such as might be used in a physician's office to hold diagnostic or surgical instruments. Facing one of the partitions was a large tripod-mounted portrait camera and one of the small cabinets which held a stack of photographic negative plates. At several of the stations around the perimeter of the room there were groups of four to six men watching demonstrations of the measurement procedures.

As though addressing a school children's tour group, Bertillon made a sweeping gesture with his arm inviting Holmes and Watson to glance about the entire room. "This, gentlemen, is our training facility." His tone of voice was just patronizing enough to reassert his position without being patently offensive. "It is here that we train clerks for all twenty *arrondissements* of Paris and from all of Metropolitan France as well. As you might surmise, since we deal with a large number of very fine measurements, precision and uniformity of technique are crucial. Under the guidance of a staff instructor, each clerk-trainee learns by observation and practice upon his fellow trainees until the staff are satisfied as to his competence. Since my schedule does not permit me the luxury of accompanying you to an *arrondissement* police station to observe an actual measurement process, I beg you to allow me to provide you with the equivalent experience here at the source."

With Bertillon leading the way, they began walking clockwise around the room. At the occupied stations, they would watch the particular measurement being demonstrated, and at the vacant stations Bertillon himself, using Holmes or Watson as a subject, would demonstrate the specific technique. Under Bertillon's tutelage, Holmes measured Watson's head, both back-to-front length and its width at the mid-point above his ears, and Watson reciprocated measuring Holmes' left forearm and right ear. They completed the circuit with Holmes and Watson eschewing the opportunity to be photographed. As they left the training room and were walking back to Bertillon's private office Holmes began, "Tell me, *M'sieur* Bertillon, how do you provide training to those who have or may wish to implement the *Bertillon* System," Holmes emphasized the name in order to demonstrate that he had gotten the message, "in some far-off land such as, for example, say, Canada or even Australia? Once a trainee is out from under your exacting and watchful eye, is the quality of his work ever double-checked?"

Bertillon smiled broadly as he leaned back in his desk chair, "Elementary, my dear Mr. Holmes, elementary." Holmes silently clenched his teeth, while Watson masked his own grin by fiddling with his pipe. "The answer to both questions is the same: my book. It contains not only minute, step-by-step detailed instructions, including dealing with total or partial amputations, scar tissue and other anomalies, but also clear drawings illustrating the proper technique for each measurement. With my book and the proper instruments in hand anyone above the level of simpleton can become proficient in the measurement techniques."

"But why then..." Holmes caught himself before asking the obvious question, "Ah yes, *M'sieur* Bertillon, it's just as you say. I was so fascinated by the actual demonstrations that I quite forgot that in its field your book is not unlike the Holy Bible; it contains all the wisdom that one needs to know in order to get on in life." The irony was totally beyond Bertillon's grasp. Watson, however, although the tobacco in his pipe was already well-lighted, struck another match and quickly cupped it in front of his face and managed, just barely, to convert his snicker to a throat-clearing cough.

"As I mentioned earlier, I am curious about the application of the Bertillon System in cases where identification is not in issue, but the case turns on legal proof of guilt. Take for example the recent case of the Bank of Liverpool forgeries. Let me briefly place before you the salient facts and circumstances.

"The bank clerk, one Goudie, carried on a successful series of forgeries over a two-year period to support a gambling habit. He also kept a mistress who, in the end, treated him even more cruelly than lady luck. Goudie's bookmaker, one Trask, soon figured out how Goudie was raising the money to make good his bets. Had Trask not made two mistakes which ultimately caused the scheme to be exposed, he might yet be alive and might have continued to milk Goudie into the coming century. Trask, so it was later revealed, in order to further ingratiate himself with his naive victim, introduced Goudie to one MaryJane Carmody who by design became Goudie's mistress and Trask's partner in crime as well as occasional lover. The introduction of Carmody, a rather pretty, if foolish and greedy, twenty-two year old girl was his first mistake."

"Ah yes," Bertillon nodded knowingly, *"cherchez la femme."*

86

Sensing that Bertillon was now solidly hooked Holmes continued. "This cozy *menage a trois* continued for over a year. Goudie was clever and the bank's internal auditing procedures were deficient in several ways that Goudie was able to exploit. Trask was careful to see that Goudie won occasionally and that his defalcations did not reach beyond prudence. MaryJane, who was from a poor but honest country family, insisted on acquiring a small flat in Mersey-side only a short distance from the main office of the bank where Goudie was employed in order, so she explained to the bewitched Goudie, to facilitate their liaisons. Once installed in the flat it was not long before MaryJane began to acquire 'just a few things' for the flat and developed a preference for silk lingerie—which Goudie was of course only too happy to indulge—as well as for the latest fashions to wear over the new under-garments.

"Housing and clothing MaryJane, as you might suppose, was becoming some what problematical without Goudie either increasing his defalcations or reducing his wagering. The first alternative was calculated to be too risky, and the second would have, in Trask's mind, defeated the principal reason for the scheme. Never-the-less, Trask, as MaryJane related in her statement to the police, was able to keep things fairly well in hand, at least temporarily by threatening to carve up her face with a long-shoreman's knife." Holmes paused to light a cigarette.

"This expedient, as I say, was only a temporary one. Within a few weeks after Trask's *tete-a-tete* with MaryJane, Goudie was compelled, although un-beknownst to him, to take on another mouth to feed. As fate would have it, MaryJane's older brother John—'One-Eyed Jack Carmody' as he was known in the *demimonde* owing to his having lost an eye in some long-ago affray—was released from Wandsworth Prison upon having completed his sentence for aggravated assault. The occasion of his latest incarceration was also a bar-room brawl—he seemed to have a proclivity for such events—in which he ripped the peg-leg off a one-legged man and using it as a bludgeon nearly beat the victim to death. While the Court directed a verdict in his favor on the charge of mayhem, His Lordship was unmoved by the plea of Carmody's counsel that the assault could not be classed as *aggravated* because his client had only one eye and was thus at least as disadvantaged physically as his victim. He was sentenced to two-years' penal servitude. Upon his release it did not take 'One-Eyed Jack' long to look up his younger sister and to wheedle out of her the source of her up-scale living standard. Now Trask was fully capable of intimidating MaryJane but he was no match for her big brother who soon reduced the bookmaker to a servile cur. It seems, so MaryJane related, that brother Jack threatened to take Trask's fearsome knife—an implement which Trask tearfully confessed to Jack existed only in his own imagination—and use it to convert him, if I may put the matter delicately, from a baritone to a soprano. Jack, being a man of simple needs and pleasures came directly to the point: for the modest price of, say, a 'tenner' a week, payable each Friday, if you please, Mr. Trask could for the foreseeable future remain as one with his masculine appendages.

"Trask fancied himself a ladies' man, and having no wish to be violently separated from such an essential body-part he soon devised a second scheme which, were he after-ward to have been in a position to benefit from hind-sight, he would have at once discarded and instead given serious thought to taking up a cloistered life. Trask in his desperation hit upon what he thought was a perfect way to keep his golden goose productive while at the same time pacifying the Carmody siblings." Holmes paused to tap the ash off his cigarette. "I trust I'm not boring you, *M'sieur* Bertillon?"

"No, no *M'sieur* Holmes. Please continue. Your little melodrama quite fascinates me. I can hardly contain myself in contemplation of the *denouement.*" Bertillon lighted a cigarette and leaned back in his chair blowing a stream of smoke toward the ceiling.

"Among the small, 'retail' bookmakers," Holmes continued, "the practice is to 'lay-off' their book with large, well-capitalized bookmakers retaining for themselves only a small percentage, in the nature of a commission, from each bet. In Trask's case, his 'wholesale' bookmaker was one George 'Jock-the-Butcher' Drummond, who had worked his way up by either intimidating or murdering his rivals in most unpleasant ways from dock-side brawler to small time bookmaker and shylock to perhaps the most feared and powerful criminal king-pin in Liverpool. Trask's brilliant scheme was to turn in to Drummond only

Goudie's winning bets and retain for his own account Goudie's losers. But since Goudie's winning bets were relatively few and far between, he, Trask that is, began to supplement them on a regular basis with bets, always of modest amounts so as not to call attention, by placing extra winning wagers in the delivery pouch after the race results were known. In this manner Trask kept Goudie's *detournement* at the same apparently undetectable level, whilst mulcting Drummond for Jack Carmody's weekly tenner. Jack, for his weekly stipend kept his sister in line, and MaryJane, in return for her flat and silken knickers, kept Goudie in line. And Trask, at least for a while, was, as they say, 'sitting pretty'.

"While Trask had a well-founded dread of Drummond's violent reputation, in his hubris he failed to give Jock-the-Butcher his due as a business-man or as an astute observer of human nature. Drummond had for over a year been aware that Goudie was Trask's best customer in that he was good for a steady ten to twenty 'bob' per week and almost never picked a winner. It therefore piqued Drummond's curiosity when almost over-night Goudie began picking winner after winner, yet—and this was the tip-off—he never let his winnings ride or increased the size of his bets. Drummond knew, although he would be un-able to state the concept in scientific terms, that gamblers such as Goudie suffer from a powerful compulsion just like, as I'm sure Watson would confirm, an alcoholic or dope fiend. This compulsion either arises from or breeds, I'm not sure which, an irresistible impulse toward self-destructive behavior. Drummond, as I say, knew this and found it implausible that Goudie first of all would suddenly go on a winning streak and secondly would not give free rein to his self-destructive impulse by greatly increasing his betting activity.

"So Drummond did a little independent checking on Goudie whom he had until then assumed to have inherited capital. He must have learned that Goudie rather than being independently wealthy was a humble bank clerk earning at most seven pounds, two and six-pence each week. Then it didn't take him long to find the little love-nest and the delectable if vacuous MaryJane. It probably took only a disappointingly brief working-over by one of Drummond's enforcers, an ex-pugilist I believe, to get the rest of the story out of Trask. Although sorely tempted to make good on One-Eyed Jack's earlier threat, the nature of which Trask must have blurted out during his 'interrogation', Drummond decided instead to take Goudie over for himself. However, while the fruits of Goudie's larceny as augmented by Trask's little embellishment were enough, albeit barely so, to keep Trask and the Carmodys contented, the whole lot was merely pocket-change to Drummond. Moreover, Drummond must have intuitively known with certainty what the others would not admit: that Goudie would be caught out with the result that they too might end up in durance vile for a long, long time.

"With this thought in mind, Drummond, one surmises, determined that his role in the affair must be kept from Goudie and the Carmodys and that since the scheme was probably going to un-ravel soon anyway, it would be best to grab as much as could be grabbed in the shortest time possible and 'devil take the hindmost.' To implement his plan, Drummond needed certain information which only Goudie, of those involved, had access. He wrote out a list—a *bordereau*—of what he wanted: the names of major depositors, their highest balances and when during the month they were likely to occur, and the names of those to whom the large depositors wrote checks in substantial amounts on a recurring basis. This list he gave to Trask, with instructions to obtain the information and report back immediately.

"In the meantime, Drummond, unwilling to trust Trask with large sums of money, in order to facilitate the funneling of the embezzled funds into his hands had his bookkeeper open an account with Goudie's employer in the name of a trading company chartered in the Channel Isles and owned by a Liechtenstein korpenschaft—holding company—whose shares were bearer shares and whose managing director was a Swiss lawyer. Drummond, using an assumed name, was the sole signatory. His scheme was to have Goudie, under Trask's supervision, write checks on the accounts of the large depositors made payable to the order of the regular payees. Trask would then turn these checks over to Drummond after first endorsing the name of the unsuspecting payee. Drummond would then deposit the checks to his bogus account always using the night-deposit box and a day or two later transfer the funds to other accounts in Switzerland and the Cayman Islands, whose bank-secrecy laws are impenetrable.

"Drummond's scheme succeeded beyond even his own expectations. Only Trask knew that Drummond had taken control of the enterprise, and he knew his life would be forfeit should he talk. Goudie was kept in line out of his fear of Trask and prison. The Carmodys were merely kept in the dark. During the nearly two years before Drummond had taken charge, the sum total of Goudie's thefts came to something like two thousand pounds; so skillful was Goudie that the exact amount will probably never be known. But in the space of less than two months with Goudie harnessed directly to Drummond's wagon the total came to more than one hundred sixty thousand pounds."

"*Incredible! M'sieur* Holmes. How is such a *fantastique* thing possible? "Bertillon was practically bouncing up and down in his chair. "How were they caught and brought to justice?"

"As is usually the case in these crimes, quite by accident. A posting error by another clerk having to do with one of the accounts from which Goudie had been abstracting triggered an unexpected audit one Friday afternoon. The auditors worked over the weekend and by the time the bank opened on the following Monday, the Liverpool constabulary had taken Goudie into custody. Scotland Yard was called in. Under questioning, Goudie, who by this time was sick of the whole affair, gave up Trask and MaryJane. Drummond, who knew what was going on at police headquarters sooner than even the chief inspector, immediately drew out the balance in the account and sent his bookkeeper to Mallorca for a lengthy holiday in the Mediterranean sunshine.

"Trask was taken into custody late that same evening. In the course of preliminary questioning, he gave up Jack Carmody and actually began to implicate Drummond. In fact, almost all that I have related regarding Drummond's involvement came from the Scotland Yard initial interview of Trask. He hinted that he had much more information to give, but he refused to say more without first speaking to his solicitor. Most probably he realized that Drummond would never trust him to remain silent so his only chance of survival was to make a deal for immunity, a new identity and transport to someplace as far from England as possible. In any case, whatever his motive, he never had a chance to carry out his offer. The assize court then being in session, there was that evening the usual formal banquet of the bench and bar. Of course

91

Trask's solicitor was in attendance, and was loathe to curtail his engagement to attend his client who he supposed was in 'nick' on another of many run-of-the-mill illegal wagering charges.

"Drummond evidently was able to wield his diabolical power even within the confines of Her Majesty's Liverpool Central Prison. Trask was found next morning hanging by the neck from a cross-bar in his cell. It was made to look like suicide, but the post-mortem examination strongly suggested that he had been garroted and his neck snapped before he was hung from the cross-bar. The autopsy showed a thin indentation line in his neck inside the mark made by the strips of bed sheet used to suspend him from the cross-bar. Also, it is extremely rare for death to occur in a jail-cell hanging by violent luxation or fracture of the cervical vertebrae. Usually in such cases death occurs by asphyxiation due to occlusion of the wind-pipe, in other words strangulation.

"Acting swiftly the authorities soon had the Carmodys in custody as well. Upon learning of Trask's death as well as the massive sums that were missing and could not be accounted for, Jack quickly came to the realization that there must be a hidden master-mind, a 'king-pin' if you will, whose power and ruthlessness were far beyond anything in his extensive criminal experience. Not having anything with which to bargain, he chose to say nothing, at least until he could figure out his next move. Since he was not able to communicate with his sister, and she was a naif in the ways of the underworld, she willingly and cheerfully told all she knew, which amounted unfortunately to what I have just related." .

"And what then, *M'sieur* Holmes, of the 'king-pin' Drummond? Indeed what was the fate of the *dupe* Goudie and the Carmodys, the 'delectable', I believe you described her, MaryJane?"

"Goudie, realizing the hopelessness of his case, pleaded guilty at his arraignment, and received for his efforts a lengthy prison term. Jack Carmody entered a plea of 'not guilty' and is awaiting trial. MaryJane also pleaded guilty, and is awaiting sentencing. Owing to her relatively minor role in the affair and her lack of a prior criminal record she may not, I should imagine, be dealt with too severely. We are made to understand that she has signed a contract to sell the exclusive rights to her life story to one of the more sensational magazines for what is thought to be a tidy sum and has numerous lucrative offers to appear on stage in London and New York once her debt to society has been paid. If I were to hazard a guess, I should say that *Mademoiselle* Carmody will, all things considered, do quite well.

"And as for Drummond, well, it is he that has caused us to impose upon your valuable time. Speaking of time," Holmes consulted his watch, "we have I see already consumed a good bit of your time and I would suppose that you have many official matters to attend to before the end of the day. Let me propose then that you join Dr. Watson and myself for dinner this evening. We have heard that Maxim's in The Rue Royale is quite good and the fashionable place to dine. We would be delighted if you could be our guest, not only help us with our little forensic problem but also assist us in selecting our dinners and a suitable wine."

"Oh yes indeed." Watson gripped the arms of his chair until his knuckles turned white. "Do *please* join us. The evening will not be the same without you. I can't imagine *how* we should be able to negotiate the menu without your aid."

Bertillon clasped his hands together and resting his chin on the tips of his index fingers gazed at the ceiling as though contemplating a major career decision. "Gentlemen, I am honored that you should seek the opinions of Bertillon in matters of such importance, both forensic and gustatory. I accept of course your most gracious invitation."

Holmes rose from his seat and extended his hand. "Excellent. Then it's settled. Watson and I shall return to our hotel. We need to check for messages, and, since we *are* on holiday, perhaps relax a bit and enjoy a pre-prandial cocktail. Shall we say *'a huit heures et demi'* at Maxim's?"

"*Tres bien, M'sieurs.* Until then, *au revoir.*"

CHAPTER NINE

"It seems to me that you will get as much satisfaction out of
putting an end to Bertillon's 'reign of terror'
as you will from getting to the bottom
of this sordid mess... ".

"**B**last it all, Holmes. Why would you want to spoil a perfectly good evening by spending it in the company of that self-styled 'mathematics prodigy'? *Idiot savant* is more likely closer to the mark." Watson had held his tongue during their walk through the labyrinthine corridors to the Place Vendome entrance and from there next door to the hospitality of the Ritz. "I must say, after three hours of his self-important blather, I'm nearly tempted to plead a recurrence of my... how do you say it? Oh, yes...*mal de la tete.* Only thing that constrains me not to do so is that I too can hardly contain my curiosity as to the fate of the diabolical Drummond. Words cannot express my relief that the delectable MaryJane will not be greatly inconvenienced by Her Majesty's judicial system.

"I could not help but mark your mention of the so-called *'bordereau'.* If I rightly recall your discourse on the boat-train, a document similarly described played a crucial role in Dreyfus's conviction. As to 'MaryJane and the Forty Thieves', I feel certain that you did not weave the ballad out of whole cloth. Again, if memory serves, within just the last few days I remember reading a brief item in the *Daily Mail* the gist of which was that a small-potatoes turf accountant name of Trask apparently in a fit of despondency hanged himself in the Liverpool Central Prison while awaiting arraignment on some relatively minor charge. I must declare that I await with keen interest your confession, as it were, as to how you came to possess so many of the other, as you put it, 'salient facts and circumstances'."

"Your *opprobrium medicorum,* my dear Watson, is most apropos. Yet in this instance, I must plead extenuating circumstances. Four days ago while you were out buying the concert tickets—by the way, I still owe you for mine—I received in the afternoon's post a rather lengthy letter from Lestrade. Seems that our friend Chief Inspector Lestrade was called to Liverpool within hours after Trask's body was found to take over management of the case. Ah, here we are. Shall we take a few minutes respite? As the rest of the story following the collapse of the scheme is nearly as convoluted as the first chapters, it would perhaps best be told over that pre-prandial cocktail I mentioned as we took our leave of Bertillon." .

The two men entered the hotel lobby and headed to the registration desk to pick up their keys.

"My own prescription, Holmes, would be at least two, perhaps as many as four cocktails, at least two as an antidote to this afternoon's exposure to *M'sieur* Bertillon and at least two more in order to assure that we are inoculated against this evening's. And should your brother, or for that matter the Rothschilds themselves, wish afterwards to scrutinize our accounts I shall be most happy to oblige them with a detailed explanation. As I do not anticipate that there will be any messages for me, let me know when you are ready. I am going to freshen up a bit, and perhaps put my feet up for a few minutes."

Forty-five minutes later, they were seated in the cocktail lounge, and having ordered their first round of drinks, Holmes resumed his description of the *"Adventure of the Bewitched Bank Clerk"* as Watson had already titled it in his mind.

"From what I can gather—Lestrade's letter was typically somewhat rambling—the Bank's employee fidelity bond covered only ten thousand pounds of the loss. Thus the stockholders' capital will be charged for the remainder. The non-management stockholders are justifiably incensed at the negligence of the bank's directors and chartered accountants in not having sooner detected the defalcation, and are contemplating an action at law in the name of the bank to force the directors and accountants to make good the losses. Likewise, the fidelity bond underwriters are asserting a right of subrogation against the chartered accountants to recoup their ten thousand pounds.

"Of course all three underwriters, the fidelity bond, the director's liability, and the accountants' errors and omissions, are Lloyd's syndicates and there is no love lost among the rival syndicate managers. The regular auditing firm and the special

95

fraud auditors continue to debate the nuances of the phrase 'scope of audit', and the syndicates' respective solicitors continue to exchange increasingly strident albeit unfailingly polite letters, the kind that only the most expensive lawyers are capable of writing. In the meanwhile, the managers at Lloyd's have made common cause in trying to either trace the money or to get enough on Drummond so that he can be credibly threatened with prosecution. Their preference is for felony murder, but extortion and conspiracy to embezzle would do nearly as well. Their intention, although they would not publicly so admit, is to induce Drummond to give back the money in trade for his life or at the least his liberty."

"Sounds to me rather a typical case: the accountants come in after the battle to count the casualties, and the lawyers come in to bayonet the wounded. But pray enlighten me," Watson took a long pull on his gin and tonic, "as to how that differs from the extortion practiced by Drummond upon Trask or by Trask upon the hapless Goudie?"

Holmes pondered Watson's question for a moment. "Be that as it may, and I can't help but think you have a valid philosophical point, the subscribers to all three policy syndicates are men of substantial wealth and it naturally follows as you might imagine, men of enormous influence as well. Just as one can infer the existence of an ocean from a single drop of water, one can readily infer that the power and influence that money and position command have been brought most bluntly to bear through The Governors of The Bank of England and The Home Office on The Yard and ultimately upon the head of our benighted friend Lestrade.

"Philosophical musings aside," Holmes continued, "the reason for my somewhat laconic behavior at the Savoy was that I was mulling the matter over in my mind, and had not yet reached the point where I could put the case before you in any useful form. Of course supervening events have relegated the saga to the status of a novel that one starts and puts aside in favor of a new best-seller by some familiar and favorite author. Who for instance would continue reading the vapid rubbish that so clutters the book-sellers' stalls today, when one could instead take up a new installment of *The Adventures of Sherlock Holmes?*

"After our visit with Mycroft, while you were having your nap I hit upon the idea of using the case as a vehicle for drawing out Bertillon in the direction we want to take him. Before Mr. Churchill again intruded, I was going to go over the matter with you at dinner. And then yesterday there did not seem to be a convenient time owing to the rigors of our journey, and then to the volubility of our host.

"The key to the Liverpool business, it seems to me lies in whatever paper trail may be available. A search of Goudie's rooms turned up the list of information—the *bordereau* indeed it shall henceforth be—presumably prepared by Drummond. One could surmise that he instructed Trask either to memorize the list or re-copy it in his own hand, and upon doing so, destroy the original. Most likely Trask, with his parents' tacit blessing, had chosen in his formative years to spend his time absorbing more adult pursuits and thus eschewed the less immediately rewarding school-boy chores of learning penmanship and acquiring the mental discipline necessary to comprehend and retain unfamiliar concepts. It may be inferred that because Trask did not feel up to his homework assignment, and probably because he resented having it thrust upon himself at all, instead of doing as Drummond demanded merely gave the list in its original form to Goudie. Perhaps he used it to persuade Goudie to carry out Drummond's orders, or perhaps he thought it would make no difference.

"No doubt the bank will still have on file the signature card, and..."

"I think I see where you're going on this. If the signature card and the list—the *bordereau;* I must get used to using that term—can be identified as having been authored by Drummond, it should be more than enough to land him in the dock charged at least with conspiracy to commit theft by fraud. And with Goudie's testimony, which, having already pleaded guilty, he can be compelled to give, that should be enough to convict."

"Well put, Watson. While the learned judge may be vexed by questions as to the admissibility of the uncorroborated testimony of a co-conspirator, whoever leads for the Crown could, I think, successfully argue that Goudie was not a co-conspirator of Drummond's, but was the victim of an extortion conspiracy between Drummond and Trask. .

97

"However interesting such issues may be to the learned members of the Bar, who shall no doubt earn substantial fees arguing either or both sides of the questions, there is one further aspect of more immediate interest to us. Bertillon fears, and rightly so I should say, that ere the rest of the world outside Metropolitan France and the State of Illinois comes to recognize his genius and adopts his system as the primary means of criminal identification, it will be supplanted by some new and better system. Then 'Europe's highest expert' and his system will be relegated to a footnote in the annals of forensic science."

"From my observation of your recent non-fiction reading list, may I hazard a guess that you are referring to the art, I'm not sure that it is ready to be called a science, of fingerprint comparison?"

"Just so, Watson. If I may recall an expression favored by my maternal *grand-pere, 'on commence par etre dupe, on finit etre fripon';* 'he who begins by being a fool, ends up by being a knave.' So it is with *M'sieur* Bertillon. As unthinkable as it may seem to us Bertillon has abused his office as head of the Bureau of Identification to secretly compile *dossiers* on all the leading politicians going back through every government for at least the last fifteen years. Whenever some new Minister of Justice suggests that Bertillon's powers or prerogatives be curtailed even in the slightest an invitation to an *in camera* inspection of the upstart's dossier or even more subtly that of his predecessor, soon leads to a withdrawal of the suggestion as having been improvidently made."

"I say, Holmes, you can't be serious. What nation with a freely-elected government could tolerate such sinister behavior by one who is essentially a mere bureaucrat? Why the rogue is no better than the late, un-lamented Milverton. Besides, after listening to Ritz's discourse last night, I'm hard-pressed to think what private behavior on the part of a Frenchman should it become a matter of public knowledge could possibly cause enough of a scandal to dissuade action against such a martinet."

Holmes signaled the waiter for another round of drinks. "That exquisite bit of irony has thus far apparently escaped the attention of those most likely to benefit from it. Irony aside, Bertillon remains the immovable object against which no irresistible force has yet been devised. To anyone who has the temerity to advocate some other system, or even to propose an open, scholarly debate, he stands as an aged but still deadly lion astride the path to scientific progress. By intimidation, black-mail and any other means he silences his critics and preserves his fiefdom."

"It appears to me," Watson handed the waiter his empty glass in exchange for a fresh one, "that you will get as much satisfaction out of putting an end to Bertillon's 'reign of terror' as you will from getting to the bottom of this sordid business and perhaps even from seeing that justice is finally achieved for Dreyfus."

As he sipped from his second drink and lighted a cigarette, Holmes seemed to relax. Watson sensed that since the explosion when Churchill first made to mention Dreyfus's name, the vast reservoir of mental energy that had built up through the melancholy winter months with their self-imposed inactivity in the after-math of the Milverton misadventure had dissipated and been replaced by the focused, intense energy which Holmes brought to bear when he found a challenge worthy of his exertions. Holmes set down his drink, "If you are agreeable, in further dealing with Bertillon, I should like for you to continue to play the picador by first broaching the subject of fingerprinting."

"Although it is generally not in my nature to do so, in this instance I shall gladly make an exception. I say, you don't suppose he has files on us, do you?"

CHAPTER TEN

"Although my international reputation rests on the criminal identification system associated with my name, I have also acquired expertise in handwriting comparison.
It was I, Alphonse Bertillon, who conclusively established the guilt of the Jew-traitor Dreyfus."

Maxim's, although crowded, held a prime banquette table 'for the celebrated English Detective and his associate' as an accommodation to Cesár Ritz. The addition of Bertillon provided an unexpected *lagniappe* and caused a considerable stir among the wait-staff. A number of these were in his pay on a piecework basis supplying tid-bits of information which Bertillon fed, meticulously indexed and cross-indexed, into his *dossiers.*

Bertillon, the moment they were seated on the burgundy plush, affected the role of host, and insisted that the ordering be left to him. However, to be certain that the *ne plus ultra* of his role was clearly defined, as Hugo the head-waiter fluffed their napkins Bertillon murmured in Hugo's ear *"L' addition a M'sieur Holmes, s'il vous plait."* Holmes, perusing the prices, silently commended himself on his foresight in cashing a draft at the Ritz before they departed for Maxim's. Unburdened by pecuniary concerns—a state of mind which is as essential to the Maxim's dining experience as a knife and fork— Bertillon, as Holmes and Watson would later admit to themselves, made the most of the occasion. *Pate de foie gras* served with warm toast points and a well-chilled PerrierJouet; *consommé royale a la madrilène* with glasses of Madeira; *coquille St. Jacques* with a pleasant muscadet; raspberry *sorbet; tournedos* in a sauce of truffles with *petit pois, pome de terre* and a splendid Chateau Margaux; *un salade vert* mixed with roasted walnuts and Roquefort in vinaigrette; and finally *coupe et framboises* served with Dom Perignon.

Between the soup and fish courses, Holmes and Watson marked the entrance of *"Les Grandes Trois."* The woman who Ritz had identified as Emilienne D' Alencon, bejeweled and gowned as elegantly as the previous evening at the Ritz, clung to the arm of a tall man whose facial hair, pointed beard and heavily-waxed mustache with up-turned ends marked him as a cavalry officer. He wore a monocle and across his chest over his waistcoat, a purple sash to which was affixed a large—and to Watson's mind rather garish—medallion consisting of an outer ring of gold worked in the shape of leaves or flower petals and an inner ring of metal enameled in the form of a heraldic crest surrounded by a jeweled bezel. Noticing Holmes's and Watson's interest, Bertillon identified him as Grand Duke Nicholas of Russia who, according to that day's edition of *Le Figaro,* had hosted a truly grand party in honor of his wife's birthday at Maxim's the previous night.

"Accompanying *Mlle.* De Pougy," Bertillon continued, "is the *Comte* Chevedole, whose title dating back to the *ancien regime* is a distinguished one. *Le Comte* himself is a prominent member of the Jockey Club.

"*Mlle.* Otero, gentlemen, clings to the arm of Baron Ollstreder, a German who, one understands from the popular press, possesses wealth in proportion to his immense girth. Notice the pearl necklace gracing the throat of *Mlle.* Otero; it originally graced the neck of The Empress Eugenie. The baron presented it to *La Belle* Otero, so one hears, in exchange for a mere fifteen minutes of her favors. She maintains, also at the baron's expense, a magnificent house with a full staff of servants in the Rue Georges Bizet."

Baron Ollstreder did, Watson mused, give one cause to wonder whether the world's oldest profession was not also among its most challenging. The man's girth was indeed astounding. It would have, as Watson later observed to Holmes, made at least two of Mycroft. The annular-shaped mass of flesh that protruded from the top of his collar bore no resemblance to a human neck, but looked to Watson's professional eye like a massive goiter which pulsed hideously as its owner breathed. This anatomical wonder merged, with only the merest hint of a chin and jaw-line, into a grotesque head. The mouth was described by large, fleshy red lips that were pulled back to expose a set of tiny, spiked teeth and pale, pink gums. His cheeks were sallow and pock-marked, and the left bore a puffy white dueling scar running from the corner of his mouth to his ear. His nose seemed to be without bone or cartilage and lay like a deflated balloon between his upper lip and the junction of his close-set porcine eyes. Beneath each eye hung purplish bags of flesh. He was nearly bald, save for a few strands across the top that were plastered down with beads of perspiration. A narrow fringe of wiry black hair clung stubbornly to the back of his head behind his comose ears. The hair's coarse texture matched the tangled mat on his wrists and the backs of his hands where they protruded from his shirt-cuffs.

Watson considered asking Bertillon how it was that he was so familiar with the make-up of *Mlle. Otero*'s household. Instead, remembering that they were there to flatter Bertillon, not antagonize him, he contented himself with commenting on the enormous mound of caviar that had arrived at *Les Grandes Trois'* table. The delicacy had appeared, along with magnums of champagne, nearly as soon as the party was seated, and even before Hugo had concluded his examination of the women's *décolletage* as he fluffed their napkins in his most elaborate manner.

When the *tournedos* were nearly gone, the Chateau Margaux down to the last few sips and before Holmes could inflict another of his *"bon mots,"* Watson judged the time propitious to begin bearding the lion in his den. "I was so absorbed with the tour of your splendid facility, *M'sieur* Bertillon, that I quite forgot to ask you how acceptance of the *Bertillon System* was faring outside your own bailiwick? In the forensic science literature much has been made of late regarding the use of fingerprints as a means of identification, and..."

Bertillon's features grew hard. "Nonsense, gentlemen. Sheer nonsense. This finger-printing business is but a passing fad. Nothing will come of it. On that you have Alphonse Bertillon's highest assurance." Bertillon slammed his fist down on the table so hard that it rattled the china and crystal and caused the conversation at the adjacent tables to come to a halt.

"I'm sure you're quite correct in your analysis," Watson pressed on. "However, I must say that the work of Sir Francis Galton and Sir Edward Henry, both of whom have expanded on the original research done by Herschel—what was it Holmes, over forty years ago?—is at least to my in-expert eye, rather impressive. Indeed, since I'm in fairly constant contact with the publishing world, I've heard some trade gossip to the effect that Sir Edward is bringing out a book either later this year or perhaps early next year.

"The publisher, I'm made to understand, is taking unprecedented pains to have a draft of the work reviewed by other leading experts even before it goes to press. Once it is released I was thinking I might have a go at reviewing it for the benefit of the general reader."

"Take my advice, Dr. Watson; do not squander your time and reputation on such a worthless endeavor." Bertillon wagged his finger in Watson's face. "The publisher will, I am certain, as you English put it: 'lose his shirt'. And everyone associated with the enterprise will suffer eternal embarrassment."

Warming to his task, Watson continued. "As I say, I claim no expertise in such matters and in this company it would be presumptuous of me to state otherwise. However, I can't help but observe that finger-printing would appear to have some features to commend it. For one thing," Watson ticked his points off on his fingers, "the equipment is as simple as can be, and for another, I would think that owing to the simplicity, the process would be quite low-cost as well as fostering economy of effort. I also suppose that elaborate training of personnel would not be required. Since but one process is involved, unless the subject has no fingers from which to take the prints, there is little likelihood that a crucial measurement could be unavailable or distorted."

As Watson paused to finish his claret, Holmes, who'd been twirling the last of his wine around his glass entered the fray. "I'm made to understand that theoretically no two persons' finger-prints are identical..."

"Ah, Ha! *M'sieur* Holmes," Bertillon smiled. "Though your powers are formidable, you too often confuse certainty with presumption. How can one be sure that no two people have the same finger-prints? Wouldn't it be necessary to obtain the prints of every living person in the world in order to be sure?"

Under Hugo's supervision the waiters cleared the meat-course dishes and served the salad. Choosing to ignore the slur on his deductive reasoning capacity, Holmes replied, "your point is theoretically irrefutable. But if one allows for the laws of probability, I'm inclined to think that finger-print comparison is not entirely wanting in forensic utility.

"With exceptions, the propensity of criminals generally is to commit their crimes in places that are familiar to them. This fact alone would allow the elimination of all but a tiny percentage of the earth's population as suspects. If one grants the benefit of a doubt to those whose circumstances—say incarceration or physical incapacity—render them unlikely perpetrators, and if one rules out women and children who statistically commit relatively few serious crimes, one would be left with a fairly manageable universe of suspects.

"Consider Drummond's *bordereau* which I mentioned this afternoon." Holmes went on to repeat the remainder of the story as he had related it to Watson earlier that evening. "Suppose that the police were able to obtain images of the residual finger impressions of those who had handled the document. And suppose that they were able to obtain a set of finger-prints known to be those of Drummond. If the two sets of impressions were to match, would that not be sufficient proof to connect Drummond to the *bordereau* and eventually to a long, long time as a guest of Her Majesty's penal system?"

"Sheer fantasy, *M'sieur* Holmes. And, may I add, entirely superfluous." Bertillon pushed away his empty salad plate.

"Superfluous?" Holmes paused with a bite of salad in mid-air. "Why superfluous?" .

"Handwriting, *M'sieur* Holmes. Handwriting. To the expert eye, no two people have the same handwriting." Bertillon leaned back against the banquette and laced his fingers over his middle. "In its narrower sphere, handwriting comparison rivals even *bertillonage* in infallibility. In France, as I'm sure is the case in England as well, the vast majority of crimes do not lend themselves to solution by hand-writing comparison. But with this limitation, handwriting comparison can be an invaluable tool."

During the pause in the conversation while the salad plates were cleared and the dessert and champagne served, Watson considered pointing out that a skilled forger can frequently confound even the highest expert. But just as he was about to speak, he was struck sharply on the shoulder by a small, hard object. In virtually the same instant, another small object clinked off Holmes's champagne flute and came to rest in his dessert plate.

"What the devil..." Watson looked up at the ceiling and then turned his head sharply in an effort to locate the source of the bombardment. The small orchestra which had been playing quietly in the background struck up a lively piece by Offenbach which it continued to play at the maximum sound level of which it was capable as the room was suddenly filled with small objects hurled through the air in all directions by the male diners.

Several more of the missiles arched toward their table. Holmes quickly caught two on the fly. *"Louis d' or,* if I'm not mistaken." Holmes, being without his reading glasses, held one of the gold coins, which was about the size of a shilling, nearly at arm's length. "A most curious custom, I must say. Is it a regular occurrence, or is this some special occasion that our guide-book failed to mention?"

Watson reached down with his right hand to pick up the coin that had first struck him in the back. As he did he noticed that Bertillon, while affecting above the level of the table an attitude of bored disinterestedness, was energetically groping his hand along the banquette seat in an effort to capture several of the coins that had landed there. Glancing about the room Watson noticed that the wait-staff were as nonchalantly as possible sliding coins that landed on the floor into inconspicuous corners and under tables to be retrieved after closing time. Even several of the female patrons could be seen discreetly extending a dainty foot in order to slide a coin or two under their chairs to be carefully picked up when leaving.

Having assured himself of a profit for the evening as well as an excellent dinner, Bertillon drained his champagne glass. "It has recently become, I'm sad to say, a nightly custom of the house. Such wretched excess! And in public too! One may, I suppose, expect such disgusting behavior among the lower classes, but to see it occur among the elite of cafe-society, why..."

"It is, all in all, quite *outré,* " Holmes agreed. "But it seems to have passed as quickly as a spring shower. And the musicians, I perceive," Holmes nodded in the direction of the orchestra, "have apparently quite exhausted themselves and have declared an intermission. Hopefully Mardi Gras is over for the evening and you can continue to enlighten us on the science of handwriting comparison. Incidentally, I must confess that I was unaware of your expertise in the area.

"I also perceive that we've run out of champagne. What say, Watson? Can you manage another glass? *M'sieur* Bertillon?" Just as Holmes was about to look for a waiter, Hugo appeared, jinni-like, with a fresh magnum of Dom Perignon.

"Compliments, *M'sieurs,* of Baron Ollstreder. He sincerely hopes that *M'sieur* Holmes and *Docteur* Watson have a most enjoyable stay in Paris, and earnestly wishes, if your schedule permits, that you spare him an hour of your time at your convenience."

Sensing that Watson was about to say something appropriately inappropriate, Holmes quickly responded, "please thank the baron for his most gracious gesture. While I believe that our schedule is committed for tomorrow afternoon, if the baron will receive us in the morning, we would be glad to call on him then. Is that al-right with you Watson?"

"I say, Holmes. I thought we were on holiday."

"True, old man. Quite true. But there's nothing like an amusing little problem to keep one's wits sharpened. Look here. I've been to the Louvre I don't know how many times. Why don't you go ahead as we'd planned, and I'll deal with the baron myself. We can then meet for lunch, and I'll fill you in. If there's any substance to the baron's problem we can both tackle it from then on. And if there's nothing of interest, you will have seen the Louvre, and I, well..."

"Very well, Holmes. I defer to your wishes, albeit reluctantly. But I refuse to do so without at least commenting on the irony. According to our distinguished friend *M'sieur* Bertillon, the baron was more than willing to part with a small fortune to purchase a mere fifteen minutes of *Mlle.* Otero's professional time. But he is able to purchase an entire hour of the time of Sherlock Holmes, the world's greatest consulting detective, for the price of a mere bottle of wine. I do believe that *M'sieur* Ritz has a point, although I'm beginning to think that he may have understated it."

"Good. Then it's settled." Hugo expertly extracted the cork and refilled each man's glass. Holmes turned in his chair toward the baron and raised his glass in a silent toast to seal the bargain. "Hugo, please tell Baron Ollstreder that I shall be happy to call upon him in the morning, say around *dix heures et demie?* Ask him to please let me know where." Holmes picked up the gold Louis that had landed in his-dessert plate, wiped it off and gave it to Hugo.

"Merci M'sieur Holmes." Hugo pocketed the coin and scampered off to report to the baron, who, Watson noticed, handed Hugo another gold Louis as well.

Bertillon during this time had been sitting with a bemused look on his face. With Hugo dismissed, Holmes turned back toward Bertillon and tipped his glass slightly in Bertillon's direction in a sort of toast. "To forensic science, gentlemen, and especially *bertillonage.* " As Bertillon and Watson raised their glasses in acknowledgment of Holmes's toast, Watson managed a faint "hear! hear!"

Holmes set down his glass and extracted his cigarette case. He offered one to Bertillon, who accepted, and to Watson, who declined, preferring instead a cigar which he took from a leather case in his breast pocket. When cigar and cigarettes were lighted, Bertillon arched his back against the banquette cushion. "Although my international reputation, such as it is," Bertillon modestly lowered his eyes, "rests entirely upon the criminal identification system which the forensic science community has graciously associated with my name, in the discharge of my duties as the head of the Bureau of Identification I have of necessity also acquired expertise in handwriting comparison. Indeed it surprises me that you do not recall that it was I, Alphonse Bertillon, who conclusively established the guilt of the Jew-traitor Dreyfus."

Watson puffed his cigar and furrowed his brow. "Ah yes. You remember, Holmes. About five years ago, wasn't it? Something about passing military information to the Germans. Haven't we read something in the papers recently about a new trial or some such business?"

"I must confess," Holmes interjected, "that I'm quite cold on the details of the case, *M'sieur* Bertillon. I'm afraid we Londoners are not nearly as cosmopolitan as you Parisians, and as often as not we remain in blissful ignorance regarding matters abroad."

"The story of the traitor Dreyfus, *M'sieurs,* " Bertillon leaned forward and lowered his voice to a near whisper, "the

'Dreyfus Affaire' as it has come to be called in the Jewish-controlled mongrel press, is perhaps Bertillon's greatest triumph. Greater even than the celebrated case of the anarchist Koeningstein, or 'Ravachol' as he preferred to call himself, in 1892. It was in that case, I, Alphonse Bertillon, using the *Bertillon System*, identified the bomber. That coup led to my appointment to my present position and established beyond question the validity of *bertillonage*. Perhaps, Doctor Watson, if *M'sieur* Holmes runs out of interesting cases, you might consider writing up the Dreyfus and Koeningstein cases." Bertillon straightened up in his seat as though posing for a front-piece portrait. "All in the interest of the advancement of forensic science of course."

As one of the assistant waiters topped off their champagne glasses, Holmes held his up to catch the light and for several seconds watched the bubbles climbing from the bottom of the flute. "Although it has been some years," Holmes lowered his glass, "I remember reading something about the anarchist 'Ravachol'... is that what you said he called himself? Wasn't he turned in by a waiter or some such?"

"That is true, *M'sieur* Holmes, but it was I who determined his real identity, upon the strength of which his guilt was established and his bomb-throwing days brought to an end."

"And what of Dreyfus?" Holmes asked. "How did you bring him to book? I say, Watson, didn't we read something about his confessing his crimes?"

Before Watson could reply, Bertillon resumed his lecture. "Yes, it was reported by Captain Lebrun-Renault of the Section of Statistics, the counter-intelligence body of the French Army. Lebrun testified in a deposition that as he was guarding the wretched dog prior to the degradation ceremony, Dreyfus tried to tell him some fantastic tale about exchanging worthless information for vital intelligence regarding a giant siege-gun our own experts believed the Germans were trying to build. Of course it was only a clever fabrication in a last-minute effort to save his miserable Jew-skin, and as such it was superfluous since I had already proven his guilt beyond any question."

Watson, holding his cigar between his index and middle fingers, hunched his shoulders and leaned forward, his elbows and forearms on the table. "And how, *M'sieur,* were you able to do that? If I may say so, the world-wide forensic science community, not to mention the public-at-large, should be made aware of such a singular piece of work and all due honor should be yours."

Bertillon helped himself to another of Holmes's cigarettes. "Ah ha, *mes amis*. The little Jew was clever, but not so clever as to deceive Bertillon. It was by careful examination of a copy of the *bordereau* written by Dreyfus at the dictation of Commandant du Paty du Clam on the day of the traitor's arrest along with a version which the traitor was compelled to write while in Cherche-Midi Prison awaiting his court-martial. I determined that in writing the *bordereau* the scoundrel Dreyfus had imitated his own handwriting so as to make it appear that someone else had forged his handwriting in order to cast suspicion upon him. In other words, *M'sieurs*, it was a self-forgery calculated by Dreyfus to divert suspicion from himself. He thought that by implicating himself through a document that every expert would expose as a forgery, he would be exonerated and would thereafter be above suspicion and thus able to continue his nefarious work without further risk.

"And, I must say, *M'sieurs*, had it not been for Alphonse Bertillon, he very likely would have gotten away with his perfidious scheme." Bertillon drained his glass, and as peroration allowed himself a small, self-laudatory belch.

Holmes raised his glass, "Amazing, *M'sieur* Bertillon, amazing. Don't you agree, Watson?"

"Absolutely, Holmes, absolutely amazing." Watson raised his own glass to meet Holmes's, "Indubitably the most singular piece of work in the annals of forensic science."

"Pray tell, *M'sieur* Bertillon," Holmes continued, "Once you had hit upon the self-forgery thesis, what proofs did you use to support it?"

Bertillon beamed. "The first clue was that the *bordereau* was written on onionskin paper, so as to make it appear to be a tracing. This clue led me to examine not only the two writings known to have been done by Dreyfus, but handwriting samples of his family as well. I was able to conclusively establish that in his cunning Dreyfus 'borrowed' certain writing characteristics from his brother and even his sister-in-law. In some instances I was able to show that he would trace letters or words as many as seven or eight times until there emerged a clear pattern of deviations, shifts or displacements from which he created a veritable 'citadel of graphic rebuses' which defied the assaults of the then foremost handwriting experts in all of France. And only I, Alphonse Bertillon, was able to trap him in his crafty lair.

"Once I was sure of my position, I went straight to Mercier, The Minister for War. So impressed was he that he took me directly to the President himself, *M'sieur* Casimir-Perier who, owing to the importance of my findings received me twice. Why on the second occasion he even went so far..."

"Excusez-moi, M'sieurs," Hugo bowed obsequiously, "but there is a uniformed *gendarme* at the entrance and he insists that I give *M'sieur* Bertillon this note immediately."

Bertillon seized the folded paper from the waiter and quickly read it. *"M'sieurs,* you must forgive me. I shall have to finish our discussion at a later date. There's been an apparent homicide in the Rue de la Paix, and I am called to the scene." Bertillon snapped his fingers. "Wait. I have a most excellent idea. Perhaps you gentlemen would like to accompany me?"

"Yes, of course. We should be honoured, shouldn't we, Watson."

"Then we must leave at once, *M'sieurs.* I want to get there as soon as possible, before the police go trampling through the crime-scene like a herd of stampeding buffalo."

CHAPTER ELEVEN

"If M'sieur Bertillon says it's murder, then murder it is. If M'sieur Bertillon says that the fellow is only taking a nap and will wake up shortly, then who am to contradict?"

*E*xpecting to hail a cab, Holmes and Watson were surprised when the gendarme directed the three men to a motor-car parked at the restaurant entrance. The gendarme started the engine, and with a clash of gears they pulled away from the kerb. They turned at once into the Rue de Fabourg St. Honore where they picked up speed heading toward the Place Vendome.

Watson, with one hand clamping his hat to his head lest it be blown away, and the other hand clutching the seat to keep from being thrown about as the vehicle careened through the traffic at top speed, leaned toward Holmes. "I say, Holmes, these fellows have the right idea. Equipping the police with their own vehicles. Think how efficient, how much time is saved..."

"True enough, Watson," Holmes shouted in order to make himself heard over the roar of the engine exhaust, the screech of the rubber tyres and the clatter of traffic as other drivers frantically tried to get out of the way, "assuming, of course, that the driver does not get us killed in the bargain."

They flew through the Place Vendome and up the Rue de la Paix coming to a screeching halt in front of the pharmacy of Henri Lambert. As soon as Bertillon had mentioned the Rue de la Paix, Holmes and Watson had exchanged apprehensive glances. When they arrived at the location, they knew that their worst fear had come to pass. As they clambered out of the vehicle and followed Bertillon inside, Holmes placed a finger to his lips indicating to Watson that they should say nothing about their visit earlier in the day.

Lambert lay, feet together and arms pressed to his sides, as though in his last sentient moment he desired to make removal of his corpse and placing it in his coffin easier for those upon whom such burdens would fall. He was lying in front of the counter where Holmes and Watson had stood earlier in the day. He was wearing the same white laboratory coat over a white shirt with celluloid collar and the same beige and brown checked trousers as when he had greeted Holmes and Watson in the last hours of his life.

As Bertillon along with Holmes and Watson entered the pharmacy they passed through a crowd of civilian on-lookers who were peering intently through the plate-glass windows which flanked each side of the front entrance. It was the same crowd, Watson thought to himself, that he had seen at each of the countless similar incidents which he, either in his capacity as a physician or as Holmes's companion, had attended over the years. The faces and hushed conversation were always the same: "who was he? how did he die? can you see his face? was it a robbery?" The male gawkers acted as though this were a familiar occurrence. Patiently they would explain to enthralled female companions each detail of what the authorities were doing, interpreting each gesture or movement to fit their notions of proper crime-scene procedures. Unconstrained by any formal responsibility or training, they would concoct the most plausible explanations for every action and would to their own satisfaction have the crime solved even before the corpse had been removed.

Then too, there were those who felt it their duty to criticize every official action and took the position that those feather-heads inside hadn't the faintest idea what they were doing. "No wonder," they would proclaim, "that crime is rampant and murderers walk the streets with impunity. Why that bunch," they would shake their heads in disgust, "couldn't catch the murderer if he handed them the weapon and confessed on the spot. Nothing but a drain on the public purse, that lot." Unfortunately, Watson thought, all too often those sentiments were largely accurate.

Inside, the situation was also a familiar one. Half a dozen uniformed gendarmes stood around enjoying the change from the tedium of their usual duties, unawed in the presence of death. Since the body did not display any horrific wounds—indeed, he may not have been murdered at all; *M'sieur* Bertillon will tell—the older officers satisfied themselves with a cursory glance and got on with making the most of their good fortune at having been in the vicinity and thus first on the scene when the alarm was raised. The younger officers, although desperately curious about everything

112

and looking forward to seeing the great Bertillon at his work, affected the blasé attitude of their seniors, lest their callowness be noted and become the subject of barracks-room comment at the end of their shift. So after little more than a perfunctory glance, they too contented themselves with strolling about the shop pausing now and then to read the label of some unfamiliar patent medicine and exchanging knowing comments at the display of condoms in a rear corner of the shop.

A gaggle of plain-clothes officers, *Sureté* they turned out to be, poked about in the various drawers and cabinets. As they recognized Bertillon making his way toward the back, they quickly formed ranks at Lambert's head. Holmes and Watson were introduced, and after "how-do-you-do's" and *"comment alles vous"* were exchanged, the senior detective, introduced as Inspector Loiseaux, a small ferret-like man with crooked, yellowed teeth and a thin, heavily-waxed mustache with up-turned ends made his report to Bertillon: "The proprietor of the millinery shop across the street was working late, and closed his shop about ten-thirty. He noticed the lights on in here, and became curious as the establishment does not normally stay open after nine o'clock. He looked through the glass door and upon seeing the lower portion of the deceased's body lying on the floor, called the police. The uniformed officers responded to the call, and upon entering the shop found the deceased as you see him now. Evidently the door was locked and had to be forced open—kicked open—according to the first men to arrive. Because of this and the fact that the lights were on, coupled with the some-what unusual position of the body, the *Sureté* were summoned. The detectives, being themselves unsure of what to do, did as they have been instructed: they summoned *M'Sieur* Bertillon."

The millinery shop proprietor was questioned and sent home upon his promise to make himself available tomorrow should the need arise. He related that to his knowledge, nothing of an unusual nature occurred during the day, although he of course was busy with the running of his own business and could not possibly have seen everything that went on. However, he did relate that one of his clerks reported to him in the afternoon that a somewhat unusual incident that occurred as she was cleaning and rearranging the merchandise on display in the front window during the late morning hours. According to the clerk, she noticed two foreigners—she was quite sure they were foreign—who seemed to have spent an inordinate amount of time apparently just looking in the window of the pharmacy. One was tall and rather thin, and the other of slightly more than average height and somewhat on the stout side. Beyond that the clerk could not describe them as their backs were mostly to her, and she was too far away to see their faces reflected in the glass of the shop-window.

"The milliner identified the deceased as one Henri Lambert, the pharmacist and proprietor of the shop."

Bertillon, his hackles rising, intervened. "Until we can take his *bertillonage* measurements, Inspector, the identification must be considered as preliminary only. Do you gentlemen have any questions to put to the detectives before we examine the body?"

"Not at the moment," Holmes responded, "but with your kind permission, Watson and I may have one or two later on. I assume that these gentlemen will remain until the body is removed?

"Why don't you have a look," Holmes motioned to Watson, "along with *M'sieur* Bertillon. As a physician you're apt to notice more than me. If you don't mind, I think I'll walk about the shop for a bit. See if I can learn anything that way." Holmes then ambled off toward the front of the store, pausing now and again to examine a shelf of merchandise, or to peer at the floor. When he reached the front door, he paused and bent down to examine the door jamb which had been splintered where the strike plate was screwed into the wooden door frame. Evidently the door had been kicked open as the Inspector had related. The top screw had ripped completely out of the wood, so that the strike plate was hanging loosely by the bottom screw. He briefly tested the door handles and peered through the keyhole which was situated in the metal plate beneath the handles. Returning his attention to the broken door jamb, he noticed that the wood strip which is fixed to the outer half of the door jamb and prevents the door from opening outward, had not been damaged nor did it appear that the several coats of paint in the joint between the strip and the jamb had been cracked. Turning to the other side of the door frame, he briefly inspected the hinges and determined that the pins were in place and had been painted over by several coats of paint that were also intact.

Eventually, as Bertillon and Watson proceeded with a superficial examination of the body, Holmes made a complete circuit of the room and disappeared into a rear storeroom. The curtained entrance to the room was situated directly behind the counter in front of which lay the late pharmacist, or in deference to Bertillon, the body of the deceased. Holmes poked his head through the curtains into the dark room. He turned around, and since Bertillon and Watson were out of sight bent over the body in front of the counter, he motioned to the chief detective. "Has anyone yet inspected this room?"

"Non, M'sieur Holmes. When the uniformed officers first arrived, the room was dark just as you see it now. One of the *flics* used an electric torch to have a look from the doorway just to be sure that there were no more bodies or in case the officers had arrived before the perpetrator had made good his escape..."

"Then you are certain that the pharmacist...what was his name...oh yes, Lambert; then you think Lambert was murdered?"

The detective moved closer to Holmes and lowered his voice to a whisper. "In a case such as this, *M'sieur* Holmes, *that* is for *M'sieur* Bertillon to say. I am merely an Inspector of Detectives. I worked my way up through the ranks. I don't have any political friends or patrons, but I do have only a few more months until I retire. So if *M'sieur* Bertillon says it's murder, then murder it is. If *M'sieur* Bertillon says the fellow is only taking a nap and will wake up shortly, then who am I to contradict?

"On the other hand, if Lambert died—assuming, of course, that he *is* Lambert and *is* in fact dead of natural causes—I would say that in all my years of experience, I've never seen a body position itself so meticulously."

Despite the Inspector's physical resemblance to Lestrade, Holmes sensed that underneath the shabby-looking derby hat, and behind the ridiculous mustache, there was a first-rate policeman's mind: the kind that didn't jump to conclusions, but took in every bit of information and patiently processed it until the right answers started to come out. "Perhaps suicide, Inspector?"

"Perhaps, M'sieur Holmes, but *'perhaps'* may, at the moment, be too strong a word. I, myself, might be more inclined to

say *'possible'*. Where is a suicide note? Why pick such an odd spot? Women commit suicide lying down; men sitting down. Hopefully, *M'sieur* Bertillon will not dwell overly long on the business of taking Lambert...I mean, the deceased's...*bertillonage* measurements and will instead devote his energies to determining the exact cause of death as well as the approximate time. I should like also to interview the millinery shop clerk, and if her description of *les etrangers* has any basis beyond a shop girl's active imagination, perhaps someone of interest will turn up in the record of passports from the last few days. I don't know if you're aware, but owing to the uncertainty of the times, we have made it a practice to..."

"Oh yes, that was explained to us by the clerk at our hotel..."

Loiseaux gave a typically Gallic shrug. "As a policeman, I suppose it is my job to meddle in the business of others. Yet I wonder, always to myself of course, whether we sometimes go beyond what is appropriate, even in times such as these. It would not surprise me to see that one day soon we shall be examining train passengers' baggage looking for bombs and weapons. Just think of the effect that will have on the railway time-tables, which are already a scandal. Give me a nice, simple murder case—with no politicians, generals or foreign agents—and I am perfectly content."

"Possibly, Inspector, that's what we have here. Do you think we might borrow the electric torch and have a look about for ourselves?"

The request was passed down the chain of command, and presently one of the young *flics* produced the light which he handed to the senior detective who in turn handed it to Holmes. The store-room, as it was revealed in the light from the electric torch, was as wide as the main part of the shop and was between four and five meters deep ending in a back wall of exposed brick. In the center of the back wall, there was a wooden door which was fastened by a lock set in the door and by a metal bar three centimeters high and, as Holmes estimated some twenty millimeters in thickness. The bar rested on open brackets in the door and was inserted into an enclosed bracket mounted on the wall next to the door just above the lock mechanism. Lining each

116

of the demising walls from floor almost to the ceiling were open wooden shelves, about one-half meter deep, that were filled with cartons of merchandise.

On the interior wall, on one side of the curtained doorway, was a deal-topped work table above which was a row of glass-fronted cabinets. These contained various bottles, vials and boxes of what were undoubtedly part of the drugs and medicines which formed the pharmacist's stock-in-trade. On the other side of the door was a similar table and cabinet arrangement, only this table was finished with a zinc top over the wood. Situated on the zinc-topped table there were a pharmacist's scale, a mortar and pestle and small machines for forming pills and filling capsules. Suspended by insulated wires above each work table was an electric light. Over each light there was a metal shade with a white-enameled under-surface designed to reflect the light and direct it downward to the work surface. Using the light from the torch to follow the metal conduits from the ceiling down the wall, Holmes located the switches and turned on each of the lights.

With the room now brightly lighted, Holmes and the Inspector moved toward the zinc-topped table. Holmes had not yet extinguished the torch which he continued to play along the floor. When they had moved a few steps from the door, Holmes suddenly stopped and held his arm out to the side in order to stop the Inspector. On the floor in the area just in front of the table was a fine dusting of powder covering an area about one meter square. "Rather curious, wouldn't you say, Inspector? I should think that an experienced pharmacist such as Lambert—there, I've done it once more: jumped to a conclusion—would be more careful with his mortar and pestle."

"Unless he was in an exceptional hurry, or was working under duress. Or, as your self-remonstrance suggests, the author of the spill was not Lambert, but in fact was someone else. Someone who lacked Lambert's practiced hand."

"Or..." Holmes stroked his chin pensively as the two men squatted on their haunches in order to more closely inspect the powdery film.

"What do you make of these marks, *M'sieur* Holmes? Loiseaux pointed at two parallel strips visible in the powder. The strips were each about one centimeter wide, and were uniformly

117

spaced about twenty-five centimeters apart. They started at the edge of the spill nearest the table and ran for its entire width. "Looks as though something, possibly a chair, was dragged through the spill. I'm sorry I interrupted you. You were about to advance another possibility as to who may have created the spill, and..."

Still on his haunches, Holmes turned and duck-walked a few steps along the directional line indicated by the parallel marks. "Oh, it was nothing; just more useless speculation. These marks may prove to be far more interesting. See how they point in the direction of the rear door. If something was dragged, evidently it was dragged outside. And one might, with due regard to *M'sieur* Bertillon's admonition not to confuse presumption with certainty, conclude that whoever did the dragging it was not the recumbent gentleman in the next room."

Holmes dropped to his knees and put his face close to the floor. There was another set of parallel marks, so faint as to be nearly invisible. But instead of being indentations in the powdery film exposing the floor beneath, they were composed of the powder itself faintly covering the bare floor. They were like a positive photographic print made from a negative. There were, Holmes discovered, two sets of these strips, the second even less distinct than the first. The first set was about six centimeters in length, and the second only perhaps two or three. The second set began about thirty centimeters beyond the first and that much closer to the door. "Do you think that it would be possible, Inspector, to have a photograph made of the powder spill showing the indentations. I doubt that the powder will remain undisturbed for very long and I think you may want to preserve the marks for further investigation."

Loiseaux stood up, groaned and massaged his hamstring muscles. "I trust you found nothing further of interest on the floor, *M'sieur* Holmes. At my age I much prefer finding my clues at the level of my desk-top back at headquarters. Too many damp cold nights spent bending over bodies lying in gutters and alley-ways finally begin to take their toll. It is, I think, too late tonight to summon a photographer. But I will do so in the morning, that is, of course, if *M'sieur* Bertillon concurs." Loiseaux turned toward the table, taking care to step around the powder spill. "Let us have a look at the tools of *M'sieur* Lambert's trade."

"By all means, Inspector. I quite agree with you. At our age, that which delights the mind is often anathematic to the body." Holmes, still on his knees with his face pressed close to the floor, made a three-quarter turn and shined the light under the table. "Wait a moment. What's that under the table?" Holmes half rose from his squatting position, and thus bent over retraced his steps back to the table. "No, no, Inspector; let me get it. No use both of us having to act like a side-show contortionist." Holmes went down on his knees again as he reached the table. "It appears to be a box. Can you perhaps find a rod of some kind with which to pick it up?"

Loiseaux rummaged about in a box of instruments. "I don't see... um... aha! Would a tweezer do?" He placed the implement in Holmes's extended hand.

"Yes. Perfectly." A moment later Holmes backed out from under the table and stood up holding in the tweezer a small paste board box which he placed on the table. He began to brush the accumulation of dust from his knees. "Would you happen to know of a good cleaner nearby? I'm afraid that I shall have to have at least these trousers cleaned. And one more dinner like the last two, I shall probably need a tailor as well." Holmes symbolically patted himself in the region of his waist-coat buttons.

"No. I'm sorry... I could perhaps inquire..." .

"Oh no, don't go to any trouble. I'm sure that the concierge at *M'sieur* Ritz's hotel will be able to accommodate me. But thank you anyway. Now, what have we here?" The empty box bore the trade-name "Bayer" and beneath it the word "Aspirin".

Loiseaux, using the tweezer gingerly picked up the empty box and regarded it through narrowed eyes. "I see it's German. What is it *M'sieur* Holmes? Some deadly poison? Is that the reason for the tweezer? Should I send for some rubber gloves? I'm sure we can find some around..."

"Actually, Inspector, I'm made to understand that the product is essentially harmless and indeed is quite beneficial as an analgesic. It's presence may have nothing whatever to do with the business at hand, yet it bothers me. My brief tour of the public portion of the shop left me with the distinct impression that, in keeping with the demands of his profession, *M'sieur* Lambert was precise and orderly in his house-keeping."

"And if he were going to take his own life," the Inspector picked up immediately Holmes's train of thought, "he assuredly would not have wanted to be found with his shop in even the slightest state of disarray. But if this 'Aspirin' product is harmless as you say, why must we handle it with a tweezer, especially as the box appears to be empty?"

Holmes took back the tweezer and held the box up at an angle to the light. He twisted it around looking at its different facets and at various angles. "Until the cause of death is determined, I would encourage you not to rule out anything as lacking in evidentiary value. If 'Aspirin' is somehow implicated, you may wish to subject the box to a test for latent finger-prints and..."

"Please, *M'sieur* Holmes, do not utter those words so loudly. How I wish I could subject that box—or anything else for that matter—to a test for latent fingerprints." Loiseaux shook his head sadly. *"Mon Dieu...* Please, *M'sieur* Holmes, you retain the box."

"Very well, Inspector. Shall we have a quick look outside the rear door? I suppose we'll need to locate a key."

Moving to the curtained doorway to the front part of the shop, Loiseaux summoned one of the detectives and in a moment the key-ring was produced. Loiseaux tried one of the keys in the rear door. "See, *M'sieur* Holmes, the door is un-locked."

"Yes," Holmes replied, "but the metal bar is in place."

"Oui, M'sieur Holmes. And, according to the first men on the scene, the front door was locked with these keys fitted in the inside lock."

"That would appear to rule out anyone exiting by the front door," Holmes mused.

"And," Loiseaux took out a pack of *Gauloises,* offered one to Holmes. After lighting both cigarettes, he continued, "since the rear door is barred from the inside, it would also appear to rule out anyone other than *M'sieur* Lambert having a hand in his death. Unless, of course, *M'sieur* Lambert, in his fastidiousness, let his killer out before conveniently lying down to await our arrival." .

Holmes, holding his cigarette so as not to allow the ash to fall on the floor, handed the electric torch to Loiseaux. With his free hand he slid the metal bar clear of the wall mounting and opened the door. "You are, I'm sure, quite right in your analysis, Inspector, even though it is wholly at war with your earlier thoughts based on the position of the body and your anecdotal gender comparison."

Loiseaux took a deep drag on his cigarette and stroked his chin.

Holmes glanced at the Inspector and repressed a smile. "Never-the-less, in the event *M'sieur* Bertillon should inquire, let us have a look outside, just in case there's anything to be seen. Would you mind terribly bringing the torch?" Holmes opened the door wider, and gestured for Loiseaux to precede him outside.

They found themselves in a courtyard of sorts which evidently ran behind the buildings on the adjacent parallel streets. It would perhaps have served as an alley, but for its ending at the rear of the building facing the Rue Danou, the street which ran perpendicular to the Rue de la Paix and formed the intersection one store-front down from the entrance to Lambert's shop. As far as could be seen in the paltry light of the electric torch, its length was interspersed with doors similar to the one through which they had emerged, and there were a few windows each of which was either barred or shuttered. Even though it had not rained for several days, the brick was cool and damp, almost slimy to the touch, making it evident that sunlight's appearance was brief and largely ineffectual. But for the narrow gap between the roofs of the flanking buildings, the alley would have been virtually indistinguishable from one of Paris's infamous sewers. As Loiseaux played the torch-light along the ground, Holmes noticed a residue of damp silt running down the middle of the courtyard its entire length.

"See here, *M'sieur* Holmes. More of those parallel track marks." Loiseaux held the light focused on the silt in the center of the courtyard at a point opposite the rear door to Lambert's shop.

Holmes got down on his knees once again to examine the marks. "Just so, Inspector, just so. Whatever was in the shop also moved past here."

"If I am able to obtain the services of a photographer, I shall have these photographed as well. But I think, *M'sieur* Holmes that we had best report back inside. It would not do at all for *M'sieur* Bertillon to question our absence. Then too, I am most anxious to hear whatever Dr. Watson may have learned from his examination of the body."

"You're quite right, Inspector, on all counts." Holmes grasped Loiseaux's outstretched hand and pulled himself back to a standing position. "Including, not least of all," he again brushed off the knees of his trousers, "your observations regarding the effects of a career spent bending over in dank alleys. Let us have a quick look 'round the courtyard, and then I am prepared to place myself at the disposal of our colleagues inside."

Returning to the front of the shop, Holmes observed that the crowds of spectators, both official and unofficial, had thinned substantially. Some of the detective squad had left, and only two uniformed officers, including the youngest whose principal duty seemed to be as custodian of the electric torch, remained. Inspector Loiseaux returned the light to the young officer while Holmes pondered the irony of the police being equipped with their own motor transport, yet they seemed to have but one electric torch for the entire department, whereas the Metropolitan Force provided a torch to every uniformed officer, while requiring that the detective force play catch-as-catch-can for transportation. Watson stood smoking his pipe and leaning on the counter where they had spoken with Lambert earlier in the day. Or rather, as Holmes glanced at his watch, yesterday. Bertillon was also leaning on the counter writing on a set of what Holmes recognized as the pre-printed *bertillonage* cards.

Bertillon looked up. "Ah, *M'sieur* Holmes, Inspector. What have you found? Dr. Watson and I eagerly await your report."

"Please, Inspector Loiseaux," Holmes turned toward the policeman, "it is you who should make the report. It is your investigation and I am merely on a 'busman's holiday.' Moreover, you are experienced in reporting to *M'sieur* Bertillon and know what it is that he will want to hear."

After lighting a cigarette, a bit of temporizing which also served to conceal his smirk at Holmes's ambiguous suggestion, Loiseaux proceeded to report what he and Holmes had observed.

He mentioned the white powder offering that it was merely a harmless analgesic sold under the trade-name "Aspirin" which probably was spilled accidentally and had nothing to do with the matter at hand. He omitted any reference to the empty box or to its disposition, and appeared relieved when, at the conclusion of his report, Bertillon did not inquire as to how he knew that the material was as he described.

"As yet, I'm afraid we have little to report." Bertillon finished his note-writing, capped his fountain-pen and placed the cards in his breast pocket. "We shall do a meticulous search of our files and certainly confirm his identity. But as to the cause of death..." Bertillon shrugged.

"That is," Watson interjected, "somewhat problematical at the present time. From the stage of *rigor mortis* and the coolness of the body, I would say that death occurred four or five hours ago. It would be helpful if we could get a rectal body temperature, but this seems hardly the place. Based on palpation of the abdomen, I expect that if we remove the clothing, we would find that the blood has all pooled in the portions of the body nearest the floor. This would tend to corroborate my estimate of the time of death.

"As you can see, we have not removed all of the clothing. I merely unbuttoned the laboratory coat, vest and shirt. I have seen no evidence thus far of a gunshot or other penetrating wound, and, as we have all seen, there are no bloodstains in the vicinity of the body. Of course until we examine the body completely, we cannot rule out the hypothesis that he was shot or stabbed elsewhere and brought here after the haemorraging had ceased. I suggest this as a possibility based upon the rather remarkable positioning of the body.

"The only unusual findings, apart, that is, from the body's position, are what may be ligature marks on the wrists and a rime of dried blood around the inside of the nostrils. This could indicate either internal bleeding from natural or other causes, or it could be the product of *peri-mortem* trauma. While the evidence is inconclusive, it is possible that his nose was broken. No bruises had formed, which indicates he may have been involved in a violent struggle immediately preceding his death. Oh, yes, and then there's the unusual odor emanating from the mouth. It..."

"Unusual odor?" Holmes and Loiseaux both asked at once.

"Yes, smell for yourselves, gentlemen. Tell me what you think it is. The aroma is nearly as familiar to me as my own briar, but I do not want to prejudice your own observations."

Holmes and the Inspector both got down on hands and knees and sniffed the corpse's mouth.

Loiseaux spoke first. "My senses deceive me, Dr. Watson. While I know almost nothing of animal husbandry, I would swear that the only time I've experienced that smell is when horse liniment is in use. But surely..."

"Your senses do not deceive you, Inspector." Holmes rose and once again attempted to dust off his trouser knees. "It's unmistakably oil of wintergreen which is one of the principal active ingredients in horse liniment, although, owing to its analgesic properties, it can be used in a number of externally applied balms. Because it has been in such use for such a long time, I expect that Dr. Watson's familiarity goes back to his days as an army surgeon."

"Right you are, Holmes. Many's the time I was called upon in the heat of battle to minister to the horses as well as the men. Seems that the army had a chronic problem recruiting veterinarians. Too much money to be made in civilian private practice. Why between horses and dogs,...."

Loiseaux, impatient to explore the ramifications of this new bit of information, interrupted, "But what are the consequences, Dr. Watson, of this chemical being ingested by mouth?"

"Off hand, Inspector, I cannot say. All analgesics, it is generally agreed, are absorbed into the bloodstream, whether they are ingested by mouth and then absorbed through the digestive system, or are applied externally and absorbed through trans-dermal capillary action. The problem is no one knows with certainty how they work. It is enough for most purposes merely to know that they do work, and in different ways. For example, if you have a headache, a *mal de la tete,* I would not suggest that you rub liniment on your head, but would prescribe something to be taken orally.

"But to address your question directly, I know of no reported study nor do I recall any incident in my own practice to which I can refer regarding the consequences of oral ingestion of wintergreen oil. Perhaps you might consult the faculty at the Pasteur Institute, or..."

Bertillon yawned conspicuously, whether from the lateness of the hour or boredom, one could not be sure. "Gentlemen, I see nothing more that we can accomplish here tonight. There is no conclusive evidence that the little Jew died of other than natural causes, and even if he did, more likely than not it was by his own hand. As you have yourselves observed today, the workload of my department is so great that if I do not give priority to those cases of the gravest public concern, why my resources..."

Holmes, standing next to Loiseaux thought he heard the Inspector mutter *"merde"* under his breath and motion to the uniformed officers.

Stubbing out his cigarette, Loiseaux asked, "Shall I then see to the removal of the body, *M'sieur Directeur?* And would it be appropriate to notify the deceased's family?"

"That, *M'sieur Inspecteur,* must be your decision and responsibility. I have not made my formal ruling on identification. Should it prove to be the case that this is not Lambert," Bertillon pointed to the corpse, "and the real Lambert perhaps is engaged in a late night dalliance with a woman other than *Madame* Lambert, I should not wish to be involved in the scandal that would ensue from such a farce."

Holmes touched Watson's sleeve, indicating that they should take their leave. *"M'sieur* Bertillon, thank you for a most instructive learning experience. You too, Inspector Loiseaux. It has been a pleasure observing you at your work. I believe that our hotel is but a short distance away, and I'm sure that Watson and I can find our way without putting you to any further effort on our account." .

"However," he continued, "there is one small matter that you mentioned a moment ago upon which I wish you would elaborate."

"Mais oui, M'sieur Holmes, and that would be?"

"If you have not as yet formally ruled that the deceased is indeed the chemist Lambert, how are you able to determine positively his religious affiliation?"

"The science of *bertillonage, M'sieur* Holmes. There can be no doubt that whatever the deceased's true name may be, his mother was a Jewess. It's in my book, *M'sieur* Holmes. I shall send you and Dr. Watson each a copy with my compliments."

CHAPTER TWELVE

"But Holmes we cannot, no matter what our sensibilities may be, let this unfortunate coincidence distract us from our mission."

*W*atson clipped the end off a cigar and rolled the cigar between his thumb and forefinger. He and Holmes were seated at a sidewalk café at the edge of the plaza in sight of the entrance to the Ritz. When they left the hotel, Holmes had instructed the *concierge* to apprise him of any message from the baron. Although their table was under an awning, the sun was making Watson uncomfortably warm as he a Holmes finished their breakfast coffee and croissants. Last night on the brief walk from Lambert's shop to the Ritz, Watson had observed the determined set of Holmes's jaw. He knew that he could sooner expect the Sphinx to break into song than he could expect to get any intelligible conversation out of Holmes about either the Lambert case or the matter which had brought them to Paris. At breakfast, for a half hour or more Holmes had scanned the Paris newspapers presumably, Watson thought, for articles about the murder. Evidently owing to the lateness of the hour when the body was discovered and the authorities summoned there was insufficient time for the story to have been included in the early morning editions. He was therefore startled when Holmes put down the last of the newspapers signaled the waiter for a coffee refill and spoke.

"Watson, you've scarcely said a word since we took our leave of Bertillon and the clever Inspector. Surely you have reached some conclusion, some inspired insight. I could certainly use a dose of your lucidity just now."

"I can see that Lambert's death has you puzzled." Watson took a thoughtful puff of his cigar. "But shouldn't we leave it in the hands of the official police for the time being? That Loiseaux chap seemed to be not only quite competent, but also willing and able to work around Bertillon as necessary. If left to his own devices, and Bertillon seemed quite prepared to do just that, perhaps he will bring the case to a successful conclusion. I quite liked the little chemist, and his murder, for surely he *was* murdered, raises my gorge as much as I'm sure it does yours. Add to it Bertillon's disgusting anti-Semitism and I'm prepared to do whatever it takes to see that justice is done. But Holmes we cannot, no matter what our own sensibilities may be, let this unfortunate coincidence distract us from our mission. Don't forget you're to meet with Baron Ollstreder in," he drew out his pocket watch, "little more than half an hour.

"I'm sorry, old man." Watson, declining more coffee, continued. "My thoughts are in a state of confusion even greater than your own, and in consequence I did not directly answer your question. For what it may be worth, my opinion is that Lambert did not die of natural causes. Consider the position of the body, the possible ligature marks on the wrists, the broken nose. Then there's the oil of wintergreen. I can think of no medicinal purpose for which it is taken internally, yet to my almost certain recollection, my pharmacopoeia does not mention that it has any conspicuously toxic properties. The only rational explanation which I can derive from these disparate and apparently contradictory facts is that the oil of wintergreen was administered as a means to cover up some other more obvious poison such as arsenic with its signature burnt-almond odor. But what purpose would that serve? .

"As to the identity of the perpetrator or perpetrators, I must confess I haven't a clew. And as to how they, or he, exited from the shop with the only two exits fastened from the inside, well..."

Holmes lit his own cigar. "Watson, how do you have the equanimity to endure my pedestrian brain? In all the years of our association, and in all of your chronicles of *my* cases, you have managed to under-state your role thereby deceiving both myself as well as your readers into thinking that it was me, Sherlock Holmes, consulting detective, whose plodding methods were responsible for solving the problems brought to our notice when all along it is you who figured out the solution in an intuitive instant. Then with infinite patience you bided your time and did my bidding—no matter how fatuous it may have seemed to you—until I worked out the solution using my puny intellectual tools."

"I say, Holmes, I appreciate your..."

Holmes held up his hand. "No, no dear friend, hear me out. Like you, I too now know the identity of the perpetrators of this foul murder."

"You...I...I mean...we do?"

"Don't be coy, old chap. You know as well as I that it was us, Sherlock Holmes, and John H. Watson," Holmes's voice and demeanor assumed the role of Queen's Counsel making his opening statement to the jury, "who brought about the death of the chemist Lambert just as surely as if we'd held him down and administered the fatal dose with our own murderous hands."

"How...what on earth are you talking about, Holmes? In one breath you pay me what from you is an un-paralleled compliment, and in the next you accuse me of murdering a man whom I met yesterday for the first time and who was guilty of no offense toward me save that he cured my rather vicious headache. Really, old man..."

"Please, Watson, have I not confessed? What more do you wish me to say? You know as well as I that Lambert's murder was no coincidence; his death was nothing more or less than a fiendish warning to us..."

"A warning? My God, Holmes, surely not!"

"Surely so, Watson, surely so. Obviously it was not a crime based upon pecuniary motives, nor does it appear to be one of passion. Although anything is possible in affairs of the heart, I can't think of a less likely candidate for the wrath of a cuckolded husband than the late Lambert. Loiseaux may poke about looking for a disgruntled business associate. He will probably intrude upon Madame Lambert in her grief searching for some indication that she had caught her husband in *flagrante delecto,* or that it was she, seeking to rid herself of an inconvenient husband, who was the perpetrator. However, I don't think that he'll have any success pursuing those lines.

"My guess is that he will assign the most junior of the men under his command to review the passport records looking for foreigners matching the description given by the shop-girl. If he gets lucky, in a few days he may come up with our names..."

"And what shall we do if that should come to pass? Do we confess, or do we make up some fantastic story about having been sent over here by Her Majesty's Government to stick our camel-like noses under the tent of French politics because your brother whose existence is unknown outside Whitehall, Number Ten Downing Street and his Club has become obsessed with the notion that the Bosch, who've been up to dastardly things for the last millennium, are once more up to something nasty?"

"Among the numerous, if sophomoric, aphorisms which you've seen fit from time to time to attribute to me, is the one to the effect that when you have discarded the impossible, what remains must be the truth. As I say, I think we can as a practical matter rule out greed and passion as motives. Nor does the crime have any of the markings of a murder committed by a crazed dope-fiend in search of drugs.

"If this were a 'garden-variety' murder, would the killer or killers have left us such a neat locked-room-type mystery to solve? Just the type that you and I have come to relish so much? Have you ever seen such an abundance of clews? And none of which make the slightest sense to anyone save ourselves and those who are discommoded by our presence."

"Since you put it that way, Holmes, I cannot but agree. Who but the killers and ourselves would have associated 'Aspirin' with our visit to Lambert? No doubt they wheedled out of him that he'd given me the drug for my headache. They probably didn't believe that our visit had no greater purpose than my seeking relief from my self-inflicted indisposition. Dear God. The poor man. What have I done?"

"Don't blame yourself. It was I who dreamt up this tragi-comic plot, and it is I who must bear full responsibility. Although it is a terrible price to pay, we now know that we have at least begun to succeed. For not only have we been warned off, we now have the added distraction of Loiseaux who is already sniffing the air and all too soon will pick up our scent. But I pledge to you this: at the *denouement* of this matter, Captain Dreyfus shall have his justice and his tormentors—Lambert's killers— shall be made to account to us for their crimes.

"I think it's time to move things to the next level. I see there's a rather large motor-car waiting at the hotel entrance and one of the porters seems to be heading this way."

"I say, Holmes, do you mind if I tag along? I really don't feel like looking at a bunch of old pictures nor do I relish the idea of being alone with my thoughts just now."

"Of course, old man, I was just going to suggest that you do so. It may be that all the baron has in mind is a bit of harmless ego gratification. On the other hand, as we've just seen there are no coincidences. Whether it's the Dreyfus business—and the baron being involved would not surprise me—or it's something else, it's almost certain to be interesting."

CHAPTER THIRTEEN.

"I have spent a small fortune on every private enquiry
agent in the city. I've placed countless newspaper
advertisements. I've even showered bribes like
gold Louises at Maxim's."

A chauffeur in lavender livery having confirmed that *M'sieur*
Holmes was in fact *M'sieur* Holmes, and having with great
reluctance come to accept the proposition that *M'sieur* Holmes was
not going anywhere—regardless of whether the baron's
instructions included picking up anyone besides *M'sieur* Holmes—
other than in the company of Dr. Watson, ensconced them in the
passenger compartment. After a few minutes' drive, he deposited
them, to neither man's great surprise, in front of an elegant private
house in the Rue Georges Bizet. As another servant in the same
garish livery assisted them from the vehicle Holmes speculated to
himself as to how the street's namesake would have compared the
resident gypsy queen to his own celebrated heroine.

Inside they paused in a circular entry foyer as yet another
liveried servant relieved them of their hats and walking-sticks and
led them down a hallway which appeared to run the length of the
house through its center. Presently the servant opened a pair of
paneled sliding doors on the left side of the hall and bowed them
into a sizable room, perhaps eighteen by thirty feet. Gesturing to a
pair of Louis XIV gilt-trimmed brocade-covered settees, he bade
them be seated and informed them that the baron would be joining
them momentarily.

Waiting for the baron, Holmes and Watson had an
opportunity to study the room. If it was the decorator's intention to
recreate the inside of a Wedgwood bowl he, or she, had succeeded
admirably. The walls and ceiling were painted in the pastel blue
instantly identified with the "Wedgwood" name, and all the
woodwork, from the baseboards to the exposed joists and
crossbeams, was painted in a brilliant white enamel. The floor, at
least that portion which was not covered by several what appeared
to be Aubusson, Oushag and Mohtashem rugs all in hues of gold,

was oak parquet in a herringbone pattern. There were three floor-to-ceiling windows, also trimmed in white, that lighted the room pleasantly with the mid-morning sunlight. Outside the windows, there was a narrow landscaped side-yard between the house and a tall privacy wall that separated it from the adjacent property.

The rest of the furnishings were also Louis XIV or XV, else clever reproductions. At the end of the room nearest the front of the house there were a few pieces which clearly showed the influence of the Empire period, if indeed they were not authentic. Except for a series of half a dozen framed etchings, almost certainly the work of de Goya, the walls were entirely devoid of any graphic art.

As Holmes and Watson were studying the etchings, each of which depicted an especially gruesome battle scene, a door concealed in the back wall opened and the baron gingerly yawed his vast girth through. The baron had incongruously small feet, clad this morning in velvet Persian-like slippers, which propelled him in tiny mincing steps toward his visitors. The rest of him was dressed, from the slippers up, in black trousers, which strained at the mid-section while flapping loosely about his ankles. The trousers were surmounted by a smoking jacket of claret-coloured watered silk, which was held together at the mid-line, "waist" in the case of the baron being a misleading term, by a thick, braided cord that could easily have served in an emergency as a ship's hawser. The ensemble was completed by a paisley-print ascot wrapped around the baron's remarkable neck and a terra-cotta coloured fez perched atop the baronial head like an inverted flower pot.

"*Herr* Holmes, *Herr Doktor* Watson, welcome, welcome. So good of you to come. I'm such an admirer of your exploits." As he pumped each man's hand in greeting, Holmes thought, and as they discussed it later Watson concurred, the baron's hand felt quite like gripping a piece of day-old raw *fleisch* in the meat market. Holmes and Watson seated themselves on one of the settees with room to spare. The baron who eased himself down the other, occupied nearly the entire width.

From a cedar-wood cigar box on the low table between the two sofas the baron offered each man a cigar. Selecting one for himself, he put a match to it, smiled and informed his guests,

133

"fresh from Havana, *mein herren,* Romeo *y* Juliettas. Please feel free to help yourselves to a supply. I'm given to understand there's something of a shortage these days in London, not to mention Paris." The rear door opened again to admit two servants, one bearing a coffee service and the other a tray with a sherry decanter and glasses. Holmes and Watson each requested coffee, and the baron, after eyeing the sherry, opted to play the gracious host and followed suit.

With the coffee poured and tasted, the baron tapped a bit of ash off the end of his cigar. "I asked for an hour of your time, *Herr* Holmes, so I'll be brief, or at least as brief as the matter I wish to put before you will permit. Although my title is a relatively old one," he began, "my baronetcy is not especially large, nor are its estates overly prosperous. I have never much cared for the bucolic life, preferring instead to operate in a more cosmopolitan venue. After my time at university—Heidelburg as you've no doubt discerned—I began a career as a trader..."

"In?" Holmes interrupted.

Ollstreder took a sip of coffee. "Various things, *Herr* Holmes, commodities, metals, both industrial and precious, whatever is bought and sold. However, my means of livelihood have nothing to do with my little problem, the specifics of which I shall now proceed to put before you. I mention my background only because it is a matter of my family's honor that compels me, although the duty is not in the least bit difficult given my unbridled admiration for your accomplishments, to call upon your services. I mention my occupation only as assurance to you that I am able and willing to pay whatever fee you think appropriate.

"That having been said, *mein herren,* let me place before you the matter which vexes me so. Perhaps you are familiar with a religious society in England known as the English Order of St. John of Jerusalem?"

"Why yes," Watson responded, "I believe they operate hospice-type facilities for the care of the chronically ill. Splendid fellows, dedicated, capable..."

"Yes, yes, *Herr Doktor.* Those are the ones. And, as you may be aware, they are virtually destitute, especially by comparison to the better known orders. Their Order is also established in my country where they are known as the *'Prussian*

Johanniterorden' and where they are equally revered for the very reasons you mention. I should also add that in my country they are just as impecunious as they are in yours. Both branches of the Order, as you may know, are descended from the original Order, the Order of the Hospital of St. John of Jerusalem, which later changed its name to the Knights of Rhodes, and yet again to the Knights of Malta."

Holmes, puffing occasionally on his cigar remained impassive while Watson shifted restlessly, feigning polite interest. The baron, pausing for a sip of coffee, continued, "It is during the Malta phase that the object of this somewhat terse history lesson came into being. During the mid-sixteenth century, the Order found a benefactor—how that came to pass is not a matter of record—in Charles the Fifth of Spain. King Charles leased the Mediterranean Island of Malta to the Order for the token rent of one falcon per annum, the bird to be delivered to him each year by a representative of the Order.

"As it happened, at the time the initial year's rent came due, the Order's fiscal circumstances were flush, 'engorged' might be an even better description. Indeed this brief, glorious moment marked the high tide in the Order's financial affairs. It has, as I mentioned earlier, been all down-hill ever since. Well, in a collective fit of gratitude, the governing council of the Order determined that in lieu of a live bird, they would instead present their temporal savior with a bird fashioned of solid gold and encrusted, beak-to-claw, with the finest jewels from their coffer chests. And may I add, sirs, that the finest of the Order's jewels ranked them among the finest in the world. After all, the Saracens, from whom they'd been won by superior force of arms, had been looting them from the ancient mines of Africa for centuries. As they say, to the victor go the spoils.

"Seldom, as I need not remind you, do the affairs of men go as planned. So it was that the finished statue, more beautiful, and I dare say a good deal more valuable, than even the golden calf of the Hebrews' Bible, was entrusted to a brave and thoroughly reliable member of the Order whose duty was to carry it by galleon to the Spanish ruler. However, as best can be determined, the vessel was set upon by pirates operating out of Algiers and the ship was lost with all hands, as of course was the statue.

135

"Toward the end of the last century, and again around 1840, rumors began to be heard, chiefly among that rather small, but cosmopolitan coterie of immensely wealthy collectors of *objets d'art,* those few who have the wealth and power to acquire whatever may strike their fancy, that the bird, which theretofore had been considered merely a grail-like legend, did in fact exist and was for a time in England. Well, sirs, you can imagine what a frenzy this news set off. This entire elite group had heard the rumors, and each was determined to best the other competitors by obtaining the article for himself. After all, what was the point of owning such a rare and precious object if its ownership did not engender bitter jealousy on the part of one's rivals? *Ja?"* The baron favored his guests with a lewd wink.

"*Ja,*" Holmes replied in his driest manner, "something akin, one supposes, to having a beautiful young wife or mistress."

The baron, oblivious to Holmes's *mot just,* continued, "as it came to pass none of the pursuers was successful. A member of the German branch of the Order, believed to be a descendant of the original courier, and who, like his forebearers had devoted his life to redeeming his ancestor's honor by restoring the statue to the Order, discovered its whereabouts and came into possession of the bird by what must, admittedly, have been felonious means. He swiftly made plans to return with the statue to Germany. Knowing that ports both in England and everywhere on the Continent would be under the most intense surveillance, he disguised both himself and the bird, the latter by application of numerous thick layers of black paint, so that he looked, of all things, like a member of the Hassidic Sect of the Hebrew Race, and the bird looked like a cheap souvenir purchased for a pittance in some East End curio shop.

"Needless to say neither the hapless courier or his prize ever made it to Germany. He evidently arrived in Paris late at night. Since his coach to Germany did not leave until the following morning, he determined to allow himself a few hours sleep. Thinking it would be the safest and least conspicuous place, he sought lodging in a cheap inn near to the coach yard. Disguised as he was, however, he appeared as easy prey to a band of apaches who had no need for people of his apparent race, and at the same time found themselves with an acute need of funds with which to purchase a few litres of the *vin ordinaire* of which they were so fond. Although totally without fear, and not without experience as a street brawler, because there were four or five to his one, and he was further encumbered by having to maintain possession of the cherished object of his lifelong quest, he was eventually overcome and left to die in the gutter. Having no idea of the value of their booty, the murdering thieves quickly pawned it for a few francs which they soon drunk up and went on in search of their next victim.

"For the last almost sixty years, then, the falcon has resided here in Paris, passing from one ignorant owner to the next, surfacing from time to time in the shop of some disreputable dealer in forged antiquities and worthless art objects, always eluding its true owners, sometimes by only a few months, and in one instance, by a matter of days. And this, gentlemen is where I, and hopefully you, enter the picture."

"How so?" Watson asked, his curiosity aroused in spite of himself.

"As to myself, *Herr Doktor,* I am bound to search for the statue as a matter of family honor. My father, the late Baron Ollstreder, was afflicted in his declining years with various debilitating ailments." Reaching into the folds of his smoking jacket, the baron extracted a silk handkerchief and actually daubed it at the corners of his eyes. "I shall not pause to catalog them for you as the recollection is still too much for me to bear, even though it has now been many years since his passing. During those years which were so stressful to us all, and even unto his final illness and merciful passing, he was cared for by *der broders,* as we affectionately called them, of the very *Johanniterorden* who are the rightful owners of the statue.

"During their caring for him, my father learned the story of the falcon and of their ancient quest. From his deathbed, in his very last words to me, he made me promise to continue the efforts to recover the falcon and to see that it is restored to the selfless men to whom we owed so much. And this filial duty, *mein herren,* is why I spend so much time in this loveliest, and yet cruelest, of cities."

"And what might you have in mind for us?" Holmes asked.

"I freely confess to you, sirs, that like so many before me, I too have exhausted every means to capture this elusive bird." He grinned in what must have been intended to be a self-deprecating gesture. But the sight of his tiny, spiked teeth made him look more like a bloated crocodile approaching its dinner. "I have spent a small fortune on every private enquiry agent in the city; I've placed countless newspaper advertisements. I've even showered bribes like gold Louises at Maxim's. I must admit that I'm at the point of despair. Frankly, gentlemen, at present this duty's become something of a burden to me, and I long to be discharged from it."

"When I heard of your arrival in the city, I was struck immediately with the idea to engage your services. I don't know what business it is that brings you here; certainly the city has more than its share of crime. *Ach!* Why just last night there was a shocking murder in the Rue de la Paix, which like so many others will probably go unsolved by the official police. But whatever your business may be, when it is concluded, if you could possibly extend your visit and undertake this engagement, I shall gladly pay whatever fee you require, place at your disposal my motor-car and driver, and do whatever else you may ask. If anyone can find this bird, surely the great Sherlock Holmes and the stalwart *Doktor* Watson are the men for the job. Having engaged the world's greatest detective, and made available to him all of my resources, regardless of whether you are successful, I shall be able, finally, to rest easy, content in the knowledge that I have done all that is within my power to carry out this testamentary mandate."

Holmes finished his cigar and ground out the remains in the ashtray before him. "Your problem, Baron Ollstreder, tugs at the heartstrings quite as much as it teases the intellect. Yet I can hardly see how Dr. Watson and I can be of much assistance to you. If there's been a crime committed, it's over three hundred and fifty years old."

"If there's been a crime, *Herr* Holmes? Was not the forcible wresting of the statue from the hands of the emissary on the high seas not crime enough?" The baron sat back, attempting to look wounded.

"Perhaps so, sir, if you discount the claims of the Saracens or even the Africans. But isn't the statue's rightful owner the Spanish Throne? If by some chance we were successful, wouldn't there be a duty to complete the delivery begun so long ago?"

"Nein, nein, Herr Holmes. The object belongs, under the law of the sea—believe me, as I have also spent a fortune on lawyer fees to have this matter researched—to the successors-in-interest of whoever last legally possessed it. *Ach! Gott in Himmel, Mein herren.* If the cursed statue is worth the legal fees I have paid just to find out that one cannot acquire good title from a pirate—an opinion reached no doubt without regard to professional courtesy—then it is surely the world's most valuable object. Sirs, if the statue is recovered, *der Johanniterorden* will never again have to be concerned with the state of their finances."

"If the law is as you say, and of course I do not doubt your word," Watson interjected, ·why doesn't the English branch of the Order have a claim at least equal to that of the German one?"

"Well, I..."

"No, no dear Baron, do not commit yourself just yet. As far as Watson and I are concerned the question is purely academic until such time as we do obligate ourselves to undertake the engagement. And that's a decision which we're not prepared to take at this moment. The matter does, as I say, have its interesting features; yet there are so many demands on our time that... let me suggest that if you have a detailed *dossier,* you send it 'round to our hotel. As much as our schedule permits, we will look over what you send us and possibly make preliminary inquiry in whatever directions seem most promising."

Rising, Holmes extended his hand. "I cannot promise you more than that. If we do undertake a full-blown effort, we can agree on compensation at that time. And now if you would be so kind, we have another engagement this afternoon and need to return to our hotel as soon as possible." ...

"Ach. Ja, Herr Holmes." The baron struggled to his feet and pulled a bell cord next to the fireplace. "What you propose would be quite satisfactory. I shall send the *dossier* to you as soon as possible. But my offer of my motor-car and driver still stands. I would be most happy to have him drive you to your next appointment and then return you to your hotel or wherever you may wish to go from there."

"Thank you, dear Baron," Holmes said with elaborate courtesy. "We could not possibly impose. The Ritz will do quite as well."

The front-hall servant bowed his way into the room bearing Holmes's and Watson's accouterments. The baron instructed the servant to direct the driver to return the visitors to the Ritz. Turning to Holmes and Watson, he offered his hand once again, *"auf Wiedersehen, mein herren.* I hope that we shall be able to do business, and in any case I wish you *bon chance* in yours, whatever it may be."

CHAPTER FOURTEEN

"As to his tale of a priceless statue... who
could invent such an epic out of imagination alone?"

*I*n a short time the driver had deposited them back at the Ritz
where over a light lunch they rehashed their meeting with the
baron.

As soon as they had ordered, omelets with mushrooms and
fine herbs and another bottle of the Montrachet, Holmes asked,
"Well, old man, what do you make of the baron's tale?".

"It did not surprise me," Watson began, "that the baron
made no mention of his mother. No doubt the poor woman took
one look at the infant baron in his swaddling clothes and went
straight-away to hurl herself from the highest parapet of the
'Schloss Ollstreder', assuming of course that such an edifice in fact
exists. As to the late Baron Ollstreder, if the current lord is any
reflection of his sire, I would venture that he succumbed not from
one of the deadly sins, but from the ravages of all seven at once.

"As to his tale of a priceless statue, pirates and ruthless art
collectors, I would speculate that it is at least in part true. I mean...
who could possibly invent such an epic out of imagination alone?"

As Watson paused to take a bite of his omelet, Holmes
asked, "And what part of the story aroused your scepticism?"

Suspecting that Holmes's question was rhetorical, Watson
took a couple more forkfuls of omelet and took a leisurely swallow
of his wine before responding. "The history of the statue from its
inception up until modern times is, in its essentials, probably true,
although one would be hard pressed at this late date to confirm any
of the intermediate details. Where I think the baron parts company
with the truth is in his motive for seeking the statue. If the statue is
anything close to what he described, why it must be worth a
million at the least. And the baron, not to speak ill of our recent
host, did not impress me as a fellow who, if he came to possess
such an object, would gladly part with it without any thought of
recompense beyond the satisfaction of having discharged his filial

responsibility. After all, the man is, by his own description, a trader in every sort of commodities.

"What I'm unsure about is whether the baron wishes to enlist our services for reasons relating to recovery of the statue—for his own benefit or in fact for the benefit of the impoverished monks—or for some other reason."

"I concur in your assessment that there may be some truth to his story. And I was no better able to swallow his reasons for wanting to locate the statue than I am able to swallow the cold remnants of this omelet." Holmes pushed his plate away. "However, it is far too early to say whether the baron is involved in the Dreyfus business, or is up to something else. Even though the problem of locating the statue could have provided a few days' interesting diversion, unless you strongly disagree, it must remain for some other consulting detective to pour salt on the tail of the elusive bird, and for someone else to chronicle his doing so. However, I do think it can cause no harm to find out a bit more about *Herr* Baron. So I propose that we have a look at his dossier, assuming that he does send it 'round, and perhaps make an inquiry or two."

Watson chewing a last bite of omelet, nodded his head in agreement. "I quite agree, old man." Watson took a sip of his wine. "But why then not avail ourselves of the luxury of his motor-car? I must say I'm becoming rather fond of them as a means of getting about. In fact I'm of a mind to look into purchasing one when we return home. Who knows," he held his hands out as though gripping a steering tiller, "I might even learn to operate it myself"

Holmes appraised his friend from beneath an arched eyebrow. "Yes, I think you'd cut quite a dashing figure in a duster and goggles seated at the controls careening about the streets of London at break-neck speed. But to answer your question, I thought that the baron pressed his offer rather too earnestly. Indeed, his doing so is one of the reasons for my suspicion that his offer of employment was, if one can even metaphorically quantify such matters, a few bushels short of *bona fide*. No, dear fellow, if our would-be patron wishes to keep track of our whereabouts, he shall have to exert himself a little more than that. Especially since our whereabouts this afternoon will be of more than passing interest to him and those with whom he is involved."

"I was beginning to wonder when you were going to share with me our itinerary for this afternoon. I assume it has something to do with the second envelope which you received in the Ritz's dining room. But I suppose I can contain my curiosity on that subject a bit longer if you will first tell me what else it is about our interview with Ollstreder that leads you to conclude that his motives run deeper than recovery of the statue."

"Did it not strike you as curious," Holmes poured the last of the wine, dividing it between their two glasses, "that the baron was informed about the murder of Lambert? If I recall, the baron's party had not yet even made it to the soup course when we took our leave of Maxim's last night. We were virtually the last to leave Lambert's shop, and I should think that if for some reason his dinner party ended early and on his way to his little *pied-a-terre* or to some other destination he happened on the scene while we were still there, his presence—for he is after all not inconspicuous— would not have gone unnoticed or un-remarked.

"As to this afternoon's itinerary, we are invited to call upon *Madame* Dreyfus, *et famille,* where we shall no doubt have our ears bent nearly off with protestations of *Le Capitaine's* innocence, and perhaps in the course of our ordeal pick up some useful information which we do not already have. Quite honestly, I'm beginning to wonder, *entre nous,* what we might do next to move this business along."

CHAPTER FIFTEEN

*"Mark the occasion well, my friend. It's likely to be
the last cooperation we get from the military
in this matter."*

*O*ver coffee and tobacco, the two men decided to take a brief
walk, both to counteract the effects of the wine, and to determine
whether their watchers, who were undoubtedly lurking somewhere
about, were the same pair as yesterday's. This information, Watson
suggested, might give them a crude gauge of the manpower pitted
against them. As they walked, they debated whether to give the
watchers, who did prove to be the same pair as the previous day,
the slip, but finally decided that to do so might be unnecessarily
obvious and therefore precipitous. That determined, and having
completed a circuit of the plaza, they had the doorman summon a
cab from the waiting rank.

As the cab reached the front door a woman and man, he in
the day uniform of an army colonel, emerged from the hotel. From
their appearance, it took no great deductive powers to conclude
that they were of the class of short-term guests who had been the
subject of Ritz's post-prandial discourse of two evenings' past. The
colonel looked at no one, hoping that if he did not make eye-
contact, he would be invisible to others. Or perhaps he was merely
scanning the field to make sure that there were no irate spouses, his
or hers, awaiting their emergence with a heart fatally bent on
mischief. *Madame,* for she did indeed wear a wedding band,
although elegantly dressed and coifed, displayed a few unseemly
wrinkles in her gown and a few wisps of hair not quite right. She
had about her that certain look—a slight flush to the cheeks and
look about her eyes that no cosmetics can either duplicate or
conceal—that spoke unmistakably of her recent exertions.

"Apres-vous, Madame, Colonel." As the doorman opened
the door of the cab, Holmes made a sweeping gesture with his arm.
"Please, you take this one. My companion and I are in no great
hurry, and will gladly take the next."

Such a gesture being virtually unknown among Parisians, the colonel hesitated a moment, and finally concluding that Holmes was sincere, and not deranged, gave a stiff little military half-bow along with a curt *"merci"* and followed *Madame* into the carriage. The cabby turned half-round in his box, gave Holmes a withering look and started off with a jerk even before the door had closed.

"I say, Holmes, that was certainly *tres gallant.* But the cabby evidently didn't appreciate your gesture. Are French officers bad tippers, d'you suppose?"

Holmes handed the doorman, who was standing with his mouth half-agape, a five-franc note. "Another cab, my good man, *s'il vous plait."* Turning to Watson, he chuckled, "I really don't know, Watson. Never studied the subject. It's just that I decided the fellow was perhaps a bit too eager for our business. Did you not notice the purple stocking peeking out from between his boot and trouser leg?"

"Then the appearance of the colonel and the lady was quite fortuitous, I should say."

"Indeed you should, Watson. Mark the occasion well. It's likely to be the last help we'll get from the military in this matter."

CHAPTER SIXTEEN

"It does not come as a surprise to us that
you and your family have felt constrained to
consult mediums..."

*L*ucie Dreyfus, rather than plying Holmes and Watson with protestations of her husband's innocence, plied them with a passable English tea and a withering cross-questioning. "I trust, gentlemen, that you do not find my scepticism regarding your accomplishments in this matter to be a manifestation of ingratitude. I assure you that it is not. It is at worst a product of our long and bitter frustration. We've had our hopes rejuvenated so many times and then crushed again and again..." she paused, her large black eyes luminous with anger, her voice unsteady as she grasped for an appropriate English adjective..."by my husband's *beloved* military." Her pronunciation left nothing of her own feelings or sense of irony to the imagination.

"My dear brother in law," she turned her head slightly in the direction of Mathieu Dreyfus, her husband's older brother, "considered contacting you to enlist your services many times over the years. And when we learned a few weeks ago that you had offered your assistance through the British branch of the Rothschilds, that, coupled with the change in the French government, acted like a bellows to our faintly glimmering hopes and fanned them once again into a raging inferno. Yet all that you have accomplished since your arrival—I shall not dwell upon the death of the chemist Lambert—I could have told you in less than half an hour. Bertillon is a pompous idiot, and is no more than a tool in the hands of those who are responsible for the persecution of my husband. As for that licentious *schwein* Ollstreder, although he is a relative new-comer to the game, he is, as *Herr* Schwabach," she gestured toward the rather small man seated stiffly on the edge of the sofa next to Mathieu Dreyfus, "will presently tell you in great detail, a major player, although by no means is he at the apex. Indeed, Mr. Holmes, for all your legendary skills and your undoubted good intentions, I think that we have gotten more useful information from the gypsy spiritualist Leonie." As though to signal that she'd had her say for the moment, Lucie raised her teacup to her wide, rather sensuous mouth.

"I say, madam, we've come here at the insistence...er, that is...as volunteers at considerable inconvenience and, may I add, expense..." Watson started to come to the defence of his own and Holmes's efforts.

"Please, please, Dr. Watson..." Mathieu Dreyfus, his face flush with embarrassment, interrupted. "My dear sister-in-law," he leaned forward and placed his hand on Lucie's in a gesture calculated to both soothe and restrain, "is understandably distraught, as are we all. I assure you that whatever may be the outcome of your endeavours, the *entire,*" he emphasized the word as he squeezed Lucie's hand, "Dreyfus family owes you both an enormous debt of gratitude which we can only hope to someday repay."

Before Mathieu Dreyfus could continue, Holmes turned to Lucie Dreyfus. "I must confess, *Madame* Dreyfus, that I cannot hope to compete with one who communicates with and through spirits. Indeed I would forsake every bit of the scientific knowledge which I have devoted my life to acquiring if I could speak just for a mere minute with *M'sieur* Lambert.

"Captain Dreyfus is after all your husband, even if his plight has become a *cause celebre* to countless groups and individuals, each with their own agenda. And it is you who must make the decisions upon which your husband's fate may ultimately depend." Holmes rose from the sofa where he and Watson had been sitting and made as though to leave. "If you feel that his interests are best served by relying upon the 'spirit world' to bring about his exoneration and freedom, then that is certainly your choice, and it would be—forgive me—mean-spirited of me to contradict you. So Watson and I shall take our leave and wish you a most sincere *bon chance.*"

Before Watson could join Holmes, Lucie got up quickly and put her hand on Holmes's arm as though to restrain him. "Please Mr. Holmes, Dr. Watson, do not go. You must not let a mere woman's emotional outburst give you offense." She lowered her eyes affecting a look of contrition. Clasping both her hands around Holmes's upper arm, she gently guided him back to his seat

147

which, to Watson's amazement, he re-took, his face a stone mask save for a furious grinding of his jaw muscles discernible only to Watson.

Lucie re-took her seat, a straight-backed chair situated between the two opposing sofas occupied by the men. She straightened her skirt, and patting the heavy, looped braids into which she had arranged her hair on the sides of her head, she leaned toward Holmes who was seated nearest to her on the right-hand sofa. "Please accept my apology, gentlemen. My comparison of Mr. Holmes to the Gypsy woman was singularly in-appropriate even, if I may borrow Mr. Holmes's *mot just,* mean-spirited." She managed a wan smile, while Holmes remained impassive, his hands resting on his knees, looking straight ahead at Mathieu who was seated opposite him on the sofa to Lucie's left. "This horrible business is like some Greek tragedy, Mr. Holmes. And I look upon you as a *deus ex machina*, arriving at the critical moment, just when it looks as though all is lost, to make things right and save the day.

"I know—or at least my rational side knows—that we must be patient. Even your formidable skills cannot always produce results as quickly as others would like. But this wretched *affaire,"* she emphasized the word which had become a short-hand for the Dreyfus case, "has dragged on now for nearly five years. Five...long...years...that my children have been without a father, and my miserable self has been without her husband." She dabbed the corners of her eyes with a dainty handkerchief as she continued speaking, her face still only inches from Holmes's. "And I sense, Mr. Holmes, that the *denouement* may be close at hand."

Holmes had by now stopped clenching his teeth. He leaned back in his seat, crossed his legs and addressed Lucie. "It does not come as a surprise to us," he turned his head slightly in the direction of Watson who was seated beside him on the couch to Lucie's right, "that you and your family have felt constrained to consult mediums and whatever others of that ilk that may have been pressed or pressed themselves upon you. You would not be the first in dire circumstances to have done so. What does come as rather a surprise is your statement that this person had somehow provided 'useful information' to you. Pray do elaborate."

"Allow me, *M'sieur* Holmes," Mathieu Dreyfus interjected. "The Gypsy woman was first brought to us by my friend Dr. Gibert, a physician of Le Havre. How the woman came to his attention, whether as a patient or a research subject, I do not know."

Watson, to whom medical ethics were sacrosanct, asked, "research subject, Mr. Dreyfus?"

Dreyfus, noting the edge to Watson's question, replied, "Dr. Gibert has for a number of years been conducting research into the realm of the super-natural in its many forms. His investigations in this area parallel the work of, among others, Dr. Conan-Doyle of London. Perhaps, Dr. Watson, Dr. Doyle is an acquaintance of yours? In any case, Dr. Gibert's particular area of interest is somnambulism, and it was in this connection that the *'demoiselle* Leonie was first brought to him. I am made to understand that research subjects come only on a voluntary basis, and are not mistreated in the slightest manner.

"Be that as it may, she has on several occasions made known to us facts regarding Alfred's condition that were previously unknown to us. For example, it was through Leonie that we first learned that Alfred had exchanged his *pince-nez* for regular spectacles. And it was through a vision of Leonie's that we first found out that a stockade fence had been erected around his miserable prison hut thereby cutting off any view of the ocean or breeze to alleviate the stifling heat. When she was first brought to me, her first words, without having been apprised of my identity, were to the effect that I had a brother who was in prison, and he had a wife and two small children."

"How," asked Watson, "can you be sure that she was not given this information for the purpose of deceiving you as part of the scheme against your brother?"

"The thought of course occurred to me immediately as well, Dr. Watson. But in the first place, Dr. Gibert is a highly respected physician, as well as a friend of many years. He is most sympathetic to our plight, and even if he were not, his professional integrity would not allow him to be used as the implement of such a vile plot. In the second place, Leonie, while of Gypsy ancestry, is a simple peasant woman, possessing neither the ability to read nor write. She may in fact have been the *only* person in France who had not heard of my brother's misfortune.

"At our first meeting, I was so taken aback at her knowledge of the details of Alfred's imprisonment, that I brought her to Paris that very evening and put her up in the home of my sister in the Rue de l'Arcade. After Dr. Gibert taught me how to induce a trance, I moved her to my own home where she is still in residence. Indeed, if you wish, I can have her brought here within the hour and you may then judge for yourself whether she is genuine or some cruel hoax perpetrated upon us by my brother's enemies."

"I have learned through long experience, *M'sieur* and *Madame* Dreyfus, that at this stage of an investigation the benefits of keeping an open mind by and large outweigh the detriments. Accordingly, I accept your proposal. Please send for her at once, and in the meantime let us hear what information has prompted the left-handed *Herr* Schwabach to forsake the comfort and convenience of his Berlin banking house for the rigors of a journey to Paris."

"One moment, gentlemen." Mathieu Dreyfus got up from his seat and rang for a servant who appeared almost instantaneously. "Let me send for her now." When Dreyfus had returned to his seat, Schwabach spoke for the first time.

"Ach, Herr Holmes, it is you who are the clairvoyant. How could you possibly know that I'm from Berlin, much less that my occupation is that of banker? Or for that matter that I'm left-handed? Is there some sign about my neck that is invisible to all but you?"

"Perhaps, Herr Schwabach, you should spend less time reading the financial journals and take up reading Dr. Watson's accounts of several of my cases. I understand that they're now translated into German and available everywhere from booksellers to railway stations. But to answer your questions, it was simply a matter of observation. When we were introduced and shook hands a while ago, I noticed that while your grip is firm, your right hand is soft and betrays not the slightest trace of your calling. Your left hand, however, is not only slightly larger than the right, but there is a distinct callous on the inner aspect of your middle finger. Such a growth may be attributed, more than ninety-nine times out of a hundred, to the constant use of a writing implement."

"While there are several occupations which require a great deal of writing, as a working hypothesis I narrowed the field down to four: physician, lawyer, journalist and of course banker. I ruled out physician when you chose not to enter the discussion regarding the ethics of experimentation on human subjects. I also ruled out lawyer for approximately the same reason; no lawyer can resist a good argument, even if he knows nothing about the subject at hand. Since our business, yes even our very presence here today, was to be kept in the strictest confidence, I was also able to rule out journalist."

"You were unmoved by any of our discussions save in one instance, and that is when Watson made mention of the cost of our little sojourn. You probably oversee your firm's letter of credit department. Although you have recently returned from Turkey, generally you do not travel all that much. However, by reason of your supervisory duties, you are no doubt quite familiar with the cost of modern travel. So during what must, in candor, be looked upon as rather heated discussions between myself and *Madame* Dreyfus, the only time you reacted was in the instance I've just described."

"Yes, but..." the banker stammered.

Holmes held up his hand palm outward. "I assure you, *Herr* Schwabach, it is merely a matter of training oneself to observe even the smallest details. Like so many others today, I too believe that after inherited wealth, capital appreciation is the next best thing. Indeed, if one believes the advertisements for new securities issues with which we are bombarded on a daily basis, investing in stocks and bonds is as much a civic duty as voting or jury service. Thus from time to time, even I have been known to invest a few pounds in some promising offering or other. And, like every other investor who hasn't the foggiest notion of what he's invested in or why—save that it seemed a good idea at the time—I devour all the news of the financial markets like a punter his racing form.

"So it was that when I observed on your watch chain the small medallion enameled with the distinctive logo of the Turkish National Railway, I recalled reading in the last fort-night, I believe it was, that a consortium of German banks had underwritten a rather large offering of bonds issued by that same railway. I also remembered that a firm headquartered in Berlin managed the consortium. From that intelligence, it was not difficult to conclude that your firm, though the name eludes me at the moment, was the offering manager and that you had received the medallion as a memento of the transaction. I do confess, however, that my assertion that you had been to Turkey was at best a two-to-one gamble. You may have gone there as part of a due diligence protocol, or in connexion with the initial *tranche,* or you may have merely received the token in your office through the mail."

"Very impressive, Mr. Holmes," Lucie Dreyfus remarked with just a lingering trace of asperity in her voice. "Would only that such parlor games could restore *Captiane* Dreyfus to his wife and children."

"Rest assured, *Madame,* that what you are pleased to describe as *parlour games* shall indeed, hopefully sooner than later, accomplish just that. And now, by your leave, I should very much like to hear what *Herr* Schwabach has come to tell us. And while he does so, would it offend you if we smoke?"

"Do feel free, gentlemen," Lucie replied. "My home is yours. If it would bring my husband back to me even five minutes sooner, feel free to loosen your collars and take off your shoes if you wish. But since I do not care for cigarette smoke and I've already heard what Herr Schwabach has to tell you about the odious Baron Ollstreder, I should like to prevail upon Dr. Watson to allow me to consult him in private regarding a small medical matter." As she rose the men all scrambled to their feet. She walked over to Watson and took his arm. "And," she said to Watson as she led him from the room, you may rest assured that my aversion to cigarette smoke does not extend to pipe smoke as well."

CHAPTER SEVENTEEN

"And should my fears prove to be true,
then my husband may become nostalgic
for the comforts of Devil's Island."

She brought him to a small, less formal room which in England would probably have served as a withdrawing room, and bade him be seated in a comfortable chair upholstered in what Watson took to be a tasteful compass rose pattern. She seated herself in a matching chair at right angles to Watson. Even though the window curtains were open, the mid-afternoon sun left the room in deep shadows interspersed with bronze light patterns on the cream-colored wall and shafts of light reflecting here and there off a polished piece of furniture or *objet d' art*.

Once seated, Watson reached in his pocket for his briar. "Would you please, Dr. Watson," Lucie gestured toward the *beaux* arts-style floor lamp next to Watson's chair. He obliged and resumed filling his pipe. As he did so, Lucie reached for a mother-of-pearl in-laid box on the small table between the two chairs. She took out a cigarette and held it to her lips, waiting for Watson to light it for her.

Watson struck a match, and when the phosphorus had burned off held it to the tip of Lucie's cigarette and then to his pipe. "But I thought, Madam, that you had an aversion to cigarette smoke...?"

Lucie sat back in her chair and took a deep drag on her cigarette. "I trust, Dr. Watson, that your professional duty to maintain as confidential what passes between physician and patient extends to minor vices as well as to medical problems. Mathieu would no doubt be scandalized, and I can hardly bear to imagine what Mr. Holmes would think of me, especially after the wretched way I've treated him this afternoon."

"I take it, Madam, that your exchanges with Holmes were some sort of test? You do not appear to me to be a woman much given to hysterics, although heaven knows you've just cause." Watson paused, took a puff of his pipe and smiled. "It is a rare

153

client who has the courage to stand up to Holmes, and frankly I think it does him good for that to happen from time to time. You may of course rely upon my discretion. But do we have a physician-patient relationship? Why Paris is the very epicenter of modern medicine, and I should think that you would have your pick of Paris's finest..."

After another long drag, Lucie ground out the remnant of her cigarette in a crystal ashtray on the table next to the cigarette box. "When I first learned that you and Mr. Holmes might take up my husband's case, I immediately set out to learn everything I could about you both. Although I knew of you, I must confess that at first lack of interest, and then in the last five years my preoccupation, have kept me from reading any of your accounts of Holmes's cases. However, I can now boast that I have read every word that you have written regarding your celebrated companion. I did not have to go very far in my reading to form the impression that you are a most perceptive student of human nature. I see now that I was not mistaken in this impression. You are quite right; I was in fact testing Mr. Holmes," she paused, "and, I suppose, you as well. I had to satisfy myself as to the depth of your commitment to securing my husband's freedom.

"Mr. Holmes put the matter quite succinctly; it is ultimately I who must make the decisions upon which my husband's fate may rest. And it is true, as Mr. Holmes says, we've had all sorts of people pressed upon us, some well-intentioned, but others merely preying upon our misfortune for pecuniary or other gain. As to those who have made common cause with us, well, tomorrow some other great cause, providing a newer fresher challenge may come along to occupy their attention and energy. Meanwhile my husband continues languishing on that miserable little rock, the unremitting sun baking his brain every day, as we pine our lives away waiting in vain for his return.

"As to my self-control, I assure you it is but a thin veneer, no more than a woman's make-up, as it were." She reached for another cigarette, for which Watson dutifully produced a match. Taking. the cigarette from her lips and holding it up to eye-level, she continued. "I said, if you will recall, that 'I did not care for cigarette smoke', and I assure you that statement is literally true. It's only in the last few months that I've taken these up. Odd as it may seem, when things appeared to be hopeless, I could cope, day-to-day, without assistance of any kind. But now, now that there's real hope at last, I find that my ability to carry on varies in inverse proportion. So it was either these, or cognac or laudanum, and I chose these.

"What you say regarding the *Parisiene* medical establishment is, I suppose, true. But then you should be flattered that of all the brilliant medical minds at my disposal, I've chosen to place my trust in you. The fact of the matter is, Dr. Watson, given who I am and the nature of matter about which I beg to consult you, I fear that should I seek the advice of a local physician, professional ethics notwithstanding, the matter would inevitably become known at the very least to our enemies, and quite probably become public knowledge."

"But surely you can see, Mrs. Dreyfus, this is neither the appropriate time nor place for me to examine you, er..." Watson fidgeted in his seat, "should an examination be necessary, that is. Why I don't even have my medical bag, much less a female nurse to be present."

"It is my fervent hope, Dr. Watson, and not merely for reasons of modesty, that an examination will not prove to be necessary. Whether it will depends entirely upon the advice which I anticipate you will be able to give me. The advice which I seek....," she paused. "I hope you are not easily shocked, Dr. Watson."

Watson shook his head. "I assure you, Mrs. Dreyfus, between my professional practice and my chronicling of Holmes's cases, I am quite shock-proof. Please feel free to speak whatever is on your mind."

"Very well then," she began again, "the advice which I seek has to do with diseases—I understand there are several—that are transmitted through," she paused, drew a breath and averted her eyes from Watson, "sexual congress." Making eye contact again, she continued, "I trust that I've not given offence, Dr. Watson."

"No, no, dear lady, please continue." Watson shifted uncomfortably in his seat and re-crossed his legs.

"Prior to my husband's first so-called trial, there were accusations made of certain...how shall I say it... libertine conduct on his part."

"Meaning..."

"...that he had relations of a most intimate nature with prostitutes, both before and after our marriage. I am made to understand that such women receive many, many men of all stations, and that the incidence of such diseases among these sad creatures is virtually universal."

"What you say, Mrs. Dreyfus, is generally accepted as true by those in the medical community who concern themselves primarily with matters of public health. I myself do not claim any expertise in the area, although during my tour of duty as an Army physician I did have occasion to observe a number of cases among the ranks. Do you have any specific reason to believe that your husband is infected? Has he said anything to give you cause for concern?"

"No, when the accusations first were made, he was already under arrest and being held, as far as his family was concerned, incommunicado."

"Are you symptomatic?" Watson asked.

"I do not believe so, Dr. Watson, at least so far as I know. But for five years now this possibility has been a Damoclesean sword hanging over me. Am I going to wake up one morning covered with hideous sores? Is it possible that my children may have been infected before birth?

"I care about my husband very much and I firmly believe that he is innocent of the charges laid against him. But even if they were true, it would not make the slightest difference to me." She paused and took out another cigarette, but when Watson reached for his matches, she smashed it unlighted into the ashtray. "But I must have the truth about this, Dr. Watson. I must know!" Her eyes welled up with tears as she struggled to retain her composure. "And for that reason, as much as any, I want him brought back to me."

Her eyes now dry, she continued, her voice hard-edged. "And should my fears prove to be true, then, Dr. Watson, my husband may very well become nostalgic for the comforts of Devil's Island."

"I'm sorry to have used you in this manner, but I simply had to share my torment with someone. And for reasons which I'm sure are now apparent, you are the only person to whom I could turn."

"Please, Madam, I understand completely. Again, while I'm not a specialist in these diseases, if you've been a-symptomatic for all these years, I..."

The door opened and a servant came in, "*Madame, M'sieur, M'sieur* Mathieu begs to inform you that the *Mademoiselle* Leonie has arrived, and as soon as it is convenient, they wish you to join them in the parlor."

Lucie inclined her head slightly in the direction of the ashtray. The servant produced from behind his back a covered silver box with a wooden handle. He opened it and emptied the contents of the crystal ashtray into the silver box and closed the lid. *"Merci,* Maurice. That will be all. Dr. Watson and I shall return to the parlour immediately."

As they rose from their seats, Watson touched Lucie's arm, and as they walked toward the door whispered to her: "Do not despair, Mrs. Dreyfus. As I was about to say, of the known diseases of this genre, I can think of only one that might not have manifested itself during an interval of five years. Judging from what I have seen of your demeanor and intelligence, I think it extremely unlikely that you are infected. And if you are not, your children are safe as well. However, if you need further assurance I would suggest that as soon as you can discreetly do so you should come to London where I can have a colleague who is more knowledgeable in the field than I examine you and put any lingering fears to rest."

"Thank you ever so much, Dr. Watson." She pressed her hand gently on Watson's forearm. "You have brought me the first peace of mind that I've had since this business began. And now," she paused as they came to the parlor door, her hand still on his arm, "unfortunately, it is time for us to turn from the sublime to the ridiculous."

CHAPTER EIGHTEEN

"Believe what you will, but do not believe that
I have wrought any miracles."

She was seated in the chair that Lucie Dreyfus had occupied earlier. Her appearance, thought Watson, was not unlike the women in paintings by Vermeer, or by Millet or Van Gogh. Her dress was a plain, dark gray of some coarsely woven woolen fabric, and was characteristic of her class. She also wore the huge bonnet that is the sartorial trade-mark of the women of Normandy. Her facial features, except for an odd arch to her eyebrows, were unremarkable and betrayed nothing of her Romany heritage. She was staring straight ahead, and did not appear to notice when Watson and Lucie walked into the room.

Mathieu Dreyfus held a finger to his lips, indicating that they should be silent. He whispered to Watson, "As you can see, Dr. Watson, I have placed her in a trance-like state using the techniques of Professor Mesmer, as taught to me by Dr. Gibert. Actually, I've become quite adept at the science, or art, whichever you prefer. At this stage she hears and responds only to my voice, although any loud or unusual noise may serve to interrupt her somnolent state. This much I have learned through prior experience.

"The next part is the most difficult. I shall, if all goes well, transfer her concentration to Mr. Holmes so that she responds to his interrogation. I am not always successful in this endeavor, so let us all hope for a good result."

"Oh yes," Lucie contributed, "do let us hope for a good result."

Mathieu gave her a quizzical look, and went to stand behind the Gypsy woman who had yet to move or betray any sign of life, save for a shallow, rather rapid breathing. Another straight-backed wooden chair had been placed in front of the woman, barely a foot away. Mathieu motioned for Holmes to seat himself in the vacant chair and again placed his finger to his lips to call for silence. He placed his hands lightly on her shoulders and, speaking to her in French, said in a quiet, steady voice, "Leonie, do you see the gentleman seated before you?"

"Oui, M'sieur," she responded in a child-like voice which, since it was coming from a distinctly middle-aged woman, startled Watson and almost caused him to snicker aloud. With her elbows rigidly at her sides, she held her hands out, palms up. Mathieu nodded his head indicating that Holmes should place his hands in hers. As soon as he had done so, she placed her thumbs firmly over Holmes's knuckles and proceeded to rub them back and forth for what must have been more than a minute.

Finally she spoke. "There is heavy fog; I cannot see. Why have you come here? Is it to help he who is imprisoned? Yes, I can see more clearly now. There is an old woman dressed in black. She sent you here. But why? You are a policeman, but the other policemen fear and shun you so you must work alone.

"I see water—rushing water. Now the prisoner comes across the water. But there is someone else; no...you seek someone else. You ask the prisoner, but he can tell you nothing. To find the one whom you seek, you must go to the one who rises from the grave." The woman gave a deep sigh, her eyes rolled back in her head and she fell to the floor in a deep sleep.

Watson rushed forward and kneeled down next to the woman to try to revive her, but Mathieu put a hand on his shoulder. "It's al-right, Dr. Watson. She is not in danger. She will now sleep for several hours and suffer no ill effects. This has happened on other occasions, and it is on these occasions that she has been her most prescient."

"Did you hear, Lucie...Gentlemen?" He clasped Lucie by the shoulders. "She said that 'now the prisoner comes across the water'!" Turning loose of his sister-in-law, he grasped Holmes's hand and began pumping it up and down. Finally, our prayers are answered; at long last Alfred's coming home! I don't know what miracle you've wrought, Mr. Holmes, but..."

As Holmes tried to extricate his hand, Lucie intervened, taking Mathieu by the arm and steering him back to the couch. "Please, Dear Mathieu, let us not make too much of this." Lucie pulled the bell-rope and in a moment Maurice appeared with two other servants who among them managed to half-carry, half-drag the unconscious woman from the room. She turned to Holmes, "what do you make of it, Mr. Holmes? How could she know these things about you? Is my husband really coming home? I do so want to believe that it's true, but I..."

"Believe what you will, *Madame* Dreyfus, but pray do not believe that I have wrought any miracles." Holmes frowned and for a moment rubbed his chin. "I'm afraid that I must continue to view the woman's 'gift', if that is the proper term, with some scepticism. I should have liked for Dr. Watson to perform one or two harmless neurological experiments while she was in the somnolent state."

"If in fact she was," Watson interjected.

"Dr. Watson is quite right, *Madame,*" Holmes continued. "Assuming that your brother-in-law's home is comparable to yours in appointments and staffing," Holmes made a broad sweeping gesture with his arm, "she has lived in considerable luxury for several years, and without having to do anything more to 'earn her keep', as it were, than to swoon upon command from time to time and mutter a few cryptic phrases which she could have gleaned from any number of quotidian sources."

"But what of her knowledge of you, Mr. Holmes?" Mathieu interjected, indignation notable in his voice.

"Probably the same explanation," Holmes responded. "Please do not take my remarks as a remonstrance, Mr. Dreyfus, but could she not have overheard you discussing our impending visit? Or is it not possible for her to have gotten the information secondhand from one of your household servants? As you know, thanks to Dr. Watson's literary efforts, my name and methods are, for better or for worse, not unknown among all levels of society. So it would not come as a surprise to find that even she is aware of who I am and that my methods often bring me into conflict with the official police."

"And as to 'the old woman in black'?" Mathieu asked.

"Can you say with absolute certainty that your foreknowledge of our taking up the case has not somehow been shared with others in your household?" Holmes arched an eyebrow in Mathieu's direction. "While I still have an open mind regarding extra-sensory perception, spiritualism and the like, I've yet to be made aware of any genuine instance of its occurrence. Again, Mr.

Dreyfus, without wishing to appear unduly cynical or harsh, I think it highly likely that *Mademoiselle* Leonie is a fraud. Whether she practices her deception for her own account or for that of someone else is, I would say, the more intriguing question."

Mathieu shrugged his shoulders acquiescently. "I concede, Mr. Holmes, the possibility that your scepticism is well founded. But how, I must ask, do you account for the fact that up until a few minutes ago, when she spoke to you in perfectly intelligible English, this un-educated peasant woman had never been known to utter a single word in English or any other language save her native Norman-French?"

CHAPTER NINETEEN

"I assure you, Mr. Melmoth, *your forbearance will be well rewarded."*

*U*pon returning to the Ritz, Holmes and Watson had gone out again and were now seated in a quiet neighborhood bistro, Holmes sipping a Pernod and Watson nursing a bottle of *eau minerale.* But for a couple of cheap posters advertising Peugeot bicycles and Michelin tyres, the establishment was devoid of any decor. It was likewise devoid of patrons, save Holmes and Watson, and a pale and somewhat seedy looking man who sat immobile at a nearby table staring blankly into the dregs of an empty absinthe glass.

Watson leaned close to Holmes. "I say, Holmes, I don't know how it's possible, but that fellow looks awfully familiar, doesn't he? Do we know him? Someone ought to warn him off that absinthe. It's deadly. No wonder he looks as he does."

Holmes rubbed the sides of his nose with his index fingers. "For a chap on holiday I'd say you're developing quite an active medical practice. Isn't one consultation enough for the day? If you're not careful, the local medical society may get after you for taking away all their custom..."

"You're in rather a droll mood." Watson fiddled with his empty glass, and continued to obliquely watch the absinthe drinker. "You should really consider writing for the stage. One of these days I shall finally persuade you to join me for luncheon with Shaw. Wait, that's it. I knew that fellow was familiar." Watson let go his glass and leaned toward Holmes, "It's Oscar Wilde," he whispered. "You remember that ugly business with the Marquis of Queensbury. I met Wilde several years ago. He used to hold court at the Cafe Royale in Regent Street. I went once with Shaw and he introduced me. Delightful chap, Wilde, but then..."

The disheveled man got up and walked the few unsteady steps to Holmes and Watson. Placing his hands on the table for balance he leaned down toward the two men, his red-rimmed eyes blazing. "You are quite mistaken, *M'sieur. Je m' appelle*

'Sebastian Melmoth'. The 'Oscar Wilde' of whom you speak in hushed tones—lest the name be taken as a curse upon thine lips—died in Reading Gaol two years ago." He quickly placed his hands over his mouth to stifle a fit of coughing. As he gasped for air, his matted, shoulder-length hair fell in front of his face like a pair of bead curtains.

Watson got up and taking a chair from the next table pushed the man down into the seat. When the coughing had subsided, he handed him the half-full bottle of mineral water. "Here, drink this, Mr. Wil... er... 'Melmoth' did you say?"

"Yes, that is the name by which I am known here." Wilde put down the water bottle. "A few friends from my former life..."

"Frank Harris?" Watson asked.

Wilde nodded, and glancing down at his dirty fingernails self-consciously put his hands in his lap. "Harris and a handful of others. They help out from time to time when I'm too sick," he looked over at his empty absinthe glass which he'd left on the other table, "to work." He coughed again into the sleeve of his frayed jacket. He drew a couple of sob-like breaths and when he'd regained his composure signaled to the barman.

Holmes turned to the bar-man. "*Trois cognacs, s'il vous plait.*" He turned back to Wilde and Watson. "Don't let me intrude on your professional prerogatives, Watson, but don't you think that a dollop of brandy would be better for *M'sieur* 'Melmoth'?"

As the bar-man placed the drinks on the table and accepted the proffered ten-franc note from Holmes, Watson asked, "Then I take it you're writing again? That's wonderful. A play? A novel?"

Wilde drained his glass and wiped his mouth on his sleeve.

"No, Dr. Watson, I'm afraid not. My sole livelihood today is serving as a guide for rich foreigners wanting a tour of *Pere Lachaise.*"

"The cemetery," Holmes interjected, noticing Watson's puzzled look. Holmes turned to the bar-man and held up one finger.

His glass refilled, Wilde continued, "Yes, the cemetery. It's my favorite place in Paris. There I can have the most entertaining conversations with the most interesting people. Think of it: Moliere... Balzac... and never a word whispered behind my back. The English tourists are rare. The Germans are most knowledgeable, but they part with their francs only with the greatest reluctance. The Americans are the best tippers, but they are, as a race, appallingly ignorant."

Holmes lit a cigarette. "I'm somewhat surprised, *M'sieur* Melmoth..."

"It's quite al-right, Mr. Holmes," Wilde leaned forward, shoulders hunched, his forearms again on the table, "for you to address me as 'Wilde'. After all, Dr.Watson and I are friends, are we not?" He placed his right hand over Watson's left forearm, and then, somewhat sheepishly pulled it away. Turning to Watson, tears welling in his heavy-lidded eyes, he asked, "We are friends, Dr. Watson, aren't we?"

"Why yes, yes, of course we are. In fact I had luncheon with Harris and Shaw but a few weeks ago, and..."

"I'm quite surprised," Holmes began again, "Mr. Wilde, that you remember Dr. Watson from, as Watson recalls the occasion, a brief meeting some years ago. At that time I must assume his star was but a minute twinkle in the firmament of the London *literati.*"

Wilde said nothing, his eyes lowered, as he pressed his glass with the tips of the fingers on both hands.

Watson reached for his pipe. "Really, Holmes, must you? I mean, can't you see..."

"I think perhaps Mr. Wilde has had your name brought to his attention much more recently. Indeed, I suspect our meeting up with Mr. Wilde was not altogether serendipitous."

Watson struck his match sharply on the ceramic ashtray. "Holmes, that's preposterous. How in the world could Wilde have known that we were going to come to this rather obscure little bistro? It was pure chance. Of all the bistros in all of Paris, why would he pick this one in which to wait for us? We had no idea ourselves that we were coming here until we walked in the door. And then how would he know that I would recognize him? Especially in his present state... er... no offence, old fellow..."

"Mr. Wilde" Holmes asked mildly, "would you care to elucidate?"

Wilde took a nervous sip of his drink, and then finished it in a single gulp that brought on yet another coughing fit, during which he managed to gesture for a refill. Holmes held up his hand in the direction of the barman making a circle with his thumb and forefinger. The barman, correctly interpreting the gesture, brought over a fresh bottle of cognac which, along with an indifferent *merci,* he exchanged for Holmes's hundred franc note.

"I take it," Holmes began as he passed round the bottle, "that you are 'the one who rises from the grave'?"

Wilde gave Holmes a puzzled look. "I don't think I understand. While I may look as though I have been recently exhumed, and indeed wish that my former self had in fact died in prison, I assure you, with my hand upon this sacred bottle, that neither is the case. Tell me, Mr. Holmes, if you were given the opportunity to rise from your grave, would you want to come back as the noxious phantasm you see before you? Please, sir, do not ply me with your riddles.

"There was a time, as you know, when clever words exuded from me like minted breath. A *mot just* from Oscar Wilde reverberated through the salons and clubs of London like thunder in a summer storm. Now words merely pass between my ears in meaningless juxtaposition. I'm at a loss, sir, to comprehend the import of your question."

"Do forgive me, Mr. Wilde. Evidently I've misjudged you. Your role in this affair is simpler and yet at the same time far more complicated that it first appeared. Let me approach the matter another way.

"You did in fact plan to meet Watson and myself, but did not mean to do so here. You intended to wait for us in the lobby of the Ritz, but owing to your appearance, you never made it past the *chassuer.* In order to re-group, so to speak, you repaired to this establishment whose sartorial standards are far less demanding than those of the Ritz. And by coincidence, Watson and I came along and fortuitously solved your problem. Am I correct so far?"

Wilde nodded in affirmation and took another sip of his brandy.

Holmes continued. "Now with all due respect to Dr. Watson, whose formidable literary skills were not nearly so well known then as they are today, I rather suspect that you had no more recollection of having met him in some cafe in Regent Street than you might remember bumping into a stranger in Picadilly Circus."

Wilde nodded again. "You were described to me by the man who sent me."

"And who might that be?" Holmes asked.

"I'm sorry, I do not know his name. I took him on a tour of the cemetery. He was dressed like a tourist, but he seemed somewhat odd, as though he'd been to Pere Lachaise before. He spoke to me in French, but with an unusual accent. At times he sounded like a Frenchman, and at others like a German. My ear for accents was never as good as Shaw's, and now..."

"Could he have been a Frenchman who wanted to sound like a German speaking French? Did you speak to him in English?"

"No, not at first. In fact, he asked me if I spoke English. I told him that I had for a time lived in England and could still, with effort, make myself understood in that tongue."

"Did he appear to know you, I mean your real, that is your *former* identity?

Wilde hesitated, willing his fogged brain to recall every detail of the interview. "I do not think so, Mr. Holmes. Apart from an occasional quizzical look from a stranger passing on the street, and former casual acquaintances such as Dr. Watson, only a dwindling roster of friends know who I am. And for the most part, other than Harris, they prefer to be discreet in their liaisons with me. They give me the use of their apartments in the City when they are away at their country houses, and they invite me to their country houses when they are in the City. I have a room in a small *pension* in Montmartre where I spend the early morning hours—as you can no doubt tell, I do not sleep much—when no one has remembered to invite me over 'for a few days'. The landlady, a war widow, has no sense of humor when it comes to the timely payment of rent, so there are also those 'friends' whose society consists of dropping off a few francs just when the rent comes due. Thus I think it safe to say, Mr. Holmes, Dr. Watson, that the instigator of my meeting with you has no reason to believe that I am anyone other than 'Sebastian Melmoth', the Charon of Pere Lachaise."

"Can you describe this person?" Watson asked.

"Yes, I believe so. He was rather elegantly dressed in the Continental fashion. Definitely not Savile Row. Stood perhaps sixteen, seventeen hands, and weighed," Wilde shrugged, "nine or ten stone. He had a large, aquiline nose and an enormous drooping moustache. I also remember his ears being rather prominent, making set-pieces with his remarkable nose.

"His eyes were close-set and very dark, and I must say, they frightened me. When we spoke he would not look directly at me, but kept shifting his gaze in all directions as though he were expecting to be attacked."

"Excellent, Mr. Wilde, excellent." Holmes laced his fingers together, a gesture which Watson recognized as his way of resisting lighting a cigarette. "We should introduce you to our friend *M'sieur* Bertillon."

"Bertillon?" Wilde asked. "I don't..."

"Pay no attention, Wilde. It's Holmes's lame attempt at humor. Accept my assurance, based upon personal experience, that you do not want to be introduced to *M'sieur* Bertillon, either in this life or the next."

Holmes took out a cigarette. "Since the 'risen from the dead' phrase has no special meaning for you in the context of your meeting with this Daumier caricature come-to-life, perhaps you should discharge your commission just as it was given to you."

"I was told to seek you out at the Ritz, and offer to give you a tour of the cemetery tomorrow morning, as early as I could persuade you to come. I was given one hundred francs, and promised another hundred if successful."

"And what," Holmes lit his cigarette, "would happen if we were so stiff-necked as to resist your blandishments?"

"Then I was to give you this." Wilde reached inside his jacket and removed a photograph that he laid on the table. Holmes picked it up, holding it at arm's length to accommodate the absence of his reading glasses, looked at it and then passed it to Watson.

"I say, Wilde, what is it. Looks like a man rising from..."

"The grave, Watson," Holmes completed the sentence, "rising from the grave."

Wilde took the photograph back from Watson. "It is, in fact the tomb of the poet George Rodenbach."

"The French poet?" Holmes asked. "I didn't know he'd died."

"He was Belgian actually. He died, let me think," Wilde paused and took another sip of brandy, "perhaps a year ago. He was," Wilde continued, "a bit of an eccentric. If," he paused, "I am permitted such an observation. You're familiar with his work?"

Watson rolled his eyes and took out his pipe. Holmes stared at the ceiling for a few moments. "A follower of Mallarme. Symbolism School, I believe." Wilde rolled his glass between his palms,

> *"Ah! mon ame sous verre, et si bien a l'abri!*
> *Tout elle s' appartient dans 1' atmosphere encloses;*
> *Mon ame est devenue aquatique et lunaire*
> *Elle est tout fraicheur, elle est tout clarte*
> *Etje vis comme si mon ame avait ete*
> *De la lune et de l'eau qu'on aurait mis sous verve.."*

"Actually, "Holmes interrupted, "I prefer his later works, *'Les Vies encloses', 'Le Miror du ciel natal'*... let me think..."

"Le Miror was his last, I'm afraid."

"Do you think, gentlemen," Watson lighted his pipe, "we might continue this fascinating discussion of minor French...er Belgian...poets at some more propitious time?"

"Certainly," Wilde, who for a moment appeared his former self, grew serious once again. "The photograph is from a collection sold by a concessionaire whose kiosk is at the main cemetery entrance on the Boulevard de Menilmontant. As you can see, the tomb is of rough-hewn granite. The top was carved to appear as though it were cracked and partially raised. A bronze sculpture of Rodenbach appears to be lifting the broken portion of the top with one hand so as to permit him to emerge from the lower portion of the sepulchre. Is it of some significance to you?"

Holmes glanced about the room. "It's starting to get a bit crowded in here. Perhaps we should conclude our business with Mr. Wilde before we arouse any unwanted curiosity."

Eyeing the half-full bottle of cognac, Wilde said, "As I have no more pressing engagement this evening, I wonder if I might just stay a bit and..."

"I would strongly advise against it," Holmes replied sternly. "I assure you, Mr. *Melmoth,* your forbearance will be well rewarded. As for now, do you know the rear entrance to the Ritz in the Rue Cambon?"

Wilde nodded.

"Good," Holmes said. "We'll..." Holmes looked at Wilde, and then at the bottle,"...no, you had better leave first. Go directly to the door, but do not try to go in. Watson and I will follow in a minute or two. I think it best if we keep you company for the rest of the night." Wilde started to pour himself another brandy, but Holmes gently took his hands and removed the bottle and glass. "Are we agreed, Mr. *Melmoth?*"

CHAPTER TWENTY

If we eliminate any Mediterranean ports...
that leaves us only every deep water port from
Tallinn to Lisbon. "

"*I*mpossible! *mes amis,* impossible!" Cesár Ritz stamped his foot. "What if he's seen? The man's a pariah. And the way he looks and smells, reeking of drink! What if he passes out, or worse, in my lobby?"

Watson turned to Holmes, "I say, Holmes, is this the same Cesár Ritz we once knew in London?"

"Can't be, old man. That Cesár Ritz was legendary for catering to his guests every whim. Remember the story he told over and over about the maharani who used to stay at the Savoy for weeks at a time with her pet mongoose and cobra? Must have been pulling our legs."

"Yes, and what about the Sultan with his seven wives, or the American cattle baron and his Indian brave, or..."

"Enough! Enough! Gentlemen." Ritz held his hands over his ears. "What do you want me to do?"

What they wanted was soon accomplished. Wilde, his coat collar turned up to cover his face was quickly led in through the kitchen, taken up-stairs in the service lift and ensconced in a vacant room. As he obligingly passed out the moment he lay down on the bed, the stationing of a sturdy young *portier* in a chair inside the door proved to be an un-necessary precaution.

Standing in the hallway outside the door to Wilde's room, Ritz rubbed his palms together and turned to his guests, "Well, gentlemen, I am I still the Cesár Ritz you once knew? Do you have any other little whims to which I may cater?"

"In fact, old friend," Watson took Ritz by the elbow as if he were about to confide some great secret, "the exertions of the day and the lateness of the hour have left Holmes and me a bit hungry. Speaking for myself, 'ravenous' might be more descriptive."

Ritz beamed. "That I can solve. Auguste, I'm sure will be delighted to see you both."

Actually," Holmes interjected, "neither Watson nor I are much inclined this evening to dress for dinner, as fond as we both are of Auguste's table. Besides, it seems we have an appointment by dawn's early light and therefore need to retire early. Under the circumstances, do you think it possible for us to have something brought up to our rooms?"

"You want food service in your room?" Ritz rubbed his chin. "Hmmm, food service in guests' rooms. Why not?" He grasped Holmes by the shoulders. "My friend, you are a genius. Food service coming up, *tout de suite!*"

A short while later, Holmes and Watson were comfortably seated at a small table brought for the occasion to Holmes's room, dining on cold *saumon fume* with *aioli, croque-monsieurs* and a *gateau* with a *chantilly* topping. The table and repast had been brought to the room by a cadre of bewildered waiters under the auspices of a beaming Ritz.

"Evidently you were right in your assessment of the Gypsy woman's extrasensory powers."

"Either that," Holmes set down his sandwich, "or our scepticism regarding the so-called 'para-normal' is about to undergo an agonizing reappraisal."

"Surely, Holmes, you don't believe..."

"Of course not, Watson. But then what are we to believe?"

"Clearly someone wants us to visit the cemetery... what was the name?"

"Pere Lachaise," Holmes replied with an exaggerated accent. "But why? To inspect some bizarre tomb?"

Watson swallowed a mouthful of cake. "Someone evidently wants to meet us, I would say. And, although I would describe the venue and time as a bit on the melodramatic side, perhaps they are best suited to his purpose."

"His purpose? Or *their* purpose?" Holmes pushed back from the table, unbuttoned his vest and reached for his cigarette case. "That was excellent, but I think I'll decline the *gateau."*

"Ritz seems quite enamored of the idea of in-room food service. No doubt he'll soon be offering it as a standard feature along with his beloved bathrooms."

"Indeed. I hesitate to mention to him that Mrs. Hudson has been doing it for years."

"Then you think there may be danger?"

"I would certainly be remiss if I did not enjoin you to bring along your revolver."

"Let me have one of those cigarettes, if I may. This pipe is starting to taste over-smoked, and at the moment I'm too full to contemplate getting up and fetching a fresh one from my kit. Thank you." Watson lit his cigarette and dropped the spent match in the ashtray which Holmes had reached back and gotten from the bedside night table. "Tell me what the German banker had to say."

"Herr Schwabach is in fact the managing director of Samuel Bleichroder & Co., a venerable Berlin banking house, which, he was proud to tell me, has been the Berlin correspondent for the French branch of the Rothschilds, *de Rothschild Freres,* for something over seventy years.

"More to the point is that under the late managing director, Gerson *von* Bleichroder, the firm, although owned and managed by Jews, are the principal bankers to the Kaiser in connexion with his personal holdings. In addition to giving them a competitive advantage in the bidding for underwritings such as the Turkish National Railway bonds—to which I made reference in what *Madame* Dreyfus was pleased to call our 'little parlour game'—the relationship also offers them unparalleled access to information."

"Such as?"

"The entrepreneurial ventures of our would-be client Baron Ollstreder. The baron, it seems, is among the largest private purchasers of weapons, from side-arms to artillery, on the Continent."

"I assume that he does not need them for boar hunting on his 'modest' estates?"

"That would be a safe assumption, but then no one seems to know exactly where they end up. All Schwabach's sources can tell him is that every few months, a freighter is loaded and departs Hamburg for unknown ports. When it next makes port, it is invariably riding high in the water and its manifest shows no discharge of cargo since leaving Hamburg. The vessel was libeled once—in fact just this past November—at Boston for non-payment of stevedoring charges. The money did eventually show up and the ship was released. Through the American court it was learned that the ship, the *Aegean Star,* is of Greek registry. Then through

172

the Greek maritime officials, ownership was traced to a Netherlands Antilles company thought to be a subsidiary of a Liechtenstein corporation. But, as usually is the case, the company's shares were all in bearer form and its registered agent proved to be a Swiss lawyer who declined to further identify his clients."

Watson stubbed out his cigarette. "You indicated over lunch, that there was nothing to implicate the baron in the Dreyfus business. And even with the banker's information, I still do not see the connexion between the baron's arms-trading—despicable though it is—and the misfortunes of Captain Dreyfus and his family.

"Nor do I, my friend, *as yet.*" Holmes stifled a yawn. "Despite *Madame* Dreyfus's somewhat extravagant representations, *Herr* Schwabach is short on hard intelligence and long on conjecture. The consensus is that after von Schwarzkoppen's recall or withdrawal—which is the truth will probably never be revealed—the German espionage apparatus needed a new on-site manager here in Paris. Having learnt their lesson from the initial implication of a high embassy official in the Dreyfus case, they wanted someone outside their diplomatic contingent, so that they could preserve deniability should another scandal erupt. They chose, according to the speculation, Baron Ollstreder because his sleep is never troubled by matters of conscience. Their *quid pro quo,* according to *Herr* Schwabach, is that the German Government ignores his arms trafficking and indeed would deny that it occurs.

"The only other non-conjectural information which Schwabach could provide to us is that shortly before each shipment, the baron makes a substantial deposit to his account, and then makes another deposit of approximately the same amount usually within a week to ten days, never more than two weeks, later."

"Obviously payment for the arms, I should think. One-half when the vessel sails, and the balance on delivery. Assuming that the interval corresponds to the time in transit, the port of destination can only be in Europe."

"My own conclusion exactly, Watson. So if we eliminate any Mediterranean ports, and if we accept that the ship does not head out to sea only to return after a suitable time to Hamburg, that leaves us only every other deep water port from Tallinn to Lisbon."

"I concur. But then, after all that, we've hardly advanced matters in the slightest."

"True enough. However, the rest of what Schwabach had to say about the payments may give us a bit more with which to work. The payments are always in sterling which must by law be cleared through the DeutschBank, the German central bank, and converted into marks. I surmise that *Herr* Schwabach must have agents in the DeutschBank, and this is how he came to possess the information that he related to me. It probably has something to do with the status of Bleichroder as the Kaiser's personal bankers, but Herr Schwabach grew quite reticent when I pressed him on the point, partly out of curiosity—evidently the universal bankers' code of silence can be bent when the occasion demands—and partly to test the validity of his information."

"It would not surprise me," Watson interjected, "to learn that Wilhelm personally profited from *Herr* Schwabach's throwing the Bank's weight around from time to time. But I rather doubt that he would be entirely pleased to learn the other uses being made of the relationship."

"Which understandably accounts for Schwabach's unwillingness to be more forthcoming. But be that as it may, the last link which *Herr* Schwabach could provide is that invariably, as soon as the baron's account is credited for the equivalent sum in Deutsche marks, the baron's bank receives a draft drawn on the account by one 'P. Villeneuf' for fifty percent of each deposit to be paid in French francs and transferred to a numbered account in a Zurich bank. So it would seem then that the baron has a partner. The 50/50 division indicates that the baron is absorbing the entire cost of the inventory out of his share alone. From what we know about the baron, it seems that his partner has a great deal of leverage."

"Do you actually think that *Herr* Schwabach will be able to work his way around or through the Swiss bank privacy laws?"

"Actually not. But I do not think it will be necessary." Holmes smiled. "I think there may be a better way. Incidentally, *Herr* Schwabach was also kind enough to agree to make inquiries through a customer in the pharmaceutical industry and obtain for you all the most current information on 'Aspirin'. You might profitably spend some time looking through the material to see if you can find anything that might be of help to Inspector Loiseaux in his investigation of the Lambert murder. Although the Bayer research people are being somewhat closed-mouth about it, evidently the 'Bleichroder' name opens a great many doors."

CHAPTER TWENTY-ONE

"...it is you sir who are the real disgrace to your uniform.
How could you do a thing like that to one who had
befriended you?"

*W*ilde, to no one's surprise, and to Ritz's hand-wringing consternation, was indisposed when Watson sought to awaken him at five o'clock in the morning. But through Watson's ministrations, first of ammonium carbonate and then of two cups of strong black coffee, all provided by Ritz along with a running remonstrance, Holmes had finally gotten him to divulge the location of a little-used entrance to the cemetery. Wilde remained sentient long enough to provide a crude map showing the way to the Rodenbach sarcophagus. The effects of the stimulants soon wore off, and Wilde, his absinthe-addled brain unable to distinguish himself from his creation, fell back to sleep mumbling that he was *Dorian Gray.*

It had rained during the night and in the half-light of the pre-dawn, the chilly, mist-shrouded streets looked to Holmes and Watson like the London they'd just left. As Ritz had predicted, there were no cabs about. After little debate they agreed to use the hotel's Benz and driver. Ritz agreed to pack Wilde off to Holmes's relatives in the South of France accompanied by the young *portier* and the chauffeur for a fort-night's holiday at full wages and at Holmes's expense. "I will not," he told Ritz adamantly, "put any more lives at risk. I assure you, my friend, you do not want to know why, but there are those," he pointed into the impenetrable mist, "who would shrink from nothing, not even torture and murder, to learn what Watson and I are up to this morning. Watson, you've brought your revolver?" Watson nodded. "Good, then let's be on our way."

At the driver's suggestion, they drove toward the Seine and then turned left on the Rue de Rivoli. By the time they reached the Boulevard Menilmontant the mist was still as thick as when they'd stood outside the hotel making their bargain with Ritz. They had the driver stop at the intersection and let them out, though they were still some blocks from the cemetery. The driver made a U-turn and started off toward the Place De La Bastille in order to confound any unseen pursuers. Holmes and Watson, after waiting a few minutes without hearing the sound of a horse-drawn or motor-driven vehicle or even so much as a footfall on the pavement, started in the opposite direction toward the southeast side of the cemetery and Wilde's gate.

As Wilde had described, the gate was neither fastened nor was there any sign of a security patrol. Holmes and Watson opened the gate cautiously, not knowing what to expect and fearing the slightest noise. But the hinges, although they appeared rusted and disused, opened smoothly making superfluous the small jar of kitchen grease which Holmes had, to Ritz's dismay, insisted on bringing should a lubricant be needed. Once inside, Holmes checked Wilde's map. As Watson again checked his revolver, they made their way through the still-heavy mist until they located what they hoped was the *Avenue des Acacias,* a broad path which they then followed as it curved to the west and then to the north. As Wilde's map indicated, they eventually came to a rather large roundabout pretentiously named the *"Carrefour Du Grand Rond"* where they paused for several minutes, watching and listening intently, before making a 270-degree anti-clockwise arc and setting off in a southerly direction down the *Chemin De Labedoyere.*

When they reached the *Chemin Grammont,* instead of continuing on directly to the Rodenbach tomb, Holmes wordlessly pulled Watson by the arm. They turned right until they came to a small, un-named path branching off to the left and then to the left again, ending several yards behind the Rodenbach tomb which by now was barely visible in the weak early light. Bidding Watson to remain concealed behind a near-by sarcophagus, Holmes moved up to a chestnut tree just a few feet from the Rodenbach tomb.

They remained as they were for at least twenty minutes. By now, although the fog remained, it was at least full daylight so that one could see, Holmes estimated, a dozen yards or so before the fog again turned everything into a gray, shapeless wall. Holmes, being closer to the Rodenbach tomb first heard the scrape of foot-steps moving slowly on the path in front of the tomb. Holmes stretched his arm out behind his back in the direction of Watson, his index finger extended and thumb raised. Watson instantly understood the gesture and took out his revolver which he braced on the top of a headstone, his thumb on the hammer. In a moment Holmes could discern a dark shape coming toward him out of the mist. As the figure reached the corner of the Rodenbach tomb, he was able to make out that it was a woman—at least the figure was clothed as a woman— and by her stooped posture and painfully slow gait, an elderly one at that. She walked with a cane, and in her free hand she carried a basket of flowers.

As she drew even with the tree, she seemed to notice Holmes and turned in his direction. She held the basket toward him, "Flowers, *M'sieur?* One should always bring flowers when visiting the departed."

"Thank you, but I do not come here to visit the departed. It is the one who has risen from the grave that I seek. Do you know where he can be found?"

"Hallo! Holmes, over here! Look what I've found!"

The old woman muttered something unintelligible and shuffled off down the path, at a gait much more sprightly than her pace before she had approached Holmes. Following the sound of Watson's voice, Holmes turned toward the Rodenbach tomb. Watson was bracing a man against the wall of the adjacent tomb. The man's face and hands were pressed flat against the granite. Watson touched his revolver to the back of his prisoner's head and with the toe of his boot nudged the man's feet apart and back so that he was forced to keep his hands against the stone to keep from falling down.

"When you moved out from behind the tree, I circled to my right in order to have a better line of fire. As I did, I spotted this fellow where you see him, sneaking up on you while your attention was distracted by the flower seller. Would you mind holding my revolver while I check to see if he's armed? There's no telling what he's got hidden under this cloak." Watson rippled the man's great-cloak with the barrel of the revolver.

"Excellent work, Watson. You keep your weapon at the ready, and I'll see what, if anything, he's brought to our meeting. No point in giving him an opening while we're making the exchange. As soon as I search him, we can have a look at him, although I expect we already know what he's going to look like."

Watson moved back and to his right a couple of paces as Holmes approached. Holmes expertly probed the man's cloak and suit jacket. He worked his way down the legs. "Hello, what have we here?" He pulled up the man's right trouser leg and extracted a long, thin-bladed knife. "An Italian stiletto, I believe. Deadly against an unarmed victim, but too fragile to be much use in a fair fight. What sort of person do you suppose we're dealing with here?"

"Please, gentlemen, I..."

"Do not speak," Holmes pushed the man's head against the granite sharply enough to cause his knees to buckle so that he lost his balance and sagged nearly to the ground, "until given permission to do so. If you find yourself greatly inconvenienced by our precautions, you may take it as a foreseeable consequence of your own rather bizarre behavior."

"Ah. And what else do we have?" Holmes pushed the cloak to one side and reached beneath the suit jacket at the small of the man's back. "What do you make of this, Watson?" Holmes held the palm of his hand out to Watson displaying in it a tiny, two-barrel derringer-type pistol.

"Perhaps we need to remove all his clothes. No other way to tell what else he's got tucked away in one spot or another."

Holmes replied, "No, I think he's quite harmless now. Let's turn him around and hear the reason for this rather singular *rendezvous*. However, it would be wise, I should think, if you could manage to keep your weapon at the ready for a while yet. His confederate," Holmes gestured in the direction of the path taken by the flower seller, "may be under instructions to return, and I'd not be shocked to find something more in her basket than a few day-old posies." Holmes reached out and grasped the prisoner by the shoulder and turned him around. "Really, my good man, you must learn that it does not pay to pinch *centimes* when putting together disguises. A cheap disguise is worse than no disguise at all. Next time, do try to use fresh flowers. They lend so much more credibility."

"May I reach inside my coat and get out my handkerchief?" the man asked as he turned. "My nose is bleeding and I think it's broken." .

"You may, if you do so slowly and with the utmost care," Holmes replied. "Then perhaps you will be so good as to identify yourself, and state your business with us that has necessitated this rather singular venue and led to the unfortunate condition of your nose."

After he finished daubing his nose, so that his face could be fully seen, he did prove to be the man described by Wilde. "Draw closer, gentlemen, if you please. Holmes and Watson hesitated. "The danger," he lowered his voice to a whisper, "comes not from me. I am in as much, no, far greater danger, than you. Believe me I have come here to help you. If I am found out, my life, I assure you, is most certainly forfeit.

"I am," he drew himself to attention, "Major Marie Charles Ferdinand Walsin Esterhazy." He made a small bow. "At your service."

"And what service," Holmes asked, "is it that you wish to render?"

"It is you, to tell the truth..."

"That," Watson interjected, "would be a refreshing change."

"...who can be of service to me, as well as I to you. You see, gentlemen, it was I who was the author of the infamous *bordereau.*"

"Why confess to us?" Holmes asked. "Weren't you tried and acquitted by a military court just last year on that very charge? Are you suddenly stricken with conscience?"

"The answer, Mr. Holmes, has very little to do with conscience, although Dreyfus is a fellow Alsatian and did once lend me money when I was in dire need."

"That," Holmes remarked acerbically, "was a regular circumstance with you, if I remember rightly."

"Unfortunately, you do remember rightly, Mr. Holmes. I..."

Watson, his voice rising in anger, shook his revolver in Esterhazy's face, "Then it is you, sir, who are the real disgrace to your uniform. And a scoundrel to boot. How could you do a thing like that, especially to one who befriended you? And speaking of uniforms, why is it that you skulk about without yours?"

Esterhazy recoiled against the granite block. "Please," he whispered, "I beg you, do not raise your voice or do anything to

180

attract attention. I chose this time and place because I really have no choice. My movements are watched constantly, and I have very little time before I must leave you. Otherwise I shall be missed and my life, I swear, will be forfeit.

"I did it because I was ordered to do so."

"By?" Holmes asked.

"My spy-master, von Schwarzkoppen. He did it to protect me. When the rumors of an agent on or close to the General Staff began to circulate early in eighteen ninety-four, Max... er... Colonel von Schwarzkoppen who as you may remember was the military attaché to the German embassy, devised the plan in order to protect me from possible exposure."

"How," Holmes asked, "did the rumor get started?"

"*Herr* Colonel," Esterhazy gave an almost obscene little grin, "had what must be described as something more than a professional or diplomatic relationship with Panizzardi, the Italian military attaché. I gathered at the time they'd had a most violent quarrel. It was, so I suspected, over a young junior officer attached to another legation. And in the aftermath, Panizzardi made an indiscreet remark at some reception and soon the existence of 'Max's spy' was common knowledge. It eventually even came to the attention of Sandherr and his Section of Statistics. By the way, does one of you by chance have a cigarette?"

Holmes took out his case, and as he lighted cigarettes for Esterhazy and himself, Watson commented, "so you admit to being a spy for the Germans against your own country."

"It is," Esterhazy inhaled the cigarette gratefully and then gave a small cry of pain as he blew the smoke out his nose, "considerably more complicated than that, Dr. Watson. Never in my entire tenure under von Schwarzkoppen did I as much as once pass to him a single French military secret. Indeed, it was quite the opposite."

"You mean," Watson looked sceptically at Esterhazy who despite everything looked as though he was beginning to enjoy himself, "that you passed German secrets to the French? I must say, Holmes, that I don't understand..."

"I'm afraid I do, Watson. It's so elegantly simple that I was an utter fool not to have understood it five years ago. The major was... is... a 'double agent'. The Section of Statistics thought he was working for them, and that he had somehow compromised or co-opted one of von Schwarzkoppen's staff, or even von Schwarzkoppen himself. In fact, the major was working for von Schwarzkoppen and was passing on only that information which Berlin wanted to end up in French hands. I assume that upon occasion he was given a bit of actual, if trivial, information, something like figures on the average corps' consumption of trotters and sauerkraut. But he never passed anything of real substance, or at least nothing of substance that had any truth to it. Correct so far, Major?"

"Almost exactly, Mr. Holmes. There also existed what the Section of Statistics referred to as 'the ordinary track'. This was a cleaning woman whose nightly duties included cleaning von Schwarzkoppen's office and emptying his wastebasket. This she did by placing the contents in a bag that she carried beneath her skirts. She would first remove from beneath her skirts the trash from the previous night's foraging, which she had delivered to the Section to be photographed and returned to her, and deposit it in the trash receptacle which she took with her from room to room on her rounds. Thus if her work was ever inspected, it would appear that she was in fact disposing of the Attaché's trash just as she was supposed to. She of course was deceiving no one in the Embassy, so von Schwarzkoppen's aide always removed anything of significance and burned it in the basement furnace before the charwoman even arrived. The only things left for her to 'find' were trivia of the kind you describe, and low-level mis-information. The only material of any significance was the *bordereau,* which von Schwarzkoppen wanted to put in Sandherr's hands by the swiftest, most un-impeachable means without my being involved."

"Whose idea," Holmes asked, "was it to fit Dreyfus for the frame-up?"

"Mine, I suppose. He was one of a small group whose postings were such that they would have had access to the information sought by the *bordereau.* This was the most difficult part, since no one in the Section of Statistics could be counted on as clever enough to identify a list of likely suspects in this manner. Because Sandherr's anti-Semitism was so virulent, even by army standards, I knew that Dreyfus would be appealing to him, whereas he might stick at naming a gentile officer. Finally, because Dreyfus and I both received essentially the same penmanship training it was easiest for me to emulate his handwriting."

"Holmes, I think I understand what he's saying. Evidently he knowingly, and the char-woman innocently, have been passing on useless or bogus information to the French military intelligence establishment. But if that is the case, what good would it have done to accuse Dreyfus of passing French military secrets to the Germans?"

"I will answer that, Dr. Watson, but I really must take my leave as soon as possible. I must change into uniform and report for duty," he pulled out a watch from his trouser pocket, "in less than one hour's time. If I do not, I may be dead in little more than an hour's time."

"Rubbish!" Watson snorted. "You are a self-confessed liar and a traitor to your country. What evidence do you have to convince us of your *bonafides?* " -

"I will answer that question too, if you will let me. But let me answer the first question first." Esterhazy dabbed his nose which had started to bleed again. "It proved to be virtually impossible to over-estimate the stupidity of Sandherr and the Section of Statistics. Von Schwarzkoppen told me that from time to time, just as a check on the efficiency of the 'ordinary track', he would circle an arrival entry on a railway time-table, crumple it into his trash basket, and then send someone down to the depot at the appointed time to see how many of Sandherr's men showed up to meet the train.

"But the important thing was not to convince Sandherr and his band of bumblers. They did not need convincing. Besides, they did nothing with the intelligence, save pass it on to higher authority for evaluation and utilization. This was more problematical, although not greatly so. The fear was that once started, the rumor of a highly-placed agent would never go away. This, it was feared, might lead to a thorough investigation of the Section of Statistics, and that in turn might lead to an independent evaluation of the sources of Sandherr's information. Once that were done, the game would be up, and years of pains-taking effort would be for nil. I understand that the *Sureté* was beginning such an investigation, but the military were able to bring sufficient pressure on the civilian government to get the effort quashed.

"Sandherr too did not want an investigation. He was nearing retirement and did not want his career to end in scandal so as to put at risk either his honor or his pension. He really had no idea whether there was in fact a German spy on the General Staff, and if one were to be caught out as a result of an investigation, especially by a civilian agency, it would mean at the least that he would be disgraced. But what he failed to appreciate was that if there was a German spy on the General Staff, he surely would have been privy to the 'intelligence' gathered by Sandherr's agents. Thus the only possible explanation for Sandherr's networks having continued for so long is that the material they were passing on was bogus. This was the Germans' greatest fear, and so both they and Sandherr had common cause in wanting to manufacture an 'acceptable' spy for the catching."

"Just a few more questions." Holmes offered Esterhazy another cigarette. "Why didn't the 'exposure' of Dreyfus as a 'spy' cause the very result that the Germans did not want: that is the realization that the material which you had been passing was bogus? And lastly, is there a spy on the General Staff?"

"The answer to your first question is simple, Mr. Holmes. In addition to the reasons that I've already given, at the time, Dreyfus was new to the General Staff and had to that point been given only relatively low-level field assignments having to do mainly with the state of training in the Field-Artillery Branch. Thus he had never been exposed to the existence of the so-called 'ordinary track' or to the fact that the General Staff were the recipient of German secrets from any source. Thus in all respects he was the 'perfect spy'. As to whether there is in fact a German spy on the General Staff, I do not know, Mr. Holmes. I knew only what von Schwarzkoppen wanted me to know and what I was able to piece together on my own at little or no risk to myself." Esterhazy's eyes watered as he exhaled. "I am not, after all, in this business out of an excess of patriotic emotion."

"I surmise," Holmes fixed Esterhazy with his most penetrating stare, "that your throwing yourself upon our mercy, as it were, is the product of the mortal fear to which you have alluded with such earnestness. But why are you suddenly afraid, so afraid that you would seek refuge in the embrace of your feared enemy? Would not Dreyfus being exonerated create the best of all worlds for your masters? If Dreyfus is innocent, then the French would conclude that there was in fact no spy on the General Staff, and therefore there would be no reason for them to question the genuineness of the material which they had been receiving from you and from the char-woman."

Esterhazy shook his head. "Were that it was so simple. If Dreyfus is freed, I assure you, gentlemen, my usefulness is at an end. And I also assure you that if my usefulness is at an end, my concern for my life is not unfounded. If there is even the slightest chance of there being an inquiry into why Dreyfus was framed in the first-place, or suppose some clever journalist like Zola raises the question loudly and often enough, or suppose some highly respected if meddlesome foreigners such as yourselves should initiate an inquiry, those whom I now serve are mercenaries just like myself and will be quick to cut their losses. As mercenaries, they do not enjoy diplomatic immunity. Should I be arrested again, they have a great deal to fear from my playing the magpie. If Dreyfus is set free, or if his case is even reopened, there's too great a chance that my role will be re-examined, and I will be dead even before the first question can be asked."

"You still haven't answered my second question. And to that one, let me ask a third: what do you have to trade us in exchange for our saving your miserable hide?"

"Your last question, Dr. Watson, will have to await our next *rendezvous* should there be one. As to your pending question, part of my reason for meeting you at such an inconvenient hour is that I wish to warn you that an attempt will be made this very day on the life of a high government official, one who is thought to be sympathetic to the Dreyfus cause, although not generally considered a 'Dreyfusard'. Who the target is, I do not know; nor do I know where the attempt will be made, other than it will be a public place in order to maximize its effect.

"And now, if you will be so good as to return my stiletto and pistol, I must be on my way." Holmes broke open the pistol and removed the bullets, which he placed in Esterhazy's outstretched hand along with the pistol and dagger. Esterhazy gave a nonchalant salute and as he walked away, he turned back for a moment. *"Au revoir, M'sieurs.* Divine Providence willing, I shall be in contact soon. And by the way, tell the Dreyfuses not to fret

185

about *Mademoiselle* Leonie. She greatly needed a change anyway; the years of luxurious living were beginning to give her a bad liver."

CHAPTER TWENTY-TWO

"On a policeman's salary one does not dine at the Ritz."

"***I*** see nothing in the official gazette that would offer a likely venue." Holmes set down his coffee cup. "Anything in *Le Figaro?*"

"Sorry, old man, but as you know my French is virtually non-existent. I can make out a little of the sports news, football scores and the like. Looks like there's going to be a big horse race today at *Au...*" Watson stumbled over the pronunciation.

"Here, let me see. *'Auteuil',"* Holmes pronounced the word. "It's a steeplechase course near Longchamps...in the Bois de Boulogne."

"Holmes, maybe we should just contact the authorities, perhaps Inspector Loiseaux, tell them we overheard a conversation on the omnibus or something..."

"I suppose we could," Holmes paused, "and spend the rest of the day staring into bright lights whilst being interrogated in some dank police headquarters basement. And how long do you think it will be before the questioning will turn again to the Lambert investigation? 'Your hotel is only a short distance from Lambert's shop, *M'sieur* Holmes.' 'Did you and *M'sieur* Holmes perhaps take a walk about the neighborhood, Dr. Watson?' 'The *chassuer* thinks he remembers the two of you going out, but he doesn't recall whistling you a cab.' 'Surely two trained observers such as yourselves, *M'sieurs,* must have noticed something of an unusual nature.' 'Isn't it an odd coincidence that the only two foreigners to have registered at a Parisienne hotel in the last few days who match the description given by the shop-girl just happened to be the two of you?' 'And isn't it even a greater coincidence that the hotel is but a short distance from the place where the crime occurred?' Shall I continue?"

Watson, who was seated facing the door of the Ritz dining room, gave Holmes a warning look, "I think not, Holmes, it appears that your very words have conjured up the inspector in the flesh.

187

"Bon jour, Inspector. Holmes and I were just talking about you, wondering how the Lambert investigation was progressing."

Holmes rose and shook Loiseaux's hand. "Yes, Inspector, so good to see you. Here, please sit down. Watson and I were just finishing our *petit dejeuner."* Holmes caught the waiter's eye, *"garcon, plus cie cafe s'il vous plait."*

Loiseaux took a chair, and, somewhat to the consternation of the waiter, insisted on placing the napkin in his lap himself, "I'm afraid that I am unused to such pampering, gentlemen. On a policeman's salary, one does not dine at the Ritz. Indeed, while I've seen the restaurant before, I think that this is the first time I've sat at one of the tables.

"The investigation goes hardly at all, much less well. There are other priorities. I'm so short of men that I'm checking hotel registers myself. In fact, that's what I was just doing. On impulse, I asked the clerk whether you happened to be in and was told that I could find you in here. I dislike troubling you, and trust you will excuse my interrupting your breakfast."

Loiseaux's coffee arrived and he took a sip. "Ah. Excellent. Far superior to that wretched brew that we keep at headquarters. Alas but no, you didn't invite me to join you in order to be bored by a policeman's lament. *M'sieur* Bertillon's office," he lowered his voice, "is still shuffling their identification cards as the widow Lambert prepares to bury her husband this very afternoon. I was hoping to attend the funeral, you know... just to see who else may show up. But I've been assigned to a special security detail for an event which is to occur at the same time."

"Are we permitted to ask what that might be?" Holmes inquired.

"I see no harm, in your case *M'sieur* Holmes, Dr. Watson. But please do not assume that I make a habit of such discussions." Loiseaux pulled his chair closer to the table and again lowered his voice. "You are, I'm certain, aware of the so-called *'Dreyfus Affaire'."* Holmes and Watson nodded. "Apparently the Captain is about to be given, if not his out-right freedom, at least a new trial, an event which, given all that has come out since his first trial nearly five years ago, ought to result in his freedom in due course. I don't know how word of such things becomes prematurely known, but it invariably does. And since this particular matter is bound to arouse extreme passions on both sides of the issue, it was thought that extra precautions ought to be taken.

"You would think that those most at risk would be inclined to provide at least minimal cooperation, given how thin our resources actually are. But no, they go, it seems, where ever they are most likely to be in harm's way." Loiseaux looked at his watch. "I must be on my way, gentlemen. It seems that President Loubet has a sudden uncontrollable urge to take in the steeplechase this afternoon at Auteuil, and it has fallen my lot to supervise his security." Loiseaux laughed derisively. "As if there's anything I can do in that crowd."

"Then do not let us detain you further, Inspector. Possibly you can join Dr. Watson and myself for dinner one evening before we leave. Then perhaps you will not be so preoccupied, and you can fill us in on the Lambert investigation."

As the three men rose and once again shook hands, Watson added a peroration, "Good luck, Inspector. I trust that nothing will go amiss."

When Loiseaux was out of earshot, Holmes took a final sip of his coffee. "Well old man, are you up for a day at the races?"

CHAPTER TWENTY-THREE

"That you are safe is reward enough for us.
We acted as decent men everywhere would have done
under the same circumstances."

"*T*hanks to Ritz once again," Holmes remarked. "Without him we would be standing out like a couple of mixed-breeds at the Royal Canine Show."

"I'm amazed that in less than two hours' time he managed to turn porter's and desk clerk's uniforms into passable imitations of formal morning attire." Watson took Holmes by the elbow. "Just a moment, you've got a loose thread in the back."

"Do take care, Watson. I wouldn't want to come un-raveled as we stand here." As Watson worked on Holmes's jacket, Holmes began scanning the crowd with the binoculars that Ritz had thoughtfully provided to round out their makeshift costumes. "Why doesn't someone open a shop hiring out men's formal attire? Just think how many men have need of such attire perhaps two or three times in their lives, and find owning such a suit an impractical expense."

"I don't know, Holmes. Wearing another man's clothes makes me uncomfortable. I can't imagine—ah, there you are, good as new. As fine a surgical knot as you'll ever see." Watson released the cloth and brushed away a piece of lint. "However, I would not recommend that you raise your arm above your head unless absolutely necessary." Watson retrieved his walking stick that Holmes had been holding while he performed his repairs. "Have you managed to locate our box?"

"Box? What box? I'm afraid the best Ritz's concierge could manage on such short notice was grandstand reserved."

"At risk of appearing to have a negative attitude, old man," Watson paused to doff his top hat as a pair of comely women strolled past and smiled, "how are we going to do anything, should some untoward event begin to unfold, if we are stuck somewhere in the—what did you call them—oh yes, the 'grandstand reserved'?"

"I concede," Holmes tapped his fingers in frustration on the binoculars, "that the situation is at the least somewhat problematical."

By this time they'd reached the entrance to the rail boxes, and in the manner of French queues were pushed along relentlessly until they reached the ticket checker.

"Billets, M'sieurs, s'il vous plait." The official held out his hand motioning for Holmes and Watson to present their tickets.

Holmes shrugged, *"Je ne comprends pas. Parlez-vous Anglais?"*

"Non, M'sieur."

Just then the queue gave another surge, forcing Holmes and Watson so close to the man that they could smell the garlic on his breath along with the faint aroma of *vin ordinaire.* *"Billets, M'sieurs, je suis desole..."* Suddenly the man came to attention, *"M'sieurs, Le Presidente de la Republique..."*

As he spoke the queue parted and Emile Loubet the newly inaugurated President surrounded by a cadre of hard-faced men strode toward them smiling and waiving to the crowd as he went. The crowd's response was about evenly divided between cheers and epithets. When one of the latter was especially discernible, the President would freeze his smile in place and waive to his detractor.

"Look, Holmes, it's Inspector Loiseaux. Halloo! Inspector!" When Loiseaux reached them a few yards in front of the President, he stopped in astonishment.

"M'sieur Holmes, Doctor Watson, what are you doing here?"

"Your comments about the races today piqued Watson's and my interest. After you left, we read an article about them in *Le Figaro* and decided to come. Now there's been some frightful mix-up about our tickets, and we can't seem to make it past this," Holmes nodded in the direction of the ticket checker, "gentleman. Do you think you might..."

"Mais oui, mes amis, but of course." Loiseaux turned to the ticket checker, flashed his credentials and pushed Holmes and Watson past the barrier just as the President arrived. Once they were through the barrier, he turned and whispered, "I'm short a couple of men anyway, so just come along and act like policemen.

191

The President's box, obviously, is the one with the bunting. *Merde!* It's as though someone is trying to make an attack even easier than it is. Tell me, *M'sieur* Holmes, is security this... this *inept* in England?

"Louis!" he motioned to one of his men, "check out that fellow with the raincoat over his arm!" Turning to Holmes and Watson he muttered under his breath, *"Dupe!"* And then turning back to Louis, "Does it look like rain to you?"

President Loubet had finally reached his box. With another waive and radiant smile to the stands behind, he went in and began greeting the other guests. He had invited them at the last minute, so Loiseaux told Holmes and Watson, as though he almost wanted to make it impossible for us to check out their sympathies in the Dreyfus business.

"You would think, gentlemen, that the President of France would have at least some sense of history. Of his last six immediate predecessors, four were hounded from office by scandals. One we know for certain was murdered by a political assassin, and his immediate predecessor was, we believe also murdered, in this instance by poison, although it was made to look like he died of a massive heart-attack while in *flagrante delecto.* I pray, gentlemen, that I may never be called upon to provide security for *M'sieur* Loubet's dalliances. I've done that once or twice for his predecessor and believe me catering to the demands of the *madame* or *mademoiselle* in question makes facing down a gang of cornered bank robbers seem tame by comparison."

When Loubet finished greeting everyone in the box, he turned to Holmes and Watson with a puzzled look. *"Bonjour, M'sieurs. Comment allez vous?"* He extended his hand in Holmes direction.

Holmes took the outstretched *hand."Enchante, M'sieur le Presidente. Je m' appelle* Sherlock Holmes, *"et,"* he gestured to Watson, *"mon ami M'sieur le Medicin* John Watson."

Just as Watson was grasping the President's hand, a military color guard and small marching band walked out onto the course and marched to the rail in front of the Presidential box. On the down-beat from the drum major they struck up *'Le Marseillaise'* and the crowd came to their feet, the men removing their hats and placing them over their hearts.

When the anthem was reaching its crescendo, Holmes sensed a slight movement behind his right shoulder. Just as he did, an elegantly dressed man attempted to push him aside and force his way into the box. Standing next to Holmes, Watson also felt the man surge forward. Watson looked back over his shoulder. "Holmes! Watch-out! He's got a sword cane!" As Holmes turned to meet the assailant, Watson stepped to the front of the box, and embracing the President from behind wrestled him to the ground between the front rail and the first row of seats.

Holmes stepped forward and as the would-be assassin plunged his weapon in a downward arc, he grasped the man's wrist with his left hand and with his right drove his walking-stick deep into the man's solar plexus. The man screamed once and dropped to his knees. Holmes then raised his stick to shoulder level and brought it down on the man's right clavicle fracturing it with a distinctive crack that blended with another shriek of pain and the last notes of *'Le Marseillaise'*. By this time, Loiseaux had also reached the man in time to remove the weapon from his now useless hand.

Meanwhile, not realizing what was in fact happening, two of Loiseaux's men were attempting to pry Watson off President Loubet's back. They pulled him to his feet and pinioned him against the rail. Watson was sputtering an explanation in English, and the two officers were screaming at him in French. Finally, seeing that Holmes had completely incapacitated the assailant Loiseaux strode to the front of the box, and rescued Watson from the officers. Loiseaux then turned to President Loubet, who had by then picked himself up from his place of involuntary refuge and was calmly brushing the dust from his top hat.

He motioned to his men to bring forward the assailant-cum-prisoner, and hurriedly explained to Loubet what had happened. A pair of handcuffs was produced, and as the man's hands were manacled behind his back, he screamed again in pain, tears streaming down his cheeks. Loiseaux brought the man face to face with President Loubet. "Do you know him, sir?"

"No, *M'sieur Inspecteur,* I do not think so..." Loubet studied the young man for a few moments.

"I do, *M'sieurs.*" A woman who'd been seated in the front row of the box rose. "I am the Countess Tournielli," she addressed the Inspector, "and this pathetic creature who has so rudely attempted to spoil the pleasures of the day is Baron Fernand Chevreau de Christiani. His title goes back to the *ancien regime,* but evidently he prefers to disgrace his family's name. His poor *maman!* She will die of humiliation, I'm sure."

"Is he an anti-Dreyfusard, or is it about the Panama Canal?" Loiseaux asked.

"One or the other, *M'sieur Inspecteur.* What difference does it make?" The Countess shrugged. "If his father were still alive—but then he's not, is he Fernand?" She favored the young baron with a look of reproach. Turning to Holmes and Watson, she continued," Since his father's death, he's come to no good at all. He's fallen, like so many young men of his station and generation, under the influence of the Marquis de Dion. You know the one, Emile," she turned to President Loubet, "the president of the Automobile Club de France. The ones who go tearing about in their automobiles, turning the city streets into fume-choked death traps, and who think the entire country-side is their private race-course. I've heard they've even started something called the 'Aero Club de France'. The next thing you know they'll be tearing around in airborne carriages! Please, officers, can't you take him away? His poor *maman,* whatever shall she do?"

Loiseaux turned to his men. "Put something over his face, I don't want his identity generally known just yet. You'd best get him to hospital first, and then I want him held incommunicado. I think I would like to pay a call on the Marquis de Dion as soon as my duties here are completed. And I would rather judge his reactions without him knowing what we know."

"M'sieur le Presidente, we owe *M'sieur* Holmes and *M'sieur le Medicin* a debt of gratitude. As absorbed as we all were with the national anthem, I'm not sure that the fellow might not have gotten through and," Loiseaux held out the sword cane for the President's inspection, "done some real damage."

"Merci, M'sieurs, merci beaucoup!" The President gave each man a Gallic embrace. "Did I understand you to say you are Sherlock Holmes and *Docteur* Watson? The celebrated English detective and his associate? I am such a great admirer of yours. I've read every one of your exploits. Tell me, *mes amis,* what brings you to France? Some great case?"

"Actually no, *M'sieur le Presidente*. Watson and I are merely on holiday, and what better place for a holiday than Paris in the spring."

"Apparently you've already met *Inspecteur* Loiseaux?"

"Why yes, *M'sieur le Presidente*, in fact they have. They've been assisting me in another investigation. I believe you've been informed, sir, of the death of the pharmacist Lambert two nights ago in the Rue de la Paix."

"Terrible, terrible, business. I sent a letter of condolence to the widow." Loubet shook his head in sadness. "How goes the investigation, Inspector? Have you made an arrest yet?"

"Er... no, *M'sieur le Presidente*, not just yet. But I have every available man working on the case, and we do have some promising leads. So...."

"Excellent, *Inspecteur*. Keep up the good work. And I wish to be kept informed of every development."

"And as for you gentlemen," Loubet turned to Holmes and Watson, what can I do to reward you for your service to France? Although there are some," Loubet gestured toward the crowded grandstand, "who might take issue with my assessment that saving me from the assassin's sword was in fact a service to the *Republique*. Can you accept the Legion of Honor?"

"Well..." Watson started to reply when Holmes cut him off.

"Please, Mr. President, we seek no recognition. That you are safe is reward enough for us. We acted as decent men everywhere would have done under the same circumstances."

"As you wish, *M'sieurs*. But at least allow me to invite you to dine with me tonight at the Élysée Palace." He moved closer to Holmes and muttered almost inaudibly, "There is a matter about which I would like to consult you and *Docteur* Watson."

"*M'sieur* President." A man wearing a uniform similar to the ticket takers approached the box rail from the course. "The Chief Steward presents his compliments and begs to inquire whether it would be appropriate for the first race to commence since Your Excellency is evidently un-harmed?"

"*Mais oui*," Loubet replied with a broad smile. "By all means, let the racing begin!"

CHAPTER TWENTY-FOUR

"And it would not surprise me to learn that
Captain Dreyfus... had now become a shuttlecock
in a game between the President and the Military."

*O*ver breakfast Holmes translated the *Le Figaro* dual headline stories. ***"Assassination Attempt Foiled! Arrests Made! New Trial Ordered for Dreyfus!"*** "Evidently the Marquis was behind the attempt as the Countess predicted. Christiani was given a shot of morphine for his pain—his collar-bone was in fact broken—and in his delirium he was begging de Dion to forgive him for botching the job. Apparently de Dion was some sort of substitute father figure whose approval young Christiani desperately wanted."

"So desperately that he was willing to spend the rest of his life in prison? Good grief, Holmes, what ever was the lad thinking?"

"Obviously he wasn't thinking very clearly. But his rantings apparently under French law gave Loiseaux enough probable cause to also arrest de Dion, who at least at the time *Le Figaro* went to press, was denying even knowing Christiani. The story goes on to tell, without attribution, that Christiani was to make good his escape by vaulting over the track rail, running across the in-field and over the back side of the course to where a fast motor-car was waiting to pick him up and drive him to a place of hiding somewhere in the South of France."

"Ridiculous, Holmes. What do you suppose will happen to him?"

"I have no idea; perhaps he will be sent to take Dreyfus's place on Devil's Island."

"That would be a fitting reward. And what does the paper say about Dreyfus?"

"Reduced to its essentials, and apart from the feckless editorial comment, it details much of what President Loubet told us last night. Acting within his presidential powers as commander-in-chief of the armed forces, Loubet has set aside the eighteen ninety-four verdict and judgement on due process grounds, and ordered a new trial for which purpose Dreyfus is being returned to France even now."

"I still do not understand why he does not just grant him the outright pardon and have done with it. Even if Dreyfus did not want it, there's nothing he could do to stop it or nullify its effect. Short of confessing to the crime, that is."

"Had we put that question to him last night, I doubt that we'd have gotten an honest answer. One does not, I suspect, become President of France by being a political naif. And it would not surprise me to learn that Captain Dreyfus, in addition to his other difficulties, has now also become a shuttlecock in a game between the President and the military. Since the 'Little Corporal' became Emperor Napoleon I, the French military has assumed that it and France are one and civilian control over the military is to them as un-thinkable as appearing in public with a tarnished sword."

"So you think Loubet is trying to force the military establishment to clean its own house as a means of asserting his control? But what of Mycroft's theory that the military would sooner 'play the Roman fool' than admit they'd made a mistake in the first place?"

"I quite agree with him, I'm afraid. This 'second trial' will be an *opera bouffe* not unlike the first and in the end Loubet will have to use his pardon power."

"Why do you suppose that he wanted to, as he put it, 'consult' with us?"

"I do not doubt that he was already aware of our presence in France, even if our showing up in his box at the steeplechase course came as a surprise. I also think he knows, or at least strongly suspects, our reason for being here. Moreover, he either knows or at least has inferred that we have some connexion in this matter with the Rothschild Family. He therefore found it expedient to use us to convey the message—and I believe he is convinced that it will be necessary to do so—that in order for him to exercise his presidential pardon power after a second conviction, he will have to have some new and conclusive proof of Dreyfus's innocence beyond merely the discrediting of the evidence against him."

"Excusez-moi, M'sieurs," the portier interrupted, "these messages have arrived for you. And," the man gave them a look of mild disapproval, *"M'sieur L' Inspecteur* Loiseaux wishes a word with you."

"Ah, yes, by all means show him in," Holmes took the messages. *"Merci."*

"I swear, Holmes, I'm beginning to understand how Raskolnikov felt."

"Bonjour, gentlemen." Loiseaux hesitated.

"Please, Inspector, do join us. Indeed we are honored." Holmes held up the newspaper. "Excellent work yesterday."

This time the waiter ignored the napkin ritual and immediately brought another cup and a fresh pot of coffee.

"Unfortunately, gentlemen, for reasons 'of national security'," Loiseaux used the phrase contemptuously, "I can tell you little of the aftermath of yesterday's *'affaire at Auteuil'* beyond what you've evidently already learned from *Le Figaro.* De Dion refuses to speak about his involvement or to name others involved in the plot. And—mind you this is merely one indifferent-to-politics policeman's opinion—I think there's more to this than the acting out of some lunatic fantasy by a clique of right-wing zealots.

"But there is news, of sorts," Loiseaux took a pleasurable swallow of coffee, "in regard to the Lambert case."

"Oh," Holmes peered at Loiseaux over his reading glasses, "then it has definitely been established that the victim... excuse me... the deceased is *Lambert?"*

"Well, actually not Mr. Holmes," Loiseaux paused, "sorry, I didn't mean to stare. I was unaware that you wore glasses. The magazine illustrations..."

"That's quite al-right, Inspector. I'm afraid the magazine illustrations flatter me even more than Watson's words. Actually, I've only been wearing them for a few months. A concession to middle-age, I suppose."

"As to the deceased being *M'sieur* Lambert, no, not yet officially. At the moment *M'sieur* Bertillon is working on the theory that the deceased is in fact the artist Toulouse-Lautrec. While it is not my place to interfere with *M'sieur* Bertillon's work,

I do assure you that the famous artist is quite alive and working in his studio, perhaps even as we speak.

"We did, however, manage to get an autopsy performed, and it establishes, at least within a reasonable degree of medical certainty, that he died of heart-failure."

"Caused by?" Watson asked.

"That we cannot say, Doctor Watson. The gross anatomical findings on examination of the heart muscle itself were in fact at odds with the heart-failure diagnosis."

"In what way?"

"Well, the most notable is the absence of any evidence of pre-existing heart disease. To be certain, we even checked with Lambert's physician who told us that Lambert, to his knowledge, had never exhibited any symptoms of a heart condition..."

"Prior, that is, until three nights ago," Holmes observed.

Loiseaux paused long enough to take another sip of coffee, and Watson asked, "Was there anything else?"

"The chemical analysis of the blood, *Docteur* Watson. The technicians could not get a pH reading above zero. They wondered for a time whether their instruments were malfunctioning. But evidently the acid level in the blood was so high as to register near absolute acidity on their equipment. Have you ever encountered a similar pathology, *Docteur?*"

Watson, his fingers steepled and his chin resting on his thumbs, asked, "Anything further on the oil of wintergreen?"

"Yes, there were traces, mostly by smell, in the esophagus. So evidently he'd ingested some quantity peri-mortem. However, they were unable to detect anything in the blood, since there is no specific reagent, and owing to its alkalinity, it was probably absorbed entirely by whatever acid caused the extra-ordinary pH reading."

"Were the stomach contents examined?" Holmes took out his cigar case, and offered it 'round.

"*Merci, M'sieur* Holmes. Coffee and cigars at the Ritz; I'm afraid I could get used to this quite easily," In deference to his surroundings Loiseaux used his pen-knife to trim the end of his cigar, and after lighting it continued, "Yes, they were. However, the report noted nothing of an unusual nature."

"Interesting," mused Watson. "Evidently, since almost no absorption occurs in the esophagus, the wintergreen was absorbed into the blood immediately upon reaching the stomach. Except for the most potent alkaloids, which attack the central nervous system, I know of nothing that would take effect that quickly. Holmes, this is your field..."

"Actually, I can't think of anything to add to your precis of the situation, Watson. Are there any developments in tracking down the two men seen earlier in the day?"

"No; again the lack of men to check the hotel registers. But there is some more physical evidence, or I should say, what possibly may be physical evidence." Loiseaux reached in his suit-coat and produced a small, oil cloth envelope and a tweezer.

"What do you make of these, gentlemen?" Loiseaux opened the envelope and removed two cigarette stubs.

Holmes took the tweezer and brought one of the stubs close to his nose.

"Gauloises, wouldn't you say, Inspector? Definitely not a woman's cigarette."

"I quite agree, Mr. Holmes, but in this instance, judging from the lip rouge stains, certainly smoked by a woman."

"Where were they found? It disturbs me to think that I overlooked them myself."

"Do not be distressed, *M'sieur* Holmes. They were found under the body, which you will recall was not moved until after you and Dr.Watson left. I was my intention to ask your opinion about them when I intruded on you yesterday. But fortunately for all concerned we got involved in discussing my security assignment and I quite forgot to mention them."

"What do you make of the lip-rouge?" Holmes passed the tweezer and stub to Watson for his inspection.

"It's not a shade we have in our files, *M'sieur* Holmes. Of course when it comes to ladies' cosmetics we are probably hopelessly out of date anyway. It is my intention to carry the cigarette ends around to several shops and see if the color matches anything available in Paris. If it does, perhaps we can do something with the information, although I confess that seems unlikely unless it is some custom shade worn by only a limited number of women."

"The hotel registry lists, Inspector. Do you think Watson and I might have a look at them? It's equally long odds, I suppose, but perhaps we will recognize some name or something else may come to mind."

"I don't know, *M'sieur* Holmes. Certainly I trust you and Dr. Watson as much as anyone in the entire *Sureté,* especially after yesterday. But those lists are by law supposed to be kept confidential."

"What about passenger manifests, Inspector? Does Customs obtain these from each vessel when it makes port? Could we see those?"

Loiseaux regarded his cigar for a moment. "Yes, I suppose it could be done, *M'sieur* Holmes. Do you want to see every one? How far back?"

"Oh, I think just from the time of our arrival, Inspector. It is after-all something of a blind-pig search, and I'm sure Watson and I don't wish to spend the remainder of our holiday perusing shipping records."

"What? Oh yes... Holmes is quite right, Inspector. It would be a shame to clutter up our holiday with such a potentially unrewarding task."

"I shall try to obtain them for you as soon as possible, gentlemen. I do appreciate your taking an interest in this matter. And of course I shall be grateful to you for the remainder of my life—which, thanks to your swift actions yesterday—may not have to be spent in pension-less poverty. Incidentally, what will you be doing with the remainder of your holiday?"

"Ah, Inspector, isn't that part of the joy of a holiday? Not knowing what you're going to do until you actually do it. As for today, who knows? Perhaps take in a museum? Climb to the top of the *Tour Eiffel?* I don't know..."

After the *au revoirs* were said and the Inspector had taken his leave, Watson leaned back in his chair and rubbed the top of his nose between his left thumb and forefinger. "I think he's on to us, Holmes. Yesterday and today, today especially, I had the feeling that he knows more than he's willing to share with us."

"I quite agree. I don't think he suspects we actually had a hand in Lambert's death, but I do think he suspects that we know a good deal more than we've seen fit to share with him. And if I'm

201

correct, I don't believe that he'll do anything aggressive. Besides, I sense that his 'burnt-out' attitude is merely an affectation and he's really enjoying the game. Nothing, not even his longed-for pension, would give him greater satisfaction than solving the Lambert case before we do."

"Were you serious about the Eiffel Tower?"

"As serious as this." Holmes slid a post-card across the table.

"What are you doing with a post-card depicting the Eiffel Tower? Planning to send it to Mycroft: 'Having a wonderful time; wish you were here'?"

"It was in one of the envelopes the portier brought in when Loiseaux arrived."

"Then it's from Esterhazy?"

"Unless someone else has decided to join our little game and this is his ante."

"So I assume we'll be making our way to the top of the tower some time today." Watson turned the card over and examined both sides carefully. "Do you see anything on here to suggest a time for our *rendezvous?* I trust he's something in mind besides the predawn hours."

Holmes gave a small self-satisfied chuckle. "Look carefully, it's as obvious as Esterhazy's nose. Why I didn't even need my reading glasses."

Watson picked up the card turned it over a couple of times, held it this way and that to the light and ran his fingers over the surfaces and edges. "I give up, Holmes, where do you see a clock that I can't?"

"Look at the picture and tell me what you see."

"I see the Eiffel Tower."

"And?"

"And what? I see the Tower against a background of sky."

"And what is it about the sky..."

Watson slammed the card down in disgust. "Blast it all, Holmes, it's a sunset sky. He wants us to meet him at sunset."

"There you are, well done. What do you think about this?" Holmes handed Watson the second envelope which he'd opened while Watson was examining Esterhazy's post-card.

"The Dreyfuses are understandably delighted with yesterday's announcement. I do not relish the thought of having to tell them that the Captain's ordeal is not yet over. Although Mathieu's naiveté seems to know no limits, Madame Dreyfus strikes me as being a good deal more clear-eyed. Evidently Mademoiselle Leonie has decamped. Such a shame, and at the moment of her greatest triumph no less."

Watson handed Holmes back the Dreyfus letter. "What do we do with Herr Schwabach's information regarding the *Aegean Star?* You said yesterday that you had a better way than trying to penetrate the Swiss bank-privacy laws. If his intelligence is right and the vessel has already gained the North Sea, we don't have much time before 'P. Villeneuf' makes his move."

CHAPTER TWENTY-FIVE

"I can't think of a better way to confound our watchers. I wonder what sort of place Esterhazy has arranged for our meeting?"

"Map, M'sieurs?" The old hag tugged insistently at Holmes's sleeve as he and Watson attempted to run the gauntlet of snack and souvenir vendors at the base of the tower. "The finest map of Paris to be found at any price; for you only five francs."

Holmes finally stopped and took out his wallet. "Five francs. Here you are, *petite maman.* Truly a bargain for such an invaluable specimen of the cartographer's art." Holmes took the map and the old woman scuttled away without so much as a *merci* just as they reached the ticket kiosk. As Holmes purchased the tickets Watson stood at the foot of one of the tower legs, his head tilted as far back as possible. When Holmes made his way over to where Watson was standing, Watson asked, "I trust you bought lift tickets? I must say that I don't relish the prospect of walking all the way up. How far did you say it is?"

"Nine hundred eighty-four feet to the very peak. However, the observation platform is eighty-five below that. And yes, I did buy tickets for the lift. But if you prefer we can climb the steps as high as the second level; after that the lift is the only way."

"What do you think Esterhazy has in mind for us, will he meet us at the top or on one of the lower levels?"

"My supposition is that our means of ascent is a matter of utter indifference to the major. In fact I doubt if he's even here, although he may be observing us at a discreet distance."

"What then are *we* doing here? I confess to a certain boyish curiosity, but..."

"You were too far away to clearly see the flower seller at the cemetery yesterday. But it should not surprise you to learn that she's expanded her entrepreneurial horizons to encompass souvenir maps as well. I expect that when we examine the map, we'll find another message from the reticent major suggesting a meeting place more conducive to our purposes. For the benefit of our watchers, I think we'd best go up and have a look about. We are tourists after all."

In spite of the seriousness of their business, the two men could not help being awe-struck by the view from the observation platform. Directly below, the Seine made a lazy arc to the south. Already the running lights of the river barges could be seen as the wide, high-prowed vessels negotiated the turn. To the southwest the sky was a deep orange blending into blue-black as the last of the sun disappeared beyond Versailles and the Bois de Boulogne. To the east, the street lamps were coming on and in the restaurants, hotels and shops as well as in the homes of the affluent, the brighter steadier glow of electric lights punctuated the darkness. In the wide boulevards and avenues the headlamps of the vehicles conflated into a steady river of light. Holmes took out the map and the two men attempted to correlate various concentrations of light to places on the map.

"Look here, Holmes, there's a pin-prick in the map. The *rue*…how do you pronounce it?"

Holmes adjusted his reading glasses, "Rue *Doe-noo.*" Holmes said the word exaggerating the last syllable. The *'d-a-u'* is pronounced like 'doe' and the *'n-o-u'* sound, 'noo'."

"I remember seeing that street name somewhere. Oh, yes. Isn't…wasn't Lambert's shop near the intersection of the street and the one that runs from the Opera Square to the Ritz?"

"The Rue de la Paix. Let's see if he gives us any further clew as to the exact address. I should hate to go banging on doors 'till we find the right one. Ah. Here it is." Holmes pointed to two more pin holes through the numeral eleven delineating the area of the eleventh *Arrondissement.*

"What about a time? He certainly made a point of it the other day."

Holmes examined the map on both sides for a minute or two. "Unless I've missed something, time does not appear to be of the essence. What do you say to a cocktail and something to eat? I think we'd be remiss if we did not allow Auguste to feed us."

"I can't think of a better way to confound our watchers. I wonder what sort of place Esterhazy has arranged for our meeting?"

CHAPTER TWENTY-SIX

*"If you'll pardon the cliché.., what's
a nice girl like you doing in a place like this?"*

*T*he facade of No.11 Rue Daunou offered no clew as to the sort of place it was. Over Escoffier's protest, they'd ordered dinner from the regular menu. They did not protest, however, when the sommelier opened a bottle of claret laid down not long after Watson's mustering out and while Holmes was still causing havoc in the chemistry laboratory at Bart's. After dinner, they prevailed on the Chef to give them a tour of his kitchen and at its conclusion, they slipped out the delivery door into the Rue Cambon and from there to the Rue Daunou.

Watson gripped his revolver and held it inside his cape as Holmes rapped on the door with his walking stick. After a few moments a viewing slit opened and a pair of rheumy suspicious eyes stared out at the two men. Through the narrow slit the faint sound of phonograph music borne on the perfume-scented air protruded tentatively into the street. Holmes stepped closer to the aperture, "Major Esterhazy..."

The slit slammed shut, and immediately the sound of stout locks being turned could be heard through the thick door. The door was opened just wide enough to admit the two men. They found themselves in a dark foyer leading to a gloomy corridor lighted only by a single gas lamp flickering weakly inside a dirty glass. The doorman proved to be a squat, swarthy man with a badly pock-marked face. He was dressed in a collarless shirt that looked as though it had once been white but was now discolored with age, lack of care and the remnants of badly eaten meals. Below the shirt he wore a pair of nondescript trousers held up by both braces and a belt over which his massive gut protruded.

After re-locking the door the man grunted indicating that Holmes and Watson should join him in following his stomach down the short hallway toward the source of the music. At the end of the hallway they came to another door. As the doorkeeper fumbled in the near darkness for the appropriate key, the music could be clearly heard along with the sound of female laughter. The door opened outward, so the men had to step back. As they did, Holmes nudged Watson, "Scott Joplin, wouldn't you say? What do you suppose..."

"Good Lord, Holmes, it's a bawdy house!"

"Steady, old man. Stiff upper lip. Remember we're here for Queen and Country, and we must do our duty no matter how shocking or distasteful the circumstances."

Watson discreetly transferred his revolver to the waistband of his trousers at the small of his back beneath his dinner jacket and mumbled something about finding a smaller version for occasions such as the present. They allowed a uniformed maid to relieve them of their cloaks, hats and sticks as they took in more of their surroundings. The room was fairly large and yet crowded with furniture grouped into several seating areas. Taking up most of one wall was a staircase leading to a balcony that ran the length of two intersecting walls. Opening on to the balcony were a number of doors which could be readily supposed to lead to bed chambers. Fitted beneath the balcony on one wall was a small bar presided over by stout woman of beyond middle age whose garish make-up did little to conceal a wispy, black moustache and several curling chin-hairs.

The woman behind the bar, presumably the proprietress of the establishment, looked the two men over with her one good eye the other being clouded over by a cataract film. From the mirrored bar-back she produced a bottle of armagnac and two tolerably clean glasses which she thrust across the bar in front of Holmes and Watson. As she poured a stingy measure in each man's glass she leaned toward him, her ample bosom pressing on the surface of the bar. "Compliments of the military gentleman, *M'sieurs*. He awaits you upstairs. For the sake of appearances, he asks that you enjoy yourselves here for a while and then two of the girls will take you upstairs to your *rendezvous. Comprendez vous?*"

Both men nodded and turned around, glasses in hand, to observe the room. Across the room in one corner, four men and a woman were seated at a table playing cards. Standing between two of the men a woman stroked the back of the neck of the player on her right while leaning toward the player on her left and providing him with a close-up view of her décolletage. Another woman—

more a girl actually—stood between the other two players, her thigh pressed firmly against the shoulder of one, as she topped off their champagne glasses. The female card-player, judging from the large stack of chips in front of her, was winning.

The phonograph was situated beneath the stairs. The furniture had been arranged just in front of it so as to provide a small dance floor. Two of the establishment inmates were dancing together, doing what appeared to Watson to be a version of the American fox-trot. On a near-by sofa a man with a monocle watched them all the while licking his lips in erotic rapture as he stroked the exposed thigh of a rather stout girl seated on the sofa next to him.

When the song was over, the two women, to the evident disappointment of the monocled customer, approached Holmes and Watson. One of the women, whose tall, buxom form, blue eyes and high-piled blond hair bespoke her German or Scandinavian heritage, ran her fingers over the lapels of Watson's dinner jacket as she pressed her body ever so slightly against his. The other, slender, with dark hair and dark, luminous eyes approached Holmes and deftly plucked from his lips the cigarette which he had just lighted. As the blond led an un-protesting Watson to the phonograph, the dark-haired girl exhaled a stream of smoke and looked up at Holmes contritely. "I trust it was not your last one, *M'sieur?*"

"And if it was?"

"I should have taken it just the same."

Holmes took out his cigarette case and extracted one which he lighted for himself. "Why would you do that, *Mademoiselle?*"

As he started to put out the match, the girl took his hand and drew it close to her face where she held it until the flame had all but reached Holmes's fingers when she gently blew it out. "Because, *M'sieur,*" she smiled demurely, "why else are you here but to partake of all that I have to offer? And after all, as you English say, 'turn-about is fair play'. *N'est-ce pas?*" She picked up Holmes's brandy glass, sniffed the contents and wrinkled her nose. *"Phui!"* She set the glass back down on the bar. "Compliments of the major, I presume."

She gestured to the madam, *"cognac, s'il vous plait.* No more of this. It's fit only for rubbing down horses." She slid the bottle of armangac along the length of the bar.

After rummaging under the bar for a few moments, the proprietress produced a bottle labeled "Napoleon" and the name of a venerable house and handed it to Holmes to inspect. He nodded his assent as the woman held out her hand rubbing her thumb and forefinger together in a universal gesture. Holmes took out his wallet and produced a hundred-franc note, and as the rubbing continued, another hundred followed by another fifty which finally caused the rubbing to stop as it paused briefly before following its predecessors down the front of the woman's bodice.

Fresh glasses in hand, Holmes and his evident companion *de la nuit* turned to watch Watson and the blond dancing a decorous fox-trot. The dark-haired girl ground out her cigarette and adjusted the closure of her embroidered silk kimono. "Your friend is an excellent dancer."

"I'm sure he would be flattered to hear you say so."

"And you, *M'sieur?"*

"My friend, I'm afraid, suffers from incurable tarantism. I, however, would be prevaricating should I attempt to include the terpsichorean arts in my *curriculum vitae."*

The young woman looked at Holmes quizzically for a moment. "What, then, would you include?"

Holmes sipped his cognac and offered the girl a fresh cigarette which she declined. "Nothing that would be of interest to *Mademoiselle,"* he paused, "except possibly one rather arcane faculty acquired, I must own, from bitter experience."

The girl moved closer to Holmes so that they were standing hip to hip with her head resting on his upper arm. "And what, *M'sieur,* would that be?" She smiled as though anticipating his answer.

Turning his head slightly toward the girl, Holmes lowered his voice to a near whisper, "It is the art, for want of a better term, of recognizing young women who find it convenient to go about dressed as young men."

Picking up the cognac bottle in one hand, and grasping Holmes's arm with the other, she led him toward the stairs. "Please, Mr. Holmes," she whispered urgently in his ear, "do not resist. Act as you would if our purpose were what it appears to be." She smiled broadly and gestured toward Watson and the other girl who were still dancing. Lowering her voice even more, she continued, "It is arranged. The other girl will bring Dr. Watson along presently."

She led him up the stairs, and along the length of the balcony to the second room from the corner. As Holmes closed the door behind them she turned up the bedside lamp.

"The doors do not lock from the inside, Mr. Holmes." She gestured toward an upholstered armchair for Holmes and she seated herself on the large metal-framed bed which took up most of the room. In addition to the chair and bed, the other furnishings consisted of an armoire, a night table and in one corner a wash stand on which stood a ceramic basin and water pitcher. "How did you recognize me, Mr. Holmes? I took the greatest pains with my disguise."

"I assume, however, that you did not plan to have an attack of sea-sickness. From observing you that day in the mirror behind the saloon bar, I rather suspected that your shipboard attire was not in keeping with your gender. Although, I must say, at a distance, the moustache and beard were effective. But as I admitted downstairs, such observations are an art acquired from painful experience.

"If you will pardon the cliché," Holmes paused, gallantly averting his eyes, as the girl shifted her position on the bed causing her kimono to slide open exposing an expanse of pale thigh above her dark stockings. "What's a nice girl like you doing in a place like this?"

She smiled weakly at his lame joke. "Thank you for the compliment, sir." She self-consciously rearranged her skimpy attire. "Truthfully, I'm not sure I know the answer to your question. I am employed by an… an investigative agency. More than that, I'm not at liberty to say. You understand these things, I'm sure, Mr. Holmes."

"So you're a consulting detective then?"

"Not exactly; but as I say, I cannot disclose any more about my employer than what I've already said."

"Since I'm no more at liberty than you, I respect your reticence. But since you apparently know what I'm doing here, in order that neither of us shall have the advantage you must at least answer my question. You may be in grave danger."

Holmes extended his cigarette case and she took one. "That's interesting, Mr. Holmes," she accepted a light and smiled enigmatically as she exhaled. "I was thinking the same thing about you and Dr. Watson. When I overheard 'Madame' instructing her husband regarding your arrival, I made 'certain arrangements' to substitute for another girl as your companion in order to warn you."

"Arrangements?"

She studied her cigarette for a few moments. "A stout dose of purgative slipped into her luncheon wine glass, I'm afraid."

"And what...or perhaps I should say, who...is the source of the threat against us that caused you to so discommode the young lady in question?"

She wrinkled her nose slightly at Holmes's crude choice of words. "I may rely upon your discretion?" When Holmes nodded his assent, she continued, "The man who is my quarry, an obscenely fat German by the name of Ollstreder."

"Indeed, Miss... Miss..."

"Pippen, Mr. Holmes, Fiona Pippen."

"Well then, Miss Fiona Pippen, who is this corpulent German? Why should he be a danger to Dr. Watson and myself, a pair of middle-aged English gentlemen taking a bit of a walk on the wild side whilst on holiday?"

"Please, sir, such dissembling does credit to neither of us." She put down her cigarette and took a small sip from her glass of cognac. "I would not be doing too much violence to your celebrated methods were I to leap to the conclusion that your comically clandestine meeting with the major is not for the purpose of discussing his putative ancestor Atilla the Hun."

"Without conceding the point, Miss Pippen, let us assume that you are correct. In the spirit of the game I am prepared, as I have already intimated, to assume that your presence in this establishment is no more volitional than mine or," he hesitated for a moment, "Dr. Watson's. What has this Ollstreder done to cause you to subject yourself to this form of degradation?"

"Thankfully, so far I've been spared at least that. I've been here only since you and Dr. Watson were so kind to me aboard the boat. And so far I have been able to avoid the disgrace to which you allude by pleading my monthly female indisposition. In another day at most that excuse will have worn itself out and my welcome along with it. Then," she paused and gave a convulsive shudder, "I suppose I shall either think of some new gambit, or do what must be done.

"Ollstreder is suspected of illicit trafficking in armaments, a matter of great concern to my employer in these uncertain times. In fact, when we had our shipboard encounter I was on my way back from rendering what I must confess was a rather unsatisfactory report to my employer. Since I'm called upon either to report or to be briefed somewhat frequently, I find it prudent to travel in disguise. Sometimes I travel as an elderly woman, and sometimes as a young man such as on the occasion of our meeting.

"Obviously my purpose in being here," she swept her free hand in a derisive circle, "is to catch the eye, so to speak, of the baron. Oh," she paused, "I failed to mention that Ollstreder holds some sort of minor baronetcy. I'm not even sure it's genuine. However, it does provide him a palpable basis for his claim—along with the claims of dozens, if not hundreds of others—to the Schleswig-Holstein throne. But in any case he seems to have an inexhaustible supply of money, the source of which is most probably his dealing in armaments. My employer has reason to suspect that the German government turns a blind eye to Ollstreder's activities so that the baron's able to purchase whatever he wants from German manufacturers who, of course, are only too willing to sell to him. What is missing to make the picture complete, is where and to whom he resells his purchases."

"Am I to understand that your employer is a competitor seeking *entre* to some lucrative new market? And your mission is to charm your way into this baron's confidence and thereby learn his most closely kept secret? Your naiveté, Miss Pippen, is certainly not the least of your many charms." Holmes stood up and walked to the window next to the bed and pulled aside the curtain so as to be able to look out. "All of which, my dear young lady, is quite beside the point."

"Which is, Mr. Holmes?"

"Why you are so urgently of the opinion that Dr. Watson and I are in, as you so earnestly put it, such 'grave danger' from the Baron Ollstreder?" Holmes replaced the curtain and stood beside the bed.

"My employer believes that Ollstreder may in fact be, in addition to his other odious enterprises, the secret owner of this establishment. He is a notorious libertine, and is known to come here quite often."

"Perhaps he is no more than a satisfied customer?"

"I think not, Mr. Holmes. There is evidence that suggests more than a mere 'customer' relationship. I learned of this place by discreetly following the baron here several nights running. I made the acquaintance of one of the girls and as we became friends she told me that he comes here not only at night but frequently during the day as well. And on the occasion of these daytime visits his behavior is much more in the nature of a proprietor. He does things such as going over accounts with *Madame,* inspecting the girls' rooms, and the like. I neither know nor care to know the nature of your business with Major Esterhazy, who in his own way is as disgusting as the baron. However, should Ollstreder learn that you have been here—or find you here in person—he will automatically assume that you are on to him and he will either go to ground, or worse, strike back in a deadly manner."

"Is there some connexion between this baron and Major Esterhazy?"

"Perhaps there is Mr. Holmes. My new friend, the one who was suddenly indisposed for this evening, also tells me that the major comes here quite as frequently as the baron, although never at the same time. And he obviously was able to arrange his liaison with you. But as of now, I really have no more information. So please, I entreat you, complete your business as quickly as possible and be on your way. If I learn anything that may be of use to you, so long as my sharing it with you will not jeopardize my own mission, be assured that I will somehow get word to you. Now please come with me. We've used up quite enough time as it is." She held out her hand for Holmes to help her up from the bed, and after he'd done so she continued to hold his hand leading him in an about-face in front of the armoire. Still holding his hand she opened the doors of the armoire and stepped inside. "This way, please, Mr. Holmes."

CHAPTER TWENTY-SEVEN

*"If it were up to me, I should give serious thought... to
wringing your miserable neck myself"*

*T*he back-panel of the armoire proved to be a sliding door leading
to an opening in the wall which separated the bed chamber from
the one next door. On the other side of the wall there was a similar
wooden panel which served as the back of an armoire situated in
the next room and the reverse image of the one into which Holmes
was now gingerly stepping. As Holmes stepped in, Miss Pippen
rapped lightly with her free hand on the back panel of the armoire
in the adjoining room. In a moment the second panel slid back
revealing the blond-haired girl, standing with one foot inside the
second armoire, peering back at them through the opening. Beyond
her, Watson could be seen sitting on the bed with his back propped
against the headboard, rearranging his tie and waistcoat. Quickly,
he swung his legs over the side of the bed and sat upright. "I say,
old man, I was beginning to wonder what happened to you."

"I perceive, however, that concern for my well-being did
not occupy your entire time and attention." Holmes dead-panned.

Miss Pippen motioned to the other girl. "Irmgaard,
Kommen schoen. Let us leave the gentlemen to their business."

Holmes took out his wallet. "Shouldn't we...?"

"Oui, s'il vous plait." Miss Pippen held out her hand.
Seeing Holmes hesitate, she added, *"cinq cent francs, M'sieurs."*

Raising an eyebrow, Holmes removed a five-hundred franc
note and put it in her outstretched hand. She looked up at him
smiling demurely, and continued to hold out her hand. "Each,
M'sieurs. Five hundred francs," she paused, "each."

"Why, yes, of course. Five hundred francs *each,*" Holmes
replied through clenched teeth as he handed her another note.

She took Irmgaard, who'd been watching the transaction in
wide-eyed amazement, by the arm and propelled her into the
armoire. *"Merci, M'sieurs. Merci beaucoup.* Irmgaard and I will
await your further pleasure in *my* room. When you are adjourned,

merely rap on the panel and we will take you back downstairs. In the meantime, I'm sure you won't object to our having another sip or two of your cognac. Would you mind, *M'sieur,* closing the outer doors of the armoire behind us?"

Watson took out his handkerchief and mopped his perspiring forehead. "Rather warm in here, don't you think, Holmes? I wonder where Esterhazy is?"

"I think," Holmes walked round the front of the bed to the curtained window which was in the same relative location as in the first room, "that I shall be able to address both your questions with a single response." He parted the heavy curtains, and instead of a window, found a glass-paned door. He turned the knob and opened the door part way. "Do join us, Major. Dr. Watson was just inquiring as to your whereabouts." Holmes opened the door fully and Esterhazy came in, dragging with him a small stool on which he'd evidently been sitting.

"What the devil!" Watson jumped up from the bed and reached behind his back thinking to take out his revolver. "Where was he? Holmes, how did you know he was out there?"

"Not terribly difficult, my dear fellow. As you can see, this is the last room in the house. I briefly toyed with the idea that he might be under the bed, but decided that would be too *outré* even for Esterhazy. This entire business bears enough resemblance, as it is, to the bedroom comedies for which the French seem to have such an insatiable appetite. So unless he was prepared to cling by his fingertips to the window-sill for an indeterminate length of time, I had to assume that the window was in fact a door which led to a balcony overlooking the courtyard which I had observed from the window of the other room." Holmes seated himself in the arm chair and took out his cigarette case. "Would you be so kind, Major, as to pass me that ashtray there on the night table, and begin by telling us why you chose this establishment as the venue for our rendezvous?"

"Indeed, Major," Watson resumed his seat on the bed. "Your propensity to conduct your business in places where everyone around you is in a horizontal position is becoming somewhat un-nerving. Although I must hasten to add that at least the residents of this establishment are a good deal livelier than the last." Reaching in his coat, he took out a cigar. "By the way, is there another ashtray about? As Rudyard Kipling so succinctly put it, 'a woman is only a woman, but a good cigar...' Ah, thank you." Esterhazy opened a drawer in the night table and produced an ashtray which he handed across the bed to Watson.

Esterhazy pulled his little wooden stool closer to Holmes and took out a cigarette, a 'Players' Holmes noticed. "My intention was, Mr. Holmes, that in case you are being watched what could be more in keeping with expectations than for a couple of English gentlemen on holiday to patronize an establishment such as this? It is after all Paris, and..."

"But why this one?" Watson interjected.

"As you have no doubt concluded, Dr. Watson, I am not unknown here nor without some influence."

"Then you are the proprietor; the man behind the madam presiding at the bar?" Holmes asked.

"Unfortunately not, Mr. Holmes. That distinction belongs to the gentleman who is the principal subject of our conversation."

"That strikes me as rather odd..."

"Reckless, I should say, Holmes."

"...Major. Watson is quite right. Why would you risk our being discovered? Is that in fact what you want?"

Esterhazy, with the blue-black bruises under his eyes, looked almost feral in his terror of being once again man-handled by Holmes. He held up his hands, palms outward, preparing to ward off the expected blows. "Please, please, Mr. Holmes. We are quite safe. The individual in question is, to my certain knowledge, hosting a private dinner and will be so occupied for the entire evening."

"And what of the priestess of Ishtar downstairs?" Holmes asked. "If she owes her position to this person, do you not think that she will report this rather singular occurrence?"

"Once more, Mr. Holmes, there's nothing to fear. When the person whom I shall describe momentarily decided that he wished to own such an establishment as this, it was I who was bidden to made the necessary arrangements," he paused, looking somewhat pleased with himself, "including obtaining the services of an experienced madam." He leaned forward, hands on his knees. "The charming *Madame* to whom you allude is in fact my mother-in-law, and I assure you our relationship is not only cordial, but I'm

216

sure she would gladly eat her grandchildren for breakfast before she would jeopardize her position as mistress of the house."

"Good grief, man," Watson jabbed his cigar in the direction of Esterhazy, "how many female confederates do you have?"

"You refer, I assume, to the Gypsy woman called 'Leonie' lately in service to the Family Dreyfus?"

"And the flower-seller, and the map-seller," Holmes added.

"One and the same, Mr. Holmes. But," he paused, "I'm sure you were aware of that. She is, truth-be-known, my first cousin on my own dear mother's side. And, lest you think me a fraud, she actually is one-quarter a daughter of Romany. Whether by reason of her ancestry, or from some other cause, I cannot say, but she does seem on occasion to possess an extra-sensory gift of sorts. And rather than waste such a talent reading palms and doing a 'mind-reading' act in cheap dance-halls, she was grateful for the steady comfortable employment and no one can say that she did any worse by the Dreyfuses than to help keep their hopes alive when no one else was able to do so." Esterhazy sat up straight and puffed out his chest as though about to receive the Legion of Honor.

Holmes re-crossed his legs. "Your grand gesture of compassion moves both myself and Dr. Watson most deeply. But tell us Major, whilst she was busily engaged in bolstering the Dreyfuses' spirits, did your cousin by any chance pass on to you each and every development in the family's quest for justice for Captain Dreyfus?"

"It would not be in keeping with this evening's spirit of candor were I to deny categorically that from time to time a tid-bit of information of the nature you describe did leak out in that manner. But please, gentlemen, in the minuscule chance that I have miscalculated our unwitting host's itinerary, let us proceed with the main business at hand."

"Which is?" Holmes and Watson chorused.

"Your arranging for myself and my companion to emigrate, secretly of course, to England and once there for a sum to be settled upon us sufficient to care for our modest wants."

"Preposterous!" Watson snorted. "Who would possibly consider funding you for life, even if you did have something to barter?"

."Come, now, Dr. Watson. Such a sum would be but a trifle to the Dreyfus family. And, from what little I know of the matter, one could reasonably suppose that certain of their co-religionists would not find such an undertaking beyond their means."

"Even if the Dreyfuses could be persuaded," Watson continued, "I cannot imagine that they would also be willing to provide as well for Madame Esterhazy and I suppose sundry cousins and whatever assorted relatives you plan on bringing along."

"I don't recall hearing him say, Watson, that his companion was necessarily his wife."

"Esterhazy, you are even more despicable than I thought upon hearing your account of your perfidious foisting-off of Dreyfus. If not your wife, then who did you..."

Esterhazy shook his head sadly. "My dear Dr. Watson. For a man of the world... what can I say? You have seen *Madame* downstairs. Can you imagine what her daughter will look like in a few short years? Would you prefer to spend your retirement years with her as opposed to, say, the delightful young *fraulein* Irmgaard, whose close acquaintance you have also so recently made?"

"Cad!"

"Spoken like a true English gentleman, Dr. Watson. I accept your rebuke. But nevertheless, those are my terms."

Watson started to say something else, but Holmes gestured for him to stop. "Let us suppose, just for the sake of conversation, that what you demand is feasible. We've heard the price, but we've yet to inspect the goods."

"As you wish, Mr. Holmes. Since the departure of the lamented *Graf* von Schwarzkoppen, my instructions have come from none other than the proprietor of this establishment, one Baron Ollstreder, a German national with whom I believe you are already acquainted." Esterhazy smiled. "You see, gentlemen, I too have my sources. As you were meeting with the baron, I was being fully briefed by Bertillon regarding your gala evening at Maxim's.

"I must also confess that it was I who first suggested to Bertillon the infamous self-forgery theory, although I must admit that the 'citadel of graphic rebusses'—whatever that may mean—is an embellishment for which *M'sieur* Bertillon may claim all the credit. At the time I was desperate. No respected handwriting expert was willing to say the *bordereau* was written by Dreyfus, and without it the case against Dreyfus was in serious jeopardy despite the hysteria whipped up by the anti-Semitic press and the willingness of the military to offer him up as a sacrifice.

"Bertillon, as you well know, remains convinced to this day that the author of the *bordereau* was Dreyfus. While time and his sense of self-importance have dimmed his memory as to my role in concocting the self-forgery theory, I remain his confidant and unofficial liaison to the Bureau of Statistics. So it was that when he reported to me the following morning that he'd had the pleasure of instructing you in the finer points of *bertillonage* and that you'd invited him to dinner at Maxim's afterward, I took an immediate interest. Like everyone else, Mr. Holmes, I've read each of Dr. Watson's reports of your cases and have come to have the utmost respect for your formidable abilities. It therefore struck me as curious that you, of all people, would seek out Bertillon at all much less invite him to dinner—at Maxim's no less—after having been exposed to his rantings for the better part of an afternoon.

"He was of course eager to share with me the details of your conversation. By the way, if it would not be too much to ask, do you think that you might be able to arrange for me to meet *Mademoiselle* MaryJane when I arrive in England?" Holmes and Watson both glared at him. "Well, never mind." He shrugged indifferently. "It was just a passing thought."

Esterhazy lit another cigarette. "I'm sorry. Let me continue. When Bertillon related the dinner-table conversation about the Dreyfus case, I of course immediately surmised your true purpose in seeking Bertillon out. Am I correct, Mr. Holmes?"

"Continue," Holmes said coldly.

"Yes, yes, of course. Be that as it may, as I've already related to you, I fear my usefulness to the baron and his superiors may come to an end at almost any moment, and when that comes about, I hardly need tell you that my retirement is more likely to be a knife slicing through my windpipe," he drew his index finger across his throat to illustrate the point, "than a villa on the Cote d' Azur and a nice pension to go with it. So if you were—are— interested in the Dreyfus case, we have the basis of a bargain— Dreyfus's freedom in exchange for mine."

"And don't forget the pension, Major." Watson ground out the stub of his cigar in disgust.

"I should think it only fair, Dr. Watson. After all, Dreyfus will be well provided-for. Why shouldn't I be as well? Not to mention the fact that his exile will be over, whereas mine will just be beginning."

"You mean exile from France, the country you have so cavalierly betrayed for all these years?" Watson got up from the bed and stretched. "If it were up to me, I should give serious thought to sparing the baron the trouble, and wringing your miserable neck myself."

"And I would cheerfully hold his coat and hat while he did so, Major. But, again for the sake of conversation, let us assume that Dr.Watson and I have something more than mere idle curiosity regarding the Dreyfus case. Tell us more about the baron. Did Bertillon babble to him as well? I rather doubt that his desire to arrange a meeting with us was a mere spur-of-the-moment gesture on his part."

"I can no more than speculate, Mr. Holmes. With the exception of indulging his numerous vices, the baron is not—how should I say it?—a spontaneous person. When it comes to business, the baron is all business. For the very reasons that brought about our meeting, I have not discussed your being in Paris with him at all. Nor do I think that Bertillon has done so. So far as I know, Bertillon is not in the baron's pay. I can only guess that Ollstreder's seeing you in Bertillon's company at Maxim's was truly a coincidence, but that he immediately suspected your purpose, just as I did. In all other respects Baron Ollstreder may be ridiculous, but I would not underestimate either his intelligence or his ruthlessness."

"What proof do you have to convince us that Ollstreder is the source of the bogus information you've been passing to the French military?" Holmes asked. "Your story could be true, or you could be using Ollstreder just as you used Dreyfus. Equally important, of what possible use would there be in validating your story insofar as clearing Captain Dreyfus is concerned? As unlikely as it may be, if we could somehow arrange for you to be spirited off to England to live in exile with a new identity, it is doubtful that you would be willing to come back to testify at a second Dreyfus trial, and even if you did, it would be even less likely that anyone would believe you."

"I think that I shall be able to satisfy you on all counts, Mr. Holmes. However, my doing so must await our next meeting which in turn must await my being summoned by the baron."

"Why is that?" Holmes asked, getting to his feet. "I thought your life was in such great jeopardy that you cannot afford even an hour's delay."

"Two reasons, Mr. Holmes. First, I must have your assurance that satisfactory arrangements have been made regarding my, shall we say, 'resettlement'. And as to that, I shall have nothing more tangible than your word as an English gentleman, with no witness other than Dr. Watson who, with all due respect," he turned and bowed slightly toward Watson, "can hardly be classed as unbiased. I assume that before you give such assurances you will need to confer with others. Is that not so?

"Second, the proof which you seek will not be in my hands until the night-after-next at the earliest. I have been instructed by the baron to call upon him not earlier than two nights hence in the Rue Georges Bizet—I believe that you know the house—to receive a 'shipment' as he refers to them, for delivery to the Section of Statistics. So I feel sure that my usefulness is not yet at an end. I am hoping that the 'shipment' contains further 'evidence' against Dreyfus which will somehow be 'miraculously' discovered by the Section of Statistics in time to condemn him at his up-coming retrial. If that is the case, you shall have your proof, and at the same time have the tools with which to clear Dreyfus's name.

"In order that you can satisfy yourselves that whatever I shall bring you came to me from the baron, before I go to him I shall come to your hotel room so that you can search me. You can then accompany me to the Rue Georges Bizet and remain in the cab while I go inside. When I come out I will have the 'shipment' which you can then be sure came into my hands from but one source. Unless you can think of a way to be present when Ollstreder hands me the package, I can't think of any better way for you to satisfy yourselves that I am telling you the truth.

"And now, gentlemen, if you please. Sitting so long on this stool has so affected the muscles in my back that I am scarcely able to stand erect." To illustrate the point, he rose with a pained expression to a hunched-over position. "Fortunately, Irmgaard, in addition to her other skills," he placed his hands behind his lower back and forced himself to an upright position, "is a trained masseuse. I shall contact you at your hotel as soon as I have the particulars of my rendezvous with the baron. In the meantime, you will, I assume, have many arrangements to make." He made it to the edge of the bed, and with a sigh lay down. "If you will retrace your steps, *M'sieur* Holmes, the new girl will see you back downstairs. Dr. Watson, if you would not object, you can exit through the door to this room. *Au revoir,* gentlemen, until our next meeting."

Holmes opened the door of the armoire and rapped on the back panel. In a moment, Miss Pippen stuck her head through, her forearm held up to her chest to cover her décolletage. "Watch your step, *M'sieur.* I will accompany you back down to the salon." Setting one foot into the meeting room, she smiled wistfully at Esterhazy. "I'm sorry, Major, but it appears that Irmgaard has drunk a bit too much of the cognac supplied by your guests, and has fallen fast asleep."

CHAPTER TWENTY-EIGHT

"While your modus operandi *may in time have produced the
desired result, time is a luxury we can no longer afford."*

*H*olmes and Fiona Pippen had carried the unconscious Irmgaard
through the armoires and placed her on the bed. While Esterhazy
proceeded in vain to try and awaken her, they returned to the first
room. The young woman sat demurely on the edge of the bed. "I
trust that your meeting was productive, Mr. Holmes?"

"And I in turn trust that you already know the answer to
that question, Miss Pippen. Judging from the redness of your left
ear, and the faint odor of naphthalene which emanates from your
costume, I would say that you've spent a good portion of the last
hour kneeling on a bag of mothballs in the bottom of the armoire,
with that glass tumbler pressed against the back-panel and your ear
pressed tightly to the glass."

"Why Mr. Holmes..."

"Please, young lady," Holmes held up his hand bidding her
to be silent. "Your disingenuousness is both tiresome and
unbecoming. You have conducted yourself admirably up to this
point. However, your mucking about in this affair has reached the
level of being a danger to all of us as well as to the success of the
enterprise, so it's time to change your role."

"*My* 'mucking about', Mr. Holmes?" She leaned forward,
her clenched fists resting on her knees, "You've no warrant to
accuse me of 'mucking about', much less to order me around like
some defenceless shopgirl. I'll have you know..."

"Careful, Miss Pippen. I'm sure that '*M*' as you and your
associates are pleased to call him, would consider it a serious
breach of etiquette for you to willy-nilly give out the identity of
your employer. And in any case, I'm not, as you so petulantly put
it, ordering you about 'like some defenceless shopgirl'. It is not my
purpose to demean your professional capabilities, nor for that
matter, to offend your feminist sensibilities.

"As you have learned through your eavesdropping, Miss
Pippen, we do indeed have a common quarry. While your *modus*

operandi may in time have produced the desired result, time is a luxury we can no longer afford. Moreover, I refuse to believe that if all else had failed you would have done what you intimated earlier you were prepared to do to gain the baron's confidence. And I know to a moral certainty that my brother, who both enjoys and takes seriously his role as surrogate *pater familias,* would never condone such an initiative on your part."

"Granting that we have, as you put it, a 'common quarry', what are *we* going to do from this moment forward, Mr. Holmes? Although we're both after the baron, it would appear to be for two entirely different reasons. You wish to clear the name of the unfortunate Captain Dreyfus, and I want to shut down what is possibly a large-scale, ongoing international arms trafficking ring, that must inevitably constitute a threat to British interests somewhere in the world. Evidently the baron is deeply involved in both, but are they connected? Somehow I must find out where Ollstreder is sending the arms purchases and by what means. And other than the fact that Ollstreder is the facilitator of the Captain's persecution, I do not see how the Dreyfus case is connected to the arms trade. The baron's capacity for mischief-making appears to know no bounds. He may be involved in the Dreyfus business for pecuniary reward or merely because it amuses him to do so."

"I know the answer to the means question, Miss Pippen, and I'm reasonably sure I know where the shipments are going. As to whether these seemingly disparate enterprises are connected, that question too shall be answered in due course. As far as what *we* are going to do next, Dr. Watson and I, our carnal appetites", Holmes gave a brief, sardonic smile, "satiated for the moment, are going to return to the Ritz, which is where you're going, too. Now get dressed..."

"I don't know, Mr. Holmes," she ran her fingers self-consciously through her hair. I've never been inside the Ritz..."

"Do not be concerned about your welcome, Miss Pippen. We shall see to that. Besides, from what I understand, ladies of the *demimonde* are quite a usual sight at the Ritz. When you arrive, merely tell the desk clerk that you want Mr. Sebastian Melmoth's room. We will join you as soon as you are safe in the room. Then I will tell you what you do next."

CHAPTER TWENTY-NINE

"Is my new assignment to be a higher class of trollop,
or did you perhaps have in mind utilising that portion of my
anatomy which rests above my shoulders?"

*W*hile waiting for Holmes to come down the stairs, Watson had managed to insinuate himself into the card game which was still in progress, although there'd been a turnover in the male participants. He was seated to the right of the female player and had a moderate stack of chips in front of him. Whether the stack was the remnant of a larger one, or the increase of a more modest initial stake, was impossible to discern as Watson was wearing his best poker-face. Evidently the game was draw poker, because Watson held five cards in his hand. In his other hand he held a champagne flute along and a cigar nestled securely in the *V* between his index and middle fingers. Seeing Holmes and the purposeful look in his eye, Watson glanced wistfully at his hand, folded his cards and picked up his chips. These he took to the bar where the madam converted them back to cash.

As they retrieved their cloaks, hats and sticks Watson turned to Holmes, "I say, Holmes, you certainly seemed to hit it off with your young lady. For all the fun I had, I might as well have stayed downstairs and taught those Frenchmen a lesson or two about poker. By the way," he took out his wallet, "here's my five hundred francs. Not that I got anywhere near my money's worth, but that's less than half of what I was ahead at cards."

"What is it they say: 'lucky at cards, unlucky at love?' But do not despair, Watson. The night is young, and the lady in question may yet provide you with an evening's entertainment, although it's unlikely to be exactly what you had in mind." As they sauntered back down the Rue de la Paix to the front entrance of the Ritz, Holmes filled Watson in on what had transpired between himself and Fiona Pippen.

"Holmes, I knew there was something not quite right about that 'young man' on the ship. The bone structure was too fine, and when we picked him up he weighed less than he ought to. I thought perhaps he was one of those effeminate types, you know. By the way, what is it that seems to attract you to these cross-dressers anyway?"

"If you are alluding to 'That Woman', my recollection is that just like Miss Pippen, she found me and not vice versa. And may I add that in her attire this evening, no one is likely to mistake Miss Pippen for a young man. Indeed after seeing her and meeting Miss Davies, I cannot fail to remark upon this newly-discovered aspect of my elder brother's personality."

A short while later, Miss Pippen had made her way to the room still booked in Wilde-"Melmoth's" name where she was joined by Holmes and Watson. Still slightly blushing from the leering inspections by the *chassuer* and desk-clerk, she did a graceful pirouette which ended with her sitting on the edge of the bed. "This bed..." she bounced on the mattress, "...and its very own water closet. I could certainly get used to this. Who, may I ask, is this Sebastian Melmoth who has so graciously lent me his magnificent room?"

"Mr. Melmoth is a long-time friend of Dr. Watson's, Miss Pippen. As it happens, he suddenly developed an irresistible impulse to tour the South of France and begged us to use his room in his absence should we have need to do so."

"And exactly what *need* might we have for the room, Mr. Holmes? Is my new assignment to be a higher class of trollop, or did you perhaps have in mind utilising the portion of my anatomy that rests above my shoulders?" To emphasize the point, she stood up. "Would you mind switching places with me, Mr. Holmes? Somehow it seems that whenever I'm in your presence, I end up in a horizontal position. Thank you, sir." She seated herself in the chair just vacated by Holmes who moved across to the bed. "Before you sit down, could you spare another cigarette? That is," she laughed, "unless it's your last one."

Holmes produced the requested cigarette, and Watson a match. She exhaled a stream of smoke as she leaned back in the chair and crossed her legs at the knee. Noticing the two men intently observing the gesture, she quickly un-crossed them. "It's a habit I've been practicing for months, gentlemen. For when I go about in my 'manly attire'. I've by now gotten so used to doing it, that I quite forget how un-ladylike it is. But then how lady-like is it

226

for me to be sitting smoking a cigarette in a Paris hotel room with two men, neither of whom is my relative or husband? When papa finally relented and allowed me to matriculate, I rather doubt that this is what he had in mind for a career."

"You earned your baccalaureate?"

"Yes, I did, Dr. Watson. With a first in chemistry. In fact, before I was recruited for my current occupation, I had hoped to follow in your footsteps at Netley and become an army surgeon." She arched an eyebrow in Watson's direction. "Don't look so aghast, Dr. Watson. Is there some reason a woman cannot be a surgeon? Or a military surgeon, in particular?"

Watson squirmed. "Er, none that I can think of, Miss...Miss Pippen. It's just that I cannot think of anyone of your gender who has ever applied to be one. It can, after all, be a somewhat hazardous occupation, as I can well attest."

"More so than my present employment, Dr. Watson?" She smiled demurely. "In any case, I sent in my application and heard nothing for months. I was then called in for what I thought was to be a personal interview as the last step in the admissions process. As it turned out, however, I ended up being interviewed by a certain 'minor treasury official' whose blandishments I was wholly unable to resist. And so here I am."

"I assume that along the way you acquired the knowledge of pharmacology which accounts for your facile use of purgatives," Holmes remarked. "What, may I ask, did you use to render fraulein Irmgaard insensate?"

"Chloral hydrate, Mr. Holmes. It mixes so well with alcohol, don't you think? I'm made to understand, however, that it does leave its victim with a rather severe *mal a la tete* upon awakening. Alas, poor Irmgaard." She shrugged and pursed her lips. "Maybe some good will come of it. Perhaps Esterhazy will become disenamoured with her and leave her behind, although the thought did cross my mind that with her obvious physical attributes, not to mention her reputed skills as a masseuse, she might make an excellent recruit for our little cadre."

"I see that you are as remorselessly manipulative as your mentor, Miss Pippen. It would not surprise me to learn that he's grooming you for a role in politics when your usefulness as a field operative is over. Who knows. Someday you may be the first female prime minister."

"I shall, I suppose, take that as a compliment, sir. But if I may return to the present, Mr. Holmes, you told me that you knew how and where Ollstreder is delivering his arms purchases. I am willing to accept your premise that time is of the essence. And to a point, I'm willing to place myself at your disposal. But that information is of vital interest to our Country. I must insist that you share it with me and let me pass it on to those who may be prepared to act on it."

"As you wish, Miss Pippen. The means of transportation is a vessel named the *'Aegean* Star' which sails under the Greek flag. While I'm not privy to its exact itinerary, I would suggest that it can probably be found somewhere off the west coast of Ireland as early as tomorrow. And I rather doubt, owing to its cargo, that it will be berthed in a major port."

"Perhaps a fishing port, Holmes? If I were her captain, I'd anchor at sea and off-load at night onto fishing boats which customarily go out at night and return at dawn and are not likely to engage the scrutiny of port officials or the Royal Navy. Although, I must say that my hypothesis becomes problematical when one considers that the baron's purchases are thought to include artillery pieces as well as small arms. I've seen first-hand how difficult it is to manhandle even the smallest field guns of my era. It's hard to imagine the difficulty of dealing with anything larger, especially if there's any sort of a sea running. And what sort of fool would risk an off-loading operation in heavy seas? A small, wooden-hulled vessel along side something as large as an ocean-going freighter... Not to mention the risk of having a ton and a half of cannon lashed on your aft deck. They must be madmen."

"Just so, Watson. But would your thinking be the same if you assume that they dismantle the artillery pieces?"

"And if you assume, gentlemen, that the baron's customer is the Sinn Fein or some other Irish independence group, then your characterizing them as 'madmen', Dr. Watson, is not far off the mark. What makes you so sure, Mr. Holmes, that it's Ireland? The thought of modern artillery, heavy machine guns and such in the hands of those fanatics is chilling to say the least. Why it can mean nothing less than an impending revolution!"

"Or, some might say a 'war of independence,' Miss Pippen. It all depends on one's point of view."

"'Just what, may I ask, is your point of view, Mr. Holmes? I must say that I've quite lost my capacity to be shocked by anything you say, but after all...'"

"Merely an abstract philosophical point, Miss Pippen. As Dr.Watson will no doubt attest."

"Um...yes, quite so, Miss Pippen, quite so."

"Then by all means please continue, Mr. Holmes. You were about to tell me why you are so certain that Ireland is where the baron is flogging his wares."

"I do not recall indicating that I was *certain* of anything, Miss Pippen. Your taking my suggestion as a certainty is perilous at best, and once again illustrates, as Dr. Watson will further attest, the folly of presenting the solution before one is prepared to articulate all the intervening steps.

"Based upon reliable information, Dr. Watson and I have deduced that Ollstreder's customer is European, and takes delivery at some port between Tallinn and Lisbon. Now one may, I should think, safely assume that the German government is not looking the other way while the baron foments either revolution or war of independence—whichever you prefer—in his own land. And if you are willing to also assume that the Danes, Swedes and Norwegians are neither a race of malcontents, nor, Ibsen notwithstanding, collectively angst-ridden, that leaves one with a much narrower universe of possibilities. It might be the French, but if recent events are any indication, making exception of course for the hapless Baron Christiani, the French with their impeccable civility, at least since the end of the Napoleonic wars, make war mostly with words and take up arms only upon the rarest of occasions."

"I thank you for the geo-political *tour d' horizon*, Mr. Holmes, but..."

"But nothing, Miss Pippen. I've said all that I intend to say on the subject for now, and you and my brother will have to accept that fact. Whether you choose to act on my suggestion is of course up to you. However, I have a commission for you that you must discharge in the morning. I do not think you will find it onerous, as I'm sure it fits exactly in with your plans."

"Obviously I have no choice but to accept, for now, the finality of your decision not to fully disclose what you know or surmise regarding the baron's customer. I do however reserve the right to determine when, and indeed whether, I shall discharge your commission. I must consult immediately with my employer, and that compels me to return to London by the swiftest available means. That will be the morning Paris-to-London boat train. So unless your commission may be discharged in that manner, I'm afraid that I shan't be able to accommodate you." She folded her arms across her bosom and glared at Holmes.

"My commission may indeed be discharged in exactly that manner, Miss Pippen. For it is to be you that is going to convince the inscrutable *'M'* that the execrable Major Esterhazy and his entourage of one deserve to become the permanent house-guests of Her Majesty's Government."

"Surely not, Holmes. You can't be serious. That slug living a life of luxury at the expense of the British taxpayers. Why if word ever leaked out, I should hate to be in Mr. Baldwin's shoes on question day."

"As serious as can be, Watson. And I would quite agree with you but for the likelihood that his endowment will be funded by certain *private* sources, and not the public fisc."

"Do you really think that the Rothschilds—I assume that's who you mean— would agree to such an arrangement?"

"Knowingly, Miss Pippen, I hardly think so. But when it suits his purposes, if you aren't already aware, that certain 'minor treasury official' so beloved by us all can be a grand master at dissembling. He will no doubt find the right combination of half-truths to wheedle what is needed. Besides, I am confident that the major will have to do a great deal more to earn his daily bread than submit to having his back massaged by the enchanting and reputedly nimble-fingered Irmgaard. Moreover, I don't recall the major stipulating any minimum sum, only some rather vague generality about 'a sum sufficient to provide for our modest wants'. I believe I quote him accurately, Miss Pippen. Isn't that what you recall?"

"His words exactly, Holmes." Watson interjected. "You know I have a photographic memory when it comes to dialogue.

And I will gladly attest to the accuracy of your recollection, although I doubt that it will be necessary."

"But what else shall he be required to do?"

"I should think, Miss Pippen, that like Scheherazade he shall spin his captivating tales, not only of the disinformation foisted on the French military but also of the trade-craft of the espionage business, to generations of eager young minds as well as to grizzled veterans such as yourself for years to come. Short of getting his hands on the baron, I can't think of anyone that Mycroft would rather have pinned in his specimen box than Major Esterhazy. No, Miss Pippen, I do not think that your commission, should you see fit to accept it, will be in any way burdensome to you."

"Why yes, of course, Mr. Holmes. I shall leave in the morning and return the evening of the next day in time for your rendezvous with Esterhazy. Is there anything else?"

"The only thing I can think of at the moment is that you ought to bring back some sort of papers for Esterhazy," he paused, "and I suppose for Irmgaard as well. As the situation is obviously still quite fluid, I'm really not sure how we'll manage to get them out of France, especially if Ollstreder, the Section of Statistics and probably the *Sureté* are all in hot pursuit. I will leave it to whoever my brother employs in matters such as these to come up with a flag of convenience as well as suitable pseudonyms. When you return, call at the front desk and leave the documents in a package for 'Mr. Melmoth'. If all goes according to plan, the clerk will in turn give you an envelope with your further instructions. If anything is amiss there will be no envelope. In that event you must immediately change your disguise and return to England at once."

CHAPTER THIRTY

"When you said we were entering deep waters...
you neglected to say that it was a veritable
Loch Ness."

"**Y**ou were quite right in your prediction last night, Holmes. The young lady did after all provide an evening's entertainment, and I must readily confess that it was nothing like what I expected. It's certainly easy to see why Mycroft was so eager to recruit her. I suppose she got off al-right this morning. Must have left before we came down."

"Actually, did you happen to notice that rather stout dowager going out the door just as we came down the stairs?"

"You mean the one with the advanced case of osteoporosis? That was her... I mean that was Miss Pippen?"

Holmes nodded as he folded his newspaper and set it on the table. "According to this account," he gestured to the newspaper, "the light-cruiser *Sfax* sailing out of Fort-de-France, has embarked Dreyfus and is proceeding on a course for Metropolitan France. Evidently the re-trial, for reasons understood only by the French military mind, is to be held at Renne." .

"*Pardon, M'sieurs.* The police inspector left this envelope for *M'sieur* Holmes." The waiter appeared at Holmes's side. "Would the *M'sieurs* care for more coffee?"

"Yes, please," Watson responded. "It appears that we may be in for a somewhat tedious morning. And would you also bring back the cigar humidor? It seems I've quite run out."

He turned to Holmes. "Those I assume are the passenger manifests. I'm only too glad to do my part, old man, but that does appear to be a rather formidable stack to work, especially when you don't know what it is you're looking for."

"Actually, I'm only looking for one name on one vessel. But I didn't see any reason to let Inspector Loiseaux know that, so..."

"And the name, I take it, would be 'P.Villeneuf' and the vessel the one we too were on. What makes you think..."

The waiter returned with more coffee and the cigar humidor. While Watson busied himself choosing from the paltry selection, Holmes, peering through his reading glasses at the fine print, began perusing the stack of documents. As soon as Watson had endorsed *l' addition* with his name and room number and the waiter had departed, Holmes permitted himself a small smile of satisfaction and passed one of the manifests to Watson.

"I say, Holmes, good show. You surely must have suspected, but why? Until our meeting with *Herr* Schwabach, we'd never even heard of the mysterious *M'sieur* Villeneuf."

"You are quite correct, Watson. To my knowledge, we'd never heard the name 'Villeneuf' before it passed the lips of *Herr* Schwabach."

"Then it was merely a lucky guess on your part?"

"Call it what you will, old fellow."

"Which one was he?" While I don't remember all the saloon passengers, I do recall a couple of rug merchants, a Hassidic diamond merchant, a couple of Church of Rome clergymen. Of course the lad whom we now know as *Miss* Fiona Pippen... and let me think," he paused, "Oh yes. There was that ancient invalid in the wheel chair and his callous nurse. Some nurse. I should have gotten her name and reported her to the Nursing Credentials Board. Surely you don't think it was the old man, do you? Why he didn't look to me like he was capable of breathing, let alone master-minding an international arms-trafficking ring. Do you think it was he who sent the telegram to Ritz on our behalf?"

"See for yourself." Holmes reached inside his breast pocket and extracted a folded telegraph message sheet which he handed to Watson who glanced at it and handed it back. "Sorry, old man. Forgot your French isn't up to it. It says," Holmes adjusted his reading glasses, "It's dated yesterday. *'Dear Sir: In response to your inquiry, please be advised that according to the counter clerk on duty at the time the message about which you have inquired was taken for transmission, it was written out in English and translated by the clerk into French. The message was written and paid-for by a large woman dressed in the attire of the nursing profession. This person merely presented the hand-written message to the clerk, paid the charge and left without saying anything. Trust this responds fully to your inquiry. Thank you for the opportunity to be of service, et cetera'*, and it's signed by the general manager, Boulogne-sur-mer Station."

"Obviously he must have recognized us. And if so, why not speak to us aboard ship rather than acknowledging our acquaintance by sending that gratuitous telegram purportedly on our behalf? And how, come to think of it, did he know we'd be stopping at the Ritz? How could anyone who does not know us well have known of our long-standing friendship with Cesár Ritz? And if he knows us that well, how come I did not recognize him?"

"Perhaps he did not want to be recognized."

"If you're correct, then we've been under surveillance since before we arrived in Paris. Do you think it was he that sicced those two footpads onto us in the Rue de la Paix outside Lambert's shop?

"I recall thinking that Mycroft was carrying his security-consciousness to absurd extremes, but now I'm not so sure. Do you think there is a spy in Mycroft's 'little cadre'? Surely it can't have been young Churchill. I must say he's as talkative a fellow as we've met in a good while. Even so, he was able to understand the importance of secrecy to the success of this project, especially after all the admonitions you gave him. That there could be a traitor in the Royal Household is unthinkable. And that leaves only the Rothschild...or the Dreyfus households.

"Oh, yes. I suppose we'd best not leave out the *'mademoiselle* Leonie'. But if she was the tool of Esterhazy, why did he tell us that he learned of our being here, and guessed our purpose, only as a result of his conversation with Bertillon—a conversation that took place on the morning of the second day after our arrival? And the major's knowing would not account for Ollstreder's approach at Maxim's the night before. Unless Esterhazy's lying to us about his relationship and his wanting to escape the baron's clutches." Watson relighted his cigar, which had gone out during his discourse.

"Excusez moi, M'sieurs." The waiter reappeared. "A gentleman, a German I believe, is here and wishes to see you. He says he is expected." He handed Holmes a calling card and then emptied the ashtrays into a salver with a hinged metal top and a short wooden handle.

"Merci. Ask *Herr* Schwabach to join us. And please bring another coffee setting and perhaps a plate of brioche and croissants."

"Oui, M'sieur Holmes. *Immediatement."*

"Guten morgen, Herr Holmes, *Herr Doktor* Watson." Schwabach pulled his chair up and set a worn leather brief-case on the table. As he started to open it, Holmes laid a hand on the banker's wrist.

"We've taken the liberty of ordering coffee and a plate of breads, *Herr* Schwabach. Perhaps we should let the waiter serve before you begin your report. Dr. Watson and I were just in the midst of a rather convoluted discussion of whether the confidentiality of our enterprise has been compromised."

"Isn't that issue moot at this point, *Herr* Holmes? I mean now that Captain Dreyfus is to have a new trial, is there any doubt that he will be acquitted? Surely with all the so-called evidence against him thoroughly discredited, the re-trial will be merely a formality. That's certainly what the Dreyfuses expect. Even I, a confirmed Franco-sceptic, am inclined to agree. Indeed, were it not for the opportunity to put an end to Baron Ollstreder's nefarious dealings, I would have thought our business concluded."

"Why is it," Watson asked, "that you're so eager to put the baron out of business? I would think that the baron's trafficking would be welcomed. After all, it must, to a certain extent, provide jobs for German workers and earns foreign exchange which is the life-blood of any modern industrial economy..."

"Gott in Himmel, Herr Doktor Watson. Do physicians pray for war so that the techniques of surgery may be more rapidly advanced? *Nein?* Then it is the same with bankers, at least some bankers. I dare say probably the majority of bankers and I will certainly vouch for the bankers at S. Bleichroder. Military weapons have but one practical use, *Mein Herren,"* he leaned forward, his hands tightly fisted on the table in front of him, "and that is war."

Pointing a finger at no one in particular, he continued, "It is I think inevitable. If you give the generals their toys, they will find a way to put them to use. And it is just as inevitable that one day they will become bored with dress parades and tired of mock battles. 'Look here,' the generals say, 'we have all these lovely weapons and no battles to fight!' And the *hauptmanns und der*

235

obersts—all of whom want to be generals—reply *'Ja Wohl, mein general!'* And on it goes from there until you have one horde of peasants trying their best to kill some other horde of peasants and the opposing governments bankrupt themselves fiscally and morally in the bargain.

"But this, for whatever it may be worth, is merely a moralistic view. From a more pragmatic perspective, the problem is that once the dogs of war are unleashed, no one can say for sure which horde of peasants will prevail, and which will be the vanquished. In these days of secret alliances and conflicting treaty obligations, who can say what spark will set off an apocalyptic conflagration that may, like a medieval plague, wipe out entire populations? And that is only the beginning. If you kill off a generation of able-bodied youths, who will breed the next generation? When there are no workers to man the mines and mills and factories, when there are no young men to plow the fields and bring in the harvest, who will produce the food and goods that make up the economy? With nothing in the shops to buy, and nothing to export, how will you control inflation? And you know what inflation can do: you lend out a mark, and with inflation you get back a pfennig. No, my friends, no banker in his right mind condones the likes of Baron Ollstreder.

"You speak of creating jobs. It is true that many skilled workmen find jobs in the manufacture of armaments, and high paying ones at that. But those same skilled workmen could also find work building machine tools or motor cars. So these jobs go begging while machine guns and artillery pieces are produced in abundance because in our scheme of values an ingot of steel fashioned into a cannon barrel is worth say, ten, twenty or a hundred times as much as an ingot of steel fashioned into a motor-car chassis. And what of the engineering and scientific minds that are wasted dreaming up new ways of exterminating large populations more efficiently than a year ago.

"As for foreign exchange, as best I can determine, the entire armaments industry benefits a relatively small clique of people: the factory owners, the politicians who look the other way, and" he paused and drew a deep breath, "those such as Ollstreder and this P. Villeneuf, whoever he may be, that make it all possible. And these men return relatively little to the economy from which they take so much. They tend to leave the greatest part of their wealth in Swiss banks who either hoard it in the form of bullion or gemstones, or they invest it in large real estate holdings in the states of Texas or California or some other part of the Western United States. What little is invested domestically is in the form of conspicuous consumption, which affects the average man in the street in a manner greatly disproportional to the actual effect on the economy. No wonder people continue to listen to the rantings of lunatics such as Karl Marx.

"*Ach*, forgive me *Doktor* Watson, and also you, *Herr* Holmes. I did not mean to respond so volubly to your question. However, it is a matter which causes me great consternation made all the worse because I dare not speak my mind anywhere but in the most trust-worthy of circumstances. Those who espouse views such as I have just expressed to you have been known to vanish in the dead of night without a trace."

"*Danke,*" he thanked the waiter who had returned with a fresh pot of coffee. As the waiter withdrew, Schwabach glanced at his briefcase.

Holmes broke open a croissant. "Perhaps you would like to show us what you have brought. Watson and I can peruse the material while you drink your coffee. Please help yourself to the breads; they are quite delicious."

Schwabach put down his cup. "As you wish, *Herr* Holmes. But I'm afraid there isn't much to see." He reached into the briefcase and extracted two sheets of paper which appeared to be enlarged photographic negatives. "These were all we were able to obtain in such a short time. They are called 'photostats'. Each is a reverse-image photograph. The first is of the most recent draft drawn by P. Villeneuf on his account. The second is a deposit slip showing the most recent sizeable deposit to the baron's account. Notice that the deposit slip coincides with the date of the *Aegean Star's* most recent sailing. I trust that these will serve your purpose." The banker tugged at his collar and looked around nervously. "Whatever that purpose may be." He held up his hand, his half eaten brioche held delicately between his thumb and forefinger. "And, considering your concerns regarding security, I'm quite sure that I have absolutely no need whatsoever to know any further details regarding that purpose.

"We were unsuccessful in obtaining any of the information you requested, *Herr Doktor* Watson, regarding the Bayer 'Aspirin' product. We learned that their research medical staff have done an extensive study of the effect of this drug in combination with other drugs and compounds. We made an effort to obtain a copy both through overt and covert channels and were unsuccessful in each instance. The medical director declined to provide a copy stating that the study was incomplete and consisted only of uncorrelated anecdotal data. Our, shall I say 'informal' source, essentially contradicted the medical director as to the state of completion, but owing to the sensitive nature of the material, it is kept under lock and key and he could not obtain access to it."

"The 'photostats' will suit our purposes quite admirably, *Herr* Schwabach. And just as you disclaim any need to know our purpose for wanting them, I'm sure that Dr. Watson and I have no need to learn precisely how it is that you came by these documents. As to the pharmaceutical study, I suspect that Dr. Watson and I have been privy to a macabre and lethal validation of a portion of the so-called 'anecdotal data', within the last few days. However, I find it exceedingly difficult to refer to our experience as 'anecdotal' inasmuch as it is entirely devoid of humor."

"Well, I'm glad to have been of some service to you. If Ollstreder is involved in Captain Dreyfus's misfortune, and you can expose him or better yet put him out of business, I should think that by doing so you would greatly enhance the chances of Dreyfus being acquitted at his retrial."

"Even if we were to succeed on both counts, *Herr* Schwabach, were Dr. Watson and myself sitting on your loan committee, we should probably recommend against making any sizeable loans on the collateral of Dreyfus being acquitted this time around."

"I fervently hope that you are wrong, Mr. Holmes. But if your skill at reading the political scene is as formidable as your reputed skill at reading a crime scene, then I despair for the Captain's fate. And poor *Madame* Dreyfus and her children. But I must return to Berlin where duty once again calls. I leave with a heavy heart, yet I cannot entirely disabuse myself of the notion that things will come right in the end. Now I must bid you both *auf Wiedersehen*. It has been my pleasure to meet you, and I dare to hope that S. Bleichroder and Company and myself have been of some service. I only wish we could do more. Perhaps our next meeting will be under happier circumstances." The banker closed his briefcase, rose and shook each man's hand. Then with a small shrug he turned and made his way out to the lobby.

Both men remained standing after shaking hands with Schwabach. As soon as he was out of earshot, Watson rubbed his hips. "As we've been sitting for quite a while, I wouldn't mind a short walk. If you're agreeable, perhaps you can confirm what I think you're about to do with those bank documents."

"If you've already figured out what we're going to do with these," Holmes gestured with the photostats before carefully rolling them into a cylindrical shape and placing them in his breast pocket, "then I hope you won't mind if we go our separate ways for a while. We must avoid being followed, and to best ensure that we are not, I suggest a diversion. You really ought not miss the Louve, and it's only a short walk from here. The doorman can point the way. In the meanwhile, I shall somewhat alter my appearance and head in the opposite direction to Montmartre. I will meet you at the main entrance to the Museum in say four hours' time."

CHAPTER THIRTY-ONE

"Bloody hell, Holmes! Where the devil have you been?"

*W*atson emerged from the museum, and shading his eyes from the bright sunlight, glanced around the U-shaped courtyard looking for Holmes. The grounds were crowded with groups of tourists clustered about their guides like ants around a dollop of marmalade at a picnic. The members of those groups that had completed their tour were all clutching their souvenir guide books as though trying to absorb anything which their eyes may have missed. More accustomed to the stodginess of the great London museums, Watson was struck by the curious practice of allowing artists— perhaps painters would be a better term—to set up their easels in the galleries and paint reproductions of the old masters hanging on the walls. He was curious to learn whether they wrought their forgeries for commercial purposes or simply for their own amusement. He thought about approaching one of the painters who were set up in the vast courtyard critically appraising their own works and those of their fellows, but owing to the language barrier decided it was not worth the effort. After glancing at his watch, he found a vacant bench. More than three hours of shuffling through the endless galleries craning his neck to look at paintings stacked row upon row to near ceiling height, and which after a while began to look alike, had quite worn him out.

Lighting his pipe, he allowed himself to review the progress they'd made and to speculate on what strange twists the case would take from this point to its *denouement.* Clearly Holmes's ploy had worked, although no one could have foreseen the role of Esterhazy or the pervasive, enigmatic presence of the baron. Bertillon was, as Holmes predicted, a pompous fool, or *dupe,* Watson recalled the French word that seemed to suit Bertillon better than the English version. But whose *dupe* was he: Esterhazy's or Ollstreder's?

And if the murder of Lambert was in fact intended to warn himself and Holmes off, who was responsible? Bertillon certainly seemed surprised at being summoned to the scene, but why was his investigation taking so long? It might be worthwhile to ask Inspector Loiseaux whether this was typical. Whoever was behind the murder of the little chemist had to know that Bertillon would be dining with them that evening, otherwise they would not have been invited to go along to the crime scene and thus the killing would not have served its despicable purpose. So far as Watson was aware, the only persons who knew that they were coming to Paris and when, were Bertillon and the Dreyfuses, and only Bertillon could have known that they would be dining together at Maxim's that night. This alone would tend to rule out an information leak in the Dreyfus household and compel the conclusion that Bertillon must have informed someone else besides Esterhazy. Given, according to Holmes, that there are no coincidences, it is unlikely that Ollstreder's forcing his attentions on them at Maxim's was a mere happenstance, no more than the phantasmal P. Villeneuf was their accidental fellow traveler aboard the boat-train.

Plainly Holmes was going to forge P. Villeneuf's name to a draft in proportion to the most recent draft drawn by the baron and divert the funds before Ollstreder's nefarious partner could get his hands on them. In one way or another this would force Villeneuf's hand, perhaps by precipitating a confrontation between him and Ollstreder. But how would Holmes know where or when the confrontation would occur?

Admitting to himself that he was stumped by this last question, Watson paused in his musings to look once again at his watch. It was a good half an hour past the time when Holmes said he would meet him, and nearly forty-five minutes since he'd emerged from the museum. The mid-afternoon sun was uncomfortably warm. Watson began to think that since Holmes had obviously been delayed, he'd just as well await his return in the cool comfort of the Ritz bar with one hand wrapped around a gin and tonic and the other dipping from time to time into one of the ubiquitous bowls of shelled almonds that seemed to gratuitously appear with each drink order. As he rose from the bench to retrace his route back to the hotel, a short muscular man in an ill-fitting suit and derby hat approached him. From just the few steps he made as Watson became aware of his presence,

Watson discerned from the man's rather odd gait that he'd at least some time in his life been a seafaring man.

"Are you *M'sieur le Medicin* Watson?" The man tipped his hat, and as he did Watson noticed the powerful-looking hands and thick wrists protruding from the too-short sleeves of his suit. He had short, bristly hair clumped in patches behind a high, receding forehead. With heavy brows, a flat, flared nose and prominent chin, his overall appearance was startlingly simian.

"And why, my good man, would you be wanting to know that? If indeed I am Dr. Watson, whom do I have the honor of addressing?"

"My name is 'Richard', *M'sieur*. Antoine Richard." He reached inside his breast pocket and extracted a thin wallet. He it flipped open to display an official-looking credential card which he held out for Watson's inspection for only a moment before snapping the wallet shut and returning it to his pocket. "You are the *Docteur* Watson who is the friend and travelling companion of *M'sieur* Sherlock Holmes?"

"Yes I am. In fact," Watson glanced around hoping desperately to catch sight of Holmes, "he's meeting me here any moment. What is it that you want?"

"You are to accompany me, *M'sieur,* at Inspector Loiseaux's request. I am to inform you that there has been a sudden development in the case of the pharmacist Lambert and your presence is urgently needed."

"But what about Holmes," Watson protested. "He was to meet me here some time ago. I was just going to return to our hotel to see if he's left a message."

"Oh, do not be concerned, *M'sieur.* *M'sieur* Holmes is already there."

Wishing that he'd brought his revolver, Watson gave a final glance over his shoulder in the direction of the museum courtyard hoping to spot Holmes, or perhaps at least a gendarme who could somehow validate the man's credentials. Although there was still a large crowd of tourists milling about the courtyard, there was no officer in sight, only a superannuated museum guard evidently sneaking a cigarette break in the shady recess of one of the doors. Other than the guard, there was no one even in hailing distance save one of the pseudo-artists dressed in a paint spattered smock and a ludicrously large beret carrying a canvass and a rickety-looking easel under one arm, and a box of paints and a palette under the other. Torn between his intuition, and his fear of being made to seem ridiculous if the man was genuine, Watson shrugged and gestured for the man to lead the way. "Very well, Mr. Richard, I shall do as you ask. But if this is some hoax, be assured that I shall not consider the matter to be amusing in the slightest degree and will deal with the situation accordingly."

"As you wish, *M'sieur*." The man pointed toward an ornate stone monument in the shape of a free-standing arch beyond which lay the gravel path into, as Watson remembered Holmes pointing out to him, the Tuileries Gardens. *"Apres vous, M'sieur."*

They walked straight along the central path through the garden in the direction of the Place de la Concorde. Continuing to temporize in every possible way, Watson paused once to check the lacing on one of his boots and another time, to Richard's obvious irritation, to light his pipe. Each time they would stop, Watson would take a surreptitious look back, but to his growing consternation, there were very few people walking in either direction.

They circled the Musee de L'Orangerie in an anti-clockwise direction, coming at last to the broad Place de la Concorde. Although the vehicular traffic was heavy in all directions, there were few pedestrians, and again not a police officer—unless Richard was what he'd represented himself to be—in sight. As they entered the plaza, Richard gestured toward a motorcar that was facing in the direction of the Quai des Tuileries which runs along the right bank of the Seine. The vehicle, Watson observed, appeared to be the same model as the one that had driven him and Holmes to their meeting with Baron Ollstreder. He could see the driver sitting at his open compartment in the front, but could see nothing of the inside, as the window curtains were completely closed.

The closed passenger compartment, to Watson's thinking, was more than enough for his intuitive sense of danger to overcome any lingering concern about being made to appear foolish. Without Watson's being aware of it, they'd picked up the pace of their walking so that they were now within a few feet of the vehicle. Richard placed his hand behind Watson's elbow as though to propel him the last few steps to what Watson now concluded was a trap of some kind, and what ever kind of trap it was, he made up his mind that he was not going to find out by meekly falling into it.

When Richard took Watson by the elbow, the driver got down from his bench and started to open the door to the passenger compartment. Sensing that he must act at once, Watson stopped abruptly and with all his strength jammed his elbow into Richard's midsection. Caught completely by surprise, the man let out a grunt and doubled over at the waist gasping for air. As soon as he did, Watson kneed him viciously in the face while at the same moment bringing both fists down as hard as he could at the base of the man's skull. As Richard crumbled to the pavement, apparently unconscious, Watson pivoted in the direction of the automobile and lunged, driving his shoulder into the other man, just as the passenger compartment door was beginning to open and the hand of someone inside emerged between the door and the body frame. The force of Watson's charge smashed the driver into the door slamming it shut on the hand. This brought a scream of pain and rage from inside the passenger compartment that was not quite loud enough to drown out the sickening crunch of the driver's head against the top of the vehicle. Recovering his balance, Watson brought his knee smartly into the man's groin, but it proved to be a useless gesture. As the man slumped to the pavement, Watson could see from the vacant stare and lolling head that the man was already beyond feeling the effect of any further blows.

Fearing that the owner of the damaged hand and outraged voice might also be the owner of a weapon, Watson started to back away. Remembering Richard, he started to turn when he heard a sound like fabric ripping and at the same instant the clap of a revolver discharging and a bullet whistling past his ear to bury itself in the side of the automobile. Thinking to rush whoever the gunman might be before he could get off another shot, Watson completed his turn and saw Richard on his knees, his arms pinioned to his sides by the wooden frame of a painting which had been smashed over his head. Behind Richard stood one of the artists Watson had seen in the Louve and later in the courtyard as he'd waited for Holmes. Quickly the man bent down and removed the weapon from Richard's limp fingers.

244

"Oh well," the artist put the revolver in the pocket of his smock, "I doubt that great-uncle Horace would have thought very much of my feeble effort at duplicating the Mona Lisa anyway."

"Bloody hell, Holmes! Where the devil have you been? You look positively outlandish in that costume. I take it you've been..."

"Look out, Watson!" Holmes, who'd been standing to Richard's right and facing the automobile, reached across the top of the man's head and gave Watson, who was on the other side of Richard with his back to the automobile, a violent shove just as another shot rang out, this time from the automobile. Watson, as he'd done so many times in combat, hit the ground and rolled to his right, away from the line of fire. Holmes quickly drew the revolver he'd just put in his pocket, dropped to one knee and brought the weapon up in a two-handed firing grip aiming in the direction of the automobile. He pulled back the hammer, hesitated and then lowered the weapon to his side. He then slowly rose, revolver still cocked and ready to fire and walked toward the car.

Watson, meanwhile, had gotten to one knee and was crouched at the front of the automobile next to the kerb-side wheel. The opening of the automobile door pushed the body of the driver away and it rolled face down in the gutter behind the front wheel. Richard had remained on his knees just as he'd been after being disarmed by Holmes. Cautiously Watson peered over the fender as Holmes approached the passenger compartment door. "Careful, Holmes." Watson got to his feet, prepared to rush the door again, should a weapon appear. Holmes transferred the revolver to his left hand and stood at the rear corner of the compartment. He motioned for Watson to remain below window level and to open the door. Taking the meaning of Holmes's gestures Watson slowly edged along the side of the machine gingerly stepping over the driver, who was evidently only stunned by Watson's charge, until he could reach the door handle. At Holmes's signal, he jerked it open. As he did, Holmes pivoted around the rear and threw open the other door. After a few seconds both men cautiously looked inside to find only themselves looking at each other.

"Where in the..." Watson turned and looked back over his left shoulder. The driver, having regained his feet and having no more stomach for the fray, took off in the direction of the river.

Watson turned back to the inside of the vehicle. "It was the driver. I thought his neck was broken. Who ever it was must have fired the shot and escaped while you and I were still recovering. Well at least we've got his confederate, the fellow who calls himself 'Richard'. Maybe we can get something out of him."

"I'm not at all sure that we'll be able to learn much from him, Watson. See for yourself."

Watson turned to the man who appeared at first glance to be unharmed beyond the damage already inflicted by Watson and then Holmes. However, as Watson squatted down in front of him he saw the neat, round hole just above the top button of the man's suit where the bullet had entered his chest and pierced his heart. There was almost no blood, indicating that the heart had stopped instantly. Even though Watson knew the man was dead, he placed his fingers on the man's neck to feel for a carotid pulse. The slight pressure from Watson's two fingers caused the body to topple over in the opposite direction.

As soon as the shooting started, the few pedestrians nearby scattered in all directions. But now a crowd was beginning to gather. Holmes made a cursory search of the automobile as he crawled through the passenger compartment. He reached Watson's side, bent down and whispered, "Quickly, Watson, let's get him into the automobile. You get in the back with him. One of us has to drive this infernal thing, and since at least I know the streets, we may end up in the Seine, but at least we won't get lost."

Watson gave him an incredulous look. "When did you..."

"Back in March, old man. Remember when you were under the weather for several days? I was going mad for something to do, and the smell of those awful poultices you were inflicting on yourself—I detest menthol vapours—were just too much. So for lack of anything better to do, I took a couple of driving lessons. Come on, let's get out of here. I'll give you the rest of the story later."

CHAPTER THIRTY-TWO

"Should such a nexus become indubitably apparent,
be assured that we shall bring it to your immediate attention."

"**G**ood grief, Holmes. I thought I was back in the midst of the battle of Maiwand." Watson held his whisky and soda in both hands as he took a long sip. "A gun battle in the heart of Paris. It's beyond belief. If someone wrote an acccunt of it, they'd be lucky to sell it as a work of fiction. In a way, I almost pity that poor fellow 'Richard', if indeed that is, or rather was, his true name. Good thing the one in the automobile, whoever he was, was such a poor marksman. A few inches either way, and it could have been you or me instead."

"Actually, old fellow, I expect he's rather an excellent shot."

Watson looked at Holmes dubiously. It was the cocktail hour, so the Ritz bar was crowded with businessmen, some relaxing after a strenuous day of deal-making, and others deep in earnest conversation still trying to consummate the day's business. It was early yet for the *'demoiselles de la soir* to make their appearance. So while there were also a number of female patrons daintily sipping their sloe-gins and martinis, they all appeared to be merely enjoying a pre-prandial cocktail after a strenuous day of shopping along the Rue de la Paix.

Holmes chewed for a few moments on a couple of almonds, and continued. "I think the bullet went just where the shooter intended. While someone may very well wish us dead, is does not suit his purpose just yet. No, the purpose of the shot was to assure the late *M'sieur* Richard's total and permanent silence. As you so shrewdly discerned, the plot was to kidnap you, either to be held hostage in return for my non-interference in the Dreyfus retrial, or to lure me into a trap in an effort to rescue you."

"And if the plot had been successful?" Now Watson took a handful of the nuts.

"Fortunately, Watson, you were too quick for them. And as for your taking on both of them, I must say 'splendid job.' I never knew you to be such an accomplished street-fighter. Such moves. A veritable ballet of the martial arts."

Despite the warm glow brought on by his second whisky and Holmes's sincere praise for his hand-to-hand combat skills—he found the term 'street-fighting' to be decidedly less than appropriate—Watson was not in the best of moods. The death of the man 'Richard' bothered him nearly as much as his anguish over the thought that he'd nearly killed the driver. These morbid thoughts were made all the worse by the painful throbbing of his war wound as a result of the collision of his shoulder with the driver and the un-yielding automobile body. Thus he responded with candor, "I appreciate your flattering words, and certainly I once again owe my life to your welcome intervention, but for the sake of all concerned, I do wish it had been a minute or two sooner. Had I not..."

Holmes signaled the waiter for another round of drinks. "You're quite right of course. I must admit that I was anticipating them making their move somewhere in the park, and so I was following more or less along side you throughout the park, but staying off the paved path so that my progress was at times somewhat slower than yours. I thought that you'd certainly spotted me when you stopped to tie your boot, as I was only a few feet away behind some bushes. I was sure that you'd seen me when you looked back to your left.

"It was not until you reached the round-about that I realized they'd be waiting until transportation was close at hand before trying to incapacitate you. I decided to go around in the opposite direction, just in case anyone had been observing and seen me in the park. It was then that I was accosted by a couple of silly dowagers, Americans I'm sure, who insisted that I show them my painting. That cost me nearly half a minute, and of course during that interval you'd evidently picked up the pace of your walking, so by the time you'd nearly reached the motor-car and made your move, I was, I suppose, better than half a minute behind and you were left to your own more than ample resources. What, by the way, tipped you off that they were up to no good?"

Watson smiled slightly at Holmes's confession of human frailty. And after taking a sip of his fresh drink and a satisfying puff on his small cigar, he replied, "Why Holmes, didn't you notice? The driver was wearing those same lavender hose."

Holmes lit a cigarette. "I noticed them as he was lying on the ground. The baron really should consider a more conservative livery, although I suspect the household color-scheme is a concession to *Mademoiselle* Otero."

"Well, at least we now know almost to a certainty that Ollstreder is connected somehow to the murder of the chemist."

"We do?" Holmes arched an eyebrow.

Watson thought for a moment. "Sorry, Holmes. In the excitement, I must have failed to mention that 'Richard' induced me to accompany him in the first place by telling me that there'd been an important development in the Lambert case, and my attendance upon Inspector Loiseaux was required immediately. When I told him I was waiting for you, he told me that you were already with the Inspector. While there may be some other and wholly innocent explanation, today's events, coupled with his having commented on the murder even before there had been anything about it in the newspapers, certainly raises at least a strong inference of his involvement."

"Don't you find it incongruous that on the one hand he has Lambert murdered as a warning to us, and on the other hand he invites our attention with his tale of the missing falcon?"

"Yes, but..."

"Enough of speculation for now. I expect that we shall learn the extent of the baron's culpability in due course. Tell me what else 'Richard' said to you. Evidently you were not immediately persuaded..."

"Well," Watson reached inside his jacket and took out the credential wallet, "he showed me his credentials. I managed to retrieve them from the body just before we stopped and abandoned the automobile."

Holmes looked at the card which Watson passed to him and chuckled. "Watson we must do something to improve your French. It appears that *M'sieur* 'Richard'—for that is indeed the name as it written here—is a duly licensed river boat pilot."

Watson sputtered, "What sheer brass, Holmes. What if I'd—in fact I started to ask one of those artists—say, I suppose it was you, was it not?—or one of the museum guards to translate what the card said. Good Lord, if only I had..." He winced in pain and rubbed his shoulder. "Perhaps I should take a few of those Aspirin."

"I don't know, Watson. You've no idea how they'll mix with alcohol, and in view of what happened to Lambert, it may not be worth the risk."

"You're no doubt right. I probably should have it checked by someone, but what if the police are watching the hospitals? If I can persuade Ritz to find some, I'll just rub in some oil of wintergreen before I retire. But what about you? What were you doing in the museum in that ridiculous costume? I thought you said you were going to Montmartre. Were you successful in diverting Villeneuf's funds?"

"Very perceptive, Watson. The draft is being processed through banking channels, I presume, even now. If it arrives ahead of the genuine instrument, then *M'sieur* Villeneuf's share of the profits from this shipment will be far less than he anticipated."

"Good show, Holmes." Watson laughed and slapped his knee. "Ow! Blast! I forgot about my knee. Must have bruised it when..."

"Good evening, *M'sieurs.*" Inspector Loiseaux approached their table. "I hope you will forgive my intruding once again. Is something wrong with your knee, Dr. Watson? I don't mean to be... how do you say... ah yes... 'nosy'. ... but you look like you are in considerable pain. Did you injure yourself? Perhaps you should have another physician look at it."

"Oh, no. Thank you for your concern, Inspector, but there's really nothing to be done. It's an old, old war wound. It acts up from time to time. I spent the entire afternoon enjoying the treasures of the Louve, and I'm afraid that so much walking and standing tends to aggravate a weakness in the anterior cruciate ligament."

"Ah, yes, Dr, Watson. An old war wound. Just like wearing one's service uniform; with each passing year it becomes less and less tolerable. I trust you found the Louve worth the discomfort. Which of its treasures did you enjoy the most?"

"That's hard to say, Inspector. One afternoon is hardly enough time to do it full justice. There was the... the..." Watson paused.

"'Winged Victory', the 'Venus de Milo' and of course da Vinci's incomparable portrait..." Holmes, mindful of Watson's indifference to great works of art, came to his rescue.

"Then you were together at the museum all afternoon?"

"Nearly so, Inspector. I had a small matter of business to attend to. We arranged to meet at 'Winged Victory' when my business was concluded."

"And what time would that have been, Mr. Holmes?"

"I say, Inspector," Watson interjected, "Is there some reason that we should be required to account for our whereabouts this afternoon with such precision?"

"My apologies, gentlemen. I am merely making a routine inquiry. I take it you've not heard about the sensational business in the Place de la Concorde late this very afternoon. It was like something out of one of those penny-novels set in the American West."

"Do tell, Inspector." Holmes motioned for the waiter. "Perhaps a glass of something? Would an aperitif do?"

Loiseaux sat down and lit a cigarette. "All that is known as of the present time is that gunshots were exchanged between the occupants of an automobile and three men on the sidewalk. The occupants of the vehicle fled, and then two of the men who had been on the sidewalk bundled the third man—evidently he was struck by one of the shots—into the automobile and drove away at a high rate of speed."

"How extraordinary, Inspector. Watson and I left the Louve around... what was it, Watson... four o'clock?"

"Er... why yes it was, Holmes. Four o'clock almost exactly. 'Remember looking at my watch. I even remarked, if you'll recall, how time flies when one is so thoroughly enjoying one's self."

"What is even more extraordinary, Mr. Holmes, is that two of the men on the sidewalk matched generally the description given by the shop-girl of the two men she saw loitering outside Lambert's shop on the day he was murdered."

"'Generally', did you say, Inspector?" Holmes asked.

"Yes, unfortunately. If you will recall, the shop-girl saw only their backs and a brief profile. So she could only describe with any certainty their heights and builds. The descriptions given by the witnesses to today's altercation were almost exactly the same, the only notable difference being that the taller of the two today, instead of a conventional day-time suit, was attired in what appeared to be a smock such as those frequently worn by artists, and instead of a regular hat, he was described as wearing a large beret which flopped down over his ears.

"To your health, gentlemen." Loiseaux raised his glass.

"And to yours, Inspector," Holmes replied as he and Watson raised their glasses. After the obligatory sip, Holmes asked, "Do you think there's a connection between Lambert's murder and this afternoon's occurrence?"

"It would be most premature to speculate at this time, *M'sieurs.* Would you tell me, *M'sieur* Holmes what was the nature of your business matter to which you attended before meeting Dr. Watson?"

"Isn't that..." Watson interrupted.

"It's quite al-right, Watson. I don't mind. After all we are guests here, so we should be obliged to aid the Inspector in his inquiries as much as we possibly can." Holmes took another sip of whisky and turned toward the police officer. "I was attending to some banking business. I deposited for collection a draft which I had received in connection with a matter upon which Watson and I have been recently consulted. Should you wish, I'm sure the bank manager will be happy to confirm the truth of what I have just told you. The bank in question is Rothschild *et Frere.* I selected them because the draft was drawn on a foreign bank, and they have by far the best correspondent relationships in Europe."

"I do not think further inquiry will be necessary, *M'sieur* Holmes, unless, of course, your Paris engagement is somehow connected to the Lambert case or to this afternoon's affair."

"I'm afraid, Inspector, that it would be premature at this time to speculate that such a connexion exists. But should such a nexus become indubitably apparent, be assured that we will bring it to your immediate attention."

"I appreciate your candor, *M'sieur* Holmes. It certainly helps to put my weary brain at ease. To my knowledge, you're well aware how the official policeman's mind works. While I have not exhausted my inquiries, it seems that you gentlemen are the only two men in English-cut clothes in all of Paris who match the general description of the two men seen lingering outside Lambert's shop earlier on the day he was murdered. Then two men, quite possibly these same two men, are involved in a gun-battle only a short distance from where you spent most of the afternoon.

"Based on what we know, it seems certain that Lambert was poisoned in some manner. It seems equally certain that his murder was a crime of calculation and not of impulse. No money or valuables appear to have been taken. So given the means by which the crime was committed and that robbery was not the apparent motive, it seems reasonable to conclude that Lambert was killed by or on behalf of someone he knew and for a reason as yet unknown."

"You have..."

"Oh, indeed we have, Dr. Watson. From all reports Lambert and his wife were both happily married, and neither was notorious for having extra-marital romantic interests. While the *pharmacie* was not overly prosperous, it provided a decent living, and was debt-free. Lambert had one employee who was out of the shop at the time the two men were noticed by the milliner's shop-girl. The employee, a young man also of the Jewish persuasion, and devoutly so, so we are told, both liked and was liked by his employer. Lambert had no former partners, and was highly regarded, we learned, by his customers, his competitors and the medical community as well."

Holmes asked, "Was he active politically? A Dreyfusard, perhaps?"

"We've discovered nothing that would so indicate, although, given his religious affiliation, it is not unreasonable to assume that he would have been counted in the Dreyfus camp. However we have learned nothing to suggest that he was unusually out-spoken in his views on that or any other subject of a political nature.

"As you might imagine, we find it necessary to gather intelligence from time to time regarding various domestic groups, or movements, if you will. In order to do so, we find it expedient occasionally to engage in covert operations such as having men infiltrate these groups so that we can be apprised in a timely manner if any group seeks to advance its cause by inappropriate means. We have called upon these sources and none have reported any knowledge of Lambert prior to his death."

"So you are of the view," Holmes asked, "that Lambert's death was not related in any way to the Dreyfus case?"

Loiseaux shrugged, "Who can say, *M'sieur* Holmes, what is or is not connected to the Dreyfus case? It is all that anyone speaks of these days. Even in the jails and prisons, the inmates are just as likely to break into riot over the Dreyfus case as they once did over bad rations or some other grievance. The Chamber of Deputies is so caught up in debating each and every nuance, that all other issues are put aside." Loiseaux lowered his voice, "In this latter respect, the case may be a blessing, but that, I suppose, is for others to say."

"I wonder, Inspector, did the uniformed officer who forced open the front door of Lambert's shop make a written report, and if so might I be permitted to review it?"

Loiseaux leaned forward and lowered his voice. "It is remarkable you should ask that question, *M'sieur* Holmes. I, too, was curious about the door earlier today. I looked for the report in the file which is, of course, where it should be. However, I examined the file page-by-page several times and was unable to locate such a document. I assume it is merely mis-filed and will turn up in due course. We have such a terrific turn-over in clerical employees, it is a constant source of wonder that anything gets properly filed at all. Then too, I must allow for the possibility that no report was ever made and I shall have to waste who knows how much more time tracking down the lazy flic who found it too inconvenient to do his job properly. If that proves to be the case, he most likely got engrossed in listening to the inane braying of the that pompous jackass..." Loiseaux paused and looked about the room, "...well, you know, *M'sieurs,* to whom I refer. But tell me, *M'sieur* Holmes, what is it about the door that compels your attention?"

"Once again, *Inspecteur,* mere curiosity, nothing more. When it turns up, if it would not be too great an imposition, I should like to see if there's anything interesting to be made of it.

But in regard to this afternoon's curious business," Holmes, his face a bland mask, continued, "have you traced the ownership of the motorcar ? Do you think the Marquis was involved?"

"The Marquis remains in custody, but I would not rule out involvement on the part of his fanatical band of followers. However, we have already established ownership of the vehicle."

"I say, Inspector, jolly good work!" Watson interjected.

Loiseaux held up his hands, palms outward. "No, no, Doctor Watson. "I wish I could accept your praise. However, it was not brilliant detective work that led us to the owner of the vehicle. It was the other way around."

"I don't..."

"It was the owner who came to us, rather than our locating him. It seems that the owner, a Baron...." The Inspector consulted his notebook, "Ollstreder... contacted us to report that the automobile had been stolen."

"Was the report made before or after the incident in the Place de la Concorde?" Holmes asked mildly.

"As usual, *M'sieur* Holmes, you ask the most penetrating questions. Unfortunately, I am unable to provide you with a satisfactory answer. It seems that the officer who initially received the report failed to make note of the exact time." Loiseaux rose to his feet, "I must take my leave almost at once so that I may interview this baron before he goes out for the evening."

Holmes and Watson rose to shake hands with Loiseaux. "Do you suppose," Holmes asked, "that we might come along?"

Loiseaux scratched his moustache thoughtfully. "I'm not sure, *M'sieurs.* An official police investigation..."

"You are aware, of course that Holmes and I quite often assist the Metropolitan Police in London. And certainly Bertillon's inviting us to join him at the Lambert crime scene would serve as ample precedent..."

"I think, in candor, Inspector, we should also apprise you that Watson and I have already met Baron Ollstreder and are considering undertaking an engagement at his instance."

"Do you think the matter about which you have been consulted is possibly related?"

"It is most unlikely, Inspector. But then one never knows..."

"Precisely, *M'sieur* Holmes. Just as in the case of Lambert's murder." Loiseaux eyed both men narrowly. "Very well, *M'sieurs*. Doctor Watson's point is well taken. The Lambert investigation is a precedent. Perhaps your presence would be of benefit. Yes, please do come with me."

CHAPTER THIRTY-THREE

*"Thank you Doctor Watson, you've
evidently averted a terrible tragedy."*

"**M**r. Holmes. Dr. Watson. To what do I owe the pleasure? Surely the gendarmes have not enlisted your aid in the matter of my purloined motor-car."

"Just so, my dear Baron," Holmes replied as the three men handed their hats, and Holmes and Watson handed their sticks to the parlour maid. "Do allow me to present Inspector Loiseaux of the *Sureté*. We were introduced to the Inspector not long after our arrival, and as luck would have it, Watson and I were of some small assistance to him in connexion with one of his assigned duties. So knowing our interest in unusual criminal investigations, he consulted us in regard to this afternoon's sensational business. When he learned that we were also acquaintances of yours, he insisted that we come along in the hope that we might be able to provide some helpful insight based on the information you may provide."

"Very well, then, *M'sieur* Inspector. Please proceed." Ollstreder gestured in the direction of the hallway. When they'd taken seats in the main parlour, he continued. "I'm afraid, Mr. Holmes, that this matter will challenge even your formidable skills. As much as I would like the thieves brought to justice, I'm afraid that my information is not at all likely to produce any, as you put it, 'helpful insights'."

"Perhaps the baron will favor us with the answers to a few questions, and we can then see whether such insights will manifest themselves." Loiseaux took out his pocket note-book and placed it on his knee, with his pen poised. "What time was it when the machine was first discovered missing?"

The baron shrugged and stuck out his lower lip. "That, *M'sieur* Inspector, I cannot say. I was evidently notified some time after the initial report was made to the police. I was occupied with some correspondence much of the afternoon, and when my labors were done I allowed myself the indulgence of a short nap. As I had instructed the servants not to awaken me before six o'clock, they did not do so. Thus I learned of the machine's disappearance and that you wished to interview me in that regard at exactly that hour."

"Then," Loiseaux completed his note taking and looked up, "who..."

"I am made to understand, Inspector, that it was one of the servants who made the report to the police. Apparently my chauffeur was cleaning and polishing the vehicle as he is required to do each day at the garage where it is stored when not in use. I am told that he was set upon by two or more assailants who beat him into unconsciousness and made off with the vehicle. The chauffeur, when he partially regained his senses, managed to make his way back here. He reported what had occurred, and owing to the severity of his injuries immediately collapsed once again."

"Please summon him, Baron Ollstreder, so that we may have his first-hand account."

"Alas, Inspector, I'm afraid that is not possible. He was in such pain from his injuries that he was given a sedative, laudanum, I believe, and put to bed. Perhaps in the morning..."

Watson jumped to his feet. "Good grief! You gave laudanum to a man with possible closed-head injuries? Quickly, take me to him. Have someone brew up some coffee, and make sure it's strong. Do you have any ammonium carbonate?"

Like an enormous walrus leaving its perch, Ollstreder slithered off the sofa and waddled to the bell pull which he proceeded to subject to several earnest yanks. As the result of his exertions, before the fourth or fifth pull had been completed, the room was filled with half a dozen or so servants. Addressing an older man who appeared to be their leader or manager, Ollstreder barked out his orders in German: "Heinrich, take Doctor Watson and the other gentlemen to see Andre immediately. Have one of the maids go to the kitchen and instruct the kitchen staff to brew some strong coffee. As soon as it is ready it is to be brought to Andre's room. Dispatch another to the medical supply cabinet to fetch some what did you ask for, Dr. Watson? Ammonium..."

"Ammonium carbonate, man. Hurry!"

The lead servant looked puzzled. Watson made a ring with his thumb and forefinger which he held up to his nose and sniffed loudly. "Am-mon-ium car-bon-ate," he pronounced slowly. "Smelling salts!"

Heinrich nodded his head up and down. *"Ach! Ja, Herr Doktor.* Smelling salts." He pointed to a young porter and issued some instructions in German. *"Mach schnell, Klaus, mach schnell!"* Turning to the visitors he bowed toward the door, "This way *Mein Herren.* If you will permit, I will lead the way. The servant quarters are on the fourth floor and can be reached most rapidly by the back stairway."

Ollstreder stood aside as Heinrich led the entourage toward the rear door of the parlor. "Please forgive me gentlemen. Because of my somewhat delicate health, I find climbing stairs too much of a challenge. The house is equipped with a small, but rather slow-moving lift which I will use and join you in just a minute or two."

With Heinrich leading the, way, they quickly clambered up the steep, narrow flights of stairs and proceeded along a dimly-lighted hallway with a ceiling so low that Holmes twice scraped the top of his head on what were probably roof joists that transected the hallway at intervals. There were a number of doorways on both sides of the hall. In a few moments Heinrich stopped at one of the doors. He opened it and stood aside for Watson, Holmes and the Inspector to enter. Evidently the servants' quarters had not been electrified with the rest of the house as the room was illuminated only by a wall-mounted gas-light and an oil lamp which stood on a small night table next to the single, narrow bed. In addition to the bed and night table, the only other furnishings were a straight-back wooden chair with a woven seat and a bachelor's chest on which were a ceramic wash basin and water pitcher along with a shaving mirror with attachments for a shaving brush and lather cup. The fourth floor was evidently built into the cavity of the Mansard-type roof so the rear wall of the room was slightly concave and fitted with a small, recessed window.

Lying on the bed was the man whom Holmes and Watson at once recognized as the driver of the automobile at the Place de la Concorde that afternoon. Although the room was oppressively warm, he was covered by a heavy quilt which made it impossible to determine whether he was breathing. In spite of the feeble light, as soon as Watson approached the bed, he could see the cyanotic

259

lips and concluded that the man was near to death, if not already dead. Putting aside the thought that this same man was an active participant in a plot to kill or at the least kidnap him only a few hours ago, Watson placed his fore and middle fingers against the man's carotid artery in the hope of finding even the faintest pulse.

After a few moments Watson threw back the quilt and placed his ear against the man's chest. "Quickly! He's still alive! Help me stand him up. Where are the blasted smelling salts?" Holmes and Heinrich rushed to the bed-side as Watson threw off the quilt. First they lifted the chauffeur to a sitting position. Then with Holmes on one side and the servant on the other, with each man draping one of his arms across their own necks and shoulders they stood him upright.

In a moment the servant addressed as "Klaus" appeared holding a vial which he proffered to Watson who removed the stopper and held the container under the still-unconscious man's nose. After a few seconds the man groaned. "Good, keep him upright." Watson took away the smelling salts and re-stoppered the vial. "Watch his head, Holmes. Don't let it fall backward as it may cause him to swallow him tongue."

"Thank you Doctor Watson. You've evidently averted a terrible tragedy."

"You're quite welcome, Baron Ollstreder." Watson responded. "But it's Divine Providence to whom you should be giving thanks. My contribution was minimal at best. What, by the way, is the name of the incompetent bungler who prescribed a sedative for a man with a probable concussion? He should be reported immediately to the Medical Society and his credentials taken away before he can do any further damage. This man needs to be given digitalis, and should be gotten to hospital immediately. Inspector, can you summon an ambulance? No, wait. Better yet, Inspector, can we take him in your automobile?"

"Oui, yes, of course, *Docteur* Watson," Loiseaux turned toward the baron.

"Would you show us to the lift? It would be much safer if we took him down that way instead of using the stairs."

Ollstreder beckoned to Klaus, "Take Mr. Holmes's place holding Andre. *Herr Doktor* Watson, I trust you will remain in attendance. *Ja?"*

"Yes, yes, of course. But please hurry, Baron. The man's barely alive. Holmes, let's you and I take the stairs and meet them in the front hall."

"*Sehr gut.* Since we cannot all fit in the lift, Inspector you go with Heinrich, Klaus and Andre. As you were informed, I have a previous engagement, and in any case, I've told you all that I know regarding this unfortunate matter. I've no doubt that *Doktor* Watson's timely intervention has saved the man's life and when he is restored to sentience I'm quite sure that Andre will be of far greater assistance to you in your investigation. The stress and excitement have quite taken their toll, I'm afraid." The baron took out a handkerchief and mopped his visibly perspiring brow. He lowered himself onto the flimsy chair which creaked and groaned as it strained to support his crushing weight. "I will just rest here a few minutes."

Holmes and Watson retraced their steps to the stairway. As they were descending, Watson reached into his pocket and removed the vial of smelling salts. When they reached a landing he stopped and whispered, "Holmes, stop. Look at this." He handed the vial to Holmes. "I swear, Holmes, this is the same vial that I borrowed on the ferry-boat. Look, it's got a Booth's label. And what are the odds of two vials from Booth's having a chipped rim? Why there's even a small smear of blood on the corner of the label."

"Good eye, Watson. And what would you say the odds were that the baron's lift also regularly serves another passenger?"

"You mean his partner in crime? What's his name? Villeneuf? You mean that decrepit old man on the boat is in this house? Should we not confront him?"

"Not just yet, old man. Soon enough he will be seeking us out. Come, let us make haste lest the Inspector and his make-shift ambulance depart without us."

CHAPTER THIRTY-FOUR

"I think it would be wise for a gendarme
to be posted next to Andre's bed just as
a precaution."

With the semi-conscious Andre wedged between Holmes and
Watson in the rear seat, and Loiseaux all the while goading the
young uniformed gendarme-driver to even greater speeds and
reckless careening around corners, the vehicle clanked across the
Pont Notre Dame and arrived at the entrance to the Hotel Dieu, the
great hospital of Paris. Once inside they encountered a near-fatal
delay explaining to the ancient nun in charge of the admissions
desk that the patient was not in fact in police custody and that the
Ministry of Justice was not going to be responsible for the hospital
charges. The fiscal impasse was finally resolved by Holmes putting
up a one-thousand franc deposit, and providing the name and
address of the baron as the party responsible for the charges.
Eventually staff were summoned and the patient taken away to one
of the emergency treatment rooms.

 As soon as the foxglove elixir was administered, Andre's
breathing returned to normal and the cyanosis disappeared.
Loiseaux adamantly wanted to stay and question the man, but the
physician-in-charge, with Watson's emphatic concurrence, made it
plain that any attempt at interrogation would be useless until the
patient had been fully restored to his senses, a condition which was
unlikely to occur before morning. Once persuaded, Loiseaux's
truculent mood abated and it being near enough to the dinner hour,
at Loiseaux's suggestion they had the driver leave them at what
proved to be a noisy brasserie off the Place de la Bastille.

 "Absolutely amazing, gentlemen. The extremes of medical
practice in this City. On the one hand you have a blithering
incompetent: someone who would administer laudanum to a
patient presenting the symptoms and history of a closed-head
injury and resultant probable concussion. And on the other hand
the brilliant—and probably lifesaving—technique of administering
the digitalis by intravenous injection. No need to worry about

trying to get an effective dose down the throat of a semi-conscious patient; no long delay while the elixir is absorbed into the blood-stream. I must find out what the dilution factor is, and how to determine what dosage is appropriate."

"While I cannot but concur in the latter part of your assessment of the state of trauma medicine in Paris," Holmes paused to take a sip of his preprandial Kir, "I'm not sure that the first part is necessarily on the mark."

"Why not, *M'sieur* Holmes? Even to my layman's mind, what *Docteur* Watson says about a practitioner who would make such an obvious mistake is a mild rebuke in comparison to what I will have to say to this quack when I confront him."

"I quite agree with you both. If it was a physician who prescribed the laudanum, then his credentials should be revoked immediately. However, I did not hear the baron acknowledge that it was a physician who was responsible."

"You mean that the baron deliberately ordered that the narcotic be given knowing that it would be fatal." Loiseaux sat back in his chair and took a nervous puff of his cigarette. "In my long career as a policeman, *M'sieur* Holmes, I have learned that the wealthy and powerful do for the most part what they please, while the rest of us do whatever necessity commands. But to order the certain death of a servant merely because, through no apparent fault of his own, an article of his master's property has been forcibly stolen, why even I find that difficult to accept."

"How very French," Holmes raised his glass in an informal toast, "to be at the same time both cynical and able to maintain one's faith in human nature. No, Inspector, there's no evidence to suggest that the baron ordered the drug to be given. Most likely, when you inquire, no one will remember who suggested or administered the laudanum, and Andre, if he remembers anything of today's events, will recall that it was he who asked for the drug to ease his pain."

"Never-the-less, *M'sieur* Holmes, *Docteur* Watson, please excuse me for a moment while I use the telephone. I think it would be wise for a gendarme to be posted next to Andre's bed just as a precaution. Perhaps it is the cynical side of my brain that has taken control." Loiseaux shrugged his shoulders as he scraped back his chair. *"Excusez moi.* I shall return in a moment."

"Why not just tell Loiseaux that you suspect that the laudanum was administered at the express direction of the baron?"

"Come now, old man. Are we quite ready to explain the basis of our suspicion?"

"I suppose not, Holmes. But how could you be so sure that Loiseaux would react as he did? What if he'd merely shrugged-off the idea that the drug was administered for the express purpose of silencing Andre?"

"Your point is taken as well, Watson. Indeed I could not be sure how the Inspector would react, so before we left the hospital I slipped a few francs to the orderly on duty in the ward where Andre was placed to make sure that no one other than the attending physician so much as approached the man's bed. Even so, I'm glad that Loiseaux's putting his own man in place as well. Ah! here he comes. And from his self-satisfied look, I assume that he was successful."

Just as Loiseaux resumed his seat, the food arrived, and for a few minutes, all three men busied themselves with their dinners: coq au vin for Holmes and Watson, and a cassoulet for Loiseaux. Nearly done eating, Holmes lay down his fork. "Is there any word yet on the automobile, Inspector?"

Loiseaux took a sip of his wine, "Indeed there is, *M'sieur* Holmes. When I called my office to direct that a man be sent at once to the hospital, I was informed that within the last hour it was found abandoned in an alley in Les Halles. And one of the three men seen on the pavement was discovered dead inside the vehicle; shot once through the heart. In fact as soon as I finish my dinner, I'm going to have a look at the vehicle and then at the body, although I doubt that there will be anything to be learned by viewing either. We know the owner of the vehicle, and the body, so it has been reported to me, was stripped of any identification when it was left. Perhaps *M'sieur* Bertillon can apply his wondrous system and in this instance actually produce some useful information."

"May Watson and I..."

"Yes, yes, of course gentlemen." The Inspector sighed in resignation. "You are most welcome to come along. Perhaps your—what is the German word?—oh yes, your 'doppelgangers' will have left behind some more tangible clue this time." Loiseaux caught the eye of their waiter, *"L 'addition, sil vous plait. "*

The waiter, pleased that he might be able to turn a four-person table once more that night promptly complied. He started to hand the check to Loiseaux, but Holmes intercepted it. "Please, Inspector, allow us..."

"M'sieur Inspector," the restaurant maitre d' approached the table, "there is a telephone call for you from one of your officers. He says he's calling from the Hotel Dieu and that it's urgent."

"Perhaps Andre has regained consciousness sooner than expected."

"Hopefully that will be the case, *Docteur* Watson. Excuse me again. I'll be back in a moment and then we can be on our way."

In a few minutes the Inspector returned, his face an open book of anger. Taking a long drag on his cigarette, he leaned forward, his elbows and forearms planted on the table and his fists clutched in rage. "Your doppelgangers have struck again, gentlemen."

"Meaning exactly what, Inspector," Watson asked mildly.

"Meaning, *Docteur* Watson, that Andre is dead!"

"Good heavens, man, tell us what happened." Watson snatched up the pack of cigarettes which Holmes had laid on the table, and after lighting one turned to Holmes, "Excuse my manners, Holmes. May I?"

Holmes ignored Watson's belated courtesy, and focused his piercing eyes on the Inspector. "Yes, Inspector. Please tell us what happened."

"When my man got there, Andre was already dead. The orderly who was on duty in the ward stated that within a few minutes after our leaving, a nurse—or at least a woman in a nurse's uniform—came into the ward and presented a letter advising that she'd been engaged by the English physician—evidently a reference to you, *Docteur* Watson—to watch over the patient through the night. Since this practice is not uncommon, the orderly apparently acquiesced and went back to his station at the front of the ward.

265

"As you observed earlier, surrounding each bed there is a curtain hanging on a rod which is suspended from the ceiling. In order to afford the patients a modicum of privacy when being examined by the *docteur* or when being bathed by the nurses or orderlies, this curtain may be drawn so as to encircle the bed. The orderly states that shortly after the nurse's arrival, she partially drew the curtain so that the orderly's view of the patient was obscured. A few minutes after doing this, the nurse approached the orderly's workstation and through gestures—evidently she does not speak French—asked him the location of the women's water closet. He gave her directions and then went back to his work which evidently consisted primarily of reading risqué novels, a number of which were found in the back of a cabinet at the workstation.

"Shortly after that, when my man arrived, the orderly noticed that the nurse had not returned. My officer went immediately to check on Andre, whose bed had been pointed out to him by the orderly, while the orderly went to summon the head nurse to report what had occurred and to have her check the women's water closet to see if the private duty nurse was still there. Of course she was not, and of course Andre was dead; most likely suffocated by a pillow being pressed to his face."

"Did the orderly give a description of the 'nurse'?"

"Yes, he did. She was tall and heavy-set. According to the orderly, she had the broadest shoulders he'd ever seen on a woman."

"And do you believe, Inspector, that Watson and I had anything to do with this most singular occurrence?"

Loiseaux hung his head for a moment and then looked up; his gaze steadily meeting that of Holmes. "I frankly don't know what to believe anymore, *M'sieur* Holmes. No, no I do not believe that *Docteur* Watson would have intervened this evening to save the man's life, only to have him killed by one who is obviously a professional killer mere hours later."

"But if not you, then who?" Loiseaux signaled the waiter and ordered three cognacs. "Obviously that leaves only the baron. But why would he want the man dead? Anger at Andre's having been the victim of car thieves? One cannot help but dislike the baron at sight, but that's a long way from believing him a murderer."

"And what do you make of the affair in the Place de la Concorde this afternoon?" Holmes asked. "Is it possible that Ollstreder was involved in that as well?"

"I have considered that a possibility since this evening, *M'sieur* Holmes, when you asked me what time the initial theft report was made. If the baron were involved, it would certainly give him a motive to silence the chauffeur. And who but the baron knew that we were taking the man to hospital? It is virtually impossible for anyone to have followed us."

"That is true, Inspector," Watson interjected, "but I do not recall that you mentioned which hospital. When you told your driver where to go, we were already pulling away from the kerb and Ollstreder's two men were going back inside with their backs to us. Also taking into account the noise made by the automobile engine, it is most unlikely that they were able to overhear your instructions."

"Watson is quite right, Inspector. It is perhaps just as likely that someone else connected with this afternoon's business had the baron's house under surveillance, saw the injured man brought out, and from our hasty departure deduced our destination. Even if one did not know in advance which hospital, the range of possibilities is fairly limited, and I should imagine that a few discreet inquiries would have confirmed our destination within a relatively short time. If indeed there are two men going about masquerading as Watson and myself, it is obviously to cast suspicion upon us, and what better way to do so than to say that Andre's killer was sent by Doctor Watson."

"Why is it, *M'sieurs,* that someone would want to cast suspicion on the two of you? You have represented to me that you are here on holiday. I am inclined to take you at your word, if for no other reason than my great respect for what you have accomplished in the application of science to police work. Yet of the three sensational, violent and apparently unconnected incidents which have occurred since your arrival, you have been somehow involved in each. Please forgive me for asking, but does such carnage follow in your wake as you perambulate the streets of London?"

"Would that there was some way to determine what happened in the Place de la Concorde this afternoon. Based upon the eyewitness accounts, it seems likely that the altercation was between the occupants of the vehicle and the three men on the sidewalk. But why did the occupants of the vehicle, after shooting one of the men on the sidewalk abandon the vehicle rather than merely driving off leaving the other two men on the sidewalk to cope with their mortally wounded companion as best they could? Abandoning the vehicle makes no sense, especially if the original occupants were the baron's men."

During Loiseaux's soliloquy Holmes sat, elbows on the table, his chin resting on long, steepled fingers. After a long silence, he lighted a fresh cigarette and replied, "A worthy question, my dear Inspector. But if one applies the philosophical principle known as 'Occam's Razor', abandonment of the vehicle makes perfect sense. It is not unreasonable to assume that an automobile as distinctive as the baron's is recognizable by a great many people as belonging to him. It is entirely possible that the occupants of the automobile were dispatched to a rendezvous with the men on the sidewalk, either for the express purpose of murdering one of them, or for some other equally craven purpose that went awry and resulted in gun-play. The occupants of the vehicle, whoever they were, had the presence of mind to allow for the possibility that the vehicle might be recognized and therefore their best course was to abandon it and to report it as stolen."

Loiseaux clasped and unclasped his hands in frustration. "If your hypothesis is correct. *M'sieur* Holmes, then it clearly points the finger of guilt of the chauffeur's murder directly at the baron. I hope Baron Ollstreder will not find my humble vehicle too uncomfortable during the ride from the Rue Georges Bizet to the Ministry of Justice where he can plan to spend at least the next several days answering questions about these matters."

"You may question him from now until you receive your gold retirement watch. But I rather doubt, Inspector, that you will get him to admit to anything."

"I concede that to be possibility, *M'sieur* Holmes. But what other choice do I have?"

"What you do, Inspector, is of course entirely up to you. But, were I conducting the investigation, I would do nothing, at least with respect to Baron Ollstreder. You've no proof that the chauffeur was in fact murdered, or that the automobile was not stolen as the baron claims. Perhaps an autopsy will yield a cause of death. Perhaps *M'sieur* Bertillon's 'wondrous system' will, as you put it, this time 'actually produce some useful information' as to the identity of the fellow found in the automobile. These things always take time, and leaving the baron alone may be the best way to deal with him, at least for the time being."

Loiseaux sighed, "Perhaps you're right *M'sieur* Holmes. I am called upon to attend court at the Palais de Justice most of the day tomorrow anyway. The Marquis de Dion's lawyers have made application for bail, and I am directed to oppose it. The examining magistrate..." Loiseaux paused, a small smile briefly crossing his face. "You don't suppose, *M'sieurs,* that there is a connection between what happened this afternoon in the Place de la Concorde and the *Affaire* at Auteuil? Perhaps some bizarre plot to effect the escape of de Dion and that *dupe* Christiani?"

"Most provocative, Inspector." Holmes returned the Inspector's smile. "There is, after-all, the circumstance that an automobile was involved in both incidents."

"You English refer to it as 'killing two birds with one stone', do you not?"

"Just so, *Mon Cher Inspecteur,* just so."

After Loiseaux took his leave, Holmes and Watson lingered over coffee and cigars. Watson leaned back in his chair. "It's interesting, Holmes, the contrast between this fellow Loiseaux and the chronic bumbler Lestrade. On his best day, Lestrade would never have taken your hint, but would have gone rushing off to arrest Ollstreder without the slightest chance, even under the French judicial system, of making the charges stand. And I shrink from the contemplation of what that move would have done to our own endeavours. The automobile connexion will undoubtedly give him added leverage in opposing bail for de Dion and Christiani, while at the same time Baron Ollstreder will be convinced that he has succeeded in deflecting suspicion from himself. Moreover, even if the legalities are not quite above question, I don't see it as anything that would compromise a prosecution should one be warranted by further investigation.

"But speaking of our own endeavours, I must admit that as wildly improbable as it sounded back in London, your plan has thus far succeeded. But what next? Surely you do not plan to rely on Esterhazy. If I ever have the opportunity to publish an account of this matter, I doubt that there are adjectives in the English language up to the task of describing his character, or perhaps more properly, lack of character."

"While I have in the past accused you of sensationalizing some of the problems which have commanded our exertions over the years, I must admit on the whole to a certain satisfaction in and admiration for the forthright, lucid manner in which you have reported them. And it cannot be doubted that the reading public share my opinions. So were our roles reversed, I should think several times over before I would risk my reputation by publishing an account of this business. You admit that words are wholly inadequate to describe Esterhazy; so how would you describe Ollstreder or 'Sebastian Melmoth'? I'm afraid that if you can manage to overcome those problems, absolutely no one is going to believe that this fantastic tale is anything other than the product of your own imagination.

"But be that as it may, you are correct in assuming that I think it unwise to rely on Major Esterhazy."

"Then you propose to ignore his plan and abandon him?"

"Certainly not abandon him; if for no other reason than his potential utility to '*M*' and his little cadre. But as for his plan, there may be a better way. I think it may be time for us to begin tracking down the baron's peripatetic bird."

CHAPTER THIRTY-FIVE

*"Obviously recent events have placed your
faculties under too great a strain."*

"*O*llstreder, despite his grief and his exhaustion from last night's exertions, will see us at seven o'clock this evening." Holmes stifled a yawn with the back of his hand, and handed Watson the telegram brought to Holmes's room by a bellman.

"Good," Watson stood and flexed the muscles in his back and shoulders, "that will give us a bit of time to freshen-up and perhaps get a few hours' sleep. Like the baron, last night's, and may I add yesterday's, exertions have quite taken their toll. My shoulder and knee are much more the worse for wear than I thought. I've not felt this sore since the last time I was in the middle of a scrum-line. Add to that staying up all night going through Ollstreder's records, looking for what I haven't a clew, and I too am quite exhausted."

"Well, old fellow, if you'd prefer to stay here and rest..."

"No, no. I'm as up to it as you are. But even you must concede that a decent night's sleep would have been preferable to reading, or in my case mostly listening to you chortle over page after page of enquiry agents' reports and lawyers' briefs. Probably most all of it was made up in the first place just to justify the fees. And after all that, what have we learned?"

"I should say a good deal. First, in all likelihood the statue did at one time exist. Indeed, there are several good descriptions of the statue. Second, and of paramount importance, the baron is convinced of its existence. From all indicia, it appears that he is genuinely obsessed with finding it. Whether that obsession is the product of a sense of filial duty as he would have us believe, or stems from some overwhelming urge to acquire something no one else may possess, I am not yet prepared to say."

"But did you really expect to find some clew in that repetitious mass of reports and lawyer-jargon?"

"That would have been, I admit, like finding a four-leaf clover growing in Trafalgar Square. And those lawyers' briefs, I must say…" He paused leaving the thought to be completed as Watson saw fit. Holmes rubbed his temples with the tips of his fingers. "Why must they use two or three words when one— English, French or even Latin—would do quite as well? However, all I wanted to do and what I hope we have accomplished, is to learn enough about the statue's putative provenance to sound convincing when I tell the baron that we've located his precious bird and are prepared to deliver it under the 'right' circumstances."

Watson leaned back in his chair and peered at Holmes over the tops of his spectacles. "As your physician and friend, Holmes, I strongly suggest, no 'prescribe' would be a better word, that you lie down and get a few hours rest. Obviously recent events have placed your faculties under too great a strain. If you are correct in your conclusion that the baron is indeed obsessed with obtaining the statue, I cannot imagine that he will be able to appreciate your rather puckish sense of humor when you inform him that you are after all unable to produce it as promised."

"I would gladly take your advice, but I'm afraid we've much to do. Especially if we're going to convince the baron that we can indeed produce the object of his quest.

"However, an hour to freshen-up does sound like a good idea." Holmes stood and stretched. "A pot of coffee and a brioche or two would do wonders toward restoring mind and body. I wonder why Ritz didn't think to put telephones in the rooms. Now that he's offering in-room food service, it would be so much easier and efficient to be able to call down one's order rather than to have to push the electronic switch to summon a bellman, give him your order, wait for him to go back down, place the order with the kitchen and then bring it back up to the room."

Watson rose and picked up his suit jacket. "Capital idea, Holmes, I'm quite sure. If and when we successfully conclude our business with Baron Ollstreder, I suggest that you press the notion upon Ritz straight-away. Better yet, why don't you open a hotel of your own. Given your evident aptitude for it, inn keeping would be more likely to suit you in your retirement than becoming an apiarist as you profess to want to do. By the way, please do not order anything for me. I shall be in my room. If you will but knock on my door when you are ready to leave, I shall join you immediately."

CHAPTER THIRTY-SIX

"That is my offer,
and I think you shall
find it more than a fair bargain."

"*W*e were most distressed to learn of the chauffeur's death," Holmes spoke to the parlour maid as he and Watson handed her their hats and sticks.

The servant-girl, her eyes red-rimmed, curtsied, "*Merci, M'sieurs, merci.* We all appreciate the efforts which you made to save his life. Please follow me. Baron Ollstreder is expecting you." As she bowed them into the now-familiar room her eyes welled up again with tears. She managed an *"Excusez moi, M'sieurs"* before she ran off down the hallway sobbing audibly.

"Ah, my dear Baron," Holmes paused and regarded the freshly-lighted Romeo *y* Julietta which he held between his thumb and forefinger, "I am tempted to say that I place myself in your service for no compensation beyond access to your cigar humidor."

"I assure you, *Herr* Holmes, that my entire supply is at your disposal if you have even the slightest glimmer of hope that I may acquire…or I mean recover the statue. May I inquire as to the contents of the package?" He gestured toward a cardboard carton that Watson had placed on the coffee table.

"In due course, Baron, in due course," Holmes responded as he enjoyed watching the baron eye the package like a child eager to open a longed-for gift on Boxing Day. "First, is there any news regarding the theft of your automobile or the death of your chauffeur?"

"*Ach, Mein Herren. Das ist ein verdamter schande. Der poleizi…* first my property is stolen. Then it is used in the commission of some terrible crime. Then it is found, and now I am advised that the *Sureté* is holding it for an indefinite time as evidence in the case. And when I ask them, 'what case?' they shrug their shoulders and tell me that they will keep me informed. I'm almost tempted to bring a legal action to get it back." The baron paused to wipe his perspiring forehead. "But then I think to myself, even if I could find a competent *advocat,* one whose fees would not exceed the value of the automobile, by the time such a proceeding was concluded, the vehicle would probably be a rusted-out hulk, were I to live long enough to see the matter through. *Vey ist mir, Mein Herren, Vey ist mir.* But please, I beg you, no more of this depressing subject. And by the way, please feel free to dispense with my title. I am simply 'Ollstreder' and I in turn shall take the liberty of addressing you as 'Holmes' and 'Watson.' After all, we are now good friends."

"Indeed, Bar...um, Ollstreder, so we are. And I hope that we shall remain so after you've heard and seen the results of our enquiries. Watson, if you would be so good as to hand our friend the package, I'm sure that he'll want to open it himself."

Watson slid the cardboard box across the coffee table. Ollstreder, his hands shaking with anticipation un-did the twine wrapping and clawed open the box. Quickly he threw aside the crumpled newspaper pages lining the inside and extracted the contents. Slowly, reverently, he held up a black statue, the unmistakable likeness of a falcon. It was about fourteen inches in height, including the attached base that was about four inches square. *"Gott in Himmel,* gentlemen, you've done it! At long last the falcon is mine."

He set the statue down, fished around in the pocket of his waistcoat and extracted a small silver penknife. He opened the knife and scraped the blade along the side of the bird's beak revealing the white of the plaster of Paris which under-lay the heavy coat of black paint. He did the same thing along the tail and then on both wings. Angrily now, he continued a frenzied scraping until the statue showed nearly as much white as black. Finally, the blade of the penknife broke and he slumped against the back of the sofa, his chest heaving from the exertion and his mouth a hideous rictus. *"Vas iss los, Herr* Holmes? Is this some cruel practical joke which you Englishers play on me? If so, I must tell you that I am greatly offended."

Motioning to Watson, Holmes stood as though to leave. "Kindly spare us further display of your wounded dignity, Baron Ollstreder. It is we who should be offended. Indeed who in all these years has as much as produced what even you concede is an exact replica of the falcon? And is it not obvious that such an imposter could have been produced only from a mold made from the original?"

"*Bitte, bitte, Mein guten freunden.* Please excuse my bad manners." The baron regained his composure and gestured for Holmes and Watson to resume their seats. *"Setzen Sie sich.* It was most foolish of me to think that you would bring the genuine article with you." He rubbed his hands together vigorously. "First we must *handel* over your *fee, ja?* But tell me, how did you locate the statue so quickly? *Gott in Himmel!* This comes as such a shock." Ollstreder slumped against the back of the sofa and mopped his glistening brow. *"Herr Doktor* Watson, *bitte,* would you be so kind as to ring for the servant. I feel an overwhelming need for a cognac to restore my equilibrium."

"Why, er...yes, of course." Watson rose and tugged vigorously on the bell-pull next to the mantle-piece. In a few moments the servant Heinrich appeared, and shortly thereafter returned with a venerable "Napoleon" along with snifters and a small alcohol lamp for warming the glasses.

"To your health, *Mein gutenfreunden. "* The baron lifted his glass in the direction of his guests and then took an unseemly swallow. "Now, *bitte,* I must know all the details of this most remarkable feat."

"According to the *dossier* which you provided to us," Holmes paused to take another satisfying puff of his cigar, "the last credible Paris sighting of the statue in its disguised form was in a shop in the Passage des Panoramas in... what was it Watson, November ninety-seven?"

"Er... yes, yes it was, Holmes. November ninety-seven. Indubitably."

"Ja? Und then..."

"Then, from the public records we were able to locate the landlord of the shop who was able to provide us with the name of his tenant, the owner of the shop at the time. He is now deceased, but his daughter, who worked with him in the shop, remembered the statue and was able to produce the shop ledger in which the sale was recorded. She recalled that the buyer particularly wanted a receipt showing the purchase price in order to support the declaration on the customs form."

"You mean that the statue is no longer in France? How did you locate the owner?"

"It was not too difficult. The shop-keeper's daughter was also able to say that the purchaser was dressed as an English gentleman and spoke with a British accent, although his complexion and demeanor did not appear to her to be typical of the English upper class. Indeed, because her father had concluded that his customer was someone of wealth, he asked three times the price that he would have asked from someone of less obviously advantaged circumstances. And the purchaser paid his asking price without the slightest haggling. Your last enquiry agent would, through the exercise of even the most minimal diligence, have discovered at least as much as I have related so far."

"But evidently you have been able to trace the current owner, *ja Herr* Holmes? How so? Who has the statue now? Is it Archos, the Athenian? What is his price?"

"Patience, Ollstreder, patience," Watson interjected, "remember your delicate physical state."

"We indeed have located the current owner of the statue, who for our purposes we need identify only as the scion of a wealthy English family whose branches are equally established in several countries on the Continent."

"*Ja,* who can this be? Lyndhurst? Pemberton? *Nein,* they have no family connections on the Continent. *Ach!* I know." Ollstreder favored his guests with a hideous smile, "de la Noye. Yes, that's who it is, de la Noye."

"Does it matter to you who owns the object if he is willing to part with it?" Watson asked.

Ollstreder was silent for a moment. Then he picked up his snifter, inhaled the bouquet and raised it in a perfunctory toast-like gesture. "*Ach,* once again I lose sight of the fact that we are in a negotiation. You need not fear, *Mein Herren,* that I will seek to go around you and jew you out of your fee. I mean we are, after all, men of affairs and as such men of honor. Is that not so?"

Holmes who had also been enjoying his cognac pointedly put down the glass. "We do not wish, Baron Ollstreder, to make an issue of your cultural prejudices. But I can assure you that the owner of the subject of our discussion would take strong exception to your choice of verbs."

The baron looked genuinely puzzled. "I'm afraid that sometimes *Herr* Holmes the subtleties of the English language elude me. I don't think I... Oh! *Herrgott!* You are telling me that the owner *ist ein Jude?"*

"Just so, Baron Ollstreder, and a devout one at that," Holmes replied.

"And he knows you act for me?"

"Actually not..." Holmes started to respond.

"Ach, sehr gut. I assume you will continue to act with discretion in this regard?"

"You may *always* assume, Baron Ollstreder, that Watson and I will act with suitable discretion in *all* matters. But that is entirely beside the point."

"Which is?"

"That Watson and I are *not* acting for you in this matter."

"But you said..."

"If you will recall, *Herr* Baron, we said we would review your *dossier,* and if we were of a mind to look into the matter further, we might make some preliminary enquiries. But we deliberately refrained from accepting an engagement to act on your behalf and made no commitment beyond what I have just reiterated. As it happens, our preliminary enquiries were more productive than could have been anticipated from your anguished narrative."

"Then who..."

"In point of fact, Watson and I are *acting,* if that be the correct term, on behalf of neither you nor the claimed-owner of the statue, but on behalf of yet another party who insists upon anonymity."

The baron shifted his bulk and re-lighted his cigar. As he contemplated the half-burned cigar he picked a small piece of tobacco from his front teeth and placed it in the ashtray. "A year ago, *Mein Herren,* it would have been unthinkable for me to re-light my cigar; if it went out before I was through smoking, I would merely light a fresh one. Now, just like the falcon statue, decent cigars are becoming more and more scarce and nearly as dear. So tell me your price, *Herr* Holmes. How much must I pay to be rid of the burden of this statue?"

"Before responding to your question, I must tell you that acquiring the statue may relieve you of the burden of searching for it, but owning it will impose even greater burdens."

"How so, *Herr* Holmes?"

"Evidently our enquiries concerning the statue have piqued the interest of others. I suspect that someone with whom we spoke in the course of our investigation is in the pay of some rival of yours who will evidently stick at nothing to obtain the object. Whoever this person may be, we think that he is responsible for the theft of your automobile. If you have read this morning's newspaper accounts of the affair in the Place de la Concorde yesterday afternoon, you have undoubtedly been struck by the fact that the descriptions of two of the men on the sidewalk bear a striking resemblance to Watson and myself. It is our belief that we were the target of what was evidently a plot to kidnap us and force us to tell what we had learnt in the course of our investigation. Indeed, because we suspected that something was afoot, Watson set himself up as a stalking horse conspicuously perambulating about the Louve, while I, in that some-what outlandish but apparently effective costume, played the role of the hunter.

"The mastermind behind the attempt either knew that we had been in contact with you, or made that assumption based upon your by now notorious efforts to find the statue coupled with our arrival in Paris ostensibly 'on-holiday' and our 'serendipitous' encounter at Maxim's restaurant. And in all likelihood, your vehicle was stolen for use in the crime in order to cast suspicion on you with all the inconvenience at the hands of the police that such suspicion would entail. By keeping you occupied in this manner, he evidently thought he would at least buy enough time to act on whatever information he was able to extract from us. If you ended up being charged with our disappearance, it would make his besting you all the more poignant."

"*Gott in Himmel!* This is monstrous beyond belief. And who was the third man, the one on the sidewalk who was killed? That Inspector.. .Inspector..."

"Inspector Loiseaux," Watson supplied.

"Ah yes, *danke Herr Doktor* Watson. Inspector Loiseaux. He was not terribly forth coming when interviewed by the press. Have they identified the third man? Obviously Loiseaux does not suspect that the two of you were the intended victims and it was you who drove the machine away."

"To our knowledge, not yet. However, Inspector Loiseaux has the utmost confidence that *M'sieur* Bertillon, through his *bertillonage* system will soon at least solve the mystery of the identity of the dead man, assuming of course that his measurements are a matter of record."

"If I may be permitted a deduction of my own, *Herr* Holmes, am I correct in thinking that your accompanying the Inspector here last night was something more than detached professional curiosity?"

"That is certainly true, Baron Ollstreder. We had to determine for ourselves that it was not you who was the instigator of the plot as a ruthless means of learning what we knew about the statue without having to deal with our compensation."

"Since the Inspector does not as yet share your views regarding yesterday's incident and the involvement of my automobile, what does he think?"

"As we speak," Holmes replied, "the good Inspector is in court opposing bail for the Marquis de Dion and Baron Christiani in connexion with the attempt on the life of President Loubet at Auteuil. Loiseaux is of the mind, so we are made to understand, that your automobile was to be used in some dare-devil plot to break the two out of jail and carry them into hiding."

"For that, at least, we can be thankful. This Inspector Loiseaux appears to be as much an incompetent as that English inspector whose misadventures you have so hilariously chronicled from time to time, *Doktor* Watson. If there's a lesson to be drawn from yesterday's business, *Herr* Holmes, it is that whoever possesses the statue is in danger from this interloper. Do you have any idea as to his identity? I am prepared to take the necessary precautions, but it would certainly be helpful to know my adversary. He may have some vulnerability that can be exploited to neutralize if not eliminate him entirely."

"You understand me rightly, *Herr* Baron. I doubt that the statue is worth your life, but that is for you to decide. As you can see from yesterday's events, this person will stick at nothing to have his way. Watson and I count ourselves lucky to be alive."

"Sorry we can't say the same for the chauffeur and that other chap," Watson muttered.

"What's that *Herr Doktor?* I didn't quite understand what you said.

"Oh nothing, Baron. Just a little sidebar. I quite agree with Holmes. We're lucky to be alive, if slightly the worse for wear."

"You mentioned several individuals whom you thought might be the current owner of the statue. Can you think of anyone who might want it that badly and who would have the resources and cunning to attempt such as feat as that which occurred yesterday?"

Ollstreder stroked his chin. I don't know, *Herr* Holmes. If de la Noye is not the owner, then perhaps it could be him. Or it could be the American, Gould. Or it could be the Armenian, Boyajannian, or Archos the Athenian." Those are a few that come most readily to mind. If any of them is in Paris, that would make him the most likely candidate. I will check with my sources. If any of them is here, he would be at the Ritz, the Crillon or perhaps the Georges Cinq."

"A most interesting list, *Herr* Baron, most interesting. Especially Boyajannian. The last we'd heard, he was in a Turkish prison."

"Ach, you should develop better sources *Herr* Holmes. He bribed his way out six months ago. The Grand Vizier, I am told, has been in an apoplectic rage ever since, probably because his share of the bribe was not sufficiently large." Ollstreder laughed his barking little laugh as he contemplated in his mind's eye Suliman, Pasha, in a paroxysm of anger over being done out of his more than fair share of the bribe-money.

"We had in mind another name, *Herr* Baron. A Frenchman, we believe. While the name is new to us, perhaps you've heard of him." Holmes turned toward Watson, "what was that name, Watson?"

"Do you mean that 'Vill'.. .something?"

"Yes, yes that's it. 'P. Villeneuf' Have you heard of him, Baron? Don't know what the 'P' stands for, probably 'Pierre' or some such. May I?" Holmes reached into the humidor and took out another cigar.

For a long while, Ollstreder said nothing, his porcine eyes simply staring first at Holmes, then Watson and then back again. A deep red almost purple flush began to spread from his collar up the great mass of his neck, then to the top of his head where the few remaining strands of hair appeared to stand on end. Gripping the edge of the sofa cushion to keep his hands from shaking, he finally leaned forward and spoke in a low voice. *"Ach, ja, Mein Herren.* I have heard rumors of this mysterious Frenchman, but I do not know him. *Und ja,* if the rumors are based upon even the smallest kernel of truth, he could well be capable of sponsoring yesterday's occurrence. But until now, I was unaware that he had any interest in the statue. The others, the names that I mentioned, have all been after the statue for years just as I have. So he must be a new player in the game. Now that I know this, I assure you that proper precautions will be taken. However, until such precautions are in place our business must remain absolutely secret."

"In that regard, Baron Ollstreder, you may rest assured. Both the owner of the statue and the party for whom we act, demand exactly the same condition. If this transaction were ever to be disclosed the consequences could be ruinous for all concerned. If I may, I should go so far as to suggest that you allow Watson and me to turn the object over to the *Johanniterorden* on your behalf while you remain an anonymous benefactor."

"A most worthy suggestion, *Herr* Holmes. And one to which I shall give most earnest consideration, especially since it seems not to take cognizance of the superficially conflicting claim of the British Branch of the Order which you took such pains to point out in our first conversation. But first I must obtain the statue, is that not so? And in order to do that I must know the seller's terms beyond the demand for confidentiality."

"Very well, Baron, you shall be pleased to know that the object of your long quest will cost you not a single mark, not a single pfennig."

Ollstreder's eyes narrowed until they were mere slits above his flattened, pockmarked nose. *"Ja, Herr* Holmes, how can this be? In my long experience as a trader I have learned that everything has its price and nothing is exchanged for free."

"For the most part I agree with your philosophy, and in your *demi-monde*, I agree with it totally. That's why I was careful to say only that the statue will cost you nothing in terms of money or money's worth.

"The current 'owner', if that is the correct term, acquired the statue for the purpose of trading it to the Caliph of Jerusalem in exchange for a few hundred hectares of land which were to be used to establish a communal refuge for Jews who are the victims of persecution in other countries. Understandably, and fortunately for our particular enterprise, the negotiations have been stalled with little hope that they will ever come to fruition. Because of this we have been able to persuade this person to part with the statue in exchange for what is hoped will provide a respite from the persecution of his people: a respite of sufficient duration to permit the mobilization of international sentiment in favor of establishing an even larger refuge in the territory of what was the Jews' ancient homeland."

"A noble objective, I'm sure, *Herr* Holmes, but what has it to do with me? I command no armies; I have no voice in the international councils of government. I am a mere trader in goods, and as you have discerned, I harbour no sympathies either for these people or for their cause."

"We would not dispute what you say, but what you say is not, do forgive me, *Herr* Baron, the entire truth. The whole truth is that you do in fact wield considerable influence in the councils of your own government." Holmes held up his hands palms out facing toward Ollstreder. "Please, *Herr* Baron, do not interrupt. If I may borrow a passage from our Shakespeare, although I'm sure Goethe has said something similar, 'methinks thou protesteth too much'. While our information resources may have overlooked the redoubtable Armenian's latest caper among the sons of the Prophet, I'm confident that the consideration for the statue is well within your capacity to pay."

"I would admit, I suppose, that one or two of his Imperial Highness's ministers do not return my letters unopened. But as for influence, I doubt it *Herr* Holmes. What's more, I'm certain that it is beyond my power to influence the German Government to act contrary to its own best interests."

"You certainly don't..." Watson started to respond, but Holmes cut him off

"That is, *we* certainly don't expect you to compromise your position by importuning something that is not possible, *Herr* Baron. However, it seems to us that what our party-in-interest seeks with the concurrence of the statue's owner is not inimical to the interests of your government."

"You seem so sure of yourself, *Herr* Holmes. So tell me then, what is it that you would have me do in order to pay for the statue?"

"Very well, Baron. You are, of course, well familiar with the Dreyfus Case..."

"Nein, nein, Gott in Himmel! Nein! Bitte, Herr Holmes, anything but that." Ollstreder held his face in his hands and began moaning loudly, his head lolling from side to side. "Not that, *Herr* Holmes, anything but that. That most accursed member of that accursed tribe. Oh *vey ist mir, vey ist mir."*

"I'm afraid, Baron Ollstreder, your involvement in the Dreyfus Case is the price for the statue. And I assure you that it is non-negotiable. Come, Watson, it appears that the baron has suddenly lost his enthusiasm for collecting unique *objets d' art*. We shall be at the Ritz for at least another day or at most two should you change your mind. Good evening, *Herr* Baron. Thank you for the excellent cigars and stimulating conversation. Oh yes," Holmes gestured toward the mutilated statue, "Do keep the replica as a memento of our meeting. You really should consider having it re-painted. Actually, it is quite handsome, even if it is only plaster of Paris. We'll send your *dossier* 'round in the morning by messenger."

"Ach", the baron sighed wearily. *"Nein, nein, Mein Herren.* Do not go. *Setzen Sie Sich.* You have won, *Herr* Holmes. I shall do whatever it is that you ask. Even if it means that I must become—what do they call themselves? 'Dreyfusards'?"

Holmes and Watson returned to the sofa. "Ah so, Watson, it seems that in our new friend's world not only everything has its price, but every man as well." Turning to the baron, he continued, "I do not think, *Herr* Baron, that you will be required to go quite so far.

"All you need do is persuade His Imperial Highness, Kaiser Wilhelm, to send a letter in his own hand disavowing Dreyfus as a German agent. Since the case against him is now so thoroughly

284

discredited, it is entirely likely that the military tribunal will finally be convinced of his innocence. In the worst case, assuming no new and damning evidence is presented against him and the court-martial finds him guilty yet again, the letter will provide ample basis for a presidential pardon."

The baron looked stunned. "I'm afraid, *Mein Herren,* that what you ask is quite beyond my modest means. Indeed, I fear that it is beyond the means of anyone, in or out of government. Kaiser Wilhelm—may his dynasty reign for a thousand years—so I am made to understand is quite enjoying the spectacle the French are making of themselves. It takes no brilliant statesman to discern that the 'Dreyfus Affair' has caused a great schism between the military and the church on the one hand, and the civilian authority, along with a large segment of the population, on the other. And, apart from its entertainment value, I would say that it suits his Imperial Highness's strategic purposes to have France in a state of turmoil at the present time. It would only be sheer supposition on my part, but it is not unlikely that he is, even as we speak, planning some—shall we say 'initiative'—that is best executed while France is distracted by its own domestic problems.

"But if what you're after is freedom for Captain Dreyfus, there may perhaps be another way."

"Namely?" both Holmes and Watson asked in unison.

"Suppose that I could provide you with a substitute for the hapless Captain together with incontrovertible proof of his culpability?" Ollstreder smiled and selected a fresh cigar. "Think of it, *Mein Herren,* what could serve your purpose better? Better even than a letter such as you have described; a letter whose authorship could never be publicly acknowledged, and the authenticity of which would therefore remain in doubt."

"Well, I don't know...what do you think Watson?"

"I say Holmes, Baron Ollstreder does make a valid point. If the authenticity of the letter cannot be established beyond cavil, it is not likely to accomplish its intended purpose. I suppose that we should hear more of what the baron has to say, and at least not dismiss his proposal out of hand."

"I quite agree, Watson. Now, Baron..."

"Nein, Herr Holmes. I will provide you with no more detail at this time. That is my offer, and I think you will find it more than a fair bargain."

"I'm afraid, Baron, that Watson's and my sentiments carry little if any weight. It is for others to determine. But I will make you this proposal in return: we were empowered to deliver the statue upon receipt of the letter, regardless of its efficacy. However, since the letter is no longer the basis of the bargain, if you are able to deliver the *true* traitor along with proof of his crime beyond a reasonable doubt and as a result Captain Dreyfus is freed, then the statue shall be delivered to you at that time. But if your candidate is not elected, so to speak, then the statue will be put up for auction on sealed bids and you will be given an equal opportunity to bid. If you are the successful bidder, then the statue shall be yours by the fairest and most equitable of means."

Ollstreder puffed his cigar thoughtfully. "Very well, *Herr* Holmes. I can see no flaw in your proposal, and I accept. I shall contact you within a day or two at most, and I shall perform my end of the bargain at that time. You know, *Herr* Holmes, should you ever contemplate giving up the trade of 'consulting detective' you ought to give serious consideration to taking up the occupation of trader in goods."

CHAPTER THIRTY-SEVEN

"...I had a nasty vision of our spending to-night, and the foreseeable future in that dank jail cell you mentioned..."

"I must say, Holmes, your idea of pitting Ollstreder against his partner Villeneuf is an absolute master-stroke. And making a model of the statue, as clever a ploy as I've seen. Besides your own desire to become an apiarist, my suggestion that you open a hotel and Ollstreder's suggestion that you become a merchant, perhaps you should also consider becoming a sculptor. But I'm constrained to ask: what are you going to do if the baron actually makes good on his end of the bargain?"

"A fair question. But if things go as I anticipate, the baron will be rather like a rat in a trap; he will be interested only in getting out of the trap, and will quite have forgotten about the cheese."

"Whom do you think he will nominate as Dreyfus's replacement? Esterhazy?"

"Can you think of a more fitting candidate?"

"No, but as you have other uses in mind for the major, I'm only wondering how it will be possible for him to serve in both capacities? Moreover, as I observed at our last meeting with the major, it is extremely unlikely that anyone will give the slightest credence to his confession.

"And speaking of the major, I wonder how Miss Pippen has faired in her mission? If she's not been successful in persuading your brother, or if he in turn has been unsuccessful in raising the necessary capital with which to endow the major's tenure as lecturer-in-residence, how are we going to get him out of the country? On the other hand, if she and Mycroft have succeeded so that we're in a position to get him out of the country, and I presume the beguiling Irmgaard as well, then how in the devil are we going to get hold of whatever it is that Ollstreder intends to place in Esterhazy's hands so that we can use it to help clear Dreyfus? After all, President Loubet did make it absolutely clear that if the court-martial found against Dreyfus a second time he would not issue a presidential pardon absent a letter from the Kaiser absolving Dreyfus of any culpability.

"I say, Holmes, there are too many loose ends. Who is this P. Villeneuf fellow any way? And what about Lambert's killer or killers? We know that the baron was at the very least a conspirator. Do you plan to let Loiseaux continue in his benighted state? Is there a German spy high up in the French General Staff? Why did the baron try to kidnap me and then murder his henchman to prevent his talking?"

As their cab pulled to a stop in front of the Ritz's awning, Holmes lay his hand on Watson's arm. "Steady on, Watson. All will be answered in due course. Hopefully Miss Pippen has returned in our absence. If the boat-train was running on schedule she should have arrived in the early evening. I will enquire at the registration desk, and perhaps then begin to answer at least some of your questions."

"What further instructions did you leave for her, if I may ask?"

They passed through the front door held open for them by the *chasseur.* Holmes smiled somewhat malevolently. "Why none, of course. Since there are no upcoming elections to occupy her attentions as in the case of young Mr. Churchill, can you think of a better way to get her out of our hair and to a place of relative safety? Why don't you go ahead to the dining room, and I'll join you in a moment just as soon as I see what, if anything, she's left for us."

Watson managed to work his way 'round *"Avez-vous une table pour deux?"* and even an *"apportez-moi un* 'martini' cocktail" and was contemplating the menu when Holmes made his way across the room with Inspector Loiseaux obediently heeling like a particularly affectionate terrier.

"Look who's here, Watson. Inspector Loiseaux's been waiting for us since early this evening. And since we've caused him to miss his dinner, I've invited him to join us."

"Watson rose and grasped the Inspector's hand. "Why yes, Inspector. Delighted you are able to join us. Couldn't bear for a dedicated police officer to go hungry, especially on account of having to wait for me."

Holmes gestured to the maitre d' for another place setting, and the three men took their seats. After additional aperitifs were ordered, Holmes turned to the Inspector, "You've quite the full plate of cases, Inspector: the murder of Lambert; the attack on President Loubet; the theft of Baron Ollstreder's motorcar, and the bizarre incident in the Place de la Concorde; the murder of the chauffeur Andre..."

"Not to mention two mysterious English-looking gentlemen whose descriptions more-or-less match yourselves," Loiseaux looked at Holmes and Watson and raised his glass in a somewhat world-weary, if not cynical toast. "Not to mention a Valkyrie-like nurse who must slay her own warriors in order to keep busy, and a barge captain with no apparent ties to anyone else."

"A barge captain?" Holmes and Watson asked simultaneously.

"Yes, *M'sieurs.* That is one of the things I came to discuss with you. *M'sieur* Bertillon, whose office has responded with uncharacteristic alacrity, has identified—with absolute confidence may I add—the man who was mortally wounded on the sidewalk and whose body was later found in the baron's automobile. His name is 'Antoine Richard' and his occupation is...was...river barge captain. In his lifetime his name was not unknown to us but his police dossier does not contain any convictions."

"Watson chewed a moment on his martini olive and asked, "In what connexion was his name known to you?"

"Several times he was interrogated in connection with trafficking in stolen goods, and in at least one case of kidnapping for ransom. But as I say, not enough evidence could be developed against the man to warrant even bringing him to trial, much less securing a conviction."

Watson urged Loiseaux to continue," What do you make of his involvement in the...the Concorde business? Do you think it was some sort of kidnapping plot gone awry?"

"I'm afraid, *Docteur* Watson, it's too early to say. But to be frank, with two of the participants dead and two others who appear and disappear like creatures from another world, I am unable to say when the case will break."

"And what of the pharmacist Lambert?"

"That was the other matter I came to discuss with you, *M'sieur* Holmes. When last we spoke of that subject you inquired about the written report of the uniformed officer who was first on the scene and who forced open the locked front door. I mentioned to you my own interest in that particular document, and reported that I had been unable to locate it either in its proper place in the case file, or for that matter anywhere else. I suggested, based on past experience, that the report, owing shall we say to 'bureaucratic inefficiencies', had probably been mis-filed and would turn up momentarily. However, it appears that my optimism was misplaced."

"Indeed, Inspector." Holmes signaled for another round of cocktails. "How so?"

"It appears, *M'sieurs,* that there never was such a report, nor shall there ever be one. I have interrogated every uniformed officer on duty that night in the Second, Eighth and Ninth Arrondissments and none admits to being the first on the scene nor to knowing who was. Evidently, whoever this officer was, his capacity for seizing the initiative is exceeded only by his aversion either to recognition for his improvisation or to doing the required paperwork. Another possibility is that he was involved in the commission of the crime, but I discount that hypothesis because the of the advanced state of post-mortem lividity indicating that Lambert had to have been dead for some time before the door was forced and the first group of officers arrived."

"There is perhaps yet another paradigm, my dear Inspector, that might explain this seemingly inexplicable set of circumstances." Holmes finished his drink and picked up one of the menus which the waiter had brought along with the second round of drinks.

"But let us first enjoy whatever Escoffier has conjured up in his kitchen this evening. After we have dined, I will place before you my own view of the matter."

Despite his agitated state, the Inspector did ample justice to his Supreme de volaille a la Provencale which earned him an introduction to Escoffier who promised to name the dish in his honor. With the plates cleared, coffee and cognac poured and cigars lighted, Holmes leaned forward and lowered his voice. "As promised, Inspector, I will now lay before you what is admittedly only a theory—a theory for which I have no conclusive proofs. Indeed, it may be that it never can be proved."

Loiseaux likewise leaned forward, his voice scarcely more than a whisper. "Anything you may suggest *M'sieur* Holmes that would provide a new direction for the investigation is most welcome, even if it proves to lead to yet another blind alley. Please proceed."

"Is it possible, Inspector, that one who is not a member of the force can obtain an authentic gendarme's uniform?"

The Inspector was in the process of taking a satisfying drag on his cigar as Holmes spoke. He drew a sharp breath and began choking on the cigar smoke so violently that Watson had to pound him on the back to restore his breathing to normalcy. After a long sip of brandy he regained his composure. "You mean, *M'sieur* Holmes, that the man who forced the door was not a *flic?*"

"Probably not, Inspector."

"Then why would anyone pretend to be an officer of the law in order to break into a shop under the very noses, not to mention with the assistance, of several other genuine if incompetent officers?"

"Firstly, Inspector, you should re-examine your premise that the door was necessarily forced."

"But I saw with my own eyes that the key was fitted in the lock on the inside, and the door jamb was heavily damaged as though it had been kicked open. Moreover, each of the officers who admitted being among the first to arrive said that he clearly observed the door frame being kicked several times to force it open."

"And what they observed did in fact occur. However, my point is that kicking the door open was entirely unnecessary. It is my opinion that the door was not in fact locked and could have been opened from the outside in quite the ordinary manner. If you will recall," Holmes paused to take a sip of his cognac, "the strike plate was torn loose from the door jamb only at the top portion where the spring-loaded catch is inserted. The lower portion of the strike plate—where the locking bolt fits when the key is turned—was still, albeit somewhat loosely, attached to the door jamb. Had the key been turned so as to insert the locking bolt into the strike plate, when the door was kicked it would have torn the entire strike plate loose, and not merely the upper portion. You see, Inspector, in the annals of true crime there are no genuine locked rooms, only 'locked-room' mysteries. There is always some other explanation if one examines the facts persistently enough."

"So Lambert was murdered, and the perpetrator simply left by the front door?"

"Yes," Holmes replied, "that would be one explanation that fits the known facts."

"But why create the illusion of—as you describe it—a 'locked room' mystery? And of course the ultimate questions: who killed the pharmacist and why? If I accept your hypothesis, *M'sieur* Holmes, it raises at least as many questions as it answers."

"According to the officers whom you interviewed, what did the man who kicked in the door do once the door was open?" Holmes flicked the ash from his cigar as Loiseaux leafed through the pages of his pocket notebook in search of the answer.

Finding the desired page, Loiseaux responded, "It appears that he simply stepped aside as the other officers went in. No one recalls him being inside the shop, and no one recalls seeing him anywhere after the door was opened."

"And who was it summoned *M'sieur* Bertillon?"

"Most probably, the senior officer on the scene prior to my arrival. Standard operational procedure mandates that *M'sieur* Bertillon be notified whenever there is a death with some unusual circumstance and the causal agent is not immediately identifiable. The locked door and position of the body were certainly enough for the officer to invoke the procedure. As you know, *M'sieur* Bertillon's offices are in the Ministry of Justice which is in the Place Vendome immediately adjacent to this hotel, and thus but a short distance from Lambert's shop in the Rue de la Paix. Undoubtedly, a *flic* was dispatched to the Ministry where he was informed as to *M'sieur* Bertillon's whereabouts."

Loiseaux paused pensively and then continued. "If your hypothesis is correct, *M'sieur* Holmes, it is surely to be inferred that those responsible for Lambert's death were aware of the standard procedure and wanted to create a set of circumstances that were calculated with the utmost certainty to cause *M'sieur* Bertillon to be summoned to the scene when and as he was. And if one takes the hypothesis one step further, may it not be concluded that the perpetrator or perpetrators somehow gained the knowledge that *M'sieur* Bertillon would be dining with yourselves and it was you and *Docteur* Watson that he or they wanted brought to the scene?"

"But," Watson interjected, "how could they be sure that Bertillon would ask us to accompany him?"

The Inspector turned to Watson and jabbed his cigar in the air as if to emphasize the point, "that, *Docteur* Watson, is the variable least open to doubt." He glanced about to be sure that no one was in earshot. "While I'm sure that *M'sieur* Bertillon is not alone in this regard, every time a new account of *M'sieur* Holmes's cases is published over your name, *M'sieur* Bertillon will quickly point out to all with whom he comes in contact that he could have solved the case much more quickly using the bertillonage system. That he would fail to invite you to accompany him to the crime scene is to my mind completely unthinkable.

"If my assumptions are correct, *M'sieurs,*" Loiseaux's voice took on something of an edge as he shifted his gaze from Watson to Holmes, "I am compelled to ask why would someone want you to be brought into the investigation? What horrific game is being played in which an utterly inoffensive and apparently wholly innocent man is sacrificed like a pawn in a chess match?"

"To fully respond to your question would require that we breach a client confidence, a step which neither Watson nor I am prepared to take."

Loiseaux stiffened and replied with a formal deliberateness that left no room to doubt his resolve, "I assure you, *M'sieurs,* that I take no pleasure in what I am about to tell you. However, unless you disclose all you know regarding this matter, I shall have to ask you for your passports and you will find it necessary to prolong your Paris sojourn until I am satisfied that you have placed at my disposal all information in your possession."

"I do not think that would be necessary nor is it likely to be productive, *Inspecteur* Loiseaux. If you wish for Doctor Watson and me to remain in Paris against our wills, you will have to take us into formal custody and you will be required to do so here in the center of *M'sieur* Ritz's dining room." Holmes ground out his cigar and held his arms across the table. "Do you want to place us in handcuffs?"

Loiseaux stared for a long while at Holmes' outstretched arms. "Please, *M'sieur* Holmes, you've made your point. The Government has enough on its hands with the *Dreyfus Affaire* once again consuming the Nation's as well as the rest of the world's attention. France does not need, nor do I intend to provoke, another international incident by taking into custody two of Britain's most celebrated citizens. Tell me, please, as much as you are willing to say at this time. And if you will give me your assurance that you will provide me with as much additional information as you can and you deem will be of aid in my investigation, I shall not detain you for even a moment."

"A sound choice, Inspector." Holmes held out his right hand and Loiseaux clasped it firmly, thus sealing the bargain. "I earnestly hope that your forbearance will be rewarded to your satisfaction." Taking back his hand, Holmes summoned the waiter. *"Garcon, encore cognac, s'il vouz plait."*

"About our engagement, Inspector, I can only tell you that we are seeking to locate a certain artifact, one that dates from the time of the Second Crusade. It..."

"Merde! Please do not tell me, *M'sieurs,* that you've been seduced into looking for the lost falcon statue." Loiseaux looked at both men incredulously, and then smiled.

"I'm sorry, Inspector Loiseaux. I must have missed the joke. Did Holmes say something amusing?"

"Both amusing and at the same time appalling, *Docteur* Watson." Loiseaux folded his hands across his waistcoat, pursed his lips as if lost for a moment in nostalgia and then continued. "When I first joined the force so many years ago, it was a rite of initiation to be assigned to the 'case of the missing falcon'. The callow farm-boy from Brittany, the raw, wide-eyed cow-herder from Gascony, the too-sophisticated city-boy such as myself, all were given the opportunity to solve the great un-solved case and restore the statue to its rightful owner. I cannot tell you how many hours I wasted—how many thousands of hours those before and after me wasted—looking for the notorious statue. Some it took weeks, others months, for the truth to dawn. But until it did, and then you worked up the courage to take the file and lay it quietly on the commandant's desk, you were allowed to do no real police work. Even today, when a detective becomes totally baffled by a case we refer to it as 'being off on a falcon hunt'. That's the amusing part.

"The appalling part, *M'sieurs,* and the one that accounts for my vulgar language, is the fact that a decent man such as Lambert had to die, as did Richard and the chauffeur, whatever may have been the degree of their culpability, all sacrificed on the altar of this legendary statue. I cannot tell you how much it pains me to learn that this wretched Phoenix has arisen once again to bewitch even the world's greatest consulting detective and his redoubtable companion. Tell me, *M'sieurs,* have you found the statue, or even confirmed whether it does or ever did exist?"

"I cannot say that we have *Inspecteur,*" Holmes replied ambiguously.

Loiseaux arched an eyebrow, but decided not to press the question. "Then can you tell me how the pharmacist Lambert was involved in the matter?"

"So far, our enquiries have not revealed any connexion what ever."

"Well what," Loiseaux asked with more than a little exasperation resonating in his voice, "if anything, can you tell me that will be of even the most trivial assistance in *my* investigation? I have paid my dues to the missing falcon society, and resigned my membership some time ago; at the moment I have three murders to solve and I mean to do so."

Holmes summoned the cigar humidor and made his selection, which the waiter clipped and then lighted a match for Holmes to apply to the cigar. When the Uppmann was started to his satisfaction, Holmes rested his head against the back of the chair and savoured the cigar's cedar and chocolate flavours for a while as he contemplated his response. "May I take it that your enquiries regarding the lip rouge on the cigarette stubs found beneath Lambert's body have produced no useful information?"

"Yes you may, *M'sieur* Holmes. The shade is a common one, found in shops all over Paris."

"And I dare say London as well. Besides determining that the lip-rouge-wearer shops amongst the hoi polloi, have you made any other deductions?" Loiseaux shook his head.

"Watson, you examined Lambert's body much more closely than did I. How would you describe him?"

"As you both no doubt observed, he was very short; an inch or so less and he would easily have been classified as a dwarf. But he was also powerfully built in proportion to his stature. His neck was muscular and his upper body very well developed. If he'd been of average height or better, I'd say that he would have given a good account of himself in any sort of scrap."

"And if he knew that he was struggling for his life?"

"Then I would say that despite his diminutive stature, he would have been extremely difficult to subdue."

Holmes paused and puffed his cigar, while Loiseaux absorbed Watson's answers. "And what, Watson, would you say about the chauffeur Andre?"

"I don't know, Holmes. I was so preoccupied with keeping the chap alive, that I had no real opportunity to make many observations about his physique." Watson finished off his cognac and for perhaps half a minute rolled the empty glass between the palms of his hands. Setting aside the glass, he took off his spectacles and cleaned them with his table napkin. At last he continued, "I think I see, Inspector, where Holmes is going with this."

Loiseaux asked meekly, "Do you think it possible that I might have some more coffee, and perhaps even another cigar? I must confess that I've not yet seen the light. Perhaps the stimulus of coffee and tobacco will enable me to grasp the relevance of your recollections of the dead men's bodies. I mean no offense, *M'sieurs,* but this conversation is taking on all the coloration of one of *M'sieur* Bertillon's interminable lectures on his infallible system."

When a fresh round of coffee and cognac had been poured, and Loiseaux supplied with another cigar, Watson continued. "Every living organism resists its own destruction—its death, if you will—with all its might and resources. Man is no exception; suicides are an anomaly. Men will do heroic deeds and are capable of incredible feats in the heat of combat. And often they die in the process. But they do not undertake these actions out of a desire to die, they are driven by a will to live." Loiseaux looked completely perplexed.

"The point, Inspector Loiseaux," Watson started to jab his finger in the direction of the officer, but caught himself and picked up his coffee cup instead, "is that the will to live is so strong that even an unconscious man will not easily give up his life. In such circumstances, automatic body responses will take over in an effort to prevent its own death."

"Very interesting, *Docteur* Watson, but what...?"

"In the case of the chauffeur, even though unconscious, he would have fought for his life. Quite probably he thrashed his head from side to side, arched his back, tried to roll over, in short did everything possible to stave off his attacker. In the midst of it all, it is not unlikely that he even regained consciousness. Although the case was not widely reported owing to the personalities involved, you may have read about the 'Sloane Square Strangler,' the Marquis of Bletchley, who went about smothering his neighbors' house-maids in their sleep. In his confession he related how they would struggle up until their very last breath. He, may I add, did his own struggling at the end of a rope not long after his confession.

"But whatever may have been the state of the chauffeur's consciousness, he's sure to have put up some sort of struggle against his assailant. And given how soundlessly and quickly it was over, I think it fair to assume that the murderer was powerfully built and possessed more than average strength. Such strength as would also have been needed to subdue the presumably conscious pharmacist."

The Inspector slapped his forehead with the palm of his hand. *"Merde!* Again pardon my bad language, *M'sieurs.* The 'nurse' was not a woman, but a man dressed as a woman. This would account for the orderly's curious description. And it was this same individual, dressed as a woman—wearing lip rouge, but smoking a brand of cigarette favored almost exclusively by men—who entered Lambert's shop and killed him by some unknown agent as well.

"But that will make the search infinitely more complicated. Obviously the only description we have is the one supplied by the hospital orderly who saw him only in his female disguise. If he sheds that disguise, he will be unrecognizable. We need yet more information, *M'sieurs.* If only I could establish some connection between the business in the Place de la Concorde and the murder of Lambert besides the involvement of this *bete noir* who hides inside a woman's skirts, then perhaps that would provide some means to run him to ground. Can you tell me anything further?"

Holmes took a sip of his coffee. "I say, Watson, don't you remember seeing someone who may have been this person somewhere recently?"

Not sure how Holmes wanted him to respond, Watson temporized, "I'm not sure, Holmes, but.. .er..."

"That's it!" Holmes snapped his fingers causing the waiter and maitre d' to rush to their table. "No, no. *Pardon-moi.* We are quite al-right." Holmes motioned the staff away. "It was merely a gesture. *Merci, merci beaucoup.*"

Picking up his train of thought, he continued. "I remember, Watson. It was on the cross-channel ferry. We had a rough crossing, Inspector. For the most part we, along with the other passengers, were quite preoccupied with either not succumbing to, or in many cases attempting to recover from mal-de-mer." Holmes smiled ruefully. "But for all that, I seem to remember seeing a large person dressed as a female nurse attending an elderly gentleman in a wheel chair. Perhaps if you were to re-check the passenger manifest you might be able to come up with a name, even if by process of elimination alone."

Loiseaux took several long puffs on his cigar, and from the way he looked at Holmes and Watson, it was obvious that he was reconsidering his decision not to take the two men into custody after-all. "Why..."

"Please, Inspector." Holmes affected a contrite look. "It was unspeakably careless of both Watson—no, not Watson; I must accept the entire blame—for me not to have recalled sooner. All I can say in my defence is that I do not remember seeing the pair board the train at Boulogne-sur-mer and I suppose I assumed that they'd taken another train to a different destination, perhaps to Spa or some other resort. I understand that the high season is just about to begin."

"Do you think it possible *M'sieur* Holmes that some epiphany may come to you such that you may be able to supply some connection between the death of Lambert and the automobile incident?"

Holmes once again leaned his head back and gazed at the ceiling while taking a long puff on his cigar. When no bolt of lightening appeared, he straightened his posture and shook his head. "*Je suis desole, M'sieur Inspecteur.* Nothing comes to mind. Perhaps the two incidents are entirely unrelated. One cannot rule out the possibility that the 'automobile incident' as you now call it is connected to the baron and to the artifact, perhaps a rival of the baron's seeking to carry out some nefarious plot. However, it is also a possibility that the murder of Lambert was nothing more," Holmes paused, "I do not mean, to minimize the monstrosity of the crime, but could it have been merely a spur-of-the-moment act—a crime of opportunity?

"Anything is possible, *M'sieur* Holmes. But it should not take much effort on my part to persuade you that Lambert's murder bears none of the common attributes of an impulse killing."

"Point well taken, Inspector. But let me pose this paradigm: suppose that the killer intended to poison someone else using whatever poison was used on Lambert. Assume that the poison was not one with which the poisoner was familiar, but for some reason its use was required. Assume also that he purchased the ingredients from Lambert, and then desired to test the compound's efficacy. Lambert was certainly convenient, and because of his diminutive stature appeared to be an easy victim. Evidently it must have taken some time for the poison to do its deadly work and that would account for the cigarette stubs found under the body; apparently the killer was timing how long it took for Lambert to die."

"I'm afraid that your paradigm, *M'sieur* Holmes, while theoretically possible presents far too many assumptions to provide a working hypothesis for a mere policeman. In keeping with your own famous dictum, I will rule out nothing at this time. But I shall also continue to pursue the possibility that there are more connections between the two cases than the apparent fact that one man was involved in both. I am therefore compelled to pursue this new information which you have provided to me and also to continue to focus my energies on Baron Ollstreder." Loiseaux stifled a massive yawn. "Forgive me, *M'sieurs,* but I've had an unusually long day. What with the excellent dinner, wine and cognac, I find that I've reached the limit of my capacity to absorb any additional information. If you will excuse me, I shall bid you a grateful *bon nuit.*"

After the three men shook hands and the Inspector had left, Holmes and Watson resumed their seats and clicked glasses in a wordless toast. "I say, Holmes, that was rather a close call. For a moment or two I had a nasty vision of our spending to-night if not the foreseeable future in that dank jail cell you mentioned the other day. What do you think Loiseaux will do next? Do you think he'll have any luck in running Villeneuf to ground? And speaking of Villeneuf what are we doing about him?"

"I do not think, Watson, that Inspector Loiseaux will have much success in tracking down Villeneuf. I'm sure he will exhaust every means to do so once he works through the passenger manifest and eliminates every other name. I expect that will keep him fully engaged for the immediate future."

"And out of our way as well, I presume. But what shall we be doing to find this fellow and his deadly servant?"

"Not very much I should say. I fully expect that *M'sieur* Villeneuf is as anxious to find us as we are to find him. And in that vein, I strongly urge you to keep your Webley close at hand at all times. Now I too feel the need for a few hours sleep. Let us see if our own chameleon has returned, and whether she was successful." Holmes signaled the waiter, *"L addition, s'il vous plait."*

After Holmes signed for the check, he and Watson made their way to the lobby and the front desk. "Have you any messages for *M'sieur* Sebastian Melmoth?"

The clerk checked the pigeon hole above Wilde's room number and extracted a thick manila envelope. *"Oui M'sieur* Holmes, there is this package. But..."

"Oh it's quite al-right. *M'sieur* Melmoth's out of the City for a few days and asked us to pick this up. We will see that it is delivered to him as soon as possible."

"Well..." the desk clerk hesitated.

"Please, if you have any question, I'm sure that *M'sieur* Ritz will authorize you to do as we ask."

"If you wouldn't mind, *M'sieur* Holmes. Even though it is you and *Docteur* Watson, and I'm sure that *M'sieur L' Directeur* would give permission, it might mean my job if I should fail to seek his authorization."

"Very well," Holmes replied kindly. "Rules are, after all, rules. If *M'sieur* Ritz has not yet retired for the night, we would appreciate your undertaking to secure his permission immediately."

"I'm afraid, *M'sieur* Holmes that *M'sieur* Ritz did retire for the night about one-half hour ago. If it is a matter of extreme urgency, I can send a bellman to *M'sieur* Ritz's apartment with the package, and..."

"No," Holmes shook his head, "I do not think it will be necessary to disturb *M'sieur* Ritz's sleep. I'm quite sure that it will keep until tomorrow morning. But if you will see that he is apprised of the matter first thing in the morning, we shall be most grateful, as will be *M'sieur* Melmoth as well. By the way, can you tell me when the package was delivered?"

"Oui, M'sieur Holmes. It was just within the last hour. It was delivered by a young man accompanied by a rather large woman dressed as a medical nurse. Indeed, the young man looked somewhat pale and sickly, as though he were in need of medical attention. I thought it rather odd that someone in his condition would be out delivering a package. I even asked the young man if he wished to sit for a few minutes, or if I could get him a glass of water or something, He started to respond, but his nurse handed me a gratuity, a gold Louis in fact, and quickly led the young man away."

"Good heavens, Holmes, that means..."

"That means, old man, that *M'sieur* Melmoth will have to wait until tomorrow for his package. Come, Watson, I think it's time we followed Ritz's example and called it a night." As they turned away from the registration desk Holmes added, "It also means, Watson, that *M'sieur* Villeneuf has already begun seeking us out."

CHAPTER THIRTY-EIGHT

*"...to my mind that makes it all the more
imperative that we have some
sort of plan."*

"Bloody hell, Holmes!" Watson slammed his fist on the hand-written message which lay on the table in Holmes's room among a packet of cut up newspaper, evidently substituted for the original contents of the package left by Miss Pippen for 'Sebastian Melmoth'. "Who is this 'Villeneuf'? What does he mean, 'You've inconvenienced me for the last time, Mister Holmes'? I tell you, Holmes, we should have attempted to do something last night as soon as we found out. That poor young woman. To think of her in the hands of this monster who's already foully murdered at least two that we know of. Why..."

"Probably three, if you count Richard," Holmes replied testily. "What should we have done? Rousted Loiseaux out of bed and thrown ourselves on his mercy? Storm the *Schloss* Ollstreder, and demand that she be released? I don't know about you, but as much as it pains me to admit it, I stopped believing that I was a character out of Mallory or *The White Company* some years ago." Holmes whipped off his reading glasses and strode angrily about the room as he spoke.

Watson slumped wearily in his chair, elbows on the table, running his fingers through his hair. "I suppose you're right, Holmes. But I must tell you that I've developed rather an intense dislike for this transvestite who masquerades as a practitioner of the healing arts and yet kills and kidnaps without the slightest compunction." Watson paused and looked at Holmes, "Do you think he's the one who shot Richard?"

"I doubt that it was Villeneuf inside the automobile. Obviously neither you nor I was in a position to see who fired the shot and then exited the vehicle by the right-hand door. I do, however, recall the Inspector saying that the occupants of the automobile fled the scene. If Villeneuf was among them, I find it difficult to imagine that he'd have gotten very far in his wheel chair, even propelled along by his 'nurse'."

"You mentioned storming the '*Schloss* Ollstreder.' I assume you mean the house in the Rue Georges Bizet and not some stone heap somewhere across the Rhine. Do you think that's where he's holding her?"

"I think not, Watson. I expect that if he's been the baron's—or more accurately *Mademoiselle* Otero's—guest these past few days, he has by now most likely worn out his welcome. I take some comfort contemplating in my mind's eye the confrontation between Villeneuf and the baron: Villeneuf accusing the baron of stealing his share of the profits from their enterprise, and the baron accusing Villeneuf of attempting to steal 'his' statue. Villeneuf, clearly the more clever of the two, eventually figured out what had happened. However, the baron, for whom the statue plainly is an obsession, refuses to believe that the statue is not almost in his grasp, and absolutely will not trust the word of anyone who tries to persuade him to the contrary."

"Then you think it was Villeneuf who tried to kidnap me?"

"I would say so. Apparently Andre was in his pay as well as the baron's, and we've no proof to contradict the baron's claim of innocence. I would also suggest that it was the same 'nurse' who administered the laudanum and, as we know with greater certainty, later finished the job at the hospital. But as you so acutely observed, the smelling salts bottle strongly points toward his presence in the house at some time since our arrival in Paris."

"If we're not going to succumb to my rasher impulses— and on reflection I quite agree that they were just that—I assume that you have in mind a plan which offers at least a glimmer of hope that we shall be able to accomplish our original mission, whilst also managing to rescue Miss Pippen and somehow getting Esterhazy and I suppose *Fraulein* Irmgaard out of harm's way as well. I would say, my dear Holmes, that for the moment at least you've got enough of a puzzle to keep even your mind occupied." Watson sat back in his chair, his arms crossed tightly across his chest.

"Your synopsis of the circumstances in which *we* find ourselves is as always succinct and dead-on. And for lack of a better plan, I contemplate allowing *M'sieur* Villeneuf to call the tune for the time being trusting that in the end it is he rather than we who shall be compelled to pay the piper. In the meanwhile, I think that Miss Pippen is at least safe if not quite comfortable. Plainly she has been kidnapped for ransom much as I suppose they intended in their aborted attempt to kidnap you. So until a demand is made and the ransom paid, I doubt that she's in mortal danger. Villeneuf will anticipate that we would not be so naïve as to comply with his demand without irrefutable proof that she's unharmed."

As unsettling as Holmes's words were, Watson managed to find a degree of comfort in them. He unclasped his arms, and began to fill his briar. "And what of the major? Whose side do you suppose that he's on?"

Holmes chuckled as he leaned forward to light his cigarette off Watson's match. "That's relatively easy; Major Esterhazy is on the side of Major Esterhazy. In whatever the circumstances, the Major Esterhazys of the world place their own self-worth above all else and have an extra-ordinary instinct for self-preservation. No, I should not expend a great deal of emotional capital on the plight of the major. I expect he's gone to ground and will emerge only when he's sure that it's safe to do so. As he made us aware the other night, he evidently is not without collateral resources. I entertain no doubt that among Irmgaard, his mother-in-law, the woman we know as 'Leonie', and perhaps even Bertillon, Major Esterhazy will somehow manage to find a measure of succor."

"That would leave only the minor problem of what to do about Captain Dreyfus, who—even if one makes allowance for a somewhat lackadaisical attitude on the part of the French Navy— will quite soon reach these godforsaken shores and whatever fate awaits him at…where did you say? Oh, yes, Renne."

"In compiling your *bordereau,* if I may be permitted to use that term, do not fail to include a line-item for whatever it is that Villeneuf intends to demand as ransom in exchange for the erstwhile if overmatched Miss Pippen."

"I was coming to that; do you have any suggestions?"

"Apart from the obvious one, that we pay over his share of the last shipment's profits, my imagination fails me utterly."

"What if his demand is something with which *we* are unable to comply?"

"That raises an interesting point: what difference does it make whether we are able to comply?"

Watson puffed thoughtfully on his briar for a moment, and then peered over his glasses at Holmes. "I'm afraid, old chap, that I'm not much in the mood for one of your Socratic exercises, and thus I am unable to see what great philosophical conundrum lurks beneath the surface of my seemingly straight-forward question or your interrogative response."

Sensing that the stress of the situation was beginning to wear away at the edges of his friend's normally genial disposition, Holmes quickly lay aside his pedagogue's mantle and responded earnestly, "what if his demand is for the money, the falcon statue and half the tea in China? Even if we were willing and able to comply, do you think he'd release the girl?"

Mollified by Holmes's simple answer, Watson said evenly, "I suppose not, Holmes, but then to my mind, that makes it all the more imperative that we have some kind of plan. Anything is better than nothing. I agree; we certainly can't go to the French authorities. At least if we were at home, as much as you'd dislike doing it, given the circumstances, in the end you would call in The Yard, or your brother Mycroft, or..."

Holmes jumped up from his chair and grasped the startled Watson by the shoulders. "That's it, Watson. You've done it again. Come along, it's time my dear brother got a status report from his field operatives. We are about to find out whether Mycroft truly is 'the Government' or merely a minor cog in its machinery as he professes to be. We must make haste. Our report is bound to be somewhat lengthy, and I want to have it in his hands before his mid-day constitutional. We probably haven't much time before Villeneuf contacts us. If Mycroft's to be of any help, he'll need to put things in motion at once."

CHAPTER THIRTY-NINE

"Do then what you think best, but
in all likelihood it will be too little, too late."

After exiting the hotel through the rear door into the Rue Cambon, Holmes led Watson through a maze of back streets, in and out of shops and cafes, for the better part of an hour until he was sure that they'd shed any watchers sent to observe their movements by Villeneuf, Ollstreder, Loiseaux or whomever else may have wished to do so. It took another long while to send the encoded telegram to Mycroft and to walk several more blocks before catching a cab to return to the hotel so that if the cabby were to be questioned, he could provide no useful information. As they entered the lobby they were approached by a young man wearing an anxious expression and a cheap suit. *"Excusez-moi, M'sieurs. Je m'appelle* 'Blanchard'." He produced a credentials wallet which he showed to Holmes. "I am most sorry to disturb you," he said in English, "but it is a matter of the utmost urgency."

Reminded of his recent experience with the impostor Richard, Watson glanced at Holmes and at the young man apprehensively. Holmes, sensing Watson's concern took the officer by the elbow and led him toward an unoccupied settee and chair group. "Yes, yes, Officer Blanchard. I remember you from the pharmacist's. You're one of Inspector Loiseaux's men. How can we be of assistance?"

"Inspector Loiseaux is missing. He did not check in with his office this morning as is his custom. When we called his home, *Madame* Loiseaux stated that he had not been home last night. Inspector and *Madame* Loiseaux have been married for many years, and she did not think it especially out of the ordinary for him not to come home. This was a regular occurrence whenever he was involved in a major case. However, as I say, his not checking in with his office to review what progress has been made during the previous day and to issue new instructions is entirely out of character. Naturally we are by this time quite concerned. I was aware that he intended to see you here at the Ritz yesterday evening, so—I hope you will forgive the intrusion—I took it upon myself to approach you to learn if you did in fact see Inspector Loiseaux yesterday evening as he had intended."

"This is most distressing news, *M'sieur* Blanchard. Doctor Watson and I share your concern and will do anything in our power to be of assistance in your enquiries. We did indeed see Inspector Loiseaux here last night. We had an early evening engagement and did not return to the hotel until around nine o'clock. The Inspector was waiting for us in the lobby much as you were just now. Since we'd inconvenienced him by making him miss his own dinner, and since Watson and I had not eaten either, we invited him to join us in the hotel restaurant. He'd mentioned several days ago that he'd not had the occasion as yet to experience *M'sieur* Escoffier's culinary magic, so it was the perfect opportunity to repay the many courtesies he's shown us during our visit.

"We had a long and most cordial dinner. Inspector Loiseaux mentioned briefly how the Lambert case was going, and I think we may have discussed the incident in the Place de la Concorde, but I frankly cannot recall what was said. Most of the evening was spent in exchanging reminisces, and enjoying the food and drink. The Inspector left at about...what would you say, Watson, midnight?"

"Yes, it must have been about then. Perhaps a few minutes before. Holmes and I stayed on a while longer to finish our cognac and cigars. We of course have not seen nor heard from him since."

"Did he happen to say where he was going, *M'sieurs?*"

"Not that I recall," Watson responded. "Do you remember anything else, Holmes?"

"Only that he indicated that he'd had rather a long day. And while he did not say as much, I took that to mean that he was going to go home and retire for the night. I certainly had that impression; if he did not do so, your concern may be entirely justified. I wish we could tell you more." Holmes stood, followed immediately by Watson and then, somewhat reluctantly, the young officer. Holmes held out his hand which Blanchard took, again with a moment's hesitation. "Please express our concern to your superiors and to *Madame* Loiseaux, if you happen to speak with her. And please, we entreat you, let us know the moment there are any developments."

"Er...thank you, *M'sieurs. Merci beaucoup.* I shall report what you have told me at once, and shall relate your kind expression of concern. I'm sure the Inspector's off following up some new aspect of one of the cases, and is merely unable to report his whereabouts. As soon as anything's learned, we will inform you as well."

When the young officer had taken his leave, Holmes and Watson returned to the settee, and ordered a pot of coffee from a passing waiter. Watson shook his head in disbelief, "This is an astounding development, Holmes. What utter cheek. Kidnapping an Inspector of the *Sureté*. Reminds me of the battle of Wadi-al-Talibani. Some bloody fool of a lieutenant, I forget his name, got his platoon trapped between the wadi and an outcropping of boulders. The mullah's men were bearing down on him, and instead of either retreating or splitting his force in order to envelop the enemy, he sent a runner back to the artillery command and called for an artillery bombardment on his own position. The attack was thwarted, but he took over ninety-percent casualties—including himself—in the process. He took a bullet in the lung, and under the conditions, I was unable to save him. I did, however, dig out the fatal projectile. It looked to me much more like it was fired from a standard-issue British infantry weapon, rather than one of the hand-molded bullets used by the mullah's forces.

"Reminiscence aside, it seems to me that Villeneuf has made an egregious mistake in snatching the Inspector. Why the entire police force will be combing the City from one end to the other and everywhere in between until he's found."

"In part, I quite agree, old man. And that bodes not well at all for either the Inspector or for our enterprise. Your analogy to calling the artillery down on one's own position is apt only to a point. My point of departure is that I cannot accept the notion that Villeneuf, un-like the late un-lamented lieutenant of Wadi-al-Talibani, would take such a step without a full appreciation of the consequences."

Watson put down his coffee cup, "What could he possibly have to gain that would be worth the risk of such an all-out manhunt? What sort of leverage can he expect to derive from a relatively low-level government employee?"

"I don't think it's leverage he's after in the case of Inspector Loiseaux. It may be that Loiseaux's learned something—obviously he chose not to share whatever it may be with us—and Villeneuf has therefore found it necessary to remove the Inspector from the case, so to speak."

"I sense you think that his 'removal', as you put it, is permanent."

"Again, as in the case of Miss Pippen, what other course makes sense? I should not wish to sound unduly fatalistic, but I think that prior to disposing of the Inspector, Villeneuf will want to extract from him whatever information he can. And I would count Inspector Loiseaux among those who are resourceful enough and determined enough to resist, for a considerable time, such means of persuasion as Villeneuf may be willing to employ. Loiseaux will certainly recognize that his usefulness to Villeneuf will at once come to an end when he gives up the information Villeneuf thinks he has. Then on the other hand, his resistance may be broken more quickly than one would have anticipated, or Villeneuf may miscalculate and inadvertently put an end to the Inspector's usefulness prematurely. I am aware how cold-blooded my analysis may seem, but there's no use our entertaining any illusions about what is in store for the Inspector, if it hasn't already occurred."

Watson lighted his pipe and puffed thoughtfully for a good while as Holmes stood at the tall windows looking out into the small garden and chain-smoked one cigarette after another. Finally Watson broke the silence, "If the baron and Villeneuf are no longer acting in concert, do you think Villeneuf's turned on him as well? If he has, then I would suggest that Ollstreder too may be in considerable danger. I do not particularly care what happens to him for his sake, but just as I care what happens to Esterhazy for purposes of whatever use your brother wishes to make of him, the baron is our only means of aiding Dreyfus. If he is forced to flee, or worse, he will be of absolutely no value to our endeavours on behalf of the Captain."

"Your concern is well-founded, Watson, and should be acted upon at once. I am going to poke about for a bit to see if I can come up with any leads on where Villeneuf's holding Miss

Pippen and hopefully Inspector Loiseaux. In order to do so, I shall have to assume a disguise. For reasons that you yourself have already pointed out, your participation in such an undertaking will not be especially beneficial. As much as I relish the peace of mind that you and your revolver bring to such outings, I think that I'm more likely to accomplish something if I go alone.

"You, on the other hand, are quite well-equipped to call on the baron. You can convey to him that we've discussed his proposal with those on whose behalf we have been treating with him. Inform him that his proposal is acceptable, as modified in accordance with our suggestion as to disposition of the statue in the event that his 'proof' is unavailing. He should also be informed, don't you think, that the risk of interference by Villeneuf is greatly increased under the circumstances. You should tell him this Villeneuf is a madman who will stick at nothing—murder in addition kidnapping —to get what he wants and that he very much wants the statue.

"When Villeneuf wants us he will probably convey a message by leaving it here at the hotel. My suggestion is that you take a cab from here to the Rue George Bizet and pay the driver to wait while you have your *tete-a-tete* with the baron. When your business with the baron is concluded, return to the hotel and wait for me."

"But what if I'm followed?"

"I expect that you will be, but it makes no difference. Villeneuf knows that we're dealing with the baron. The only risk is that he will seek to add you to his roster of captives. In an abundance of caution, you should most definitely take your revolver. And if you feel warranted in the circumstances, you should not hesitate to use it.

"Hopefully, by early evening we shall have received a reply from Mycroft as well as a communication from Villeneuf. If you return before I do, as is likely to be the case, pick up any messages left for either of us at the front desk. I will also leave at the front desk in your name a key to the code which Mycroft will be using. De-code his message in your room as soon as you pick it up from the desk, commit the message to memory and then destroy both the message and the code. If a message comes from Villeneuf, do not attempt to act on it prior to my return. If I do not return by midnight, then follow the instructions in Mycroft's message as best you can. Hopefully he will have figured out some way to get us out of France and back to England."

"And leave you, Miss Pippen and the others to whatever fate Villeneuf may have designed for you? I say, Holmes, you know me better than that. If I am able to do nothing else, at least I can go to the police. In their agitated state they may throw me in a cell, but I may cause them to re-double their efforts to locate Loiseaux, and thereby possibly the rest of you. Or better yet, I can go to President Loubet. Even with a politician's memory, he can't have al-ready forgotten that he probably owes his life to us. If he has any doubts, he can, I'm sure contact your brother."

"Bear in mind, Watson, that Mycroft cannot engage in any overt action to assist us. Remember his admonition that Her Majesty's Government can take no official cognizance of our being here other than as a couple of tourists. Do then whatever you think best and trust that it will not be too little or too late."

CHAPTER FORTY

*"I must say...that you're the first man I've ever known
to pass up that particular opportunity."*

Baron Ollstreder, please. I am Doctor John Watson." Watson
handed his hat and stick to a servant whom he'd not seen on their
prior visits to the house in the Rue George Bizet.

*"Je suis desole, M'sieur Docteur, L' Baron n'est pas a la
maison."*

Watson paused, trying to make sense of what the servant-
girl was telling him. Then, remembering out of desperation. a few
phrases of grammar school French he managed, *"Je m' appelle
Docteur* Watson. W-a-t-s-o-n." He spelled his name slowly as if
that would help the servant-girl understand. *"Je suis anglais.* Do
you *parlez-vous anglais?"*

"Anglais? Non, M'sieur. Je ne seis pas anglais." The girl
led Watson by the arm to a heavily carved chair in the vestibule
and gestured for him to sit. *"Attendez-vous une minut*e." Holding
on to Watson's hat and stick she dashed off down the hallway,
leaving Watson regretting his disdain for foreign languages, save
for medical terminology Latin and the few phrases of native
dialects that he'd picked up out of necessity in the field during his
military days.

After a few minutes, the young maid returned. As Watson
instinctively stood, she curtsied, wiped her palms on her apron and
briefly moistened her lips with her tongue.

"S'il vous plait," she paused and pursed her lips,
"um...please, *M'sieur...Docteur* Watson, *voulez-vous...voulez-
vous...*would you..." she paused again for a long moment as
Watson leaned forward straining to understand,
*"venir...*come...*avec moi...*with me?" She blushed and lowered
her eyes waiting for any sign of comprehension on Watson's part.

"Yes, er...*oui, oui* of course. What is the matter? Is the
baron ill?"

Her memorized English phrases having had the desired
effect the servant-girl smiled with relief, seized Watson by his

elbow and pulled him down the central hallway to the rear of the house and into the elevator.

"Tout droit, M'sieur," the girl pointed down the hallway. Comprehending her meaning if not her words, Watson started down the long hallway. After they'd walked about half the length on the passage, the maid tugged at Watson's elbow stopping him before one of the doors. *"Arrete, M'sieur, ici."* She knocked on the door.

"Entre." It was a woman's voice

The maid opened the door, and again propelled the startled Watson into the room. She remained in the room closing the door behind her, as though to bar Watson's escape.

Facing the door against the opposite wall was a large canopied bed of cherrywood trimmed in gold surmounted by a tapered canopy made of red and gold brocade fabric which reached to the high ceiling. The walls of the room were covered in the same fabric set between white-painted wood panels above a white wainscoting. The rest of the furnishings—a chaise lounge, large armoire, lingerie chest, night-tables, various other tables and occasional chairs—all matched the bed and were situated on a deep-piled white carpet covering the entire floor.

The canopy was drawn shut in front, so Watson could not see the bed's occupant. "Please, Doctor Watson, come take the chair here by the side of the bed. If you would care for coffee or tea, or perhaps something stronger, I will send Helene to bring it for you."

"I beg your pardon, Madam. Evidently your maid did not understand. I'm here on behalf of Sherlock Holmes to see Baron Ollstreder. I have been assisting Mr. Holmes in a matter having to do with the baron, and it is imperative that I see him at once. It is a matter of the utmost urgency. If you are ill, I strongly suggest that you send a servant to summon your own physician. I do not have my instrument bag, nor am I otherwise equipped to render either medical advice or treatment.

"I'm sorry to have intruded on your privacy, but as I say, because my French is so inadequate, apparently the girl did not understand that I'm here only to see the baron on a matter of business and not to render medical services to you or anyone else. When I introduced myself as 'Doctor Watson' because of the similarity of the word 'doctor' in both languages, she must have thought that I was here at your request to treat whatever condition it is that requires medical attention."

The woman started to laugh, but instead cried out in pain. As soon as she did, Watson quickly went to the side of the bed. In the light of the bed-side table lamp Watson recognized her from the Ritz and Maxim's as Caroline Otero, although she looked far different than she did that first evening. Her face and lips were puffed and swollen, and both her eyes were blackened. Over her left eye was a jagged cut about three quarters of an inch in length that looked like it needed stitches.

"I hope that years from now when you think back on the occasion of our meeting, Doctor Watson, you will remember me as you saw me the other night at the Ritz and not as you see me now." She tried to smile and at the same time to adjust her posture to a more upright position. This latter effort brought forth another gasp of pain, and Watson could see tears welling up in her eyes. "Forgive me, Doctor Watson, I'll be al-right in a moment. Would you be so kind as to light one of those cigarettes," she pointed to an enameled cigarette case and matches on the night stand next to the bed, "and hand it to me? I think that several of my ribs are broken, so that it is excruciatingly painful for me to inhale deeply."

Watson obliged, and after she'd taken a delicate puff, she continued. "Baron Ollstreder is gone. Either he's lying dead in the bottom of some vile *pissoir,* or if Villeneuf and his trained beast are not yet done with him, trussed up like a sausage in some secret place."

"Then Villeneuf has seized the baron already? His 'trained beast' I take it is a reference to the large man who goes about dressed as a female nurse?" Watson bent down to inspect the cut over her eye. "You really should have this attended to, Miss Otero. It's quite likely to become infected. Did Villeneuf's man by chance leave behind the medical bag that he usually carries?"

Otero spoke to the maid in French, apparently instructing her to search for the medical bag. The girl scurried off closing the door behind her. Otero took another puff of the cigarette and clasped her hand to her left side under her breast in reaction to the pain brought on by her inhaling. "It happened last night, Doctor, after you and *M'sieur* Holmes left. There was an awful row. I

314

cannot tell you much more than that. It is…or was the baron's instruction that whenever he and Villeneuf were having business discussions, I was to remain in my rooms and no servants other than Heinrich were to be about. I am sure that his concern was at least in part for my own well-being; the less I knew the better off I would be. Mostly they spoke in German. I know very little of the language—mostly terms of use to me in my profession—and the servants, other than Heinrich and Klaus so far as I know do not understand the language at all."

"Your profession, Miss?"

"Come, Doctor, Watson," she drew back her swollen lips in a gesture resembling a smile. "Surely César Ritz did not omit that detail from his discourse. Just as you have acquired the ability to diagnose patients by observing them, I too have developed a keen eye for reading people. From the learning and practicing of my 'trade', if you prefer that term to 'profession', I can tell most all of what I need to know about a man merely by watching him, even across a crowded room. I would have been blind in one eye and unable to see out of the other not to be able to read your mind as Ritz was talking. Was he not giving you his famous 'I do not wish to run a brothel' lament? Would you like to know my thoughts about your companion Sherlock Holmes? While for the most part your written observations are accurate, there are some things…"

"Er, perhaps some other time, Miss Otero. In the meantime, please tell me everything you know about last night's occurrence and the events which led up to what happened."

"Yes, yes, of course, Doctor Watson." She winced sharply as she reached for the ash tray. "I will tell you everything I know if while we talk you will apply your professional skills to doing what you can for my injuries."

"There's not much that I can do, Miss Otero. I can probably do something to disinfect that cut over your eye, but it may be that too much time has elapsed for sutures to be of any benefit. I'm afraid you may be left with a rather conspicuous scar when the wound heals. But frankly, I'm more concerned about your ribs. If any are in fact broken, there's a possibility that the jagged end will tear the peritoneum. If that occurs, your life could very well be at risk. In order to properly assess the situation, I am going to need to examine you with the upper portion of your body uncovered."

"I assure you, Doctor Watson," she again favored Watson with an attempted smile, "that you will not be the first man to see my 'upper body' in its natural state. "But you must do something about this cut," she touched the wound with the tip of her finger. "If I am going to be scarred for the rest of my life, my life may as well be over. I would just as soon that my 'per-' whatever you called it…be torn so that I might die right now." She bit her lower lip as tears began to course down her cheeks.

"I will do the best that I can, Miss Otero. But perhaps…wouldn't make-up serve to conceal…" Watson turned at the sound of the maid entering the room. "Ah, good. She's found it. Let me see what there is. What we have to work with will determine what I can do. But even if the bag contains a full compliment of supplies, you really should be in hospital. That's the only place where you'll be able to get adequate attention."

"Attention such as the chauffeur Andre received, Doctor Watson?"

"I take your point, Miss Otero. Let's see what's in the bag." He held out his hand as the maid approached the bedside. "Have her bring a basin of hot water along with some soap; I shall need to wash my hands thoroughly if I'm going to be probing your wound." He started rummaging through the bag, removing its contents and laying them on the bed beside his patient. "Hmm, tincture of iodine." He held up a small brown bottle. "That will do for an antiseptic. I must warn you, Miss Otero, this is likely to be somewhat painful."

"Please, call me 'Caroline'," she looked at him steadily. "And I shall call you 'John'. I think we shall be friends, as well as physician and patient."

"Very well, Miss…er…Caroline. As you wish. On second thought, don't send your maid for the hot water just yet. Let me first deal with your ribs. Even though, or especially because we are now 'friends' as well as doctor and patient, I must insist that she stay while I examine you. Also, since it would be best if you were standing up while I examine the affected area, and it may be necessary for her to assist you in maintaining your balance. I assume that you've been in bed since last night's incident, so you may not be as steady on your feet as would normally be the case.

316

First sit up, and then rotate your body so that your legs are off the side of the bed."

Caroline gave her maid some instructions in French, as a result of which the girl climbed up on the opposite side of the large bed and crawled across to Caroline's side. Following Watson's gestures and her mistress's verbal instructions, she and Watson managed to raise Caroline to a sitting position, her legs dangling over the side of the bed still beneath the covers. Watson stood and held out his left forearm. "Very good. Are you al-right?" Biting her lip from the pain, Caroline nodded.

"Now grasp my forearm with both hands, and when you are ready, pull yourself to a standing position. Tell your maid to support you from behind, and when you are comfortably standing, to help you with your garment. Are you ready?"

After relating Watson's instructions to Helene, Caroline grasped Watson's arm, and slid from beneath the covers and into a standing position. "There," she exhaled, "that wasn't so bad. What is next?" She ran her right hand through her hair pulling it back from her face.

"I shall need for you to turn slightly toward the light so that I can see better. It would be helpful if we could remove the lampshade. Then as I mentioned, you will need to lower the top portion of your..." Watson looked down and for the first time noticed that Caroline was wearing a silk kimono-style garment that covered only to slightly above mid-thigh, "...gown."

Sensing Watson's discomfort, Caroline squeezed Watson's arm and laughed. "I must say, John, that you're the first man I've ever known to pass up that particular opportunity." She turned her head toward Helene, *"Helene, apportez-moi le jupe noir. Vite!"*

Helene, unable to suppress a fit of giggles, ran over to the large armoire and after a moment's rummaging returned with a full black skirt with buttons down the side. She quickly unfastened the buttons and wrapped the garment around Caroline's waist, and then refastened the buttons.

"Good. Thank you, Madam. Now let's have done with it."

Caroline spoke a word to Helene who gently pulled the kimono back from Caroline's shoulders and let it fall about her waist. "The proper form of address," she paused for a moment as

Helene helped her wriggle her arms out of the kimono sleeves, "for an unmarried woman is *'mademoiselle'*.

Watson placed his hands on her waist and gently rotated her body in a clock-wise direction toward the lamp. As he drew his head closer to her body he could smell the ylang-ylang scent which had so pervaded the atmosphere in the Ritz grille-room. It mingled with the sharper scent of perspiration producing an erotic synergy that was in cruel contrast to the large blue-black bruise beneath Caroline's left breast. "It does not appear that the skin is broken. That's a good sign. I'm going to have to touch the bruised area. Would you please lift up your… " he paused.

Caroline, who'd been studying the beads of perspiration forming on the top of Watson's head, finally understood what he wanted and obligingly cupped her hand under her breast and lifted it out of the way. "Do you know that you're growing quite a bald spot on the top of your head?"

"I'm very much aware of my alopecia, *Mademoiselle,* as is my barber who takes considerable pains to conceal its existence. And I would consider it a great favour if you would desist from examining me while I am examining you. It is a most unwelcome distraction." Watson began to palpate the bruised area, perhaps just a bit harder than necessary.

"Ouch!" She stepped back in reaction to the pain. "That hurt. Now do you believe me when I say my ribs are broken?"

"Sorry. It could not be helped. Now would you please turn your back to me?"

She complied, and Watson probed the skin in the area of her kidneys. "Does this hurt?"

"No. But what are you doing? He only kicked me in front, not in my back." She turned back around to face him.

"I assume that you have used the water closet since this happened. Did you pass any blood?"

"No, no blood. But what's..."

"Again that's a good sign. He did not do enough damage to cause internal bleeding. You are, all things considered, a fortunate woman. I do not detect any fractures, although it is possible that there may be green-stick fractures of one or two of the ribs that took the brunt of the assault. I think that most of the pain is caused by the bruising of the soft tissues."

"Then there's no tearing of my peri.. .peri...?"

"Peritoneum, Caroline. No, I don't think you're in any immediate danger. The only things that can be done are to immobilise the area for at least ten days or so, and give you something for the pain. I'll see what else is in the bag, and then I can look at the wound to your forehead. You can put your garment back on now."

"Shall I have to wear some hideous plaster cast?"

"Not necessarily. Do you perhaps have some undergarment with whale-bone stays that fits around your body? I'm sure I've seen such things, but I'm not sure what they're called in English much less French."

Caroline thought for a moment. "Ah yes, it's called a corset, in both languages." She issued some rapid instructions to Helene. The maid began searching through a lingerie chest and in less than a minute returned with a black lace and whale bone garment which she fitted around Caroline's waist.

"Yes, that will do quite well. In fact, it's perfect. Tell her to tighten the laces as tightly as you can stand them. I suggest you wear this at all times for at least the next ten days, even when you are sleeping. That will give any fractures time to heal. If it becomes unbearable, take it off for a few minutes two or three times a day, and rub some lotion on your body so that the skin does not become irritated. Let me see if there's an analgesic in the bag."

He looked in the bag, and pulled out a box with the now familiar name 'Aspirin'." These seem to work well on headaches. I don't know how they'll act on muscle pain, but they're all that seems to be in here except for...." He took a small phial out of the bag and held it toward the light. "Hmm, cocaine. This will do as a topical anaesthetic, but I would not recommend that you use it for any other purpose. No, give the Aspirin a try, but let's wait until we've done what we can for your cut. It is said that the Aspirin works as a blood thinner. We shan't want it to cause excessive bleeding from your wound. Come, sit in this chair next to the lamp, and send Helene for the hot water. I'll need a basin to wash my hands, and have her bring an extra pan or something to use for washing out the wound."

While Helene was gone to bring the hot water, Caroline, now firmly cinched in her corset with her kimono back in place

319

obediently sat in a chair next to the lamp table. Watson continued looking through the contents of the medical bag, once on twice muttering to himself. "While your maid is gone, you can begin telling me what happened last night"

"Very well. I will begin at the beginning. But first, would you light me another cigarette." Watson obliged and after he'd handed the lighted cigarette to her, with her free hand she tugged hard at the black lace corset, an inch or two of which was peeking out from where her cleavage met the fold of her kimono. "God. How I hate this wretched thing. Do you have even the slightest idea what misery you've sentenced me to for the next ten days?"

Watson lighted a cigarette for himself, and drew up a chair in front of her. "Be assured, *Mlle.* Otero, that I shall lodge no objection whatever should you desire to place your need for medical attention in the hands of another physician. If you will recall, I came here for the sole purpose of communicating a warning to Baron Ollstreder. It seems that my warning was entirely in order, if unfortunately a day too late. Now if you would be so good as to begin at the beginning, I shall be glad to continue performing my end of our bargain as soon as your maid returns with the hot water."

"Baron Ollstreder, as you may have guessed, is the owner of this house, although the muniment of title stands in my name."

"Then if he's dead, the house is yours?"

"I suppose that is the case, although I must admit I have no knowledge of these matters."

Watson arched a quizzical eyebrow as he flicked the ash off his cigarette and held out the ash tray for Caroline to do the same. Observing his scepticism, she continued. "Apart from certain natural endowments," Watson involuntarily fixed his gaze on her cleavage, "one of the reasons for my 'professional success' is that I practice but one profession. When a man is with me, he does not think much less speak of other things. Some women in my line of work make it a practice of drawing out their clients on matters of business or state as the case may be and then selling the information. *M'sieur* Bertillon, I believe you know him, is a notorious buyer of such intelligence. But girls who augment their income by such means are usually found out quickly and thereby lose their best clients. Often the parting is something less than amiable and they end up as you see me now." She again self-consciously brushed her hair back from her face. "Do you think that your profession is the only one with ethical standards?"

"Please forgive me for doubting you, Caroline. I did not realize that such punctilios of honour were observed in your profession. You were mentioning that the baron is the true owner of this house..."

"Yes and over the two years of our association he has, on the whole, treated me quite well. Our relationship is not constrained, either by formalities or empty promises. He does as he pleases, as do I. Naturally, however, I always put his wishes ahead of any others, whenever possible."

"And Villeneuf?"

"That execrable creature? He comes here every few months with Gerald...or 'Geraldine'...as he sometimes prefers to be called. Villeneuf and Ollstreder have some kind of joint business enterprise. Something to do with importing or exporting. Of what, I do not know, but evidently it is most profitable. Whenever a transaction is to take place, Villeneuf comes here during its consummation."

"You mentioned 'Gerald' or 'Geraldine'. Is he the brute who goes about dressed as a nurse?" Why does he prefer to be called 'Geraldine'?"

"The first time he arrived, in an effort to be—shall I say 'hospitable'—I tried to seduce him. All I got for my effort was my first beating at his hands. I think he is...how does one say it... *homosensual?* He prefers a male companion for his physical gratification. And from what I've observed, he likes little boys around the age of twelve. But whether he's interested in little boys, big girls, or small ones, or for that matter barn-yard animals, he apparently receives his greatest gratification from inflicting pain. Once, when a servant spilled a plate while serving him at dinner he nearly beat the poor man to death. The baron had to pay an enormous amount just to keep the incident from being reported to the police. Since then he's taken his meals in the servants' quarters. He must prepare his own plate, as no one will serve him. Even Heinrich and Klaus, both of whom the baron recruited from the Hamburg waterfront, are deathly afraid of him."

"What happened last night?"

321

"In keeping with the baron's wishes—as well as my own preference—I remained here in my room while Villeneuf and the baron discussed their business. They of course did not begin their discussion until after you and *M'sieur* Holmes had left. The baron had promised to take me to the theatre and I was concerned that we would miss the entire first act. I thought they were having one of their usual discussions, so I made the mistake of going downstairs. They were in the parlor; I believe you are familiar with the room. I stood at the door for a minute or two, trying to decide if I should interrupt or simply wait and have a tantrum later expecting that Ollstreder would buy his way back into my good graces in the usual fashion with some gaudy and obscenely expensive bauble from Cartier's. In fact I rather had my heart set on one of those 'dog collars' designed by *M'sieur* Lalique. They're all quite the rage."

"Dog collars? Indeed," Watson gave her a disapproving look. "Please continue."

"I heard Villeneuf mention you and *M'sieur* Holmes several times. And there was something I did not understand about the baron's obsession with the falcon. It seemed that Villeneuf was doing all of the talking, and the baron responding only with 'yes' or 'no'. I must have scraped my shoe along the floor, or perhaps my gown rustled against the door, and Gerald or 'Geraldine' must have heard me. Just as I made up my mind to knock, Gerald threw open the door and violently pulled me into the room.

"I shall never forget the sight. The baron was seated in a chair, his arms bound behind him. His face was a bloody mess— even worse than mine—from the beating he'd been given. The baron, as you may yourself have observed, is not the most attractive of men to begin with, and after Gerald was through with him he looked like something left over from the *charcuterie.*"

"The what?" Watson asked.

"The *charcuterie...* how do you say in *anglais?*...the 'pork butcher'."

Watson imagined the scene in his mind's eye. "Why was Ollstreder being beaten? Why were you assaulted as well?"

"They were trying to get the baron to tell them, as best I could make out, the location of some documents; Villeneuf referred several times to a 'portfolio'. Oh, John, it was simply awful! Poor Ollstreder!" She clasped her hands to her face as though to blot out the memory. "One time Gerald kicked him in the stomach and it made the baron throw up. Most of it landed on the front of Gerald's shirt. Gerald then took off his shirt and rubbed it in the baron's face.

"Ollstreder stubbornly would not tell them what they wanted to know, so then Gerald started beating me. He slapped and punched me a few times, and still the baron refused to tell. I was of course crying and screaming by then, and I begged the baron to tell them. He only shook his head. I'm certain that I saw tears in his eyes, but I was not sure at first whether they were from his physical pain, or from seeing me being tortured. I think it was in his mind that if he gave in, it would mean death for both of us."

"It's al-right, dear girl. You're safe now. Watson reached out and clasped Caroline's hands. "Where were Ollstreder's men... Heinrich and Klaus?"

"I do not know. All of the servants except for the two of them and Helene are gone to Andre's funeral which was in a small village half a day's train ride from Paris. Heinrich and Klaus did not go, but Helene has not seen them since you were here yesterday evening."

"Obviously they finally let you go. What happened to Ollstreder? Did he reveal the location of the portfolio?"

"Please, John, I beg you; do not force me to tell more. It's simply too horrible." Caroline withdrew her hands and held them again to her face as she began to cry.

"Be strong, Caroline. I must know what happened. It's the only way that Holmes and I can do anything to help the baron and the only way that you can get a measure of revenge for what Gerald and his master did to you."

Caroline continued sobbing for a while longer. Finally she lighted another cigarette, and after coughing twice she continued, "I too came to realize that if the baron gave them what they wanted, they would probably kill us then. So I spit in Gerald's face to let the baron know that I understood. I think Gerald would have strangled me where I stood but Villeneuf stopped him. Villeneuf correctly interpreted the baron's tears and realized that the only way to get the baron to talk was by threatening harm to me.

"On Villeneuf's orders, Gerald ripped off my gown. Then he slowly, almost tenderly, removed all my under-garments until all I was wearing was my stockings and my shoes. Even though the room was quite warm, I was freezing with fear and from his touch. My body was all goose-flesh. You should have seen my...," she paused, willing herself to continue.

"I don't know why I noticed, perhaps force of habit, but I could see that Gerald was aroused. Anyway, he forced me to bend forward over the back of one of the sofas so that my derriere was facing the baron. Out of the corner of my eye I saw him go over to the fire place and pick up the metal poker. Whether he meant to beat me with it, or..." she hesitated, "something worse, I do not know. Villeneuf had read the baron's thoughts accurately. As soon as Gerald picked up the poker, the baron said 'Enough! I will tell you what you wish to know, but only once we are gone from here and Caroline is harmed no further.' Apparently Villeneuf knew the baron's mind so well that he knew that Ollstreder would keep his word, and that if any more harm came to me, he would never reveal the location of this portfolio.

"Villeneuf then told me that I could get up and put back on the remnants of my clothing. I could see the disappointment on Gerald's face, but he dared not contradict his master. Gerald put the poker back in its stand and when he turned around again, I kicked him in the groin. I don't know why I did it, but I assure you it was worth the price. I think that he would have torn my leg off, but Villeneuf again forced him to retreat. However, he was so enraged that Villeneuf could not control him completely. I think he meant to kick me in the same place, but his aim was high resulting in the injury to my ribs that you have so ably tended."

"I take it that Ollstreder left with Villeneuf and Gerald. You have no idea..." The door to the room burst open and crashed against the adjacent wall. Watson, facing Caroline had his back to the door. "Wha..." He fell sideways off the chair and rolled toward the bed reaching for his revolver. Before he could draw it from the waist-band of his trousers, he realized that it was only Helene, who ran screaming and crying, incoherently in any language, across the room. She collapsed at Caroline's feet and rested her head in Caroline's lap as she continued to sob uncontrollably. As Watson regained his feet and his composure, Caroline spoke soothingly to the terrified girl and stroked her head tenderly.

After a few minutes the sobbing was reduced to whimpering, and the girl's laboured breathing began to return to normal. "What is it Caroline? Can't you get her to tell you what has happened? Has Villeneuf returned? If he has, I assure you that he and his androgynous monster are in for an unpleasant surprise." Watson took out his revolver and rotated the cylinder for perhaps the twelfth time that day to confirm that it was fully loaded, and on this occasion to assure the two women that he was capable of defending them if need be.

As Caroline continued to comfort the hysterical girl, Watson strode rapidly to the door. He stepped into the hall and walked a few paces as softly as he could in each direction listening for any sound that would indicate the presence of others in the house. Satisfied that the only sounds were the laboured breathing of the servant-girl coming from the room behind him and the sound of his own pulse thundering in his ears, he returned to the room his revolver still at the ready. "Do you know how to use this?" He thrust the revolver, handle first toward Caroline.

"Yes, I think so. The baron once took me to his hunting lodge for a boar hunt. I became, shall I say, 'friendly' with the head gamekeeper's son. I was not permitted to accompany the men on the actual hunt, so while they were in the field, to keep myself amused, I taught the lad a few things, and he taught me how to shoot a handgun."

Giving her his most reproachful glare, he handed her the weapon. "I'll get her up and onto the bed. You keep your eyes focused on the doorway. If anyone comes into your line of vision shoot him. We'll look later to see if there's any identification on the body. You'd best grip it with two hands, as the recoil may be rather much for you. Do you have any brandy close-by? If I can get her to take some, it will help to steady her nerves. I'd rather give her that than a dose of laudanum from the bag." As Caroline obeyed his orders, Watson pried the girl's arms from around Caroline's legs, and carried her to the bed where Caroline had been laying. She was conscious, but evidently in a state of hysterical shock.

"There should be a bottle in the nightstand on the opposite side of the bed. I will take a draught now and then to help me sleep. And I use it as a form of 'Dutch courage'—I do not much care for the taste of gin—when the baron comes to exercise his 'conjugal rights'. As often happens, the spirit is willing but the flesh is weak and he is unable to rise to the occasion, so that I'm forced to provide some additional stimulus."

"Caroline," Watson shook his head in exasperation, "if someday the reading public tires of the adventures of Sherlock Holmes, so that I am forced to make a living by writing about other subjects, and if the Crown censors will sufficiently relax their standards, I am sure that I shall want to write your biography, including every salacious detail. But until then, keeping in mind the circumstances in which we find ourselves, please try to avoid explaining yourself to me each time I ask you a simple question and just tell me where I can find the bloody brandy!"

CHAPTER FORTY-ONE

*"...like politics, international intrigues
such as the one in which we find ourselves
now engaged, make for strange bed-fellows."*

"I can well understand her becoming hysterical." Watson for a moment looked over his right shoulder to check on Helene who was sitting on the bed, her arms clasping her knees, softly crooning little songs to herself. "It was just as she described. Heinrich and Klaus both dead. Because of the rigor mortis, I could not be sure, but I think that he must have broken every long bone in both their bodies in order to stuff them in the dumbwaiter like that. And the stench, good God, this house will never be rid of it. I did not see any penetrating wounds, so I assume that he killed them both with his bare hands. I can easily imagine her horror when she opened the dumb-waiter to send up the bucket of hot water. Poor child."

"How utterly disgusting." Caroline grimaced. "While I shall not greatly miss them, I would not wish such a horrible fate on anyone, save perhaps Gerald and his master." She sat rigidly in a chair next to the nightstand while Watson worked by the light of the unshaded lamp to repair the damage to her face. "Do you think," she tried to glance over at the servant girl, "Helene's had too much brandy?"

"She is a little drunk, but after what she's been through, that's probably a good thing. She be al-right..."

"Ouch! You're hurting me!"

"Be still. I'm almost done. Aren't you the one who assured me that women are far more able to endure pain than men? Evidently the cocaine is beginning to wear off. Just let me tie this one stitch off and we're done. There, not a bad job if I say so myself. I think a small gauze bandage, and..."

"No! I want to see." Caroline, momentarily forgetting her ribs, sprang up from the chair and went around to the other side of the bed to examine the results of Watson's suturing efforts in the pier mirror which stood against the opposite wall. "My God! What have you done to me? I'm disfigured for life. It looks like I have three eyes and one of them is winking. What man will ever want to look at me again?" She strode back across the room, her fists clenched. When she reached Watson she thrust her face toward his, "Want to kiss me, *mon cher?*"

"Caroline, stop it. I assure you that once the wound heals and the stitches are removed, it will not be at all noticeable, even in the most intimate situations. I was able to completely debride the wound, and I believe that the iodine will take care of any possible infection. I cut away the scar formation in the tissues beneath the surface of your skin, so I was able to get a nice regular margin. I used a large number of stitches—that's why it took so long that the anaesthetic was beginning to wear off—so as to hold the tightest possible closure. Believe me, I have stitched up far worse wounds than this one, and under far more difficult circumstances, trying as these may seem.

"Now hurry along, we've no time to spare. Holmes is expecting me back by six o'clock and," he pulled out his watch, "it's almost that now. Tell Helene that she must pack only as she would if she were accompanying you to an assignation. We do not want to draw any more attention than necessary. When the other servants return tomorrow, they will find the bodies and of course call the police. If all goes as planned your account with Villeneuf and Gerald, along with the due-bills owed numerous other people, will have been settled for good in just a few short hours from now. In a few weeks' time you can return to France and tell everyone how this wealthy, impetuous English gentleman insisted on taking you to London where he kept you in luxury at the Savoy, and took you 'round to all the finest salons where you met and mingled with the elite of London society."

"If I'm having such a grand time, why did I return to France?" Caroline asked sarcastically.

"Oh, I don't know. We'll think of something. Maybe you discovered that your paramour was merely a second son and thus was not going to inherit the title and estates. Perhaps his widower father fell in love with you as well, and forced to choose between *pere et fil,* you decided to choose neither. What difference does it make? The police will ask you a few questions, but you will be as mystified as they regarding what happened while you were away. You'll shake your head sadly, and bemoan the fact that it is so difficult to get reliable help these days. They'll no doubt ask Scotland Yard to corroborate your story, but we'll see that the proper response is sent. Hurry and get dressed. We can't be late."

"John, I cannot go with you. I..."

"Don't be absurd, Caroline. You not only can, you must. Have you suddenly developed amnesia so that you do not recall what has occurred in this house in the last twenty-four hours? Why can't you?"

"Look at me!" She stamped her foot and shook her head. "I can no more go into the Ritz looking as I do, than you would appear before your Queen wearing only your regimental small-clothes. Look at my hair! And what about my face!" She glared at Watson. "Are you sure you don't want to kiss me?"

"Caroline, stop being foolish. You know you can't stay here, or even in Paris, or anywhere in France, for that matter. How are you going to explain the two bodies that are now smelling up your larder downstairs? Are you going to explain your black eyes and bruises by telling them that you ran into a door? Even worse, what if, heaven forfend, something's happened to Holmes so that Villeneuf and Gerald remain at large? Do you think they'll leave a loose end like you laying about? For God's sake, woman, don't you have a hat with a veil? If you're not ready in ten minutes, I'm going to drag you out of here dressed just as you are. Now get along with you. Helene, up."

During the carriage ride neither woman said anything. Helene dozed, her head resting on Watson's shoulder, and Caroline alternated glaring at him while attempting to put on make-up using a small mirror which she carried in her reticule. Her grooming efforts were not aided by the clattering of the coach over the rough streets. Finally she gave up and confined herself to pouting and staring out the window.

As the carriage turned into the Place Vendome, Watson tried to awaken Helene who had fallen into a deep sleep and was snoring contentedly, her head still resting on his shoulder. His efforts succeeded in provoking a nightmare, in which, she later related, Heinrich and Klaus were reaching out trying to pull her into the dumb-waiter with them. She awoke with a scream that immediately turned into a new outbreak of hysterical sobbing. Even over the sound of the carriage and the noise of the traffic in the long plaza, the driver heard the commotion from within his vehicle and threatened to drive them into the courtyard of the Justice Ministry instead of their destination next door. Finally Caroline, aided by a gold Louis, persuaded the driver that one of his passengers was not being raped or murdered. In fact 'their daughter' was given to spontaneous fits of hysterics for no apparent reason, and would recover shortly. His concern was assuaged by Caroline's explanation along with the generous compensation. He remarked that he also had nubile daughters, and that they too were given to inexplicable fits of weeping so that he understood completely. He even continued to drive them 'round the plaza until Caroline assured him that everything was under control, whereupon he deposited them at Ritz's door and bade them a sympathetic *"bon soir"* as the *chassuer* assisted them from the carriage and smirked them through the glass revolving door.

To Caroline's relief, the lobby was relatively deserted, although there was a roaring torrent of conversation and laughter emanating from the salon as the cocktail hour was by now in full swing. Her fleeting hope that Watson could quickly negotiate the front desk was shattered almost instantly because the regular clerk who knew Watson and Holmes by sight was not on duty that evening. The replacement clerk's understanding of the English language was about on a par with Watson's French. An impasse of glaring punctuated by conflicting bursts of unintelligible conversation soon resulted and gave every indication of lasting until *M'sieur* Ritz could be summoned. Out of desperation, Caroline intervened and through a combination of threats and flattery, eventually managed to get Watson's room key along with an envelope addressed to him and a telegram and another envelope both addressed to Holmes.

Once inside Watson's room Caroline took off her hat and lay down on the bed, her forearm over her eyes. "What have I gotten myself into? That fat *schwein* Ollstreder, if I ever see him alive again, he'll wish that Gerald had finished him off. And as for you and your supercilious *M'sieur* Holmes...Oh God! How I detest men and their silly games. If by some chance I manage to survive this ridiculous farce, I swear I'm going to give up everything and become a nun. Yes, from now on, chastity and poverty and itchy underwear."

She got up and walked over to the mirror. Looking intently at her reflection in the glass she laughed. "Here I am, *Mlle.* Caroline Otero, one of *'Les Grandes Trois'*, courtesan *extraordinaire,* captive in a room at the Ritz with a priggish English doctor and a twit of a chamber-maid whose been frightened half out of her wits." She glanced in the mirror at Helene who was slumped in a chair, her legs splayed out in front of her and a silly grin on her face.

As soon as they got to the room Watson had opened the envelopes, first the one addressed to him, and then the telegram addressed to Holmes that proved indeed to be from Mycroft. Even with the key left by Holmes, the coded telegram proved difficult, but eventually he was satisfied that he'd gotten it correctly translated. During Caroline's tirade, he went into the water closet, tore the telegram and translation key into shreds and flushed them down the commode. By the time he'd returned, Caroline had turned around and was standing hands on hips glaring at him. "What were you doing? I was speaking to you..."

"Come over here, and have a look at these." Watson walked over to the table and picked up the third envelope. "They appear to me to be tickets—er, what's the French word? Oh yes, *'billets'*—to something or another, but I can't make out what."

"Here, let me have them." Caroline snatched the envelope out of his hand and extracted the two tickets. She glanced at them for a moment and handed them back to Watson. She lay back down on the bed, her head propped against the headboard. "They're tickets to a concert tonight at Saint Chappelle. Vivaldi's *'Four Seasons'* Concerto. I'm afraid, however that *Mlle.* Otero is quite indisposed this evening and shall be unable to attend. She sends her regrets, and hopes that you will invite her again on some more suitable occasion."

"Caroline, stop it. You simply must go with me; there's no other choice. Holmes obviously is not back or he would have picked them up at the front desk. Villeneuf must have left them for Holmes and me. Plainly this concert hall, wherever it may be, is where he plans to meet us either in person or through an emissary to present his kidnapper's demands. I need for you to accompany me because as you know my French is practically non-existent. Villeneuf may now have Holmes, as well as Miss Pippen and

Inspector Loiseaux, and possibly even Esterhazy and Ollstreder, if he's still alive. This may be my only means to save them. If I don't go..."

"His *what* demands?" Caroline sat upright in the bed. "Who are Miss... what did you say her name was? And Inspector Loiseaux? Isn't he the one who came to the house about the stolen automobile? Did you mention Esterhazy?" She shook her head in disbelief. "What's that lascivious worm got to do with this?

Watson stripped off his suit jacket, hung it in the closet and began laying out his evening clothes on the side of the bed opposite where Caroline was sitting. When he was done, he went around to her side of the bed. "My dear Caroline," he grasped her gently by the shoulders, "like politics, international intrigues such as the one in which we now find ourselves engaged make for strange bed-fellows. I must ask you to take me at my word for the moment. I assure you that all of the people I've named are in one way or another involved in this business. I cannot tell you everything, but I promise you that at the very least, the honour of your Country is at stake, not to mention the possibility that we may postpone if not entirely avert a major war. I'll explain more in the cab on the way to the concert. Now if you'll excuse me for a minute, I'll go in the bathroom and change into my evening clothes."

"I don't know why, but I half-way believe you." She got up from the bed and walked stiffly to the closet where Helene had stowed her small suitcase. As she made her way across the room she massaged her fingers into her rib cage. *"Merde!* My ribs are starting to hurt again. Do you think it too soon to take some more of those pills?"

"I suppose not. Why don't you loosen the corset for a few minutes while I'm in the other room dressing?"

After Watson finished dressing, Caroline took over the bathroom. While she was ensconced Watson summoned a bellman, and enjoined him to ask Ritz to come to the room immediately. Ritz arrived just as Caroline emerged from the bathroom. After a suitable amount of head shaking and tongue clucking, he agreed to move Helene to *"M'sieur* Melmoth's" room for the night and in the morning see that she got on a train to her home village in Provence.

332

As a result of the skilled use of make-up and strategic placement of her veil, Caroline was much less annoyed with her appearance. She even remarked what a handsome couple they made as they promenaded through the lobby and into a cab. In route, Caroline explained to Watson that Ste. Chapelle was a small church built in the thirteenth century and was now attached to the Palais de Justice on the Ile de la Citi. It was built to house what are thought to be some of the most venerated relics of Christianity. However these, along with the dependable stream of donations which they propagated, had been moved to the larger and more prestigious Cathedral of Notre Dame but a short distance away. So while Ste. Chappelle still functioned as a church, in order to remain self-supporting, it was now also used as a concert hall for small ensembles such as chamber orchestras and the aggregation of strings who would play tonight's performance. They arrived just in time to dash through the small wooden gate that served as an entrance to the courtyard, and up the steps of the chapel. They found seats at the very rear of the nave just as the small orchestra, which had arranged themselves in the chancel, had gotten their key from the first violin who served as both concertmaster and conductor.

They played a brief opening piece, and then moved directly to the Vivaldi. Watson and Caroline both looked about the smallish nave for anyone familiar but the chairs were arranged in regular rows all on one level, so it was impossible to see more than two or three rows ahead, and only a few seats from side to side in either direction. By the time the introductory piece was concluded, they'd all but given up looking. A few measures into the "Spring Season", they were caught up in the music, and for a time all but forgot why they were there.

As many seats as possible were fitted into the nave, and all were filled. The evening was seasonably warm, and inside the chapel the mass of people made it even warmer. Lighting was provided by relatively few candles arranged in sconces on the walls between the magnificent stained-glass windows, and by a few tall candelabra mostly at the front, illuminating the orchestra. The candles provided more heat than light, so that the nave was in virtual darkness. The combination of the warm, dark room, the vibrancy of the violas and double bass playing the intricate melodies, and perhaps a sense of peace and security after her ordeal, caused Caroline to link her arm through Watson's and to take his hand, and in a few minutes she was fast asleep, her head resting on his shoulder as had Helene's earlier.

Not wishing to disturb Caroline, whom in spite of everything—including her calling him a prig—he found himself growing to like, Watson remained motionless. Even though the familiar music was soothing to the senses, his mind was racing. He realized he'd made a mistake in not heeding Holmes's admonition to do nothing in his absence and had probably made things worse by bringing Caroline with him. Villeneuf was clearly expecting him and Holmes to show up at the concert. He supposed that he could have dissembled his way through Holmes's absence, but there was no way to explain Caroline's presence. Her being with him would leave no doubt that he knew most if not all of what had transpired in the Rue George Bizet last night, and Gerald's nurse persona would be of no further utility. On the other hand, left to his own devices and unable to speak the language, there was probably little chance of his saving anything or anyone, including himself. So on balance, he concluded, he was better off with Caroline, than without her.

Trying to figure out what Villeneuf was up to was infinitely more problematic. The "portfolio" which had been the cause of so much grief and pain to the baron undoubtedly contained some French state or military secret. It was evidently Ollstreder's plan to deliver the document and Esterhazy to Holmes and himself for them to turn over to the French Government and thereby establish Dreyfus's innocence. But of what use were they to Villeneuf? Was he also the baron's partner in the espionage business? Could his plan include taking over not only Ollstreder's share of the arms trafficking business but also the manipulation of Esterhazy as a conduit for feeding bogus information to the Section of Statistics? All of these questions might have made for a two- or three-pipe problem for Holmes, and Watson, indulging a brief maudlin twinge, thought to himself how interesting it would be to hear his friend articulate the solution. But the overarching problem was not a Baker Street arm-chair intellectual exercise; it required bold action as well as careful thought. That brought him back to the business at hand. Assuming that they were still alive, Villeneuf had at least two people, Miss Pippen and Inspector Loiseaux, as his captives. He also most probably had Ollstreder and Esterhazy, assuming that they too were still alive. In the cases of the Inspector and Ollstreder, their still being alive was at best a questionable assumption. And what of Holmes? What if his reconnoitering had gone awry and he too was now in Villeneuf's clutches? How can I, he mused, assisted only by Caroline, whose dedication to the enterprise might wane at any time, expect to find Villeneuf's lair and once it is found get past the formidable Gerald?

These last thoughts caused him to shudder involuntarily. His sudden movement startled Caroline from her sleep, and as she came awake she let out a small gasp of surprise. This brought a chorus of fingers-to-lips disapproving glares from those around her. The "Winter Season" was at its coda and in a few moments the concert was completed. The audience rose as one and gave the musicians a prolonged standing ovation, during which Watson took the opportunity to look about in the hope of spotting someone or something that would indicate the direction of his next move. In response to the audience's appreciative gesture, the musicians resumed their places and began an encore. As the audience resumed their seats Watson took Caroline's arm and began edging her toward the aisle, much to the displeasure of those whose feet they trod upon and whose enjoyment of the music they interrupted as they made their way out.

"Well that was certainly exciting," Caroline stifled a yawn as she descended the steps on Watson's arm, "not to mention utterly unproductive."

Watson gave her a reproachful look. "Let's wait here a bit. Since we were so late in arriving, and whoever was on the look-out for us was expecting Holmes and myself, I wouldn't be surprised if they failed to identify us and are equally bewildered. You'd not believe how often rendezvous such as these get bollixed up in the carrying-out, no matter how precise the planning."

"You don't say," Caroline remarked, the sarcasm obvious in her voice. "I have not eaten since noon yesterday and I'm ravenous. I will wait until the main body of the audience has left and after that you may take me to Maxim's, or I shall go there myself in the hope that some arch duke or other takes pity on me and buys me a morsel of food. Or perhaps I shall emulate some of my less esteemed sisters and grovel about the floor looking for stray Louis when they begin to toss them about."

"I should have thought that you were above such solipsism. I'm most disappointed to learn that you are not. Perhaps it was a mistake to involve you in this business to the degree that I have." Watson briefly grasped her upper arms, and then resignedly let his hands fall to his sides. "I thought that I'd managed to fan a spark of patriotism; you are after all a 'national treasure'. Or at the least you cared about what has or may yet happen to the baron. But it seems that I've mis-judged..."

"John, look." Now Caroline grasped Watson's upper arms. As they were standing, his back was more or less turned toward the chapel entrance. Caroline turned him partially around so he could see the concert patrons coming out the door and down the steps. She let go his arms and held the back of her hand to her mouth as though to suppress a scream. "It's... it's..."

"Gerald and Miss Pippen. Thank God she's alive." Gerald was now dressed in gentleman's evening clothes. Fiona, her hair freshly coifed, was dressed in a white empire-waist evening gown made of silk with bits of tulle at the bust line and around the short sleeves. Her arm was linked inside Gerald's, and as they descended the steps he held her hand as Watson had held Caroline's during the concert. When they reached the bottom of the steps Watson could see a wan smile frozen on her face.

"Who is she?" Caroline whispered. "Surely she has no idea who she's with. How can she be smiling? I thought you said she was one of the ones Villeneuf kidnapped. Evidently her captors have a rather enlightened idea of confinement. Obviously she does not find Gerald's attentions nearly as wearying as do I."

"Quiet, Caroline, please." I need to think." Watson turned so that he was again facing away from the steps. "Keep your eye on them, but don't let them see you staring. Let me know what they're doing."

"They're walking out the gate, John, which is exactly what I plan to do if you do not provide me with an extremely good reason to stay."

"Come along, Caroline." Watson seized her arm, and they started after Fiona and Gerald who by now had passed through the gate to the street where they turned toward the Palais de Justice and headed toward the Pont Au Change. "We must follow them. It's our only means to track Villeneuf to his hiding place. Couldn't you tell she was drugged? I mean she moved as though she were in a trance. Most likely a combination of drugs and hypnosis."

Watson and Caroline by then had reached the street. They also turned left, falling in behind Fiona and Gerald. They followed along about twenty-five paces back, liberally sprinkling *"excuzes-mois"* and *"pardons"* as they threaded their way through the leisurely-strolling concert patrons. As they walked, Watson continued, "Because you were wearing a hat with a heavy veil that covers most of your face and since my back was to them, in the dim light Gerald did not recognize us. As I said before, they were expecting Holmes and Watson. By letting us see her at the concert they were going to prove that Miss Pippen was still alive and relatively unharmed. They figured that by now we'd know that Gerald killed Andre. So having her appear in Gerald's company sends the simultaneous message that her relatively unharmed status could change for the worse at any moment in the event that we do not meet their demands.

"When they did not see both Holmes and Watson, they assumed that neither of us was here and so now Gerald is returning Miss Pippen to wherever they've been holding her. If we're able to follow them and if we're in luck, we'll be able to take Villeneuf and Gerald by surprise and free not only Miss Pippen, but whomever else's being held captive."

"This is madness," she hissed in Watson's ear. "What if we lose sight of him? What if he sees us? He could kill her in an instant and escape. Or he could turn on you."

"If that occurs, have no fear. Even Gerald is no match for my Webley." As a precaution, Watson transferred his revolver from the rear to the front of his waist-band.

"Then why don't we confront him now. What if he has confederates wherever it is that he's going? At least you could rescue your precious Miss Pippen."

"That's an appealing thought, Caroline. But let's go on as we are for a while. If our luck holds, we may yet save the whole lot."

By this time, Gerald and Miss Pippen had reached the other end of the bridge and had turned right in the direction of the Hotel de Ville. The pedestrian traffic by now had thinned to only an occasional passer-by, so Watson let the distance between themselves and their quarry widen even more as he and Caroline tried as much as possible to remain in the shadows. When they reached the edge of the bridge on the right bank, Gerald and Miss Pippin were not in sight. Watson took out his revolver, and with his other hand took Caroline's hand and pulled her along as he quickened his pace. "Hurry," he whispered, "I've lost sight of them. Perhaps you were right. We'd best confront Gerald now, while I've got him one-against-one."

"That is," she whispered breathlessly, "if we haven't lost them already. Oh!" Caroline stumbled and broke Watson's grip. "I can't go any faster. These shoes were not made for this sort of activity." Caroline regained her footing and made her way to the low parapet-like wall at the edge of the river embankment. She stood looking over the wall, one hand on the top of the wall supporting her upper body and the other holding her ribs as she tried to catch her breath. "I'm..." she gasped for breath, "sorry." She paused while she took up her veil and rolled it over the brim of her hat. "I've made you lose them."

"Don't feel badly. I let them get too far ahead of us. I can't imagine where they could have gone. They were in sight and in the next moment they disappeared."

Caroline continued leaning over the wall. "Why don't you go on. Maybe someone noticed them, and..."

"And how would you suggest that I conduct my enquiries? I don't..."

"John, down there along the walk." She pointed to the broad stone path running along the riverbank about twenty-five feet below. "See, next to that barge. Someone moved."

Watson peered in the direction that Caroline pointed, shading his eyes from the street lamp at the end of the bridge. "You're right, old girl. There must be stairs farther down. Come along. We can keep them in sight as we go." He grasped her elbow and started in the direction of the stairs.

"Who?" Caroline jerked her arm away. She sat down on the top of the wall, her arms folded. "What did you call me?"

"What did I... Oh for heaven's sake, Caroline, it's only an expression." Caroline remained where she was, her arms folded and her mouth set in a defiant pout. "Look here, I'm sorry." He held out his hand once more, but she twisted her upper body away from him. "Very well," he bowed from the waist, "would the youthful and lovely *Mlle.* Otero graciously consent to accompany Dr. Watson whilst he places his life at risk and attempts to rescue a damsel in distress as well as sundry others?"

"That's much better." She held out her hand for Watson to take. "*Mlle.* Otero, would be delighted."

With revolver in hand, Watson led as they quickly made their way along the wall until they came to an opening leading to a set of stone steps descending to the water side. Below street level it was completely dark, the nearest illumination being the street lamp at the foot of the bridge, now above and behind them. Mid-way down there was a landing, no more than the width of half a dozen steps. They paused, straining in the darkness and the silence to see or hear anything. Watson pulled Caroline against the rough stone of the embankment wall. He gestured toward the river with his revolver, "There, look." There was a faint amount of light reflecting off the water against which the silhouette of a barge could be made out. "Listen. You can hear the creak of the hawsers. There. Did you see that?" For an instant there was a sharp shaft of light emanating from a porthole amidships. "They must have gone aboard. Stay here; I'm going to get closer and try to hear what's going on inside." Watson started down the lower flight of steps and in spite of his instructions, Caroline followed a step behind him.

They continued to edge their way down the steps, their backs pressed against the embankment seeking the darkness to cover their movements. As they neared the bottom, Watson started to cross over to the outer rail. "Be careful, John," Caroline whispered.

As Watson reached the last step, he stopped and turned to Caroline who was standing on the next step up so that they were face to face. She reached out and put her arms around his neck pulling him toward her until their lips met. Their embrace lasted only for a few seconds, and then Caroline pulled away and put her lips next to Watson's ear. "Please don't do anything foolish. I've never been to London, and I'm so looking forward to it."

Gently Watson pressed a finger to her lips. "S-h-h-h. No more talking. Don't worry about me. I'm not going to try to take

339

the vessel single-handed. I'm just going along side to listen and try to tell who's on board. Count to three hundred. If they're not on the boat, or if I can't tell with certainty, I'll come back and we can decide on some other course of action. I'm not back by the time you're through counting, then I will have determined with certainty that they are in fact on board. In that case, you should summon the police. You only need to tell them that you've located the whereabouts of Inspector Loiseaux and they will come at once and in force. Do you understand?" Caroline took Watson's free hand and pressed, it to her cheek, and then kissed the tips of his fingers. Just as she released Watson's hand, even in the poor light Watson could see a look of utter horror cross her face. "No! Please, no!" She stumbled backwards and sat down hard on the steps.

"Caroline, what is..."

"Do not turn around, Dr. Watson." Watson felt the unmistakable shape of a large calibre gun barrel in the small of his back. "Raise your hands slowly. Yes, there's a good chap. I'll have your weapon now, if you please." Watson complied, allowing the Webley to hang by the trigger guard from his index finger. "Thank you." He felt the weapon being lifted from his hand. "And now, if you'll both come with me, there's an old acquaintance of yours on board, Dr. Watson, and he's most eager to renew your relationship. You've much to catch up on, not to mention chatting about good times past. Would you be so kind as to assist Miss Otero to her feet?"

"Gerald, no! I beg you, let Dr. Watson go! You've got his weapon, he can do you no harm. He can't even speak the language. Please, I'll go with you. You can finish what you started last night. I know you wanted me, and I wanted you. Yes, it's true. I adore it when my lovers play rough. Remember how I looked when you removed my bustier, when you bent me over the sofa?

"Caroline, stop it. Don't..."

"Shut up, harlot!" Gerald shoved Watson aside and slapped Caroline hard across the face. Watson regained his balance and lunged at Gerald throwing a roundhouse right which struck the much taller man on the shoulder, doing no damage. Watson's momentum carried him past Gerald, and he landed heavily against the embankment wall. In an instant Gerald was on him, the barrel of Watson's own revolver pressed under his chin, the hammer back. "Steady on, mate. On your feet, nice and easy. This is your lucky night. My instructions are to deliver you in one piece." Watson picked up his top hat and got slowly to his feet. He started to put his hat back on, but when he touched the side of his head he felt the sticky wetness of his own blood as well as a flap of torn flesh from his head striking the rough stone.

Once Watson was back on his feet, Gerald glanced over his shoulder at Caroline who'd landed against the stair railing where she lay crying softly. "Get up, you worthless slut!" Gerald waived the revolver at her. She got to her feet, and trembling with fear edged past Gerald. When she reached Watson's side she took his arm with both her hands. "There, now that's better." Gerald gestured again with the gun. "This way if you please."

CHAPTER FORTY-TWO

"How can you sit here and carry on a civilised conversation with this monster who in a very little while is going to have us killed simply because it pleases him to do so."

As they walked toward the boat, Caroline clung tightly to Watson's arm. With his free hand, Watson pressed a handkerchief to his scalp wound and tried to ignore the brassy taste in his mouth that was the result of the dizziness and nausea caused by striking his head. He was sure that he'd sustained at least a mild concussion. Gerald stayed a few paces behind them, perhaps anticipating that Watson might try and swing 'round on him catching him off guard. It was not that he feared Watson as a hand-to-hand combat opponent, but he'd been made to give his word that he would capture them and bring them aboard without doing any more damage than absolutely necessary. Usually he was able to keep his rage under control, if just barely so. However, Caroline, both last night and tonight, had pushed him over the brink. But he knew that his guv' would be displeased with him if he did anything now, rather than waiting until he was given his leave. He was still sore where she'd kicked him, and when she mentioned last night, he felt an excruciating pain that began in his groin and stabbed all the way up into his gut.

When they reached the gangplank, it proved to be just that: a single wooden plank about ten inches wide. Watson stopped, not trusting himself to walk so narrow a path, especially with the boat rocking in the wake of another barge which had sailed past as they were walking from the steps to the edge of the water. "'Ere, what's this? Get a move on." Gerald barked.

"I can't make it. I'm too dizzy from striking my head. Let me stand here a moment until my head clears. Caroline, can you tear off a strip of petticoat that I can use as a bandage? I need to tie something around my head to stop the bleeding, and my handkerchief is already soaked through." Caroline let go her grip on Watson's arm and started to lift the hem of her gown.

"Never mind that," Gerald barked. "If you don't get a move on right now, it's not your head that you'll be worryin' about; it'll be my boot up your arse that'll be botherin' you." He took a menacing step toward Watson and then stopped. "Ladies first, isn't it? Not that you are one." He waived the gun at Caroline. "You get your arse up there first and help him across. And if 'e ends up in the bloomin' drink, I swear I'll shoot 'im like a fish in a barrel."

Caroline did as she was told. When she reached the gunwale, she stopped and turned around stretching out her hand toward Watson who'd mounted the plank and taken a couple of hesitant steps. Slowly, agonizingly, he made his way forward until he was finally able to grasp Caroline's hand. As he reached the end of the gangplank, Caroline stepped aside, and stood delicately on the gunwale until Watson inched past her and stumbled forward onto the main deck of the boat. Then she gracefully hopped down into his waiting arms. Gerald lumbered up the gangplank, his gun leveled steadily at Watson. As they stood waiting, Caroline murmured, "When I was a little girl, I'd hoped to become a ballerina. Oh John, how I wish I were that scrawny eleven year-old right now. What's going to happen to us?" She began to tremble as tears welled up in her eyes.

"'Ere, that's enough o' that for now," Gerald dropped from the gunwale onto the deck causing the boat to list to its mooring side. "One more word, and I'll forget me manners. It's inside with you now, so move along.

"You first Doc; remember I've got your revolver stuck in your playmate's back. Try anything, and at this close range, the bullet's likely to pass clean through her and end up in you. And if it didn't kill you, you might get to spend the rest of your days in a chair just like me guv'. That's it, nice and easy. Just open that door and step down into the 'allway."

Watson and Caroline did as they were told, and found themselves after stepping down three small steps, standing in the front of a companionway that apparently ran the length of the vessel's superstructure along the port side, much like a first-class railway carriage. On the outer wall there were small windows that provided a view of the black river and a few lights coming from buildings on the far bank. On the inboard side, there were a series of doors leading, Watson surmised, to cabins and common rooms

343

for the crew and any passengers. Mounted in sconces on the wall between the doorways were dimly-lighted oil lamps. Gerald pulled the outer door shut behind him. "You," he poked Caroline in the back with the revolver, "lie down on the floor, face down." He reached behind his shoulder and grabbed a length of hemp that was hanging from a steel peg on the inside of the companionway door. The rope was about five feet long and fashioned into a simple slip knot at one end. "'Ere, Doc," he tossed the rope to Watson, "slip the loop 'round 'er neck and tie 'er hands nice and secure behind 'er back. Be sure there's no slack in the rope, so that if she's a mind to try and work loose she'll only end up 'angin' 'erself."

Watson glared at him briefly, and then did as he was instructed. As he bent over Caroline's body he started to whisper in her ear, "Don't..."

Gerald prodded Watson hard in the back of the neck with the gun. "That's enough o' that, mate. No time for whispering love words in 'er ear. No more talking 'till I say so." He poked Watson again. "Got it?" Watson nodded. When he was through tying her hands, he started to stand up and again. Gerald prodded him hard in the back of the neck. "Not so fast, mate. Now it's your turn. Lie down on top of her with your hands behind your back."

Watson turned his head trying to look back over his shoulder and for his trouble received a vicious swat on the ear with the barrel of the gun. He bit his lip to keep from crying out. His head throbbing from the pain, he felt the warm trickle of blood in his ear. He sensed Gerald standing astride his hips. Then Gerald grabbed Watson's hair and jerked his head back so that he could slip the second rope around his neck. In an instant, Watson realized the Gerald must have put down the guns so as to have both hands free. Just as the rope began to slip over his forehead, Watson pulled his right leg back until his instep was cradled in the palm of his hand. Tensing his thigh muscles as tight as he could, he released his doubled up leg driving his foot into Gerald's groin. Gerald let out a high-pitched shriek as the toe of Watson's boot bore deep into his crotch crushing the already inflamed and tender tissues.

The force of the kick drove Gerald backwards. He let out a second scream as he smashed into the door and was impaled through the shoulder by the peg on which he'd earlier hung the ropes. With one hand still clutching his groin, he reached the other across his chest and grasped his impaled shoulder. Just as he did, one of the guns fell out of his waist-band, and clattered to the floor. As soon as Watson delivered the kick, he rolled off of Caroline and scrambled to his feet. He saw the gun, his own Webley, lying at Caroline's feet. Instantly he picked it up. As he fitted his finger on the trigger and started to thumb back the hammer, there was a tremendous explosion behind him. A heavy calibre bullet roared past his ear and struck the door, barely an inch from Gerald's head.

"That will be quite enough, Doctor Watson." The voice behind him, although soft, was as clear and piercing as a glass cutter slicing a window pane. "Do put down your revolver. Guns are so uncivilised. Don't you agree?" Watson stood up straight and let his gun hand fall to his side. "There, that's better. Now just set it on the floor next to *Mlle.* Otero, and since you seem to be so agile with your feet tonight, kick it backward along the floor in this direction."

Watson hesitated. Even though the companionway was narrow, he could dive one way or the other, creating a fifty-fifty chance that his opponent would shoot instinctively and guess the wrong direction. But then, he thought, I will not be in a very good position to return fire and I'm just as likely to miss, even at this range. As if he could read Watson's mind, the man behind him spoke evenly. "It won't work, Doctor Watson. I'll take my chances on your first shot not finding its mark. Mine, however, will not be aimed at you. My next shot will be at a stationary, somewhat smaller target: namely, the top of *Mlle.* Otero' s lovely, if rather disheveled head."

Unwilling to risk Caroline's life against such poor odds, Watson did as he was bidden. He knelt on his right knee and placed the gun on the floor. Then standing back up, he pushed it with his toe until he was sure that it was past Caroline's head, and then gave it a stronger prod so that, judging from the sound, it slid along the floor nearly the length of the companionway. "Very sound judgement, Doctor. Once again, *Mlle.* Otero is indebted to a gallant man who is so smitten with her charms that he would place her well-being ahead of his own life. *Mademoiselle,* how do you do it?" He laughed, although it sounded more like a cackle, as Caroline began to struggle to her feet.

"Gerald, if you can tear yourself away, perhaps it would be best if you would complete your restraining of Dr. Watson. It would be so much more pleasant if we could have our little conversation without the distraction of wondering what fool-hardy feat he will attempt next. Doctor, if you would be so good as to turn around this way..."

With another shriek of pain, Gerald tore himself loose. "Please, guv', just let me..." Gerald began to cry. "He...he...he kicked me in my...and...and...I'm stuck in me shoulder like a bloomin' pig, I am..."

"Enough, Gerald! Stop that blubbering at once! If you do not control yourself, you'll not get your play time later. Is that what you want?"

Sniveling all the while, Gerald slipped the loop over Watson's head tightening it so much that Watson could barely draw breath. As Gerald began to bind his wrists, Watson remembered a magazine article he'd read about the American escape artist Eric Weiss. In it the author had revealed that Weiss flexed the muscles of whatever part of him that was being bound, so that when he relaxed, there would be just enough slack that he could work himself free. Watson tried to do the same and when Gerald was through, he found that there actually was the minutest bit of slack, should an opportunity later arise to take advantage of it. Gerald tested the tension of the rope between Watson's neck and wrists and being satisfied reported, "All done guv'."

"Very good, Gerald." The man pivoted about in his wheelchair, "Bring them along to my stateroom, and we'll have our little chat. And while we do, perhaps you'll look in on our other guests and make sure that they're not wanting for anything, at least insofar as circumstances permit." He wheeled through an open door at the far end of the companionway and Gerald prodded Caroline and Watson along, stopping to pick up Watson's revolver as they walked past.

The room was fitted out much like a sea captain's quarters on an ocean-going vessel. There was a comfortable-looking bunk bed built into an alcove in the stern wall, and in front of that, a heavy wooden table that could serve as either a desk or dining table as needed. The man wheeled himself to the side of the table nearest the bunk and poured a glass of clear liquid from a decanter setting to his right on the table-desk. Gerald seized Watson and Caroline by their ropes and jerked them down in the two armless wooden chairs that were situated on the opposite side of the table-desk.

"Thank you, Gerald, that will be all for now. Before you attend to our other guests, you perhaps should pour some brandy in your wound. I'm sure that Dr. Watson would be glad to treat it, but he's tied up at the moment and quite unable to be of any assistance." He smiled delightedly as Watson grimaced in pain. "Besides, it appears that you've mislaid your medical bag, although I suspect that Dr. Watson may know something of its whereabouts. Perhaps later on he will tell you where it is, so that you can go and fetch it and then you and he can play with the implements until your heart's content.

"Welcome aboard." He held up his glass in front of Watson and Caroline in a mock toast. "Vichy water," he gestured with his glass. "It's quite healthful, I'm made to understand."

"You, I assume, are 'P. Villeneuf'. I recognize you from the channel crossing. And I gather we're aboard the late Captain Richard's river barge."

"Actually, to respond to your second statement first, the barge belongs to me; the late Captain was my employee. Such a shame, his demise I mean. It's so extremely difficult to find good help these days. Regarding your first statement, as *Mlle.* Otero will confirm, I am indeed 'P. Villeneuf'. However, although we've never actually met, you've known me for many years, albeit under a different name."

Watson looked puzzled. "What does the initial 'P.' stand for?"

He sucked in his gaunt cheeks and slowly turned his head toward Caroline.

"Perhaps *Mlle.* Otero will assist you in a brief French lesson, Doctor Watson. *Mademoiselle?*"

Caroline steadily returned his look, her eyes narrow and her nostrils flared in hatred. "What is it you wish? Why don't you just kill us and be done with it? I hope you rot in hell, you flaccid bag of bones!"

"Please, *Mlle.* Otero. Is that what you really want? Do not make such categorical presumptions regarding your fate. Now if you please, *Mademoiselle,* would you kindly assist Doctor Watson by translating the words *'ville'* and *'neuf'* into English?"

Caroline shook he head defiantly. "You miserable excuse for a man sitting in that chair. I'll bet you couldn't satisfy a woman if you tried all night. Is that what your precious 'Geraldine' does for you?" Caroline spit at him and her saliva landed in his water glass. "There. Does 'Geraldine' have to hold it for you when you..."

"Caroline, control yourself!" Watson leaned toward her so that their shoulders were touching.

Villeneuf took out a pocket handkerchief and wiped a drop of spittle from his wrist. "You must be more understanding, Dr. Watson. You've no doubt heard the maxim 'when the only tool you have is a hammer, all problems look like nails'. In *Mlle.* Otero's case, her hammer... well, I'm sure you grasp the analogy. *Mlle.* Otero," he shifted his gaze to Caroline, a slight smile at the corners of his mouth. "Now that you've had your little say, would you be so kind as to oblige Dr. Watson and myself?"

"I do not wish to play your silly word games." Caroline glared at Villeneuf defiantly.

"Then perhaps you would prefer to join the others. While the hold is not fitted out nearly as comfortably as this cabin, I'm sure that you and Gerald will find ways to keep one another amused. I'm certain as well that the others would welcome a fresh face, especially one as lovely as yours, *Mademoiselle.* And as for Dr. Watson and myself, we'll just muddle through on our own. However, be assured that as we do, our thoughts will be with you, especially in case you should find Gerald's attentions unbearable and therefore feel compelled to scream. No, on second thought, I'd best ask Gerald to fit you with a gag. We shouldn't want your cries to attract the curiosity of some passer-by."

As Villeneuf started to pull back from the desk to reach for the bell pull next to the bunk, Watson turned toward Caroline. "Caroline, don't be a stubborn fool. Do what he says. At least you'll be spared the depredations of Gerald—or Geraldine—whichever it is?"

"Gerald or Geraldine, either will do, Dr. Watson. My ward's gender role—how shall I say it—is something of an unresolved ambiguity."

"Your ward?" Watson echoed.

"Yes, Dr. Watson, I am Gerald's legal guardian. But more of that in a moment. *Mlle.* Otero, have you decided to continue favouring us with your charming presence?"

Caroline glared at Watson as if to say "How can you sit here and pretend to carry on a civilized conversation with this despicable monster who in a very little while is going to have us killed simply because it pleases him to do so?" Determined not to betray the terror that clutched her stomach, Caroline sat up straight in her chair. "Very well, *M'sieur,* say again what it is you wish me to do."

"Translate the words *'ville'* and *'neuf'* into English for Dr. Watson."

Caroline thought for a moment. "*Ville'*... a *'ville'* is a city. And *'neuf', 'neuf'* means 'new'. Your name in *anglais* means 'city new'? Why do you not just call yourself 'Rumpelstiltskin'? This is ridiculous."

"Patience, my dear. You've almost got it. What do you call a smaller city?"

His impatience growing as well, Watson interjected, "A small city? A village? A town?"

"Excellent, Dr. Watson. Your facileness with words never ceases to amaze me."

"Then your name is 'Town new'?"

"No, wait. I've got it. It's Newton. That's it, your name is 'P. Newton'. But what does the 'P.' stand for? Peter? Paul? Percival? Pierre?"

Villeneuf drummed his fingers impatiently on the desk, "Try a title, Dr. Watson."

"A title? Hmmm." Watson, his head throbbing, tried to concentrate. Finally he asked, "Is it 'Professor' Newton? Aren't you almost two centuries too late?"

"Yes and no, Dr. Watson. While the late Sir Isaac first postulated the binomial theorem—and may I add reaped all the glory—it was my proofs that..."

"No! It can't be...You're...I mean...Moriarty is dead. He died eight years ago..." Watson shuddered and stretched his wrists against his bonds causing the slip knot to tighten around his neck resulting in his gasping for air and turning red-faced.

"Mlle. Otero, perhaps you should get out of your chair and walk around behind Dr. Watson. With your fingers I'm sure that you'll be able to loosen the knot around his neck sufficiently to allow his normal breathing to be restored." Caroline sat still, looking from one man to the other. Villeneuf-Newton-Moriarty clapped his hands together sharply. "Quickly! Do it at once, *Mademoiselle.* Can you not see that he's choking?"

Caroline, still not comprehending the reason for Watson's paroxysm, got up and standing behind his chair managed to get her fingers on the noose and loosen its death grip on his throat. Watson's face, which had begun to go from red to blue, began to return to its normal coloration. Finally he stopped gasping and managed to ask for water. "In the cabinet to your left, Mademoiselle. You should be able to open it and remove a fresh glass. Or perhaps Dr. Watson would not object to drinking out of this one." Moriarty held up the glass which he'd poured for himself just a few minutes ago.

Giving Moriarty her most contemptuous look, Caroline went over to the cabinet and managed to secure a glass which she set on the edge of the desk nearest to Moriarty. "Here, *M'sieur* whatever your name is." She started to return to her seat.

"Attendez une minute, Mademoiselle." Moriarty placed his bony, claw-like hand on Caroline's wrist. "Dr. Watson shall also need your assistance in bringing the glass to his lips." He poured a nearly full glass of the Vichy water and set it back on the edge of the desk.

"Will you stop these childish games and say what you want of us? Are you going to force us to bob for apples next?"

"Caroline, please," Watson gasped. "The water..." Caroline managed to pick up the glass, and without spilling too much walked around to the side of Watson's chair. With her back to him she was finally able to maneuver the glass so that he could drink the water. Spilling more down the front of his shirt than he was able to swallow, Watson finally managed a few sips and indicated to Caroline that he was done. After she set the glass back on the desk, she returned to her seat.

"As you can plainly see, Dr. Watson, I am quite alive. However, as you know, I suffered an accident mountain-climbing in Switzerland a little more than eight years ago. I was able to drag myself down from the accident site and since then I've been more or less as you now see me." He turned his head toward Caroline. "You see, *Mlle*. Otero, for many years now a state of rather bitter enmity has existed between Mr. Holmes and Dr. Watson on the one hand, and myself on the other. And in recent years, since his coming of age, my ward—or I suppose I should now say, former ward—has joined me and helps somewhat to maintain the delicate balance of forces between the two sides."

"Your ward?" Watson asked. "Who..."

"Gerald Moran, Dr. Watson. I believe you were acquainted with his late father..."

"You mean he's the son—or whatever he is—of Colonel..."

"Yes indeed, Dr. Watson. Gerald is none other than the son of the late, lamented Colonel Sebastian Moran. When the good Colonel met his untimely death, he made me promise to take in his only child and see to his proper upbringing. This I was only too glad to do. My one regret is that Gerald's intellectual capacity does not match his impressive physical stature.

"Early on in our relationship, I realized that Gerald was probably not going to live up to my hopes for him. My plan was for him to take over where I left off in my investigation of the properties inherent in the binomial theorem. Newton barely scratched the surface, and my own accomplishments opened numerous promising areas of inquiry, awaiting only some eager, brilliant young mind to take up where my own efforts were so cruelly attenuated. Even though my work was warmly received on the Continent..."

"I take it that Alphonse Bertillon was your acolyte?" Watson interjected.

"Very perceptive, Dr. Watson. Even today he is one of my closest colleagues. In his case as well, I also had hopes for a brief while that he would carry on what I'd begun. His best work, however, was done, like so many other mathematicians, before he turned thirty. He shrewdly built on his celebrity from the Koenigstein case, then the Dreyfus case, eventually turning his energies almost exclusively to his *'bertillonage* system'.

"But to continue my thought, in contrast to the reception my work received on the Continent, I was subjected to nothing but ridicule throughout Britain. I applied to every college and university in the land for either a teaching chair or research grant so that I could continue my work. Most of the 'learned' professors who even bothered to look at my work were incapable of understanding it and the rest thought me a plagiarizer like Lobachevsky. Sooner or later every door was closed to me. You see I was but a poor Irish lad from a large family. No titles, no lands, and mainly self-educated in the bargain. I was not one of the old-school chaps, not part of the clique whose families had known one another and intermarried for generations. Chairs and grants are awarded, I eventually came to find out, based not on what you know, or what promise you show, but on whom you know.

"In any case, denied the career of choice, I like Bertillon after me, turned to criminology as a career."

"Criminology?" Watson asked.

"Whom do you know, beside your prejudiced choice of Holmes, that knows more about crime and the criminal mind than myself?"

"You had a chair, if I recall rightly. And I assume that it was you who assisted Bertillon in securing his first teaching post."

"Your memory does not fail you, Dr. Watson. Yes, it was I who first opened the world of academe to dear Alphonse. My application for tenure had not been given favourable consideration, so my 'chair', such as it was, was at best a precarious perch upon which to continue building a career. When I was not awarded tenure, I knew that my own career as an academician was on the down-slope and that I would never be given the recognition that I deserved. I had already settled on what my new career would be. I had further decided, not yet having built up a network of at least sometimes reliable henchmen, that my first criminal enterprise would be in the field of extortion—'blackmail' to use the more vulgar term. One person acting alone can bring it off, and the risk of being caught and prosecuted is virtually nil.

"For sometime prior to my receiving Bertillon's plea for assistance, I'd been working on setting up my first endeavour in my new field. The then-assistant headmaster of the public school in Smithwyck had a fondness for young boys which extended not merely to their eager young minds, but to their bodies as well. I managed to come into possession of a number of letters written to youngsters whose welfare, in addition to their education, had been placed in his hands by their trusting or, as often as not, indifferent parents. The British upper classes, and you should know this better than me, are like amphibians in the rearing of their offspring; they hatch them, and then leave them more or less to fend for themselves. The letters were shockingly explicit in content, such that even if they were fictitious, their delivery to the authorities would have earned the worthy master a long stretch in Reading Gaol for sending obscene material through the Royal Post."

In spite of his predicament, Watson had to ask, "How did you..."

"Elementary, my dear Watson," Moriarty cackled and rubbed his hands together as Watson winced. "It's amazing what a bag of treacle candy, or in the case of the older boys, a pack of cigarettes, can purchase. Holmes spends far too much on his 'street arabs'. A handful of hore-hound drops is more than enough. Ah, but I digress..."

Caroline, who'd been sitting silently, her head tilted back and staring at the ceiling, sat upright at the mention of cigarettes, "Speaking of cigarettes, if I'm to sit here and listen to you tell us your life story—which Dr. Watson may find totally absorbing but I do not—I should at least like to have a cigarette."

"I am truly sorry, *Mlle.* Otero, both that I'm evidently boring you and that I cannot accommodate your wish for a cigarette at this very moment. Perhaps later..."

"You mean when I'm given a blindfold as well?"

"Please, *Mlle.* Otero...by the way, since Dr. Watson addresses you as 'Caroline', do you mind if I take the liberty of doing so as well? Do not let yourself think such morbid thoughts. If all goes as planned, I cannot picture you by dawn's early light in front of a firing squad, at least not one assembled by me."

Caroline's nostrils flared in anger, "You may call me 'mother dearest' if that is your wish. But if you're not planning to do away with me, why am I trussed up like a pheasant about to be cooked for dinner? I have nothing to do with this business of yours, this export-import whatever it is..."

Moriarty put his hands over his mouth in mock horror. "Oh dear me, Caroline. I'm afraid you've said just a bit too much. The baron assured me that you had no knowledge whatsoever of our little business arrangement. Now that I know that his representation to me in this respect is in error, Gerald and I shall have to rethink your role. At the very least, I shall have to be persuaded that your knowledge is not of such a nature as to pose a threat to my interests. And I'm afraid that will mean getting Gerald more involved than either you or I would want." He wheeled himself back and tugged on the bell pull.

"No!" Watson shouted. "Leave her alone! Your business is with Holmes and me."

"Very touching, Dr. Watson. Essentially the same sentiments were expressed to me by the baron only last night. But alas, I'm afraid that's not the case. While it is true that you, Mr. Holmes and I have a great deal of unfinished business, there are other issues which must be dealt with and they are of no concern to you and Mr. Holmes. Ah, Gerald. Thank you for responding so quickly."

Gerald entered the cabin, revolver in hand. When he saw Caroline and Watson still bound and seated where he left them, he looked puzzled. "Everything al-right, guv'?"

"Everything's fine, Gerald, everything's fine. Dr. Watson and I were just catching up on old times, and *Mlle.* Otero has become quite bored and more than a little restless. Why don't you take her below, but keep her separate from the others. Oh yes, and since she's most desirous of having a cigarette, I suppose there would be no harm in your lighting one for her and holding it while she smokes."

Gerald seized Caroline by her rope restraint and led her toward the door. "That's it, Missy. Come along with Gerald, just like the guv' says. You 'n me'll have lots of fun soon as we gets down below."

"Gerald! That's quite enough of that for now. Do exactly with Miss Otero as I instructed you."

"But guv'" Gerald started to protest.

"But nothing, Gerald. Now do as I say." After a long pause, Gerald shrugged and led Caroline out of the cabin, closing the door behind him.

"I do so wish that I could dissuade him from calling me 'guv', it's so unbecoming, don't you think?"

"I've really no opinion on the subject, Professor Moriarty, other than to mention that I could, if pressed, think of a few terms with which to describe you that one might find far more pejorative. You mentioned some 'unfinished business', I believe."

"In due course, Dr. Watson, in due course." Moriarty, instead of wheeling himself back to the desk, went instead to the china cabinet and took out another glass. He returned to the desk and filled the fresh glass from the carafe. "First, I need to take my pain medication." He opened a drawer in the desk and took out a bottle of the now familiar white pills. He downed several, followed by a long drink of the Vichy water. "What a blessing these Aspirin have been. As a result of my 'accident' I sustained a rupture of one of my spinal disks, evidently where the sciatic nerve branches out..."

"Then you still have the use of your legs?" Watson's professional curiosity got the better of him.

"To a limited extent, yes. With leg braces and canes, I can manage to get about for short distances. But since my physical activity is minimal anyway, I do not find the wheel chair to be that great an inconvenience. Were it not for the pain, I suppose that I should be relatively content."

"Relatively?"

"I am reminded daily, after all, that my one and only attempt at strenuous physical activity ended rather badly. Would you not agree?"

"You will forgive me, I trust, if I maintain an air of professional detachment in regard to your condition?"

"That would not surprise me in the least, Dr. Watson. And more's the pity that you chose to throw in your lot with Holmes. All these years listening to Holmes's execrable fiddle-playing and having to write about his 'amusing little problems' most of which he made unduly complicated by his self-important pontificating."

Angered by Moriarty's slander, Watson began getting red-faced again. "I say..."

"Steady on, Dr. Watson. You don't want to strangle yourself. That wouldn't do at all. Just think of all the fascinating stories you could have written if you'd been privy to some of my exploits. If one is going to write about true crime, what better way than to have the perspective of one who is indeed Europe's 'highest expert'?"

"You mean you want me to write your biography?"

"Perhaps at one time, that would have been feasible, Dr. Watson. But by now, we've far too much history between us. Actually, what I had in mind is for you to write about a rather sensational double murderer, and from the perspective of the culprit himself."

"Moriarty, you're mad, mad as a..."

Moriarty slammed his fist on the desk so hard that the carafe and glasses nearly overturned. His tone turned cold, "It would be very much in your own interest, Dr. Watson, if you would refrain from making ill-informed diagnoses regarding the state of my mental health. Should you survive this night, in the weeks and months to come, you will think upon our conversation many times. In your ruminations you may think of me as diabolical, cruel, remorseless or any of those other 'pejorative terms' to which you alluded earlier. You may also call me 'old', you may call me 'a cripple', you may even refer to me as bald-headed," he ran his hand over his nearly hairless pate, "but under no circumstances will you ever again refer to me as a madman!"

"As you wish, Professor. In my present incapacitated state, your wish, I'm afraid is my command. But if not you, who is this double-murderer whose foul deeds have thus far escaped my attention?"

Moriarty cackled and rubbed his hands together in his familiar gleeful gesture. "In due time, Dr. Watson. First we must speak of other things."

"Namely?"

"To begin with, who set you and Mr. Holmes to meddling in my affairs?"

"Your affairs, Professor? And what affairs would those be?"

"Your coyness is most unbecoming, Dr. Watson, and is beginning to try my patience."

"I assure you that Holmes and I came here for no better reason than to escape the ennui that accompanies a damp and dismal London spring-time. Being desirous of meeting in person the celebrated Alphonse Bertillon—of course being at the time ignorant of his connexion to you—Holmes arranged to meet him strictly as a matter of professional curiosity. As far as our becoming involved with Baron Ollstreder, it was he that

356

approached us with his fantastic tale of the jewel-encrusted statue, and not vice versa."

"You really should confine your story-telling to the *Strand Magazine,* where you're more likely to find an appreciative audience, Dr. Watson. Time grows short, and I've had quite enough of your dissembling. What about your visit to the Dreyfus residence? Was that merely a social call?"

"Dreyfus?" Watson drew a deep breath and looked up at the ceiling. Dreyfus. "Oh yes. Madame Dreyfus. Charming woman, Madame Dreyfus. Lays on a lovely tea..."

"I'm sure the cucumber sandwiches were delightful." Moriarty dropped his hand in his lap and brought it back up clutching a large revolver. "A Colt .41 calibre, Dr. Watson. This model's been in manufacture for some three years now. They make it for the United States Army. Quite the equal, I would say, of your own trusty Webley. The stainless-steel finish is most attractive wouldn't you agree?" He caressed the hammer with his thumb. "It's a single-action. Makes for more rapid, if less accurate shooting." Instinctively Watson recoiled backwards nearly tipping over his chair. "Do not be alarmed, Dr. Watson, hopefully we're not yet at that point. I display this weapon so that you'll keep its presence in mind when I summon Gerald and have him bring back *Mlle.* Otero."

Moriarty began to slowly wheel back toward the bell-pull. "If you can maintain your 'professional detachment' I think you'll find Gerald a rather interesting study. It seems that one evening when the late Colonel was out conducting some business, Gerald, who was then at very impressionable age, came upon his mother and a gentleman, not the Colonel, in flagrante delicto. He must have spoken of it, in his own halting way, to his father who in a fit of anger beat Gerald's mother rather badly. And now, whenever Gerald tries to relate to a mature woman, he too becomes frustrated and angry and relieves his anger in the only way he knows—by replicating his father's behavior toward his mother. I also expect, although not every alienist would necessarily agree, that his penchant for young boys is an attempt on his part to regain his own youthful innocence, so cruelly taken from him. But whatever personal demons drive Gerald to do these things, it is not a pleasant diversion either for the other participant or any spectator, myself included, who does not share Gerald's proclivities. So for that reason, while Gerald has his 'fun' I will keep this weapon at the ready, lest you be overcome by the urge to interfere despite your restraints."

Sensing that Holmes was not among the 'others' whom Moriarty had in captivity below deck, Watson played for time. "Despite your professed distaste for your ward's despicable behavior, I expect that you derive a macabre form of pleasure from it as much as he does. Caroline... I mean *Mlle.* Otero... has an uncanny knack of reading a man's personality. I think that in just a few minutes, she's most likely learned more about you than a room full of alienists could expect to know after years of examining you. Using my own comparatively feeble diagnostic skills, may I venture a guess as to some of the secondary symptoms associated with your neurological condition?"

"No, Doctor, you may not. The only part of my anatomy that need occupy your attention at the moment is my right index finger which at present is relaxed against the trigger guard of my revolver. However, should you continue to bait me, I may succumb to the temptation and use it to reopen your old war wound. With such a large calibre projectile, one could scarcely avoid 'nicking' the sub-clavian artery as happened once before."

Watson looked steadily back at Moriarty, and with great deliberateness replied, "I rather doubt that you'll be doing any such thing. If you were going to do away with me precipitously you would already have done so. I'm sure that you've something else in mind."

"If you continue to provoke me, I assure you that I will alter my plans, much as I shall dislike doing so. In that event we both shall be the poorer for my having done so, although it is you who will most keenly bear the loss." He thumbed back the hammer part-way and raised the gun to eye level. Knowing that his life hung in the balance, Watson steeled himself, and continued his unwavering, defiant stare. After what seemed to Watson a lifetime, Moriarty lowered the revolver and carefully let down the hammer. "No, Dr. Watson, I shall not allow you to provoke me to rash action. Holmes did that to me once, and my life changed unalterably as a result. Either you will tell me what you and

Holmes were doing at the Dreyfus residence, or I shall resummon Gerald and give him carte blanche with *Mlle* Caroline."

Sensing that Moriarty could no longer be dissuaded or distracted, Watson shifted in his seat, "Very well, professor. I shall tell you everything I know, but I cannot see how the information will be of the slightest use to you." Willing telepathically that Moriarty would not ask who was present at their meeting with Madame Dreyfus or any other hard questions, Watson began. "Obviously you recognized Holmes and myself on the boat-train, although neither Holmes nor I, since we both thought you dead, recognized you. I had my doubts about Gerald. His rather remarkable appearance, and his unfamiliarity with the contents of his medical bag, marked him as being not what he appeared to be, although I must confess that it was Holmes who much later hit upon the notion that Gerald was in fact of the masculine gender. If," Watson added parenthetically, "that is indeed the case. I assume that your sending the telegram to the Ritz was intended as a distraction, or as some sort of joke. Whichever it was, it served neither purpose.

"As I have previously chronicled, after surviving his rather Wagnerian duel with you in the Swiss Alps, Holmes traveled extensively. Just prior to his re-emergence in London, he happened to be in France and became interested in the *Dreyfus Affaire*— although it had not been given that appellation inasmuch as Dreyfus had not yet been implicated—and in fact spent some time in consultation with the French authorities. His endeavours obviously had no bearing on the initial outcome of the case. At a later date, however, Holmes exchanged some correspondence with Madame Dreyfus as a result of his earlier involvement. Since we were in Paris anyway, he decided that we should call and pay our respects. We hoped to hear from the most authoritative source the latest news regarding the Captain's fate, and to provide whatever comfort and encouragement we could. Our visit to the Dreyfus home was no more than a social call.

"Madame Dreyfus, along with Captain Dreyfus's brother Mathieu, graciously had us to tea. We spent a cordial afternoon where we learned nothing that was not already or has since become public knowledge. The Dreyfuses—Madame and brother Mathieu—are just as courageous and determined as the captain himself and one cannot help but think that things will come right for them in the end."

"And they all lived happily after. Bravo, Doctor. It's too bad you never turned your hand to writing children's fairy tales. Are you sure you don't ha' just a wee drop o' Irish blood in ye? You've th' gift of th' Blarney sich as I've n' heard since last I downed a pint in th' tavern near me childhood home in Dublin. An' I suppose now you'll be tellin' me th't yer little tete-a-tete with Bertillon was no more th'n payin' homage to Europe's 'highest expert'. Come now, Dr. Watson. My legs are not so far gone that I can't tell when one's being pulled."

"That, Professor, is the absolute truth. It was Bertillon himself that first brought up the subject of the Dreyfus case. Neither Holmes nor I thought to bring it up because we assumed it would be such an embarrassing topic that Bertillon would not want any mention made of his role. We merely sought his views on the subject of finger-printing as a means of identifying criminals. It's something that Holmes and I are both interested in and we simply wanted to know how, in Bertillon's view, it compared to his system. It was he who first mentioned the science of handwriting comparison and used as an example the Dreyfus case. Since you're his close friend and mentor of sorts, do you happen to know what he means by the term 'citadel of graphic rebusses'? It sounds like a term that may have its origins in some abstruse branch of mathematics."

"I'm afraid, Dr. Watson, that I am unable to be of much help to you in that regard. It must remain for some high expert— higher even than *M'sieur* Bertillon—to explain its mysteries. Except as it evinces a once-promising mind gone to atrophy, I frankly have no interest in the 'citadel of graphic rebusses' whatsoever. What interests me more, at least at the moment, is how Holmes managed to ingratiate himself with Baron Ollstreder. Are you going to tell me that was purely happenstance?"

"Nearly so, Professor. Much of what I can tell you is at best an informed guess on my part. Evidently, in Paris at least, the rumors of this long-lost statue are well-known, as is the baron's own obsession with finding it. Given Holmes's insatiable appetite for the bizarre, I would find it odd that he would not at some point have heard about the quest for the artifact and possibly even

Ollstreder's prominent role. It is not impossible that at an earlier time Holmes may have considered a commission on behalf of some other eccentric collector, although I cannot agree that he would have accepted such an engagement and then at a later time accepted a second commission from the baron.

"Be that as it may, when we arrived in Paris, we dined that first evening at the Ritz. During dinner, *Mlle.* Otero and two of her colleagues—I believe they are referred to as 'the grand something or other'—were seated at a nearby table. Although we were not introduced, Ritz identified them to us, and I'm sure they must have asked their waiter who we were, since it's most unusual for Ritz to join his guests at table. The next night, as you know, we dined with Bertillon at Maxim's. Prior to that occasion, neither I, nor to the best of my knowledge had Holmes, ever set eyes on the baron. It was Bertillon who told us who he was. He was seated at an adjacent table, in the company of *Mlle.* Otero and the other ladies, and two other gentlemen whom Bertillon also identified. It is merely an assumption on my part, but probably *Mlle.* Otero informed the baron as to who we were. He sent over a bottle of champagne by way of introduction and asked that we call upon him the following day. Holmes agreed to accept the baron's invitation, although he did not tell me why. I had made a rather sarcastic remark about the relative value of his time and perhaps he was piqued at me. Possibly he did not wish to discuss the matter in front of Bertillon. I simply do not know. All I do know is that we did call on Ollstreder the following day and Holmes agreed to consider the matter without any firm commitment."

"There are simply too many coincidences for my taste, Dr. Watson. Who is the young woman who goes about dressed as a man? First she is seen on the boat where she feigns an attack of sea-sickness. Her fainting was an obvious signal to Holmes having to do with me. She miraculously recovers and continues her journey to Paris where she immediately disappears. Sometime after that she returns to England. Then she comes back to Paris intending to deliver a package to Holmes at his hotel. The package contains two passports, a man's in the name 'de Becourt', and a woman's in the name 'Irmgaard Siegerson', a surname which Holmes himself has utilised in the past. What does she have to do

361

with Holmes and how did Holmes acquire the information to enable him to forge my name to the bank draft?"

"Your benighted state will have to continue until Holmes himself can enlighten you; I cannot. Moreover, even if I were able to do so, in drawing my last breath, I would take great satisfaction in having denied you that information. The fact is, as you well know, during the course of an investigation Holmes never fully confides in anyone, myself included. All I know about your export-import business is what *Mlle.* Otero told me this afternoon as I tended her wounds. And apparently the baron is as close-mouthed as Holmes, because she was able to tell me nothing." Watson stood, and Moriarty warily brought the revolver up from his lap. "And now, Professor, I've quite had my fill of questions. Evidently your plans do not include doing away with me, at least yet. Accordingly, if you will be so kind as to summon Gerald—I assume that your condition makes it impossible for you to negotiate stairs or ladders—I should like to go below and join your other 'guests'. Perhaps, if you will have Gerald undo my bonds, I can make up a fourth for a game of whist. You do keep playing cards aboard?"

CHAPTER FORTY-THREE

"...I will admit that Paris is an enchanting city...
But I must say that much as I've enjoyed the sights
and the food, I'm more than ready to finish this
business and go home."

Watson could not tell how long he'd been sleeping. Moriarty, concluding that his verbal duel with Watson was at a stalemate, summoned Gerald and had him take Watson below. As instructed, Gerald had fitted a heavy cloth sack over Watson's head and placed him in a hold or compartment below the main deck. It took Watson only minutes to determine that he was alone and that he must be below the water line in one of the bilges since he could feel the seat of his trousers becoming wet from the seepage. He worked himself into a squatting position and then leaned back fitting his spine more or less to the curvature of the outer hull. He then was able to stand almost upright so that only his feet were in the water. However, he could not stand completely straight without pressing his head, which hurt badly enough as it was, on the floor-plate of the deck above him. His head was throbbing and his thigh muscles and knees were burning with pain from having to bear his full weight in an awkward semi-crouch.

The compartment was not large. He inched his way around the perimeter and eventually stumbled over a wooden box. He maneuvered the box so that it was resting directly over the keel and a few inches from the bulkhead separating the compartment from the adjacent one. Sitting on the box, his back to the bulkhead and his feet splayed in front of him resting on the curve of the hull just above the pool of bilge water, he had fallen asleep.

For a few moments before becoming fully awake Watson could not recall where he was. He could feel his upper body being pushed forward so that he was bent at the waist. He pushed back against the bulkhead until he realized that there must be a door in the bulkhead and someone was trying to open it. He dug in his heels and stiffened his leg muscles, pressing his back against the door as he frantically picked at the knot between his wrists. His mind flashed back to the hours and hours spent during his training at Netley practicing tying surgical knots while wearing a blindfold and with his wrists pressed together inside a leather sack. This, he told himself optimistically, was not any different, save for the fact that his hands were tied behind him and it was his life rather than some hypothetical patient's that hung in the balance.

Finally he found an end loop and within a few seconds had loosened his bonds enough to slip one hand free. He brought his hands to his head and removed the blindfold and then the noose around his neck. Whoever was on the other side of the bulkhead door was aware of his presence since the pressure against his back had ceased. The hold was in total darkness, so Watson could not see anything, even without the blindfold. Whoever was on the other side of the bulkhead, it obviously was not Gerald. Thinking that it might be Loiseaux, Watson pressed his ear against the wood.

"Who's there?" he whispered.

As he spoke, shafts of light penetrated the hold through several thin spaces between the boards of the bulkhead. Because he'd been in total darkness for so long, the rays were like looking directly at the sun so Watson had to turn away and shield his eyes until they adjusted to the light. He stumbled toward the opposite end of the hold away from the light source.

"Quiet, Watson, or you'll have your over-size friend back down to check on you."

"Holmes. Thank heaven it's you. Where have you been? Can you turn off that blasted light? It's blinding me."

Holmes immediately switched off the electric torch and pushed the bulkhead door open a few inches until it was blocked by the box that Watson had been sitting on. "There's something blocking the door. Can you..."

Watson, still blinded, inched his way back and tipped the box over a couple of times until it was clear of the door. Holmes bent nearly double to get through the small door and closed it behind him. "Close your eyes and turn away. I'm going to turn on the torch again." Holmes placed the torch inside his coat and turned it on.

As Watson blinked rapidly adjusting to the light, Holmes played the torch along the overhead planking looking for a hatch.

He located one at about the middle of the hold and gently pushes against it to see if it was fastened from above. Seeing that it was not, he turned the light in the direction of the fo'c'sle and leaned against the bulkhead through which he'd just entered. "Looks as tho' the Professor's man got a bit careless leaving the hatch cover unfastened."

Watson resumed his seat on the small crate and peered up at Holmes. "Then you know who's occupying the master's cabin?"

"I've been aware of his presence since the boat-train crossing and I suspected it for some time even before that."

"There was, I'm certain, a good reason for your not seeing fit to share your awareness with me some time earlier?"

"Only your scepticism regarding his existence. You were already thinking that I'd taken leave of my senses, so I thought it best to leave things be until I had some definite proof. I knew that he would find some way to insinuate himself into our affairs, whatever other business may have motivated his crossing. So it was only a matter of time. By the way, you don't happen to have a dry cigarette, do you?"

"Holmes, you're soaked from head to toe. How did you get on board? How long have you.... I... we... been here?"

Holmes pressed a finger to his lips and whispered, "Take it easy, old man, your liable to have Moriarty's man-servant down on us before we're ready. I located the barge some hours ago, apparently between the time he took Miss Pippen out—to where ever it was that he took her—and his return with you and the Otero woman hot on his heels. Until his return there had been no movement on board, so I had no way of knowing who, other than Moriarty and his man-servant, was here, who was not, or what was going on."

"Then you do not know the identity of Moriarty's 'man-servant' as you describe him?"

"Should I?"

"His name, so Moriarty informs me, is Gerald..." Watson paused and looked at Holmes in the eerie light, "Moran."

"Related to..."

"The son of the late un-lamented Colonel Sebastian Moran." Watson went on to relate all that Moriarty had told him.

"As for Miss Pippen, he drugged her and took her to a concert in some church which is part of the judicial court complex across the way from that hospital where we took the chauffeur. He left two tickets at the Ritz, intending them for you and me. Evidently, just as you predicted, Moriarty wanted us to see that he had her and that she—and we—were at his mercy." Watson continued, briefing Holmes on what had transpired since they'd gone their separate ways so many hours ago.

"I saw your first go-round with young Moran on the steps and almost interceded then, but I couldn't take the chance of trying to disarm him. There was too great a risk. I'm sorry I missed the second round."

Watson snorted. "I'll be most happy to give you the honors next time. I assure you, I shall never forget the sight of Ollstreder's two men stuffed in that dumb-waiter."

"Don't sell yourself short, Watson. I've a feeling that before we're finished with this business, one or both of us will be having another go. While you were taking your penalty-shot at Gerald, I was trying to find a way on board other than the obvious one, since, as I say, I had no idea of who else might be standing watch. There is a small hatch in the stern just at the water-line. It is used to service the steering mechanism. After you and *Mlle*. Otero went aboard, I slipped into the water and got aboard through that hatch. The engine and drive shaft are located in the compartment just aft of this. My guess is that this compartment is just abaft of 'midships."

"To get here I was led down one flight of rather steep stairs. There were eleven steps not counting the deck-plate. I don't recall Moran opening the hatch. I then went down a four-rung ladder which must have been in place in the hatch opening. It was not the easiest of feats descending that ladder trussed and blind-folded. I must have hit my chin on at least two of the rungs. Evidently, once I was down Moran pulled the ladder up and closed the hatch.

"Besides Caroline... er... *Mlle*. Otero, Miss Pippen, ourselves, Moriarty and Moran, I've no idea who else may be aboard. I'm sure that there are others, but I don't know who, where they are or what their condition may be. From what Moriarty said, the wheel-chair is not merely a stage-prop. While he retains some use of his legs, apparently the chair is his chief means of locomotion. Moran the younger, in addition to the damage inflicted to his groin, first by *Mlle*. Otero and later by myself, has a nasty puncture wound in the region of his right infraspinatus muscle. By now he's probably in a good deal of pain unless Moriarty's given him something for it. Incidentally, Moriarty's quite familiar with Aspirin. Seems he takes them for his own sciatic pain."

Holmes nodded. "That doesn't come as a surprise, considering that he was present while Moran poisoned Lambert with it."

"How can you be sure of that?"

"You did not inspect the back room of the shop nor the alley behind. They must have ground a box or more of the Aspirin tablets using Lambert's mortar and pestle in the rear of the shop. There was a fine coating of white powder on the floor next to one of the work tables. There were impressions of the Bath-chair wheels in the powder and then leading toward the rear door. There were more impressions in the alley. The alley dead-ends at the rear of Number Eleven Rue Danou. Most likely there's a rope and pulley on the roof of the house which Moran used to haul Moriarty up to the balcony where Esterhazy waited for us the night of our meeting with him. Probably Moriarty was sitting in the window watching Loiseaux and me making fools of ourselves in the alley below."

"Then you were right; he killed the pharmacist for no better reason than as a warning to us. But why? He must have suspected that you'd recognized him on the boat. And then he sent that anonymous telegram to Ritz..."

"Perhaps to make a stronger point, Watson. Or perhaps he has something else in mind."

"Well whichever or whatever, I hope that you're now ready to settle your business with the Professor and his ward once and for all. I've had quite enough of sitting in the dark—both literally and figuratively—and in a puddle of bilge-water, even if it is the Seine. No... especially because it is the Seine. Holmes, I will admit that Paris is an enchanting city; the travel guide-books hardly do it justice. But I must say that much as I've enjoyed the sights and the food, I'm more than ready to finish this business and go home."

"Not so fast, Watson. From what you say, Ollstreder's folio must have some bearing on the Dreyfus case. And we still don't know what Moriarty has in mind for the Inspector. Moreover, if I've heard you rightly, our enemies have at least three handguns between them and we've nothing to oppose them save a length of rope and this." Holmes dug in the pocket of his jacket and extracted a folding knife hardly larger than a pen knife.

"Hardly an arsenal, I must agree." Watson glanced at the knife which Holmes proffered for his inspection. "Then what do you propose?"

"That I replace your bindings so that you can remove them easily enough. I should imagine that Moriarty'll be sending Gerald for you presently. In the meantime, I'll have another look about and see if I can locate the others. I sense that Moriarty is enjoying himself too much to do anything precipitous. Then too, he's bound to assume that I will be making every effort to locate you, and whatever his other plans may be, the only thing that really matters to him—I trust you will forgive my seeming arrogance—is besting me in this demented chess game that he calls his life.

"As soon as you're keeping Moriarty occupied, I'll deal with Gerald and then join you for a little chat with Professor 'Villeneuf.'" Holmes spoke the name derisively. "'Villeneuf indeed. How utterly sophomoric."

"Quickly, Holmes! I hear footsteps. And don't forget the bloody blindfold."

CHAPTER FORTY-FOUR

*"Promises, Dr. Watson. I always
keep my promises."*

*T*hey were back in the master's stateroom, seated once again across the desk-table. "I trust you took the opportunity to sleep, Dr. Watson. Unfortunately, I could not oblige your desire for a game of whist."

"Presuming that you've not had occasion to visit below the 'promenade deck', I beg to advise you that the accommodations are far inferior to those of Mr. Ritz's hotel." Watson, his head throbbing, his arms and legs stiff and his bladder uncomfortably full, replied with more insouciance than he felt.

Moriarty bristled noticeably at Watson's oblique reference to his incapacity. "Your next accommodations, my dear Doctor, are likely to make you nostalgic for my bilges, much less the Ritz. The French authorities, I'm made to understand, do not take kindly to double murderers. Especially when one of the victims is a respected police official."

"You'll never get away with it, you monster." Watson stood and started to come across the table.

"Do sit down, Dr. Watson." Moriarty produced his Colt from his lap and aimed it between Watson's eyes. "If you're so certain that my little plot won't work, why not stay around to find out? Perhaps with a good team of lawyers...who knows? But one must admit that your prospects do not appear all that promising. When the police find certain material in your room at the Ritz and then find the Inspector shot through the heart with a .450/.455 calibre bullet...why even the most gullible examining magistrate will find it difficult to believe your protestations of innocence. You'd agree, would you not, that only a Webley military-issue revolver fires a bullet of that unusual calibre. And how many of those do you suppose are to be found in France at the moment?"

"What is it that the police are going to find in my hotel room?"

"Come, come, Dr. Watson, I thought you were keeping up with me." Moriarty tapped the barrel of his revolver against the open palm of his hand and slowly shook his head in mock disappointment. "Concealed in the lining of your portmanteau is a faded but still legible copy of an unpublished monograph by one 'S. Siegerson' reporting on the deadly results of combining a certain coal-tar derivative—acetylsalicylic acid—and oil of wintergreen."

"Non-sense. Holmes never wrote anything of the sort. It was you and Moran who killed the pharmacist and I shall prove it to them."

Moriarty chuckled, "How do you propose to do that, my dear Doctor? I've been dead over eight years, at least according to your own writings. And who was it that wrote that Holmes adopted the name 'Siegerson' and did research on coal-tar derivatives? Do you think that the eminent questioned document examiner, 'Europe's highest expert', will have even the slightest difficulty in identifying Holmes's handwriting? Do you think that the shop girl will have any hesitancy in identifying you as one of the two men lingering outside the shop on that fatal day? And how will you explain the small paste-board package of Aspirin bearing the same lot number as those in Lambert's shop which will be found in the trash can in your room?"

Watson slumped back in his seat, his mind reeling. "Have you already done away with the Inspector?"

"No, he's in the hold. I dislike such unpleasantness and Gerald's been preoccupied with other matters. Why do you ask?"

"I'll make you a bargain. I will turn myself in and confess to Lambert's murder, if you will release the Inspector and *Mlle.* Otero unharmed."

"Very noble, Dr. Watson, but even if I am willing to assume that you'll honour your word, I'm afraid that leaving the Inspector to continue his investigative efforts could ultimately negate your confession. But if it will give you any comfort, I can tell you that my plans for *Mlle.* Otero do not include letting Gerald completely have his way with her."

"Completely?"

"Promises, Dr. Watson. I always keep my promises. Gerald's kept his end of our bargain, so I must keep mine. But if you give me no more difficulty, I'll let you tend to her afterward. I understand that Gerald managed to recover his medical bag from your room."

Watson fought to keep from lunging across the desk. "And Inspector Loiseaux? You'd just murder him in cold blood?"

"Kindly explain the term 'cold-blood', Dr. Watson. Does the lion or the leopard kill in cold blood, or in a fit of passion? What of the military commander who orders his troops forward knowing that a goodly number of them will never again answer to roll call? Is that chauvinistic passion or 'cold blood'?" Moriarty tapped the barrel of his revolver against his open hand again. "And how would you taxonomize the execution of a convict by the state?"

"I admit that 'cold-blooded murder' is neither a legal term nor a precise one. But a lioness kills to feed herself and her young. Animals kill by instinct, not by rational thought. The military commander does not send him men out to be killed, but to kill the enemy. He acts in self-defence; it's kill or be killed. That's in essence the same reason the state executes a murderer, to protect society. But be all those examples as they may, I assure you, that no matter what I thought of someone, I would not shoot a defence-less man regardless of what he's done to provoke me."

"I'm sorry that time and circumstance do not permit us to further debate this fascinating topic, Dr. Watson. Let me simply conclude by asking: does it matter to the Inspector whether he dies as the result of a random act, or as the result of a fit of passion on someone's part, or as the result of a deliberate design? Whichever way, he's just as dead."

"That, Professor, is a certainty with which I cannot argue. But after Gerald's had his fun with *Mlle.* Otero, what will become of her? And what of the baron...I assume that he's also one of your guests?"

"Such inquisitiveness, Dr. Watson. I will only tell you that there are at least as many forms of purgatory as there are human vices. The baron, even as we speak, is aboard the afternoon train from Gare Du Est returning to his rather derelict estate in Germany, after having signed over to me all his liquid assets as well as his property interests in France as compensation for his bungling having brought about the dissolution of our partnership.

Mlle. Otero has...or soon will...consent to join him as his devoted *hausfrau* and live out her days in genteel poverty. Sentimentalist that I am, I did allow the baron to retain the plaster statue of the falcon as a souvenir of happier days."

"I can see Ollstreder willingly returning to his ancestral home, but *Mlle.* Otero married to him and living in squalor in some primitive, crumbling castle? And even they both did go, why would they not return to France as soon as they think it safe? I cannot imagine either of them adapting to the bucolic life, especially in a state of impecuniousness. And in any case, with the baron's contacts in the government, how long will it take for him to begin rebuilding his fortune? What is there to prevent him from repudiating the conveyance documents and stopping payment of the bank drafts?"

"Ah, Dr. Watson, what a team we'd have made. If there's a flaw in any plan you have the unerring capacity to expose it. Why do you continue to allow Holmes to take all the credit? Such a pity. However, I have considered all those possibilities and assure you that none of them is likely to occur. How eager do you suppose the baron will be to explain the rather gruesome deaths of three of his servants in the span of two days? Or to explain certain documents which will no doubt be found in his wall-safe?"

"To a degree, I am counting on Ollstreder's tender feelings for *Mlle.* Caroline to act as a counter-weight against any temptation on his part to reconsider his decision to liquidate his holdings. And to guard against the possibility that I have misgauged the depth of his feelings toward the *mademoiselle,* I took the further precaution of sending the two men assigned to watch you and Mr. Holmes—obviously they won't be needed for that purpose any longer—to accompany the baron back to Germany until he's, shall we say, 'settled in'. As far as re-building his fortune, you've rubbed elbows with a sufficient number of politicians that frankly your naiveté surprises me. In the political *demi-monde,* no one is forgotten more quickly than a benefactor who's run out of beneficence. Were I Baron Ollstreder, I would not waste what little money I had on calling cards.

"As far as *Mlle.* Caroline," Moriarty paused over the name, "after she goes on a little honeymoon cruise with Gerald, we shall see that she joins the baron. After a few weeks at sea in Gerald's company, I expect that she will readily accept the baron's proposal of marriage. And as to her returning to Paris any time soon, between her association with the baron and—no insult intended—yourself, do you think her former illustrious clientele will continue to patronize her? Indeed, she'll be fortunate if she can find employment at Number Eleven Rue Danou, or some similar establishment in the event I am unable to find a place for her."

"All very clever as usual, Professor Moriarty. But, once again you've not accounted for one critical variable. Is that why you were so unsuccessful as a mathematician? It seems to be a common failing of yours."

Moriarty's face reddened, the tiny vessels in his cheeks engorged beneath the translucent, parchment-like skin. He'd lowered his revolver as he was describing the fate he had planned for the baron and Caroline. Now the barrel tapped violently against the edge of the table as his hand shook in anger. "You taunt dame fortune once again, Dr. Watson. As you shall see soon enough, the 'variable' to which you refer, Mr. Sherlock Holmes, has more than been accounted for."

"Meaning, of course, that you haven't a clew as to his whereabouts..."

"I warn you, Dr. Watson," Moriarty raised the weapon again, holding it in his right hand, and clutching his wrist with his left hand to steady it. He flicked his tongue between his thin white lips. With his heavily lidded eyes and high forehead, he looked like a venomous serpent about to strike. Instead, he wheeled backward and tugged violently on the bell rope.

"We shall see in a few minutes whether I've accounted for the 'Holmes variable'. I assure you, however, that I know precisely what he's been up to. Since you did not return from your little adventure last night, I should think he's been out frantically looking for you, while at the same time doing his best to avoid the police who, having nothing better to do, are searching for Inspector Loiseaux by retracing his steps in connection with his pending cases. As they do, they shall no doubt be struck by the fact that those steps seem to cross those of yourself and Holmes a remarkable number of times. With their policemen's inveterate propensity to cynicism, I'm sure they'll find it exceedingly difficult to accept your explanation of how Inspector Loiseaux came to be shot dead with your revolver, and how you came into possession of an unpublished monograph on such an exotic and deadly combination as Aspirin and oil of wintergreen.

"But I digress. Back to the peripatetic Sherlock Holmes. Without you as a sounding-board, I hope that he will be able to function at nearly the level of efficiency that you ascribe to him in your accounts of his cases. If he has been, he's no doubt learnt that you and *Mlle.* Otero went out last night in evening clothes. Knowing of your aversion to the company of women of dubious character, he'll no doubt wonder what prompted such a scandalous relaxation of your usual high standards. Discarding the less savory explanations, he will have concluded that you invited *Mlle.* Otero for the dual purposes of acting as your interpreter, should the occasion arise, and to call as much attention to yourself as possible in case of another kidnap plot being afoot.

"The cab rank outside the Ritz, like similar facilities in London, is ordinarily staffed day-in and day-out by the same drivers. Pressing his inquiry in that direction, I would say that by now he's found the one who remembers driving you and your companion to the concert. He then will have wondered why, even though you are a music aficionado, with so much other pressing business you would have decided rather impetuously to attend a concert.

"Adhering to his own dictum, he would have decided that your attendance at the concert was no mere whim and therefore you went with some other purpose in mind. He will have surmised that you were enticed there by someone; he may or may not know whom. But in any case, he would have discerned that it probably had to do with the young woman and that you'd gone off on some courageous but ill-advised attempt to rescue her. In his conceit, he surely would have concluded that instead of rescuing the maiden in distress, you'd fallen into a trap. And now, like some Nietzschean *übermench,* it will be up to him to save the day.

"However, from that point the trail will have gone cold. It is unlikely that he will have access to Toby the celebrated tracking dog or any of its French canine cousins, so he will have to find some other means. He will pay a surreptitious visit to the Rue George Bizet, perhaps in the disguise of a tradesman. But all he will find is a house swarming with police in the first stages of

374

investigating the horrific deaths of two more of the baron's servants.

"At that point, he will do one of two things: suspecting that he's being lured into a trap, he'll return to the Ritz to await being contacted, or he will remember the recently deceased Captain Richard and his involvement in the bungled attempt to kidnap you from the Place de la Concorde. Once he begins looking for Richard's barge, it will be easy enough to find. One merely looks up the registration number at the Hotel de Ville, and then hires a launch to search up and down the river from, say, the Pont D' Austerlitz to Pont de Sevres."

"And when he locates this accursed vessel, do you suppose that he'll come charging up the gangplank and into Gerald's waiting arms?"

"Actually, I expect that he's already aboard. If he's found us, he cannot have failed to notice the small hatch at the rear of the vessel where the drive shaft emerges from the hull. I would be keenly disappointed if he did not locate it, inasmuch as I directed Gerald to leave it unlatched for just that eventuality.

"Good, here's Gerald. Gerald, my lad. Is our extra guest aboard? Have you battened down the bilge hatch?"

"Aye, aye guv'. 'eard 'im scrapin' about as I was fastenin' the hatch cover."

"And the young lady who accompanied you to the concert last night, she's in her cabin and properly tranquilized?"

Gave 'er the injection just like you said. She was tied-up, gagged and sound asleep when I left 'er."

Watson, when he heard Gerald's report, had to fight off a growing despondency. Whatever they were planning, they were taking Miss Pippen as well as Caroline with them. He shuddered at the thought of both women at the mercy of Gerald and began to delicately feel the knot Holmes had used to re-tie his hands. If Holmes really is trapped like a cod in the hold below, then, Watson thought, it'll be up to me to do what must be done.

"Gerald," Moriarty extracted a watch from his waistcoat and checked the time, "it will soon be dark and time for us to get underway. You may have twenty minutes with *Mlle*. Otero. I'll ring the bell for you when it's time. You will then bring her up here along with the medical bag. I promised Dr. Watson an opportunity to say *au revoir* and to put his medical skills to use once again. After all, it may be for the last time as I rather doubt that the French prison authorities will allow him to possess any sharp implements or narcotics." He favored Watson with a malevolent smile.

"Don't be so disappointed, Gerald. The good Doctor will patch her up good as new. You wouldn't want her under the weather for the duration of our cruise, would you? Besides, while he's attending to the *mademoiselle,* you can go below again and dispatch the Inspector."

His chin sunk down to his chest, Watson struggled to maintain his self-control. "Clearly, Professor, you plan to leave me here to stand trial for the murders of the pharmacist Lambert and Inspector Loiseaux. You're kidnapping *Mlle.* Otero and Miss...er...the young woman...and taking them with you. But what of..." Watson paused, debating whether to mention Esterhazy and Irmgaard, "...what of Holmes? If he's really your prisoner aboard this vessel, you're not going to leave him on the boat to be found by the police. On the other hand, I cannot see you just gunning him down. You've waited too long for your revenge to let it be over with the single pull of a trigger. What Dantean fate have you in store for him?"

"In due course, Dr. Watson, in due course. But first, you must tell me what you know of the young woman who refuses to identify herself. You started to mention her name and then thought better of it. I shall learn it soon enough, so you may as well spare her the unpleasantness of having the information extracted under 'physical compulsion'. Or is it only *Mlle.* Caroline who is to be the beneficiary of your gallantry?"

"Even if I knew her name or how she came to be mixed up in this business, I would not tell you..."

Gerald!" Moriarty spoke sharply. "Don't go just yet. Dr. Watson seems disoriented and suffering from memory lapse. Perhaps he needs something to remind him of where he is and to help focus him thoughts."

Quickly Gerald stepped behind Watson and struck a savage open-handed blow to Watson's already injured ear. "There you go, guv, 'ow's that?"

The force of the blow knocked Watson's chair over side-ways so that his head struck the floor with nearly the same force as Gerald's blow. Taken by surprise he grunted in pain. He lay on the floor, both ears stinging with pain and his head feeling as though someone had split it open with an axe. As he lay, his body still molded to the chair, he felt two more sharp blows, one to his bad knee and the other to his chest. Nearly unconscious, he vaguely realized that Gerald was kicking him. Dimly he was aware of Moriarty shouting at Gerald to stop. He could not tell how many more kicks Gerald had got in before reaching down to grab him by the hair and pull him along with the chair to an upright position. After perhaps a minute, he began to recover his senses. He could see light and shapes, but everything was a blur. He choked back a sob. "My God!" he thought to himself. "He's damaged the optic nerve. Shall I be spending the rest of my life a blind-man in some French prison? Or maybe they'll send me to Devil's Island in place of Dreyfus. How ironic that would be."

"Give Dr. Watson back his eyeglasses, Gerald. He's quite unable to see much of anything without them. Well, Dr. Watson, has your memory improved in response to Gerald's stimulus?"

Glasses restored, Watson gave a silent prayer of thanks, managing a contemptuous laugh which turned into a gasp as pain radiated throughout his rib-cage. "I'm pleased to report, Professor, that it has not. Try Gerald as he may, I can't seem to recall a thing about the young lady in question. Since I know that you will not let Gerald inflict a mortal injury, I am impervious to any sub-lethal form of torture. I will at some point lose consciousness, thus rendering further exertions unproductive. It's rather like trying to teach a pig to whistle. It's frustrating for you, and all it accomplishes is to make the pig angry."

Moriarty wheeled back to his place at the desk-table, and placing his hands flat on its surface leaned forward. "A brilliant *mot just,* Dr. Watson. Worthy of the great Oscar Wilde at his best, if I'm any judge. I don't know whether the French prison wardens allow their charges to possess writing implements. If they do, perhaps you'll produce something on the order of *Reading Gaol*. I shall faithfully scan all the literary magazines in anticipation of seeing it."

He slapped his hands on the table. "Gerald, be off with you now. There's a good lad. Mustn't keep *Mlle.* Caroline waiting. Run along and have your fun, while I fill Dr. Watson in on what we've in mind for his celebrated friend. We'll have plenty of time to deal with the young woman. And Gerald..." he paused, "remember twenty minutes only. And by all means do control yourself. It wouldn't do in the least to have her expire on us. After all, she is a national institution."

As Gerald bounded off like a school-boy released from classes early, Moriarty turned his attention back to Watson. He rested his elbows on the table, his long, bony fingers steepled as though he were lost in thought. Watson thought how odd it was that Moriarty's hands were so like Holmes's and that they used them in virtually the identical gesture.

"I'm sure you've noted my mention of a little cruise. In addition to this worthy vessel, I also own two others. Being a shipping magnate does have its advantages in connexion with my other enterprises. In addition to its cargo uses, it's so nice to have a full-size vessel at one's beck and call and fitted out to one's own taste and specifications. Indeed, I'd invite you along, but I cannot afford to alienate the French Government by aiding and abetting a fugitive to escape justice. Unfortunately, Dr. Watson, if you're going to escape you'll have to do it on your own."

"You disappoint me, Professor. Think what a gripping story it would make: a respected physician unjustly accused of murder. He makes good his escape, and spends years eluding pursuit by the authorities while at the same time pursuing the true murderer. But let me ask you this: if you have this yacht—for I presume it is that—ready to sail at your whim, what pray tell were you doing on the boat-train?"

"Business before pleasure, Dr. Watson. The vessel, which I assure you is much larger than a mere yacht, was needed in connection with a commercial matter and was required to be in another port when I found it necessary to be in Paris. So I sacrificed my comfort for the sake of yet another business transaction. It truly is remarkable, Dr. Watson, how once one acquires a bit of money one can never thereafter have enough."

Moriarty smiled almost benignly. "You asked about Holmes's fate. You will be gratified to know that I've decided to spare him as well. In fact, he'll be accompanying us on our cruise, at least for the first week or so. In addition to my other enterprises, I've also branched into resort properties, albeit very few in number and only for a very select clientele.

"We shall, as you may have gathered, begin our cruise right here aboard this very vessel. With Holmes and our other guests stowed securely, if not exactly comfortably, we shall disembark the late Inspector leaving him on the *quai*. You will accompany us downstream for at least a few hours and will be disembarked at a suitable spot, perhaps Argenteuil. The rest of our gala little company will continue to the mouth of the Seine at Le Havre where we shall transfer to the larger vessel.

"There's an island in the far South Atlantic, only a few hundred miles east by southeast of Tierra Del Fuego. It's uninhabited and not to be found on any nautical charts. Indeed, it's hardly more than a speck of lava rock, perhaps five miles end-to-end, and at its widest, perhaps a mile or at the most two. It's at the tip of a small archipelago. There is a tribe of stone-age aborigines on the northwestern-most island. In their religious liturgy, the island of which I speak is the home of their god, some sort of half-man, half-beast.

"They've ceded a small portion of their Mt. Olympus to me in exchange for a yearly ration of tobacco and Irish whisky. I've used my concession to build a small stone hut which shall be Mr. Holmes's place of residence most probably for the rest of his life. As part of my bargain with them, they'll keep the island supplied with potable water along with dried fish and some sort of edible root that forms the principal staple of their diet. They will also keep the place guarded and drive away any stray vessels from the modern world. I'm sure that Mr. Holmes will be quite comfortable there, even if he is not overly stimulated intellectually."

"You'll never get away with it, Moriarty. As long as I draw breath, I'll fight you. Someday, somehow, you'll be brought to book."

"There's an ancient Arab proverb, Dr. Watson: 'be careful what you ask for, as you may get it.' You would do better to wish me a long and prosperous life. Only I know the exact coordinates for my island paradise. If I die, they die with me. If I'm in prison, what incentive do you suppose I'd have to release Holmes from his? And who's to say whether the aborigines, deprived of their annual stipend, will not revert to their cannibalistic practices and boil Holmes up as the main course on one of their feast-days?"

As they sat across the table, Moriarty continuing his gloating prattle. Watson, trying not to think of the depraved torture to which Caroline was being subjected as they spoke, or of the wretched, cruel fate awaiting the Inspector in but a matter of minutes, worked on the knot binding his wrists behind his back. It was, Watson thought, an unconscionable dilemma, one that only a fiend like Moriarty could think up: every tick of the clock brought Loiseaux a second closer to his last living moment, and at the same time prolonged Caroline's torture by an equal measure. Which was preferable, that Loiseaux's life, or Caroline's torture, end quickly? It was clear to Watson that he'd best do what ever he was going to do before Moriarty summoned Gerald back up. Banking on Moriarty's promise and Caroline's resiliency, he decided that the longer Moriarty allowed Gerald to have his way with Caroline, the better the chances that he could free himself and come to her and Loiseaux's aid, not to mention the faint hope that Holmes might somehow work himself out of his own singular predicament. He continued to work on his bonds, thankful that Holmes did not try to be too clever by half in using some arcane conjurer's knot that would, if inspected, appear incapable of being untied, and as a practical matter would be so.

Moriarty leaned forward, resting his hands on the table, and stood up. "What's the matter, Dr. Watson, are your bonds too tight? I should imagine that by now, your arms would be so stiff as to be nearly useless. Yet I see your shoulders moving and your upper arm muscles flexing. You wouldn't be trying to..."

"Would that I could, Professor. Indeed, I've been trying since last night without success. Now I'm just trying to keep the circulation going before gangrene sets in."

"Then by all means let me summon Gerald at once. I should not want you to be incapable of carrying out your professional duties when *Mlle.* Caroline arrives."

"Not to mention what my losing the use of my hands would mean to your little plot."

Moriarty slapped the table. "Excellent, Dr. Watson. Your mental acuity continues to dazzle me."

"My current predicament, if I may paraphrase, has tended to marvelously focus my mind. However, much as I would like to be shed of this rope, I wonder if I may first prevail on your hospitality to furnish me with a couple of those Aspirin pills and a glass of water to wash them down? Our little conversation, and especially the part in which Gerald participated, has give me quite a headache."

"Of course, Doctor." Moriarty sat back down on his wheel chair. "I shall summon Gerald, and then pour you a glass of water myself."

As Moriarty rolled backward to pull the bell rope, Watson worked at his bonds, willing his numb and swollen fingers to do their task without betraying their effort. Just as Moriarty wheeled next to the side of the table, Watson felt the rope give way behind his back. When Moriarty was even with his own chair, Watson hurled himself sideways into Moriarty's chair tipping it over and sending both of them crashing to the floor. The Colt, which had been in Moriarty's lap clattered away coming to rest against the wall just out of both men's reach. Watson's head and heart were pounding; his arms and legs weak from inactivity. Moriarty's upper body, although appearing frail, was wiry and deceptively strong, no doubt from propelling the wheelchair. Watson could not overcome the older man's vise-like grip around his waist. Desperately he tried to gain purchase with his feet on the slick wood floor.

Then Moriarty removed one hand from Watson's body, reached up and knocked off his glasses which ended up against the wall next to the revolver. He clawed Watson's face with his fingers in a macabre reprise of his death-dance with Holmes on the verge of Reichenbach Falls eight years ago. Moriarty's move freed up Watson's right arm. With his eyes tightly closed against Moriarty's powerful probing fingers, Watson managed to wedge his forearm under Moriarty's chin. He pressed his wrist with all his strength against the other man's neck. He could feel his wrist bone pressing against the windpipe. The tighter Moriarty clutched him, the greater the pressure.

Realising his predicament, Moriarty quit clawing at Watson's face and began frantically pushing Watson's head back with his open hand. The two men were lying nearly side by side, with Watson slightly on top. Moriarty's left arm had been around Watson's back at the waist. He moved his arm around to the front, and began trying to push Watson away with both hands. When he did, Watson was able to arch his back and then get to his knees. He then shifted his right forearm so that instead of pressing Moriarty's windpipe with his wrist, he now had it clasped in his hand. Still clutching Moriarty by the throat he began inching toward where he last saw the revolver before Moriarty had torn off his glasses. Moving on all fours, a few inches at a time, he slowly made his way along the floor. Moriarty now had both hands around Watson's right arm, trying to break the grip on his throat. With each movement of Watson's right arm, he lifted Moriarty's head slightly off the floor and brought it back down with a satisfying crunch. In a few moments, he reached the wall. He blinked rapidly, adjusting his eyes to the light. In another moment, he located the Colt which he picked up by the barrel. In a fury he smashed the butt into the side of Moriarty's head catching the tip of his ear and stunning Moriarty long enough for Watson to transfer his grip on the revolver to the handle, his thumb on the hammer. He rose to his feet, transferred the Colt to his right hand, and with his left grabbed Moriarty by the shirt front, intending to prop him up against the wall.

As he began to lift Moriarty, the door to the stateroom was flung open. Gerald burst into the room propelling Caroline ahead of him. She was wrapped in a filthy piece of tarpaulin with a length of rope wound from her neck to her knees. "What's the prob...", Gerald started to ask.

Watson reacted instantly. Instead of pushing Moriarty against the wall, he wedged his left forearm back under his chin and pulled him in front of himself as a shield. Moran reacted almost as swiftly. Just as Watson was thumbing back the hammer of the Colt, Gerald pulled Caroline in front of himself and drew the Webley from his waistband. Caroline, who had been all but unconscious anyway, fainted, leaving both men holding dead-weight human shields and pointing large-calibre revolvers at one another.

Gerald had not yet realised that Watson was without his glasses. Watson thought momentarily about taking a head shot at Gerald since Caroline with her head slumped to her chest came to barely above Gerald's waist. At a distance of at least fifteen feet, and with an unfamiliar weapon, it would have been a difficult shot even with his glasses on. But then what if he did hit Caroline? She might already be dead or at least dying. And as things now stood, if he were to be disarmed, Moriarty would probably kill them all anyway. No! Watson shook his head, disgusted with his own thought process. Just then, Moriarty groaned, evidently regaining consciousness. Watson tightened his choke hold slightly, lifting Moriarty nearly off the floor. He placed the muzzle of the Colt in Moriarty's right ear as Gerald began cautiously inching back toward the door, trying to get a clear shot at Watson's left side.

Watson thumbed back the hammer, and remembering that safe-handling dictated that one keep an empty chamber under the hammer of a single-action revolver, prayed that Moriarty was not well-versed in weapon safety. "Stop where you are, Moran. All I have to do is release my thumb and your master's brains will be splattered all across the cabin. So if you shoot, even if you hit me instead of the Professor, it's him you'll be killing. Now throw down your gun and then lower Miss Otero gently to the floor."

"Never, mate. You drop yours or I'll finish the bitch off good 'n proper, I will." He adjusted his grip on Caroline, moving his hand from her breast to clutch her by the throat under her chin so that her body was fully extended, her head just below his shoulders and her feet barely touching the floor.

As Gerald slowly circled to his left, Watson shifted his angle so that his right shoulder was against the wall, and Moriarty was directly between himself and Gerald. "How do I know that she's not already dead?"

Gerald cupped his hand under Caroline's chin and shook her head back and forth. "Speak up you bloomin' slut. Tell th' doc 'ere that you're not dead, just resting after 'aving a good time with young Gerald. Bet she'll not be 'aving it off with nobody for a while."

Watson could feel Moriarty beginning to regain his senses and knew that with him fully conscious it would be impossible to hold him effectively as a shield. He jammed the barrel of the revolver hard into Moriarty's ear. "Speaking of 'having it off' with someone, Gerald, I've just been learning about you from your guardian. In all these years, have you never once suspected the truth?"

Gerald came to a stop and adjusted his grip on Caroline. "An' what truth's that, Doc?"

"Who do you think was 'having it off' with your mother that night? Who was your father's employer? Who do you think sent him out on some pretense to keep him out all night so he could have his way with your poor, sweet mum?" Lest the answer to these questions prove too much of a challenge for Gerald's intellect, Watson shifted the gun barrel to the back of Moriarty's head and uses it as a prod to move his head back and forth.

Slowly the light of comprehension began to dawn. "You mean…. no, he's me guv' 'e is. An' 'e's been takin' care of me ever since me da got himself snackered in that old empty house." Tears began to well up in Gerald's eyes.

"I'm afraid it's true, Gerald, every word. Why do you think he sent your 'da' to that 'old empty house'. Go ahead, Professor," Watson nudged Moriarty again with the revolver barrel, "deny it. I dare you."

Moriarty held out his hands toward Gerald who was standing completely still, holding Caroline as though he'd all but forgotten about her. He lowered his weapon so that it was pointing directly at Moriarty's mid-section. "What's 'e sayin', guv; tell me 'e's lyin'."

"He is lying, Gerald. I swear to you, he's lying. It's not true. The man whom you saw with your dear, sainted mother that night was none other than the man you have locked in the bilges this very moment. None other than Sherlock Holmes himself. Why do you think that the colonel, your own father, went to that house the night he was captured? As his closest friend, as well as his employer, I tried my best to conceal the truth from him because I knew that he'd try to do something rash and place himself at risk.

"And that's exactly what happened. That's why I lured Holmes to Switzerland. I tried to dispose of him myself, so that your father would not expose himself to capture and trial. I thought I had succeeded until Holmes re-emerged back in his old rooms in Baker Street. I had obviously failed. And since even the intervening years had not dimmed your father's desire to avenge what had been done to you, he could not be dissuaded from going after Holmes—the destroyer of his family—himself."

Gerald stood dumbfounded, not knowing whom to believe. He looked pleadingly at both men, hoping for some sign. The tableau continued no one daring even to breathe. Just as Gerald had about decided to solve the dilemma by shooting both Watson and Moriarty, the boat creaked loudly and began listing to port. Moriarty was the first to realize what was happening. "It's Holmes, the fiend! He'll kill us all! He's opened the sea-cocks. Gerald, do as I say. Lay down Doctor Watson's revolver, he'll not harm us." He twisted his head around, "I take you at your word, Doctor Watson, that you'd never shoot an unarmed man. Besides, if you're going to save your companion—who evidently cares nothing for your life or the lives of the others—you don't have time to debate or negotiate. Now when Gerald sets down your Webley, you set me in my chair."

There was a loud hiss as the cant of the vessel extinguished the boiler. "Hurry, you fool, or do you have the same death wish as Holmes? I will wheel myself to the door. As soon as I'm out the door, Gerald, you put the woman down and follow me. Are we agreed, Dr. Watson?"

Watson gripped Moriarty across his chest and under his arms. Watson sidestepped in the direction of the chair. "Do it Gerald. Put down the revolver. I cannot pick up the chair with you still pointing the gun at me." Gerald kneeled down and placed the gun on the floor. "Good. Now slide it toward me and then start toward the door." The boat listed even further so that it was becoming difficult to stand upright. As soon as Gerald toed the gun toward Watson and started backing toward the door, Watson released his grip on Moriarty. "Professor you lift the chair, I want to keep my eye on Gerald."

"As you wish, Doctor, Watson. I shall not take time to debate good manners with you." Moriarty righted the chair and pulled himself into the seat. As he wheeled himself to the cabin door he motioned to Gerald, "Put the woman down, Gerald. Doctor Watson's kept his end of the bargain and now we must keep ours." Gerald did as he was told, depositing Caroline just outside the arc of the open door. As Moriarty reached the door he wheeled around in the doorway so that Gerald could take his grip on the chair.

From his waistcoat pocket he extracted a key and with the other hand took the doorknob and started to pull it closed behind him. "Adieu, Dr. Watson. I must say it's been interesting knowing you, especially these last few hours. I understand that drowning, if one has to die—shall we say 'prematurely'—is not all that unpleasant; it's rather like going to sleep in a nice bath."

"Moriarty, wait! We made a bargain!"

"Yes we did, Doctor Watson. And I've kept it. I recall nothing being said about our leaving the door unlocked. "Quickly, Gerald. I've no wish to learn whether this chair is capable of flotation." He pulled the door to, and turned the key in the lock just as Watson began firing the big Colt in the direction of the door.

CHAPTER FORTY-FIVE

"If I'm going to die, let me at least be with you."

*I*n a panic, Watson threw the empty revolver against the wall and began hunting for his glasses. He quickly located them and put them back in their accustomed place. Although the ear pieces were hopelessly askew, at least the lenses were not broken. The list of the vessel was now even more pronounced. He bent down to pick up his own revolver and felt a stream of cold air coming up through the joints in the floor, evidently being forced up as it was replaced with water in the holds below. Caroline worked herself into a sitting position. "John, do something! Has your friend Holmes gone mad? Get us out of here!"

"Quiet, Caroline. I cannot get us out, much less the others, unless I first get out of this room." He leaned down and helped her to her feet and approached the door. At least two of his shots with the Colt had struck the door and not penetrated. "Damnation," Watson muttered, "it's solid oak. Impossible to kick in. Back away from the door," he ordered. As Caroline scuttled toward the rear of the cabin, Watson positioned himself at an angle to the door and transferred his Webley to his left hand. He brought the muzzle to within a few inches of the lock and thumbed back the double-action hammer. Gritting his teeth, he fired into the lock. At point-blank range, the noise was deafening and muzzle flash blinding. The effect of the round on the lock, however, was essentially inconsequential. It ricocheted off the metal plate and buried itself on the cabin wall next to the door.

"John, what about the windows?"

Watson turned and stumbled to the back of the cabin where there was a heavy curtain above the bunk bed. He tore it aside and reversed his grip on his revolver in preparation for breaking out the glass. He drew back his arm and started it forward, stopping in mid-arc. He turned around and sat down on the bed, his head in his hands.

"What is it? Hurry! Break the glass! Shoot it out, if you must!"

"It's no use, Caroline. Look for yourself. Behind the glass is a metal grate, and outside that solid shutters."

Caroline made her way to the bunk bed and sat down beside him leaning her head against his shoulder. Watson noticed that she was shivering. He put his arm around her shoulders and pressed her to his side. He set his revolver down and located the knot holding the rope around her body and untied it. Caroline shook the rope loose and clutched the tarpaulin closed around her body. Realising the ambiguity of his action, Watson stood up. "Stay where you are. There's a wardrobe just here," he pointed to a tall door next to the bed. "Let me see if there are any garments that you can put on. At least you won't have to be found that way." He nodded toward the filthy rag which Caroline still clasped tightly around her.

"Oh John. Only an English gentleman." She stood up and managed a wan smile. "I'll look; you work on getting us out of here." She shouldered him out of the way, and opened the wardrobe door which fell back with a thud.

Remembering Holmes's dictum regarding locked-rooms, as Caroline perused the contents of the wardrobe, Watson began looking about for another means of egress. Except for the built-in wardrobe and the main door, the only other door in the cabin was the double-doors of the cabinet from which Moriarty had produced the water glass. Watson opened the right-hand door and found several shelves containing glass-ware and china. He opened the left-hand door and looked back over his shoulder. "Caroline, see here. There's a dumb-waiter. The galley must be just below."

Caroline was in the process of fastening the top button of a pair of man's trousers which she'd found in the wardrobe. She turned her back, covering her bare torso with both hands. "Turn round for a moment, will you?" She bent her head back into the wardrobe and in a few seconds emerged with a man's shirt which she quickly put on, and since there were no studs, she tied the shirt tails in a square knot below her ribs. "God. How do you men wear these things all day?" She tugged at the waistband of the trousers. "I feel like a sausage."

"Caroline, could we please discuss gender-related sartorial issues at some other time? The ruddy boat's sinking, and you're worried about your costume. Come here, please. There's no way that I'm going to fit in here—at least not without some help from Gerald—so you'll have to do it." Hastily Watson told Caroline what little he knew about the layout of the vessel and where to find Holmes. He enjoined her to first locate Holmes, since he was probably still in the lowest level, and then to locate Inspector Loiseaux. She should tell them to find something to use as a battering ram, since it was unlikely that Moriarty had been sporting enough to leave a key in the door. Finally, he told her, while Holmes and the Inspector are getting me out of here, she must locate Miss Pippen and if she were still unconscious, get her out of her cabin.

"What if I get stuck?" Caroline grabbed Watson's wrist as he started to pull the rope to lower Caroline down the chute.

"If you get stuck, then it is likely that we all shall drown, Caroline. Don't worry, just keep clasping your arms around your knees, and you've room to spare." He removed her hand from his wrist and placed it on her knee. He pressed his left hand over her hands and with his right began playing out the rope lowering the box to the deck below.

In a few seconds the rope went slack. "That's as far as it goes, John. What do I do next? I cannot get out. There's an outer door and it's closed."

"Feel along the edges to find the catch."

"There's nothing, I'm trapped in this horrid box just like the baron's men! Please, pull me up. If I'm going to die, at least let me be with you."

"Caroline, don't panic. It must open somehow." Watson paused, his mind racing trying to recall the mechanics of such a common-place household appliance. "If there are no latches... wait! It's probably a sliding door. Push yourself away from the door and try sliding it upward."

"Yes, yes, that's it! I'm out."

"Good work, Caroline. Now go quickly and release Holmes. He's bound to be up to his neck by now." With Caroline gone, Watson turned and went to the desk. He found a drawer on the side opposite where he'd been seated and in it the passports for Esterhazy and Irmgaard. He scooped these up along with the few other bits of paper in the drawer and stuffed them in a leather portfolio which he found in the back of the drawer. The boat meanwhile was continuing its list, and was also beginning to settle by the stern. He heard a loud creak and then a loud report—like a gunshot—evidently one of the mooring hawsers giving way, no longer capable of withstanding the weight of the sinking vessel. Unable to maintain his balance, he sat down on the floor. He reached around his back with the portfolio and stuffed it into the top of his trousers.

Realizing that the boat was going down by the stern, and possibly being in danger of rolling over keel-side up, he began trying to make his way up the slope of the cabin floor to the door. He picked up the length of rope that he had been tied with and wrapped it around his upper arm. He inched his way along lying flat on the floor in order to provide as much traction as possible. After a minute's struggle, he was within a few feet of the door. His breath coming in laboured gulps, he leaned back against the port wall and closed his eyes, preparing himself either for rescue or for death.

His momentary reverie was interrupted by the sound of the chairs and table sliding across the cabin floor and crashing into the wall next to him. The only illumination in the cabin had come from a large alcohol lamp which had been on the table. As the table started sliding, the lamp fell over spilling the liquid which was instantly ignited by the last flicker of flame from the wick. The heat of the flame was intensified by the streams of air coming through the floor joints. In a few seconds the dry wood of the table and chairs were engulfed, and in a few seconds more, so was the cabin wall. Watson recoiled back from the spreading flames, but found that he could barely move because of the sharp slope.

The intense heat caused him to break out in perspiration. The glue in the furniture joints was hissing and popping sending embers in all directions. As the fire began to spread along the wall, Watson removed the length of rope from his shoulder and fastened a slip knot. He made a wide loop and twirled it around much as he'd seen American cowboys do with their cow ropes. He flung the loop toward the door handle, cursing silently as it missed by at least two feet. He reeled the rope in and tried once more, without success. The fire was now a roaring conflagration, consuming the oxygen in the cabin faster than it was rising up through the floor. The room was now thick with smoke, although by ducking down as low as possible, Watson could avoid most of it. The cabin was now an inferno. He inched another foot closer to the door and tried the rope once again. This time, it caught the handle and just as the flames reached where he'd been sitting, he managed to pull himself upright. He rappelled up to the door wrapping the rope around his wrist as he went.

"Watson! Are you there?" It was Holmes. "Stand away from the door if you're there. We're going to break it open." Watson tried to answer, but by now he was choking on the smoke. He felt a jarring vibration in his hand and wrist from a heavy object being smashed into the door. He was now light-headed from lack of oxygen. There was another crash, and he could see the door frame beginning to splinter. Finally overcome by the heat and lack of oxygen, he fainted and crumpled to the floor, his wrist still tied to the door handle.

He felt the cool wetness of the cloth on his face even before he fully regained his senses. He was sitting with his back propped against the stone wall of the embankment. Caroline was bathing his face with a piece of cloth that looked as though it had been torn from Miss Pippen's evening gown. In the distance he could hear the clang of the fire-wagons. The part of the boat that was still above the water line was now fully engulfed in flame. A noisy crowd had gathered at the top of the embankment. Nearby Holmes and Inspector Loiseaux were engaged in an animated conversation, their angry faces and gesticulations illuminated by the roaring flames making a Mephistophelean tableau. Watson started to speak, but could manage only an unintelligible croak which became a fit of coughing. As soon as the coughing subsided, he managed to rasp "Caroline, help me to my feet. I must tell Holmes..."

Caroline took Watson's hands and pulled him to his feet. He put his arm around her shoulders and leaning on her hobbled over to Holmes and the Inspector on rubbery legs. When her reached them, Holmes turned and grasped him by the upper arms. He held him for nearly a minute, neither man speaking. The flames from the burning boat were beginning to diminish for having run out of fuel. In their uneven light as Watson returned Holmes's gaze, he thought, just for the briefest moment that he saw a bit of moisture forming in the corners of Holmes's eyes. He dismissed the thought as simply a trick of the light from the fire. "Thank heaven you're safe, old fellow."

Unwilling to expose his true feelings, especially in the presence of others, Watson removed his glasses and wiped his own eyes with his coat sleeve. "Must have gotten a cinder in my eye. Can't see a blasted thing." Turning to Inspector Loiseaux, he shook his hand. "Glad you made it out, Inspector. None the worse for wear, I trust?"

"Merci, Dr. Watson. *Mlle.* Otero has told us of your courage and resourcefulness. It seems that I am indebted to you not only for saving my pension, but now my life as well. As soon as I bring in this fiendish professor, I shall look forward to enjoying both."

"I am pleased that I was able to do so, Inspector, as it was very much in my own interest as well as yours." Both men looked at him quizzically. "Caroline...er *Mlle.* Otero was not present when he informed me of the fate he had planned for us. He was going..." Watson paused for another fit of coughing, "to have Gerald shoot you with my revolver, and frame me for both your murder and for the murder of the pharmacist Lambert."

Loiseaux clutched his fists in anger. "But why, Dr. Watson? To what end?"

Out of the corner of his eye, Watson noticed Holmes pursing his lips, signaling him not to say too much. "I'm afraid it's all rather convoluted, Inspector. He's evidently quite mad and has some inexplicable fixation with reenacting the *Divine Comedy."* To change the subject, he turned back to Holmes. "I say, Holmes, next time you're of a mind to go swimming in some river, I do wish you'd let me in on your plans."

"Sorry, Watson. After Moriarty's bully-boy locked the bilge hatch, there was nothing else I could do. Before I could go back through the door in the bulkhead between the bilges, he got there first and locked the other hatch as well. As you know, my only weapon—or tool as it were—was the small folding knife. I admit it was a calculated risk, opening the seacocks, but there was no other choice. I took a chance that Moriarty, unable to use his legs, would have a fear of drowning far keener than those who are not so incapacitated."

"I am delighted, Dr. Watson, that you too have escaped without serious injury; my delight is even greater since learning of the fate in store for me had you not acted decisively as you did. But just as a precaution, as soon as we arrive at the Ministry, I will have the police surgeon summoned to have a look at you."

"Please Inspector. You've got to believe me. Watson and I know this man. He is the arch criminal of this century. I assure you that by now he's gone from Paris, on his way to some *pied a terre* kept for just such an emergency as this. But even if he's remained in Paris, you'll never find him. But I doubt that he's here. He will surely make his way to the coast. He owns an ocean-going ship which almost certainly is lying off the Normandy coast awaiting his arrival."

"What Holmes says is true, Inspector. The professor told me exactly the same thing in our final conversation. It was his intention to kill you and leave your body on the quay. He was going to let me out downstream and proceed with Holmes locked safely in the hold until the rendezvous with his larger vessel somewhere on the coast."

"Well even if that is the case, that is all the more reason for you to come with me to my office. There are still many, many details regarding which I shall be needing your full account. Those two have murdered at least five and possibly six men—if you include Ollstreder—on French soil. They will, I pledge to you, be captured and tried under French law."

"If he escapes, Inspector Loiseaux, it is no exaggeration to say that he may cause the deaths of five or six thousand, or even five or six *hundred* thousand. I tell you, and without the slightest hyperbole, that this man is the most dangerous creature on the face of the earth."

"And you *M'sieur* Holmes are the only agency in the world capable of stopping him? I thought *M'sieur Bertillon* had..." Loiseaux paused and made a face as he felt through all his pockets for a cigarette. *"S'il vous plait...* please..., *M'sieur* Holmes, do give us some credit. I will notify the naval and port authorities in every port from Cherbourg north to Belgium. After all, I would say that a man in a wheelchair accompanied by a huge man dressed as a woman, would not be exactly inconspicuous." He drew himself up and glared at Holmes. "In spite of what you must think of the abilities of the French military and civilian law enforcement authorities, we are quite capable of dealing with this professor. Besides, *M'sieurs,* if they have indeed escaped from Paris and are making their way to the coast, what can you do to stop them? Do you have an army or navy at your command? So far as I can tell, you have your own formidable selves, *Mlle.* Otero—whom I suspect would much rather be sipping champagne and nibbling caviar at Maxim's just now—and, lest we forget, the young woman in the evening gown who..." He paused and looked about, "Where is she, by the way? I distinctly ordered her to remain here as soon as she returned from summoning help."

"I would not rule out any possibility in the case of Miss Pippen, Inspector. But in the present circumstances, I would speculate that she's gone to answer what in her mind is a higher imperative."

"Thank you for such an enlightening explanation, *M'sieur* Holmes. It confirms my determination that we must continue this discussion in my offices. I would not want anyone else to be overcome by an irresistible impulse to determine their own priorities in this investigation. I do not wish to appear an ingrate, *M'sieurs,* but in the nadir of my despair, the thought did cross my mind that our recent predicament may at least in some part be attributed to your—shall we say—disingenuousness?"

"As you wish, Inspector. While you continue to ply us with questions, Watson and I shall continue to ply you with 'disingenuous' responses. And in the meanwhile, Professor Moriarty—or as you know him 'Villeneuf'—will continue making good his escape. If you are so confident of your ability to apprehend him, why not let us be on our way. In the off chance that you may actually take him into custody, Watson and I can be back on twelve hours' notice to give evidence any time you wish."

Loiseaux looked as though he was beginning to waiver in his resolve. "And what of *Mlle.* Otero?"

Watson stepped in front of Holmes. "Caroline...er...*Mlle.* Otero is coming with us, Inspector. Admitting the possibility that Moriarty may yet be in the city, or have left henchmen behind, the risk to *Mlle.* Otero is entirely too great."

"In addition to being unable to conduct a manhunt, are you also of the view that we are incapable of protecting the *Mademoiselle?*"

"Forgive my bluntness, Inspector," Watson brushed away Holmes's discreetly restraining hand on his elbow, "I'm sure you are sincere in your desire to see that she comes to no further harm. But do you propose to protect her with the same diligence as was employed in the protection of President Loubet at the racetrack the other day? And what sort of uniform was it that the imposter wore breaking in the door of Lambert's shop the night of his murder? Not to put too fine a point on the matter, what of the baron's chauffeur?" Watson burst into a new fit of coughing, and both Holmes and Loiseaux had to hold him to keep him from collapsing. When he regained his balance he held out his hand to Caroline. "If *Mlle.* Otero is willing, she's coming with me. I've promised her a visit to London. She's suffered more than the rest of us combined at the hands of Moriarty and his ward. If anyone deserves an opportunity to be in on his capture, it is she. After that, you may contact her at the Savoy, The Strand, London."

"But, John, I've heard the Savoy..."

"What? Oh yes, Caroline, you're quite right about the Savoy. Then make it the Connaught, in Park Lane, Inspector. Come, Caroline, let's be on our way. If Inspector Loiseaux wishes us to remain in Paris at his disposal, he shall have to clap us in irons. Perhaps we can arrange for one or two of those newspaper reporters who seem to be heading down the steps, their notebooks poised and at the ready, to be present while he does so. Holmes, are you coming, or is it your intention to meet the press with Inspector Loiseaux?"

CHAPTER FORTY-SIX

"I think, old fellow, we'd best leave that decision to
a certain minor Treasury official in Her Majesty's Government."

"I think I could tolerate a little more of that champagne, Holmes. Would you be so kind?" Holmes, his nose buried in the papers from the portfolio, reached out and slid the silver ice bucket across the cocktail table in Watson's direction. "The chilled liquid has a wondrously soothing effect on my throat." Watson sat back in his club chair looking yearningly at the box of Romeo *y* Julietta double coronas. He toyed with the idea of giving one a try, but decided that his throat was not yet up to a cigar and it would be a shame to waste such a luxurious one if he were unable to do it full justice. In anticipation of the moment when he deemed himself sufficiently recovered, he did, however, slip three into the pocket of his coat.

"*Mlle.* Otero, I take it, was not severely injured?"

"It's difficult to say, Holmes. I could do nothing more than a perfunctory examination. It's too early to tell whether she sustained any internal injuries. She seems to be sleeping normally. Miss Pippen will, I'm sure, keep a close watch and inform me should there be any cause for alarm. How much longer to Boulogne?"

"According to the head porter, we should be there in less than an hour, depending on whether the east-bound Venice-Simplon-Orient Express is on time. He tells me that the French National Railroad regulations require that private trains yield the right-of-way to the public carriers. Evidently this rule is un-waivable, even for the Rothschilds' private train."

"You would think that with this much traffic on the line, the French National Rail System would have put in a double track"

"One would think so, but then I suppose that such an installation requires a good deal of capital. The government probably has none to spare, and after the Panama Canal debacle, no one, not in France, much less anywhere else, will touch a French bond issue. Until the government stabilizes and gets its fiscal house in order, I'm afraid the French people are in for rather hard going. And until the government can put this Dreyfus business to rest, it's unlikely to make much progress toward solving its other problems."

"Speaking of the 'Dreyfus business', have you made any sense out of the papers in the portfolio? I must say that while I'm not the least regretful to be leaving France, I do feel a sense of disappointment that we've not accomplished anything in the way of aiding in the exoneration of Captain Dreyfus, or for that matter, in finding out what Mycroft enjoined us to discover."

"*Au contraire,* my dear Watson, quite *au contraire.* Understandably, your various pre-occupations have perhaps interfered with your usual faculty for being able to see the forest as well as the individual trees. I think we've accomplished quite a lot in both respects, not to mention the added bonus of putting Moriarty to flight."

Watson sat up eagerly. "Then you've found some linkage between Moriarty's arms-trafficking partnership and the plot against Dreyfus?"

"Merely circumstantial; nothing I would want to present in a court of law."

"Then let us convene a moot court." Watson took another soothing draught of wine. "I shall be the judge and you present the case for the Crown."

"Very well." Holmes having made note of Watson's wistful looking at the cigar box, fetched himself a fresh one and lighted it with exaggerated ritual. "In my opening statement, I will suggest to your lordship and members of the jury that the evidence will establish that once *Graf* von Schwarzkoppen's involvement in espionage became established such that it could no longer be plausibly denied, before he could be declared *persona non grata* by the French Government, he was recalled and assigned to other duties in Germany. Baron Ollstreder, who already was spending as much time in Paris as anywhere else, was recruited as von Schwarzkoppen's replacement. It is a virtual certainty that the German Government was aware of Ollstreder's arms trafficking and at least turned a blind eye, aided in this endeavour no doubt by the liberal application of eyewash in the form of Deutsche-marks paid to various officials in a position to do the baron either good or ill. It was a natural progression for the baron to expand the scope of his export license and as a quid pro quo, to stand as von Schwarzkoppen's replacement.

"However, like the hapless Trask of the Liverpool Bank frauds, the baron greatly miscalculated his co-conspirator. I would surmise that Moriarty, acting as an agent or broker for Sinn Fein, made a purchase or series of purchases from Ollstreder. Like the camel putting his nose under the tent he soon took over the lucrative arms-trafficking leg of the baron's commercial triangle. And eventually he may have subsumed the espionage business as well. You'd certainly agree that he's no slacker in spotting good business opportunities and he's certainly not constrained by such existential notions as conscience in exploiting them." Holmes paused and took a thoughtful puff on his cigar. "But I digress. That is only speculation. Since this is a court of law, I must confine myself to proof of the case at bar."

"*Mlle.* Otero, if called to the witness box would and could testify to a series of commercial transactions conducted by Moriarty—using the pseudonym 'Villeneuf'—in joint enterprise with Ollstreder, these involving the import or export of some unspecified article of commerce. She would further testify— perhaps over the objection of defence counsel—that these transactions were carried out in what appeared to her to be a clandestine manner and in an atmosphere of mutual mistrust. Although she would not know the details, she would testify regarding, to use her words, the 'terrible row' which preceded the dissolution of their joint venture, and that in the course of their rather contentious discussions, the man that she formerly knew as 'Villeneuf' and now knows to be none other than the prisoner in the dock whose true name is 'James Moriarty', quondam professor of mathematics at a certain public school in Smythwick, made repeated demands, punctuated by threats and violence, upon the hapless Baron Ollstreder to produce a certain 'portfolio'.

"Dr. John H. Watson, formerly of the Fifth Northumberland Fusiliers and presently celebrated author, after taking the witness oath, would give evidence as follows: whilst on holiday in Paris, through a convoluted set of circumstances, the retelling of which need not detain your lordship and members of the jury, he found himself the victim of a bizarre plot involving not only the kidnapping of himself, Mr. Sherlock Holmes, as well as others, but also the murder of one French citizen and the near murder of another, namely a high-ranking inspector of the *Sureté*.

"After his lordship had admonished the gallery against any further outbursts, the witness continues: 'while I was captive aboard a river barge moored along one of the quays on the right bank of the Seine, my captor, the prisoner in the dock, identified himself to me as Professor James Moriarty, admitting as well that he was one in the same as 'P. Villeneuf', a name which he used when in Paris. He remarked on the fact that although I had written much about him, we had never actually met face to face. He took considerable satisfaction in reminding me that I had written of his death—as it turns out prematurely—some eight years ago. Thinking that he'd gotten the best of my-self and Mr. Holmes— whom he believes, and rightly so, to be his mortal enemy—he revealed that he owned three ships: the river-barge in whose main cabin the conversation took place and which, I should mention with your lordship's permission, now lies, so much of it as remains, at the bottom of the aforementioned river; an ocean-going vessel larger than a private yacht, fitted out to his specifications; and a third vessel which he neither named or described. I should add, again with your lordship's permission, that the prisoner made the cross-channel passage on the regular boat-train ferry at the same time as Mr. Holmes and my-self. When I asked him, the prisoner, that is, why he had not used his own ship to make the crossing, he told me that it was at the time engaged in a commercial transaction and was thus unavailable.'

"Pausing to take a few sips of water, owing to the fact that his throat is still somewhat raw and parched from his ordeal in escaping from the barge, Dr. Watson further testifies that in the course of effecting his escape, he managed to save from the burning and rapidly sinking barge a leather portfolio—'Yes, m'lord, this is the one; Crown Exhibit number one'—which contained various papers. These papers are variously marked as Crown exhibits as well. They consist of an empty envelope bearing on its broken seal what may possibly have been the German Imperial crest; some maps—large-scale ordnance maps by the look of them—of what appear to be portions of the Continental coast between Cherbourg, France, and Rotterdam, The Netherlands.

There were some other documents written in what appeared to him to be French and others that appeared to be in German. He glances at his lordship apologetically, 'Since I am versed in neither language, I am unable to describe the contents of these documents.'

"After a perfunctory cross-questioning calculated to emphasize the long-standing enmity existing between the witness and the prisoner in the dock, which relationship ought to be taken into account by the members of the jury in weighing the credibility of the witness, and some further questions to establish that even if the witness's testimony is to be believed, the only crime thus far proved occurred on French soil and therefore beyond the jurisdiction of this honourable court, the witness is excused."

"I quite agree, Holmes, there doesn't seem to be a provable case against Moriarty under British law. But if that's the legalistic situation, assuming that we are successful in effecting his capture, what about handing him over to the French? Inspector Loiseaux would surely be delighted."

"Indeed he would. But I've not yet finished putting on the case for the Crown. I should next call an army officer, fluent in the German language. He will be shown one of the exhibits comprising the contents of the portfolio. He will identify it as a copy of a cargo manifest, or ocean bill of lading, from the vessel *Aegean Star*. He will proceed to read into the record the text of the document, both in the original German, and translating it to English as he goes along. It reads, if I may..." Holmes adjusted his spectacles, "... two-thousand, four-hundred Mauser carbine-type rifles; two hundred thousand rounds of ammunition for same; four, eighty-eight millimetre field artillery pieces; twenty thousand rounds of ammunition for same; fifty heavy machine guns—calibre not stated—and another one hundred thousand rounds of ammunition for same.

"A separate manifest, written in English, calls for some fifty hogs-heads of Irish whisky and another fifty casks of tobacco, American in origin."

"The whisky and tobacco match what Moriarty described to me as the annual 'rent' for the use of his island 'paradise' where you were to be imprisoned. And the arms: why there's enough there to equip a brigade. But it still would not be enough to account for her riding low in the water as she's been described. What else could there be?"

"Quite right, Watson. There's no accounting for the discrepancy. It could be anything from extra ballast to a company of cavalry—men and horses."

"And how is the vessel linked to Moriarty? My recollection is that its registry is Greek, and it's owned through a Netherlands Antilles company by a Liechtenstein korpen..."

"Korpenshaft. As you may further remember, a holding company, which in turn is organized with bearer shares that are owned by whomever possesses them at a given moment. You may also recall that such an entity was involved in the Liverpool Bank forgeries. Apparently their use is becoming a common occurrence among those who wish to conduct their business without the constraints of official scrutiny. We could link the vessel to Moriarty through Herr Schwabach, but the price of his testimony, as you can imagine, would be too dear.

"Instead, we shall call next an officer serving in Her Majesty's Navy. He will tell the court that while on routine patrol off the west coast of Ireland, a frigate under his command spotted at first light a vessel matching the description of the *Aegean Star* riding at sea anchor. At that early hour there was still a good bit of surface fog. I must interject at this point that the *Aegean Star* was built in one of the Clyde yards in 'eighty-five, so its dimensions and other specifications were readily obtainable by investigators from Admiralty House. That information having been established by stipulation, the officer continues his testimony. Thinking that the vessel was either in distress or up to some clandestine activity, the Navy ship changed course in the direction of the anchored vessel. Before the deck officer could use his loud-hailer to demand that the other ship stand by to be boarded, it quickly hauled in its anchors and got underway full speed ahead. Evidently she had steam up al-ready. Apparently her captain knew the waters well, because he dashed shoreward, still at full speed, and concealed himself in a fog bank. The commander of the naval vessel was unwilling to risk his ship and crew in such treacherous conditions, so he lay off-shore for more than hour until the fog had lifted. But by then, the other ship had made good its escape."

"Remarkable, Holmes. Do you suppose the *Aegean Star* had already off-loaded its cargo of death?"

"It's impossible to say, Watson. There was apparently a moderate sea running, so the Navy look-out was unable to tell how the vessel rode in the water. But what is even more remarkable is that the officer will testify he was following the other ship through binoculars, and as it went into the fog bank, he's quite certain that he saw mounted on the aft deck a cannon with a muzzle-bore at least as large as any of his own armaments. This would account for some of the modifications that were made to the vessel about five years ago. According to the Clyde yard's records—again by stipulation—the *Aegean Star* was in dry dock for a complete refitting. Among the modifications were the installation of a second engine and propeller; reinforcement of the aft deck plating; enlarging the master's cabin and up-grading its furnishings; widening of certain doorways; increasing the size of the coal bunkers; addition of a heavy-duty boom and steam driven windlass over the fo'c's'le hold; and installation of a passenger elevator."

Noticing Watson's bemused look, Holmes paused and puffed his cigar for a few moments. "I've not been hoarding information again, old fellow. Miss Pippen was the source of the Royal Navy intelligence. My brother was able to act immediately on the information which we provided to Miss Pippen. He must have guessed that the vessel was built in Scotland, and either telephoned or telegraphed some Admiralty personnel who were already there on other business. The events that I have just described occurred the morning of Miss Pippen's departure from London. Mycroft received the information from Admiralty House and informed her so that she could in turn inform us. Of course she never had an opportunity to do so until a short while ago. She told me while you were tending to *Mlle.* Otero."

"Then obviously you were right about the ship's destination. Moriarty's evidently in league with Sinn Fein. I never took him to be an Irish patriot. I would have thought him incapable of any emotion such as patriotism."

"Do not let yourself be persuaded to the contrary. I doubt that Moriarty cares any more for the isle of his birth than Captain Dreyfus cares for Devil's Island. If he's driven by any thought other than money, it would only be his obsessive hatred for all things British. I would go so far as to say that revenge against the land that refused to recognize his self-proclaimed genius as a mathematician is the motivating force behind his entire criminal career. Condemned to live in anonymity without the honours and accolades that he thought were his due, he became the anonymous master-criminal, with each successful crime sapping the wealth and morale of the land and people he'd come to hate. And at last, for his magnum opus, he foments an Irish uprising and at the same time turning a hansom profit in the bargain."

"What do you make of the ordnance maps? I make so bold as to assume that our brothers across the Irish Sea are not planning an invasion of the Continent. Are they the link to the Dreyfus case?"

"They do appear to lend themselves to that office. Notice the leather binding of the portfolio, how old and weathered it looks. Of equal or greater significance, look at the date on the maps—March, 1894. Evidently, it was intended that the portfolio be fortuitously 'discovered' just on the eve of Dreyfus's new trial, and that it be linked to him as conclusive 'new' evidence of his guilt."

"Good grief, Holmes. How clumsy can they get? The appearance of the leather could be easily simulated: a few days' immersion in water; a few drops of bleach spread here and there; rapid drying in front of an open fire. And as for the maps, why you could probably find maps that out-dated in half a dozen of those booksellers' stalls we saw along the quay a few days ago. All that's missing is Dreyfus's initials on the outside of the binding. Why any decent barrister would make this so-called 'evidence' a laughing-stock in front of any fair-minded jury."

"And therein, my friend lies the rub. I think you assume too much when you hypothesize a 'fair-minded jury'. It would not suit the purposes of the French military to make even the smallest concession to due process in the case of Captain Dreyfus."

"Then you're convinced they intend to railroad Dreyfus yet a second time?"

"Apart from a small cadre of officers who are generally considered misfits and malcontents, the military establishment is by no means in a mood to admit that it may have been mistaken in regard to Captain Dreyfus."

"Then aren't they playing right into the hands of President Loubet?"

"My supposition is that they mean to do just that. He is newly installed in office, and they sense that he's not yet consolidated his power-base. Applying the lessons learned at the Ecole Militarie, they mean to attack their perceived enemy when he is most vulnerable—before he has time to build his strength."

"What was going to be done with the portfolio? I mean how was it going to be 'discovered', and by whom? Now that we have it, can we not establish that it is a fraud? And once that's proven, does it not necessarily follow that if someone is trying to frame Dreyfus now, he must have been innocent five years ago as well as now? Have these people no sense of decency and fair-play?"

"Esterhazy told me that he was not sure what he was to do with the portfolio. Obviously the baron never had an opportunity to give him his complete instructions. Most probably he would have been told that he should come forward, claiming that Dreyfus on the eve of his arrest had entrusted the portfolio to him enjoining him to destroy it in exchange for Dreyfus's forgiving the loan he'd made to Esterhazy. He would have been instructed to say that he'd given his word as an officer and a gentleman, but when he examined the contents and realized their significance, he'd breached his promise and hid the portfolio away, always intending to bring it forward should it appear that there was any danger of Dreyfus being acquitted. While he might have received a 'slap on the wrist' for withholding evidence, he would probably also have received a good deal of sympathy for his effort not to appear to have broken his word to Dreyfus."

"Moriarty mentioned documents which were to be found by the authorities in the baron's wall-safe and that they would have a prophylactic effect on Ollstreder's ever returning to France. I wonder what they are? Do you suppose that they would have lent any credibility to this other garbage?"

"I hope that we shall find out in due course. Inspector Loiseaux promised to cable us in care of the Boulogne station-master."

"And what do you think we ought to do with this bogus 'portfolio'?"

"I think, Watson, that we'd best leave that decision to a certain 'minor Treasury official' in Her Majesty's Government. Besides, I think we're slowing down. I hope that it's because we're approaching Boulogne, and not because we're being shunted off to some siding waiting for the morning milk train to amble past. I'll rouse Esterhazy and *Frauline* Irmgaard; you tend to *Mlle.* Otero and Miss Pippen. We shan't want to waste any time."

CHAPTER FORTY-SEVEN

*"It's a good thing I do not believe in the old
superstition about women aboard a ship
bringing bad luck."*

"Is this how I'm to arrive at Connaught's—smelling of dead fish? Marie Antoinette at least had an open-air tumbrel and clean straw on which to sit."

"Caroline, be patient."

"Watson's advice is sound, *Mlle*. Otero. Each of us has the same problem."

"Mr. Holmes is quite right, Caroline." Miss Pippen, who was seated on the floor opposite Caroline leaned forward to reassure her. "I'm certain that some arrangement can be made to provide us with presentable clothing and an opportunity to..." she lowered her voice to a whisper, "bathe."

Neither Esterhazy nor Irmgaard had joined in the conversation. They huddled together in a rear corner of the van, Esterhazy looking sullen, and Irmgaard looking like she was having second-thoughts about the wisdom of her decision to accompany Esterhazy to what he'd promised would be a life of security and luxury.

They had in fact arrived at Boulogne, but instead of the main passenger terminal, their train had been routed to a remote corner of the freight yards where they were transferred to a horse-drawn lorry whose mephitic interior made it obvious that its usual service was hauling fish. At Holmes insistence—the driver having made it clear that his instructions did not include detours and that he was placing himself at some risk by transporting them at all—they stopped at the telegraph office where Holmes retrieved the promised message from Loiseaux, and were now clip-clopping through the central district toward the port area.

"John, can I have some more of those pills, my rib feels like it is about to poke through my... my... peri... whatever you called it."

"My own ribs are in sympathy with yours, Caroline. But we'd best wait until there's water available to swallow them with. I think it helps to dissolve them more rapidly so that they take effect that much sooner. Besides, you remember how bitter they taste on the tongue."

"I do not think you'll have long to wait; I believe we're here." Holmes rose to his feet, bumping his head on the low roof. The lorry had come to a stop as Watson was speaking. They could hear the driver dismount from his bench, and could hear the crunch of his gum boots on the road surface as he came around to the rear of the wagon. Esterhazy, who was a good bit shorter that Holmes, stood and arched his back. He held out his hand and helped Irmgaard to her feet. Holmes held out his hand to assist Miss Pippen, and Watson got to his knees and then to his feet.

Caroline held out her hand, expecting Watson to assist her. "Caroline, this is not a cotillion. You'd best do as I did. Get to your knees first. Otherwise you may do further injury to your ribs, or at the least cause yourself a good deal of unnecessary pain."

"Thank you for your advice, Doctor," Caroline muttered as she followed Watson's instructions. "Thank you very much. First you drag me through the lobby of the Ritz looking like I've been run over by an omnibus; now you're going to drag me through the lobby of the Connaught, smelling like a fish-wife. I wonder what Emilienne and Liane..."

"I'm sure *Mlles.* d' Alencon and de Pougy would be beside themselves with envy, *Mlle.* Otero." Holmes completed her thought—not necessarily as she would have—and making no effort to conceal his exasperation. "Please do hurry along." As if to make up for his harshness, Holmes uncharacteristically grasped Caroline by the waist and lifted her gently to the ground from the back of the lorry. "If we miss the tide, we may very well have to cross the Channel in the hold of a French fishing boat, rather than on the bridge of one of Her Majesty's ships of the line."

Once Caroline and Watson were out of the lorry, the driver wordlessly closed the rear door and as quickly as he could, drove off leaving the six bedraggled travelers standing in the dark, their pitiful collection of luggage piled at their feet. They were standing on a broad path made of crushed oyster shells. Following Holmes's lead, they picked up their luggage and started down the path toward the sound of water lapping against wooden pilings. Behind them, the sky was just beginning to lighten, and after they'd gone about fifty meters they came to a wooden shack next to the path. The small building was of ship-lap construction, with a tin roof which at one time had been painted red. There were pairs of small windows, round like portholes, in each of the two visible sides and another in the door set at eye-level. When they reached the side of the building facing the path they could see a sign, its paint peeling. Holmes looked at the sign, "Well done, Watson. Your memory's perfect. This is the place: 'Boudreaux's Boat Yard and Pier'."

In a moment the door opened and a man stepped out. He was of indeterminate age, having the weathered look of one who has spent his life on or next to the sea. He was wearing baggy corduroy trousers, gum boots turned down below the knee and an oil-cloth coat which came to his knees. He wore a knit fisherman's cap, and in his hands he held a large-bore, short-barreled shotgun similar to the lumparo favored by Sicilian goat-herders. Evidently, he'd been told whom to expect, and before Watson could make up his mind to reach for his Webley, he lowered the weapon and broke into a broad grin displaying, even in the weak light, a set of perfect teeth set off by his deeply tanned and wrinkled face.

"M'sieur Boudreaux, I presume?" Holmes stepped forward close enough to grab the barrel of the shotgun, should his assumption prove to be incorrect.

"And you'd be Mr. Holmes? I was told to expect five people, not six."

"I trust that one extra passenger will not greatly inconvenience you?" Holmes took out his wallet and extracted a thousand-franc note which swiftly disappeared into Boudreaux's coat pocket.

"Well since you put it that way, I suppose not. But we need to get a move on. The tide'll be turning soon, and there's a bit of a sea running so I wouldn't want to take you all the way across."

"Nor do we want to put you to that much trouble. Lead the way, *M'sieur* Boudreaux. I think it would be in all of our interests if we clear the harbour before it's fully light."

Wordlessly, Boudreaux turned and started down the path toward a rickety wooden pier, his passengers straggling along behind. They clambered down a set of steps and picked their way among the cracked and patched boards to the end of the pier.

Moored at the end of the pier was a fishing boat that appeared to be in a state of decrepitude in keeping with the shack and pier. It had a rusty steel hull and wooden superstructure consisting of a wheel house and forward of that an enclosure over the top of the wood-fired boiler whose tin smoke-stack protruded up through an off-center hole on the port-side so as not to obstruct the view from the starboard side of the wheel-house where the steering and throttle were mounted. Booms for raising and lowering the fishing nets were mounted on each side, one set forward of the wheel house, and one set aft. The nets lay folded on the aft deck on either side of the hatch opening to the aft cargo hold.

Because of the high tide the boat's gunwales rode above the top of the pier pilings so that the charter-party had to step up to board. Once on board, Boudreaux directed the women to a narrow bench beneath the taff rail. He sent Esterhazy down to the engine room with instructions on how to stoke the boiler. Their luggage was lowered after a brief but intense debate into the aft cargo hold. In anticipation of his passengers' arrival, Boudreaux had al-ready fired up the boiler, so it only took a minute or two for sufficient pressure to build. He ordered Holmes and Watson to cast off the bow and stern lines, engaged the clutch and they chugged easily away from the pier and into the harbor.

Even in the harbor there was a moderate chop caused by a storm front blowing in off the open Channel waters. It brought with it a thick fog, but just as a further precaution against coming across a French Navy ship or Customs vessel, they took a long southwestern reach around the main roads. The fog and their luck held. Eventually they cleared the harbour and set a northwest course across the main traffic lanes. It began to drizzle, so Holmes motioned to the women to take shelter—such as it was—in the cramped wheelhouse, while he and Watson made their way back to the taff rail. Boudreaux motioned for them to lift the bench which also served as the top of a built-in tool chest. Inside they found a couple of oil cloth slickers which afforded at least some protection against the raw wind and chilling rain.

Boudreaux reached in his pocket and took out a watch. Shaking his head in disgust, he motioned to Holmes and Watson to look at their own time-pieces. They confirmed that Bourdeaux's own watch was approximately correct. He shouted to make himself heard over the sound of the engine and the rising storm, "We're running late already, my friends. I do not think we'll make the rendezvous in time. Perhaps we should turn back. I've got the throttle wide-open, and we're hardly making any headway against this sea."

Holmes and Watson made their way back to the lee of the wheelhouse. "How far to the rendezvous point?"

Boudreaux, his hands maintaining a death-grip on the wheel, shrugged, "I don't know, *M'sieur* Holmes. In this fog, there's nothing to navigate by except the compass." He pointed to a small binnacle mounted next to the wheel. "All I know is that we're on the correct heading. There's no way to know how much leeway the storm has caused. I'm almost certain I heard us pass the outer buoy marking the main channel into the harbor within the last few minutes. From the sound of the bell, I thought it was on our starboard side, about one hundred meters away."

"He's right, Holmes. I'm sure I heard it too. I didn't remark on it, thinking that I was merely experiencing an odd form of tinnitus as a result of having been struck in both ears, as well as having fired guns in enclosed spaces."

"If you and Dr. Watson are correct, where does that place us in relation to the rendezvous point?"

"If your navy ship is where it's supposed to be, we're almost exactly on course, about three or four kilometers away. Perhaps the mademoiselles have brought us good fortune." Boudreaux flashed a prurient grin in the direction of the three women. Caroline rolled her eyes, Irmgaard looked queasy, and Miss Pippen turned up her nose in disgust.

"Come *Mlle.* Otero, *Fraulein* Irmgaard, let us go below. I expect that Major Esterhazy could stand a spell of relief from his labours." She leaned down into the small companionway, "Captain Boudreaux's compliments, Major. Would you care to join the other gentlemen on the bridge?"

"Ah, *merci,* thank you, *Mlle.* Pippen." Esterhazy poked his head through the doorway. "As you know my back..."

"Please, Major, spare us at least that." As soon as Esterhazy had cleared the companionway, Miss Pippen started down. She glanced back over her shoulder, "Ladies, shall we?"

As Caroline started down, Watson put a hand on her shoulder. "Caroline, are you sure you're up to any exertion? I really think..."

"The little pills have helped a good bit. In any case, I would prefer to be doing something useful rather than standing about listening to you men playing at sailor-boy. Should we, against all odds, actually make it to England, after all this you are booking me, Irmgaard—poor *liebschoen*—and Fiona, if she'll join us, into nothing less than the royal suite at the Connaught." As she shook loose from Watson's hand, she looked up at Boudreaux. "You said maintain the boiler pressure at fifteen kilograms?"

Boudreaux gave a bewildered shrug, "*Oui, Mademoiselle,* fifteen." As soon as they were below. Boudreaux reached inside his coat and produced a pack of Gauloises which he passed round to a grateful Holmes and Esterhazy, with Watson forlornly declining.

"Does it seem that the rain's letting up?"

"Possibly, *M'sieur* Holmes, but I do not think so. I think that this is a storm front. If it were just a summer squall line, we'd have passed through it by now. I do not know what kind of vessel is being sent for you. If it is a battleship-class or other large ship, with the sea running as it is, she won't have enough sea-room to manœuvre in these off-shore waters. Her captain, unless he's a fool, will know that and will not wait around very long for us. I think we should turn back. I would be happy to take you all the way across, but I do not think we'd make it. While I have enough wood on-board to keep the boiler stoked, maintaining fifteen kilograms of pressure is going to exhaust the fresh water in the boiler and reserve tank in another," he paused to look at his watch again, "forty minutes or so. When the water tank gets too low there's also a great risk that the boiler will over-heat and shut down completely"

"I appreciate your candor, Captain Boudreaux, but we cannot afford to lose another day, if it is humanly possible to avoid doing so. In order to extend our time as much as feasible, I suggest that you reduce speed and the water consumption to just enough to maintain headway, and if we've not made contact when you reach the point that you've only enough water in the boiler to safely navigate back in, then we will turn back."

"As you wish, *M'sieur* Holmes. Would you be so good as to tell our make-shift stoker gang to belay their efforts until the pressure drops to ten kilograms, and to maintain at that level." As Holmes stuck his head down into the gangway to relay the instructions, Boudreaux cut back on the throttle reducing the engine noise to a quiet thrumming. They continued at trolling speed for another thirty minutes, the rain coming down with increasing intensity.

Boudreaux passed the Gauloises around again. When they were lighted, he turned to Holmes, "I think, *M'sieur* Holmes that we have reached the limit of our water. I'm terribly sorry, but we must turn back now, or we may not make it back to the harbor."

Holmes cupped his hands around the cigarette and took a drag. "Watson?"

"Captain Boudreaux's right, Holmes. We're doing no one any good out here. I would hate for Captain Boudreaux to complete, albeit inadvertently, what Moriarty tried so hard yet failed to accomplish. It seems to me that what's most important is that we report what we've learned and deliver the portfolio as well as the major into the proper hands. Can you not telegraph Mycroft from Boulogne?"

"You're right as usual, old..." Holmes grabbed Watson's arm. "What was that? Did you hear it, Boudreaux?"

"Yes! Who could not hear it? It's a fog horn, *M'sieurs!*" He turned away from the wheel and grabbed Esterhazy in a clumsy embrace. "We've found them!" He leaned over toward the companionway, "Do you hear, *Mademoiselles?* We've found them!"

"Well done, Captain Boudreaux, well done!" Watson clapped Boudreaux on the shoulder. "But how shall they know we've found them? How far away?"

Boudreaux's euphoria passed as quickly as it had come. He shrugged his shoulders, "One kilometer, no more. Dead ahead; possibly a few degrees to port. The wind and rain tend to distort the sound. It's your choice, *M'sieurs.*" He paused, noticing that the three women had all crowded into the tiny companionway. "And yours, too, *Mademoiselles.* Do we risk the rest of our water, or do we turn back?"

"We turn back!" Esterhazy pulled his derringer from his waist-band and pointed it at Boudreaux. "Turn this boat around now. With the papers so graciously provided by Her Majesty's Government, Irmgaard and I shall take our chances on dry land. *M'sieur* Holmes, Dr. Watson, please step back toward the stern and raise your hands. Captain Boudreaux, you will please carry out my instructions at once. I warn you..."

Reaching out from the companionway, Caroline and Irmgaard each took hold of one of Esterhazy's legs and pulled backward sending him face down on the deck. Miss Pippen threw herself onto his back and put her hand on his arm pinning it to the deck so that he could not raise the weapon. In a second Holmes reached down and pried the gun out of Esterhazy's hand and then pulled him to his feet. "I think it is you, Major Esterhazy, who should move to the stern. Do you have any more weapons? Or would you prefer that we complete your humiliation by having Miss Pippen search you?"

Esterhazy shuffled toward the rear of the boat, blood streaming once again from his nose. "No, *M'sieur* Holmes, no more weapons. I'm sorry. I panicked. I'm not afraid to die. But my concern is for the women. We must think of them."

"You miserable little coward." Caroline climbed out of the companionway. "Tell me, Captain Boudreaux, if we throw this worm overboard will it save any fuel?" Esterhazy scurried to the taff rail and sat down glaring sullenly over his forearm which he had pressed to his nose to stanch the bleeding.

Miss Pippen picked herself up off the deck and turned to Boudreaux. "I believe you have your answer, Captain Boudreaux. The glass tube mounted on the boiler next to the pressure gauge shows about one-eighth full. Do you wish to increase the pressure?"

"That's al-right, Miss Pippen. It's time I took a turn as stoker." Holmes handed the derringer to Miss Pippen. "Would you keep an eye on the major? If he gives you any trouble, you may feel free to carry-out *Mlle.* Otero's suggestion."

Miss Pippen took the pistol, and as Holmes ducked his head under the companionway lintel, she turned to Boudreaux, "Do you have any more of those Gauloises, Captain? *Mlle.* Otero, *Fraulein* Irmgaard and myself would be most appreciative if you would share them with us. I would not want to scandalize the Royal Navy by smoking aboard one of their vessels."

The fog horn sounded again, and Boudreaux pushed the throttle forward to maximum speed. The craft responded by dipping its bow and plowing ahead sending a heavy spray of water all the way over the wheelhouse. Boudreaux turned and raised his voice so as to be heard over the noise of the rain, wind and pounding engine. Holmes had taken off his slicker when he went below. Watson took his off and handed it to Caroline and handed the one worn by Holmes to Irmgaard. He started to take off his suit jacket to give to Miss Pippen. "Wait Dr. Watson, help me off with mine and give it to the *Mademoiselle*. I'll be dry enough in the wheelhouse."

Watson did as Boudreaux suggested, and when Miss Pippen had put on the coat he started toward the stern with her. "No, Dr. Watson, you remain here." Boudreaux put a restraining hand on Watson's arm. "You stay with me and keep a look-out for the navy ship. Watson looked uncertainly at Miss Pippen.

"It's al-right, Dr. Watson. Do as he says. We shall be fine. I would rather look like a drowned rat than be one."

"But..."

"Dr. Watson, please." Miss Pippen seized Watson by his lapels and turned him around to face the bow. "This is neither the time nor place for expressions of genteel gallantry. I assure you that the other women and I will not hold such an involuntary lapse against you. Now stay!"

They plowed ahead, for several more minutes, Watson peering through the small windows in the front and sides of the wheelhouse. He took off his glasses and wiped them with his pocket handkerchief, and put his hands to the sides of his face as though holding a pair of binoculars. "There! Captain Boudreaux. Ahead off to the left. Lying low in the water. That must be it. Holmes, I've spotted it. Less than a quarter-mile away."

"Mon Dieu! M'sieur Holmes; that's it. Just as Dr. watson says." Boudreaux leaned over to the companionway. "Is there any water left?"

"None, Captain Boudreaux, unless we use sea water. Is there a bucket aboard?"

"Sea water, *M'sieur* Holmes? Impossible! It will corrode the boiler tubes and cause too much impurity carry-over which will foul the piston."

Holmes stuck his head out of the companionway. "Captain, the measuring glass is empty. Would you not prefer to suffer corrosion now and save your passengers, your ship and yourself, or would you rather let your boiler corrode on the bottom of the Channel after we capsize and sink?"

Boudreaux pondered Holmes's question for a long moment, "You are correct, *M'sieur* Holmes. But you or whoever is paying for this will have to bear the expense." Boudreaux looked back over his shoulder, "In the chest, Dr. Watson. There are buckets. I use them for swabbing the deck and hold."

Watson made his way to the stern where by now the others had also glimpsed the other vessel. They were standing and waiving, oblivious to the fact that it was unlikely they'd be seen at such a distance in the rain and fog. Reaching into the chest, Watson extracted two tin buckets and started forward with them. Noticing what he was doing, Miss Pippen went forward with him to form a two-person bucket brigade. She dipped the buckets into the water and handed them to Watson who passed them down to Holmes. After a few rounds, Holmes climbed back up out of the hold and sat on the companionway step. "It's up to a quarter full, Captain Boudreaux. I don't think we'll need more than that, and I did not want to put in more than necessary so that it would take the least time to convert to steam. There's no pressure now. How much do you need to drive the piston?"

"At least fifteen, preferably." Boudreaux pointed ahead through the wheelhouse window. "We may be too late, *M'sieurs*. Look, they're getting under way!" He pointed to the Navy ship. Smoke was pouring from all four of her stacks.

"Quickly, Captain, do you have a lantern? Miss Pippen, would you be so good as to remove your petticoat?"

"There, *M'sieur* Holmes." Boudreaux pointed to a cabinet built into the forward bulkhead of the wheelhouse between the binnacle and the steps down to the boiler room.

As Holmes bent down to retrieve the lantern, Miss Pippen ducked down the steps into the boiler room and in a moment re-emerged and handed Holmes her white muslin under-garment.

Holmes removed the lantern fill-cap and poured the fuel onto the cloth which he then handed to Watson. "Here, Watson. I'll rotate the forward boom and lower it. As soon as you can reach the top, tie this on and set it aflame."

"The booms do not pivot, *M'sieur* Holmes. Let me have that," Boudreaux held out his hand. One of you take the helm, and one of you watch the boiler pressure. I'll rig this to the net clasp, light it and haul it up the boom." He lighted a fresh Gauloise, took the fuel-soaked cloth from Watson and made his way along the narrow, slippery deck between the wheelhouse and the starboard gunwale. When he reached the forward boom, he fastened the cloth in the metal clasp which ordinarily held one corner of the fishing net. He then unwound the lanyard from its cleat on the deck and touched the cigarette to the cloth. It instantly burst into flame and in a few strokes, he hauled it to the top of the boom.

As Boudreaux returned to the wheelhouse Watson shouted up from the boiler room, "Pressure's at fifteen, Holmes."

Holmes stepped back so that Boudreaux could re-take his position at the helm. "Pressure's at fifteen, Captain. Do you want to give it a try?"

Boudreaux engaged the clutch which resulted only in a pathetic gasp-like sound from the engine below. "Not enough pressure, *M'sieur* Holmes. You take the helm. I'll go below and rotate the fly-wheel until the pressure builds back up. When I signal, engage the clutch and it should, I pray, start up."

"Wait! Look there!" Miss Pippen pointed through the windows to a blinking light emanating from the other vessel. "The ship's signalling! They've seen us! The flame must have worked. Well done, Mr. Holmes." She turned and clasped her arms around Holmes's neck. "We're saved, everyone. Look!"

In an hour's time, after some delicate maneuvering by the two vessels, the passengers and their luggage had been transferred from the small fishing boat to the relatively enormous navy ship via a Jacob's ladder, and in the case of Esterhazy, a bosun's chair since he flatly refused to climb the ladder. Boudreaux had immediately shut down his over-worked boiler which then drained and refilled with fresh water from the navy vessel's own tanks. By the time Boudreaux had cast off the navy lines and gotten underway, Holmes, Watson and Miss Pippen had changed into dry clothing and were seated in the small ward room with the captain of the ship, Commander Rowland.

"Welcome aboard, Miss Pippen, gentlemen." He signaled to a mess steward who responded with a carafe and four coffee mugs. "I'm afraid all I can offer you is seamen's grog. This is a new ship, and in fact this is her maiden voyage. We were not scheduled for sea-trials actually for several more months. However, along with everything else that's new, we were in port testing a new gadget when, out of the blue as it were, we received orders to get under way immediately to rendezvous at sea with a French fishing vessel. We'd barely time to round up the crew, most of whom were on port liberty, and took on only such provisions as the chief bos'un was able to scrounge up in barely a couple of hours time. I dared not ask how or where he got them. He did assure me, however, that the requisition forms would be appropriately mis-filed and never see the light of day." Smiling ruefully, he poured generous measures for Holmes and Watson, and when he reached Miss Pippen he paused.

"Yes, please, Commander." Miss Pippen held out her cup.

"Yes, yes, of course. Please forgive me. I did not intend to be rude. Having a woman on board, not to mention three, is quite unsettling. It's a good thing I do not believe in the old superstition about women aboard a ship bringing bad luck. I should be loath to have something go awry on the first voyage of my first command."

Watson took out his briar. "Do the regulations permit smoking, Commander Rowland? I'm an old army man myself, you know. Never could resist a good pipe with my daily ration."

"Yes, in the ward room for the officers and in the seamen's mess. We have to be careful, since a fire aboard is about the worst thing that can happen. And you can imagine what would happen if there were a stray spark in one of the magazines." Rowland signaled again and the steward brought a pair of ash trays made from the bases of brass cannon shells.

Holmes took out his cigarette case and looked over at Watson. "Do you think you should, old man?"

"Don't know, Holmes. At least with my pipe I do not need to inhale."

Before removing a cigarette for himself, Holmes offered the case to Commander Rowland, and then to the Commander's

417

jaw-dropping amazement, to Miss Pippen who smiled discreetly at Holmes and took one also.

"I say, Miss..." Rowland began.

"You'd best say as little as possible, Commander. Miss Pippen has but little use for many of the social conventions that men of our generation take for granted. And from what little Watson has been able to tell me, *Mlle.* Otero by comparison..."

Miss Pippen blew out a stream of smoke. Maintaining her same demure smile, her eyes changed from amusement to menace. "Perhaps you and Dr. Watson would like to share your observations not only with my-self, but with *Mlle.* Otero as well. Commander," she turned toward Rowland, "would it be possible for you to send the steward to ask *Mlle.* Otero to join us? I'm quite sure she would be as fascinated as I to hear what you *gentlemen,"* she forced the word out between clenched teeth, "have to say on the subject of women's behaviour."

"Oh no, Commander. As her physician, I quite forbid it. *Mlle.* Otero has suffered a good deal of trauma, both physical and emotional, and more than anything she needs as much rest as possible."

"Are you sure, Dr. Watson? I should think that she would find the conversation most stimulating." Miss Pippen smiled maliciously and flicked an ash from her cigarette. "Very well, gentlemen, if I am to be denied the singular opportunity to eavesdrop on your card-room chatter, perhaps Commander Rowland will tell us about his ship. I must confess I've not seen one like it. I thought I was familiar with every class of ships of the line, but I do not recall a warship riding so low in the water. And that strange cowl over the forecastle; even if it is non-functional, it certainly is menacing looking."

"I assure you, Miss Pippen, it is indeed functional as well as menacing looking." Commander Rowland shifted uneasily in his chair. He stubbed out his cigarette. "I suppose there's no harm. I presume that you've all signed the Official Secrets Pledge." He paused as all three nodded affirmatively. "In any case, I understand *Jane's* already has the pertinent data. The ship is a new version of the destroyer class. Designed for anti-submarine warfare."

The Commander's voice took on a tone of pride as he grew more at ease. "She's been christened the *'Viper'.* I suppose the name was suggested by the cowling which you mentioned. It does, if one is given to flights of imagination, suggest some deadly jungle snake. Actually, the cowling's function is to prevent our taking on water when at full power in heavy seas. As you accurately observed, she does ride uncommonly low in the water. Which is, after all, understandable considering that she's estimated at 344 tons."

"Must be all engines." Holmes interjected. "I noticed four stacks, but very little in the way of armament. Is she heavily armoured below the water-line?"

"You sound like one of those reporter-chaps from *Jane's*, Mr. Holmes. Actually, she's not all that heavily armed or armoured. She's built for speed and maneuverability. We've got one twelve-pounder aft, and one in front of the bridge, plus a few heavy machine-guns. The builder and our own engineers say that she can do at least thirty-four knots in a moderate sea. Most of the weight is in the engines and fuel bunkers. She burns better than six tons an hour at flank speed. Takes thirty-two stokers just to keep her boilers lighted. The engines are of a radical new design. They're four-shaft turbines built by Parsons."

"Turbines?" Miss Pippen raised an eyebrow.

"Indeed," Rowland continued, eager to display his own knowledge, while at the same time intrigued by the thought that a woman, particularly a young attractive one, would be interested in so arcane a subject as the difference between piston and turbine marine engines. "Rather than a piston, which must 'recover' from each compression stroke, the engine has blades or vanes arranged 'round a cylindrical shaft. I believe the engineers refer to them as 'buckets' owing to their curved shape. The steam is passed from the boiler and expelled under pressure through a nozzle against the blades causing the shaft to rotate continuously.

Actually, the *Viper's* engines combine the two types of turbine, the 'impulse'-type that I've just described and the 'reaction'-type which makes use of Newton's Third Law of Motion. In this type the nozzles are at the end of two opposing arms that rotate 'round a shaft. The speed of the rotation is a function of the volume of steam, and of course the load. The reaction turbine functions well at lower speeds, and the impulse turbine functions best at high speeds. So they work well together but require a rather complex gearing system so as not to create a cavitation problem with the propellers. But you'd be amazed at the amount of torque that can be generated by the continuous pressure. Each of the two engines is rated at over 4,000 shaft horsepower. And the rotations per minute... one of the biggest problems is how to keep the bearings sufficiently lubricated so that the friction does not cause the shaft to overheat. I'm afraid I'm not as well informed in that area as perhaps I should be. But when the engineers and metallurgists start talking about metal-fatigue and coefficients of friction and such, my eyes tend to glaze over a bit."

"You mentioned that you're testing some new 'gadget'. You mean there's something beside the engines? Does it also have wings so that it can take off and fly when necessary?"

"Not quite that miraculous, Dr. Watson. I..." Rowland turned as the steward handed him a folded paper. He read it briefly and refolded it. "It seems that you shall have the opportunity to observe the new 'gadget' first hand, Dr. Watson. And you and Miss Pippen as well, Mr. Holmes. If you all will come with me. It seems that Mr. Mycroft Holmes would like to have a few words with you."

Even the normally taciturn Holmes could not conceal his amazement at the Commander's statement. "That would indeed be a miracle, Commander. My brother aboard a navy vessel? Take care, I warn you. I would stake my life that whomever he is, he is not Mycroft Holmes. I assure you with all earnestness that Mycroft Holmes has not set foot on an ocean-going vessel in thirty, probably closer to forty years."

Rowland chuckled. "I will gladly accept your word on the matter of Mr. Mycroft Holmes's antipathy toward travel by sea. And to my almost certain knowledge, I can assure you that he's not on board."

"Then are we to exchange greetings through some enormous loud-hailer, or is this wonderous new 'gadget' some sort of ship-to-shore telephone?"

Holmes put a restraining hand on Watson's arm. "That's close, Watson. Remember Mycroft's meeting at Admiralty House the day before we left for Paris?"

Watson pursed his lips, engaging his near-photographic memory for conversations. "Oh yes. The Italian chap with the wireless telegraph. I honestly thought your brother was having a bit of fun with us. You mean there really is such a device?"

"Not only is there such a device, Dr. Watson, the blood...er...bloomin' thing actually works as represented." Rowland blushed deeply at his careless use of course language which Miss Pippen graciously feigned not to have heard.

The wardroom was on the main deck level. They followed the Commander along a short interior companionway, at the end of which there was a steep stairway, almost a ladder, leading to the bridge which was the highest part of the superstructure except for a tiny crow's nest. They emerged from the stairwell on to a narrow platform which protruded from the front and sides of the bridge. The top of the stairway emerged on to the port side of the bridge.

A face appeared for an instant at the porthole set in the door to the bridge. The door was opened immediately and they were greeted by a smart "Captain on the bridge!" The small room was barely able to hold the four of them in addition to its regular compliment consisting of the watch-officer, the quartermaster-helmsman, a navigation officer and two ordinary seamen. Along with the usual instruments and equipment, a small portable table had been placed next to the starboard door. This table held the navigation charts. The young lieutenant navigator was bending over the charts with his compass and straight edge.

When Commander Rowland entered he and the others came smartly to attention. Rowland responded with a perfunctory "As you were" and walked over to the small table. "Sorry we had to appropriate your normal work station. Are you able to do your work on that small surface?"

"Aye, Sir. Although I'm glad we've a bit more sea room. It could be a bit tricky trying to read those large-scale coastal charts without being able to spread them out. But we'll manage al-right.

"Very good, carry on then." Rowland turned to the watch-officer. "How's your speed, Mr. Hemphill?"

"Indicated eighteen knots, Sir. And I'd reckon that's pretty close to true."

"Any problems reported from the engine room?"

"No Sir. I checked with Mac...I uh, I mean Mister MacGregor, Sir, less than half an hour ago. The bearings are running hot as usual, but not so as to be cause for alarm."

"That being the case, Mr. Hemphill, let's run 'er up to 24 knots. Our passengers are no doubt weary of travel and in any case I assume they have pressing business ashore. So let's get them home as soon as possible. Besides, I'm sure that Admiralty House would be glad to know what *Viper* can do in a...what would you say, Hemphill, a force two storm?"

"Aye, aye Sir. At least a force two, perhaps a three, if I may say so Sir."

"And tell Mr. MacGregor he's to use his judgement in regard to the shaft bearings. If he thinks they're running too hot, he may ease off at his discretion." As Hemphill reached for the engine room communication tube, Rowland turned toward the rear of the bridge. "Mr. Holmes, if you would be so good as to step away from that door in the back wall there, we can get to the navigator's quarters. That's where they rigged up the contraption. Had to be at the highest point on the ship. It's a mass of knobs and wires. Some even running out the roof. Well, you'll soon see for yourself."

Holmes stepped aside, and Rowland opened the door leading to the chart room which was appended to the rear of the bridge. The cabin was smaller even than the bridge, so all of them could not be accommodated inside. Holmes followed Rowland inside, while Watson and Miss Pippen remained on the bridge peering through the open door. Most of the chart room was taken up with a map table built into one wall and surmounted by cabinets. Instead of the work table being covered by maps and charts, there was a wooden box from which protruded various sets of wires. One set ran up through the roof, and another set led to a telegraph key.

When Rowland and Holmes entered, the young seaman who was occupying the room stood to attention. He had been seated at the map table, writing out a message as the telegraph key clicked out the familiar pattern of short and long key strokes—dots and dashes—that comprise the international Morse code. Instantly Rowland gestured for him to resume his seat and to carry on. When the incoming message was completed, the telegrapher tore it from the message pad and handed it to Commander Rowland. He glanced at it only long enough to see that it was addressed to Holmes.

As Holmes read the message, Watson managed to squeeze into the cabin in order to more closely inspect the device. Sensing Watson's curiosity, Commander Rowland addressed the telegraph operator. "Seaman Sparks, explain to Dr. Watson how the device operates."

The young seaman identified as Sparks rose and came to attention. "Aye, Aye, Sir." Addressing Watson, the young man pointed to the set of wires running out through the roof of the small cabin. "Those wires there, sir. They intercept electromagnetic waves that pass through the ether. Then somehow, I'm not sure about this part, Sir, the components inside the box convert those waves to electrical impulses which activate the telegraph key just like a common wire telegraph."

"Can one see these waves? Does the weather have no effect?"

"No sir. Being electromagnetic, they can neither be seen nor heard by the human eye or ear. And weather seems to have little effect. The quality of the transmission seems not to be affected by the rain or anything else, save perhaps distance from the transmitting station. I'm made to understand that the waves can even pass through a vacuum, although no one has been able to test this with certainty because of the practical difficulty in achieving a perfect vacuum."

"You seem very knowledgeable, Seaman Sparks."

"Thank you, sir. I had hoped once to go to university and study the physical sciences. But my family was not able to afford to send me, so I took Her Majesty's shilling instead." Commander Rowland arched an eyebrow. Noticing, Sparks continued, "I've been in now a little more than two years, Sir. It's been just fine. I couldn't ask for better. And if the Navy starts equipping all ships with the wireless, perhaps I'll be able to make them my career. At least that's what I'm hoping." The telegraph began to clatter announcing a new in-coming message. Sparks turned to Commander Rowland. "New incoming, Sir. By your leave..." He gestured toward his stool.

"Yes, yes, Sparks. By all means do carry on."

Sparks re-took his seat. He noted the time by a wall-mounted clock, picked up his pad and pencil. There was a long pause, and then the key began tapping out the message in the familiar longs and shorts. After less than a minute it stopped. Sparks, wide-eyed, tore the page from his pad and handed it to the Commander. Rowland read it briefly. "It seems, Mr. Holmes, that I'm to place myself, my ship and its crew at your disposal."

"So it appears, Commander. I hope I'm not guilty of some serious breach of etiquette, but I could not help but translate the message in my head as it was coming in. In any case, it confirms the instructions contained in the message addressed to myself."

"Please have Seaman Sparks send a reply message to Admiralty House confirming receipt of their messages to us and advising that we are acting in accordance with their instructions. Once that is done, please have your man stand by for further messages, either in-coming or out-going. It would be best if we could retire back to your wardroom. I can then share with you, and of course Watson and Miss Pippen, the rest of the message addressed to me. It would also be helpful if you could have your navigation officer calculate our current course and position and join us in perhaps a quarter-hour's time with his charts for the Channel Islands and adjacent French coast waters."

After the necessary orders were given, they returned to the wardroom. Holmes adjusted his reading glasses and glanced once more at the telegraph message. "We are to seek out and capture a Greek-flagged merchant vessel named the *'Aegean Star'*. Naval Intelligence is reliably informed that it is making its way on a course to intercept and sink the French light cruiser *Sfax* which should be approaching the vicinity of the Channel Islands in a very short while."

"A...a merchant vessel is going to sink a French cruiser?" Rowland looked at Holmes. "Perhaps Seaman Sparks is wrong and the weather does in fact interfere with the transmission of the...what...oh yes, the electromagnetic waves. And why this particular warship?"

"As to your first question, Commander, I'm inclined to side with Seaman Sparks. If the message were garbled in the transmission, it is likely, given that it is sent in groups of impulses each equating to a single letter, the words or letter groups would be non-sensical, not entire sentences. And regarding the *Sfax,* the press of your official duties has no doubt kept you from reading the news of the day with much attention to trivial details. The *Sfax* carries Captain Dreyfus back from his Devil's Island exile to France for his new trial which is to be held at Renne."

"You are quite right, Mr. Holmes. I think we, that is my officers and myself, were aware that Dreyfus was to be given a new trial. Indeed word even filtered up from the fo'c's'le that there was a pool started among the ratings on whether he'd be acquitted or convicted the second time around. But gambling, even in port, is inimical to maintaining good discipline aboard a fighting ship, so much as I like to allow the men a little lee-way, I had to put a stop to it. In any case, you're correct; I don't remember reading anywhere the name of the ship that was commissioned to transport him back. Is there any way to judge the reliability of the intelligence? I mean how is a merchant vessel going to attack and defeat a fully-armed naval vessel?" He paused, "Even a French one?"

"The *Aegean Star* is a gun-runner, the flagship, as it were, of an insidious cartel of international arms-traffickers. Within the last few days, thanks in part to Miss Pippen's courageous efforts, the vessel was thwarted in an attempt to disembark a shipment off the west coast of Ireland." Holmes lit a fresh cigarette, and consulted the wireless message. "Apparently one of the shore-party was not quick enough getting back to the beach when the alarm sounded, and as a consequence was left ashore when the rest of the lot returned to the ship. According to his story—told to the local constabulary who'd captured him within a few hours—his job was to climb the cliff and act as lookout for the caravan of lorries sent to meet the ship and receive the cargo. It seems that he'd ducked behind a boulder to..." Holmes paused, looking first at Miss Pippen and then at the ceiling, "er... attend to a matter of personal necessity, and..."

"And was caught with his trousers down, Mr. Holmes?" Miss Pippen smiled demurely.

"Just so, Miss Pippen, just so. But whatever the circumstances of his capture, evidently his loyalty to his former master was less than tenacious, and in exchange for a reduced sentence, he told all he knew. While I'm given to understand that he's much more to tell, for our immediate purposes he did provide the information regarding the impending piratical attack on the *Sfax.*"

"But why, Holmes?" Watson asked. "What advantage would there be in murdering Dreyfus?"

"I am inclined to think," Holmes answered, "that he meant to do so all along. I expect that he plans to see that the French blame the Germans. With the outcome of the last Franco-Prussian war still festering in the minds of the French military, they will make the hapless captain into a martyr and a *casus belli* for the next war. And that will occur far sooner than anyone would have thought even a month ago."

"Then," Miss Pippen injected, "the torture, the murders, the kidnappings, they were all a ruse, a diversion?"

"More than that, I would say, Miss Pippen." Watson turned to Miss Pippen. "It's only conjecture, but I would say that the professor had two objects in mind: ending his partnership with the baron and providing insurance in case his act of piracy goes awry."

"You're undoubtedly right, Watson," Holmes's face grew stern. "But if he told you the truth about a rendezvous with the attack vessel, that means he plans to command the attack himself. And that can only mean that he must be absolutely confident that the attack will succeed."

Commander Rowland shook his head. "I find it difficult to believe that a freighter, even if armed with a single cannon, can take on and defeat a navy cruiser, no matter which navy it belongs to.

"Did he also provide information regarding where the attack is to occur, Mr. Holmes?"

"That much he could not say, Commander Rowland. But if the re-trial is to occur at Renne, and if we dare hope that the French military will un-characteristically think through the logistical and public-relations nightmare that debarking Dreyfus at some more distant port will entail, then the *Sfax* will surely be making for the closest suitable port..."

"Which will most likely be St. Malo," Commander Rowland completed Holmes's thought.

"I quite agree, Commander...." Holmes paused as the navigation officer entered the wardroom, a round leather map-case hanging from a strap slung over his shoulder. Commander

Rowland nodded and the lieutenant took a seat at the table and opened his case. "Lieutenant..."

"Melbourne, Sir."

"Could we please see the charts for the *Passage de la Deroute* and *Les Minquiers.*"

"Aye, Sir." The lieutenant pulled a couple of charts from his case and spread them on the table. When they were completely un-rolled and the corners held down by coffee mugs and ash trays, Holmes leaned forward and traced a line down the southwest side of the Cotentin Peninsula. "A French warship, Mr. Melbourne, returning from a destination in the Southern Caribbean to, say, St. Malo would it take the *Passage de la Deroute,* or take the southern route?"

Melbourne scratched his ear for a moment. "Hard to say, Sir. I'm sure that the French Navy has its standard navigation manuals just as we do, and perhaps our intelligence chaps have got hold of them. Now if it was a..." Melbourne hesitated as he caught a sharp warning look from Commander Rowland. "I'm sorry, Sir; it's just... I've not been briefed on them."

"Then let us approach the problem another way. Suppose you wanted very badly to intercept that French warship, and, as you admit, you don't know which route she'll take. Obviously you cannot lurk about the mouth of St. Malo harbour. So where, then, would you 'lurk' Melbourne?"

Melbourne flashed a boyish grin and pointed to a group of tiny specs on the chart about midway between Jersey to the north and the port of St Malo to the south. "Right here, Sir." He jabbed a finger emphatically on the group of dots. "Here, half-way between St. Malo and 'The Minkies'."

"The what?" Miss Pippen leaned forward to see what the lieutenant was pointing toward.

"*Les Minquiers,* Miss. That's the French name. We call them 'The Minkies.' They're a group of rocks. Some say they're the top of an extinct volcano. Others say they're all that's left of the lost continent of Atlantis. I call 'em a ship's graveyard. They barely breach the surface at low tide, and at high tide, or when there's a sea running like now, it takes a mighty brave captain to take his ship anywhere near 'em. But if I were desperate enough, that's where I'd lay up until when I estimated that the French ship was approaching. But even with that, it would still take a good bit of luck. Put a sharp-eyed lad in the crow's nest with a good glass, and he can cover about three hundred fifty square miles assuming an arc of 180 degrees. That's on a clear day and light seas. Change that equation to night-time, or add fog or rain, and...well..."

Commander Rowland leaned forward and looked intently at the chart. He ran his hand through his thick hair. Holmes, Watson and Miss Pippen sat impassively waiting for him to form in his mind the words which they were anticipating. "Do not, my friends allow yourselves to be infected with Lt. Melbourne's youthful exuberance. Her Majesty pays me a fair sum to go in harm's way, and my men and I train every day just to do so. But I must tell you that the order you're about to give, Mister Holmes, promises very little hope of success, and conversely a high risk of sending one of Her Majesty's very expensive ships, along with one hundred thirty or so of Her loyal subjects—yourselves included—to the bottom of the English Channel. If that is to be the case, may I at least be informed as to the name of the madman who commands this *Aegean Star?*"

"Fair enough, Commander. When you hear his name, perhaps the risk-reward ratio will become more balanced." Holmes paused, as if summoning the strength to once again utter the hated name. "The master of the vessel is none other than the infamous Professor James Moriarty..."

"But I thought he was... even you, Dr. Watson, wrote that he..."

"It appears, Commander, that my report of his demise was a bit of literary license, albeit an unintended one. But if we are successful, then perhaps I shall be spared the humiliation of having to confess my error to the general reading-public as well."

"Now, Commander, if you please, would you give the necessary orders to proceed with all possible alacrity to the area suggested by Lt. Melbourne?"

"In accordance with my instructions, I shall do so at once, Mr. Holmes. Mister Melbourne, have you plotted our course yet?"

"Aye, Sir. But because of the weather, it's by dead-reckoning only."

"Then by dead-reckoning it shall be." Commander Rowland turned and called for the steward. After instructing him to summon the watch-officer, he turned back to the table. "Mr. Melbourne, how long do you make our transit time?"

"I make our position just here." Melbourne pointed to a spot north by northwest of Le Harve. "Our current heading puts us on a course for Torbay, which I estimate is about eighty miles from our current position. Assuming an average speed of twenty knots, about three hours, twenty minutes. Half-way between The Minkies and St. Malo is one hundred twenty-five miles from our present position, allowing for staying outside French waters as we round Cherbourg. Assuming no change in the weather and that we maintain twenty knots, I should say seven hours thirty-six minutes, Sir, give or take."

"Mr. Holmes?" Commander Rowland shifted his gaze to Holmes.

"Time being so much of the essence, Commander, I must urge you to push your ship and crew to the limits of their capabilities."

"I am perfectly prepared to do so, Mr. Holmes. But while I know my men, this ship is an unknown quantity. As I mentioned earlier, this is her maiden voyage, a voyage whose purpose is to determine her capabilities and deficiencies, but under controlled, not virtual combat conditions. You've heard concern expressed regarding the shaft-bearings and their tendency to overheat. If we push things too far we could lose our entire propulsion system. And who knows what else can go wrong."

"I take your point, Commander, so I will leave it to your best judgement. However, you now understand the urgency of our mission. If Moriarty is successful in sinking the *Sfax* and Dreyfus along with her, the French military, as I said, will no doubt blame the Germans. The French government is weak. I would expect at the very least a military coup d' etat, and quite possibly a war with the Germans within six months after that. Would you not agree, Miss Pippen?"

"I quite agree, Mr. Holmes. And I would only add, Commander, that it would be exceedingly difficult for us to stay out of the fray."

Hemphill, anxious for having been summoned from the bridge, came in and reported. He listened gravely as Lieutenant Melbourne gave him the new heading and destination. When

Commander Rowland instructed him to increase speed to thirty-three knots, he nearly bit through his lip resisting the temptation to question the order of his superior officer. His instructions having been completed for the time-being, he came to attention, turned smartly on one heel and charged back out the door. Commander Rowland shrugged and turned to Melbourne. "Lieutenant, you return to the bridge as well. Perhaps the weather will break and you'll be able to get a fix on where the devil we are. I'm going down to the engine room, since that's where I'll likely be needed most. Gentlemen, Miss Pippen, you're welcome to join me. Indeed I think you should see firsthand that The *Viper* and her crew are doing all that is expected of us. This way, please."

Commander Rowland led them through a series of hatches and companionways, descending several ladder-like flights of stairs until they were three decks below the topside deck. It began to be uncomfortably warm and the vibration of the engines was a noticeable thrumming beneath their feet and in the handrails of the stairways. Finally they paused in front of a closed hatch. Through the small porthole, they could see a bright red-orange glow which told, even before the Commander could speak, that they'd arrived at the engine room. Commander Rowland began to turn the wheel to open the hatch. When the bolt was undone, he stepped through the opening. He turned and motioned the others to follow. "Please mind your step, and take care not to touch any of the metal surfaces with bare hand, especially as we near the boilers and engines. They're quite hot, and can cause rather a severe burn."

Following Rowland through the portal, they were each struck in turn by the heat emanating from the maws of the four great furnaces. Perspiration immediately burst forth on all their faces. Breathing the fetid, coal dust-laden air was like sipping scalding-hot soup laced with ground pepper. There was a string of incandescent light bulbs along each wall and overhead, but they may as well have been turned off, because of the intense light produced by the furnaces. The roar of the flames made shouting the only means of communication.

The new Parsons-built engines were mounted between the immense boilers. There was a manifold atop each boiler from which a conduit ran to a second manifold fitted to the side of each engine. Aft of each engine was a gear box from which protruded the drive-shafts which ran to the stern plates and thence through the hull to the propellers. Because of the great length of the shafts, between the gear boxes and stern plates there was a series of three racks each holding ball bearing rings through which the shafts passed. At each of these stations there were seamen holding large, long-spouted cans of lubricant which they poured in steady streams over the bearings with the residue dripping into collecting pans fitted beneath the racks.

Along the hull even with the furnaces were slanted openings leading down to the coal bunkers, one for each furnace. The openings were rather narrow. Presumably there were two or more sailors down inside the bunkers themselves, and a couple stationed on each of the steep, narrow stairways. Their function was to haul up filled coal scuttles and pass back down the empty ones. They would hand the filled scuttles to another seaman who was stationed on the engine room deck at the mouth of the stairway, and his job was to pour the coal from the scuttles into wheel-barrows. The filled wheel-barrows were then wheeled the short distance from the mouths of the coal bunkers by yet another man who dumped the coal at the feet of the furnace stokers who then shoveled the fuel into the insatiable mouths of the furnaces. The sailors on coal detail moved like automatons, never breaking their pace. They worked stripped to the waist, their faces and bodies streaked with coal dust and sweat. Miss Pippen remained impassive as she watched the frenetic ballet.

Standing in front of a rack of gauges were two ordinary seamen and a tall heavily-built rating with copper-red mutton-chop whiskers running up from his chin to a Clan MacGregor tam-o'-shanter perched atop his head. His uniform blouse was open at the neck and nearly everywhere else was stuck to his body by perspiration. One of the seamen was the first to spot Commander Rowland, and came smartly to attention. "Captain on deck!"

Rowland gave a perfunctory salute, "Carry on. Mister MacGregor, if you please."

The giant Scot folded a notebook in which he'd been writing. "Aye, Sir."

"Mister MacGregor, this gentleman is Mister Sherlock Holmes. This is Dr. Watson, and this is Miss Pippen." MacGregor nodded to each in turn.

As the presence of civilians, especially a woman, became known to the crew, they paused in their various duties, staring in amazement. MacGregor turned and bellowed over the din of the furnaces, "Back to work, or I'll have the lot o' ye up before a Captain's Mast. Move along now."

Commander Rowland continued, "For reasons which I'll explain later, Admiralty has placed us under Mr. Holmes's orders, Mr. MacGregor. And if Lieutenant Melbourne knows his business, we're now on course for The Minkies on an urgent mission to interdict an act of piracy against the French Navy. That's why I've asked you to give us all you have. How are the men and equipment holding up?"

"I could feel her heel pretty good to port as we turned, Sir. And when the bridge ordered up thirty-three knots, I figured something must be a-foot. So far the men are holding up just fine. But if were going to be at this for awhile, I would suggest that you have the off duty crews stand by. If we can make up three shifts, I would prefer to work the men n' more than thirty minutes at a time, half an hour on and an hour off. They're a good bunch of laddies, Sir, but if we don't give 'em a wee bit of breathing spell, they'll start falling out no matter how hard they try. As for the equipment, Sir, I kin na' say. As you can feel, the vibration is getting stronger. I've na' been topside since we got under way; has the weather let up any?"

"Not as of a few minutes ago."

"No insubordination intended, Sir, but can th' Frog—er...beggin' your pardon, m'am—the French Navy, that is to say; can th' French Navy nay take care o' its own?"

"Evidently not in the present circumstances, Mister MacGregor." Holmes replied. "Excuse me, Commander. I didn't mean to butt in."

"Quite al-right, Mr. Holmes. Under the present circumstances," Rowland paused for a brief moment, "you are more than entitled to do so."

"Thank you, Commander. However, it's your ship and I shall intrude no more than I have already done. Would you be so kind as to inquire of Mr. MacGregor our current speed?"

"Mr. MacGregor?"

"We can nay tell from down here, Sir. Without knowin' windspeed and direction, I can only estimate based on the shaft rotations-per-minute. Based on that, I'd say thirty-three perhaps thirty-four knots, Sir."

"Can you give us any more, Mr. MacGregor?"

MacGregor pulled on his chin. "Again, no insubordination intended, Sir, but come and see for yourself." He pointed toward the propeller shafts. "By your leave, Sir. Come this way."

They made their way between the engines, balancing precariously as the deck plates viabration became more intense. MacGregor paused at a joint between two large plates. "Look here, Sir." He pointed to the joint. "See how the plates are rubbing. And look at the rivets; they're bouncing around like they were set in there loose. These plates are over an inch thick, and are laid over cantilevered spars anchored to the hull. I'm no' a religious mon, but I kin nay help wonderin' whether th' good Lord intended that monkind build engines as powerful as these." When they reached the first row of ball bearing racks, he stopped. "See for yourself, Sir." He took an oil can from one of the oilers and squirted a short stream directly onto the rotating shaft. In a few seconds the oil evaporated into a puff of vile-smelling black smoke. He handed the can back to the oiler. "The lubricating oil's breaking down already. If these bearings go, we're dead in th' water, and th' Frogs... er I mean th' French'll have to fend for themselves. If that's all that happens, we'll be lucky, I'd say. The way these deck plates are going, if I gie ye any more, ye best pray that these engines can float, because they'll nay longer have any ship left around them."

Commander Rowland watched the rotating shafts for a while, and finally turned to the Scotsman, "Carry on as you are, Mister MacGregor. I will return to the bridge and issue the orders to establish three shifts. You are to notify the bridge if you determine that you cannot maintain present speed. I will send a survey party to maintain a constant watch for any serious vibration damage.

"Mr. Holmes, would you please join me on the bridge? Miss Pippen, Dr. Watson, there is nothing that requires your presence on the bridge. However, our medical officer was on leave when we sailed and we did not have time to obtain a replacement. There is the distinct possibility that we will take some casualties and we will certainly need your expertise in that event. I will have someone show you to the infirmary. They will also see that you are outfitted with life vests and shown to your lifeboat station."

"Anything to help, Commander." Watson, sensing Miss Pippen's indignation, turned to her, "I'm quite used to working alone, Miss Pippen. So if you would prefer to return to the bridge, I'm sure I can manage..."

Realising that she'd been outflanked, she looped her arm through Watson's. "Oh no, Dr. Watson, I shall be delighted to serve as your nurse...or is the correct term 'dresser'? After all isn't that the most appropriate role for a woman?"

CHAPTER FORTY-EIGHT

*"Forget about The Minkies and put us on
a course for St. Malo."*

Once Rowland and Holmes had returned to the bridge, the commander quickly issued his orders. The rain had mostly abated, but they were still running in heavy seas. As they crashed through each wave the ship shuddered ominously. "Is the cowl doing its job, Mr. Hemphill?"

"Aye, Sir. We're still taking a bit of water on the largest waves, but the fo'c's'l scuppers seem to be taking care of it."

"Mr. Melbourne, have you a fix on our position?"

"I make it east by nor'east of Guernsey, Sir. Had a glimpse of sun a few minutes ago. If I'm right, we should be abreast of Jersey in about two hours, assuming that we maintain present speed. Oh! Beg pardon, Mr. Holmes." Melbourne apologised as the ship rolled with a particularly big wave causing him to lose his balance and fall against Holmes.

In addition to the now teeth-chattering engine vibration, the ship was now rolling heavily as the helmsman fought to keep the ship on course. Just as the ship rolled deeply to port, the port door to the bridge opened. The seaman who was trying to enter was thrown back against the outer rail. As the keel righted, he managed to stumble into the cabin, slamming the door behind him. Coming to a semblance of attention he reported. "Survey party report, Sir. Vibration's pretty bad, Sir, but so far the hull plates are holding below the water-line. Some of the deck-plates are in bad shape and getting worse, and some doors and hatches are sprung. As long as the hull plates hold, the main worry is the engine room deck and the gun mounts. Mister MacGregor had to pull one boiler to replace a manifold gasket, but says he'll have it back on line in thirty minutes or less."

"Very good." Rowland nodded. "Carry on. Report back again as soon as Mr. MacGregor has his boiler back in operation."

Holmes stood with his legs braced against the ship's roll stroking his chin thoughtfully. "Commander, if you were going to engage an enemy in the present circumstances, how would you do it?"

"It would depend on the enemy, Mr. Holmes. As I've already pointed out, we're not heavily armed in the way of cannon. I could not expect to come in first in a gunnery duel with even a light cruiser. In seas like these, however, the outcome would depend on who has the best gunnery officer. But my main armament is not cannon, it's torpedoes. I would attack head-on at top speed, trusting that I could get close enough to launch, before the enemy got my range and blew me out of the water."

Holmes continued stroking his chin. "Torpedoes. Interesting. How do you assess our chances of finding what we're looking for?"

"Virtually nil, Mr. Holmes, virtually nil. I'm sorry, but I assume you want my candid opinion."

"You assume rightly, Commander, and I appreciate your honesty. Is it also your opinion that the *Aegean Star* is having the same problems?"

"I cannot imagine otherwise, Mr. Holmes."

"That being the case, if you were in command of that vessel, what would you do?"

"I would head for the harbour at St.Malo. I'd anchor in the outer part of the harbour keeping my boilers stoked. In this weather, it's unlikely that the harbour master will come calling. But if he should, I would claim a mechanical problem, and invoke the right of safe-harbour. Under the law of the sea, I would have the right to lay up to make repairs, so long as I did not transact any business other than as necessary to effect repairs."

"Any port in a storm?"

"Just so, Mr. Holmes. In any case, as soon as the weather let up, I'd clear the harbour and wait in the roads. I'd want to make my attack as far out to sea as possible, so as to minimize the chance of survivors making it to safety. But you're forgetting one crucial difference between the *Viper* and the *Aegean Star;* I've got torpedoes. Two good hits amidships below the water line, and I've got almost a certain kill. What does the *Aegean Star* have? One cannon?"

"That we know of, Commander. How do you launch the torpedoes?"

436

"Launch racks amidships. We cannot chance arming them until just before they're launched." Rowland paused as the ship slammed down in a trough between two huge waves. "Especially in heavy seas like these."

"What do submarines do?"

"The newer ones have tubes fitted into the bow, and the torpedoes are forced out by compressed air. The older ones used limpet mines or even a long spike or lance fitted onto the bow."

"Do those not require a stationary target?"

"Precisely, Mr. Holmes. That's why the older submarines were so impractical. They could only attack a surface vessel riding at anchor, or, I suppose, one moving very slowly. I suspect that our own warfare planners have done some experimenting along these lines, but we blue-water sailors haven't yet been made privy to their thinking."

Holmes clutched at the cabin wall as the ship crashed with teeth-jarring force through another set of waves. "Could we perhaps adjourn to the wireless room? I'd like to send a message to Admiralty, if you please."

In a few minutes, the message was sent. When they'd returned to the bridge, Rowland asked, "Do you think this Professor Moriarty has actually gotten hold of a submarine, Mr. Holmes?"

"I would certainly like to rule out the possibility, Commander. However he did tell Dr. Watson that he had a third vessel which he did not further describe. And as you may recall, the *Aegean Star's* modifications did include enlarging the forward hold and adding a heavy-capacity windlass."

"Then you think he nipped a sub off some navy or other and keeps it in his fo'c's'le hold? Surely, Mr. Holmes..."

"Bearing in mind the intellectual risks of quoting one's own dicta, Commander, when you eliminate all other possibilities, the one that remains is likely to be the truth."

The port door opened and the survey party messenger fought his way in. "Chief's compliments, Sir, ship's condition report."

"Proceed," Rowland replied brusquely.

"Aye, aye, Sir. Hull plates are still holding, but the engine room deck—and these are Mister MacGregor's very own words,

Sir—'is goin' to end up in the bilges. The plates are screechin' an' wailin' like an Englishman tryin' to play bagpipes'. He lost two men to heat exhaustion. They'll be al-right though with a bit of rest. Another man, one of the oilers, lost his footing when the deck heaved. He grabbed on to one of the shafts to catch his balance and ended up getting a nasty burn on his hand, arm and part of his chest. 'E was took to infirm'ry, Sir, and the civilian doctor and his nurse are takin' care of him. We're starting to hold water under the fo'c'sle cowling, but we jury-rigged a spare bilge pump, and that's takin' care of the problem, at least for now."

"Does Mister MacGregor think we need to reduce speed?"

"No, Sir. He assumed you'd be askin' that, Sir. And he said to tell you—and again these are his own words, Sir—'Tell th' Cap'n we'll hold 'er t'g'th'r if we 'av to do it with rope and caulking tar.' Those were 'is words, Sir."

"What do you make our speed, Mister Hemphill?"

"It's amazing, Sir. Forty, even forty-one knots!"

Commander Rowland looked at the wall clock, took out a fountain-pen and made a notation in a small notebook which he kept in the pocket of his blouse. "Mister Hemphill, please tell Mister MacGregor, since we've little rope and no caulking tar aboard, he'd best reduce speed by five knots." He turned to the messenger, "That will be all. Tell your chief 'well done' and to carry on."

Holmes and Commander Rowland returned to the wireless room to await a reply to Holmes's message. When it arrived, Holmes translated the message as Sparks was writing down the letters. "It seems, Commander, that there may be a submarine unaccounted for. Within the past year, the Italians de-commissioned four of their older ones, and this has been confirmed by our own attaché. The French reported one lost at sea, and from all the evidence, the report is genuine. We know next to nothing about the Kriegsmarine nor about the Americans. However, neither are known to have any miniature sub-surface vessels in active service. The Union forces employed a crude version during the American Civil War, but have not utilised them since."

"So your theory evidently cannot be substantiated, Mr. Holmes?"

"According to *Jane's* it appears that it can, Commander. It seems that an American firm with yards on the Mystic River in Connecticut built two vessels—both miniature submarines—in the early 'Eighties. They were ordered by none other than the Sinn Fein. The American government, no doubt under pressure from our own, refused to allow them to be delivered. The designer named them both *'Finnian Borer'*, evidently because their principal weapon consists of a long pointed steel pike which was intended to ram enemy—presumably English—warships. One of the vessels is apparently still on the *Jane's* lists, but the other was reported cut up for scrap in December of last year. However, no independent agency has verified that to be the case, and the *Aegean Star* was known to be in Boston harbour during the preceding month."

"Then you believe that this Professor Moriarty somehow got his hands on one of these *Finnian Borers*, did you say?"

"Obviously it is only speculation at this point, Commander, but there does seem to be a good bit of circumstantial evidence pointing in that direction. One might suppose that Moriarty persuaded the Sinn Fein to pay for the modifications to the *Aegean Star*, telling them that the alterations were necessary so that she could accommodate the submarine in her hold in order to avoid detection whilst clearing American waters, or in the event a British ship should spot her on this side. He may have even talked them into paying for the submarine a second time, or more likely talked them into having their American sympathisers come up with the money."

"Knowing Moriarty, one can envision the dilemma he created for himself: shake more money out of the Fennians as the price for the vessel, or keep it for himself and use it to precipitate a pan-European war that will surely involve Britain. Possibly he promised to deliver it after a brief period of sea trials, not unlike what you're doing with the *Viper*." Holmes pounded his clenched fist into the palm of his open hand. "Commander, that's it. Forget about 'The Minkies' and put us on course for St. Malo."

"Very good, Mister Holmes; St. Malo it is. Do you think we should signal Admiralty so that they can alert the French?"

"Absolutely not, Commander. I'll not risk the French setting off an alarums and excursions which will serve only to warn Moriarty off."

439

"As you wish, Mister Holmes, but I..."

"Don't worry, Commander. I shall be pleased to put my instructions in writing. By the way, I trust that you did manage to load some torpedoes aboard?"

"Only two, Mister Holmes. And we've got only the new timer fuses. They're not as reliable as the old contact fuses, but they are a good deal safer."

"Forgive my ignorance, Commander, but I should think that one torpedo would do quite well, considering the size of your target."

"It's the size that's the problem. I would like our odds much better if we could catch the *Aegean Star* with the submarine hanging from the boom half-way out of the hold. Once a torpedo is launched, we cannot control its course. So the larger and more stationary the target, the better my chances of hitting it."

CHAPTER FORTY-NINE

*"I'm inclined to think, if you're
asking my opinion, that Admiralty House
will not take well our putting one of Her
Majesty's ships on the bottom."*

Commander Rowland ordered the necessary course change. Mr. MacGregor reported his fourth boiler back on line. There was little abatement in the vibration, even though their speed had backed off in accordance with the Commander's instructions. Watson had given the injured seaman a hypodermic of morphine, and Miss Pippen, wearing a gauze mask, was bathing his burns with cold compresses. They'd swabbed the infirmary with disinfectant, and rigged a gauze curtain around his bunk to further minimize the risk of the open wounds becoming infected. Watson expressed his prognosis that if the man managed to avoid contracting a fatal infection, he'd likely make a satisfactory recovery, although he would probably not regain full use of his left hand.

Less than an hour had passed when the survey party messenger made his next report. "We've got leaks between four of the hull plates just abaft of the port bow, Sir. One's below the water-line. We're taking a moderate amount of water, but the pumps were handling it when I was sent top-side to make my report. The plates are where the forward spars supporting the engine room deck plates are anchored to the hull, Sir. Chief thinks that the combination of the vibration from the engines and the pounding we're takin' from th' heavy seas are more than the structure can take. Sir," the seaman paused, "Chief says if th' port plates go, we'll lose the bow and with it th' ship!"

Rowland turned to Holmes, "Well, Mr. Holmes, as de facto commanding officer, it's your decision. Do we risk being late for the party, or do we risk not getting there at all?"

Holmes pulled on his chin for a long moment. "Whatever the goodly sum Her Majesty pays you to go in harm's way, Commander, I'm bound to say it isn't enough. Last night, I risked the lives of several people, including myself, in scuttling a barge in

441

the Seine. This morning I risked those same lives again in pushing the Frenchman's fishing boat far beyond prudence.

"I'm inclined to think, if you're asking my opinion, that Admiralty House will not take well our putting one of Her Majesty's ships on the bottom."

"Thank you for your candor, Commander Rowland. For the time being let's cut back one-third, and see how things go for a bit. Would you ask Lt. Melbourne to calculate our current position and estimate our time of arrival at St. Malo if we're able to maintain twenty knots?"

"As you wish, Mr. Holmes." Commander Rowland gave the necessary orders, and in a few minutes they could feel some lessening of the vibration as well as the shock caused by the vessel ploughing through the waves.

When Lt. Melbourne gave them their present position and estimated time of arrival, Holmes turned to the commander, "I wonder if it would help if you had Mr. MacGregor shut down one of the two engines. What kind of speed can you maintain on only one engine?"

"We've not tested that, Mr. Holmes. However, Parson's specifications predict twenty knots. Shall I give the order?"

"If I recall, Commander, we were making one hundred fifteen percent of the predicted maximum speed utilising both engines. And that was in heavy seas. If Mr. MacGregor can coax twenty-three or twenty-four knots out of one engine and keep us afloat, he may yet get us there before Moriarty has a chance to strike. So give the order, if you please."

"Gladly, Mr. Holmes. Mister Hemphill, tell Mister MacGregor to idle the port engine and give us all he can out of the starboard. If it starts running too hot, then he is to switch over to the port for as short a time as will allow the starboard to cool down. I'm going below to assess the damage in the bow. You and Mister Melbourne are to take your orders directly from Mr. Holmes as though they were coming from me.

"Mr. Holmes, should we come in sight of the *Aegean Star,* I request that you summon me back to the bridge and do not yourself give the order to engage. Lt. Hemphill, should the vessel be sighted, you are to at once give the order to man battle stations. In the meantime, Mr. Holmes, as we seem to have thrown all protocol and regulations overboard, I urge you to consult Lt. Hemphill and Lt. Melbourne and consider their advice before you give any other orders."

"You have my assurance on both counts, Commander."

"Very well, then. Gentlemen, carry on. Good hunting, Mr. Holmes."

Melbourne looked up from his charts. "Mr. Holmes, if Mr. MacGregor can maintain twenty-four knots, we should be in the roads leading in to St. Malo in approximately one hour, twenty minutes. May I suggest that we go ahead and send a man aloft now?"

"Yes, Lieutenant, by all means."

The order was given for a crow's nest detail. For the next hour, Holmes paced back and forth, unable to contain his excitement. Every second or third round he would pause and ask Hemphill their speed, or ask Melbourne for a position update. Sensing that he was becoming a nuisance, he picked up a pair of binoculars and went out on the catwalk in front of the bridge to scan the horizon for himself. The passing storm had cooled the ambient air. With the spray blowing back from the bow, he soon caught a chill and retreated back inside. Just as he turned to go he noticed two men rolling the portable bilge pump back inside the superstructure.

"Mr. Hemphill, shouldn't Commander Rowland have returned by now?"

"No way to tell, Sir. We have voice communication only with the engine room and the gun turrets. If you wish I can send a man down to ask Commander Rowland for a report."

"Please do, Mr. Hemphill. I..."

"Mr. Hemphill, Sir." The seaman stationed outside the bridge to relay signals from the crow's nest burst into the cabin. "Crow's nest reports a ship, Sir."

"Where away?"

"On the horizon, Sir. Ten degrees off the starboard bow. Too far away to tell anything about her, except that he thinks he can make out two funnels, just like we're looking for, Sir."

"Keep a sharp eye and report as soon as you have any more information."

"Aye, aye, Sir."

"Flemming," Hemphill turned to one of the seamen stationed on the bridge, "report to Commander Rowland and let him know that we've spotted a ship and it may be the *Aegean Star*. Also present Mr. Holmes's compliments and state that Mr. Holmes would appreciate a report on the seaworthiness of the ship."

"Mister Hemphill, Sir." The helmsman called over his shoulder. "Beg pardon, Sir, but I'm getting a strong pull to starboard. I'm having a hard time keeping the rudder amidships."

"Does it feel like it's fouled?"

"No, Sir. If we'd run across a stray fishing net or something, it most likely would have caught one of the props."

"Mister MacGregor!" Hemphill picked up the voice communication tube.

"Reduce speed to dead slow immediately. We're shipping water in the forward holds.

"It's not good, Mr. Holmes. From all indications they've not been able to staunch the leaking and it's getting worse. I was concerned when I saw them take in the portable bilge pump, but I did not want to say anything prematurely. I think we'd best sound general quarters."

The ship became a swarm of activity as soon as general quarters were sounded. Sparks stuck his head out on the wireless compartment doorway. "Mr. Hemphill, Sir. Do I go to my general quarters station, or stay with the wireless?"

"What is your station?"

"Aft gun mount, Sir. I'm a loader."

"You shan't be needed there. Stand by the wireless. I'll inform your chief when we stand down."

"Aye, aye, Sir." Sparks retreated back into the wireless compartment, relief evident on his face.

"Speaking of the wireless, Mr. Holmes, do you think it advisable to send a message to Admiralty House informing them of our evident predicament?"

"If we do so, they'll almost certainly order us to break off the chase. Let us wait until we have further word from Commander Rowland in regard to our seaworthiness."

"Report from the crow's nest, Sir. She definitely a freighter, and a large one at that. Carries two stacks for sure. Can't make out what flag she flies. She's blended in with the shoreline,

444

so's it's hard to see any more detail. Doesn't seem to be in any hurry to make port. It's almost as though she's waitin' for someone to either enter or clear the harbour."

Holmes rubbed his hands together in anticipation. "That's it, Hemphill. It's got to be. Please sound battle stations at once. Where's Seaman Flemming? We need Commander Rowland back on the bridge."

Melbourne stood up from his make-shift chart table. "I say, Hemp. If you can maintain present course and speed, I can be spared for a few minutes. I'll nip below and have a look-see. I'll be back in plenty of time to break out the harbour charts if we're going in that far."

"Thank you, Lt. Melbourne. Please proceed with all celerity. And when you've done with that, also direct—is it the gunnery officer?—to arm his torpedoes." As the lieutenant dashed out the door on his self-appointed mission, Holmes turned to Hemphill. "Lieutenant, please have Mr. MacGregor add a few turns..."

"But Mr. Holmes, it's too dangerous. Who knows how much more pressure the bow plates can stand before they give way?"

"Helmsman, how's she feel?" Holmes put his hand on the helmsman's shoulder.

"I can hold 'er steady as she goes, Sir, but I'll not be likin' 'er chances if we push too 'ard."

"We must take the chance, Lt. Hemphill. Please give the order at once."

"Mr. 'olmes! Lt. 'emphill, Sir!" Flemming burst back through the door. "'ere's a message from Commander Rowland. 'e's gone and closed the water-tight door, so I couldn't see or talk to 'im direct-like, Sir. 'e sent the message out in Morse code by tappin' a spanner against the steel door, an' I wrote it down in me message pad."

"I'll take it, Seaman Flemming." Holmes took the pad from the seaman's tentatively out-stretched hand. "Well done, sailor. Now stand by. We may need you to take back a message to the Commander."

Holmes donned his reading glasses and rapidly scanned the message. "It seems, Lieutenant, that they've rigged some sort of brace between the starboard and port hull plates using some old scaffolding that was left on board by the construction crews."

"Oh, yes, Mr. Holmes. I remember." Hemphill smiled. "Commander Rowland gave the contractor's man a right proper dressing down for not having removed it two weeks ago. I'd been told that they were going to get it done by today, but then of course we sailed before they could."

"Shall I continue, Lieutenant?" Holmes arched an eyebrow. "Apparently they've managed to substantially reduce, if not wholly eliminate the leaking. However, they'd taken a good bit of water—over two feet it says—but now that the plates have been stabilised the pumps are managing to stay ahead of the leaking so that the water level has gone down a bit.

"As for Commander Rowland, it seems that he's sealed himself in with the damage-repair party. He intends to keep the hold partially flooded, since the water inside serves to equalize the pressure on the hull exerted by the water on the outside."

"A clever but rather dangerous gambit, Mr. Holmes. It will work as long as we do nothing to upset the equilibrium."

"We shall have to chance it, Lieutenant. Please give the order at once. Please send Seaman Flemming below and have him inform Commander Rowland that we have what we believe is the *Aegean Star* in sight and have ordered battle stations. Also inform him that we've increased speed just a bit. If he is of the opinion that the hull cannot withstand the additional pressure, then we'll reduce speed to dead slow once again. Is your Morse code up to that, Seaman Flemming?"

"Aye, Sir."

"Good. Then be on your way."

"Lt. Hemphill, what is the maximum effective range for your torpedoes?"

"Effective, Sir? No more than a thousand yards."

"And your cannon?"

"By naval standards it's no more than a pop-gun, Mr. Holmes. Fifteen hundred, at most two thousand yards."

"Can we have a report from the crow's nest?"

As Hemphill opened the door to summon the look-out messenger Melbourne slipped in. "Torpedoes are armed and at the ready, Mr. Holmes. Look-out says the *Aegean* Star—assumin'

446

that's who she is—is headed this way. Look's like they've been sailing a triangle, holding in the same general area. It appears I was wrong, Mr. Holmes. From all indications, they're doing just what Commander Rowland thought they'd do."

"Do you think they've spotted us as well?"

"Hard to say, Mr. Holmes. Riding as low in the water as we are, it would take a good set of eyes. And even if they've seen us, like as not they think we're an over-size trawler. But I wouldn't rely on they're mistaking us for too long. There aren't any trawlers that mount cannon on the foredeck, carry four funnels and fly the Union Jack from the fore mast."

"Can you tell the distance between us and them? How long before we're in torpedo range, Mr. Melbourne?"

"I'd say four thousand yards, Mr. Holmes. But as to torpedo range..."

Hemphill cut Melbourne off, "As to torpedo range, Mr. Holmes, that's much more problematic. If both vessels continue their present course and speed, I would expect closure in less than fifteen minutes. Agree, Melbourne?" Melbourne nodded and Hemphill continued. "However, Mr. Holmes, unless they fire on us first, under no circumstances will I give an order to torpedo an unidentified civilian vessel. Either Commander Rowland will have to give that order or you'll have to launch the bloody torpedoes yourself!"

"Hemphill's quite right, Mr. Holmes." Melbourne shifted his position so that he was standing shoulder to shoulder with his fellow officer in a not-so-subtle emphasis of his agreement. "If the First Sea Lord himself gave the order, I can't see myself carrying it out."

"Stand at ease, gentlemen. I will not ask you to execute an illegal order. Let us continue our present course and speed until we have confirmation, one way or the other."

The crow's nest messenger came in, "Bryson, Sir...er...'e's in th' nest, Sir. Seaman Bryson says to tell you that th' other ship must be some kind of a whaler. They've got a good size 'un that they're 'aulin' aboard into the fo'c's'le 'old."

Holmes pounded his fist into the palm of his other hand. "There, gentlemen. What do you make of that? When's the last time you saw a large whale in these waters? Sailor, tell Seaman Bryson to look sharp. Is it a whale, or is it a submarine?"

"A submarine, Sir?"

"Yes, a submarine," Melbourne answered. "Now move! Be quick about it!

"Certainly they've seen us, Mr. Holmes. And it looks like they've mistaken us for the *Sfax*."

"That I doubt, Lt Melbourne. We could hardly be taken for a cruiser-class vessel at this distance. I suspect that Moriarty's figured out that we've guessed his plans. I would say that he plans to engage us, and once we're disposed of, he'll ambush the *Sfax* at his leisure."

"Just like Reichenbach Falls, only more water."

"What... oh. Watson, I didn't notice you come in."

"Miss Pippen's doing all that can be done for the chap with the burns. We've got four cases of heat exhaustion, but the only thing for them is rest and some time to cool down. In fact I sent them out on deck where it's cooler. They'll be al-right. Tough bunch o' lads, gentlemen. I gave Miss Pippen my solemn oath that I'd only stay a few minutes, just long enough to get briefed on what's going on. Promised her I'd come right back with a full report."

"To be as concise as possible," Holmes began, "we're but a few miles off the French coast. We're virtually dead in the water and slowly sinking by the bow. Moriarty's about to attack us with a submarine against which we have no defence, save a couple of torpedoes which no-one seems willing to launch, and which probably won't detonate were someone to actually heave them overboard, and in the unlikely event that they should strike their intended target.

"Does that about sum things up, gentlemen?" Holmes turned to the two officers.

"I say, Mr. Holmes..." Hemphill began a rejoinder just as the crow's nest messenger once again burst into the crowded cabin.

"Sir," the seaman addressed Holmes, "you're right, Sir. It is a bloomin' submarine; tiny one at that. Hold n' more th'n two, three men. Got a long snout good for rammin' I'd say, Sir. But it's also got what look like torpedoes strapped to either side of the hull."

448

"Range, Lt. Melbourne?"

"Three thousand yards, Mr. Holmes, possibly a little less."

"Full speed ahead, Lt. Hemphill? Or would you prefer to remain a sitting duck?"

Hemphill was already reaching for the annunciator. "Full ahead it is Mr. Holmes. By your leave. I'll now take charge of the attack."

"Please do Lieutenant. By your leave, however, Dr. Watson and I shall remain on the bridge."

"You may do so, gentlemen. However, I must insist that you stand back and that you put on your life-vests." Hemphill looked back over his shoulder, "Mr. Holmes, would you ask Seaman Sparks to report to me immediately."

Holmes did as he was asked and in a moment Sparks appeared. "Sparks, send the following message to Admiralty House: 'Have located vessel believed to be *Aegean Star* off French coast near port of St. Malo. Hostile vessel has launched small submarine apparently armed with torpedoes. We have sustained hull damage in the bow due to excessive engine vibration and heavy seas, but are still sea-worthy. We are counter-attacking hostile vessel, closing at two thousand yards.' Have you got that Sparks?"

"Aye, aye, Sir."

"As soon as it's sent, if Seaman Flemming isn't back, you are to go below and relay the same message to Commander Rowland."

"Wait, Lieutenant." Holmes stepped forward. "I can send the message to Admiralty House. Let Sparks go below now. We need to inform Commander Rowland as quickly as possible, and we need to know how his repairs are holding up."

"Excellent suggestion, Mr. Holmes. Sparks, on your way. And if you come across Flemming, have him report to the bridge double-quick."

Sparks dashed out the door, bumping into the crow's nest messenger as he did so.

Once the messenger had regained his balance, he reported, "Enemy sub's in the water, Sir, and under power. Its course appears to be making right for us. The freighter, Sir, she's turning

180 degrees. Bryson says she's mounting a cannon on her aft deck."

Hemphill reached for the forward gun turret communication tube. Just as he started to speak the air was rent by the unmistakable whine of a heavy cannon round. This was followed by a deep rumbling sound and a geyser of water exploded on the port side just a few yards from the ship causing everyone to instinctively flinch. Hemphill shouted into the communication tube, "Return fire! Fire at will!"

With the cannon barrel already elevated for maximum range, the forward turret responded instantly, getting off two quick rounds. The voice communicator light for the forward gun illuminated and Melbourne picked it up and listened for a moment. He put it back in its clip beneath the window and turned to Hemphill, "Says we're out of our range, Hemp; just wasting ammunition."

Hemphill nodded and turned to the helmsman. "Standard evasive manœuvres, quartermaster!"

"Aye, aye, Sir, standard evasive manœuvres." He repeated the order just as another round passed directly overhead and exploded astern. "Sounds like they've got our range, Sir." He brought the helm smartly to port. ·She's steerin' heavy again, Sir."

The ship heeled to port as another round landed a few yards to starboard even with 'midships.

"Seaman Flemming reporting as ordered, Sir. Commander Rowland says the plates are holding, but the leakage is getting worse. The water level in the hold's risen some, maybe two or three inches. He thinks there may be some seepage around the bulkhead into the coal bunkers. Says you should have Mister MacGregor check them out."

"Melbourne, will you have a word with Mac?"

"In a sec, Hemp." He picked up the forward gun communication tube. "I make it fifteen hundred yards and closing, Chief. Let 'em know what real naval gunnery's about." He replaced the tube and picked up the tube for the engine room. It a few seconds he relayed Flemming's report and replaced the tube. Just as he did another round whistled directly overhead followed an instant later by a tremendous crash that shook the entire ship dashing everyone to the deck except the helmsman who calmly brought the ship back hard to starboard. Melbourne scrambled to his feet and picked up the communication tube for the aft gun mount. "Damage and casualty report!" Holding the communicator to his ear and with his other hand holding his binoculars to his eyes, he waited for the reply. "Al-right. Get your casualties to the infirmary at once, and get the fire out with the rest of your crew."

He turned to Watson, "Doc, we've taken some casualties. You'd best get back down to the infirmary. One man's unconscious; the concussion smashed his head against a steel bulkhead. Another man may have a broken leg."

Instinctively, Watson came to attention, saluted and dashed out the door.

"How bad's it, Melbourne?"

Melbourne watched through his binoculars as two rounds from The *Viper* bracketed the stern of The *Aegean Star*. "Look's like we're getting their range as well. It could have been much worse. Clipped the aft funnel and exploded just above the quarter deck. Took out the funnel and tore up some deck planks, but that's about it. There's a small fire, but they'll have it under control in no time. Let's just hope that was their best shot."

"Except for the submarine," Holmes reminded. "We should be in torpedo range by now."

"True, Mr. Holmes, their range as well as ours. But I don't think they'll risk a shot at this distance. They've got only two torpedoes..."

"So do..."

"That's true, Mr. Holmes, but they don't know that. Besides, they'll have to try a bow shot which has exactly no margin for error."

"Thousand yards, Hemp." Melbourne had been peering intently through his binoculars suddenly shot a fist in the air. "Yes! Good show!"

"What? What happened?" Holmes and Hemphill both peered through the bridge windows.

"We got 'er. Direct hit on the gun mount. Wow! What a shot! Just about put it right down their cannon barrel!"

"I would say that evens up the odds a good bit, does it not, Lt. Hemphill?"

"Indeed it does, Mr. Holmes." Hemphill turned and clasped Holmes's hand, pumping it vigorously for several seconds. "Look's like it's us against the submarine."

"Helmsman, break off evasive manouvering and set a course straight for the submarine."

"Aye, aye, Sir. Ceasing evasive manouvering and setting course directly for the submarine. Could use a bit o' help in that regard, Sir. She's too low in the water for me to see. Can you have Bryson give me a heading?"

Keeping the door to the bridge open, Hemphill relayed instructions to the helmsman as they were shouted down from the crow's nest. Melbourne maintained voice communication with the torpedo gunnery officer.

"Come left five degrees; five hundred yards and closing. Melbourne prepare to fire on my instructions!"

"They've launched! Both their torpedoes!"

"Five degrees to port, Sir."

"Fire both, Melbourne! Now!"

"Any course change, Sir?"

"No steady as you go! They fired both thinking that we'd manœuvre either to port or to starboard. That way, they'd be almost certain of one hit. And if they get that, they'll finish us off with the ramming pike."

"Hemp, ours are away and running. Estimate forty-two seconds to target."

"Crow's nest, where are theirs?"

"Can't see 'em, Sir."

Melbourne intoned, "Twenty seconds, gentlemen."

"Two torpedoes, Sir!" The messenger burst in. "One hundred twenty yards dead ahead! They're running just a few feet apart, Sir, and veering slightly to port!"

"Helmsman, right full rudder!"

"Right full rudder, Sir!" The ship heeled sharply to starboard as the order was executed.

"Brace yourselves, gentlemen." Hemphill spread his feet wide apart.

"Ten, nine, eight, seven..." Melbourne counted down the seconds until their own torpedoes should find their target.

The force of the concussion heeled the ship heavily to starboard knocking everyone off their feet. They ended up in a heap thrown against the starboard cabin wall on top of the make-shift chart table. Melbourne was the first to recover his balance, "two, one... bloody hell. We've missed. Both shots."

"Evidently our adversary did not." Holmes sat on the floor, his back against the rear bulkhead, and his arms wrapped around his knees.

"Helmsman! Is the steering responding?"

"Aye, aye, Sir."

"Then let's show those blighters how to ram. Left full rudder! When you've got 'em dead ahead maintain course and" run 'em over."

"Left full rudder. Aye, aye Sir."

"Melbourne, will you have a look-see as to how badly we're hit?"

"On my way, Hemp. Don't let 'em get away!"

"Mr. Holmes, will you use the wireless and let Admiralty know where things stand?"

Holmes struggled to his feet. "Yes, of course. What about the freighter?"

"Submarine dead ahead, Sir! Brace for collision!"

As the *Viper,* her engines still at full speed, dipped her bow into a small wave, the men on the bridge caught the briefest glimpse of the rusted conning tower and sail of the submarine. "Steady as you go!"

They felt rather than heard the collision. It was like a carriage crossing over railroad tracks. The *Viper's* bow struck the small submarine amidships on the port side, connecting first with the conning tower and sail. It heeled the vessel over on its starboard side and then crushed the hull under the *Viper's* keel. Hemphill cranked the annunciator back to dead-slow and picked up the engine room communicator. "Mister MacGregor..." He listened for a few moments and returned the communicator to the rack.

"Sir, the three-mile marker buoy ninety degrees to starboard," the helmsman reported.

"Reduce speed to dead slow and remain steady as you go. I'm going to try and make St. Malo harbour if we can stay afloat that long."

"What about the *Aegean Star,* Lieutenant?"

The crow's nest messenger staggered into the cabin, his head bleeding from a sizeable gash over his left eye. "Sir, crow's nest says the freighter has broken out distress pennants and is now flying a German flag from the mizzen."

"There's your answer, Mr. Holmes. We're now in French territorial waters. Unless you want to risk a war with France, we cannot fire on her or even attempt to board. I'm afraid the game's up."

Hemphill, noticing the engine room communication tube light illuminated picked up the tube and listened for a minute. He replaced the tube and turned to Holmes, "It's bad Mr. Holmes, very bad. Evidently we did not take a direct hit. However, the two torpedoes from the submarine must have collided with one another and detonated within a few feet of our port side. The concussion wave stove in part of our hull just at the water line. The port side coal bunkers are flooded and we've taken heavy casualties—more than half the port-side stoker crews—in the bargain. Mr. MacGregor managed to seal the bunker hatches, so if we don't crack apart, we can probably stay afloat, although listing rather badly to port. I told Melbourne to leave the engine room to Mr. MacGregor, and to check on Commander Rowland in the forward holds.

"The hunt for the *Aegean Star* is over, Mr. Holmes, and I no longer feel bound to place this ship and her crew at your disposal. Besides, without her cannon and submarine, I should think that the *Aegean Star* no longer poses a threat to the *Sfax*. My job at this point, until Commander Rowland relieves me, or Admiralty tells me otherwise, is to save this ship. And I mean to do just that. Now I would be much obliged if you would man the wireless as I requested; God knows what's happened to Sparks."

Noticing the still dazed crow's nest messenger, Hemphill seized him by the shoulders, "Buck up, Sailor. We've got jobs to do."

The young sailor, tears now mixing freely with the blood from his wound, came to a semblance of attention.

"Aye... aye, Sir," he acknowledged weakly.

"Get Bryson down out of the crow's nest and have him report here immediately. Then go below and locate Lt. Melbourne. Ask him to return to the bridge at once, and you remain as the communication link to Commander Rowland. In fact ask Lt. Melbourne to return as quickly as possible so that he can assist in navigating the entrance to the St. Malo harbour."

CHAPTER FIFTY

*"Come along, Watson. Now it's you
who've been bitten by the green-eyed monster."*

"I can still see that hideous face smirking at us from the bridge of the *Aegean Star* as we dropped anchor." Holmes had just shed his suit coat and hung it from the coat rack next to the door.

"I'm just as glad that I was still in the infirmary tending to the casualties." Watson raised the bay window overlooking Baker Street, and shed his own coat which he threw over the back of a chair. He sat down heavily on the sofa and made preparations to light a cigar. "At least we can take some comfort in the fact that half the fleet's chasing after him all over the South Atlantic. And if they do not run him to ground, someday he's going to need supplies or repairs. He'll have to call at a known port. Every commercial and naval attaché in every embassy and consulate around the world is on the lookout, and no nation who values her relations with Britain will dare give him sanctuary."

"Comforting as that all sounds, I still think we should have sent sappers over the side that night—before they got underway and escaped under cover of darkness—and placed a couple of limpet mines on her hull."

"You're right, Holmes, I suppose, but it was Lt. Hemphill's decision."

"Yes, and he made it."

"With Admiralty's full backing, don't forget."

"I do not forget, Watson, but I cannot help but think that Commander Rowland and twenty-four of his crew perished virtually in vain."

"Nonsense, Holmes. Such thoughts dishonor their memory. As you yourself remarked on the train as we were leaving Paris, we did shut down Moriarty's arms-trafficking ring and put him to flight. Add to that the fact that we saved the *Sfax* and Captain Dreyfus and possibly postponed, if not prevented a war. With no submarine, and her cannon out of commission—not to mention the Royal Navy hot after her—even if the *Aegean Star* had managed to encounter the *Sfax,* she was hardly in a position to do any damage."

"Speaking of Captain Dreyfus, do you suppose that we did him much of a favor even if we did save his life?"

"The answer to that question, Holmes, requires a gin and tonic. Especially in this wretched heat." Watson started to get up.

"Keep your seat, old fellow; I'll pour. Sometimes I think the Americans may have the right idea, putting ice in their drinks."

"Even in whisky? Ice in tea? Good heavens, Holmes, you begin to sound like young Churchill."

"One gin and tonic, no ice." Holmes handed Watson his drink and settled himself in one of the wing-back chairs. "By the way, did you see the letter from Hemphill?"

"No, when did it come?"

"In today's morning post. As it was addressed to both of us, I left it on the dining table thinking you'd read it at breakfast."

"I must have missed it, as I was absorbed in reading the newspapers. Did he have anything exciting to say?"

"I would suppose one might find it exciting. Seems he and Melbourne along with MacGregor and most of the *Viper* crew are transferring to the *Cobra,* a sister ship which was launched a few weeks ago."

"I pray that they've licked the heat and vibration problems; otherwise the ship'll be a death trap just like the *Viper.*"

"All in good time. I understand they're also working on replacing the voice communication tubes with an on-board telephone system. Before long naval vessels will be equipped with so many gadgets, there won't be room for armament."

"And Melbourne is still paying court to Miss Pippen?"

"Hemphill didn't mention it; perhaps he's a trifle jealous. But I did have a report to that effect from brother Mycroft. It appears that Melbourne and Pippen are quite smitten with one another."

"I'm afraid I cannot see Miss Pipen in the role of stay-at-home housewife while her husband is off to this exotic port or that."

"Neither can Mycroft. Evidently Miss Pippen has no intention whatever of giving up her career. Seems that she's become something of a mentrix to Irmgaard, who, at last report, has called it quits with Major Esterhazy and been accepted into Mycroft's 'little cadre' as he so quaintly describes his burgeoning nest of spies."

"And what of Ollstreder? Have the French yet sought his extradition?"

"No, nor do they intend to."

"Why in heaven's name not? I take it you've been in contact with Loiseaux?"

"I have been in contact with the Inspector, but he's not the source of my information regarding the baron. That again was Mycroft. The French Government fears that by requesting the baron's extradition, they will become an international laughing stock."

"Not unlike the little boy who cried 'wolf!' too often? First von Schwarzkoppen, then Ollstreder..."

"Not exactly, Watson. The request, if made, would not be founded on the Dreyfus case; they know that such a request would be rebuffed with the same haughty expression of 'righteous indignation' as in the case of von Schwarzkoppen. Instead, if they were to make the request, they would do so through the civilian authorities in connexion with the investigation of the deaths of Ollstreder's servants. However, they know that the case against Ollstreder is too weak, even under French law, to support extradition. They anticipate, and rightly so, that the Germans will know it is simply a ruse to question him in regard to the documents found by Inspector Loiseaux in the baron's safe.

"Moreover, and these are merely my own suspicions, President Loubet may attempt to lure Ollstreder back to France voluntarily with the promise of amnesty in exchange for his testimony exonerating Dreyfus."

"I can imagine such an offer would be highly tempting to Ollstreder. I expect he would jump at the chance to escape his bucolic prison and resume some semblance of his former sybaritic existence. But who would he implicate? That toad Esterhazy?"

"Who better than Esterhazy? After all, that was his plan when he thought he could secure the falcon statue."

Then 'M'sieur deBecourt' is probably better off left to the tender mercies of Mycroft. And speaking of M'sieur deBecourt formerly known as 'Esterhazy', is he earning his keep?"

"On the whole, yes. But between his making outrageous demands, grousing about the food and pining for Irmgaard, serving as his nanny has become the least desirable posting for the members of Mycroft's cadre."

"Did Inspector Loiseaux provide much information regarding the papers found in Ollstreder's wall safe?"

"No, once the Section of Statistics got hold of them, any civilian access was cut off. All that Loiseaux could determine was that the principal document appeared to be the entire battle plan for a German invasion of France through the Low Countries, with the right flank sweeping west all the way to the Channel. ' Let the right-most man's sleeve touch the ocean' it says in the preamble."

"What an extraordinary bit of luck. What do you suppose the baron was doing with such a sensitive document?" Watson's tone betrayed more than a hint of sarcasm.

"Evidently the French are asking themselves the same question, and for want of a satisfactory answer have discounted entirely the document's genuineness."

"Well at least in that respect they're finally showing a bit of common sense."

"*Au contrair,* Watson. It appears your sojourn to the City of Lights has caused you to begin thinking like the French."

Watson took a contemplative drag on his cigar. "Come now, Holmes. Surely you don't think it's genuine?"

"I am convinced it's genuine. In the first place, I do not believe the baron had anything to do with procuring it. I don't think he even knew he had it. Moriarty's behind this as sure as..." Holmes paused and drained the last of his drink, "...as sure as this glass is empty. Without a doubt Moriarty planted the document at the behest of the German counter-espionage operatives."

"I'm afraid this is a bit deep for me. Why on earth would they give away their most important military secret?"

"To achieve the very result which apparently they have achieved: to convince the French that it is a fraud..."

"So that the French will plan their defensive strategy based upon other assumptions."

"There you have it, Watson. Were that the French could so readily see the light."

"Has no effort been made to persuade them?"

"How and by whom? Even if there was the slightest chance they'd listen to the British Government, how should Her Majesty's ministers account for having knowledge of the document's existence? The French, suffering as they do from terminal cynicism regarding all things British will continue to deny the document's authenticity even when the Germans are marching down the Champs Élysées." Holmes rose to make himself another cocktail. "Another round?"

"Not just yet, thank you. I'll freshen this one up in a moment." Watson laced his fingers behind his head and stared at the ceiling. "I see in this morning's paper that Dreyfus's re-trial is to commence August Seventh. How's he holding up?"

"Quite well. As a physician you should know that hope is the best tonic."

"He's confident, then? Even without Ollstreder's testimony?"

"Mlle. Otero's testimony may be just as effective, or ineffectual, as the case may be."

"I take it, then, you're not sure that an acquittal will result this time either?"

"One may always hope. But the Dreyfus case has never been about truth, justice or due process, even as those concepts are dimly understood under French martial law. It has been and will remain about the antithesis of these values; in other words, it's about politics."

"And politics is about power."

"A wise observation, my dear Watson. Democracy, at least as practiced in *fin de siecle* France, is fatally flawed. The real power is in the hands of those who, to accomplish their aims, must first destroy democracy."

"Those," Watson rose and ambled over to the drink cart, "would be the church and the military? Or at least the right-wing extremists who seem to dominate both institutions?"

"Unfortunately, the line between 'true believer' and fanatic is a blurred one, and is quite easily crossed. Just as he who starts out a fool ends up a knave, he who starts out a true believer often ends up a fanatic."

"So the church and the military make common cause in order to destroy democracy. But why?"

460

"One would suppose that democracy is an inconvenience. The military and their allies the armament manufacturers realize that they cannot frighten the populace to the point of distraction and bribe their elected representatives all the time. After a while, the public grows weary of paying for more and more increasingly expensive weapons and fortifications. And they have a stubborn aversion to sending their sons off to be killed or maimed in some inexplicable war in some place they've never heard of."

"And as for the church..."

"As for the church, its mission—its ministry if you will—is to save mankind regardless of whether all of mankind wants to be saved in a particular way, or for that matter saved at all. By way of example, look at what they've done in Central and South America, not to mention Africa. The church sees the government as standing in the way of its bringing true enlightenment to the benighted masses all of whom would gladly see the light if the government would just stop blocking it out. Laws that permit religious liberty, scientific and academic freedom, laws which respect the individual's right to be left alone, these are an anathema to the church hierarchy. If one is free to follow the dictates of one's own intellect or conscience who knows where it could lead? And that is a risk the church is unwilling to take.

"The church and the military, they each in their own way, both pander to and prey upon the ordinary man's greatest desire, the desire for peace-of-mind. The military exhorts jingoism, which is but another name for xenophobia. And the church echoes the theme until it resonates against not only 'foreign devils' but those among us whose behavior is thought to be unacceptable, or who worship in a different manner, or chose to worship not at all.

"If one will only conduct one's life according to the tenets of the church, then one shall be blessed with prosperity and contentment, if not in this life, then surely in the next."

"Rather a sharp view, wouldn't you say, old man? Do I detect a touch of personal animus?"

"Perhaps, Watson. My family were Huguenots, and even today one does not mention in the presence of my aged relatives either the Edict of Nantes nor the 'Sun King'. But personal feelings aside, have you not observed that it is the wealthy who build churches, and the poor who most frequently attend them?"

"Point taken, Holmes. But will the military and the church be content to share power, or will they inevitably turn on one another?"

"Who can say, Watson? No historical paradigm comes readily to mind. Possibly we shall learn from the impending example of France; possibly the answer will not come until the next century, or the new millennium after that."

"Speaking for myself, all this philosophizing has given me something of an appetite. Are you interested in dinner?"

"Capital idea, Watson, provided that it doesn't involve getting dressed."

"I quite agree, Holmes. I quite had my fill of London's finer restaurants while Caroline... *Mlle.* Otero was here. I was thinking more in terms of Limehouse. Fish 'n chips, or possibly even giving your favourite Chinese a try. Your choice, old man."

"Speaking of '*la belle* Otero', have you heard from her since the telegram letting you know that she'd arrived safely?"

Watson rose and began putting on his jacket. "Yes, in fact I received a letter yesterday. She's in the process of closing the house in Paris in preparation for the August holiday which she plans on spending in the South of France. Some place called 'Cote d' Azure' or something like that. Evidently every Englishman who owns or can afford to charter an ocean-going yacht is heading for the same place."

"I take it that *Mlle.* Otero was favourably received in society?"

"Indeed she was. Not only was she 'a hit' in London, her two country-house weekends will no doubt be talked about for years to come."

"In any event, she's made a remarkable recovery, both physically and emotionally."

"Thanks in the main to your tireless efforts, old fellow. You should consider writing up the case for *Lancet.*"

"I hardly think so, Holmes." Watson peered into the mirror mounted in the frame of the umbrella stand near the door and ran his fingers through his hair re-arranging to cover his bald spot. "She also reports that Loiseaux's had his squad assigned as body-guards, and as a result he's with her nearly all the time. When he's not on duty, his place is taken by that young detective chap,

462

Blanchard, who came to see us at the Ritz. For the sake of his career, I can only hope that Caroline doesn't take a fancy to him."

"Come along, Watson. Now it's you who've been bitten by the green-eyed monster."

CHAPTER FIFTY-ONE

*"In my experience, in the Chinese Quarter, one must
learn to expect the unexpected."*

*D*uring the cross-town cab ride, they settled on Chinese. It was
nearly night-fall when they arrived in the Limehouse District. The
cabman, not wishing to venture into the area after dark, left them at
the West India Docks Road to walk the remainder of the way.
Because of the heat, those habitations having windows, opened
them to the hemmed-in dimly-lighted streets so that the sounds of
the street were interspersed with staccato bursts of conversations in
what Holmes said was the Cantonese dialect. The air was redolent
of exotic cooking. The smell of cabbage cooking in spices mingled
with the aroma of day-old fish cooking in oil. These were over-laid
with the scent of curry, a dish which Watson learned to despise
during his first convalescence.

They made their way through the twisted streets, cutting
twice through now pitch-black alleys where the cooking smells
were supplanted by the oddly cloying-yet-pungent smells of
smoldering joss-sticks intermingled with the odors derived from
the controlled burning of derivatives of the *cannabis sativa* and
papaver somniferum plants. Watson was beginning to feel light
headed from the combination of hunger, two gin-and-tonics and
the emanations from the drug dens.

They crossed over the fetid, brackish Regent Canal just
above where it empties into the Thames. From a peeling sign over
one of the shops, Watson noticed that they were on Limehouse
Causeway. At last Holmes paused before the door of a featureless
building set in the middle of a block of similar non-descript row
houses. Holmes rapped briskly with his knuckles, and the door was
instantly opened by a small wizened Chinese dressed in a crimson
pyjama-like garment whose fit was such that Watson could not
determine the door-keeper's gender. To Watson's relief, Holmes
was evidently known and they were met with an out-pouring of
greetings in the Chinese language, punctuated by many herky-
jerky bows and tooth-less smiles. Holmes responded somewhat

haltingly with a few phrases in what Watson took to be the same language, accompanied by several perfunctory bows and a nod or two in Watson's direction.

Once inside, they passed down a hallway and emerged in a kitchen at the rear of the establishment. Standing at the stove was an extremely tall Chinese man, whose height was exaggerated by a tall toque which he wore straight up on his head. He was cooking something in a large frying pan shaped like an inverted and slightly flattened dome with two handles fastened opposite one another on its circumference. The chef greeted Holmes with the same effusiveness, and Holmes answered in kind. At one point as Holmes was speaking he mentioned Watson's name. The Chinese cook quickly wiped his hand on a grease-stained apron and held it out in Watson's direction. Watson took the proffered hand and the man smiling broadly began at once to vigorously pump their clasped hands up and down until, after about a dozen strokes, Watson was able to break the grip and reclaim his hand.

Once extricated, Watson followed Holmes up two flights of very steep stairs that in the edifice's more elegant days had been used by servants. When they reached the second landing, they edged their way through a series of tiny rooms crowded with tables most of which were occupied by Chinese diners earnestly engaged in consuming bowls and platters of strange foods while talking animatedly, smoking cigarettes and waiving their odd eating utensils about in syncopated rhythm with the ebb and flow of conversation. A few of the tables were taken by non-Asian diners. These, however, appeared to Watson not to be Anglo, but Eastern European or possibly Semitic. Holmes and Watson were led to a small table next to an open window which provided a slight breeze to relieve the oppressively warm and aromatic air in the crowded dining room.

As soon as they were seated, a waiter, dressed in thread-bare but neat formal attire brought a chinoiserie jug of plum wine, which Watson found to be sweet but on the whole not unpleasant. By the second glass, Watson relaxed a bit and inquired of Holmes as to when they could expect the menus and whether they would be in English. Holmes replied that they need not concern themselves with menus or ordering, inasmuch as Chef Wu, with an imperiousness reminiscent of Escoffier, had insisted on ordering for them. Watson's apprehensiveness was eased somewhat when Holmes added that he'd informed Chef Wu that Watson was a Chinese cuisine novice, and it would be best to forgo some of the more exotic delicacies which otherwise might have made their way to table there to languish unappreciated.

The wine service was immediately replaced by a pot of steaming tea accompanied by small handleless cups. The tea had an unfamiliar aroma. Watson lifted the teapot lid in an effort to identify the source, and was unsettled to see a handful of tiny chrysanthemum blossoms peering back at him. Yet despite the flowers, the tea was quite flavourful, as were the various courses which followed. With his surgeon's hands, Watson quickly learned to wield the chop-sticks which were provided in lieu of the customary European eating utensils. Whether by happenstance, or because Holmes had informed Chef Wu of Watson's fondness for duck, the high-light of the meal was a whole roasted duck with crispy outer-skin, expertly carved table-side by their waiter.

When the duck remnants had been cleared, the waiter brought a fresh pot of tea along with two small, pouch-shaped pastries which Holmes explained, as Watson poured them each a fresh cup of tea, were customarily presented at the conclusion of a meal, and contained a printed fortune. Holmes picked up one of the biscuits and broke it open. He extracted a small piece of paper which proved to be a prediction that he would marry a fair-skinned woman and they would have twelve children, one for each of the years comprising the Chinese dodecannual cycle. Following suit, Watson picked up the remaining pastry and broke it open. He looked puzzled as he read the slim scrap of paper. "I say, Holmes, looks like I'm not nearly as fortunate as you; all I got is some sort of hand-written advertisement." Watson read aloud, "Go to shop of Tong Mon-fook. Find most interesting." Watson handed the paper to Holmes. "Bad luck, I'd say. I would much prefer to have had the one about the fair-skinned woman. What do you make of it, Holmes?"

Holmes's expression took on a serious mien. "Rather than an advertisement, Watson, I would describe it as an invitation intended for both of us."

"But how, Holmes? No one knew we were coming here. And even if they did, how could they slip something into one of these...these...fortune cakes?"

Holmes looked at his watch and leaned across the table so that he could speak in a near whisper. "In my experience, in the Chinese Quarter, one must learn to expect the unexpected. Inexplicable things happen. But in this instance, I suspect there may be a more mundane, yet sinister explanation."

"Which is?"

"That someone wants to contact us, and followed us here."

"And then bribed the waiter?"

"Or threatened him."

"I suppose we shall find out which soon enough. Where do you suppose the chap's gotten off to? He hovered over us throughout the meal, and now when we want him, he's nowhere to be found."

"Either he has de-camped—which is unlikely inasmuch as he's one of Chef Wu's sons—or he's been made to leave by force or by threat."

They made their way back downstairs to the kitchen. Chef Wu was furiously chopping at a piece of meat with a large cleaver. He looked up as Holmes and Watson reached the bottom step. He glared at them for several seconds, his face betraying a mixture of fear and anger, and then he returned to his chopping rending the meat with blows so heavy that the cleaver embedded itself in the wood of the chopping block. Wordlessly, Holmes plucked at Watson's sleeve and led him back through the kitchen to the front door. The door-keeper was absent, so they let themselves out.

With darkness, and the modest breeze off the river, the heat of the day had somewhat dissipated, and the air, though still warm was not stifling as it had been earlier. Now that the dinner hour was past, the streets were crowded. Many of the shops were still open, and lining the kerbs were push-cart vendors selling every kind of merchandise. After they'd walked about half a block, Watson stopped and turned to Holmes, "I say, Holmes, what in blazes is going on?"

Holmes lighted a cigarette, "Do you remember the ancient amah who let us in?" Watson nodded. "Well, she's no mere amah. She is in fact Chef Wu's grandmother and the head of the Wu clan.

She's also highly respected, even venerated, in the community at-large. My supposition is that she's been kidnapped to assure that the 'invitation' was delivered to us just as it was. Hopefully by now she's been released, and is none the worse for the experience."

Before Holmes put away his cigarette case he offered it to Watson. Watson selected one, and when it was lighted, he took a thoughtful drag. "I'm sure it's already occurred to you, but to my mind, there's only one man capable of such a despicable act." Holmes nodded in agreement.

"Then shouldn't we be summoning the police, Scotland Yard, The Household Guard... the..."

Holmes held up a restraining hand. "Capital ideas, all, Watson. But I think we'd best not act in haste. We are undoubtedly under observation even as we speak. If we raise a hue and cry, where shall we send the police? Do you know the location of the shop? Do you think we shall be able to find it before Moriarty makes good his escape? What if the venerable Madame Wu is still in his clutches as insurance against just such a rash act on our part? You saw Chef Wu wield his meat-cleaver; would you like to be the first to express condolences over the loss of his be-loved grandmother?"

Remembering the chef's bone-crunching hand-shake, and the violence with which the man drove the cleaver into the wood block, Watson reluctantly concurred. "Very well, Holmes, but what do you propose we do instead? Even if we somehow locate the shop, are we going to confront him by ourselves? The man's now obviously desperate as well as deranged. With every military and para-military force that salutes the British Flag on the alert for him, he somehow manages to come here and seek us out. Do you think he means merely to compliment you on your frustrating his magnum opus? At risk of being accused of cynicism, I for one do not." Watson paused to catch his breath and take another drag on his cigarette, "By the way, how do you intend that we find this shop?"

"I do not anticipate that being much of a challenge, Watson. Let us walk on. Before too long I expect that the wily merchant Tong will see to it that we do not miss the opportunity to sample the wonders of his estimable establishment." Holmes had scarcely completed his thought when they were approached by a Chinese youth who had been slouching against the building wall a few feet ahead of them, and whose appearance and mannerisms marked him as a street-tough or someone who fancied himself to be one. Despite the heat, he wore an ankle-length leather coat which he kept tightly buttoned and belted, his hands thrust deep in the side pockets. His thick, black hair was heavily pommaded and gleamed in the light from the green-grocer's shop in front of which Holmes and Watson were standing. As he drew closer, they could see that the heat had evidently begun to melt the pommade so that one heavy forelock hung down over his brow.

When he began speaking he did not remove the lighted cigarette that dangled from one corner of his mouth. Trying to ignore the smoke that was curling upward into his eyes and making them water, he addressed them in Pidgin English, "Hey you! English gents! You come Chinatown have good time? Yes? You come me. I show you where have good time. Lots pretty girls, all virgins. You come, yes?" He attempted to seize Watson by the elbow.

Watson jerked his arm away. "Get back you disgusting pimp. Get out of my sight before you get the thrashing you deserve." Watson, his right fist drawn back, took a step in the man's direction. Instantly the youth pirouetted on one foot and leaped in the air aiming a kick at Watson's head. As the manœuvre was begun, Holmes stepped in front of Watson and caught the on-coming leg at the ankle. He slipped his body to one side and the attacker sailed harmlessly past, ending up on his back on the side-walk.

He lay there dazed for a few moments and then got up. Grasping his left arm with his right hand, he rotated the sleeve of his coat. The left elbow had a large tear where it had scraped along the pavement. "Look! You make Chan tear new coat. You pay fix!"

"Why the nerve..." Watson took a step toward the young man.

"Steady on Watson." Holmes placed an arm in front of Watson's chest. "Perhaps young Mr. Chan will lead us to where we want to go. That was your purpose in accosting us, was it not?"

Chan, still looking at his damaged coat replied, "Chan tol' look two English men look like you. If ask way to shop of Tong Mon-Fook, Chan bring you there. You must ask first; otherwise maybe wrong Englishmen."

"Then how do you know we're the 'right Englishmen'?" Watson asked.

"English gentleman come Chinatown, always want girls. So I ask, you want girls? If say yes, you wrong man. I tell you go away. If not ask girls, you right man. I take you Tong Mon-Fook. Maybe later you want meet girls?"

Chan, muttering to himself in a Chinese dialect, led them through a maze of streets and alleys until even Holmes was unsure of his bearings. They slipped single-file through the aptly-named Narrow Street. As they walked along they became conscious of the sounds and smell of the river. After a few minutes they came onto a street identified as Ropemaker's Fields by a chipped and rusted metal sign high up on the side of a corner building. They stopped in front of a three-storey building with a green ceramic tiled roof which curled upward at the ends in the fashion of Chinese construction. The door was of solid red-painted wood. Over the door was a wooden dragon mounted by its tail perpendicular to the face of the building. From its jaws hung a flickering gas lantern. Next to the door was a plate-glass display window. The dim light reflected off a few Ming-style porcelain plates and vases which shared window space with a cloisonne tea-set and a few crude-looking jade and ivory carvings. The Chinese ideography, which Holmes translated, read: "Tong Mon-Fook, Dealer in rare and valuable antiquities and other objects." When he and Watson turned around, Chan was gone. The two men peered into the darkness, and then turned toward the door. As Holmes tried the handle he asked, "I don't suppose that you happened to bring your Webley?"

Watson patted the pockets of his suit jacket, hoping that somehow he'd brought the weapon and had merely forgotten about it. "Sorry, Holmes, I thought we were just going out to dinner."

Not surprisingly, the door was un-locked, so they walked inside. In the faint illumination provided by a couple of gas lamps set in wall sconces, they could see a knee-high pile of oriental rugs next to the door beneath the window. Scattered about the room was a small inventory of carved wooden furniture, perhaps a dozen pieces in all. There were rows of wooden shelves along the two demising walls. These displayed more of the same goods as those in the window. Holmes walked to the first row of shelves and blew out his breath causing a small cloud of dust to rise from one of the shelves. "Hmm," he mused aloud, "looks like the estimable Mr. Tong could stand a lesson or two in merchandising from Mr. Harrod of Knightsbridge." He picked up a vase, held it to the dim light and then tossed it to Watson, who taken by surprise, had to lunge to catch it. "Don't worry about dropping it, old fellow. From the weight of it, and the lack of translucence, I cannot imagine that it's genuine."

"You have an excellent eye, Mr. Holmes. Most buyers do not know the difference. As long as I keep the prices ridiculously high, they think they're getting authentic Ming." The familiar voice raised goose-flesh on Watson's arms, and caused Holmes's jaw muscles to tighten.

After a moment, Holmes replied, "And the arms you sell to the Irish insurrectionists?"

"All first-quality, Mr. Holmes, I assure you. First-quality only. After all, it wouldn't do to be selling factory rejects to one's best customer, would it?"

"And what do you have to sell us, Professor Moriarty," Watson picked up on the metaphor. "Is it gold, or is it dross?"

"That, Dr. Watson, is for you to decide. One man's trash may be another man's treasure. If you will be so kind as to join me in the rear of the shop, you shall have an opportunity to judge for yourselves."

By now their eyes had adjusted to the poor light. Looking back in the direction of Moriarty's voice they could make out the shape of a doorway. They passed through a beaded curtain and then down a short hallway at the end of which was a solid wooden door which was slightly ajar emitting a flickering glow as from a kerosene or oil lamp. Holmes motioned to Watson to stand behind him at the side of the door where the hinges were mounted. As soon as Watson had moved in behind him, Holmes reached out and pushed the door open and stood back, his body pressed against the wall.

"Do come in, gentlemen. As long as you conduct yourselves in a civil manner, I assure you that you've nothing to fear."

Cautiously they edged into the room to find Moriarty, dressed in traditional mandarin costume, nearly recumbent on a divan. In one hand he held the mouth-piece of a hookah. The other hand rested on what appeared to be a telegraph key sitting on a low table in front of the divan. The walls of the room were covered in silk and gold lamé fabrics which were bunched together in a knot hanging down from the ceiling in the center of the room. The shirred fabrics spread from the center of the ceiling to the perimeter and thence down the walls to the floor. The effect was the decorator's vision of a palatial tent from Arabian Nights. The surrealism was continued by the piles of oriental rugs on the floor and the absence of any occidental-style seating.

Moriarty replaced the mouthpiece in its mounting clip on the side of the hookah, and pointed to an arrangement of over-size cushions placed in front of the divan. "Please be seated, gentlemen. It was so good of you to come on such short notice. Gerald and I were terribly disappointed that we were unable to spend some time together in Ste. Malo. But that's the way things happen sometimes. Just two ships passing one another un-noticed in the night."

As Moriarty spoke, Gerald, who'd been standing in a shadowy corner of the room stepped forward to stand behind Moriarty. Also somewhat in keeping with the bizarre decor, Gerald was attired like some sort of mameluk in a pair of pantaloons fitted tightly at the ankles, and topped by a sash around his waist. Above the sash he wore a short, sleeve-less vest with no shirt underneath. Since their encounter on the river-barge, he'd evidently shaved his head and added a gold earring to his left ear. As Holmes and Watson seated themselves on two of the cushions, Gerald remained standing behind the divan, his arms folded across his chest, and a look of undisguised hatred in his eyes.

"I take it that in addition to being 'P. Villeneuf' you are also 'Tong Mon-Fook'?"

"Actually, Mr. Holmes, there was at one time a Chinese merchant by that name who did indeed operate an oriental

472

antiquities atelier in these premises. However, I bought him out several years ago—made him an offer he was unable to refuse—and I believe he took the sale proceeds and retired to his native land. As part of the purchased assets, I also acquired the use of the name. The seller was not especially enamoured of it, as at the time he had some twenty-seven living relatives with exactly the same name. In any case, I've found it useful in the intervening time since the transaction.

"I see that you are again taking the measure of Gerald, Dr. Watson. Let me at once discourage you from any ill-considered moves in that direction, or for that matter any other reckless action that you may be contemplating. My right index finger, as you have surely noticed, is resting on a telegraph key. On the table next to the key, I'm sure you've also noticed a wooden box from which four wires protrude. These wires, as you can see are connected to the telegraph key. If you were to look inside the box, you would find that two of the wires are connected to a storage cell. The other two wires, running from the key back into the box are connected to a blasting cap and several sticks of dynamite. If you were to look closely at the telegraph key, you would see that I have re-configured the terminals so that they are reversed. In other words, rather than the normal function of depressing the key to close the circuit, if I release the pressure of my finger on the key, that will close the circuit sending a current from the storage cell to the blasting cap. And that, I'm sure you'll agree, would result in devastating consequences for all of us."

"Diabolical..." Watson started to retort.

"Perhaps so, Dr. Watson." Moriarty compressed his thin lips into something resembling a smile. "However, it serves a dual purpose. Not only does it assure that our meeting will be conducted with the utmost civility, it also rather dramatically underscores the point I wish to make."

"Which is?"

"The symbiotic nature of our relationship, Mr. Holmes. Although, due to our similarities, 'symbiotic' may be something of a mis-characterisation."

"Similarities? How dare..."

"Please, Dr. Watson," Moriarty held up his left hand, palm outward, "if I may continue? I find that I am able to maintain an even pressure on the key for only so long. I would be terribly embarrassed were some accident to occur.

"After much contemplation of our long and always contentious relationship, I have come to the conclusion, gentlemen, that we are very much dependent upon one another. For my part, although some measure of satisfaction is to be taken from each successful coup, it is you, my dear Mr. Holmes, that brings my creativity to its fullest fruition. The knowledge that you alone are capable of appreciating my endeavours spurs me to ever more complex and subtle schemes. Without you, I should no doubt be reduced to seeking recognition for my exploits by writing letters to the *Times*. Moreover, knowing that one mis-step may bring you and Dr. Watson along with his trusty Webley down upon me at any moment adds that element of danger which makes life worth living. As you know, I neither drink alcohol, nor," he paused and focused his gaze on Holmes, "do I use cocaine. My foremost joy in life is having you as my implacable adversaries."

"And for our part?" Holmes, who had assumed the lotus position, leaned forward, clearly intrigued.

"For your part, Mr. Holmes, what would you do without me? Retire and become an apiarist as you claim you wish to do? Or will you continue to serve as court of last resort for the unjustly convicted? Perhaps you can keep yourself amused—and, if may I add, away from the cocaine bottle—by solving the 'problems' brought to you each day by the gentry with too much time and money on their hands. Without my reciting them by name, you know whereof I speak: those trivial matters which tax to the limit Dr. Watson's writing skills to make them sound both interesting and consequential."

"Some day the official police agencies may adopt your methods, but I hardly think that you'll be given proper credit. Then too, Bertillon notwithstanding, there are others who have made contributions to the field of scientific police work that are at least the equal of your own. Ballistic comparison, finger-printing... the list goes on, and in time will no doubt be added to with every advance in the physical and medical sciences. Will your life's work become, like bertillonage, a mere footnote in some future encyclopaedia of criminology? Not a pleasant prospect, and I dare say one that has not escaped your contemplation as you face the immutable verities which middle-age forces upon us.

"You knew it was me on the boat-train; why did you not have the captain take me into custody then and there? Or better yet, finish what you attempted to do eight years ago, and simply lure me to the taff-rail and toss me overboard? Were you not tempted? Why did you not act? Were you really that curious to see what I was up to, or were you overcome with joy that the game was once again afoot?

"As for you, Dr. Watson: a competent, workman-like trauma surgeon; a better-than-average diagnostician; an unpredictable 'bed-side manner'. Is that a fair assessment of John Watson the physician? But what shall your obituary say about John Watson the writer? Will the *Encyclopaedia Criminalis* devote a volume to your works? Will lecturers in criminology assign your writings as required reading? Or will future scholars and literary critics belittle your work as riddled with annoying inaccuracies and inconsistencies and lacking in substance? Fifty or one hundred years from now, will your works still be read, or will you be forgotten even before the copyrights expire?"

Watson shifted uneasily on his cushion. "Even if those matters are of concern to me, what has that to do with you? Surely you do not suggest that without you I am at a loss for subject-matter about which to write. I assure you that if I could write the final episode of your infamous career, I would cheerfully lay down my pen forever as the price for doing so."

"And what is your view, Mr. Holmes? Do you agree with your colleague's noble sentiments?"

"I expect, Professor Moriarty, that there's more to the matter than you've seen fit thus far to disclose. You know how I detest coming to conclusions before all the facts are known. I should like to know more of what you have in mind. Would you care to enlighten us?"

"I regret that I cannot share with you the specifics, gentlemen. I will tell you, however, that I've grown weary of this benighted isle. England no longer offers the challenge it once did. It suffers from so many self-inflicted wounds, that there's little more I can do to make matters worse. Through the rents in the fabric of its social system, one can already see the sun beginning to set on its so-called empire. It may yet take a war or two for the man in the street to come to the realisation, but England is no more than a shell of its former self. It is dying, gentlemen, and I for one have no taste for carrion.

"Fortunately, unlike Alexander of Macedon, there are other worlds, newer and larger, for me to conquer. You've possibly heard rumors of a society of Sicilians, mainly in the City of New York, who call themselves the 'Black Hand'. They are ruthless and well-organised; their leaders lack only the depth and breadth of vision that are my forté. I have made the *Aegean Star* into their very own trans-Atlantic luxury liner, enabling them to avoid when expedient the tedious bureaucratic formalities imposed by the United States Customs and Immigration Services. As a result, I am one of the few non-Sicilians to have entré to their inner councils. The synergistic potential of an amalgamation of my leadership skills and their organisation is, I assure you, unlimited."

"Most interesting, Professor. I take it the gist of your proposal is an offer of stalemate. What if Watson and I decline to accept? What is your next move to be? Do you really expect us to believe that you will deliberately remove your finger and detonate your bomb?"

"It would certainly relieve us all of the lassitude into which we've declined, do you not agree? But do you really wish to test my resolve, Mr. Holmes? What about you, Dr. Watson? Are you prepared to lay down your life and not just your pen?" Moriarty raised himself to a sitting position and with his left hand began to massage his right wrist as he fastened his eyes on Holmes, then Watson and then back to Holmes. In the utter stillness and silence, each man tried to read the others' thoughts, and Holmes and Watson each bore the added burden of attempting to bring some order to the chaos of his own.

Finally Holmes spoke. "We, you and I, Professor, have acted out this scene once before. I was fully prepared then to accept my own demise as the price for causing yours. When I thought that you were gone and that I had survived, my initial reaction was one of elation. Then, before I'd even made my way down the mountain, I began to doubt. In destroying you, had I destroyed myself as well?" Holmes un-coiled his legs and twisted his torso so that he was partially turned toward Watson, his left hand resting on the floor to maintain his balance.

"Watson, old friend, Moriarty's right; if he did not exist, I would have had to invent him. After our encounter at the Reichenbach Falls, by the time I returned to the lodge at the edge of the village, my doubt had resolved itself into certainty. My egocentrism had won out. I spent a restless guilt-ridden night and by morning determined that I must somehow rid myself of this Nietszchean monster within me, lest I be driven mad as Nietszche himself. In fact, since the sanitorium where he is confined was not far away, I even went to see him. They let me in, ironically on the strength of my name, but my interview was useless. I left after a few minutes, more depressed than before.

"This is the reason for my three-year hiatus. During that time I tried everything I could think of from a life of sensory and physical privation living as a hermit on the frozen tundra above the Arctic Circle, to attempting various feats of derring-do, perhaps sub-consciously hoping that I would fail. When those regimens did not produce the desired result, I began immersing myself in esoteric religions. I tried most every one from a tiny sect of Hebrew cabalists to a particularly exotic Hindu sect in a remote corner of Rajasthan whose adherents subsist on uncultivated grains and the moulted husks of insect larvae, and drink only a tea made from the dried leaves of a particular species of rhododendron. And in the last stages of my self-discovery quest I even turned to the Eastern religions—Buddhism, Shintoism, Taoism—and some I'm sure you've never heard of.

"After all of that, I found that the only cure for my affliction was to immerse myself in work. This is how and why I first became involved with this accursed Dreyfus business, as I've already related. I would have, and in retrospect should have, returned straight-away to London and placed myself in your capable hands. However, after so long an absence, and knowing what a rough patch you'd been through, I could not bring myself to do so."

Moriarty looked steadily at Holmes, "All that having been said, Mr. Holmes, may I take that you've decided to accept my offer?"

Holmes paused and again turned to Watson whose look told him that he spoke for both of them. "On one condition."

"And that would be?"

"That you turn over the letter that you obtained from the baron."

"Then you found the envelope? I was afraid that it was lost along with the barge."

Watson looked at Holmes, and then at Moriarty. "What letter?"

"The one, Dr. Watson, that you sought the baron's assistance in obtaining as the price for the apocryphal bird statue. You see, the Germans had already decided that it was in their best interest that Dreyfus be pardoned, and the letter which you and Holmes sought had even then been prepared and was on its way to Ollstreder's hands."

"But why..."

Holmes immediately grasped the import of Moriarty's statement. "Once they were certain that Dreyfus would be re-tried, their purpose was first to assure his conviction, and then his pardon. This accounts for the evidence which you rescued from the barge. They concocted the specious ordnance maps, and terrified Esterhazy into sponsoring them as evidence. Thus they all but assured that Dreyfus would again be convicted by the second court-martial."

Watson nodded his understanding and at the same time conveyed to Holmes that he was aware that no mention should be made of their meeting with Esterhazy at the cemetery, or their subsequent dealings with him. "I can understand why they should want to see him convicted yet again—presumably to deflect attention from the real spy— but why would they want him to then be pardoned? Would it not better serve their purpose for him to be returned to Devil's Island?"

"Not necessarily, Watson, especially if their purpose were a larger one."

"Indeed, Mr. Holmes. And what would that 'larger' purpose be?" Moriarty interjected.

"As you are well aware," Holmes paused, his jaw muscles clenching, "Loubet is inclined, if not committed, to pardoning Dreyfus if he is convicted a second time. And it is just as certain as

Dreyfus's second conviction, that a pardon will be intolerable to the military."

"But how," Watson shook his head in exasperation, "could the Germans be sure that the military, however grudgingly, would not just acquiesce?"

"That is simple, Dr. Watson. Loubet will not grant the pardon except on the strength of the letter. How do you suppose the military will react if the letter is denounced as a fraud? A pardon, and certainly one that is founded on a fraud, will, the Germans are convinced, lead to what they ultimately want—a military coup. The Third Republic will fall, and be replaced by a 'Restoration' or 'Third Empire' titularly ruled by whichever feckless pretender to the throne captures their fancy. But the real power will be in the hands of the military junta.

"Such a turn of events," Holmes interjected, "will create in the minds of the Junkers who rule over the German Empire 'great cause for concern for the welfare of German-speaking peoples throughout the European Continent'. A *causus belli* will, probably sooner than later, be manufactured, and if events go as planned, His Excellency Kaiser Wilhelm will, after a brief-but-bitter war, be found cantering down the Champs Élysées at the head of a brigade of Prussian Guards. Britain will surely intervene on the side of France to no effect, save the squandering of its material wealth along with a generation of its young men. And if your fondest dreams come true," Holmes pointed a finger at Moriarty, "there will be an Irish insurrection in the bargain."

"Bravo, Mr. Holmes. Disraeli could not have thought it out any better. I would applaud, but then in the present circumstances," Moriarty continued massaging his wrist, "it would be something of a meaningless gesture."

"But we've gone and spoiled all of that as well as your primary plan to sink the *Sfax*, haven't we, Professor."

"Perhaps, Dr. Watson. But if I give you the letter, what shall you do with it? If you give it to Loubet, the result may be exactly what Mr. Holmes has predicted. If you destroy the letter, then Captain Dreyfus is doomed." Moriarty reached backward with his left hand. "Gerald, the letter if you please." Gerald reached inside his wide sash and produced the document which he placed in Moriarty's out-stretched hand. Moriarty placed it on the table and gestured to Holmes to pick it up. "Well, gentlemen, which shall it be: Dreyfus or France? My hand grows weary, and I must reluctantly bring this interview to a close."

Holmes picked up the letter and placed it in his coat pocket. "I think, Professor, we will leave that decision to Captain Dreyfus. Come, Watson," Holmes rose to his feet, I see no reason to detain Professor Moriarty any longer. The consequences of over-staying our welcome are more than any of us may wish to endure."

As Watson rose to his feet, Moriarty held up his free hand. "One final thing, gentlemen, before you go. Gerald, would you please show our guests the contents of the other box?"

Gerald knelt down behind the divan and produced a pasteboard shoe box. He removed the lid and held the box up at an angle so that Holmes and Watson could see the contents. Moriarty chuckled, "If you were to examine the shoes carefully, Dr. Watson, you would no doubt be struck by the similarity in the tread pattern to a pair of tennis shoes once owned by yourself. Indeed, were you to examine the underside of the tongues, you would see your own name, written in your own hand in india ink. It seems such a waste to discard a perfectly good pair of tennis shoes, so I had Gerald rescue them from your garbage can where you deposited them January last."

"But... but... how did you..."

"Please, Dr. Watson. That scoundrel Milverton... do you think he could have carried out his despicable enterprise for as long as he did without my sanction? Have you forgotten how I got my start? He'd been in my employ, so to speak, for years. And he would still be today had he not decided, unilaterally, to alter our arrangement." Moriarty, in his characteristic reptilian manner, turned his head from side to side in mock bemusement. "And you, Mr. Holmes, thinking all these months that he'd been done in by one of his victims. The young woman in question was acting at my behest. Your bumbling on the scene, as it were, made the transaction all the more delicious.

"And no, Dr. Watson, I shall not as yet make you a gift of the shoes. It would be well for you to remember that I have them. Should the fortunes of war favour you and I am someday captured, you will find your joy on the occasion tempered by the thought that I may see that the shoes are placed in the hands of Inspector

Lestrade who will no doubt be delighted to have them at long last. I have, however, made you a gift of your tennis racquet. I purchased it at the jumble sale put on by Mrs. Hudson's church. You will find that it has been delivered this very evening to your rooms in Baker Street. Gerald was most reluctant to part with it, but in the end I was able to persuade him. And now, gentlemen, while I do not wish to appear the un-gracious host, I must bid you *au revoir*. I trust that you will be able to see yourselves out. Gerald, the lights." Gerald, in response to Moriarty's command turned a concealed wall switch and the room was instantly dark.

Holmes and Watson turned and stumbled their way to the door. Watson found the knob and quickly opened the door. They turned and looked back into the room, and in the feeble light from the front of the shop, they could see that Moriarty was already gone, along with Gerald, the divan, the shoe-box and the bomb. Watson started to go back, but Holmes took him by the sleeve. "Come, Watson, let Moriarty enjoy his night's work. I can assure you that our business with him is far from done."

They were but a few dozen steps out the front door when the force of the blast sent them sprawling to the rough pavement. A huge curtain of flame billowed over their prone bodies followed by a rain-storm of glass shards, porcelain fragments, pieces of fractured timbers and broken bricks. As the sound of the explosion reverberated through the close-set buildings lining the road, they scrambled to their feet. Dazed and nearly deafened, they made their way back to the blast site.

The main force of the explosion had been toward the rear and upward, so that the facade of the building, except for the door and window, and the front portion of the roof were largely still intact. Once past what had been the front door, the gutted hulk of the building was illuminated by the fierce blazing of the ruptured gas lines. Nearly the front third of the two upper storeys remained, with the rest having collapsed onto the ground floor. They picked their way over the rubble of shattered floor beams, remnants of lath and plaster walls and exterior brick toward the rear of the building where the office had been. Even through the debris from the two upper floors, the brightly coloured wall fabrics made it relatively easy to locate the room where they had so recently conducted their singular business. Holmes pried loose a piece of wooden crown molding and used it to probe the rubble. They could hear in the distance the sounds of the approaching fire brigade as well as the excited chatter of curious neighbors gathered in the street in front of the site. After a minute or two, Holmes left his impromptu probe jammed down into the fabric. "Come, Watson, I'd rather not spend the rest of the night accounting for our presence up until now."

"But what about..."

"He and Gerald, along with your shoes, I expect are long gone. When the fire is extinguished and the debris cleared, I doubt that any trace of the occupants will be found. My supposition is that is what Moriarty intended. Probably the divan was on a hydraulic platform; perhaps it once served as a freight elevator. When the lights went out, they simply lowered themselves into the basement. The bomb was placed on a timed fuse, giving them enough time to escape through a tunnel or passage leading, no doubt, to the river. By now they are on board a fast launch making their way down river to where the *Aegean Star,* or whatever its current name may be, lays waiting for them. If we're lucky, in ten or fifteen minutes' walking distance we may be able to catch a cab back to the West End."

"Where are we..." Watson stumbled over the remnant of a chair and paused to regain his balance "going?"

Holmes attempted to brush the plaster dust from his trousers and coat. "I could certainly stand a whisky and soda, and since it's after hours, about the only place that will let us in without too much bother is likely to be the Diogenes Club."

"Then you plan to tell Mycroft?"

"At least part, don't you think? He ought be told enough in case he feels it proper to ring up Admiralty House and inform them should they wish to alert the Home Fleet."

"Do you plan to include mention of the disclaimer letter?"

Pausing to light a cigarette, Holmes looked at his friend over the glow of the match, "What do you think we ought to do?"

"When young Churchill first mentioned Dreyfus that evening in our rooms, I was amazed at your reaction. I've never, before or since, seen you so agitated. Now I understand why. Will we never be shed of this matter and its endless riddles and conundrums? Let us await the outcome of the second trial; perhaps we are being too pessimistic. Without the bogus map evidence, and with Caroline's testimony, it is at least possible that justice will prevail." Watson shrugged his shoulders, embarrassed at his own thoughts.

"Perhaps you're right, Watson."

By then they'd re-traced their path back to the West India Docks Road. Watson raised his hand to signal a passing cab. After they'd clambered in and given the driver their destination, Watson turned to Holmes, "And now let me ask you one final question: what are you... no, what are we going to do about the professor?"

Holmes sat quietly, his hands folded in his lap and his head arched back against the seat cushion. After a few moments, he relaxed his posture and looked over at Watson. "How does autumn in New York sound, old man?"

Watson sighed, "I suppose there's no getting around having to travel there by boat, is there?"

EPILOGUE

Late September, 1918; France, near the Aire
River East Northeast of Paris

"*Y*ou've been awfully quiet for the last half-hour or so." Holmes took off his metal helmet and mopped his high forehead with a handkerchief.

Watson was seated next to Holmes in the large military staff automobile totally absorbed in thought. "Eh... what? I'm sorry Holmes, did you say something?"

"Nothing important, old fellow. Just remarking how quiet you've become since Churchill and the driver went to get directions. Actually, I've rather enjoyed the respite. He does tend to talk on a bit."

Watson fished around in his kit bag until he located his briar and tobacco pouch. "I shouldn't complain, Holmes. After all it was you that set him off about the effect that tanks have had on the war. However, I would have thought that he'd have given you more credit for their invention, since it was you put the idea in his head almost twenty years ago."

"Oh, no. Let him take the credit. First of all," Holmes ticked off the point on his finger, "he's richly deserving of it. But more important, at least it's turned the topic of conversation away from Gallipoli and the Dardanelles Commission. He's had rather a rough go, and I doubt that he's entitled to nearly as much blame as he's gotten."

"I suspect that's the reason for his inviting us to accompany him in visiting the front. I would suppose that he feels the need to justify himself to every friend he has, although what good a couple of old dinosaurs like ourselves can do frankly is beyond me."

"Dinosaurs indeed. Speak for yourself. I would have thought that the prospect of seeing some actual combat would have you feeling like a young subaltern again. That is what you were so quietly musing about, is it not?"

"No," Watson paused to light his pipe, "not that at all. In point of fact, I was thinking about when we were in France in the

484

spring of ninety-nine. It's interesting how things have turned out. Churchill, not yet forty years old, has had enough of a career to last most men a lifetime. Caroline married to Blanchard and running a small hotel on the Cote d' Azure. Ollstreder giving his estate to the Johanniterorden and then joining them himself. I wonder if he ever gave up searching for the statue or his dream of succession to the Schleiswig-Holstein throne. And Esterhazy," Watson's nostrils flared in disgust, "where was it?"

"Chicago," Holmes supplied.

"Oh yes... running a Rumanian restaurant in Chicago."

"And then of course there's Dreyfus."

"Mustn't forget Dreyfus. Never even bothered to thank us. Why if we hadn't extracted the Kaiser letter from Moriarty, Dreyfus'd probably still be back on Devil's Island, if not already dead."

"Aren't you leaving out one other crucial player?" Holmes lighted a cigarette. "Had Her Majesty not presented the letter to Loubet and convinced him that she'd shamed her grandson into writing it, Loubet never would have accepted it as genuine. And certainly grandson Willie was not going to publicly brand his grandmother a liar. So he couldn't very well repudiate the letter..."

"And since they couldn't rightly claim that the letter was not genuine, the military had no choice but to accede to Dreyfus's pardon, and in the bargain losing their justification for a coup d'etat. What continues to amaze me though is that Dreyfus chose to continue his career in the military. It's as though he forgave his persecutors, and turned his back on all those who worked so hard and risked so much to help him. Someday I'd like to meet him and ask him why."

"Who knows, my friend. Why does a cuckolded husband forgive an unfaithful wife? Ah, here comes Churchill..."

It had been raining off and on the entire time since they'd left Paris the previous night. Churchill, his trench coat flapping loosely, came clumping up the muddy road followed by the driver. When he reached the automobile he stuck his head in through the space between the door and the canvas top. "Sorry it took so long. Army field communications are a bit dicey under the best of circumstances. When you add to the normal difficulty by trying to communicate between three armies—even if they are on the same side—it becomes an utter nightmare. In any case, I finally got through to Field Marshall Haig's chief of staff. He kept me on one line while he tried to contact the commander of the American Forty-second—I believe they call it the 'Rainbow Division'— but they said he was out in the field and couldn't be reached. Finally Haig's chap got hold of another American Division, the Thirty-fifth, and they cleared us up to the front. We're supposed to meet up with a Yank chap and he'll take us to our billet," Churchill paused, "such as it is."

Churchill got back in the front seat of the vehicle and they lurched off continuing east, the tyres spinning in the mud. They continued on through the intermittent rain and lowering clouds. Off to their left they could see the sky lighten in the distance and a moment later they would hear a rumbling like the sound of thunder. "Must be quite a storm off to the North," Holmes remarked.

The driver looked back over his shoulder. "Man-made storm, Sir. Mostly German 'eighty-eights'. The Yanks are lobbing a few back the other way as well. When there's a short interval between the flash and the sound, that's the Bosch sending 'em our way. My guess, neither side's doing much damage. It's hard to hit what you can't see. The Bosch like to put on a show at night mainly because of what it does to our blokes' morale. It's hard to get a night's sleep in the trenches anyway, and when artillery shells are landing all around you, why it's no wonder lots of men go ''round the bend' after a while. 'Shell-shock' I've heard the docs call it. In my book, it's just as bad as getting hit. You see, they gets that blank stare in their eyes. Sometimes they just sits for hours; don't hear, don't see a bloomin' thing. Then all of a sudden someone will drop a shovel accidentally, or even one time I seen wi' me own eyes, a bloke struck a match behind one of 'em and th' poor blighter let out a scream, took out o'er th' top and got 'is head blowed off by a Bosch sniper.

"Sometimes they'll lay down a rolling barrage, so's to make us think they're starting a night-time assault. Everybody gets all roused up, officers running up and down the lines, and then nothing happens. Then 'alf an hour later, it starts all over again. After two or three times, you wish th' bloody bastards would come on just so you can fight something human."

"Sounds as though you've seen a good bit of action, Sergeant." Watson encouraged the soldier to continue. The driver glanced over at Churchill, clearly wondering whether he should.

"Carry on, Sergeant. Doctor Watson's seen his share of combat. Not to mention being twice wounded like yourself."

"Been in since Namur, Sir. Got a whiff of gas at 'plug street', but it weren't too bad. Flanders's where I got it the worst. Lieutenant blew the whistle, and I was 'alf-way o'er th' top when a bloomin' shell hit the trench right behind me. Nearly shot me arse—'cuse my language, Sir—clear off. Doc said he pulled half a dozen pieces of shrapnel out 'o me legs and backside. Some days it feels like he must 'ave left another half dozen in there."

"How awful, Sergeant. The pain must have been terrific."

"I was lucky, Sir. My foot slipped, so I was maybe a second behind the others. Lads next to me on both sides didn't make it ten feet before they both got cut in two by machine gun fire. Anyway, I got taken to the field hospital pretty quick, and they took care o' me just as good as if I was at Bart's back in London. Moved me to a hospital at Armentieres. Spent a month layin' on my belly, and another hobblin' around, then they cleared me to go back to limited duty. That's how come I've drivin' you gents around today."

"Two months' convalescence? For wounds that severe?"

"Two months was about all I could stand, if you don't mind me sayin' so, Sir. Armentieres weren't all that terrific. Never did see any of those mademoiselles they're always singin' about. Soon as I could walk, I started helpin' out in the surgery and in the wards. Seen all those men—boys most of them—shot up so bad, missing arms and legs, or blinded by th' gas... Th' smell when a wound doesn't heal and starts to go bad. No Sir, I got what was left o' my arse out o' there as soon as I could."

"Ow! Bugger all!" The vehicle's right front wheel thudded into a crater in the road bouncing the four men off the soft canvas top and back down onto the seats. "Sorry, gents; the hole was filled with water and I couldn't tell how deep it was." The sergeant wrenched the wheel and shifted into low gear. When he accelerated the automobile skewed sideways with the rear wheels ending up in the shallow ditch on the side of the road. The driver opened his door and started to get out. "You gents best stay here. I'll go on up the road and get help."

"How far to our rendezvous point, Sergeant?" Churchill asked.

"Not far at all, Sir." It's been more'n hour since we left the B.E.F. sector. And even with the rain and all we've been making pretty good time. I'd say no more than four, maybe five kilometers, two or three miles. Won't take me long at all."

"Wouldn't it save time if we just went along with you? We're bound to meet up with an American patrol soon enough." Watson started to get out.

"That's the problem, Sir. Four of us go sloshin' along the road, Yanks are liable to shoot first and ask questions second. They haven't been in it long enough so's you can tell what they're going to do. One bloke like me's got a better chance o' not being mistaken for a Bosch reconnaissance patrol"

"The sergeant's right." Churchill reached in his trench coat and pulled out a metal flask. He unscrewed the top and passed it over his shoulder to Holmes and Watson. "Besides, I don't much fancy the notion of slogging two or three miles in the mud and heavy rain."

Holmes took the flask from Churchill, and nudged Watson with his knee. "Whatever you think best, Churchill. Watson and I can but defer to your better judgement. Don't you agree, Watson.?"

"Hmm? Oh, yes. Quite so Holmes. Wouldn't do at all. We did come out here to see the Yanks in action, but I'm sure getting shot at by them was not what we had in mind."

Churchill continued his discourse on the finer points of the Galipoli Campaign, emphasizing each point with a jab of his cigar pausing only occasionally for a breath and to sip from the brandy flask which the three men continued to pass back and forth. Just as the flask was nearly empty, and Churchill had expounded his views on the pusillanimous Fisher for the third time, the sergeant returned waiving cheerfully from the top of an American horse-drawn caisson.

The driver, a corporal, whistled the team to a stop in front of the automobile and turned them around so that the caisson was directly in front of the automobile. In a few minutes the sergeant had attached a steel cable from the rear of the caisson to the front of the automobile. The American corporal whistled and snapped the reins urging the team forward as the sergeant started the automobile and shifted into first gear. The rear wheels at first spun in the mud. Finally they gained purchase, and slowly they eased back onto the road. The corporal disconnected and re-wound the cable, and with a wave to the automobile started back down the road.

"Well done, Sergeant," Churchill congratulated the driver. "Did you have to go far?"

"Thank you, Sir. No, not more than a mile, I'd say."

"Any idea how far to our destination?"

"Just the same, Sir. Th' Yank's from th' outfit we're suppose to billet with. All we need to do is follow him, and we'll be there 'fore you know it."

After a few minutes, they turned off the road onto a rutted path leading into a copse of trees. As they did, the sergeant turned off the headlamps and they inched forward by sound and feel. After a quarter-mile or so, their way was blocked by a pair of sentries, one holding an automatic pistol and a dim lantern open only on one side, and the other holding a rifle at port-arms. Their identities confirmed, the sentry instructed them to park their vehicle in a small clearing, and after admonishing Churchill to extinguish his cigar, motioned for them to follow him. They continued single-file along the double track, one sentry in the lead, with the sergeant and the other sentry carrying the civilians' kits bringing up the rear. The sounds of the German artillery fire were now much more distinctive, and a few times they could feel the earth vibrate from the explosions. When they'd gone another hundred yards, the trees began to thin and they could now make out a vague horizon in front of them. Off to the right, they could hear the thud of artillery rounds being fired back at the German lines. On the horizon they could see the brief bursts of white-orange light as the shells exploded.

As they came to the edge of the trees, the lead sentry led them down a narrow, sloping communication trench. A short distance into the trench, they came to what appeared to be a collapsed wall. The sentry stopped and opened the side of the lantern a little more, and they could see that the obstruction was in fact a crude hut made of bags of dirt interspersed with logs and rough-cut timbers. In the center there was a plank door, and over that a hand-lettered sign which read 'Battery D 2nd Batallion 129th F.A.' The sentry pointed to the sign and then knocked on the door. From inside a voice responded "Come."

The sentry pushed the door open and stepped just inside. "It's th' English civilians, Cap'n."

"Well send 'em on in, Corporal Don't want 'em t' think we're not hospitable. Come on in, folks!"

"Yes, Sir, Cap'n," The sentry stood aside as Churchill, followed by Holmes, Watson and their driver edged past and into the long, narrow low-ceiling room.

"Welcome, welcome." The captain rose from his seat at a camp table and strode over to his guests extending his hand. "Truman's the name. Harry Truman. Welcome to Battery D." He shook each man's hand warmly as they introduced themselves.

Captain Truman paused briefly as he shook Churchill's hand. "Churchill. H-m-m. Pardon my asking, but are you the Navy fella's been catching all that hell about the Dardanelles Campaign?"

Churchill's face reddened in the weak light. "Er, yes, that's me. But you see, Captain...".

Fearing that Churchill would launch into yet another explanation of the ill-fated expedition, Holmes stepped partially between Churchill and their host. "I'm sure Mr. Churchill would be pleased to fully expound his position, but the matter's a complex one as you might suppose. And the full story's a rather lengthy one. I assure you that when the history of this war is finally written, our good friend will be completely vindicated."

"Well," Truman removed his glasses and rubbed the bridge of his nose, "say, would you be *The* Sherlock Holmes? And *The* Doctor Watson?" Both men nodded affirmatively. "Well I'll be...I'm right pleased to meet you!" He shook each mans hand again. "Why I've read all about your cases. Could use you folks over in my neck of the woods. Come, sit down. We'll rustle up something to eat." Truman reached into an ammunition box under the camp table and removed a bottle. "Been savin' this bourbon for a special occasion. Can't be one bigger'n this. Hope you don't mind the tin cups." Truman poured each of them a generous measure of whisky and raised his cup. "To Allied Victory!"

"Hear, hear," Churchill responded somewhat grumpily. "Hear, hear." Holmes and Watson echoed.

Just as the four were raising their cups, the corporal who had guided the guests to the bunker peered out of the open door. "Cap'n, looks like more visitors. It's that general sir."

"Ten hut" Truman barked as everyone rose from their seats, the military men coming smartly to attention and saluting as the tall, lean general ducked through the doorway.

"As you were, men," the general returned the salute.

Truman lowered his cup and met the general's steely gaze with his own. "Thank you, sir. Welcome to Battery D. May I present our British visitors? Mr. Churchill, Mr. Holmes, Dr. Watson," he nodded toward each man in turn. "This is General Douglas MacArthur, commander of the U.S. 42nd Division." General MacArthur removed his heavily braided officer's hat and unwound the rather incongruous-looking long yellow scarf from around his neck. "you gentlemen journalists?"

"No, sir," Truman responded. "They're here by request from Field Marshall Haig's headquarters. Mr. Churchill's with the British Navy. Dr. Watson's a retired army surgeon, and Mr. Holmes...."

"Merely a civilian, General. A retired bee-keeper." Holmes finished Truman's sentence.

MacArthur's eyes narrowed. "Just as you say, gentlemen. I'm sure that Field Marshall Haig has his reasons, although I'm at a loss as to what they might be. But be that as it may, I doubt that you have anything to do with espionage.

"What's that you're drinking?" MacArthur turned toward Truman.

"I... uh..."Truman nervously fingered his cup.

"Tea," Holmes interjected. "Earl Grey, to be specific. Brought it along with us. Would the general care to join us?"

"No, no thanks," MacArthur re-wrapped his scarf. "Never acquired a taste for the stuff. I'll leave you gentlemen to," he again eyed the four suspiciously, "whatever it is you're doing. I'd like to take a quick look at your gun placement, Captain."

Truman let out his breath and set down his cup. "As you wish, Sir. Let me get my helmet and gas mask and I'll be most pleased to show you around. It can be a bit tricky moving around out there in the dark. You gents excuse me. Make yourselves at home. Food'll be here soon enough. All we've got is U.S. Army field rations, but at least they're filling. I'll be back soon as the general's done."

"That was a rather close call, Mr. Holmes." Churchill took a long sip from his cup. "Suppose he'd said yes?"

"Churchill's right old man. It was a bit cheeky. Gad! How do the Yanks drink this stuff?" Watson grimaced as the unfamiliar liquor passed his lips.

"A calculated risk, I admit, gentlemen. But the general didn't exactly strike me as a tea-drinker. Clearly not the diplomatic type. Moreover, once he was satisfied we were neither journalists nor spies, it was apparent that his interest in us was quite exhausted. I'm sure he had no desire to listen to me expound on the social hierarchy of the typical bee colony."

"No doubt you're right, Holmes, but I would have enjoyed seeing his reaction to the von Bork story. His rather dismissive comment about our having no connexion to espionage was almost more than one could bear politely." Watson took another cautious sip of bourbon. "Say, I wonder what's keeping the 'grub' as the Yanks call it?"

Over the sparse meal, the men continued their discussion of the von Bork case. "That arrogant swine." Churchill brandished his tin fork. "I'd have loved seeing him in the dock. I wonder how cocky he'd have been without his diplomatic immunity. I'll wager that a stout English noose about his neck would have gotten that smirk off his face."

"But that would have defeated the whole purpose of our labours," Holmes responded.

"How so, Mr. Holmes? Surely von Bork's escaping the gallows was of no benefit to us."

"Oh indeed it was." Holmes chuckled. "Had von Bork been hanged, the German General Staff would never gotten their hands on the contents of his bulging attaché case."

Watson fished around in his kit bag for his briar. "The moment we delivered von Bork on the steps at Carlton Terrace trussed up like a Christmas goose, the Germans knew that—as the Americans say—'the jig was up.'

"This part of the story you may not know," Watson continued. "Holmes, in his disguise as the Irish-American Altamont, had for some two years been feeding documents to von Bork. A few were genuine, and the others just done up to look that way.

"Holmes learned early on that von Bork was not shipping the supposedly-purloined documents back to Germany as he received them. Indeed, so Holmes tells me, von Bork was under instructions not to do so. The General Staff had their own concerns about spies in their midst, so they didn't want to chance their vile secret getting back to us."

As Watson paused to light his pipe, Holmes continued the story. "Von Bork was in fact the feckless wastrel he purported to be. It took me less than a cigarette's-worth of time to locate his wall safe and to surmise its contents. It took little more than that using a stethoscope borrowed from Watson, to gain the combination. So while von Bork was out and about playing at English country-gentleman, I was able to keep apprised of his plans whenever necessary. That's how he kept losing his other agents."

Churchill lay down his fork and finished the last of his bourbon. "Most remarkable, Mr. Holmes, Dr. Watson. But I still don't see how...."

"Elementary, my dear Churchill, elementary. When Holmes asked me to act as his 'chauffeur' that night, in addition to bringing along my Webley, he had me lash a packed leather attaché case to the extra tyres. As I was putting von Bork into the spare seat, Holmes switched the two brief cases stuffing the replacement case in with von Bork and placing von Bork's on the floor in front. So when we dropped von Bork off at the embassy, it was the substitute case that he took with him."

"And the second case, I take it, was filled with old newspapers or some such?"

"As good a joke as that would have been, it would hardly been worth the two years I spent in the persona of Altamont. The second case in fact contained genuine material, exactly the information von Bork thought he was getting during the time of our association."

"But, Mr. Holmes, surely..."

"Don't be alarmed. Here, have another tot of bourbon." Holmes reached under the table and retrieved the bottle from where Truman had secreted it. "Remember the 'Dreyfus Affair'. Remember the cache of documents found in the baron's wall safe. Turns out they comprised the very battle plan executed by the Germans at the outset of the war. You must recall the preamble, 'Let the right-most man's sleeve touch the ocean.'

"Once von Bork was exposed, whether hanged or released, none of his material was the least bit credible. The Germans, had the tables been turned, would never have let a British agent out of Germany with such material, no matter what his diplomatic status. So they found it inconceivable that His Majesty's Government would allow von Bork to leave England were his case actually filled with genuine military secrets."

"In other words," Watson injected, "we beat them at their own game. Just as the French discredited the contents of Ollstreder's safe, the German high command concluded that the contents of von Bork's attaché case were utterly worthless. Quite a proper payback wouldn't you say?"

"I'd say that was pretty risky business there with the general, Mr. Holmes." Truman reentered the bunker and pulled off his helmet. "Think I could use that drink now. The general doesn't care much for strong drink, and I'd not want to find out what he'd do to an officer caught taking a nip or two at the front. Fortunately he's gone off to inspect the French battery down the way a bit on our right flank. Doubt that he has a very high opinion of the French, the way they drink wine at every meal."

"Tell me, Captain Truman, why does he wear that—forgive my frankness—ridiculous yellow scarf about his neck," Holmes asked.

"Damn if I know, Mr. Holmes. Far as I can tell all it does is make him a target for every German sniper, or worse, their forward artillery observers. His father won a Medal of Honor in the Civil War, and I suppose he's after one too. Either he'll get one, or get himself killed trying.

"Beats me, them West Point fellas. A year or so ago Pershing gave him a chewing-out at Charmes would have singed the hide off a Missouri mule. Then, next thing you know, Washington makes him a one-star and gives him command of a

494

whole division. If it was up to me, I'd bust him down to private, or better yet sack him straight out of the army."

"I can't tell you how happy I'll be when this war is over and we...."

"In-coming, Cap'n!" The corporal stuck his head through the doorway just as a tremendous explosion shook the bunker causing the tableware to rattle off the table-top.

As shards of mud and straw rained down from the roof of the dugout, Truman fixed his helmet back on his head. Motioning to a corner of the room he called out "There's some spare gas masks over there. You'd best keep them handy. Rumor has it that the other side's using gas again. And if you've got ear plugs now's the time to use 'em. The shock waves can leave a man deaf in no time. Looks like the Bosch have got our range. Thanks, no doubt, to the general. Time for me to earn my pay and give 'em back some of the same. You gents need to stay down here. The bunker's pretty solid; it'll withstand anything but a direct hit."

"That's a comfort," remarked Holmes dryly as another shell landed near-by, this time causing the support timbers to creak and the three men to cringe involuntarily. Two more rounds exploded, it seemed, right on top of the bunker. The last one sending the men sprawling on the dirt floor amidst a cascade of dust and splinters. "Mind the lantern. Churchill, wouldn't do to have it break an engulf the place in flames."

Churchill gripped the edge of the table and began to pull himself up-right. As he was about to regain his feet another shell exploded a few yards beyond the doorway. The concussion blew the door inward and sent the three men sprawling once again as it lifted the roof of the structure several inches off its supporting timbers splintering one of the vertical supports forming the doorway. A shard from the fractured beam flew the length of the room imbedding itself in the far wall at a height where Churchill's head would have been had he managed to regain his feet before the explosion.

With one of its support beams gone, the main cross-timber supporting the roof splintered and sagged appearing about to give way entirely.

For a few more minutes the three men sat stunned and disoriented by the last concussion. Above them the shelling continued, a cacophony of rounds screaming in, mixed with the cracking of trees being torn limb from limb, their shorn trunks crashing to the ground, and the dull thud of the bare muddy earth absorbing those rounds that did not find other targets.

Still dazed, their ears ringing, the men managed to regain their feet. "I say, Watson, have a look over in the far corner. I thought I saw what I hope is a medical kit. I fear I may have taken a bit of shrapnel from that last round."

"Turn around, Holmes, and let me see in the light." Holmes did as Watson instructed. "Good God, man! Your coat is in bloody tatters. Churchill, grab the medical kit. Here, Holmes, let me help you out of your coat and suit jacket. Steady on old man." Watson succeeded in removing the coat and held the jacket as Holmes slipped his arms out of the sleeves. "There, that's got it. Now lay face-down on the table and let me see how bad the damage is."

Churchill meanwhile had located the medical kit and placed it on a stool near the table. Watson found a scissor and used it to cut away the remnants of Holmes's shirt. "Bring the lantern closer, Churchill. No, wait. Before you do that, see if there's any of that bourbon left. I need something to sterilize my hands, and I imagine Holmes could use a stout measure to provide a bit of relief from the pain."

Churchill took the lantern and knelt down under the table. "Sorry, Doctor. It appears that the blast got the last of the bourbon along with just about everything else. Just a moment." Churchill stood up and hung the lantern back on its peg. "I've got a bit of brandy left in my flask, unless the bloody Bosch got that too. Where the devil's my kit bag?" Churchill poked around in the rubble for a few moments. "Ah. Success. Here it is. But there's hardly a good swallow left."

Holmes lifted his head from the table. "You use it Watson. You know how I detest sedatives. See if there's some Aspirin in the medical supplies. I'll take a few of those when you're done."

Watson busied himself with examining Holmes's wounds. "Hmm, not too bad Holmes. Only three or four that I can see, and they all look to be splinters of wood, rather than shrapnel. I'll have them out in a moment.

"Churchill, hand me the forceps, please." Watson extended his left hand expecting to instantly feel the instrument being placed

firmly in his grasp. "There, man. The long tweezer. Thank you."
As he began removing the wooden shards, Watson murmured
under his breath, "Where the devil is Murray when I need him?
Even young—no, I suppose he's quite old by now—Stamford.
Even he'd do in a pinch."

"What's that Watson?" Holmes raised his head.

"Nothing, old man. Just mumbling to myself."

"Ouch!" Holmes exclaimed as Watson removed a jagged
piece of metal barely a centimeter to the left of Holmes's spine.

"Steady on Holmes. That's the last one, and its shrapnel
after all. Just a few good dressings and you'll be fine. I would,
however, like to find an antiseptic in the supplies. Wouldn't do for
these to get infected." Watson glanced down at the medical kit.
"I'm afraid this is going to sting a mite, old man." Watson quickly
placed several gauze pads in a metal tray and poured phenol on
them. He then applied carbolic acid to another pad and brushed a
generous measure on each wound. He placed the phenol-soaked
pads on each wound and covered them with more gauze and finally
adhesive tape. "There you are, Holmes. That ought to do for now.
I'll change the dressings in a few hours and determine whether
you'll need stitches.

"Seems the shelling has let up some," Churchill remarked.
"And it sounds like Captain Truman's lads are giving as good as
they got and then some."

Holmes eased himself to a sitting position just as another
round landed nearby causing the damaged cross-timber to sag even
further.

"I can certainly sympathise with Churchill's sergeant,"
Holmes remarked as he sat on the edge of the camp table. "Thank
you Watson. I'm glad that your field-surgeon's skills remain un-
diminished by the years. I think I'll have a few of those Aspirin
now and see if I can find a clean shirt in my kit bag."

"Take it easy, Holmes," Watson enjoined as he and
Churchill moved to help Holmes to his feet and another round
burst near the bunker sending more debris raining down on the
three men.

"I think I shall speak with Haig when we get back to the
British sector," Churchill said as he brushed a film of dust off the
sleeves and front of his trench coat. "He really ought to have a

497

word with General Pershing about this fellow MacArthur. He is simply too much to bear strutting about like a peacock in mating season. Why…"

The rest of Churchill's sentence was drowned out by the sound of a huge explosion apparently coming from the German lines. This was followed by a few moments of complete silence and then by the sound of cheering coming from the men of Truman's battery.

The British sergeant poked his head in the doorway. "Captain Truman's compliments, gents. The Captain wants to know if you're al-right. He says you're welcome to come up top if you're inclined to do so. Looks like the Bosch are done for the night."

"Gladly, sergeant, gladly." Churchill adjusted his helmet which had been knocked askew by one of the blasts. "Be along in a moment."

"Holmes, are you fit enough to make it?"

"Of course, Watson, just let me get my jacket and what's left of my trench coat back on."

The sergeant spotted the open medical kit. "Oh, and Dr. Watson, the Captain asked if you would tend to three of his men. Looks like some of them got roughed-up a bit by the incoming. From what I could see, two of 'em took some shrapnel and a third one's got what looks like a broken arm."

"Certainly, sergeant. There's a litter over there against the wall," Watson pointed. "You take that and see if you can get the wounded down here. I'll take a brief look around up-top and then come back down and do whatever I can. Also see if you can form a work-party to do something to shore up this roof. It wouldn't do to have it collapse on the wounded, not to mention myself."

"Yes, sir," the sergeant replied as he carefully prodded the shattered door-frame.

Holmes, Watson and Churchill picked their way through the blast crater and clamored up the muddy slope of what had been the trench. Following the sergeant they made their way through the wreckage of downed trees to the gun emplacements where they found Captain Truman kneeling beside one of his wounded men.

Churchill saluted and then pumped Truman's hand. "Good show, Captain. Jolly good show. Gave the Bosch more than they bargained for!"

Truman took off his mud-spattered glasses and reached inside his field-jacket for a handkerchief. "Thank you, but I can't rightly say it was all our doing. As you can see, we took some casualties and it looks like we've lost one of our guns. Truth be known, our side was getting the worst of it there for a while."

"Yes, Captain," Churchill surveyed the crippled gun as well as the close-by shell craters, "but in the end, it appears as though you prevailed."

"I'd like to take the credit," Truman responded. "My boys did themselves proud," he paused. "But what saved our bacon was that French battery over yonder," Truman pointed in the direction of the unseen French position. "Those Frenchmen, while the Germans were concentrating their fire on us, managed to sneak one of their 'eighty-eights' a ways forward to where they had a clear line of fire. Before the Germans knew they were there, they put a couple of rounds right in the middle of the German's ammunition dump."

"That, I take it, was the huge explosion we heard just before the shelling stopped?" Holmes asked.

"Indeed," Churchill folded his arms across his chest. "From my own experience, I can tell you, Captain, that no matter how much training you give a fighting man, and no matter how courageous he may be, some times—and I mean no reflection on you or your gallant men—it takes a good dose of luck to carry the day."

Before Truman could respond, Watson paused in his examination of the wounded man and stood up. "Well, I for one would be most happy to shake that Frenchman's hand."

"You'll get that chance 'fore too long, Doctor. They sent a runner over here even before the shelling stopped. They took some casualties and wanted to know if our regimental hospital'd be able to look after them. I hope its not imposing, but would you mind seeing what you can do?"

"Not at all, Captain. I'm honored to do so. Say, is that them coming now?" Watson gestured toward the tree line. There were an officer, two teams of litter-bearers each carrying one wounded man and two more enlisted men one with his head shrouded in bandages helping the other who was hopping along on one foot, the other useless.

Truman turned to one of his men standing near-by. "Sergeant Wintz, see that our wounded get down in the bunker. Send a couple of men to show the French the way and to help their walking wounded."

"Yes, sir." Sergeant Wintz saluted and began to carry out the Captain's orders. He quickly made sure that his own wounded were taken care of and dispatched two men to assist the French.

"I'd best get down there and get to work. Do you know, Captain, what anesthetics you have on hand? If I'm going to be setting broken bones, the men will certainly need something."

"I'm sure there's morphine and probably chloroform," Truman responded.

Remembering Churchill's clumsy groping for the forceps, Watson turned to Holmes, "Care to give a hand, Holmes?"

"Of course, Watson. Perhaps I can handle the morphine. I've had some experience, as you know." As Watson turned to go, Holmes laid a hand on Watson's shoulder. "Hold on, Watson. Let's stay a moment and meet our gallant saviour."

Captain Truman saluted as the French officer joined the group and returned Truman's salute.

"Captain Harry Truman, Battery 'D' 129th Field Artillery." Truman held out his hand. "Can't thank you enough for what you folks did."

"These gents are from the British sector, Field Marshall Haig's headquarters. This is Mr. Churchill, Mr. Holmes and Doctor Watson. The doctor's going to do everything he can for your men.

The French officer grasped each man's hand with a "*comment allez vouz*." Turning to Truman, he said "Major Alfred Dreyfus, at your service. I am pleased that we could be of assistance." Turning back to the three civilians, he continued, "Mr. Churchill, I've seen your name, have I not? You're with the British Government? And you, *M'sieur* Holmes and *Docteur* Watson, you are the great detective and his companion?"

Holmes and Watson nodded.

"*Tres bien.* I am delighted to meet you as well. A number of years ago, I found myself with a good deal of time on my hands during which I read of your exploits. They kept me amused for many, many a lonely hour."

"*Mon Dieu.* How shall I say it? You, Mr. Holmes are the Don Quixote of crime and you, Dr. Watson his Sancho Panza."

"You are too kind, Major." Holmes grasped Watson by the arm. "Come, Watson, I think our work on this case is finally done."